THE MAGIC ARMY

Born in Newport, Monmouthshire, in 1931, Leslie Thomas is the son of a sailor who was lost at sea in 1943. His boyhood in an orphanage is evoked in *This Time Last Week*, published in 1964. At sixteen, he became a reporter before going on to do his national service. He won worldwide acclaim with his bestselling novel *The Virgin Soldiers*, which has achieved international sales of over two million copies. His most recent novel, *Waiting for the Day*, is published in paperback to coincide with the sixtieth anniversary of the D-Day landings.

Praise for *The Magic Army*
'It's bawdy, funny, sad and sometimes sorry and it brought those times vividly back.'
Daily Mail

Praise for *Waiting for the Day*
'Thomas's characters are finely crafted, with dialogue that never misses a beat . . . It is as vivid a portrait of those crucial months as one is ever likely to read.'
Daily Telegraph

'Warm characters, immaculate period detail and dialogue that neatly evokes the wartime sense of humour as part of a story that packs a surprising emotional punch.'
Daily Mail

'Thomas is an accomplished storyteller . . . D-Day may have been nearly sixty years ago but in this lively reprise, it feels like yesterday.'
Sunday Telegraph

THE MAGIC ARMY

Leslie Thomas

arrow books

Published by Arrow Books in 2004

1 3 5 7 9 10 8 6 4 2

Copyright © Leslie Thomas 1981

Leslie Thomas has asserted his right under the Copyright, Designs and
Patents Act 1988 to be identified as the author of this work

First published in the United Kingdom in 1981 by Eyre Methuen

Published by Penguin Books in 1982

Arrow Books
The Random House Group Limited
20 Vauxhall Bridge Road, London, SW1V 2SA

Random House Australia (Pty) Limited
20 Alfred Street, Milsons Point, Sydney,
New South Wales 2061, Australia

Random House New Zealand Limited
18 Poland Road, Glenfield
Auckland 10, New Zealand

Random House (Pty) Limited
Endulini, 5a Jubilee Road, Parktown 2193, South Africa

The Random House Group Limited Reg. No. 954009

www.randomhouse.co.uk

A CIP catalogue record for this book is available from the British Library

Papers used by Random House are natural, recyclable products
made from wood grown in sustainable forests. The manufacturing
processes conform to the environmental regulations of the country of origin

ISBN 0 099 46917 0

Typeset by SX Composing DTP, Rayleigh, Essex
Printed and bound in Great Britain by
Bookmarque Ltd, Croydon, Surrey

To Zoo with love

O what is that sound which so thrills the ear
Down in the valley drumming, drumming?
Only the scarlet soldiers, dear,
The soldiers coming.

'O What is that Sound?'
W. H. Auden

THIS MEMORIAL
WAS PRESENTED BY THE UNITED STATES
ARMY AUTHORITIES TO THE PEOPLE OF
THE SOUTH HAMS WHO GENEROUSLY LEFT THEIR
HOMES AND THEIR LANDS TO PROVIDE A
BATTLE PRACTICE AREA FOR THE SUCCESSFUL
ASSAULT ON NORMANDY IN JUNE 1944.
THEIR ACTION RESULTED IN THE SAVING OF
MANY HUNDREDS OF LIVES AND CONTRIBUTED IN
NO SMALL MEASURE TO THE SUCCESS OF THE
OPERATION. THE AREA INCLUDED THE VILLAGES
OF BLACKAWTON, CHILLINGTON, EAST ALLINGTON,
SLAPTON, STOKENHAM, STRETE AND
TORCROSS TOGETHER WITH MANY OUTLYING
FARMS AND HOUSES.
Plinth on Slapton Sands, Devon

Even today there are signs to be seen of what happened in those months of winter, spring and early summer. The ribs of a ludicrously sunk landing craft lie off-shore; the outlines still show of a house, a farm, the beach hotel, destroyed and never rebuilt. A bullet is wedged forever in the church clock; men and women have odd American names; a few memories; a few graves.

It began on the final, dark afternoon of the year 1943. They came ashore at Avonmouth Docks on the Bristol Channel, and were moved at once down the West Country through the anonymous wartime night of England. There were no signposts and the conducting officer, an American captain, who had been doing the job for three weeks, got them lost. The convoy halted wearily and Schorner, in the second vehicle, a heavy staff car, waited for the captain to come back. He put the window down and the drizzle blew in. He wound it up again until he saw the man making his way back from his jeep at the front.

'Sorry, sir,' said the conducting officer. 'I guess we've gotten off course. This country . . . it seems like the British keep moving it around. Nothing's ever the same twice.'

'It *is* the right country?' suggested Schorner. 'I

mean, we *didn't* get off the ship in the wrong place?'
There were one hundred and eight men in the short
convoy behind him. They had come straight from the
troopship after a miserable, confined and stormy
voyage. He wanted to get them into camp.

'Well, it sure ain't Florida,' said the captain half to
himself in case the colonel was one who couldn't take
a joke. He nodded ahead. 'I think we'll just go as we
are, sir,' he said. 'According to my compass in the jeep
we're driving due south, so we're going in the right
direction.' He crouched and went forward through
the rain like an infantryman under fire.

'Jesus Christ,' muttered Schorner to his driver. 'His
compass. Did you hear that? His compass. I didn't
think this country was big enough to need a goddamn
compass.'

'No, sir,' replied the driver. Schorner could see his
big, young nose silhouetted in the dimness. His name
was Albie Primrose. They sat in silence until the jeep
in front began to stutter forward. The rain thickened.
'I sure wish I was going home,' said Albie.

'So do I, son,' agreed Schorner. 'So do I.'

'The quicker we get it over, the better,' ventured
Albie. He had been Schorner's driver ever since he
had joined the unit from Camp Abbott, Oregon, the
Army Engineers Training Centre, eight months
before. 'The invasion,' he added, as though the commanding officer might think he meant something else.

Schorner nodded. 'I'm with you there too, Albie,'
he said. 'Just so long as it's not tonight.'

The car jerked forward along the tight Devon road.
Albie said: 'No sir, I don't think I could handle it
tonight.'

*

At five past eleven o'clock that night Private Peter Gilman stood at the end of the jetty at Wilcoombe and gazed morosely from his greatcoat which was turned up like a wall about his neck. A New Year wind was pushing ragged clouds across the Channel and there was a timid and desultory moon. The jetty, old and wooden, had not been repaired since the declaration of war; as he stamped his army boots he was certain he felt it tremble beneath them. Dull waves, without crests, lumbered in from the open sea.

The anti-aircraft gun, which he was guarding, was positioned opposite his post, on the stone dock across the enclosed water of the small port. He was protecting it from the seaward side. In case the Germans came across and stole it, he thought caustically. The sentry on the shore side stood by a white picket gate, like that of a cottage garden, and shuffled off every five minutes to warm himself in the cosy guardhouse. The gun had been established there since nineteen-forty-one and had not been fired in anger for twenty-one months. The soldiers had settled into a life of not uncomfortable domesticity. In summer there were geraniums around the gate.

For several minutes the cloudy moon broke into free sky and shone briskly along the Devon coast. Start Bay was patched with silver and Gilman, turning half a circle, could see the strong shoulder of Start Point. Almost below his feet, small craft creaked in the comfort of the harbour. Someone opened the door of the pub half a mile away and he could hear the singing.

His relief was not due until midnight, but, to his

3

surprise and pleasure, Catermole appeared, a thick clumsy figure stumping along the jetty, dragging his rifle and small pack behind him, the rifle butt bumping on the woodwork, the pack pulled like a reluctant dog.

'I reckoned one of us might as well have a New Year drink,' he said to Gilman. 'If you slope off now you'll get there in good time.'

Gilman grinned: 'Thanks, Pussy,' he said. 'What's Bryant doing?'

'Don't worry about Bryant,' sniffed Catermole. 'He's writing letters to his missus, like he's always doing. He's been down the phone box three times to wish her a Happy New Year.'

'Three times?'

Catermole shrugged. 'She ain't at home. Once his little kid answered. He told me. He had to tell somebody, I s'pose. Poor bugger gets in a right state. She's probably out with some hairy-balled Yank. If you piss off sharp now, he won't even notice.'

Gilman patted Catermole's arm gratefully. 'I'll bring you back something,' he promised.

'That big landgirl,' suggested Catermole wistfully. He pulled his solid greatcoat collar up the sides of his head and hung his rifle clumsily across his shoulder. Gilman's boots resounded on the wooden jetty and then on the stone. Catermole snorted at the cold air. He spat experimentally at the sea and the stiff wind caught the gob and blew it unerringly back on to his nose. Philosophically he wiped it off with his rough sleeve.

He took a swig of scotch from a flask concealed in his left ammunition pouch. Then a second. Then crossing his arms over his chest, tonelessly, softly, and

4

only just catching the tune, he began to sing into the Channel wind:

'Should auld acquaintance be forgot,
And never brought to mind . . .'

At ten minutes past eleven Howard Evans, the doctor from Wilcoombe, was driving through dark and remote lanes making for Mortown Farm where Mary Lidstone was delivering her sixth child. Although he had answered the call without delay, he guessed he would be too late. Mary had a habit of doing things herself.

The sides of the lanes were steep-banked and topped with thickly knotted hedgerows, so that driving through them was like going along a trench. Where there was a break for a gate or the junction of another lane, the moonlight rolled through, golden across the narrow road. He turned on to the track that led to Mortown Farm and was at once confronted by the small herd of Lidstone cows. It was as though they had come down the track to meet him. The headlights of his car were filtered through blackout slits but the moon was sufficient. He stopped. The cows advanced and stared blankly and yet with curiosity through the windows of the car.

'Bugger off,' shouted Evans in his Welsh voice. 'Go on, clear off, you dozy dolts. Move your arses.' He tooted and revved the engine, but the animals continued to study him with the same benignity. 'Right, sod it,' he swore. 'I'll run you down.'

Since the car was old and miniature, a 1936 Austin Seven saloon, and the cows were mature South

5

Devons, big flanked and great-faced, grown on the thick pastures of that lush region, it was an unreal threat. He revved the hesitant engine again and pushed carefully forward. The cows, like a crowd of bland countrywomen, moved aside with clumsy reluctance and with eloquent hurt in their eyes. Some commenced to moo and soon, as he inched his way through, the others joined the protest. Geese, up at the farm, being disturbed from their pond, began to sound off. Evans got clear of the cows and drove up the rutted track. It had been a dry winter for Devon and the red ground was firm. He stopped in front of the farmhouse, edgings of light showing around its blackout curtains, and, as he left the car, was at once surrounded by the threatening geese. Prudently he decided not to run for it. He sidled back into the car, closed the door and sounded the horn. A boy of about five, in a nightshirt, came to the door and herded the geese away. Evans got out and smiled at him. 'You're Edward, that's right isn't it?'

'Georgie,' corrected the boy shyly. 'Edward's littler than oi be.' He moved towards the door. 'I got another brother now,' he said without excitement. 'He just come out.'

'Too late again,' muttered Evans. He went in. The Lidstone grandmother was sitting in front of the fire holding a cup of tea with both hands as though she thought it might be taken from her. 'She be upstairs, doctor,' she said unnecessarily. ' 'Tis another boy, for God's sake. Another one. B'ain't never a maid in this house.'

'Everything all right?' he asked automatically as he went towards the ancient staircase in the corner. It

6

was blackened and curled like a lock of hair.

'Same as usual,' nodded the grandmother, gazing into the tea. 'She don't have any bothering.' She swirled the cup as if it might hold secrets. ''Tis no world for little children,' she muttered dolefully.

He was not a tall man but he had to bend to negotiate the staircase. It opened out immediately into a bedroom, low, warm and dim as a burrow, lit by two paraffin lamps. Mary Lidstone was sitting cheerfully in the fat bed, her new baby in a wooden box cradle jammed between the mattress and the wall. She smiled at his obvious anxiety.

'Beat me to it again, Mary,' he sighed. 'How was it?'

''Tis easy,' she smiled. She was a broad, pleasant woman; she wore the white nightgown she always donned immediately after her births. 'Just like having my dinner, doctor. 'Twas right after I got Gran to bang the old saucepan with a poker.'

He understood. There was no telephone at the farm and it would have been arranged for the grandmother to go out and strike a heavy saucepan with a poker so that the Steers, the next family down the short valley, could send their son to the telephone box in the near village. Evans examined the baby, which awoke briefly to examine him, and then sat on the bed and held the woman's hand. 'Another son,' he smiled. 'What's Ernie going to say?'

'I don't think 'ee'll be able to say nothing,' she said practically. 'By the time they let him 'ome, this 'un will be as grown as the others.'

'I don't think so,' Evans told her kindly. He was forty and had volunteered for the services, but, ironically, had been considered unfit. 'It will all be over, finished, this year . . . you see.'

A pout of sadness puffed her face. ' 'Tis hard for me to think how far away my Ernie is,' she said simply. 'I look at the map in the *Daily Herald*, when they 'as of Burma and those parts, but 'tis hard for me to think of Ernie being there.' She looked strangely ashamed. 'There's me, I never been out of Devon, you know. Never further than Exeter in all my life. Nor had Ernie afore they sent 'im to Burma, except for the army training and that. I can't think 'ow far Burma is.'

'It seems a long way from here,' Evans agreed. 'This coming year . . . it'll be over. You see, Mary.'

'I was trying to 'ang on until the New Year, with the baby,' she went on. 'Now he's a year older than he might have been.'

Evans nodded at the odd logic. 'What are you going to call him?'

'I 'ave a fancy for Winston,' she said, folding her arms across her large rural bosom. 'But I know Ernie won't 'ave any of that. He's got no time for Churchill, not since he shot at the Welsh miners.' She glanced at him. 'You're Welsh,' she said.

'Yes, but I wasn't there at the time,' he replied shaking his head. 'I'm not all that sure it really happened. I think it's just a story.'

'You try and tell that to Ernie,' she answered stoutly. 'No, he won't have Winston, for sure. I'd like to have some name like that, though, you know, like one of the leaders. It'll show when 'ee was born.'

'Why not Stalin?' joked Evans, patting her puffy hand. 'That would be original in Devon.'

'Now there's one I don't like, myself,' she sniffed seriously. 'Never did care for those whiskers, you know. Old Daffy at Telcoombe Beach, he's got whiskers like that.' Evans tried to think of Stalin and Daffy together. Mary went on: 'And we've got to get Harold in somewhere, that being Ernie's late father's name, before he passed on. It's got to be 'is second name. Stalin Harold Lidstone don't sound right. No. I like the American one better.'

'Eisenhower?' he asked aghast. 'Dwight Eisenhower?'

'No, not 'im. He's got a funny mouth. The other one . . . Roosevelt. I like Roosevelt. I'll give it a bit of a think. I might even get a letter to Ernie and one back afore we have to make up our minds. Don't need to 'ave him christened till spring.'

Evans remained talking to her for another fifteen minutes. She was tired, and sinking down into the bed, and he settled her on her pillows. 'I'll be going,' he said. His shadow arched across the room. 'I'll be by to see you tomorrow. Any trouble before then, get Gran to bang the saucepan, or send one of the boys over to the Steers. I'll come out right away.'

She smiled mildly and thanked him. 'Get Gran to give you a cup of tea,' she said. 'I forgot, sorry.'

'No, I won't wait. I might get home for a New Year drink.'

'That's right, I be forgetting. Happy New Year, doctor.'

'And to you, Mary,' he smiled. 'And to all of us. Ernie will be back soon, you watch.'

'I do hope,' said Mary. 'There's 'im wanting a maid and 'tis another boy.'

'There's never a choice,' he said. 'I'll be going. If I can get past your geese and cows. The Germans

9

would never have got this far, not through that lot.'

'They never even tried, did they,' she said. 'Goodnight, doctor.'

''Night Mary. Have a good sleep. The boy's fine.'

He went out and down the stairs. The grandmother was asleep, sitting up before the fire. The five-year-old boy, Georgie, was asleep on the hearthrug. He wondered where the others were. Quietly he went out.

The geese began to sound, but he got in the car and started the little engine before they advanced. The car bumped in the moonlight across the rutted field track. Evans began to laugh to himself.

'Roosevelt Harold Lidstone,' he said shaking his head and smiling. 'Jesus Christ.'

Gilman left the gun-site carefully, but once he was away from the close area of the harbour he thought it was safe enough to walk openly up the hill towards the Bull and Mouth. He was conscious of the regular echoes of his boots striking from the pavement but not overconcerned. Hardly had he begun the steady ascent, however, when he heard a voice, unmistakably the officer's voice of Bryant, behind him, calling out something from the direction of the gate guardhouse. For a moment he thought he had been spotted. In the best tradition of the basic training manual for street fighting, unused until now, he froze and then dropped quietly into the darkness of a doorway. Tight against the brickwork he heard Bryant's voice again, but realized, with relief, that it was not shouting after him. He was calling to the corporal in the guardhouse. He was going to post his letter. He would be back quickly.

The post box, Gilman knew, was further up the hill on the same side as his place of concealment. With new concern he realized if he stayed where he was Bryant must see him. On the other hand he could hear the officer's steps coming up the cobbles of the street, along the flat part just before it rose to become a hill, and if he broke cover now he was just as likely to be spotted. Almost touching his nose on the woodwork of the door frame was a white-buttoned bell. Quickly he pressed it and heard it ring inside the terrace house.

Nothing happened. The regulated footfalls came rising towards him. He swore through his teeth. Desperately he pressed the bell again. This time the door opened at once. There was no time to explain. He stepped back into the tight hall. 'Sorry,' he said. 'Emergency.'

'Official emergency,' said the woman who had opened the door. 'Or one of your own?' She sounded unexcited by the intrusion. The hall was still in darkness. Gilman only had the impression of an enclosed space and of her standing near. She pushed the door closed and turned on the passage light. He saw that she was neat, dark-haired, about thirty, her face clean of make-up, lines below her eyes but the eyes unruffled. She had been in bed and was wearing an army greatcoat as a dressing gown.

'My own emergency,' he admitted. 'Sorry about this. There's an officer just come up the road and I'm supposed to be on guard at the gun. I was sloping off for a drink.' He added lamely, 'It's New Year.'

'So it is,' she said calmly. 'Happy New Year.'

'Happy New Year,' said Gilman. The awkwardness

of the situation overcame him. He said, trying to smile, 'It's a bit inconvenient.'

'That's all right,' she replied. She turned and started to walk back along the short passage. 'Come on in a minute,' she said. 'I'd give you a New Year drink if I had anything, but I haven't. I don't generally have anything in the house.'

Relieved, Gilman followed her down the close corridor. She opened a room door and switched on the light. It was warm in there although only a few red veins showed in the fire-grate. She went over and gave the dying coal an offhand stir with the poker.

'It's very good of you,' said Gilman. 'That could have been a bit nasty. Bryant – our lieutenant – was coming right past the door. He's not bad but he could be difficult.' He hesitated, then added: 'You wouldn't like to come and have a drink would you? In the pub.'

She shook her head and laughed without emphasis. She looked more weary than tired, her face was attractive but with a hardness about the mouth and eyes. 'Can't, I'm afraid,' she said. 'I've got a kid upstairs and she's poorly.' She laughed again. 'I could offer you a drink of cough mixture, if you like.'

Gilman grinned at her uncertainly. 'No thanks. Had enough of that when I was a kid. My mother was a great believer in the muck.'

'We get through gallons of it,' she said.

There was a brief silence. They continued standing. 'Do you just . . . have a little girl?' he asked.

'No, I've got another. A boy. He's sick as well. I'm bloody trapped.'

'That's rough,' said Gilman, 'New Year's Eve and all.' He glanced at the clock.

She said: 'Listen, you go on. Don't miss anything. That's if your spoilsport officer has gone now.'

'I expect he has,' said Gilman. 'He was only posting a letter. He's always writing to his wife.'

'He must be the only one,' she said strangely.

They had walked into the passage and she opened the door and looked out into the street. 'Not a soul,' she said. She opened the door wider.

Gilman hesitated. 'Look,' he said, 'I feel terrible . . . sort of just leaving you here. You've been very good. Can I . . . well, if I go up to the pub . . . could I bring you something back? You ought to have a New Year drink, oughtn't you?'

'Yes I ought,' she said at once. 'All right. I'll wait for you.'

He made to go out. 'I won't be long,' he promised. 'I'll come straight back.'

'Don't bother,' she answered practically. 'Have a drink up there first. I'll wait. I spend half my life waiting.'

He went out into the street. He said, 'Do you drink scotch?'

'Anything,' she said, grinning.

He was about to step away, but he stopped again. 'I don't know your name,' he said. 'It's all been a bit . . . well, unexpected.'

'Unofficial,' she agreed. 'My name's Mary. Mary Nicholas.'

'I'm Peter Gilman,' he said. They shook hands and she laughed. 'Funny business, isn't it,' she said.

'Right. It's the war.' He started up the hill. 'I won't be long, Mary,' he said. 'Be right back.'

'All right,' she said. 'John.'

'Peter,' he called back.

Her giggle came up the dark hill. 'Sorry. Peter.'

Wilcoombe had a single straight street canting steeply down to the rounded harbour like a leg terminating in a broad boot. At twenty-five minutes to midnight it was wet and vacant, the mild moon reflected in a fitful sheen on the pavements and making the cobbles of the road look like loaves. No lights showed from the houses. Within them, the other side of the blackout curtains, people bent to listen to the coming of the New Year on their wireless sets, waiting with a curious anxiety, counting the minutes away, as though its arrival were far from a certainty.

Such noises and excitements as there were that night in that Devon village were contained behind the bulky door and shuttered windows of the Bull and Mouth. Occasionally the door rattled open and some-body pulled the thick curtain aside, permitting the sounds to escape into the street. The inn sign, a demure sailing vessel entering a harbour, creaked in the dark breeze outside.

Tom Barrington left the bar as secretly as he could, easing and manoeuvring his way towards the door while they were all singing. He loitered by the blanketing curtain. Doey Bidgood, a ruby-faced farm labourer, was standing staunchly on a table, tankard held up like a prize he had won, performing, with actions, a South Devon song of a milkmaid and a licentious landlord. They had all heard it many times and they anticipated every verse, every chorus, every innuendo, with widening smiles splitting into

14

rollicking laughs.

> 'That b'ain't the milking stool,
> That be somethin' else!'

They were enjoying themselves as only true familiars can. Arms about shoulders, men and women rolling left and right, standing, sitting, their rural faces glowing. The people of Wilcoombe and the villages about it had known each other for generations. Barrington put down his glass and slid behind the curtain. He could smell its roughness. He opened the door as swiftly and quietly as he could and went out into the wet and empty night.

Just above his head the inn sign swung gruffly. It was as if his appearance had roused it. He glanced at it and looked out over the wide pan of Start Bay, scaly with moonlight, spread from the edge of the land to the dark horizon. Everywhere else was folded in blackness; the shoreline, the village at his feet crammed on its single hill, the other hamlets and the deep coombes, the rift valleys between the coastal hills. All around him lay ancient and settled farmland, worked by families who had occupied the same fields for centuries. He paused on the incline and shook his head. 'Hell,' he said bitterly. 'Bloody hell.'

He continued his descent down the vacant street. When he had almost reached the harbour, when he could smell clearly the sharp edge of the sea, he saw a man walking up the hill, an army officer, coming from the direction of the anti-aircraft post that had long been a fixture and become a joke in Wilcoombe. He was going towards the post box halfway up the incline.

The moon had again freed itself from the chaffing clouds and gained sufficient space in the sky to light the street. The officer put the letter in the post box. He and Barrington nodded to each other. Barrington said: 'First letter home of nineteen-forty-four.'

'Yes, that's right,' said the young man. 'Happy New Year, Mr Barrington.'

'Yes, and to you,' said Barrington. 'You're Lieutenant . . .'

'Bryant,' said Bryant.

'Yes, you played cricket against the village.'

'That's right,' agreed Bryant. 'It seems a long way from the cricket season now. It seems a long way from anything, come to think of it. Let's hope and pray it'll all be over this year. I'd like to get home.'

Barrington said wryly, 'Praying doesn't seem to do much. I think even the vicar's given it up.'

'Maybe God's got a mean streak,' said Bryant suddenly.

Barrington glanced at him and nodded. 'Perhaps He has,' he said.

They had reached the entrance to the gun-site. They wished each other a happy New Year once more and Bryant went into the guardroom. Barrington saw the sentry lurking like a suspect in the doorway. He walked along the wharf until he reached a wooden gate leading out on to the cobbles. Behind it was a pale cottage, its windows faintly outlined with seams of light where the blackout curtains failed to fit. He gave the gate a push and went in. The low front door of the cottage opened immediately he knocked.

'Happy New Year, Beatrice,' he said. He saw Beatrice Evans smile from the dimness of the hall. He stepped in. 'Your blackout curtains still don't fit,' he mentioned.

She laughed quietly. 'You *would* notice. I'm just hoping they'll last out the war.'

'Remember when they used to tell us that a cigarette could be seen by a German bomber at thirty thousand feet or something? Remember that rubbish?' He gave a snort. They had gone into the comfortable sitting-room. A fire was bunched in the grate, almost ready to go out.

'Howard's gone on a call,' said Beatrice. Without asking she poured him a sherry from the bottle on the sideboard. She replenished her own glass. 'Mary Lidstone. She won't cause him much trouble though. He'll be back in time for the New Year.'

They sat down each side of the fire. Barrington, the big awkward farmer, almost filled the armchair. The woman was slight and pale. Like her husband, she was from Wales. He said again, 'Yes, remember the cigarette end that could be seen from the German bomber? And the pots and pans and church railings that we gave to make Spitfires?' He laughed caustically. 'I bet our graveyard railings never flew anywhere.'

Beatrice glanced at him. 'You're a bit downhearted for the New Year,' she said. 'This ought to be the year the whole business ends. So they say.'

'At the beginning of the war they said it would all be over by Christmas,' he recalled. 'But they didn't say which Christmas.'

She glanced at him uneasily. 'We thought you'd be in the pub,' she said. 'We intended to come up there as soon as Howard got back. It's always a laugh, with Doey and that crowd.'

Barrington nodded. 'Doey was performing when I left. The old milkmaid song. They were all swaying about and singing. It's funny, they all know it by heart and yet it always comes fresh.'

Beatrice said: 'Something's gone wrong, hasn't it?'

'Yes,' he replied. 'I'll tell you when Howard gets back.'

She rose. 'If it's that serious perhaps we ought to have another sherry. Sorry that's all we've got. It's the good stuff we keep for weddings and Christmas and funerals. And the end of wars.'

As she poured the sherry she heard her husband's little car coming down the hill through the town. 'Here's Howard,' she said. She felt vaguely relieved. Taking a third glass she poured the last of the sherry into it. The mantelshelf clock showed twenty to twelve. 'The bottle just lasted the year,' she mentioned. 'We've got another for the rest of the war, and the last one to celebrate victory. We had a whole case in nineteen-thirty-nine.'

They heard the Austin squeak to a halt outside and Beatrice went to the door. 'Another boy,' Howard called through the wind. 'Six now.' He walked the few paces and kissed her on the cheek. 'A few hard bangs on the old saucepan to warn the Steers, up I go and hey presto! There's another Lidstone. It must be the noise that attracts them.'

She laughed merrily. 'Tom's here,' she said.

'Good. Are we going to the boozer? It's nearly midnight.'

'I don't know. I think he wants to talk about something.'

Howard glanced at her and she shrugged. He went

into the sitting-room. 'Happy New Year, Tom,' he said shaking hands with the farmer.

'Mary Lidstone was it?' said Barrington.

'That's it. Strong as an outside privy that one. I've never got there on time yet. By the time I arrive the baby's washed and dressed and sleeping it off. She's wonderful. She's thinking of calling this one Roosevelt.'

Beatrice grinned and Barrington muttered: 'Christ.'

'Harold as well,' said Howard. 'It's got to have Harold in it. Roosevelt Harold Lidstone.'

'I think that's very nice,' said Beatrice genuinely. She handed the sherry to her husband. 'It shows she cares.'

'Roosevelt,' repeated Barrington. He added: 'That's appropriate. There'll be a few more of them around before too long.'

'You wanted to tell us something,' said Howard. He pulled a third armchair towards the fire, stretched his legs and stirred the dying coals with his foot.

Barrington looked at the clock. 'I'm not supposed to divulge this until nineteen-forty-four,' he said. 'And then only to selected people, such as yourself. I'm telling you early.'

'God, it sounds serious,' said Howard.

'It is. We're going to be occupied.'

Beatrice and her husband exchanged glances.

'By the Americans,' continued Barrington.

'Jesus, I thought you were going to say the Germans,' said Howard with a puzzled grin. 'There are plenty of Yanks around already. All over the country.'

Barrington said grimly: 'This is different. They are

going to take over this entire area . . .' He paused. 'Everybody's got to be moved out, thrown out. Everybody. Thirty thousand acres, including my farm, from the sea to the Totnes road. Three thousand people. They're going to use it as a training area for their bloody invasion. They're using live ammunition. The place will be destroyed.'

Howard put his glass on the table. It tipped and he failed to catch it. The sherry ran in a pale stream towards the edge. 'Sorry,' he said to Beatrice. She rose and got a cloth from the kitchen. When she had wiped it up, Howard said: 'Here too? Wilcoombe?'

'No. Wilcoombe's all right. It's right on the edge of the area, just outside. There are six villages, Burton, Sellow, Normancroft, Telcoombe Magna and Telcoombe Beach, and Mortown. Farms, cottages, churches, the lot. The clergy were told by the bishop last week. I was told at the same time, because I'm chairman of the council. It was decided to keep it quiet until after Christmas and New Year. They're all going to be told tomorrow.'

'Mortown,' said Howard quietly. 'What will Mary Lidstone do?'

'Same as everybody else,' said Barrington. 'She'll have to clear out. Kids, cattle and everything. Lock, stock and bloody barrel. Crops, animals, old people, sick people. Then they'll start blasting the place to smithereens.'

Beatrice found herself stuttering. 'W . . . w . . . why here?'

'Because they say "here",' said Barrington. 'Some of the richest farming land in the country. What the Germans never did, the Yanks are going to do.'

20

'When?' asked Howard Evans.

'January twenty-first,' Barrington said bitterly. 'We've got three weeks to clear out.'

The inn sign of the Bull and Mouth, with its picture of a vessel entering harbour, was suspended like a stiff flag. A sailor from those parts – some said he became the first landlord – used to trade along the Channel coast as far east as the Dover Strait and he had given the inn its name. It was a corruption of the Boulogne Mouth; the entry to the port of Boulogne.

It had seen three centuries of New Year's Eves. Over the generations they had varied only a little; faces growing, changing, seasons passing, wars occurring, songs to be sung.

Gilman was near the curtain at the door. The area between him and the bar was a wall of broad backs and drinking heads. A quaintly high voice called from one of the window seats sunk into the wide bays. 'Over here, boy, come and sit down.' A full tankard of beer, one of a formation set on the table like large chessmen, was pushed in his direction.

'Thanks,' he said. 'That's very kind of you.' There were six or seven people on the window seat, crushed together, almost needing to drink in turns, but, because he was a soldier, they cheerfully moved even closer to accommodate him.

The thin arm that had propelled the beer in his direction belonged to Horace Smith, a poacher of the coombes. He had the face of his kind, worn and pointed, the lid of his left eye permanently drooped as though in readiness for a shot. Gilman recognized him for he sometimes brought game and an occasional unofficial salmon to be disposed of in the bar. Minnie, his wide, red wife sat next to him, and it was against the warm bolster of her thigh that Gilman found himself established. 'Hungry?' she shouted in his ear. 'Oi reckon you are.' She urgently explored a brown paper carrier bag held in her lap. 'There,' she said swelling with kindness. ''Ave a swan sandwich.'

She produced two portions of bread as thick as her hands and only a little cleaner. Between the slices, like mortar, was a wedge of dark meat. ''Tis all right, boy,' she said, nudging him with her powerful arm. ''Tis swan, tru 'tis.'

'Never had a swan sandwich,' admitted Gilman, hesitantly taking the offering. It filled his fist.

'I don' expect you have, my darlin',' she replied expansively. 'There's not many as 'ave.' She dropped her chin towards her small, riven husband. 'Him,' she said, but without disparagement. 'Been terrible drunk since Christmas. Shot it by mistake.'

Her potato face closed in on Gilman. Hurriedly he took a bite. The strong, strange meat and the doughy bread filled his mouth like mud. It left him no room to speak. Minnie, seeing the blockage, said it for him: 'A bit oily, but not too bad.' Horace leaned around her furtively and saw Gilman's situation. His eye drooped further as though admitting someone to a conspiracy. ''Ow it be, then?'

His wife barged him powerfully. 'There's no eating swan and talkin',' she admonished. 'You know that. Jesus, it took oi twenty minutes afore oi could say a bluddy word.'

She bellowed cheerfully and slapped Gilman on the

back. He wanted to drink but his mouth was still clamped over the sandwich. Eventually he managed to clear sufficient room to drink and then to speak. 'Never had a swan sandwich before,' he repeated ruefully. 'It's strong . . .' He glanced at the waiting Minnie and the fragile, eager Horace who still peered around his large wife. It looked as though she were carrying him under her arm. '. . . But tasty, very tasty.'

'Nearly time, 'tis,' announced Minnie suddenly. She half stood up, her huge lap pushing against the table. 'Near midnight. Oi reckon that sleepy bugger Willum is going to forget.' She bawled across the room. 'Midnight Willum! You'm missing the year!'

''Nother five minutes,' the landlord shouted back heftily. 'Nobody'll be missing it, Minnie. You just keep your Horace to order.'

The simple return provoked a great roar of approval and laughter through the bar. Gilman sat and watched. The low ceiling, dark as a storm sky from generations of smoke, the smell of beer, the tang of cider, the cheerful glasses and bottles behind the heavy wooden bar, the rough faces, the country voices.

'Ah,' breathed Minnie at his ribs. As she breathed he felt the force of her lungs. 'Now that Doey and that Lenny Birch, they be gone outside. I knows what they're at. I knows . . .' She abruptly expanded with laughter, crushing Gilman against the window. 'Look! The buggers! Oh . . . the buggers!'

The whole company heaved with mirth, holding on to each other, spilling their drinks, the landlord's protesting voice above the uproar. Gilman endeavoured to stretch to his feet. Two men, one pulling, one pushing, were manoeuvring a donkey into the bar. Patient but adamant, the beast was allowing them to push him an inch at a time. 'I do reckon he be enjoying it!' exclaimed Minnie. 'Go on, shove 'un, Lenny, shove 'un!'

When the donkey was entirely in the room, at a stance in the middle of an area briskly cleared on the flagstones, it looked about with deep unfrightened eyes. Then it laid its ears back and emitted a momentous and trembling bray before lashing back with its hind hooves. Lenny Birch moved swiftly but not enough. The right shoe caught him a blow on the thigh and he fell back howling into the hilarious crowd. The donkey returned to sedateness, looking straight ahead. Minnie gripped a slab of bread from Gilman's swan sandwich and passed it through the customers until it was offered to the donkey which munched it without expression. The door curtain rattled on its wooden rings and into the room came Tom Barrington and Howard and Beatrice Evans.

They stood laughing at the scene. Tom went to the bar and ordered two pints and a sherry. Gilman also moved forward and bought a half bottle of scotch from across the counter. Barrington said, raising his eyebrows a trifle: 'Expensive now, scotch.'

Gilman said awkwardly: 'It's for someone who can't get out.'

'Have one with me?' asked Barrington.

'Thanks. I haven't bought one myself yet.'

'Doesn't matter. You're in uniform. What is it?'

'A pint. Thank you.'

The farmer said, 'You from the gun-site? Don't answer, I might be a German spy.'

Gilman shrugged. 'It's easy to guess. We're the only soldiers in Wilcoombe,' he said.

'At the moment,' said Barrington.

Howard Evans, behind him, called to the landlord. 'Nearly time, Willum.' He took his beer from Barrington and raised it. 'Happy New Year everybody.' He glanced at his wife and she smiled seriously and kissed him on the face.

It was time. Willum had turned up the volume of the big brown-faced radio behind the bar. Like the echoes of the sea, Big Ben sounded from London. It was nineteen-forty-four.

Warmth and fellowship engulfed everyone. They joined arms across their chests and country stomachs and began to sing, loudly, raggedly, the old heart-felt chorus of 'Auld Lang Syne'. In that confined room there hardly seemed space for so much sound. There was scarcely leeway for definite movement and they had to jog by inches one way then the other, their arms going up and down like those of sailors desperately at the pumps.

Gilman found himself with Minnie Smith on one side, his hand crushed in her large, hard paw, and with the delicate fingers of Beatrice Evans holding his on the other. He smiled apologetically and made room so that Tom Barrington could take his place, so that she was flanked by her husband and their friend. Now he found himself dancing between Minnie and her poacher husband. Across the room the heads rose and fell with the voices. Doey and Lenny were standing on the bar bending under the low ceiling as they sang, and somewhere in the middle of it all was the donkey.

At the very climax of the final chorus Tom

Barrington looked around and saw a small, bespectacled American officer standing at the door. He leaned across Beatrice to Howard Evans and said quietly: 'They're here.'

Evans, hot-faced, still holding hands, turned to see the anti-climax of the apologetic man in the smooth olive uniform standing gazing nonplussed into the room. His spectacles made his stare all the more innocuous. For some reason he took his cap off. The singing had finally dragged to a stop and people were kissing each other. Howard kissed his wife again and then Barrington kissed her before quickly turning back towards the American. Gilman was released from the sturdy hug of Minnie Smith and he too saw the stranger. Others, as laughingly they released their friends and loved ones, quietened and turned towards the man. Doey Bidgood and Lenny Birch had hoisted two robust landgirls on to the bar and were the last to relax their rural embraces. When they finally did, they turned too and faced the green man with surprised silence.

'Excuse me,' he began. The accent was from Georgia but they would not have known. 'Excuse me, but I guess we're lost.'

Howard and many of the others glanced towards Tom Barrington. He moved a pace forward. 'Where did you want to go?' he asked stiffly. Gilman was surprised at the attitude and tone of the man who had a few minutes before bought him a drink because he was in uniform.

'Well,' said the American with an embarrassed smile. He unfolded a tiny sheet of paper. 'Telcoombe Magna.' He said it 'Telcoomby May-gna' and looked

26

up, hoping he had pronounced it right. 'Burrell's Farm Camp. It's a former Royal Air Force camp, I think.' He shrugged lamely. 'I'm supposed to be conducting officer.'

'What might you be conducting?' asked Barrington. 'Or is it a rude question?' The people by the window of the inn had pulled the blackout curtains aside and were peering out. 'There's those jeeps outside,' Horace Smith called to the people behind him.

'It's just a small unit of the US Army,' replied the American defensively. 'Is it possible, sir, that you could give me the directions?'

The people in the bar were looking at Barrington with as much curiosity as that with which they regarded the American. His tone was still sharp, official. 'Yes, there's no harm in that, I suppose,' he said. 'We've always had instructions here not to give directions to strangers. That was on account of the invasion threat, you understand. That's why there are no signposts.'

'I've already figured that out,' said the officer. He remained smiling politely but was not backing away from Barrington's manner. 'That's why we got lost.'

Instead of an answer Barrington turned towards the bar. 'Would you like a drink?' he called almost over his shoulder. 'It's New Year you know, yours as well.'

'Yes, I realize. I'd really like the directions.'

Beatrice Evans stepped forward, smiling. 'You continue down the hill towards the sea,' she said kindly. 'On the front you turn left and drive for about a mile along the side of the beach. It's a straight road. You'll come to some cottages and a hotel. That's Telcoombe Beach. Turn left there, going inland, and that road takes you to Telcoombe Magna. It's another half a mile up a hill. The camp at Burrell's Farm is just through the village. You'll see the nissen huts just past the church. Is that all right?'

'Thank you, ma'am,' said the American. 'That's all I need to know.' He gave a little bow in her direction and, putting on his flat cap, went out.

He went to the staff car. Albie Primrose lowered the window. Colonel Schorner looked over wearily. 'Jeeze, sir,' said the conducting officer. 'The natives are not too friendly. I thought I was going to be lynched.'

'Did you get the directions?' asked Schorner. It was all he wanted.

'Yes, I got them. In the end. It's only a couple of miles.' He hesitated at the window. 'You won't believe this, but they've got a donkey in there.'

Schorner looked sideways at him. The man was not smiling. The colonel had a sudden thought that he ought to look into the inn. 'Maybe I ought to take a looksee,' he said, more to Primrose than the officer. 'Maybe I'll get some idea of what we've got to deal with.'

Reluctantly, stiffly, he eased himself from the car. He was in his middle forties; five foot eleven. There was no rain here, but there was a chill breeze on the moonlight. He pulled his coat higher around his neck. His escort, two white helmeted military policemen, left the truck behind him and followed him towards the door of the pub. With misgiving the conducting officer followed.

Doey, who was now at the window and looking out, withdrew his head and called into the bar: 'They be coming in. Looks like the gaffer.'

The talk was squashed in a moment. All faces turned to the door. The thick curtain was agitated and in walked Schorner and the military policemen. He had not noticed they were behind him and a look of annoyance touched his mouth when he saw them. 'There now,' said Minnie Smith under her breath, but so that everybody heard. 'There's 'andsome. Oi loikes the looks of 'ee.'

It missed Schorner because he did not understand the accent. The locals scarcely grinned at it. 'Good evening,' said the American. 'And a Happy New Year to you.'

The greeting was generally mumbled back. They had taken their suspicion from Barrington. 'We'll be in this district for a while and I thought I'd just say hello.' He hesitated. 'Is there anybody . . . ?' He looked embarrassed. 'Is . . . is the mayor here, maybe?'

A genuine laugh went up. Barrington stepped forward. 'I'm the chairman of the parish council,' he said quietly. 'Tom Barrington.'

'Ha, thank you. My name's Schorner. Carl.' He held out his hand and Barrington formally shook it. Schorner looked unhappy. The people in the bar were puzzled by Barrington.

Howard Evans said: 'I'm the local doctor, Howard Evans, and this is my wife Beatrice.' Schorner's expression relaxed and he shook hands. Barrington mumbled an apology more to Evans than to the American.

Barrington looked sideways and then behind him. 'And these are the people of this village,' he said almost dramatically.

'I'd just like to say hello,' Schorner straightened up

and said firmly. 'We'll be around for a while, folks. I hope we're all going to get along.' He looked across the bar and pretended to see the donkey for the first time. 'Does he always come into the bar?' he grinned.

Beatrice smiled. 'He didn't come of his own free will,' she said.

Schorner thought: 'I know how he feels.'

Howard said: 'Will you have a drink? Can you?'

Schorner shook his head. 'I guess not right now, but thanks. I have a company of tired soldiers outside and I want to get them into camp.'

There was a commotion from the back of the room, shouts and the gush of water. Schorner and everybody looked.

''Tis all right, sir,' called Lenny Birch cheerfully. ''Tis just the donkey having a widdle.'

While everyone's attention was on the Americans, Gilman had eased his way through the crowd towards the back of the bar. There was a small door there, the one through which they had brought the donkey. Unnecessarily, he excused himself to the people standing near it and slipped out into the yard of the inn. He had the unpleasant thought that as soon as the Americans reached the foot of the hill they might stop at the gun-site to check the directions. Bryant was the sort of officer to turn out the guard for them.

The short convoy of American vehicles, their engines still running, was a few yards up the hill as he emerged into the bare street. He turned away from it and began to walk with brisk care down the incline. Behind him, to his alarm, he heard the Americans emerge from the inn and the engines of the convoy increase in volume. Keeping his eyes solidly to the front he continued down the hill, keeping as far from the gutter as he could. The leading car went by him, and the next, but the third stopped. 'Hi, soldier,' called a voice. 'Want a ride?'

The British soldier stopped and turned. The man looking out at him was, without doubt, the American colonel who had been in the inn. Gilman saluted clumsily. The jeeps in front had stopped now, some way down the hill. 'No . . . thanks . . . thank you . . . sir. It's only just down the road. It's very kind of you, but it's no distance.'

'Get in,' said the American. He pushed open the heavy door of the car. Gilman knew an order when he heard it. A final hesitation was of no use. He stumbled into the seat alongside the colonel, his rough army sleeve against the smooth uniform of the American.

The car was a left-hand drive. He could see the driver looking across, a large pair of eyes behind glasses split by a large nose. He had a smooth uniform too. In the interior light of the car, which they had switched on, he suspected, to get a better look at him, he could see the driver was wearing brown, patent leather shoes. Schorner said: 'Okay, Albie, let's go. Drop this gentleman at the bottom of the hill. Is that right, soldier?'

'Yes, sir,' swallowed Gilman. He could imagine Bryant calling out the guard and seeing him alighting from the side of a US colonel. That would take some explaining. He sat tightly like a prisoner.

'Royal Artillery,' Schorner said, reading Gilman's

shoulder flashes. They went past the house of Mary Nicholas, where he had promised to return.

'Yes, sir,' he said. 'We've got a gun at the bottom of the hill here. By the harbour. Anti-aircraft.'

'You have bombing raids here?'

'No, sir. Not for a couple of years. But the gun's here – well, just in case.'

'Good to know you're well-prepared,' said Schorner.

Gilman stared directly ahead. 'Could you drop me just before the bottom of the hill, sir, please?' he said. 'Otherwise it will be out of your way.'

Schorner smiled in the dark. 'Okay, soldier,' he said easily. 'We'll do that.'

He said to the driver, 'Stop where the soldier says, Albie.'

'Okay, if you say so,' said Albie. He glanced towards Gilman and added: 'Sir.'

The car stopped and brought the rest of the convoy to a halt. Gratefully Gilman got out. He made to close the door but Schorner closed it first. Gilman stumbled his thanks and, just as the cars were pulling away, threw up a belated salute. He stood in the shadows of the first house on the hill and watched the vehicles turn along the coast road. They had only done that so they could get a look at him. He was sure of it. Christ, what an army that must be, wearing patent leather shoes and the colonel calling a private Albie. He turned and walked cautiously back to his familiar home at the gun-site.

In the car Albie said: 'Jeeze, was that a soldier, sir?'

'A real British soldier, Albie. That's the first one you've seen. Me too. What do you think?'

'Those clothes,' whistled Albie. 'That rough brown stuff, right up to his throat like it was choking him. And did you get a look at the boots? Maybe they kick the Germans to death.'

Schorner nodded. 'He certainly looked . . . well, different,' he said.

'Sure did,' muttered Albie. 'The poor guy looked like a half-starved bear.'

Just after midnight Eric Sissons, the vicar of Telcoombe Magna, stared from his chair to the chair on the opposite side of the fireplace. From it his wife, Cecily, was quietly slipping towards the floor. Her eyes were closed tightly as though she feared the drop; the lines around her eyes were drawn together like thread, the firelight incised deep shadows in her face. Her emptied glass remained held desperately in her fingers, the last thing she would ever relinquish. The light of the fire shone through the Johnnie Walker bottle. The vicar's father, Conrad, had taken his aged stance, shoulders sloping left, staring out of the window as if his vision took him beyond the night to the far and private distances of the sea. He had pulled the heavy curtains six inches apart.

'Nineteen-forty-four,' the old man announced eventually in a tone which indicated he had arrived at the end of a complicated calculation.

Sissons knew he would expect an acknowledgement. 'Nineteen-forty-four,' he said back. 'The year of Our Lord.'

'Don't know about Him,' grunted his father. 'All I know is I'm eighty this year.' He waited, continuing to peer searchingly into the darkness. 'Is Cecily still with us?' he asked. With difficulty he looked over his shoulder. 'Did she see the New Year in?'

'Gone,' answered Sissons without emphasis. 'She missed it by one swallow. Like the summer.'

'Always said she could drink year in, year out,' joked the old man. He chortled and Sissons grinned grimly with him. They were very accustomed to it. Sissons said: 'Perhaps this *will* be the year she packs it up,' he said without hope. 'She did promise.'

Conrad Sissons gave a truncated snort. 'You'll have to lock the bottles up then,' he said. 'And lock her up – somewhere else. Not that she's a lot of good to you. You had a hole in your sock Christmas morning, you know, looking out like a blasted eye from under your cassock. Half the congregation saw it.'

'I know,' said Sissons. 'Mrs Hannaford came back with a pair of socks for me. A Christmas present and a hint combined.'

'You ought to get rid of her,' decided the old man. 'Cecily, not Mrs Hannaford.' He remained at the window but turned to face into the room as if he expected the suggestion to be properly considered.

His son had closed his eyes. 'How? How does a vicar get rid of someone?'

'Throw her in the sea or something,' suggested his father. 'Make your life a lot easier.'

Sissons nodded as though it were something he had already considered. 'Cecily says the same about you, more or less,' he muttered.

His father returned his gaze to the window. 'I'll probably be going anyway this year,' he said. 'I've got a feeling in my water. If I thought I'd be able to collect the winnings I'd go so far as to bet on it.' He brightened. 'Perhaps they let you claim things like winning bets in the Hereafter?'

'Providing there is one,' said Sissons gently.

'God, that's a fine thing coming from you.'

'I find it difficult to give guarantees about something I'm far from convinced about myself,' admitted his son. 'Would you be very disappointed if it turned out there wasn't a Hereafter?'

A half-laugh blew across the room. 'Ha! I don't think I'd be in a position to be.'

Sissons grinned at his father's back. 'I mean *now*. If you knew for sure there wasn't. How would you feel *now*? Very let down?'

Conrad Sissons turned again, with rising belligerence. '*Bloody* let down,' he said. 'Listen, there'd *better* be something afterwards. I'm not going to be satisfied with just death.' He shook his head as if ridding himself of the thought. 'All that praying on your knees, and those terrible psalms, and that freezing bloody church, not to mention the quids I've put in the plate over the years. I hope it hasn't all been some kind of fraud.' He returned to the window.

Sissons shrugged. 'Well, if it is a fraud, it's been a necessary fraud. What would people do, otherwise?'

'There's lights,' his father said suddenly and quietly. 'Lights along the beach road. Dozens, all following each other. I haven't seen lights like that for years. Look, car lights . . . shining straight out.'

Sissons stood up and took his wife's glass from her dumb hand. He set it next to the mocking bottle and walked to the window. The lights, two by two, were moving along the straight mile run of road that cut

35

between the beach and the leys, the freshwater lakes, immediately inland.

'Just like the lights of Torquay front before the war,' said Conrad Sissons, suddenly content. 'You remember, don't you?'

'Yes, I remember,' said Sissons absently. 'Wonderful, wasn't it.'

'Torquay? Yes, wonderful. I'll say.'

'These are Americans,' said Sissons nodding down at the convoy. 'That's why they're ignoring the black out. They're going to have a big operation in these parts, I've been told.'

'Why didn't you say?' The old man straightened and smiled. 'Ha, that ought to wake things up a bit,' he said. 'Americans.'

'It probably will.'

'Americans,' said Conrad with a happy grimace. 'Soldiers.' He half turned and shouted towards his sleeping daughter-in-law. 'Wake up, Cecily. Come and look. The soldiers are coming!'

Colonel Schorner slept for only three hours. It was partly discomfort, for his army cot had been set up in a corner of a nissen hut that had not been occupied for eighteen months. The tin seams were parting like lips and the bleak night air whistled through. By the time his advanced unit had located the camp and established themselves, even for that night, it was beyond three o'clock. Vehicles had to be parked, arms and supplies checked and sentries posted before he could retire. Since all the men were weary he ordered that the sentries should be changed every hour. They were young, inexperienced, boys, most never out of their home towns in the far spaces of the United States. Some did not even know where they were. Before going to sleep Schorner had made a round of the camp. One of the sentries at the vehicle park was so jittery that Schorner had to bellow at him to drop the muzzle of his rifle. He saw the young man was trembling. His eyes were points of light in the darkness.

'What's the trouble, son?' asked Schorner.

'I'm sorry, sir, I just didn't know it was you. This place sure is creepy. I never saw such a lot of dark.'

'Take it easy. What's your name?' Normally Schorner would have known the name and home town of every man in his company, but these soldiers were strangers, assembled on the troopship and put under his command only when they disembarked at Avonmouth twelve hours before.

'Wall, sir. Benny Wall.'

'Where you from, Benny?'

'Cincinnati, sir,' he said, calling it 'Cincinnata'. 'Ohio.'

'Don't you get darkness in Ohio?'

'Not like this. This is black dark.' The boy hesitated. Then bluntly, he asked: 'How far away are the Germans?'

Schorner was not surprised. 'Across the sea,' he said, nodding south.

'How far across?'

'A good distance. They won't be over tonight.'

'Maybe they'll come over to bomb,' insisted the youth. 'They *do*, sir. They've been bombing this place like crazy. All the time. I saw it on the movies back home.'

The memory of the movies back home caused his expression to sag even more. Schorner nodded but did not laugh. 'I don't figure we'll get any air attacks, not tonight,' he said as if he had planned a whole strategy around it. 'There's not a whole lot for the Germans to bomb around this area. Only fields.'

'There's us,' persisted the sentry. 'Maybe they already know we're here, sir. There's spies all over. Maybe they know we're sitting right in the middle of this shit field.'

Schorner raised his eyebrows. The fear had not gone from the soldier's face. The colonel rubbed his jaw tiredly. 'If you catch anybody spying, shoot them,' he said, trying to make it sound simple. Then, thinking again, 'No. Arrest them and bring them to me. Okay?' His voice dropped to seriousness. 'Don't, I repeat, Wall, *don't* shoot them. And in case of air attack – well, I guess you'd better duck.'

'I already thought I'd do that, sir.'

'Sure, get the hell under that vehicle.' He pointed.

'Not that one, I ain't, sir. That's the ammunition truck.'

'See, now you're thinking like a soldier. Goodnight, Wall, you'll be fine.'

He walked back towards the main camp. After a few yards only, he turned and saw the sentry standing transfixed in silhouette, his face lifted, fearfully searching the sky, rifle at the ready, Schorner shook his head. What would they be like when they got on the beaches of France?

January

The colonel lay in his cot, wanting to get up but realizing that there was no point in wandering about in the dark, especially if the other sentries were as jumpy as Wall had been. He might well become the first casualty of the invasion that was still five months away.

Lying there against the rough pillow, waiting, still in his uniform, waiting for the winter dawn, he began to think of his farm in the Shenandoah Valley, of West Virginia, his wife, Sarah, and his children Thomas and Cliff. He shut off the thought; nostalgia was too much of an indulgence. He checked the blue hands of his watch. Six-forty. He closed his eyes and dozed and then, inevitably, slept. He was awakened in early daylight by the crowing of roosters and the thin warbling of the camp bugle. He smiled with the small satisfaction. He had not been aware that they had brought a bugler with them. A moment later his driver, Pfc Albie Primrose, his nose red in the raw morning, brought him an enamel mug of coffee.

'There's some guys, some Limey guys, hanging over the gate and laughing,' complained Albie in a hurt way. 'They look pretty ugly. They're laughing at our boys.'

'Oh, that's too bad. Laughing? Well, I guess I'd

better take a look.' He glanced at Albie who, he could see, needed the reassurance. 'We didn't come here to be laughed at,' he added firmly. 'Not even by the English. But I guess I'd better shave first.'

Albie brought him a kettle of hot water and a field basin and he washed and shaved. He left the skeletal nissen hut. The air was only a little colder outside than within. A smokey dawn smudged the sky, the indistinct landscape lay like a dead fire. Schorner put a cigar in his mouth, took it out and then with a short curse thrust it back again. He could see a group of figures hanging over the farm gate at the entrance to the camp. He walked steadily towards them across the soaked grass.

There were six men, agricultural workers he could see, and a churlish-looking woman holding a thin boy by the hand. 'Good morning,' he said cheerfully. 'Is there anything I can do for you people?'

At once they seemed nonplussed by his attitude. Eventually a man in his twenties, with a heavy coat around his unshaven chin, sleep still sticky in his eyes and string around his trousers at the knees, answered: 'I don' reckon there's anything.' His fellows, all older although it was difficult to tell, looked towards the speaker with rustic admiration, not lost on him. He grinned insolently with rotten teeth. 'What you lot doin' 'ere, then?'

'I can't tell you that, I'm afraid,' answered Schorner evenly.

'Why not? It be *our* field. Well, it be Luscombe's field.'

'The farmer,' added another man.

Schorner shrugged. 'It's a field belonging to the British Air Department . . . Ministry,' he said with more confidence than he felt. 'We will be using it for some time to come.'

'Call them soldiers?' the second man suddenly said, thrusting an earth-dirty hand towards the field. 'Look at they! Just like Boy bluddy Scouts.'

Looking at him quietly, Schorner said: 'We arrived at one o'clock this morning. I guess we'll soon be straight.' He moved along the gate towards the speaker. 'I'd say you were about military age, sir.' He looked across to the first man who had taunted him. 'And you, sir. I thought all you Englishmen were in the army.'

They looked at each other. No one had ever called either 'sir' before. The younger man began to say something, then gave up in favour of the older man. He said: 'We be agricultural workers. 'Tis an essential occupation. Growin' crops, see.'

'Ah,' said Schorner. 'I get it. I guess we hear things wrong in the States. I had the picture of the men all in the army and the women working the land.' The women at the end of the gate laughed coarsely at her compatriots. 'Army wouldn't 'ave them,' she taunted. She said to Schorner, 'Mr Luscombe, the farmer, says you'll be wanting eggs and milk. Fair prices, 'ee says.' She winked. ''Ee might even get you a pig if you can keep a bit quiet about it.'

The men watched while she made the offer. They looked around at each other. Then the elder man said hurriedly: 'I got a spare pig too, zur.'

Schorner walked back towards the camp area. The field draped a slope which began some miles inland at

41

the roots of Dartmoor. He had digested that much from the maps he had been given aboard the troopship. At least, he had noted at the time, it meant that once drainage ditches were cleared, or dug (if the former occupants, the British Air Force, had not excavated them) the endemic rain of the English winter and spring would run off more easily.

Schorner knew that in the tradition of advance parties, no matter what the war or the army, his was ill-prepared. Although he had known five days before disembarking at Avonmouth that he was to command this first small contingent of engineers, his other officers and the enlisted men were put together piecemeal only hours before they came ashore into this strange, chilly country. Even as he walked towards the camp he knew that the tents which were sprouting up between the bones of the old RAF nissen huts were only suitable for summer use, and American summer use at that. His men, wearing the pre-war doughboys gaiters, erecting the tents, did in truth have a touch of the Boy Scouts about them. Some of them, he recalled sadly, had no idea where England *was*. On the ship one boy had asked if England were part of France, or an island off the coast of France, which, in a way, he supposed it was. There had been others, particularly those with Irish ancestry, whose forebears had left the British Isles with only a hatred that, far from diminishing, had been nurtured by fable and tradition over the years.

Private Albie Primrose came towards him with a mug of coffee steaming volcanically in the thin air. He took it gratefully. 'You repelled the enemy, colonel,' said Albie, nodding with satisfaction towards the gate.

Only the small boy was left now, gazing through the lower bars like a calf at market.

Schorner smiled. The familiarity between commissioned officers, no matter what the rank, and the private soldier was a hallmark of his army. 'Albie,' he answered, 'if that's the worst battle we have to fight it will be just fine by me.' He drank the coffee and wiped his mouth with the back of his hand. He handed the mug back to the soldier. 'I think it's time I took a look around,' he said. 'Just pass the word, I want all officers and sergeants in my hut in half an hour. And that guy who brought us here, the conducting officer, whatever his name is . . .'

'Hulton, sir,' supplied Primrose. 'Captain Hulton.'

'That's the guy. Ask Captain Hulton to come and see me before he leaves, will you. Right, that's all.'

Albie flapped up the languid salute of the US Army and sloped off across the cold, damp hill. He sang, loudly, defiantly, tonelessly, as he went. 'My momma done tol' me, when I was in knee pants, a woman'll sweet talk . . .' Crows flapped from the bare-boned trees at the sound of the strange song.

Schorner smiled and then, his farmer's instinct moving him as much as military practice, he walked to the highest point of the long climbing field. It rose briskly over its last fifty yards or so, forming a grass platform, a gallery from which he could look down on the camp and over the countryside beyond it – a land of red, curving earth interset with meadows like bright green banners. There were houses, farms and other buildings sunk into the sharp deep valleys. Beyond the valleys was the long vision of the sea. In the foreground, almost at his feet, more drab tents were going

43

up between the camouflaged nissen huts. Men were moving about and smoke was fingering from the cookhouse. It reminded him of an encampment of the old pioneers on the trails west in his own country, the tents, the long rounded forms of the nissen huts like the backs of the covered wagons. He noticed that the vehicles had been parked badly in the dark, but at least they were in one area. A new sentry stood at the spot where the previous night he had encountered the nervous Private Wall from Cincinnati. Even at that distance the man looked sloppy and listless. Schorner's reaction was to look towards the gate. The little boy remained, still watching, and had now been joined by four more children, sitting astride the top bar and shouting towards the sentry who waved back. Children always liked soldiers, and soldiers children. Perhaps soldiers *were* children. As the sentry waved a second time he saw a grey puff rise from his upraised hand as if he had performed some conjuring trick. 'Jesus Christ,' muttered Schorner to himself. 'The son-of-a-bitch is smoking.'

'Soldier!' he bellowed from his shoulder of hill. 'You – soldier!'

The voice sounded over the whole area. Every soldier in the camp stopped what he was doing and looked up to the broad man standing in silhouette against the pale morning sky. 'That man!' bawled Schorner again. 'The sentry!'

The GI on guard was the last to turn around. He looked up at the figure of his commanding officer. Schorner was too far away to see the puzzlement on his face. 'Yes, sir?' he called. 'Me?'

'Yes, *you*. You're smoking! Put that cigarette out!'

44

'It's a cigar,' complained the man quietly to himself. He dropped the butt into the earth and screwed his foot over it. Then he waved amiably towards his colonel and continued on his short duty walk.

Schorner clamped his mouth fiercely. He was tempted to run down the slope towards the sentry but he resisted the idea. Instead he carefully measured his paces down the incline until he arrived at the area where the tents were erected. The men stared as he walked. Mostly they were strangers, to each other and to him. He went towards the smoke of the cookhouse. Twenty men were lining up with mess-tins for breakfast. He picked up a tin plate and stood in the line with them. Nobody moved aside. Three cooks were moving in a businesslike way behind the field kitchen. He watched with admiration. Cooks were always the first to settle anywhere.

'How ya' doing, colonel?' said one of the men up to his armpits in steam.

'Just fine,' said Schorner. 'Everything okay?'

The sergeant cook sniffed derisively over his shoulder at a black stove against the wall of the hut. 'We got ourselves fixed okay now, sir,' he said. 'But that junk back there. The stuff the Limeys left. Jesus Christ, no wonder they look half-starved. All you could cook in that is mud and rocks.'

'Good thing you had the field kitchen,' nodded Schorner. Three fried eggs, four sausages, a handful of bread and butter and plum jam were put, unasked, on to his plate. A mug of coffee, trailing steam like a railway train, travelled along the table towards him. The sergeant patted the hot stove as if it were a pet. 'Made in the good old USA,' he grinned. 'The best. I guess we're going to have to depend on a whole lot of things made back home in the USA. Yes, sir. They don't look like they got nothin' in this asshole country.'

Taking his breakfast with him, Schorner returned to his hut. Private Primrose had rolled his bedding, discovered a ragged and mildewed strip of carpet and put it over the cracked concrete of the floor, and set up a trestle table and a chair as a desk. A fat and cheerful engineer was putting in a telephone which he had connected to a line at the bottom of the field. Schorner said: 'Good. That's quick work.'

'Nothin' to it, sir,' grinned the man. He had a face that beamed like a freshly-made pie. 'Telephones is telephones no matter where you go. And we invented them. Alexander Graham Bell. So we know we'll always have a phone. Just pick it up and call your wife – it's easy!'

'I just wish I could,' said Schorner, realizing how much he meant it. 'She might give me some advice on setting up house here.'

'It's something you get used to,' said the man confidently. 'This country.'

'You've been here before? In England?'

'Sure. I was here from thirty-five to thirty-nine, every two weeks. I was a steward on a liner, the *Mauretania*, so I got to know the Limeys okay.'

Schorner regarded his smile with something like relief. 'You might be the guy we need,' he said carefully. 'Somebody who knows the natives.'

'Sure thing.'

'What's your name?'

'Ballimach, sir. George A. Ballimach. Private first

class. Englishtown, New Jersey.' His face remained straight.

Schorner laughed. 'Okay. And what's your opinion of the English?'

'Weeell . . . they're okay. Sometimes, that is, and sometimes they ain't. If they can get a cup of their tea, they're generally okay. If they can't then they ain't.' He had finished connecting the telephone and now he stood regarding it as if he were considering improving its design. 'They got one big trouble,' he continued.

'And that is?'

'They think they made the world. Like they own it. The greatest people ever, they figure they are.'

Schorner grinned. 'And you don't go along with that, Ballimach?'

The fat soldier looked surprised. 'No, sir. The greatest people ever – that's us. That's Americans.'

Sitting in the bleak hut, the cold wind seeping through, with the vacant table in front of him, the telephone silent at his elbow, it occurred to Colonel Schorner that this was a strange way to begin an invasion. He picked up his briefcase and put it on the table. Somehow that made it seem more empty than ever. The telephone rang and startled him. He picked it up. It was just Ballimach, the fat engineer, testing the line.

'Colonel,' he said breathlessly, 'I need a little help. Put the phone down. It will ring again but this time don't pick it up. Just go to the door of your hut and wave at me. I'm up a goddamned tree alongside the goddamned gate. Could you do that, sir?'

47

Schorner smiled and agreed. He replaced the handset and waited. There was nothing more urgent for him to do. When the tinny bell sounded he walked out of the hut and waved. Ballimach, as he had said, was wedged like some bulky fruit in the bare branches of the tree. He cautiously waved back.

The conducting officer, Hulton, was walking down the slope of the field towards Schorner. He was well-cast, the colonel thought, for he had a slightly bowed, studious air and a habit of moving his bespectacled head from side to side like a professional guide. Schorner could imagine him airily conveying visitors around stately southern homes. They exchanged blunted salutes. Hulton looked about him with some satisfaction. 'Well, colonel, we found the place in the end. What do you do now, that's the big one?'

Schorner led him into the nissen hut. 'We'll find something to keep busy, I guess,' he said. Hulton sniffed the damp cold of the corrugated room. 'We're going to start by getting something better than this,' added Schorner, reading the expression.

'It sure ain't the Pentagon,' agreed Hulton. At Schorner's invitation he took the second metal chair and they sat formally one each side of the desk.

Schorner said: 'We'll get some quonset huts in as soon as possible and in the meantime get some fuel to use in those stoves. We're going to start this invasion by collecting wood. I'm going to try and get these huts patched up as much as possible until the quonsets arrive and can be erected. I'm not sure the tents are not more comfortable. At least they don't have so many holes in the walls.'

'Mine did,' mentioned Hulton. 'Moths, I think.'

The phone rang. Hulton jumped at the sound and looked at it in astonishment as if he had thought it was merely decoration. Schorner picked it up. 'Schorner,' he said. 'Do you want me to wave?'

Hulton's eyebrows arched. He regarded Schorner with a close and serious respect thinking this might be some message in code. Schorner leaned closer to the mouthpiece as people curiously do when they cannot hear well. 'You're what, Ballimach? Stuck? You're stuck up the tree? Christ! Hold on man, we'll have to get you down.'

He put the phone back firmly and got to his feet, glancing at Hulton. 'Excuse me, we seem to have a guy stuck up a tree,' he said. He went to the door and peered towards the gate. The dark mass was waving pitifully from the branches. 'Albie!' called the colonel. 'Albie Primrose . . . anybody seen . . . oh, there you are, Albie. Look over there, by the gate, up that tree. Got it. That is an American GI. He's got himself stuck. Get somebody to get him down, okay. Better take plenty of help. He's heavy.'

He returned to the table. 'These guys will be great in action,' he said, solemnly. 'Killers.'

Hulton said: 'I thought it was all in code. Do you want me to wave? . . . Stuck up a tree . . . Albie Primrose. I figured the invasion had already started.'

Schorner shrugged. 'Everything will get better. It needs to,' he said. 'Do you know why we're here? This particular unit, I mean?'

'Not exactly. I'm just the guy who takes everybody by the hand to their places. Just so long as they don't want me to take the army across to France . . .'

'This is going to be something very big. The last

chance to get it right before the real thing.' Schorner glanced around. 'It may not look like it, but it is. When are you leaving?'

Hulton looked at his army watch. 'In ten minutes, I hope. I have to get back to Bristol tonight to nurse another battalion or so across this fog-sodden country.'

'You don't like it? The country?'

'I prefer Georgia.'

'Right. But I wanted to ask you a couple of things. Since you've been here a while.'

'A year,' said Hulton sombrely. 'Twelve whole fucking months.'

From such a mild man the language seemed strange, almost shocking. Schorner blinked with surprise. 'I'd really like to see my mother,' added Hulton, as though justifying the outburst.

Unsurely Schorner glanced at him. 'Yes, I guess a lot of guys would.' He leaned forward over the table. 'The reason I asked you to come over is the same thing we've already talked about. I'm anxious to get things right with the British. We've got a job to do here, and it's a job that's going to make us even more unpopular than armies are anyway. I want to cut off as few toes as possible. So I need advice. For example, those people in the inn last night. With the exception of that doctor and his wife they were pretty unhelpful. Even . . . okay, hostile?'

'They are,' confirmed Hulton. 'In general, the English are. I sometimes get the feeling that, given the choice, they'd have preferred the Germans to us.'

Schorner looked at him with astonishment. 'You're kidding.'

'I'm not,' shrugged Hulton. 'That's the message I get loud and clear, colonel. It varies with the place, of course. In some parts of the country they love us – they've never been so prosperous, but there's all the usual resentments.'

'Over-sexed, over-fed and over here?' suggested Schorner.

'Sure. Even the little kids can repeat that. That's when their mouths aren't full of gum or US candy.'

The colonel whistled. 'Wow, you're serious, Hulton. I can't say you're filling me with optimism. As far as I know we're the first US troops to come to this area. I need it to be as painless as possible. We're going to have enough military problems without a hostile civilian population. You make it sound like we can expect trouble from the underground resistance.'

'You certainly might get it,' alleged Hulton solemnly. He spread his arms. 'Colonel, I just hate the goddamn place. It rains and it rains. And with all that water the people still don't *wash*. Not like we wash at home in Georgia.'

Schorner pursed his lips. He said: 'Maybe it's the war. Maybe soap is short. Maybe they get extra dirty in the plants making guns and ammunition.'

Hulton did not appear to have heard him. 'The whole country seems like it's spent the last two hundred years under a gigantic glass case,' he complained. 'Just getting anything to *move* is an impossibility.' He struck the split concrete floor of the hut with his shoe. 'Just watch a gang of Englishmen putting down this stuff, concrete, or digging a ditch. It's like something out of history. They had a war once

51

called the Hundred Years War, and I'm not surprised.'

Schorner said unconvincingly: 'Well, thanks, Hulton, I guess we'll have to keep a look out for these problems.' He stood up and the conducting officer shook hands with him and turned towards the door. 'How about London?' asked Schorner. 'I heard some of the men already asking how far we are here from London. I didn't tell them yet just how far. They seem to think they can get there by cab.'

'I got a dose of clap in London,' said Hulton reflectively. The memory of the cause, if not the effect, apparently still held some pleasure for him. 'Wonderful girl. Great complexion. They get it from the rain, you know. The complexion, I mean, not the gonorrhoea.' He shook hands again and saluted. 'I must go, colonel.'

'Sure,' said Schorner, not sorry. 'Thanks for the information.'

'That's okay. Glad to help.' He paused seriously. 'One thing's for certain – whether they like us or not. They need us. They need an *organized* army.'

As Hulton saluted and turned, a formation of US soldiers appeared from the direction of the gate. A stretcher party emblazoned with red cross emblems was carrying the limp bulk of Pfc Ballimach. Another man, this one moaning, was being borne behind. Twenty other soldiers followed like an animated funeral procession. Albie Primrose led the way importantly.

'Ballimach fell out of the tree, sir,' said Primrose as though reporting a battle casualty.

'Jesus,' breathed Schorner. He advanced on the

52

prone mass in the khaki fatigues. It was awake and gutturally moaning. 'I'll be okay, sir,' muttered the fat man gallantly. 'It was that fucking Limey tree.'

'What happened to the other man?' asked Schorner. Then he knew. 'Ballimach fell on him?'

Schorner spread a few useless pieces of paper across his table and pinned his map of the area against the only piece of wood remaining on the wall. God, he had to get some heating in that place. The wind blew straight from the cold-eyed sea, up the valley, and through the crevices in the curved walls of the nissen hut.

'Albie,' he called from the entrance. 'Private Primrose, are you around?'

'Sure, sir,' replied Albie quietly coming round the corner. He was the sort of man who appeared, materialized, at any given moment, as though he had been lying in wait for the call.

'How are the casualties?' asked Schorner.

'Ballimach, well, he ain't too bad, considering all that poundage dropping out of a tree. I guess that's why elephants don't climb trees, because it's serious when they fall. The other guy, Fillborough, he just got every square inch of wind knocked out of him.'

'We should get a doctor,' said Schorner. He was reluctant to send for a civilian doctor and they had none of their own.

Albie thought about it. 'Ballimach don't seem too bad, sir,' he said. 'Some of him's gone black. But that's about all as far as the medics can see. But they're not real medics, either. Just two guys with red cross arm

53

bands. They found them along with the stretcher. But they don't know nothing. Jesus, twice those goons dropped Ballimach off the stretcher.'

'Well, maybe we ought to get a doctor,' sighed Schorner.

'It could be you're right there, colonel. I mean Ballimach's got a whole lot of *insides*, if you know what I mean, there must be miles and miles of them. Anything could be wrong in there. In the dark.'

'Okay, get somebody in a vehicle to go into that place we came through last night, what's it called . . . Wilcoombe, and get a doctor. That nice guy in the bar was a doctor. See if he's around. Maybe we ought to send Ballimach and Fillborough down there instead of getting the doctor here.'

Albie looked doubtful. 'Gee, I don't know about that, sir. Like I say, there may be all sorts of splits and cracks inside Ballimach, things we just don't know about.'

'Okay,' agreed Schorner. 'But send some guy down who can open his mouth politely. I don't want any mutton-head upsetting people.'

'Ballimach could get a medal,' offered Albie thoughtfully. 'First purple heart of the invasion.' He sauntered away through the tents. As he went Schorner saw a group of two officers and three sergeants approaching warily as a sheriff's posse.

'Come on in,' he called cheerfully.

They trooped in. Each one looked about him, as Schorner knew they would, ascertaining whether the quarters were an improvement on their own. 'Luxury,' he said, waving his arm to encompass the bleak accommodation. 'I'm sorry I can't offer you gentlemen a seat, or light refreshments.' He sat on the table, felt it quiver and prudently went round it to the chair. 'First we have to get names,' he said. He picked up one of the pieces of paper from beside the telephone. 'Maybe you'd just let me know who you are. Since we didn't get the opportunity to be introduced yesterday.' He looked up at them and two, one officer and one sergeant, nodded as if he needed their compliance.

'Lieutenant Brunn, Harold,' he recited from the manifest roll.

Brunn was the wrong shape for an officer, stubby and wide, his shoulders falling away like folded wings. Three months back in civilian life he would be a fat man. Schorner shook hands with him. 'Glad you're here,' he said.

Doubtfully Brunn turned his eyes around the hut. 'Thank you, sir,' he said. 'I am too.'

Schorner returned to the roll. 'Lieutenant Kenholm, Conroy.'

The second officer saluted. 'From Nebraska, sir,' he said as though it might get him special consideration.

'Great,' said Schorner, mildly surprised. 'I guess this place feels pretty warm to you.'

'It feels damp and cold, sir.'

'Right. One of our priorities, today in fact, this morning, is to organize fuel. Lieutenant, I'd like you and one of the sergeants . . . what's your name, sergeant?'

'Humpchick, sir. Raymond.'

'Okay, Sergeant Humpchick. You go with Lieutenant Kenholm and organize some fuel. Get the men together into wood-gathering parties and also get on to the US Quartermaster in . . . wait a minute . . . what's the place? Yes, Exeter, which is a city not too far away. Call him and fix a supply of coal or coke, or whatever these iron stoves need. Tell him the invasion force is freezing its balls off.'

The group laughed with varying degrees of sincerity. The other two sergeants made themselves known, Perry from Illinois and Shermack from Georgia.

'Georgia,' ruminated Schorner. 'That captain who eventually got us down here last night, the conducting officer as he was called, the guy who nearly made us into the lost company. He was from Georgia. He said he wanted to get home and see his mother.'

Sergeant Shermack smiled seriously. 'I sure would too. We think a lot of our mothers in Georgia.'

'Okay, okay,' sighed Schorner. 'Now that we all know who we are . . . My name's Schorner by the way, in case nobody mentioned it. I'm from West Virginia.' He walked to the solitary map which he had himself pinned on the wooden boarding of the hut. 'Where we've come from doesn't matter right now,' he added. 'Just where we are. And this is it. This map shows part of Devon county, England. That small town we came through last night is Wilcoombe. This camp is here, at Telcoombe Magna. The beach is right along here, as you can see, and it's straight as a Texas cow fence, the ocean is there and right across there are the Nazis.' He paused and glanced back at them, five concentrated frowns. He went on: 'We are the first unit of the US Army to arrive in this section of England. I don't have to tell you what a mess everything was yesterday. That was down to some logistical genius on the troopship. I just hope to God he's not fixing the arrangements for the invasion. The task of this advance party is to first, establish this camp and attempt to make it livable. We will then go on to construct a further camp for a second company of engineers and combine with them, and a hell of a lot more who are on the way, to make this area into a very big military deal. Once our construction work is through and, the way I see it, it will *never* be through, we have to start thinking about our task, as engineers, during the projected landing in France and what follows it. Then, when we've won the war, we can *all* go home to our mothers.'

He walked back towards them and sat carefully on the edge of the table. 'What I am about to tell you is classified information – top secret. I'm giving the news to this group because it's going to make our job a little easier. But what I am about to tell you must not go beyond these tin walls for twenty-four hours. No mention must be made of it to the men and, particularly, and believe me I *mean* it, particularly to any civilians you may come into contact with. If it does get out then whoever let it out will be court-martialled. Okay?'

They regarded him with collective seriousness. Lieutenant Brunn's Adam's apple rose violently in his truncated throat. Schorner went back to the map. 'This entire area,' he said, pushing the flat of his hand across the map, 'all you see here, apart from Wilcoombe, down here, is to be evacuated of civilians. Everybody, everything goes. In three weeks. That's the time they've got to get everything together; everything, farm animals, homes, everything and quit. They're not going to feel too happy about this, any more than you would if it happened to you. But they've got to go. Six villages, three thousand people, thirty thousand acres.

'This is tough for them, but things aren't going to be easy for us either. The pre-invasion exercises conducted in this area are to be as near the real thing as makes no difference. That means *live* ammunition.' He watched their faces. Surprise, worry, a limp grin. Brunn's Adam's apple seemed to have become wedged under his chin. 'Some guys are going to get killed here, it's just about inevitable; killed before they've ever got a look at a German. And by other Americans.'

He sighed heavily. 'You just have to look around this unit, these hundred or so guys we've got here. Right now they're not fit to fight anybody, even other Americans. Christ, we had a guy stranded up a tree this morning – and he fell out of the tree on top of some other guy. So you see what I mean.'

The two officers and one of the sergeants, Humpchick, nodded sagely as if they were confident of controlling the situation. Perry was staring through a fissure in the nissen hut wall and Shermack looked as if he might be thinking of his mother.

Schorner said: 'We can anticipate a back-up unit in a couple of days, once the local population has been told what's going on, and then there'll be doughboys coming in thick and fast. There'll be a month to shake down, get everything organized. After that the battle – the battle before the real battle.'

He looked through the hut door and saw Private Primrose standing twenty yards away with the doctor from Wilcoombe. They had stopped, as though

58

unwilling to come further, and were peering towards the hut. Schorner said to the officers and sergeants, 'I'll tell all the men what's going on just as soon as I think it's the time, or I get the okay from a higher echelon, wherever that is. The English civilians must know first anyway. Understood?'

'Yes, sir,' they chorused. A succession of ragged salutes went up and down and they left the hut.

The doctor walked towards the colonel and they shook hands. 'Howard Evans,' said the doctor. 'Just in case you don't remember from last night.'

'I remember all right,' smiled Schorner. 'You were like a kind light in a difficult world.'

Evans nodded. 'And you're Colonel Schorner. I've seen your two injured men. They're all right.'

'Good,' said Schorner. 'I'm sorry to have called you out but we don't have a medical officer yet and that guy fell out of a tree for God's sake. *And* he hit another guy. We can't afford to lose good men like that.' He smiled.

'I've examined them,' said Evans. 'Nothing broken as far as I could make out. Except the tree.'

'Yes, the tree. I guess we'll have to compensate somebody for that tree.'

Evans looked at him seriously. 'I think you'll eventually have to compensate for a bit more than a tree,' he said. 'From what I understand.'

'You know,' nodded Schorner. 'I guess some folks do. It's the sort of thing that leaks out. Bad news always does.'

'Not many people know yet,' said Evans. 'Barrington, the chairman of the council, he knows. You met him last night.'

Schorner smiled grimly. 'He wasn't very pleased to see us,' he said.

'You might feel like that if you were going to have your farm blown up, or whatever the US Army intends to do,' said Evans reasonably.

'Blow it up,' confirmed Schorner grimly. 'That's the intention.'

Evans sniffed at the grainy day. The landscape rose and descended indolently like a swell on the sea. 'Pity it has to be here,' he commented. 'Lovely part of the country, lovely. Soft, don't you think, colonel, not harsh in any way? And it's a lived-in countryside, if you know what I mean. People belonging here and working.'

'Yes, I see it and I understand,' replied Schorner. He had a strange, shame-faced feeling, as if the decisions were his. 'I'm a farmer myself. In the Shenandoah Valley, West Virginia.'

Evans smiled and said: 'Shenandoah. We've heard the song here, that's all.'

Schorner responded to the smile. 'That's something I sing to myself now and again,' he admitted. 'Not when anybody's around, but I sing it. Are you from this area, this county? Devon?'

It was such an unexpected question that Evans blinked. 'God, no, I'm a Welshman.' He paused. 'But I suppose it's difficult for you to detect the accents.'

'More like impossible. In time I'll learn. And a lot more.'

'There are going to be six meetings in different parts of the area, I gather,' said Evans, looking away from him towards the modest hills. 'The first one's right here today, at Telcoombe Magna, in the church, and the others are in different villages. There's three thousand people involved, you know. Will you have to be there?'

'I don't think I'm going to find a way out of it,' said Schorner caustically. 'At the moment I'm the senior representative of the . . . well, okay, the invaders in this area. They have to throw the rocks at somebody.'

They had begun to walk back towards the gate. A thin western rain began to drift across the hill. Schorner looked up as if he wanted to detect the cloud from which it was falling but the sky was flat ash. Evans did not notice the drizzle or the look. 'I understand that some British admiral is to tell the people,' he remarked. 'Christ knows why. An *admiral*! I would have thought the Minister of Agriculture would have been more appropriate. He's the one who's been exhorting them to grow more food. Dig for Victory it was called. Good slogan, isn't it? He's the one who by rights ought to come and tell them they're being kicked out, dispossessed of their land. Or a bishop. He might convince them that it's what's known as God's will. An admiral seems to be neither here nor there.'

Schorner enlightened him. They had reached the gate now. The small boy was still bent against the bars, gazing like a sniper at the soldiers. 'The whole business is going to be under the umbrella – and maybe that's a good word also – of your Admiralty. Don't ask me why. Maybe it's to fool the Germans. The Admiralty won't be responsible for our operations, of course, but they'll be answerable for everything else. We're going to make the mess and they're going to have to take the blame and clear up.'

Evans looked up at the tree from which Ballimach had fallen. 'They're not all that strong, some of these trees,' he remarked. He looked down at the boy. 'Had much attention from the local populace yet?'

'Some were at the gate at dawn,' answered the American. 'Giving us the bird. But we expected that.'

'They're strange people down here,' said Evans. 'Warm but strange. I found that when I came here. Some of them couldn't get over my Welsh voice. They were very suspicious of a doctor speaking like a miner. Your accent will really be a novelty.' He added thoughtfully: 'They've been sheltered from change in these parts much more than most other places. Even the railway never got this far, you know. It's all going to be one hell of a shock to them, not just the evacuation and all that entails, but having strangers in the countryside. Will you be bringing any coloured troops here?'

'Sure will,' said Schorner. 'By the thousand, I expect.'

Evans nodded at the boy. 'I bet he's never seen a negro,' he said. 'Nor have any of his friends. It'll be a novelty, believe me.'

'Not so much of a novelty as having a few thousand coloured and white troops in a mock battle – but using *live* ammunition,' ruminated Schorner. 'That's going to be something to see.'

Evans said: 'Are negroes good soldiers? Do they fight well?'

Schorner shook his head. 'The US Army doesn't use them for fighting,' he said. 'Not yet anyway. Maybe one day it will. Depends on our losses, I guess. The coloured guys do the work, digging and making roads, stuff like that. Which doesn't mean they don't get shot at. But when it comes to combat – that's down to the white soldier.'

Evans had parked his small car in the lane. Schorner regarded the high-banked sides, topped with bony hedgerows. They were well above his head. 'Are all the highways like this?' he asked. 'Like trenches?'

'A lot of them,' confirmed Evans. 'You're going to have a job getting a tank along these lanes.'

Schorner shrugged. 'There are ways,' he said.

Evans looked out from the driving seat. 'How?' he challenged.

Schorner looked at the tight lane with the high entangled banks enclosing it like walls. 'We just fill them in,' he said. 'Fill them in with dirt.'

Evans shook hands with the American and started the car. As he drove away he saw Schorner talking to the small boy at the gate. He was giving him something. Chewing gum, thought Evans correctly. 'Bloody hell,' he said aloud to himself. 'What a nasty shock they're *all* going to have.'

On New Year's Day Gilman trudged up the cobbled hill from the anti-aircraft gun. He reflected that it was not possible to do very much else except trudge in British army boots. A milkman, whistling through his teeth, was delivering from a handcart halfway up the slope but there were few other people about. He wondered how long the Americans were going to stay. Captain Westerman and Lieutenant Bryant had been excited by something that morning. Westerman, who was a lazy man, had suddenly decided to inspect every-body and everything on the gun-site, from the gun itself down to the mess-tins. Sergeant Bullivant, another one for an easy life, had begun to storm about vocally like a real sergeant. Something was happening.

Because he had been on guard all night, Gilman had three hours off-duty. He walked up the street to the house where he had concealed himself the previous night. With caution he knocked on the door. It was answered immediately, almost as if she had been lying in wait.

'You're back,' she said caustically. 'Did you lose your way?'

'Sorry,' he replied. 'I would have come back, you know I would, but something happened.' He pro-duced the half-bottle of scotch. 'There, look, I didn't touch a drop.'

Reluctantly, it seemed to him, she opened the door and let him in. She was wearing a dull, flowered dress. A washed-out looking child was playing with no enthusiasm in front of the reduced fire in the grate. Gilman, who did not know what to do with children, asked its name. The woman answered: 'Karen.'

'That's an unusual name,' commented Gilman. She nodded towards the armchair on the opposite side of the fire. He sat down. 'I'm really sorry,' he repeated. 'I intended to come straight back. But a whole lot of Americans turned up in the pub. There was a convoy of them, straight off a troopship, apparently. Two officers, a colonel and another chap, came into the pub and asked the way to Telcoombe Magna. They wanted the old RAF camp there. It looked as though there was something special going on. You could tell. Anyway I thought that if Lieutenant Bryant saw this lot coming down the street, headlights full on and everything, he'd have the guard out – and I'd be missing. So I went out the side door and tried to get back.'

She had opened the half-bottle of whisky and poured out two measures. 'It's a bit early,' she said almost to herself.

'I'd just got outside the pub and the two American officers came out and got into the cars and the whole convoy started off. Then the officers' car stopped and the colonel asked me if I wanted a lift. That was the last thing I wanted, but he told me to get in. They gave me a lift down to the bottom of the town.'

'Perhaps they thought you were a general or something,' she said. 'I heard they even salute the doormen outside the cinemas in Plymouth.'

Gilman grimaced: 'I don't think so. I think they just wanted to take a *look* at a British soldier. I mean, it was very odd, sitting there in the dark and it's only a short ride, but I got the impression that they wanted to get a look at me, almost touch me to see what I was made of.' He shook his head. 'There's a difference between them and us, you know. They've got those smooth uniforms. And shoes. Not these bloody boots we have to clobber along in.'

He glanced up and saw that she was regarding him with amusement approaching disdain. It put him on the defensive. 'No, but . . . I mean, the driver . . . well he was *only* a driver so he couldn't have been anything very special in rank. He didn't have any stripes or anything as far as I could see. But him . . . he had a pair of brown shoes on, I saw them on the pedals when they turned the light on to get a look at me and, honestly, we've never had shoes like that in this country.' He glared down at his own bulging boots. 'And there's us wearing these great things. They're like the boots cripples have to wear.'

The woman erupted with mirth. He looked at her with almost a sulk. 'No, well, I mean,' he stumbled.

'You *are* odd,' she said, putting her hand across her mouth. The fingers were slim and curved, her eyes blue and mocking over the barricade they formed. 'You're a scream. Getting all worked up about shoes and boots.'

'But don't you see, that's what it all means. They put us in these damned things so that we *know*, we know from the moment we put them on our feet that we're servile – they've got us. They might as well be chains. They mean the same thing. Surely you *can* have an army without making some people feel inferior. The Yanks, they don't make their soldiers feel like rubbish by dressing them in this stuff . . .' He tugged at the rough khaki of his tunic, '. . . and with bloody clodhoppers.'

She exploded with laughter again and he had to join in. 'You're . . . you're very expressive,' she said, leaning forward with interest. 'What did you do before the war?'

'I worked in a bank,' Gilman said without pride.

'Oh, that's disappointing.'

'Yes, it was for me too. I want to write. Write anything. On a newspaper, if possible, but anything just as long as it's writing. I'm using up this war trying to teach myself. I've got a correspondence course. I'm never going back to that bank. There's nothing more demoralizing than counting other people's money. It's like working as a washer-upper in a brothel.'

She laughed outright again. He took a heavy drink of the scotch. 'Listen,' he continued, 'you don't realize the meaning of the word *envy* until you see the miserable woebegone buggers who've got all the money in the bank. They watch you like a bloody ferret while you're counting it out – and all for three pounds a week.'

The woman looked at him seriously. 'You know, I can't even remember your second name,' she said.

'It's Gilman,' he said. 'Peter.'

'Ah, that's right. And I'm Mary Nicholas.'

'Yes,' he said. 'I remember.'

'How long have you been down here?'

'Three months,' he answered. 'I hope it's until the end of the war. That would suit me fine. I'd like to leave the fighting to the Yanks.'

'You're honest about it, anyway,' she said. 'My husband makes out he's doing work of national importance. He *whispers* when anybody asks. Just as if he's in espionage or something. He's in the Ministry of Pensions, in Manchester. God, he's a wet week, believe me. He's so prissy. He even put a bloody cuckoo clock in our air-raid shelter.' She laughed wearily.

Gilman stood up. 'I'll have to be going,' he said. 'I thought I'd better come up and explain about last night.'

'That's all right,' she replied easily. 'Any time. I don't go out. Just knock.'

Gilman smiled at her. 'Thanks,' he said. 'I will. Maybe sometime you'll show me your cuckoo clock.'

*

The parish church of St Peter and St Paul, Telcoombe Magna, dated from the eleventh century and had a long, wonderful roof, ribbed like the upturned hull of a boat. Mottled slabs paved its walls listing the members of important families, dormant now beneath the chancel floor; there was a font dating from Elizabethan times; Cromwell's soldiers had cut, but not destroyed, the fine screen with their ignorant swords. On the side of one of the pews – made much of by children – was carved the demure figure of a bare-breasted mermaid.

At two o'clock on the short, mean January afternoon the first parishioners of Telcoombe Magna and Telcoombe Beach walked uncertainly into the church; Mr and Mrs George Hicks, who kept the village store at the beach, with Sammy, their fifteen-year-old son, who reluctantly helped them. They came through the rattling oak doors timidly, unvaried expressions of puzzlement nailed on their faces. Eric Sissons, the vicar, was standing almost at the altar steps. He saw them, said, 'Ah,' and walked towards them nervously.

'You're the first, I'm afraid,' he greeted them as brightly as he could. 'Still, there'll be plenty here soon.' The family were not regular churchgoers. Mr Hicks, who had a mole on his eyebrow which lent him an undeservedly devilish appearance, said: 'What be it all 'bout then, vicar? I 'ope it b'aint be just a church service.'

'Nor one of they appeals,' his wife added emphatically. 'We 'ad to shut the shop.'

Sissons said: 'It's not a service and it's not an appeal.' He felt like saying, 'It's an order.' But he only

68

added: 'It's something very important. Something which affects us all.'

He was grateful when they passed on without further words, seating themselves typically in the back row and staring, unspeaking, down the dim length of the church. The Hibberts, a family from Telcoombe Magna, were next, parents, two sons and a seventeen-year-old daughter, Tilly, who smelled of chickens. The father and the boys came in wearing their farm clothes and with mud still on their boots. 'What's all this then?' asked Jack Hibbert. 'Getting us away from work.'

'It is very important,' Sissons told him. The family, looking as if they thought he was lying, moved into the church. Sharply they nodded to the Hicks, whom they did not like and moved three rows down on the other side of the aisle.

Deaf Mrs Bewler and her son Bob, the simpleton of Telcoombe Magna, arrived next and headed, with much fuss but no questions, towards their normal pew. Sissons reflected that for years he had been trying to move them further back where their combined singing – hers loud and tuneless, his mad – would interfere less with the choir. There would be no need for that any longer. He watched them sideways as more people came through the door and saw the widow and her poor son drop to their knees and pray with rivalling fervour. They sat up and knelt down together three times. Sissons wished he could pray with so little impediment.

The people began to come through the door in greater numbers. To the vicar came the sad reflection that they had never arrived like this for services. The faces were puzzled, annoyed, worried, excited. They had been brought from their homes and their work for what? 'I heard it's the King visiting,' said Mrs Katlin, a widow who had lived, the only permanent resident, at the Beach Hotel for twelve years. 'Is it His Majesty?'

'No,' replied Sissons. 'It's not . . . not really.' He wondered where she would go when they were moved out. Where would they all go?

In thirty minutes the church was fuller than he had ever seen it, even at Christmas. The people's collective breath in the chilled air rose above the pews like a strange universal halo. Tom Barrington came through the door, set-faced, his expression hardening even more when he saw the people occupying every pew. 'Pity you can't take a collection,' he muttered to the vicar.

'I fear we might have to give it back,' replied Sissons. He felt annoyed at Barrington's bitterness because his own was just as sharp and deep. Barrington strode into the church and only then did Sissons see that Jean, his wife, and Annette his daughter, who managed the dairy herd on the farm, were behind him. They walked by dutifully like a Victorian family. The vicar imagined Barrington had told them. The girl smiled shyly at him. She was eighteen. She might be relieved to be away from the farm and the timetable of cows.

Horace Smith, the little poacher, came through the door next with Minnie, his large wife. He was nervous of the church, which he never attended, and went down the side-aisle timidly, his wife holding his hand, like a son with his mother.

Doey Bidgood and his sister, Beryl, who had been

engaged for as long as anyone could remember to Lenny Birch, came in almost last. Doey winked towards someone in one of the pews. 'What's goin' on then, reverend?' he asked. Then shrewdly: 'They Yanks going to take us over?' He went jauntily on without expecting an answer.

Almost everyone in the village was now crowded into the nave. The exception was remedied just before two forty-five when the government people were due to arrive. Sissons sensed the presence of Mrs Mahon-Feavor outside the door; it was something he had learned to know. Opening it to its fullest extent he saw that he was right.

Mrs Mahon-Feavor of Telcoombe Manor, feathered hat squatting like a tatty bird of paradise above the aloof and lined face, fur coat coming apart at the skins, and walking stick raised as if to assault the door, stood in the porch. She was regally flanked by her two sons, Jolliffe and Andrew, both Guards subalterns, and followed by her uniformed daughter Bridget, an adjutant in the WRAF. It occurred to Sissons that she looked like someone under military arrest. Without a word, and yet on some sensed sign, the echelon moved into the church and proceeded down the nave. Barrington turned with the rest of the heads to witness the entry. The two sons wore Sam Browne belts which must have belonged to their father (who had been the type to have a spare Sam Browne) because they had not been available to officers since nineteen-forty. They proceeded to the family pew at the front, under the lectern, and sat with tidy ceremony. Mrs Mahon-Feavor squatted, eyes open and unblinking, while her three children knelt for the

71

statutory prayer, apparently, Sissons thought, saying hers by proxy. When they were seated the church became restless though silent. Nobody spoke but the Devon people began to look around expectantly. Sissons remained by the door. Doey, who was in the back pew, leaned towards the front and whispered waggishly: 'What we waitin' for, reverend? Jesus?'

Sissons, smiling wanly, shook his head. 'I wish it were, Doey,' he replied. 'It might answer a lot of questions.'

'And it'd be nice for you,' said Doey matily.

At that moment Sissons saw they were coming, two black, clean cars mounting the short hill towards the church. They pulled up outside the lychgate, shiny limousines like a short but expensive funeral procession, followed by an American jeep containing three officers and a driver. From the black cars came two naval officers, one with sufficient gold braid to be the admiral, followed by various civilians, two gripping attaché cases, and three women in the green uniform of the Women's Voluntary Service. He took a step towards them, shook hands with the admiral and several others in a confused manner. He almost felt inclined to salute. He did not retain any of the names, although he knew the admiral was called Denning-Pryce. 'This way, please,' he said as though there were an alternative, and led the procession down through the packed people in the church.

The entry of the formation had an electric effect on those in the pews. Had it been a Gestapo captain at the head of his henchmen it could scarcely have caused a greater sensation. The younger naval officer led the way, following the vicar, the admiral came next, head bowed as if he spent much time gazing into deep water, with the ladies and officials wedged between him and the American officers who brought up the rear. Their out-of-step footfalls made their progress even more threateningly official. 'High-ups. I reckon we're going to see a bit o' trouble 'ere,' forecast Doey in a whisper to the people in his locality. The formation reached the chancel steps where a line of chairs had been arranged on the worn red carpet. A thick silence had covered the assembly. Then Bob Bewler, the simpleton, unable to stand the pressure, began to applaud. Several people helplessly joined in.

Admiral Denning-Pryce looked embarrassed and the three WVS ladies smiled gently and with under-standing between themselves. The clapping was smothered under a chorus of rustic shushing. Colonel Schorner, sitting on the right of the group, hardly heard what was going on. He was staring up at the lovely, simple, ancient roof of the church, the bowed rafters and ribs, black with years. It astonished him that this was, casually, a village church. The walls were thick with age and hung with memorial tablets like heavy pictures in a gallery. Through the pointed windows the tired light of the winter day softly glowed behind the reds, blues and yellows of the stained glass. He turned to look at the east window, a coloured saint on each side, a glowing Christ in the middle. Then his eyes came down to the people, row after row, worn faces looking over the worn pews, all turned eagerly, apprehensively, towards the chancel where he now sat. He felt guilty and sad.

Eric Sissons had asked Tom Barrington if he

wanted to be in the front and introduce the visitors. As chairman of the parish council it was, properly, his duty. Barrington had been blunt. 'No, I'll sit in a pew, thanks. You tell them – it's your bloody church.'

Sissons now stood haplessly before the people. He seemed to be short of breath. Why did he have to do it? Glancing around him was, he thought, like looking at a Breughel painting, the rough, thick, needful faces, each showing its own small drama. It was terrible, he thought, disgraceful. He opened his mouth but nothing happened. Again he tried. 'Lost your tongue, vicar?' called the irrepressible voice of Doey Bidgood over the heads. Some laughed a little; most turned and shushed him.

'Yes, I think I have,' confessed Sissons more loudly than he had intended. 'It's difficult to know what to say, where to begin.' He looked behind him at the visitors arranged on the chancel chairs. There was no help there. Turning back towards the congregation his eyes caught those of Beatrice Evans sitting beside her husband. She gave him a friendly nod, as if to say, 'Start now.' Encouraged, he looked up at the rest of the people again.

'Dear friends, people of this parish,' he began. 'As you may have gathered, this is no ordinary meeting. You have been told to come here for a very special purpose. Something which will, immediately, affect the lives of all of us. The officers and people you see behind me on the chairs have all come to help . . . to explain things. But first, for a brief statement on what is taking place, I would like to introduce Rear Admiral Sir Arthur Denning-Pryce . . .' He glanced at the slip of paper in his fingers. He repeated, 'Sir

Arthur Denning-Pryce, DSO, DSC and RN . . .' He fluffed. 'Royal Navy, naturally. I . . . I . . . this . . . this is Admiral Sir Arthur Denning-Pryce.'

The vicar sat down heavily, as though worn out. The admiral, a bulky grey man with a double jowl, glowered at him as he would glower at a man cowering under fire. Heavily he got to his feet and with a wounded limp moved forward to the front of the chancel.

'Ladies and gentlemen,' he began sharply. It sounded like an accusation. Schorner closed his eyes and remembered the British he had seen on the cinema screen. They were true after all. He looked up and caught the glance of a young, dark woman in the front pew, sitting next to Beatrice Evans. The admiral coughed and produced a sheet of paper. 'First of all I have something to read to you. This is a government notice which will be read at five similar meetings to this in various parts of this district over the next twenty-four hours. Please listen carefully as it affects you all.'

He fumbled and pedantically unfolded the sheet of paper like a maid opening a napkin. 'It is headed: Requisition Order.' Curiously, he turned the notice round and pointed to the words as though trying to convince them that he was telling the truth. He coughed wetly and went on: 'This order authorizes the military requisitioning of an area of South Devon bounded by the roads from Wilcoombe to the sea at Start Bay. This includes the villages of Telcoombe Magna, Telcoombe Beach, Burton, Sellow, Norman-croft and Mortown but does not include Wilcoombe. All civilians with their possessions, including livestock, must be evacuated from the area by twenty-first January, 1944.'

A dumbness fell over the church, an eerie stunned vacuum; five hundred wooden people. Some heads craned silently forward like geese as if to make sure they had heard right. Others sat blinking. A whimper came from a woman at the back; deaf Mrs Bewler turned to her fool son and made 'What? What is it?' motions with her mouth.

The first audible words came from Mrs Mahon-Feavor. Scarlet-faced, she abruptly shouted at the admiral, 'You bloody old fool!' Her Guards officer sons and her angular WRAF daughter, equally outraged, looked as though they might at any moment attack the elderly naval man. The angry return ignited the whole crowd. In an amazing moment they were shouting and howling and on their feet waving arms and fists. Sissons made flapping motions with his vicar's hands.

Schorner had never seen anything like it. He felt as if he were confronted by hostile and primitive tribes. Several men came down the aisle. Admiral Denning-Pryce, who had been at the Battle of the Dogger Bank, stood his ground, fire-eyed now, waving the piece of paper, the proclamation, before him like some invincible weapon.

Howard Evans was smartly to his feet and gently held the people who had moved forward away from the chancel. Mrs Mahon-Feavor quelled the outcry as quickly as she had begun it. Getting to her feet and clambering on to the seat of the pew, hat feathers dipping, the seams of her coat yawning beneath her waving arms, she shouted: 'Sit down! Sit down everyone! Quiet! Quiet at once!' They knew the voice of authority when they heard it. They slumped back into their seats, their protests swallowed in their scowls. Schorner watched with increasing astonishment. He had never experienced the power of the feudal system.

Within a few moments the church was almost as quiet as it had previously been, a quiet only underscored by some brittle whispering and the sniffing of women. Mrs Mahon-Feavor had climbed down from the pew, assisted by all three uniformed offspring, and now sat, ugly with challenge, facing the paled admiral. 'I will continue,' he said.

He blinked at the sheet of paper again, mouthing the opening words silently, trying to find the place he had reached. He discovered it and drawing a deep breath said, clearly as a preacher, 'This requisition and evacuation will be carried out with the assistance and direction of the military and naval personnel, the US Army and US Navy, the civilian agencies, and local government authorities. Compensation will be paid for any damage to land or other property, for disturbance and hardship. Alternative accommodation will be found for all inhabitants and assistance given in the disposal of livestock and other farm produce.' He looked up from the words. 'The order is signed by the Secretary for War,' he said. His face had lost its fight. He made to sit down, then rose and merely said: 'I'm very sorry.'

Now there was no shouting. They sat stunned, fumbling to try and understand, to take it in. Mrs Mahon-Feavor's face had dropped almost to her lap. She looked up, great hurt in her wrinkled eyes, and said, almost sulkily, 'You do realize that includes my home, Telcoombe Manor.'

'Yes, madam,' replied the admiral. 'I do.'

'It has been in my family for seven centuries,' she muttered. But said no more. Her younger son, who was at the Guards depot and had never seen action, looked as if he wanted to fight. The elder one, who was also at the depot but had gone to France just in time for Dunkirk, gave the impression he was already trying to think of a plan.

From his seat halfway down the church, Tom Barrington rose heavily. His name was whispered across the crowd, people telling their neighbours who he was, although everyone already knew. 'Are we to be allowed the privilege of asking questions?' he said. He sat down again.

Admiral Denning-Pryce nodded tiredly. Schorner, watching him, could see how much the encounter had taken out of him. 'Yes,' said the admiral. 'But individual matters must be dealt with individually. I simply cannot deal with them, nor have I any authority to do so. It was my unpleasant duty to come here to Telcoombe Magna to read that notice. That was all I was required to do by the Prime Minister, Mr Churchill, and the War Cabinet. If, however, I can help to ease matters, I would like to help, believe me.'

Barrington nodded and stood again. 'Does Mr Churchill realize that this area, thirty thousand acres, is some of the richest farmland in this country and yet he orders that it must be abandoned, just left, at a time when they're ploughing damned gravel to try and raise crops? Does he know that – or does he care?'

An assenting growl went up through the church.

Schorner watched the heads above the pews nodding as if on strings. The admiral rose and said: 'I am sure that the matter was fully discussed before the decision was taken.'

'It weren't discussed with us!' shouted Doey from the back. A rabble of voices agreed. Mr and Mrs Hicks, from Telcoombe Beach, stood up pathetically together. 'Does it mean shops as well?' she asked tremulously after he had nudged her. 'We've got the shop by the beach.'

'It does, I'm afraid,' nodded the admiral kindly. 'Everything, shops, houses, schools, churches, including this one, farms, everything.' Schorner shut his eyes and imagined the couple's shop on the beach.

Now the poacher, hardly higher than the pew, stood, his sharp face and nose thrust forward belligerently. 'You'll be taking every man's living away,' he said bitterly. 'What they going to do?'

'Jobs and accommodation will be found outside the area,' said the admiral. 'That has been undertaken.'

'Why's everybody got to get out anyway?' someone demanded from the middle of the church. Nobody stood to match the voice up. 'Yes, there's plenty of room for soldiers as well,' put in another voice. 'Nowhere else have they kicked the people out, just because of the soldiers.'

Schorner suddenly found everyone on the chancel chairs was looking at him. The admiral turned slowly and regarded him. 'Would you like to say something, colonel?' he inquired.

'I don't want to,' muttered Schorner as he stood up. He walked to the fore. His tongue felt dry. They were staring at him like an enemy. 'I'm Colonel Schorner,' he began. 'I have no authority to comment on these matters. It just happens, unfortunately for me, that I'm in command of the advance party of the US Army engineers in this district. All I can tell you is that the sooner we get this business through, the sooner we can all go home. I'd like just to say, as a farmer in the United States, how very sorry I am.'

He almost tripped over the seated admiral as he tried to retreat to his chair. 'But *why's* everybody got to *get out*?' insisted the voice again. 'That's what I want to know.'

Tom Barrington stood up. 'Since nobody else appears to want to answer the question,' he said. It was almost a snarl. '*I'll* tell you. Nobody has told *me* to keep quiet about it.' He looked around the church. A wintry bird could be heard singing in the silence. A woman near the door looked out and said, quite loudly: 'It's started to rain again.'

Barrington turned towards the platform. No one there had moved. No one challenged him. 'I'll tell you,' he repeated. 'The reason that we all have to clear out, lock, stock and barrel, is because live ammunition is to be used in these exercises, bullets, shells and bombs.'

Admiral Denning-Pryce unsteadily got to his feet. He waved the piece of paper at Barrington as if it were an indictment. Barrington ignored him. 'During the next six months or so,' Barrington went on, 'this place, this church, our homes and farms, are going to be the middle of a battlefield. Don't expect to come back – whenever you do come back – and find your houses in one piece.' He almost threw his head around in defiance. 'Somebody has to tell the truth – and that's it.'

Barrington sat down again, the force of his bulky and angry descent sounding through the church. Wearily the elderly admiral stepped forward. There was one more thing to say.

'You are all aware of the importance of secrecy in wartime,' he said like someone espousing a lost cause. 'I have been asked to point out that this whole matter must be kept as . . . er . . . quiet, as confidential as possible. The less people outside the area know about it the better for the war effort.' He made a final effort. 'Careless Talk Costs Lives.'

It was early, damp evening by the time Schorner returned to the camp. As Albie Primrose drove the jeep through the tunnel-dark, steep-sided lanes, Schorner sat back silently, unhappily. 'You'll never have to worry about the car leaving the road here,' he remarked eventually. 'This tight, it's like driving in a trench.'

'Sure is, sir,' replied Albie. He had been standing in the porch at the back of the church. 'Those folks were real sore,' he said. 'Can't say I blame them.'

'Nor me, son,' said Schorner. 'But they'll get it all back. One day. And that's the day you and me will be up to our hair in shrapnel, sitting in holes in the ground, scared as shit, and they'll be back there in their houses, good and safe. In a war everybody has to give something.'

As the lane humped before dropping again towards the camp they could see the glow of kerosene lamps fringing the wind-ragged trees on the immediate horizon. 'Look at that,' muttered Schorner. 'Just get a load of that. It's like signalling to the Germans to come in and get us.' The jeep turned into the field and Schorner leaned out and shouted to the sergeant at the gate guardpost. 'Get those lights covered, sergeant. And right now! Do you want the goddamned dive-bombers over?' The sergeant, Perry, looked with wild concern, stupidly at first at Schorner and then up into the night sky as if to check it was dark, before turning and running heavily towards the points where the lights were showing. Schorner could hear him shouting: 'Get those lights covered! Do you want the goddamned dive-bombers here? Get them covered!'

Schorner jumped from the jeep and walked across to his own hut. He was grateful that the iron stove had been lit. A cloud of warmth came from it. 'Albie,' he said tiredly, 'when that sergeant's through with the lamps and the dive-bombers, will you tell him to get the men together in the mess tent. I guess that's the best place. I'd better tell them about the situation. Yes, the mess tent. In ten minutes, okay?'

'Okay, sir,' replied Primrose. He left the hut but came back to salute, then left again. Schorner sat down on the bed and smiled at what Albie had done. It was like a gesture of sympathy.

The telephone rang, so sharply and unexpectedly that he jumped. He cursed himself, then picked it up. 'Colonel Schorner.'

'Ah good, good, right first time,' said the English voice cheerily. 'Colonel, I'm Captain Westerman, Royal Artillery.' There was a pause, an uncertainty, then: 'British Army.'

'Sure, of course.' Schorner grinned to himself. 'What can I do for you, sir?'

82

'I'm commanding officer of the unit in Wilcoombe, the anti-aircraft gun.'

'Yes, I know. I saw it when we came by.'

'I thought I'd just call and well . . . welcome you. But also, I've had instructions from way up high, God almost, that I must appoint a liaison officer to deal with matters that might come up between us. We're a sort of little outpost here, very quiet too for the past couple of years, and now it seems as though we're going to be surrounded by a few thousand of your chaps. So we've got to have someone as a . . . a go-between, I suppose you could call it.'

Schorner nodded into the phone. Outside his men were walking through the wet field on their way to the mess tent; cheerful voices in the jaded darkness. Someone set up a loud whooping. He covered the phone so that the British officer would not hear it. 'Sure, captain,' he said, pushing his mouth close to the mouthpiece. 'That's a sensible idea. If I know anything about the US Army we'll have a whole battalion of liaison officers heading this way in no time at all.'

Westerman laughed defensively, it seemed, at the other end. 'Well, from our side it will be just one chappie. Of course we're only a small unit and a small army. Small, but we like to think pretty workmanlike. A rabble wouldn't have got out from Dunkirk, would it?'

'No, sir,' Schorner agreed carefully. 'You did a great job at Dunkirk.'

'Your chaps will be learning what it's all about soon,' forecast Westerman. He sounded stronger now. 'I don't suppose many of them have ever seen a German.'

'Only if they come from Milwaukee,' said Schorner.

'Oh?' said Westerman, not understanding. 'Why if they come from Milwaukee?'

'It's a German city,' replied Schorner simply. 'It was settled by German immigrants to the United States. My family was originally from that country.'

He was sure he heard the Englishman swallow on the distant end of the phone. 'Really,' said Westerman nervously again. 'Yes . . . I'd never thought of that. No, well, of course, you might well be.' His tone brightened encouragingly. 'Still, you're on our side now. I suppose when it comes to it your German chaps will fight as well as anybody else.'

'You bet,' said Schorner evenly. 'When it comes to it. You called me about the liaison officer.'

'Oh yes, so I did. Yes, it will be Lieutenant Bryant, nice young chap. Been to America, so he understands the language and customs and everything. Can I send him over tomorrow?'

'Sure,' agreed Schorner. 'Send him over any time. We're not going out anywhere.'

There was another blank of uncertainty from the other end. Then Westerman quickly said, as if he wanted to finish: 'Right-ho, then, I'll see he gets over about ten.'

'That's fine,' returned Schorner. 'I guess we'll be up and about by then. Good-bye, captain.'

'Oh yes, good-bye. Perhaps we could meet for a quiet beer or so quite soon.'

'Right. I'd like to do that. We'll fix a date.'

Schorner put the phone down. He stared out of the

open door to the marsh of the English night. 'What a dummy,' he said quietly.

Two flaring yellow kerosene lamps were hanging over a table just inside the mess tent flap, illuminating the nearest faces, deepening the eyes and nostrils so that the men looked like Chinese lanterns. The second circle of faces, slightly away from the aura of the lights, were blurred and further behind them the men were just blots in the dimness. As Schorner entered, Sergeant Perry, trying to impress him, bawled the men to attention, but the result, muddled and muffled on the muddy ground, was like the heavy flapping of hidden bats.

Schorner said: 'Okay, thank you, sergeant.' He examined the illuminated faces in front and then peered into the shadows at the rear. 'At ease, men,' he said. There was a further dulled movement. Schorner went behind the table and leaned his fists on the wood. 'You're probably wondering what the hell you're doing in this beautiful English resort,' he began. Some of the soldiers sniggered, but others were not sure. Schorner helped them. 'I'm told,' he said, 'that it's a fine place in the summer – but nobody seems to be able to tell when the summer is. I guess the temperature of the rain goes up a few degrees.' This time most of them laughed.

'Some of you may not know exactly where we are located. All of you will have a general idea of *why* we are here. God, I hope so, anyway.' He paused. 'This area is called the county of Devon. If you look at a map of England, the leg that sticks out like it's kicking at Ireland –' some ironical laughing came from the rear of the tent. Schorner looked up but made no comment. He went on: 'If you take that as a leg, then Devon is the thigh. If you read your history books you'll know that the Pilgrim Fathers left from Plymouth, which is just down the street from here.' He glanced up. 'Any questions so far?'

There was a brief vacuum, then a voice: 'Any women around here, sir?'

Shouts of laughter went up. Schorner said: 'What's your name, son?'

'Harrington, sir.'

'You don't look old enough for women, Harrington. Where are you from?'

'Pittsburgh, sir.'

'In that case, I guess you're old enough for women.'

They all laughed now. Ribald, childish comments flew through the darkened tent. Schorner stopped them with a wave of his hand. 'Don't ask me about women,' he said. 'I'm a married man. I understand all the sort of women you guys want are in London and that's two hundred miles away. And two hundred miles in this country is a long, long way. We're going to distribute free pictures of Betty Grable and Myrna Loy.'

The boyish shouts and laughing broke out again. He waited until they had settled, then added seriously: 'And I don't want any trouble with the local women. And especially not the married women. Their husbands are fighting in Burma and Italy and they won't like the idea of Americans sniffing around their wives and their girls. And don't say they won't know because if they don't somebody else will. Got that?'

There was a mumbled assent from the men. Schorner did not believe a word of it. 'We have a difficult situation in this particular area,' he went on. 'I've just come from a meeting at the church right here in this village which is called Telcoombe Magna. This place has been here for a thousand years and the people have just this afternoon been told that they've got three weeks to beat it – to get out. Another five villages like this one are to be evacuated. Three thousand people have been told to quit. And the reason for this is that the US Army has to use this area for a series of invasion exercises over the next three months . . .' He waited, then said casually: 'Using live ammunition and including bombing and shelling.'

That silenced them. They stood motionless, the yellow faces in the front looked hollow-eyed, the mouths seemed stitched together. Then someone in the middle said: 'Why, sir? Why are they doing that? Live ammunition.' A babble of questions broke out and he stemmed them. 'Because that's the order, son,' he said. 'It's been figured that if the invasion of Europe is carried out as efficiently as the invasion of North Africa and the landings like Anzio in Italy, then we'll all be dead before we've seen our first German. It's got to be better than that. A lot better. The Nazis have been waiting for us for years. Everybody's got to know when to shoot and when to duck.'

The silence had solidified. Schorner went on: 'Our job here is as advance party to make ready certain camps and sites, hards for vehicles and tanks, and then to join with the invasion exercises as engineers. There will be a whole sequence of limited exercises, some on most days, until we've run out of time. There will also be major, all-in manoeuvres involving thousands of men.'

They were still thinking about the live ammunition. 'Sir, can I ask a question?' The man pushed his way through the first line of faces.

'Sure, son,' said Schorner. 'What's your name?'

'Kerzick, sir. Renton Kerzick.'

'Okay, Kerzick.'

'Some guys . . . some guys here in this tent maybe . . . well, some guys look like they're going to be killed by our own side. Is that correct, sir? By Americans?'

'You got it,' nodded Schorner. 'That's what I said.' He tried to grin. 'I've told the sergeants to go real careful.'

It got a laugh, but not much of one. Kerzick said: 'It's crazy, sir. It's bad enough being killed by Germans, but being killed by Americans! I mean, I didn't come into the army to have that.'

'You didn't come on any conditions at all, Kerzick,' returned Schorner quietly. 'You came because Uncle Sam told you to come.' He looked over their heads. 'Okay, that's about it, men. We have to get this camp in some sort of order and then work on another base for more GIs who'll be here in a few days. This place will be lousy with Americans within a month. My guess is that we'll be here until mid-summer, or whatever the English have instead of it.' He looked directly at Kerzick. 'You got the answers now, Kerzick?' he said.

'No, sir. But I guess I'm not going to get them.'

'Right, son,' said Schorner. 'You're not.'

*

On that same day, 1 January 1944, General Dwight D. Eisenhower was confirmed as Supreme Commander of the allied armies preparing to invade the European Continent – Operation Overlord; General Bernard Law Montgomery was appointed Commander of the British 21st Army Group and given overall charge of the assault phase of the invasion, code-named Neptune. In the late light of the afternoon of that same day a Catalina flying boat clattered in to touch down on the calm winter water of Poole Harbour in Dorset, England. It had flown from Charleston, South Carolina, via Bermuda, the Azores and Lisbon, a total journey of four days. On taking off from the Tagus River, Lisbon, it had flown in an arc, far out into the Atlantic, to avoid sighting from the French coast. It turned in over the Western Approaches, where it was joined by two escorting fighter planes, then, skirting Fastnet on the south-west coast of Ireland, it made its final approach over Land's End and across South Devon.

General Arthur C. Georgeton of the US Army was on the flight deck, sitting beside the navigator, as the inelegant aircraft dropped lower over the grey-green of England. He had asked the navigator to tell him when they were over-flying Devon. The man looked around and nodded. 'That's Devon right down there, sir,' he said. 'The city of Plymouth is right on the starboard wing.'

Georgeton manoeuvred his round figure towards the observation window and adjusted his spectacles. The navigator idly wondered how someone of that shape ever got to be a general. It must be brains, he decided. Georgeton peered through the goldfish-bowl window. The pilot obligingly banked the cumbersome aircraft to give him a better view. The sideways drop of the fuselage caught Georgeton by surprise and he stumbled. The navigator caught him by the arm. 'Don't fall out the window, sir,' he said.

Georgeton laughed good-humouredly. 'Right. Down there is where I'm headed, but I'm not in that much of a hurry.' Plymouth had almost gone behind them. He looked down at the indented countryside east of the city, the shadows showing the small folds of pleasant hills, the incisive creeks and estuaries cutting deeply into the land. There was a brief opening of sunshine and the sea below glinted like someone signalling with a mirror. There were collections of roofs stitched together by apparently empty streets. Georgeton took it in, and, taking his bearing from Start Point and its great adjoining bay, named each place in his mind as he had memorized it from the maps. Eventually he straightened up and the pilot corrected the clumsy plane's bank. 'Thanks, boys,' said the general. He grinned around the cabin. God, he thought, they were really boys, too. Clean faces almost like those of children smiled from under the flying helmets. It seemed ridiculous that they could keep such a huge machine in the air. The pilot was smaller and even more boyish than the others. The general wondered how his feet reached the pedals.

He returned to the forward passenger cabin. The plane was full of American officers of all three services. He took his seat beside Captain Oscar Scarlett, his ADC, who had taken over the appointment only the day before they set off from Charleston. 'We're just going in,' he said. 'I got a good look at Devon.'

'How did it look, sir?' asked Scarlett smiling. 'Friendly?'

'It looks okay. I like places with a sea coast. It gives them a *real* look, you know, as though they're fixed to something. That's what's the trouble with the States. It's too big. Half of it seems to be floating around nowhere.'

'Did you see the British fighters?' asked Scarlett. He was a tall man with hair greying years before time. He had been an advertising executive with a Philadelphia newspaper.

'They only came to escort us when we were over Ireland,' pointed out Georgeton. 'There didn't seem a lot of point to it then.'

'Maybe they thought the Irish might attack,' laughed Scarlett. 'It could be. I'm Irish myself, well my family are. The old folks still curse the British.'

Georgeton said: 'These times there's plenty of enemies to go around. Who needs old ones?'

'Looks like we're going in,' mentioned Scarlett. The Catalina had made a cautious circle and was now dropping rapidly, over low hills, over a headland and a hand of small islands, lower and lower, until they felt the contact with the harbour water and the spray flew up to cover the portholes and their view.

The engines of the big plane emitted a final clatter and then died, the propellers flapping around like helpless arms. 'This is England,' the pilot called back. 'At least, I think it's England. If anybody starts shooting I got it wrong.'

The camouflaged flying boat squatted on the water like a resting mallard. A naval launch put out from the distant quay, making a toenail in the limp winter

91

water as it curved towards the aircraft. Scarlett watched it, a sailor standing in the bow like a figurehead. The afternoon was too spent for him to make out anything on the shore.

The front hatch of the flying boat eased open and the cold English air rushed in, their first smell of the new country. Georgeton sniffed heavily and Scarlett grimaced. They left the aircraft first, shaking hands with the flight crew and wishing them luck. They clambered down to the trembling launch. A British naval officer saluted and introduced himself. The land all about the harbour was backing away into a short January evening. There were some seabirds swooping about the flying boat, white shadows, crying harshly in the saline air.

'I have your orders, sir,' said the British officer. He called to the man at the boat's small wheel and the vessel turned abruptly away from the Catalina and made for the indistinct shore. The Englishman handed a yellow envelope to Georgeton. He was uncertain whether to open it then. The boat was rolling with its own momentum and the lights were doused. 'I should wait until you get ashore, sir,' suggested the Englishman with a grin. 'Unless you read braille.'

'You could be right,' Georgeton returned the smile in the dark. 'What's Devon like, sir?'

The officer, unused to that mode of address from a senior, hesitated. Then he said: 'It's lovely, Devon. Small hills and red earth. The drink scrumpy – that's cider.'

'What are the people like?'

The naval man thought, then said: 'Slow and

strong you could say. Not easily pushed around.' The American nodded and tightened his lips as if committing the description to memory. 'The north of Devon is different from the south,' went on the Englishman. 'The north is rugged, the south is softer.'

'Did the war get down there very much yet?' asked Georgeton.

'The war gets everywhere one way or another,' replied the naval officer. 'Plymouth and Exeter were both knocked about in the bombing. There have been hit and run raids on small places. I've spent a lot of time there in this war. There's still a funny sort of peace there. Devon's always been like that. There's not much that would change it.'

The American did not answer. Scarlett coughed and sniffed at the air accusingly. The launch wheeled into the stone quay and they stepped ashore, walking up a length of old, cold steps set into the landing. A heavy US Army staff car with a GI driver was waiting. The Americans shook hands with the English officer and climbed into the back of the car. The vehicle moved along the dark jetty, warehouses looking on one side, fishing boats creaking in the water on the other. Georgeton switched on the interior light of the car. The driver halted, and came around to the passenger door. 'Sorry, sir,' he said. 'I'll have to pull the blinds. It's a black out.'

'How do you find your way when everything's so dark, and on the wrong side of the highway?' asked Georgeton as the man tugged the blinds down and fitted them into their retaining sockets.

'It's a matter of feel, sir,' replied the driver. 'This is a great country for feel.'

He returned to the driving seat and the car moved forward again. The American general opened the yellow envelope. He read carefully for two minutes, then said to Scarlett, 'We go to London now. Tomorrow there's a briefing. This guy Montgomery. They say he's brilliant. But objectionable.'

Scarlett lay on his hotel bed in London, sleepless despite the wearying journey. General Georgeton had gone to his room immediately after dinner. Scarlett had not undressed. The ceiling was lofty and dim overhead, beyond the perimeter of the bedside lamp. He got up and went to the lavatory, then, taking his coat, he went out of the room and down the wide stairs to the lobby.

He tugged on his greatcoat and walked out into the chilled night. Immediately he was caught in the engrossing dark; different shades of blackness, something he had never thought to be possible. A few taxis and cars crept like cats through the streets, their lights filtering through slits in visors across their headlamps. Footsteps approached him and passed by without his hardly recognizing a human form. And yet they walked firmly, unhesitatingly, people alone, people in pairs and groups, talking, laughing, but never faltering even as he approached them without seeing. Some spoke with American voices. They had also become used to the dark.

Fearing he would be lost he kept on a straight course, so that it would merely be a matter of turning and retracing his steps to the hotel. It was a long, high-built street, lined with regular trees; he could feel the dead leaves like dirt under his shoes. His eyes learned quickly; he began to pick out the lofty-roofed houses against the night sky. There came a break in the buildings, nothing more than a hole. He thought it might be a square or a small park until he realized that it was a yawning space carved by a bomb. Only a week before he had been in Washington, with his wife, in a restaurant beside the misty Potomac. The city had been flooded with its customary white light. It seemed many years ago.

He had walked, by now a little less cautiously, almost past the vacant space when he heard a sub-dued groaning. Stopping, he listened. It was repeated. It sounded to be only yards away, a woman's groan. Scarlett stopped and hesitated. There was now no other person on the pavement with him, no voices, no footsteps. The noise seeped through the darkness again, like a whimper now. 'Who's there?' he called carefully. 'Who is it?'

The sound was stifled. Two or three low words were spoken and a torch flicked. The beam struck him in his chest, enabling him to see above and beyond it to its source. There were no faces, just a heavy naked negro jacked up between a pair of spreadeagled white legs. They were lying on a piece of canvas.

'What you want, mate?' demanded a sharp woman's voice. It was she who was shining the torch at him.

'Sorry, nothing, nothing at all,' muttered Scarlett. 'I just heard you . . . that's all. I thought you needed help.'

The deep brown male voice came next. 'A don' need no help, mister. Ah is fuckin'.'

Scarlett backed away, stumbling over some loose rubble. He made various apologetic sounds as he retreated and as soon as he felt the flat pavement again he turned and went hurriedly back towards the hotel.

Behind him he heard the white woman and the negro laughing in the night. He slowed to a walk along the gritty pavement. A terrace of large houses rose on his left, their roofs outlined against the paler sky like the prows of moored ships. Abruptly, almost below his feet, it appeared, a basement door turned letting out a warm amber light. It was as though someone had opened a quiet furnace. Two men came out and from their mixed words, laughing snorts and their stumbling up a flight of stone steps, he knew they were drunk. Before the door was closed again by someone inside, he saw they were American Air Force officers.

On impulse he called, 'What's that down there, fellas?'

They halted unsteadily almost at the top of the steps and he could feel them staring at him through the dark. 'Down there?' said one eventually. He blew out wind. 'Goddamn it, this guy don't know what's down there, Harry,' he said with arch surprise.

'Down there,' said his companion heavily, 'is The Wishbone Club. It ain't officially called The Wishbone Club, but we call it that, don't we, Ferdie, pal?'

'Sure, it's just the place you might get lucky, if you pull the right bone. Okay?' He giggled. The drink and the darkness made it difficult for him to focus Scarlett. 'For US commissioned personnel only,' he said, slushing the esses.

'Off limits to all other guys,' said Harry. He gave Ferdie a tug and they rolled clumsily out on to the street, yawning and staggering through the dark, singing separate songs, neither of which Scarlett had ever heard.

Hardly knowing why, and after a moment of standing at the top of the steps, he walked down and knocked tentatively on the door. There was no response. Muffled music seeped from within. There was a brass handle on the door. He turned it and it opened easily. The warmth of the place came out on to his face. The music remained subdued. He looked in on a lobby, fluently furnished; with gentle lighting and a shadowed pink carpet. In a low alcove on his right was a male receptionist in evening dress sitting behind a gilt table, like someone performing a one-man show. 'Can I help you, sir?' he asked. The voice was cockney, although Scarlett could not recognize it as such. The man was young, incredibly sparse and wore spectacles on a nose that just escaped being mere bone. The American had the passing thought that perhaps he was too thin for military service.

'Well,' hesitated Scarlett, 'I'd like to come in.'

'You're not a member, sir?'

'No. I've just got here. I only got to England this afternoon.'

For a moment he was going to be refused entry. The man's long pink fingers were already half-raised when a woman's voice from the far side of the foyer said: 'He's all right, Jimmy. I'll sign him in.'

'Right, Mrs Manifold,' said the bloodless young man. He smiled eerily and handed Scarlett a pen. The American looked at the woman gratefully, then signed the offered book. She was wearing a slender white dress. As she walked towards him, smiling generously, the silk of the garment ruffled across the carpet. Her face was beautiful in a careful way, as though she spent a lot of time making it so. The eyes were pale enough to be fawn. The arms that came naked from the dress were shapely and pale. Scarlett began to feel happier.

'Welcome,' she said. 'Let Jimmy take your coat.'

Scarlett enjoyed letting the man take his damp greatcoat. He shrugged his shoulders and straightened his uniform. 'This is very kind of you,' he said. 'I'm Oscar Scarlett. I only got here this afternoon, to England, I mean.'

'You soon found your way here,' she smiled. 'That was clever navigation. Come in with me.'

Her fingers dropped on his sleeve as they walked from the foyer. 'It was just an accident,' he admitted. 'I was only walking by on the way back to the hotel.'

'Good,' she said so that it sounded genuine. 'I'm glad you did.' She led him into a large but intimate room, carefully lit, with a bar and tables set around a small dance floor. A four-piece band played from a dais and three couples lolled to the tune, heads on shoulders, eyes closed, each partner apparently stopping the other sliding to the ground. There were twenty or so American officers in the place, some of them with women at their tables. 'It's Mrs Manifold, I believe,' said Scarlett, smiling at her.

'Oh, so sorry, I forgot. It's Jean Manifold. Now, Oscar, what would you like to drink?'

He laughed. 'This gets better,' he said. 'Isn't it the man who buys the drinks in England too?'

'Next one,' she said, holding up a well-tended

finger. She motioned him to a table and he held her chair back while she caught the barman's eye. 'I'm the duty hostess tonight, so I buy the first drink. It's the rule.'

He eyed the place unhurriedly. 'Duty hostess?' he repeated. 'What sort of dreamhouse is this, anyway?'

'It's just a social club for Unites States officers,' she shrugged. 'The Courtnall Club. It's been going for a couple of years now.

'The Wishbone Club?' he said raising his eyebrows.

She laughed. 'That too. Some of the boys call it that. I thought you said you found it by accident.'

'I did. The two drunks who were going out called it that.'

'Yes, it's got that nickname,' she said seriously. 'But we don't let the committee know, especially Lady Courtnall, because it's named after her.' The waiter had arrived. He was old and dusty. Of course they had bourbon. Jean Manifold asked for a gin. She leaned forward. 'So you only arrived today.'

'Right this afternoon,' he said. He felt comfortable now. The atmosphere was getting to him. He sat back in the slim chair and looked at her while she spoke. She was about twenty-five, he thought, slim and she wore a wedding ring and a diamond engagement ring. 'We came on a flying boat,' he continued. 'And that's a long ride from the States. I don't think I'll ever get the creases out of my bones.

She saw he was looking at her rings. 'No,' she said, 'my husband doesn't know I come to this place.'

He said: 'I'm sorry. I guess all the guys ask you that?'

She turned the rings on her finger. 'They certainly

do,' she sighed. The drinks arrived and she told the tottery waiter to put them on her account. They raised their glasses to each other. 'He doesn't know because I haven't told him,' she said. 'He's a prisoner in Germany. The poor bastard's miserable enough as it is.'

'That's tough.'

'Especially for him,' she returned. 'I come here because it gives me company and I give company in return. Sometimes I think that's what the war's become, you know – finding someone to keep you company.'

'I think it's soon going to mean something else,' he answered.

She nodded into her gin. She was so at ease that he guessed she was merely carrying on with a conversation she had left unfinished with another man. 'That may be,' she said. 'But for the past three years, anyway since the blitz, it's been just . . . well, waiting. When the invasion starts, then it will be different again.'

'At home we still think England's in the middle of a battle every day. I've heard of GIs getting off the ships and dropping flat right there on the dock in case there's dive-bombers.'

She laughed laconically and said: 'You should see this place clear every time there's an air-raid warning. But not much is happening, is it? Not just now. It's almost as if we're all shipwrecked on a gigantic raft. All waiting for something to rescue us.' She was suddenly listening to the music. ' "Alice Blue Gown",' she said. 'I love this. Can we dance?'

'My pleasure,' he grinned. He put the glass down and looked towards her attentively. She returned the glance with a flush, oddly guilty. He held out his hand and at once she clasped it fiercely. God, he thought, I'm going to bed with her.

Immediately they were on the dance floor she moved close into him, the slim, silken body holding itself against the tops of his legs and his chest. Her full dark hair was under his chin. Without looking up she said: 'This place is going to be quiet tonight, Ossie.'

No one had ever called him that before. He told her and he felt her smile. 'I can't call you Oscar,' she said. 'That's a terrible name. It's like a cartoon name, like Walt Disney. As far as I'm concerned it's Ossie. Is that all right?'

'Okay,' he said. 'You're calling the shots.'

'This place was jam-packed last night, Ossie,' she continued. 'New Year's Eve. You couldn't move.' She paused, the band stopped playing the tune and went immediately, and a touch wearily, on to another. She remained tightly against him, her face thrust into his chest like a woman weeping. 'Where were you last night, New Year's Eve?' she asked.

'Last night, last year,' shrugged Scarlett. 'I've lost track. In a hut by the harbour in Lisbon, waiting for daylight. It wasn't a great New Year's Eve.'

The dance went on. His limbs felt stiff from the travelling. He knew his heart was beating against her face. Casually, sleepily, she took her hand from his shoulder and brought it down between their bodies until it was touching inside his trouser leg. 'Can you take me home,' she asked, quietly, still without looking up at him. 'I feel I want to go home early. It's only around the corner.'

*

101

It was not so dark when they left. A low quarter moon had moved across the sky and cast into outline the buildings and the trees of the street. He walked with his arm about her. He remembered walking home from high school dances like that once. She was almost submerged in the huge collar of her coat. 'My husband,' she said suddenly after they had been walking in silence, 'Mike. He was a pilot. Brought down over Germany. Do you know what they were doing?'

'Bombing, I guess,' he said.

'Leaflets. Dropping bloody leaflets,' she said bitterly. 'Telling the Germans they were naughty and advising them to surrender. Seven boys in that squadron were killed, including my brother. Dropping bits of paper.'

They had reached a heavy house with a flight of smeared steps reflecting a damp moon. At the top she took a key from her bag and turned to him wearing a serious smile. He thought that, after all, she was going to say goodnight.

'Will you come in with me for a few minutes?' she asked politely. 'I'd be glad if you would.'

He put his hand against her neck. It was cool, almost dank. 'Yes, sure,' he said.

She led the way into a hallway, dark and narrow, closed the door and turned on the light. A flight of stairs went up into gloom. She turned and opened a door on his right. 'It's in here,' she said. 'It's a self-contained flat. They've been quite easy to get since the blitz. I've lived here since nineteen-forty. The cat is called Morgan.'

The cat elongated his black and white stomach

along a couch of deep satin cushions. 'The cat and the settee are alike,' she smiled. 'Elderly but elegant.' Scarlett could see that despite her apparent confidence she was unsure. She had taken her coat and put it in a cupboard. 'It's quite cold in here,' she said, putting her hands to her bare upper arms. 'The coke ration gets short at the end of the month, so the radiators don't get hot. Would you like a drink?'

Scarlett moved forward and put his arms confidently about her. 'You're always offering me drinks,' he said. 'Is this some kind of ploy?'

'Yes,' she replied simply. She eased her lips towards him and kissed him with studied gentleness on his lips. He did not press her but let her lie against his neck, her ample hair under his jaw. He had a quick memory of holding hands with his wife over that table by the Potomac only a week ago. At once she seemed to detect the thought.

'You married, Ossie?' she inquired.

'Yes, I am.'

'Take off your coat. You won't feel the benefit when you go.'

'No,' he said vaguely. 'I guess I won't.' He climbed out of the coat. She had gone away to the other end of the room and was taking some glasses and bottles from a cabinet. 'How long?' she said over her shoulder. 'How long have you been married?'

'Two years. Nineteen-forty-one. A week after Pearl Harbor.'

'That was a busy time for weddings,' she smiled. 'You'd be surprised how many Americans I know were married that week.' He was looking at her from the other side of the room, still surprised at her. She

103

brought a bourbon with ice back for him. 'Adultery,' she confided, 'is, you'll find, very nearly as good as the real thing.'

Firmly he took her glass and put it on the low table by the couch. He put his next to it. His arms went around her again, resting against her backbone under the soft dress. 'Listen, now listen,' he said. 'Are you for real? I mean, things don't happen like this. Not for me. I've never been an angel . . .'

'Few soldiers are,' she said with a soft briskness. 'It doesn't go with the job.' She regarded him and he her, their eyes inches apart. 'Look,' she said, 'if you want an explanation, there isn't one. You were looking for company, you may not admit it but you were. And I'm feeling like company. Where will you be tomorrow?'

He shook his head. 'Some place . . . Devon . . .'

'Exactly. Miles away,' she confirmed. 'People can't afford just to hold hands now. I know, I've tried it. You end up writing letters. There's no time, Ossie.' She smiled slightly. 'On the other hand, if you feel you must go, go now, for Christ's sake.'

'There's no danger of that,' he said. 'I'm staying.'

She pulled away from him gently. 'Let me go and put my nightdress on, will you,' she said. 'I like to wear a nightdress!' She walked a few feet towards the door at the end of the room. Then she turned with the small laugh again. 'I do have pyjamas if you feel the same way,' she said. 'All sorts and sizes.'

He laughed and shook his head. 'No thanks. I hate second-hand clothes.'

She was not put out but turned and wriggled her backside good-humouredly at him. He shook his head

104

and sat down by the cat. The room was heavily but tastefully decorated and furnished. There was a long crack in the ceiling and another down the mirror over the fireplace, like a split in sheet ice. He drank the bourbon and put his hand on the cat. His weariness, long days of it on the Catalina, overcame him at once. Unable to prevent himself, he drifted to sleep. He toppled to one side and the cat jumped with a petulant cry which woke him.

His fatigued eyes opened to see her standing smiling at him, her naked arms held out of a long peach-coloured nightdress. Her breasts were standing out against the material. Scarlett blinked and stood up. He embraced her again and her arms went up under his and held almost desperately to his shoulder-blades.

'Don't go to sleep on me, Ossie,' she said seriously.

He shook his head. 'I won't,' he promised. 'With anybody else, but not you.'

'That crack in the ceiling,' she said conversationally, turning her head slightly to one side but not looking at it. 'That was a bomb. The same one that did the crack in the mirror.' She took her arms from him and then took his from her and went over to the mirror. She regarded herself so that the split was down her face. 'It fell just across the road,' she went on. 'Killed seven children in one house.'

'That's terrible,' he said.

'Yes, it was. Terrible.' She returned to him and put her arms lightly around his neck again and rubbed her body against him. 'Are you ready?' she asked.

He kissed her hair. 'Yes. I have been for some time.'

The remark brought a subdued laugh from her. She began to tug him gently towards her bedroom.

'Americans always have some smart answer,' she said.

'Don't British men have smart answers?'

'I don't remember. I gave them up,' she shrugged. 'They all reminded me of my husband. It didn't seem fair on him.'

'In that case I'm American and different,' said Scarlett. They had reached the far door and he saw that it gave into a bedroom, brown and fawn, with a single lamp spreading a pond of light at the edge of the wide bed.

Scarlett began to take his clothes off while she sat on the bedside looking away in thought. Then reaching below the bed she pulled out a case of red wine.

'There are some glasses somewhere,' she murmured absently, feeling under the bed. 'Ah, here they are.' She took out two goblets and held them to the light. 'They're not all that clean,' she mentioned. 'Do you mind? I don't want to have to start washing up now.'

He was naked, standing at the side of the bed. She was sitting only inches away and she leaned her head forward against his groin and began rubbing her hair against him. Her hands went around his thighs and his to the back of her bent neck. 'My father,' she said, 'went to France with the British Army in 1939. He let it be known that the whole object of the thing, as far as he was concerned, was to be able to get drinkable wines at reasonable prices. He brought back whole cargoes of the stuff when he came on leave. He was killed at St Valéry, just before Dunkirk, but he still managed to send a final consignment home before he died of wounds. This is the last case.'

He bent his knees and squatted down naked in front

of her. Her fingers lengthened and enfolded his taut stem. He kissed her urgently and rolled her back over the bed. 'Let's get inside the covers,' she whispered. 'It's more private.'

'Do you ever stop talking?' he smiled, close to her face.

'Sometimes. When I've nothing to say. Jesus, I *do* want you inside me *now*. Please do it now, right away.'

They were below the sheets. He pushed her thighs firmly apart and knelt between them, his tip running against her first and then the rest of his length hungrily entering her. She whistled like an errand boy as he did it. 'That's lovely,' she breathed against his ear. 'That feels very nice indeed. Make it last out a little while, will you. Please, soldier.'

'There's a name for ladies like you,' he said, moving into her. The arches of their legs were against each other.

'I know,' she said. 'Nymphomaniac.'

'No,' he said. 'Beautiful.'

The morning was sharp with January sunshine, without warmth, but splashed across the buildings and parks of London, touching the scarred, bombed walls with a mellowness that made them look as though they had fallen long ago in history.

At nine o'clock a US Army staff car called at the hotel in Lancaster Gate for General Georgeton and Captain Scarlett. As they drove they became silent, watching the damaged streets, people, buses, taxis, moving through the decay. Buildings were holed, stripped, some hardly more than single walls, the sun

107

on them, like gravestones. The spaces that yawned everywhere gave a view of more spaces, more devastation. Sandbags were piled in monotonous pattern high against walls; windows were blind with boards. A battery of anti-aircraft guns, their long-necked barrels stretched out, were spaced across Hyde Park like horses before a race. Georgeton looked up through the staff-car window and nudged Scarlett. Above them in a wan winter sky rode barrage balloons, great-nosed, great-eared, like silver clowns. 'War looks different from here,' said Georgeton thoughtfully. 'How would it have been if America, New York, Chicago, Los Angeles had been blasted like this?'

'There would have been bigger holes,' answered Scarlett simply. 'I guess we would have gotten by. Like the British have.'

The general did not answer. The car turned into Grosvenor Square. Split and crippled trees stood on the grass in the square. The driver took the car into the kerb outside a building half-buried in sandbags. A log-faced British military policeman opened the car door and saluted. A pale American marine at the entrance came to attention as they walked in.

Their overcoats were taken by two young Americans in civilian clothes. A third came through a pair of mirrored doors into a fine room, gilt and pale green, with a chandelier like a glass cake at its centre. There were already twenty or more officers of various services, British and American, in the room, seated on incongruously dainty golden chairs. Scarcely had Georgeton and Scarlett taken the seats indicated to them when a further set of mirrored doors opened and

General Montgomery walked in. He came in alone, with a junior officer eventually following to shut the door behind him. His battledress was well-worn, he had two cap badges in his jaunty black beret, and his medal ribbons were bright as a row of flowers. The assembled officers stood.

'Sit down, sit down, gentlemen. Good morning.' The squeaky voice suited the face.

The junior officer, who had followed Montgomery like a pageboy, opened a briefcase and put some folders on the central table. He then stood precociously, sharply surveying the assembly as if to ensure that it was paying attention. There was a blackboard on one side. Montgomery, his officer's cane giving him the air of a schoolteacher, leaned back against the table and began on a high-pitched note, almost a caricature of himself.

'Gentlemen, two days ago I was in Marrakesh, Morocco, with General Eisenhower and Mr Churchill . . . Winnie,' he glanced around and, as if it were possible that they might not have understood, emphasized, 'our prime minister. As you know, Mr Churchill has had a very nasty bout of pneumonia, but I'm sure we can all be relieved that he seems now to be well on the road to recovery. Thank God. We need him.'

He waited as if he expected some dissent, then continued.' At our meeting Mr Churchill confirmed that a provisional date for the second front, for the invasion of the European Continent, is 1 May. That particular date, May Day you see, should please the Russians, who have been nagging us for goodness knows how long to get on with the invasion, whether or not we were properly prepared. Life is much cheaper in Russia. Mr Churchill has said in the past that he has a nightmare of the English Channel being a sea of corpses. We don't want that, do we?

'General Eisenhower was confirmed as Supreme Commander, Allied Expeditionary Force. The mantle of commandant of the 21st Army Group has fallen on me. My first and major responsibility will be to get the armies ashore on the coast of France, Belgium, or wherever it may be finally decided.

'The codename for the invasion of Europe is to be, as some of you will already be aware – OVERLORD. The assault phase, which is my particular pidgin, is codenamed NEPTUNE, although I hope we spend less time in the water than that gentleman.'

There were polite smiles. Montgomery opened a sheet of paper. 'The directive outlining the objects of Overlord reads like this.' He placed a pair of reading glasses on his nose. They made him look like a small sporting dog.

'To mount,' he began, his voice a little louder but retaining its squeak, 'and carry out an operation, with forces and equipment established in the United Kingdom and with target date 1 May, 1944, to secure a lodgement on the Continent from which fuller offensive operations could be developed. The lodgement area must contain sufficient port facilities to maintain a force of some twenty-six to thirty divisions and enable that force to be augmented by follow-up shipments from the United States or elsewhere of additional divisions and supporting units at the rate of three to five divisions per month.'

As he finished he removed his glasses and folded

both them and the paper. He smiled, the smile so small it became trapped under the little brush moustache. 'Now that doesn't *sound* too difficult, does it?' he said wryly.

His sparse nose sniffed at them.

'The officers here, this morning, are or will be engaged in one aspect of preparation for the invasion, one particular and important area – an area where we intend to try something quite revolutionary. We intend, in fact we have already set the matter in motion, to take over a largish area of Devon, in the West Country, of about 30,000 acres, with the object of training assault forces to the peak of efficiency. This will not be just another military exercise, another war game as you Americans call them. The entire civilian population is being evacuated and live ammunition will be used.'

He waited again to note any reaction. He knew that many of the American officers sitting before him, fresh from their homeland, had never known a real battle in their military lives. No one moved. He continued.

'So far in this war our amphibious operations have not been the most successful. In fact, if you think of Norway, Greece and, most tragic of all, Dieppe, where fifteen hundred Canadian chaps came back in one piece out of a raiding force of five thousand, they've been no bloody good at all.' The expletive came out in a little squeal as the sharp head came forward to throw it out.

He gave his sniff again and went on. 'Even the Operation Torch landings in North Africa, against opposition far less than any we shall encounter in

111

France, were unsatisfactory in many aspects. And I don't have to mention Salerno in this company, or, for that matter, several islands in the Pacific theatre of war to cause you to agree with me that landing from the sea is both hazardous and costly. It has never worked in the history of warfare. Well, not since ten-sixty-six. The only successful amphibious operation so far has been Dunkirk – and then we were going the wrong way! Mr Churchill himself remembers, very soberly indeed, the Gallipoli operation of the First World War.

'There is only one way to make sure that his nightmare of an English Channel full of corpses does not come true. And that is to have an invasion army that is fully trained and prepared and in such force that it can establish a beachhead and reinforce it against the strongest opposition. The timing and many other factors are important. But this preparation is far and above the most important of any factor. We must have *fighting* troops.'

He waited, his little face pecking around the room. 'Tell me,' he said sharply. 'Is there any American *army* – and I emphasize *army* – officer here who has ever heard the proverbial shot fired in anger?'

An uncomfortable silence gathered. Several golden chairs scraped against the polished floor. Only one hand was up. Montgomery jabbed his finger and his face towards the man. 'Major,' he said, 'and where was that?'

'North Africa and Sicily, sir. I was with the Torch Landings.'

'Right,' nodded the British general. 'Well, that was what you Americans would describe as pussyfooting.

112

Europe is going to be a lot harder than that.' He looked around the expressions. 'I take it that the remainder of you gentlemen are fresh from the United States over the past months and weeks.'

He smiled bleakly at them. 'So, so . . .' he continued. 'Here in the United Kingdom we will have a numerically great United States force, very few of whom have ever seen a German, allied to British, French, Belgian, Canadian troops, who know a Jerry when they see one. To land this company of beginners on the Continental beaches in the face of one of the most powerful – and experienced – armies the world has ever seen would be akin to sending me to New York to box against your Joe Louis.'

He obviously hoped that the allusion would please them. A few nervous smiles broke. His eyes snapped shut for a moment, when he opened them again they were stern. 'Operations in Devon will be as lifelike – if that is the correct word – as possible. The area has not been chosen without a reason which will become apparent to you at a later time. Security considerations make it desirable that as few people know as possible at this moment. The civilian population will not like it, nor will the troops taking part find it a happy way of spending their time. All I can tell you is that this training in this essential area is of the greatest importance to our plans for the invasion.'

The British general began rocking himself to and fro on his heels, a curiously patronizing action. 'It may be necessary,' he said, 'to emphasize to those of you who have only recently arrived in Great Britain that the need for security is *paramount*.' He snapped out the final word like a drill sergeant giving an order.

'Paramount,' he repeated more quietly. He made a sharp movement, almost a stationary strut. His edged voice filled the room again: 'Already in the south of Britain a great army is beginning to assemble. By summer it will be one of the mightiest fighting forces that the world has ever seen. Everybody –' he let out a short laugh like a minor gasp '– well, everybody on *our* side anyway, everybody from the King of England to the snottiest schoolboy believes that this army is invincible, unbeatable. They think that in some magic way it is going to fly across the Channel and beat hell out of the enemy in no time at all. Let me tell you, gentlemen, that this magic army is going to need a lot of training, a lot of courage and a lot of luck. Let's hope to God we have it.'

The final sentence was barked out again. He stopped abruptly but it was obvious that he had finished. A curious thing happened. All the strength, the assurance, the arrogance, dropped from him. He stood in a vacuum, a silence, uncertainty cramming his tight, dark face. He half turned, sheepishly, and the young officer who had appeared with him and who had been hovering like a conjuror's assistant picked up a chair and hurried forward. The gaunt, thin man sat down heavily. He looked suddenly tired and sad.

By the time the car left London for the west, January clouds had moved across the buildings and drizzle smeared the streets. Georgeton spent the first hour of the journey looking studiously from the car window, first at the tired city suburbs, then at the widening countryside and smaller towns through which they passed. His rounded form twisted awkwardly in the padded seat as he sometimes tried to catch a second look at a sight which had gone by. He was like some strategist planning a campaign. Scarlett wearily leaned back and thought of Jean Manifold; how he had dragged himself from her arms and bed at seven, returning to the hotel under a sky already light at the seams.

'I called your room at seven this morning,' the general mentioned, as if he could casually read thoughts. He continued to look out of the window. 'There was no answer.'

Scarlett said: 'I guess I was in the bathroom, sir. It was along the corridor.'

'I called again,' said Georgeton. 'Still no answer.'

'I'm sorry about that, sir,' said Scarlett calmly. 'I went back to the bathroom. Maybe it was then.'

'It wasn't important, not at all,' answered Georgeton. He shrugged and extended the movement so that he leaned forward and opened the driver's panel. 'What's this old place called, son?'

'This is Marlborough, sir,' replied the driver. 'You won't believe it but this highway is called the Great West Road. I don't think it's all that great.'

'Keep trying, soldier,' said Georgeton, closing the window. He turned to Scarlett. 'Everybody's a smart-ass,' he complained. Then he said: 'What did you think of Montgomery?'

'He's like the English people you see in the movies,' replied Scarlett. 'He talks like Basil Rathbone.'

Georgeton pursed his lips. 'He's got it right, though,' he said. 'About us not knowing about warfare. I've been in Uncle Sam's army twenty years and I've never even sniffed a battle. Even Eisenhower, before last year in North Africa, had never heard a real gunshot. And he's been in the army since World War One.'

It was Scarlett who now gazed from the car window. The afternoon was dim over the grey fields; some small hills corrugated the horizon. 'The guys in the Pacific must have gotten some idea of war by now. And in Italy,' he pointed out. 'I expect we'll soon be learning fast.'

'We sure will,' agreed the General. 'But we've got a hell of a lot to learn, Oscar. The British have got this war under their fingernails, ingrained in their skin. In their eyes. Just take a look. We don't know a single thing yet.'

Scarlett lay deeper against the upholstery of the car. He was glad when Georgeton did the same. After a few more miles through the dimming countryside the general was blowing out rotund snores. Scarlett closed his eyes gratefully.

Morning came down the English Channel, an inch at a time, until it reached the anti-aircraft unit at Wilcoombe, the stealthy light growing along the resting gun barrel, affording it a faint beauty. The two sentries, one at the gate and the other on the harbour wall, banged their feet on the stones and their arms about their ribs in the manner of tribal warriors performing a regular daybreak ritual.

The unit did not possess anyone who could blow a bugle. Sergeant Horace Bullivant, an obese and ineffectual soldier, was roused by a mundane alarm clock. His fat hand flopped and fumbled from the blankets seeking out the chattel which it then struck firmly, a blow which caused the clock to fall into several disjointed pieces. It still ticked on gamely like something wounded that refuses to die. Bullivant delivered the blow with the same effect every morning. At night he reassembled the clock, replacing the bell and its small brass belfry, the minute hand and sometimes the hour hand also. Bullivant's large loose face seemed to be fixed not very securely to the front of his head. Last night's beer lay in the hollows of his mouth and sleep hung on his ginger eyelashes like sugar. 'God,' he muttered to himself. 'God.'

In civilian life he had been a physically meagre man who, contrary to the accepted and usual form, had waxed fat on the military existence. The domestic years of posting at the gun-site, of which he was the oldest inhabitant, had given him poundage.

Sergeant Bullivant had rolled from the bed on so many military mornings that the mattress, and even the iron frame, bowed to his weight. He performed it now, an almost childish roll, his huge hooped pyjamas spinning like a top. His feet found the chilly floor at the final moment of the tumble and he stood upright with a sigh. Heaving on his greatcoat and sliding his pale feet into bedroom slippers he left the hut and wobbled across the short parade ground to the cookhouse. The windows were steamed up and inside the two unit cooks, known as Mutt and Jeff, moved about like Valkyries. 'Want your gunfire, sarge?' called the sweaty Mutt.

'Just coming up,' augmented Jeff, a young, toothless and hairless man with shining eyes.

Like a man about to pray, Bullivant placed both hands around the enamel mug. It both warmed the hands and preserved the heat of the tea. He took a long, grateful suck.

'Sarge, your water,' announced Jeff handing him a billycan. The combination of the bright eyes and the toothless smile was disturbing. Bullivant took the water and waddled back towards his quarters where he washed and shaved in the hot water provided by the cooks. He pulled on his bulky uniform. His boots had been polished the previous night before he had gone to the Bull and Mouth, and the brasses on his gaiters and belt only needed a brush with a duster. Today, he hoped, his trousers might somehow stay anchored around his stomach.

He stamped his boots on the asphalt outside his quarters, a long habit which had left its mark in the form of a depression by the door, worn enough to gather in rainwater. The morning had grown balefully around the small camp by now. He glanced towards the gun, as if to ascertain that it had not vanished in the night, and then marched towards the two barrack huts where the entire unit was housed.

Throwing open the first wooden door he shouted: 'Action stations! Come on you lot, the Germans are on us! Fall in!'

'Piss off,' whispered a man from his bed just within the door. Bullivant heard him but ignored the remark. He had rarely been brave enough to charge any man with insubordination. Instead he banged the panels of the door with his pudgy fist before turning towards the second hut. He picked up a piece of wood, kept specially concealed like a secret weapon, and as he strode along outside the hut he ran it noisily along the corrugated iron wall. He smiled with satisfaction as he heard the men groan and curse.

Gilman was in the second hut. He had fallen asleep trying to write a short story, an exercise set in his journalism correspondence course, and he woke to Bullivant's summons with the paper distributed on the floor. Hurriedly he gathered it. It was a love story and he did not want the others to read it. Bullivant thrust his face through the door. 'Come on – out of those pits,' he chortled. 'Parade in fifteen minutes. Action stations today.'

Catermole scratched himself fiercely as he crouched under the covers of the next bed to Gilman. 'Christ, what's he on about now?' he grumbled. 'Action? What bloody action?'

Gilman had gathered all the sheets of paper. He pushed them almost guiltily into the bedside locker. 'Oh, it's just another lot of talk,' he shrugged. 'I suppose it amuses him.'

'It don't me,' grumbled Catermole. He got from his bed. He had a big, early-morning erection and, as though reacting to Gilman's words, he covered it, unselfconsciously pushing it into an army sock while he continued scratching pensively. 'Action,' he repeated scornfully. 'I didn't join the army to go into action.'

There *was* something happening, however, because a full morning parade of the unit was unique. Desultory pay parades, more like assemblies, took place on Fridays and there was an occasional inspection by some touring busybody officer, but to be ordered to turn out in the early light, in straight lines, was a matter for conjecture and grumbling.

'Who's he think we are, then?' demanded Killer Watts, the unit electrician. His surname had ensured him the job. Knowing nothing about electricity, he had fused the entire system on several occasions. 'Parades,' he continued to Gilman and Catermole, as they stood at ease in the short double file of thirty men, almost the whole battery. 'We ain't the Grenadier Guards. How can we *parade* with a measly few blokes like this.'

Gilman pushed his head out tortoise-fashion and peered along the line. Stomachs and heads were at random, in and out, short and tall, giving the parade the look of a carelessly-built fence.

Captain Westerman, the commanding officer, and Lieutenant Bryant were obviously taken with the same thought. They advanced across the asphalt square that did duty as both barrack square and volleyball court and eyed the two ranks dubiously. 'Haven't we got any more chaps than this?' whispered Westerman. 'It doesn't seem many, does it?'

'Only the cooks are absent, sir,' replied Bryant, eyeing him sideways. Did he imagine some were hiding? 'We've even got last night's guard detail on duty. Just to make up the numbers. And two from the sick bay.'

Westerman stopped fifty yards short of the parade and regarded them sulkily. 'Makes you livid, really, Bryant, don't you think? What we have to put up with.

When you think this place will be absolutely lousy with Yanks soon. Thousands, millions, of them. And this is the best we can do.'

Bryant, searching for the logic, merely said: 'Yes, sir.'

'One of the things you've got to impress on the Americans when you do this liaison business is that we do a good job with very small resources. They won't understand, but you can try.' He paused thoughtfully. 'Do you know,' he said unhappily. 'I've heard they get paid *monthly*. Even their rankers. Monthly.'

Bryant obligingly raised his eyebrows. Westerman sniffed and marched on. Bullivant called the men to attention, at first bawling: 'Parade!' then modestly changing it to 'Party' and finally to 'Squad!' before shouting the order. Their boots came together with only a few late or early. Bullivant bounced like a large rubber ball towards Westerman and saluted. 'Ready for inspection, sir.'

Westerman observed the sergeant's slipping belt. He wished the man could keep his trousers up. It was that belly. 'Right, sergeant,' he said, returning the salute briskly. He felt his thumb strike his ear. Followed by Bryant he strode slowly along the front rank. A wispy beer smell issued from it. Hardly one uniform fitted, hardly a cap was sitting correctly on a head. Khaki pancakes. Perhaps they could all change caps with each other, he thought hopelessly. Change around until every man had one that fitted. He dismissed the idea. He returned to the front of the two ranks and told Bullivant to stand them at ease. Hitching his lazy trousers, Bullivant did so.

Westerman braced himself in front of them like an

inadequate actor. 'This unit,' he began importantly, 'has been given a mission.'

He watched the nasty silence spread across the faces in the ranks. 'No need to fret, nothing dangerous,' he assured them. 'But it requires organization and hard work, and I know that these qualities are here, no matter how well concealed.' A smile flitted along the brown rows. 'We're going to have a few thousand Americans in this area very shortly. You will already know from your contacts with the civil population that a large area is to be evacuated so that our allies can shoot live ammunition at each other in preparation for the invasion.

'This unit must be on its toes to repel air attack from the real Germans while these Americans are settling in. They've never been in an air raid and we don't want them frightened out of their wits before they've even made themselves comfortable. They will be bringing their own anti-aircraft units in due course to protect their build-up operations.' He smirked and pointed upwards. 'We may have to show them where the sky is.' The ranks returned the smirk. Westerman went on. 'But until they do we have to provide protection.'

He pointed his cane at Bryant. 'Lieutenant Bryant has been seconded as liaison officer with the advance Yanks. The best of British luck to him.' Bryant tried a quarter smile of acknowledgement. Westerman went on. 'The other function, the mission this unit has to accomplish is a little different. Three thousand people are to be moved from the area and we have to give them a hand. As usual, there's a great shortage of transport and everything has to be cleared out, furniture, animals, stock, not to mention people. We have been instructed to use the two big lorries and the platoon truck to assist in whatever way we can. Sergeant Bullivant will be detailing the squads.'

Bullivant tried to look stern and reliable. 'The three vehicles will report to the parish hall in Wilcoombe this morning,' went on Westerman, 'where you will take instructions from the lady in charge of the Women's Voluntary Service. Good luck, men.'

Barrington left his farm early and drove in his Austin Seven down through the lanes towards Telcoombe Magna. He could tell by the feel of the air that it was going to be one of those bland, springlike days that come even in January to the West Country. He had only driven half a mile, to the crossroads on the Wilcoombe to Totnes road when, with almost a shock, he saw a line of four furniture removal vans moving steadily towards the evacuation area. They were starting already.

At Telcoombe Magna he noted at once the business-like air about the US Army advance camp – manned by an armed and gaitered GI. A sentry post had been established at the gate and there was a white barrier pole across the entrance. Next to the barrier was an oblong hut from which flew a Stars and Stripes larger than the hut itself.

He took the car along the narrow, familiar road and caught sight of a segment of sunshine lying over the Channel. Barrington realized he was a man untouched by war. He had been seventeen in 1918 so that he had missed the slaughter of those only months older than himself; the fact that he was a farmer and in the upper age bracket had excluded him from military service in this war. The only time he had ever fired a gun was at a pheasant or a fox.

The church was down the hill, towards the sea. Reaching the churchyard he saw Sissons, the vicar, standing alone by the porch, a square of paper in his hand. Barrington stopped the car and walked through the lychgate. 'What's that, the eviction order?' he said.

Sissons looked up. He smiled a half-smile. 'It might as well be,' he replied. 'It's a message from the bishop. It has to be fixed to all church doors in this area. In the hope that our allies will not plunder or wreck them.'

'What did the bishop have to say about it all?'

'What could he say? He was merely passing on a message, an order. At his suggestion we, he and I, knelt and prayed that the high explosive or whatever, would by some miracle miss our steeples, but I got the feeling that we weren't getting through very well. It's very embarrassing, you know, praying like that, with a bishop. Somehow you expect something better to come of it.'

Sissons read the notice aloud. He was wearing his cassock and as he read, Barrington thought, for the first time, that he liked him. Sissons sat on a Victorian tombstone.

'It's headed "To our allies of the USA". It says, "This church has stood here for several hundred years. Around it has grown a community, which has lived in these houses and tilled these fields ever since there was a church. This church, this churchyard in which their loved ones lie at rest, these homes, these fields are as dear to those who have left them as are the homes and graves and fields which you, our Allies, have left behind you. They hope to return one day, as you hope to return to yours, to find them waiting to welcome them home. They entrust them to your care meanwhile, and pray that God's blessing may rest upon us all."'

Barrington glanced at him. 'Very poetic and touching,' he said. 'I'll be interested to see what sort of notice the Americans take of it.'

Sissons took a hammer from beneath his cassock and tacked the notice to the church door. 'What are you going to do with your livestock?' he asked.

'Sell it, what else?' said Barrington. 'Unless I can arrange to rent some pasture outside the area, and that's going to be difficult. There's going to be some bargains in cattle going at Totnes market in the next couple of weeks. There's Hannaford's smallholding, on the Newton Abbot road. He's getting on now and I think I can buy it. I'll keep some of the stuff together at least. I can keep the pigs and poultry but there's no room for the cows.'

Dolefully Sissons smiled. 'Pigs and poultry,' he mused ruefully. 'I've got Cecily and the old man. I wish I could send them to market. Not that I'd get much for them.'

They were walking towards the church door. As they did so an American jeep drew up outside the gate and the driver called: 'Hey, lady.' They stopped and turned. Sissons realized the mistake had been made because of his cassock. The driver did not seem to be embarrassed. 'Which way's the ocean?' he called.

Sissons pointed due south. 'Keep going,' he advised

tartly. 'You'll know it when you get there. It's shiny and wet.'

The American was not put out. He waved with exaggerated cheerfulness and roared away noisily. 'I fancy our road accident figures will be showing an increase,' mentioned Sissons.

'They'll kill a few,' said Barrington. 'But they'll make up for it by fathering a lot more.' They walked towards the door again. Barrington returned to their interrupted conversation. 'A market will be just about it,' he forecast. 'Getting all these people out and farming them out elsewhere. God only knows how it's all going to work.'

'God moves in a mysterious way,' acknowledged the vicar. 'The trouble is it's sometimes so mysterious as to be incomprehensible.'

They had walked through the dim porch of the church with its old stone benches and the tatty pieces of paper fixed to its notice board. Whist drives, jumble sales, missionary appeals, precautions against anthrax and the death watch beetle, an old warning about the necessity for carrying gas masks, long ignored. They went through the oak door that had admitted centuries of worshippers and strolled into the church. Bland sunlight was seeping through the windows. The building was cold. Two men were working at the ancient carved screen in front of the chancel. 'That's going,' nodded Sissons. 'I told the bishop that if there's one thing in this church that must be saved, then that's it. They took it out when Cromwell's troops ransacked the place. It was hidden in Cornwall. And just as well too. See what they did to Sir John and Lady Gurling.' He paused by the medieval tombstone with the lord of the manor and his wife, resting in traditional effigy, stony faced, hands clasped in unending prayer, with their dog carved at their feet. Sissons touched the figures. 'They cut his toes off, her breasts and the dog's ears,' he pointed out. 'It must be a primitive man who defiles stone.'

'I've heard that US servicemen are religious,' said Barrington. 'Churches all over the country, when they have American camps near by, are packed.'

'There's a big Catholic element,' agreed Sissons. 'And all sorts of slightly lunatic sects. I'll be very happy if they just leave this church alone.'

Barrington thinned his lips. 'Take everything of the remotest value away from the place,' he advised. 'And pile sandbags around the rest.' He made to move away, but turning, he put a caustic finger to his lips. 'And not a word to anyone, vicar. Everything must be done in secret. Remember – Careless Talk Costs Lives.'

'Ridiculous, isn't it?' answered Sissons shrilly. He tried to laugh but it came out like a rattle.

Gilman drove the fifteen-hundredweight platoon truck nervously at the head of the two heavier unit vehicles. His apprehension was caused not so much by the tightness of the lane but by the small, formidable lady in the green uniform sitting beside him. She was red-faced and fiercely cheerful. 'Don't be frightened, young man,' she said. 'This challenge will be met in full, with our usual British competence.'

'It's the road,' he replied lamely. 'It's getting these vehicles along this road. It's not much more than a track and the banks are so steep.'

'Made for packhorses,' she beamed. 'That's how this region existed not long ago. In my mother's time and even after. None of these villages would have survived it if it had not been for the tinkers and pedlars and grocers with their packhorses. They managed in those days and I'm sure we will manage now.'

He could see she was going to enjoy it. Her name was Mrs Kennerly. 'Nothing,' she said strongly, 'gets in the way of the Women's Voluntary Service. We can bend rules in the way that none of your precious army or government departments could manage. We can work miracles, believe me. And we are dependent on nobody. We even pay for our own uniforms. Jolly good, aren't they? You feel that material.'

Doubtfully Gilman took one hand off the wheel and touched the rough green material of her jacket. 'That will wear forever,' she said, 'even if the war lasts a hundred years.'

'Well, I hope it doesn't,' said Gilman. 'I've got other things to do.'

She seemed surprised. 'Such as?' she inquired.

He raised his eyebrows. 'Such as getting on with my life,' he said.

'Why are you a private soldier?' she inquired bluntly. 'You seem moderately intelligent.'

Gilman said evenly: 'That's why I'm a private soldier. I have no ambitions in this war.'

'Ah, but the challenge!' she almost shouted. 'The resourcefulness that's needed. That's where we come in, you see. The WVS.' She patted his hand. 'Our unofficial motto is, "We are the women who never say no!"'

They turned a steep corner and a low row of

128

terraced cottages came into view. People were moving in the small front gardens. Mrs Kennerly said brightly: 'Let's get this lot organized. People like this just *have* to be organized. The quicker they're moved out the quicker we can get on with the next batch. I really want your chaps to pull their weight today. No sneaking off for tea and buns like the rest of the army seems to do at the least excuse.'

She jumped from the small truck almost as soon as it had stopped and went briskly across to the first of the small enclosed gardens. She began waving her arms and giving orders. Gilman sighed and got out of the cab. Catermole who was driving the vehicle behind jumped into the lane and sauntered forward. 'Blimey,' he said. 'She's a bit of a goer, ain't she?'

'She is,' confirmed Gilman solemnly. 'You might be in line for a bit of the other there, Pussy. She told me she's one of the women who never says no.'

Catermole sniffed. 'I wouldn't bang her as an act of charity,' he said bluntly. He softened fractionally. 'I quite reckon the uniform though . . . those thick stockings.'

His growing grin was taken from his face by Mrs Kennerly whirling around and hooting in their direction, 'Come on, then, come on you squaddies! There's a war on.'

They ambled towards her, followed by the rest of the army party from the trucks. The villagers were standing about sadly and helplessly in their tight gardens. Cardboard boxes of belongings were standing on the wet vegetable patches outside the low windows.

An expression of pique thinned Mrs Kennerly's mouth. 'There seems to be a shortage of suitcases,' she

129

said with brisk annoyance. 'That's going to be a nuisance.'

'They've never needed suitcases before,' said a woman's voice. 'Nobody here ever goes anywhere.'

It was Mary Nicholas. Gilman turned and saw her standing by the door of the outside lavatory of the end cottage. He smiled at her and raised his hand but she did not return the acknowledgement. Mrs Kennerly gave a short stern jaw movement. 'I am not investigating the social reasons,' she said bluntly, 'but trying to think of an alternative. We must get some cardboard boxes from the shops in Wilcoombe. From somewhere anyway.' A sound came from the end cottage whose front door was open, a thin elderly howl.

'What seems to be amiss in there?' asked Mrs Kennerly.

'An old man is amiss,' replied Mary Nicholas flatly. 'He's a relative of mine. He's eighty-two and he doesn't want to move. He says he's not coming out.'

'Oh,' said the WVS woman. 'Well, we shall see. It's no good people being stubborn. They either go or they get blown up.'

'He says he'd rather be blown up,' added Mary. Gilman grinned. She still had not acknowledged him. Mrs Kennerly sniffed fiercely and strutted along the narrow paved path that joined the cottages. Grownups and children watched with awe. 'She's a German,' whispered one man. A child began to grizzle. Mary Nicholas moved to the open door first, forestalling Mrs Kennerly. 'Don't rush him,' she warned seriously. 'He might shoot you. He's got a gun and he's in the mood.'

Gilman hesitatingly moved towards the door. 'Watch it, mate,' whispered Catermole. 'Don't go and get shot. Not by an old nutter.'

Gilman reached the door. Mary had gone in to the dim sitting-room with Mrs Kennerly just behind her. It was tight, aromatic, warm in there, like the burrow of a mole. Gilman felt the years of close habitation.

'Nobody be goin' to shift me,' the old man was protesting quietly. Gilman could see he was ensconced in a wooden chair near the small, smoky fire, a shotgun across the shawl on his knees. 'I bain't joinin' thank ye,' he repeated firmly. 'I bain't joinin'.'

With a moment of kindness that seemed to Gilman foreign to her general busy manner, Mrs Kennerly leaned closer to the old man. 'You'll be helping to end the war,' she told him sincerely. 'Then *everybody* will be able to go back to their homes.'

Mary Nicholas, herself taken aback by the approach, glanced at Gilman for the first time. Thoughtfully the old man lifted his fretted face. 'The war?' he inquired as though trying to remember. 'An' 'ow will oi be about that?'

'The soldiers need to come here,' explained Mrs Kennerly still quietly.

'Soldiers?' he asked, his creased eyes opening, brimming with tears and suspicion. 'Whose soldiers?'

'Ours,' she answered. Then: 'Well, American soldiers.'

Thoughtfully he considered her close face before turning to study the faces in the room; the soldiers and the others. 'What about my old dog?' he inquired. 'What about 'ee then?'

It was a simple, important question for which no

one was prepared. The dog, a sparse, yellowing creature, crouched under the old man's chair. The occupants of the room looked at each other. Mary Nicholas caught Gilman's eye. 'I'm taking the old man – but I can't take the dog,' she said firmly. 'You could do with a dog.'

'Me?' He was astonished. 'I can't have a dog. They don't let you have dogs in the army.' He turned on Catermole for support. 'They don't, do they?'

Catermole's grin began to wriggle across his face. 'There's no facilities, see,' he explained. 'Not for dogs.'

'Rubbish!' snorted Mrs Kennerly. Mary nodded confirmation. 'You could have a herd of cows down at that silly gun,' continued the older woman. 'It would make no difference at all.'

'We might have to go into action,' said Catermole lamely.

'Any day,' agreed Gilman.

Mrs Kennerly picked up the ratty-looking mongrel from beneath the old man's chair and thrust it into Gilman's hands. 'You've got a bloody dog,' she said firmly. 'Congratulations.'

Bryant stopped the miniature Austin army car outside the gate of the American camp at Telcoombe Magna. The outsized Stars and Stripes rolled in the Devon breeze and it occurred to him that if a marauding German plane happened to fly over the area then this would prove excellent target identification. He wondered whether he ought to point it out.

The sentry at the gate appeared casually around the

side of the guardhouse. He was rolling gum around his mouth. He stopped suspiciously when he first saw Bryant but then his expression opened out with a sort of childish amusement as he took in the tiny car. The gum hung like a stalactite from his top teeth. 'Gee . . . sir . . .' he said. Bryant did not know whether the man had recognized him as an officer or whether it was merely the general American usage of the application. 'Sir,' continued the man. He touched the car as if he thought it might be made of paper. 'That sure is cute.'

'I've come to see Colonel Schorner,' said Bryant, heightening his officer's tone. The guard said: 'Okay,' when a sergeant loped around the side of the guardhouse. He took in the scene and springing to muscular attention, he bawled: 'Turn out the guard!'

Before Bryant's bemused gaze half a dozen dishevelled American soldiers tumbled from the inside of the wooden building and another arrived languidly from around the back. The latter man was putting his shirt into his fly-buttons. They scrambled into a nondescript line. The fly-buttons of the last man were still undone, shining like medals. 'Right, you guys!' howled the sergeant. 'Att – en – *shun*!' Bryant became aware that other soldiers within the camp had begun to drift towards the gate where they gathered like sightseers. Some smiled at his little car, others regarded him reverently as if he were some suddenly-materialized front-line hero. The men of the guard stood expectantly as though they hoped he would inspect them. But at that moment the growing crowd of soldiers around the gate parted and Colonel Schorner walked through like the sheriff in a western film.

The British officer jumped from the car and came to attention. His sharp but untheatrical salute evoked a rumble of comment from the Americans. Schorner stepped forward and saluted in return, bringing a further approving murmur from the congregation. 'Real good . . . real good.'

'Good morning, sir,' said Bryant. The audience leaned forward to the words and the accent and there was another buzz. 'I'm Lieutenant Bryant.' The word 'Lieutenant' said with the British-pronunciation was mumbled through the crowd. Schorner replied with a grin and a side movement of the head: 'And I'm Colonel Schorner, commanding this rabble.'

At once the soldiers hooted and laughed like children with a joking teacher. Schorner turned and politely motioned Bryant into the camp. They began to walk and, to Bryant's added astonishment, the soldiers began to stroll with them, like disciples following a pair of prophets He glanced back and saw that the guard detail were crowded around his Austin Seven, touching it and peering under the chassis.

The two officers reached the hut which Schorner used as his office and billet. 'This is Albie,' said Schorner as soon as they had entered. 'Albie, this is Lieutenant Bryant of the British Army.'

'Yes, sir,' replied Albie, throwing up an awkward salute. Bryant returned it and, hesitatingly, took the private's proffered hand. 'Albert Primrose, sir,' said Albie. 'Glad to know you.'

'Lieutenant Bryant,' returned the Englishman clumsily. He was aware that the soldiers were still crowding outside the hut. He thought he heard his car start up in the distance. He had left the key in the ignition. 'Albie,' said Schorner. 'Tell those guys outside to blow, will you. And tell those boneheads at the gate to quit starting that car. Tell them they'll be charged with sabotage.'

Albie was not sure. He grinned first, but when the mention of sabotage was made he threw up another quick, serious salute and hurried from the hut. Schorner was about to say something but he waited while Albie's voice carried into them. 'Okay, you guys, break it up. It's only a Limey officer. You'll see plenty of those. Go on, beat it.'

Schorner smiled apologetically. He motioned Bryant to sit down and took his own chair behind the trestle table. 'You'll have noticed we have a different kind of army to yours,' he said.

'Well, yes,' hesitated Bryant. 'They're certainly very novel.'

Schorner said solemnly: 'They think they're wonderful, you know. They think they're *unbeatable*, the greatest thing ever. Immortal. Magic. I don't want to have them disillusioned too quickly. The hard part will start soon enough.'

Bryant did not know what to say. He merely nodded. Schorner saw his embarrassment. He said, 'If there's one guy we need around here it's a liaison officer. We're going to make a hell of a lot of mistakes, like you just saw. And the more you can get us out of trouble the better. If you can get us out before we're in, I'll like it even more. If you can't then you'll have to lie.'

Bryant grinned. 'Quite honestly, sir, I don't know why I got the job anyway,' he said. 'Apparently it's just because I once went to America, and I happen to be here now. And not doing very much.'

'Where did you visit in the States?'

'Only New York and Philadelphia,' said Bryant. 'I had an aunt who died over there and I had to go and clear things up.' He waited. 'Not many English people have been to America. It's still another country.'

'This is another country for us too,' said Schorner. He went on cautiously: 'The anti-aircraft gun hasn't been busy lately.'

Bryant shrugged. 'A few false alarms,' he said. 'But we haven't seen a Jerry for months. Not since I've been here, anyway. Since Dunkirk and the bombing the war's been a bit of an anti-climax.'

It sounded oddly like an apology. Schorner said: 'Well, you couldn't make the Germans come. They blew the chance.'

Bryant said quietly: 'We would have set fire to the sea with oil. It was all ready. They would have been roasted. And anyway, they didn't have the boats, the landing craft. It's all right having a big army. You've still got to get across the Channel.'

Schorner looked at him seriously. 'I think that's what we're going to find out for ourselves pretty soon,' he said.

The village school at Telcoombe Beach was romantically set almost at the edge of the sea. A brief, steep path went down from the small walled playground to an area of the beach clear of the barbed wire coils which had been there since the threat of invasion in nineteen-forty.

Bryant went in the bulky American staff car with Schorner. Albie was driving and they left him outside the greystone school and walked around to a promontory where they could see the wide arm of Start Bay opened out. The wind was sharp from the Channel and the winter rollers came headlong to the sand, shredding against the barbed wire. From the school they could hear the singing voices of children.

'It's a great name, Start Bay,' commented Schorner. 'A place to begin.'

Bryant smiled and agreed. Schorner could have been his father and yet here they were in the same war. The wind was stiff and they both took off their caps. 'This used to be mined as well,' said Bryant. 'Now they've taken them up. It was difficult to stop the kids wandering down there.'

'Show kids a beach and they'll want to be on it,' shrugged Schorner. 'I wonder how quickly the Germans would have gotten through that wire. I wonder how the GIs are going to get through it. What are the kids singing?'

'"Widdicombe Fair",' replied Bryant. 'Old Uncle Tom Cobbleigh and All. It's a Devon song.'

'Let's take a looksee,' said Schorner suddenly. He turned and walked through the low gate into the playground. He sniffed at it. 'Schoolyards look the same the world over,' he grinned. 'With the little outhouses there.'

They walked towards the school door. It was arched and made of stout, weathered wood, like that of a side entrance in a church. Schorner hesitated, then, curiously, knocked. The singing wavered and stopped. A young woman's voice called them in.

It was a single classroom, ranks of inky desks, bright drawings on the tiled walls, a blackboard like a square sail, and, in one corner, an iron stove breathing warmth into the room. The children were small, up to seven years of age, Bryant guessed. Two had stood on their desks to see the American staff car outside. They and the others turned to face the two men. The teacher, slight and dark, in her twenties, nodded to them nervously. Schorner remembered seeing her sitting next to Beatrice Evans in the church.

'I'm sorry to intrude, ma'am,' he said. He introduced himself and Bryant. She shook hands with them. 'I'm Dorothy Jenkins,' she said. 'We're having one last day at this school.'

'We're surprised that you're still here,' said Schorner.

'So be we!' interrupted a cherry-faced girl in the front desk.

'Mary Steer,' sighed the teacher. She said to Schorner, 'Everybody thought it might be a good idea to have them in school today, it all being a bit confusing with the evacuation and everything. They'd only be getting in the way. Making it worse than it's going to be.' Her voice was calm, West Country.

The American officer stepped three paces to the window. 'Sure a good place to have a school,' he said again.

He turned to the children, then quickly back to the young woman. 'Mind if I just say something to them?' he asked.

'You go ahead,' she said firmly. Her voice was simple and soft.

Schorner thanked her and faced the class again. Twenty-three round, attentive and expectant faces looked towards him. Silence settled through the room.

Mary Steer smiled wilfully at him. He leaned forward and touched her on the shiny nose. She reddened and looked around at the other children to make certain they had seen.

'Ladies and gentlemen,' began Schorner. They all giggled and put their hands over their mouths. 'I expect you all know by now that you won't be going to school here for a while.'

'We don't want to go to school in Wilcoombe,' said Mary cheekily.

'Mary Steer,' muttered the teacher. The little girl blushed. Quickly her eyes returned to the American.

'I guess you'll always have to go to school,' he answered. 'We all have to do things we don't like, at times. Me, I don't care very much about being a soldier.' He glanced mischievously at Dorothy Jenkins and added: 'I'd like to teach school.' The children laughed and the teacher acknowledged the point with a quick smile. He turned to the class again.

'No, the reason I wanted to talk to you is . . . well, it's a very serious matter, children. It's a warning. You know what a warning is?'

'Like the air-raid siren,' called a boy from the back.

'Right. What's your name?'

'Billy Steer,' answered the boy. He had a sharp face, with a tooth missing in the centre of his mouth.

'*Billy* Steer,' repeated Schorner. He looked at the girl in the front desk. 'Are you this young lady's brother?'

'Yes, sir, but I don't like 'un,' replied the girl. Billy Steer blew a raspberry towards her and she turned and poked out a cherry tongue. The teacher hushed them.

Schorner waited, then said: 'Okay, Billy Steer, you're right. It's a warning, like the air-raid alert. But it comes from me, and this might happen at any time. Okay – so remember.'

Bryant glanced at Dorothy Jenkins. She did not return the look. She was watching the American as intensely as the children. 'The whole countryside around here is going to be surrounded by barbed wire, like that down by the ocean,' he said, nodding at the window. 'It's very, very important that none of you *ever* go through that barbed wire. *Ever*, you get me? For any reason. Even if your dog or cat goes under, you stay the other side. Okay? The dog will come back.'

'How about the cat?' inquired Mary Steer. 'I've got a cat.'

'And the cat, Mary,' said Schorner seriously. The smile dropped from her small face. 'Just keep right away, because it's going to be dangerous.' He paused and looked along the desks. The children were intent on him. 'And one more thing. If any of you find in any place anything to do with the army – like a bullet or a shellcase or a grenade, that's a metal thing that looks like a pineapple –'

The teacher interrupted. 'They don't know what a pineapple is,' she said quietly. 'They've never seen one. They know what a grenade is.'

'Excuse me,' said Schorner. 'I have things to learn also.' He returned to the children. 'Any of these things. *Do not touch.* Just leave it where it is. Tell your mom or your dad. Or a policeman. Or a soldier. But *do not touch.*' He waited again and smiled. 'Okay? You promise?'

'Promise,' came the chorus from the class.

'Great. Thank you, ladies and gentlemen.' There

were more giggles. Schorner turned to the young teacher again. 'Do you think they could sing that song again? The one about the fairground.'

' "Widdicombe Fair",' said Bryant to Dorothy Jenkins. She looked surprised but she moved to the front of the class and said: 'Children, let's sing Old Uncle Tom Cobbleigh again. Our very best for the gentlemen.'

The tall, greying American, his face set, standing, hands behind back, while the Devon children stood at their desks and began to sing with loud, disorganized voices:

'Tam Pearce, Tam Pearce,
Lend me your grey mare,
All along, down along, out along, lee . . .'

Schorner grinned with delight when they drew in their breaths and launched into the lusty chorus:

'With Bill Brewer, Jan Stewer, Peter Gurney,
Peter Davy, Dan'l Widden, 'Arry 'Awk
Old Uncle Tom Cobbleigh and *all*
Old Uncle Tom Cobbleigh and all.'

When they had come to the end of the song they remained standing until a motion with her hand from the teacher sat them down with a clattering of desks. Schorner said quietly: 'Thank you. Thank you very much.'

Mary Steer suddenly beamed. 'You sing sommat to us!'

All the children cheered and shouted. Schorner

141

looked around at Bryant and Dorothy. Then back to the children.

'Children,' he pleaded, 'if you heard me sing, you wouldn't ask again.'

They laughed with delight. 'But,' he continued, holding up his head, 'I'd sure like to tell you a poem. Something from America. Something I learned in America. Just like this.'

He looked directly at the intense faces. He felt suddenly sad for them and for himself so far from his home. He recited:

'I dwell in a lonely house I know
That vanished many a summer ago,
And left no trace but the cellar walls,
And a cellar in which the daylight falls,
And the purple-stemmed raspberries grow.

O'er ruined fences the grapevine shield.
The woods come back to the mowing field;
The orchard tree has grown one copse
Of new wood and old where the woodpecker
    chops;
The footpath down to the well is healed.'

Schorner stopped. 'I can't remember how it goes on,' he smiled. The children laughed shyly in sympathy. He swallowed, and suddenly embarrassed turned to the teacher and to Bryant, both watching him seriously. 'I guess we have to go,' he said.

'Thank you,' said the young woman. 'We enjoyed that very much.' She clapped her hands and the class began to applaud with childish verve.

The sound followed them as they left the school and went out into the stiff sea wind, coming in from the west, whistling miserably through the coils of barbed wire. Behind them, the schoolroom dropped into silence. Then, when they had almost reached the car where Albie sat at the wheel, a burst of song came from the small, grey building. Schorner paused and grinned. He glanced at Bryant. Bryant said: 'It's "There'll Always Be An England!"'

Schorner said: 'It gives me more confidence hearing it from kids.'

Albie got from behind the wheel and opened the door for his commanding officer. Bryant got into the vehicle the other side. As they drove back through Telcoombe Magna Mrs Bewler, the deaf woman, and her idiot son, loaded with cardboard boxes and carrier bags, were being put into a van. A notice in large letters, 'Keep out. Back soon.' was fixed to the door of a deserted shop.

In the lanes and the fields there were also changes. Two men with a horse were turning up mangolds from a field. Another man was taking them by hand-barrow to the edge of the narrow road. On the grass banks outside a cottage were bundles of poor agricultural tools.

Schorner said: 'They do things the old way here.'

'They tell you it's the war,' shrugged Bryant. 'But if it wasn't the war it would be something else. They don't like things changing too quickly.'

'It's great farming country, though,' nodded Schorner. 'Look at that earth. It's like cream. And the livestock looks good. Makes me wonder what's happening back home.'

143

'You're a farmer?' asked Bryant, a little surprised.

'Yes. West Virginia. What do you do?'

'I was at university. Reading law at Oxford.'

'And when it's all over you'll go back?'

'I'm not sure. Things are going to change after the war. Everybody's going to change much more than we realize. I'm married too. I've got a child, a daughter. She's two. I have to make a living.'

'You're young to be married.'

Bryant grinned. 'Spur of the moment. Last leave sort of thing.'

Schorner said: 'That's what a lot of our guys did. As soon as they know they're going away – maybe for ever – they get married.' He shook his head.

They had reached the entrance to the camp now. Albie slowed the car at the gate. The sentry came confusedly to attention and George Ballimach, the rotund telephone engineer, appeared from behind the guardhouse, as if he had been hiding, awaiting their arrival. He gave a fast salute. Schorner returned it.

'You got three telephones, sir,' Ballimach beamed proudly. 'Three. And they work. They all work.'

'That's really swell,' said Schorner kindly. 'How are you feeling now?'

Ballimach's great face descended. 'Okay now, sir. Fine. I just ain't going to climb any more Limey trees.'

'That sounds like a good idea, Ballimach.'

The big soldier leaned forward. He glanced at Bryant but decided he could say what he wanted to say. 'There's been a message already on one of the phones,' he confided. 'The special line I put in. I only got it fixed a couple of minutes and it rang and there was a message.' He paused importantly. His great

144

eyes narrowed to chasms. 'From the general,' he said.

Schorner took in the bemused expression of Bryant. 'Okay, Ballimach,' said the colonel. 'Dismissed. Just keep moving.'

'Okay, sir, you bet,' said Ballimach flapping up another salute. He rolled away. 'He's a good guy,' said the American to Bryant. 'Not a great soldier, but a good guy.'

'He fell out of a tree?' asked Bryant. They had left the car and were walking towards Schorner's hut.

'Sure. But he meant well.' He pointed to the three telephones on his trestle table. 'See what I mean.' Albie had been quickly to the cookhouse and appeared with two mugs of coffee. Bryant tasted his. 'My God,' he said, 'I've never tasted coffee like this. It's wonderful.'

'We're good at coffee,' smiled Schorner. 'Albie get me Lieutenant Conroy Kenholm, will you. Or is it Kenholm Conroy, for God's sake?'

'Right first time, sir. Conroy Kenholm.'

'Okay, whichever it is, get him.'

Albie went out. 'The British have such a love affair with tea,' commented Bryant. 'It's our ambrosia.'

'Have people here been really short of food, I mean hungry?' asked Schorner. 'That's something we'd never be able to understand in America. Being hungry.'

Bryant said: 'A lot of people eat better now than they did before the war. They *have* to have their rations. Nobody would refuse them. The neighbours would talk. A lot of them made do with less in the thirties.'

Kenholm, the officer from Nebraska, came into the

hut. Schorner introduced him to Bryant. The American officer shook hands and examined the British uniform with interest, like a woman looking at another woman's dress.

Schorner said: 'We got a message from a general.'

'Oh yes, sure,' said Kenholm uncomfortably. 'I was just coming over, sir.'

He took a slip from a message pad from his tunic pocket, followed by a pair of rimless glasses which he put on his face. They made him look like Benny Goodman. 'General Arthur C. Georgeton,' he read importantly, 'is coming right over. From Exeter . . . yes, Exeter, I guess that is. He's just gotten here from Stateside.'

'Thanks,' said Schorner laconically. 'When is the general going to arrive?'

'They didn't say,' said Kenholm, allowing himself to look puzzled. 'I guess right away.'

'What time is the message timed?'

'Oh sure, I got that. Eleven thirty-four.'

Schorner glanced at his watch. 'I hope he's not expecting lunch,' he said. As he said it they heard a shout from the gate. Albie hurried into the hut. 'There's a big-time procession at the gate, sir,' he said excitedly. 'They turned out the guard.'

'That's bad,' muttered Schorner. 'I might have guessed they would.'

Albie glanced out. 'I guess it's okay, sir. They all seem to be in a line.'

'Great,' breathed Schorner. He said to Bryant: 'You'd better come too.' Then to Kenholm, 'Get around and see everything's okay. Nobody hanging about. No trash or scrap paper. Get the guys busy. If they're doing nothing get them looking for wood. Okay?'

Kenholm saluted rapidly and with a short, oddly envious glance at Bryant went from the hut. Schorner followed him and Bryant went with the colonel. 'This is the commanding general for the exercise area,' the American said as they walked towards the gate. They could see the guard drawn up and the US Army staff car waiting under the Stars and Stripes. Soldiers were drifting towards what had become a path across the field, looking towards what was happening at the entrance. 'You guys,' called Schorner brusquely, 'get busy. Go and collect wood.'

Bryant tried not to grin. He walked after the American, half a pace behind. At the gate the staff car had begun to move into the field, the driver taking it forward cautiously as though worried about holes or cow dung.

The car, with the general's white stars on its khaki mudguard, drew to a halt a few yards in front of Schorner. The driver jumped out to open the door for General Georgeton although the officer was halfway out before the man reached it. Scarlett climbed out after him. There were salutes and handshakes. 'I'm sorry to drop in like this, colonel,' said Georgeton. 'We got here last night, to Exeter, and I thought the quicker we took our first look at this area the better. I hope we haven't arrived in the middle of a military exercise.' He glanced around the field as if he doubted it.

Schorner said: 'No, sir, that's fine. We're getting settled in. I've got the men collecting wood.'

Georgeton's eyes moved fractionally. 'Good,' he said. 'Cold billets are lousy billets.'

'Would you like some coffee, sir?' asked Schorner. 'We make great coffee.' He glanced at Bryant. The general said: 'No thanks. I'd really like to take a looksee around the evacuation region. Is it under way now? Are they being moved out?'

'It started today, sir,' said Bryant. Schorner had nodded at him. 'We hope that everybody will be out, with all the belongings they can take with them, within two weeks.'

Georgeton had turned back towards his car. 'The civilian population can't be very pleased about things,' he suggested, '. . . about us.'

Bryant was careful. 'Nobody's happy about it, sir. Obviously. But they're getting on with it. It's all part of the war, most of them understand that.'

'Right, let's go,' said the general. 'Maybe we can get a bite to eat on the route. I figure we'll learn more like that than sitting with our own army.'

Bryant swallowed. 'Well, yes . . . I suppose that could be arranged, sir. I could phone the hotel at Wilcoombe. But . . . it won't be very special, I'm afraid. Not what you would get in America.'

'That's okay, son,' said Georgeton easily. 'I didn't come across the ocean to eat.'

At first Bryant conducted them along the coast road, along the elongated landing beach. They stood in a tight group, Bryant a short distance away, collars up against the rattling wind, looking out to the Channel through binoculars, as if by some chance they would be able to see their enemy a hundred and more miles away. Bryant had stood separately, out of deference, in case they should be discussing things not meant for his subaltern's ears. The general pointed out to sea and Schorner and Scarlett gazed dutifully in that direction. Bryant had a faint reminder of one of the pictures of childhood, 'The Boyhood of Raleigh'. Georgeton's voice was carried back to him by the wind. 'Start Bay, Start Point. A good place to begin.'

He heard Schorner approve and smiled to himself because Schorner had said the same thing earlier. They turned back from the beach. 'Where are the lakes?' asked Georgeton. 'The lakes are important.'

Schorner glanced towards Bryant, as if wondering how much he knew. The senior officer trudged back to the exposed road and the staff car. 'The lakes are just along behind the road, just a few hundred yards,' said Bryant. 'They're known as the leys.'

'If the GI hears that he'll think we've set up a whole load of easy women for him,' joked the general as they climbed into the warmth of the car. 'Boy, will he be disappointed.' He shook his head and laughed: 'Wow, the leys,' he repeated.

They drove for a minute with the gushing sea on one side and dark high reeds, swaying as though threatening them, on the other. Soon the car cleared the banks and the small lakes came into view. 'Hold it,' instructed Georgeton. 'Let's take a look from here.'

They left the car and leaned against it, sheltering, looking out over the ribbed and ruffled water of the modest lakes. Some geese took concern and flapped away from their habitation with a startling honking. There was a narrow bridge going across from the coast road to the further bank of the lakes, a distance of a hundred yards. It was supported on wooden piles. The wind seemed to move it.

The general studied the riffled water with care, raising his field glasses like a bird watcher, searching the reeded banks on the far side. Scarlett and Schorner both followed his gaze through their field glasses. Bryant felt a little foolish standing there with only his eyes. He put his hand up like a shield and followed the direction of their watching. All he could see was cold, trapped water and grey-green winter rushes.

Georgeton took a long time examining the water and its fringes. Then he raised his glasses to the hinterland, rising, but not steeply, up through the wooded Devon coombes. Some fields were pale, January green, others vivid ploughed red. A few cattle dawdled on a meadow across the water. The general examined each of the rifts, the coombes, that sliced steeply into the quiet landscape. 'Good,' he said. 'That's real good.'

He turned a quarter turn and took in the roofs and walls of Wilcoombe, climbing the hill to the west. The church pointed like an admonishment into the dun sky. 'That town would be outside the area,' said Georgeton.

'Yes, sir,' replied Schorner. 'Just. The boundary will be at the western edge of the lakes. That's where the wire will be.'

'I hope the gunners can shoot straight,' muttered Georgeton. 'I don't care for the idea of them massacring the English before they've accounted for any Germans.'

He turned quickly on Bryant. It was as if he had

suddenly made an important military decision. 'Lieutenant,' he said, using the English pronunciation, 'I'm hungry.'

'Yes, sir,' said Bryant. He ventured, 'I was afraid you might say that.'

The Americans laughed together. Scarlett winked at him, his first sign of friendliness. The general said: 'Like I said, son, I didn't come all this way to eat well. Maybe it will give us some idea of how you British have suffered.'

Bryant thought it might. He said: 'I tried the hotel in Wilcoombe, but they didn't advise it themselves, not their lunch. The Telcoombe Beach Hotel sounded more promising, so I've asked them to keep a table for four. I had to take it. It's necessary to make a booking.'

'They get short of tables?' asked Scarlett.

'No, food,' replied Bryant.

They laughed again and Georgeton patted the English officer on the back. 'Okay,' he said as they climbed once more into the car. 'Let them do their worst.'

'That's what I'm afraid of,' said Bryant.

The Telcoombe Beach Hotel was a raddled, once-white building, set immediately against the short sand and reed bluffs that divided the shore from the straight road. On one side it put a brave but ageing face to the sea and on the other looked over the more placid water of the leys and the elevated countryside behind them. Bryant was conscious of moving lace curtains and faces flitting against the windows as they left the car. It had begun to rain, immediately heavy, and it splattered against them as they ran to the hotel's porch entrance.

Inside they were greeted by a distraught elderly woman in the tired black and white fatigues of an English waitress. 'Mr Bonner's away,' she apologized immediately. She saw Bryant's uniform and turned to him as a compatriot. 'Would you tell them that he's had to go to Plymouth,' she pleaded as if the Americans understood only a foreign tongue. 'He couldn't put it off,' she continued. 'Even for the military.' She began to take their coats, almost staggering under the weight. Georgeton kindly told her not to concern herself and they put the greatcoats on the hooks of a fine brass hall-stand.

'Don't worry about Mr Bonner,' Bryant assured her. The Americans looked amused. 'We don't want any fuss. Just whatever you happen to have for lunch.'

There was a glass door immediately behind him. A small, crooked, black painted door, the panes half muffled with a faded flower curtain. First the curtain moved, then the door opened and an old face appeared. A nervously smiling elderly lady emerged.

'King George the Fifth once stayed here,' she announced. 'He said he enjoyed it. He wrote it down in the visitors' book.'

The officers turned and examined the shrivelled and stooped figure. 'Yes, Mrs Katlin,' said the waitress with subdued impatience. 'But I don't suppose these gentlemen would be very interested in that. They're Americans.'

'They ought to be,' said the old lady stoutly. 'If they intend to blow the place up . . . Our late gracious King

152

laid his head here. Nothing seems to matter any more.'

She closed the door with a finality which suggested she could not bear to discuss the story further. The waitress frowned apologetically. 'Mrs Katlin is our oldest resident,' she explained, indicating that said everything. 'She was actually here when the late King stayed. She's never forgotten.' The woman led them into a low dining-room. It was tatty but clean. A table with a white cloth had been set near the window. The cloth was so starched it looked like cardboard. A glass jug of water stood among the shining cutlery. 'She's our only resident now,' went on the waitress as she led them to the corner. 'And of course she will be having to move on.' She had been holding back a sniff which now escaped. 'Or be killed,' she sobbed dramatically. She turned away still sniffing.

The men grimaced at each other. 'I'm beginning to feel suspiciously like a louse already,' muttered Georgeton. He glanced at Bryant. 'Do all the folk react like that?'

'A great many,' nodded Bryant. 'But they'll get over it. Some of them may even enjoy it. Particularly the younger people. They won't feel so trapped. It's the most exciting thing that's happened around here since Drake played bowls.'

'Sure,' said Georgeton as if he personally recalled the incident. 'On Plymouth Hoe. That can't be too far.'

'About eighteen miles,' said Bryant.

'And the Pilgrim Fathers, they sailed from Plymouth, right?' put in Scarlett.

'I think they cheated,' smiled Bryant. 'Or

somebody has. The truth is they sailed from Southampton. They only put into Plymouth because of a storm.'

'I wonder how they felt,' ruminated Schorner. 'They set off for the New World and they land in their own country. I bet some of them felt like walking straight back home.'

Bryant thought a quick look went between them. He coughed and passed the menu, pounded out on a near-blind typewriter, around the table. A second waitress, a fair representation of the menu smudged on her apron, appeared and stood with apprehensive obedience at the table. 'Sprouts?' asked General Georgeton. 'I am about to display my ignorance. What is a sprout?'

Scarlett and Schorner looked towards Bryant. The young Englishman said: 'Sprouts, sir? They're green and sort of oval.'

'Like small cabbages,' put in the waitress quite briskly. 'Boiled.'

'Gee, I must taste them. And what's this "meat of the day"?'

'Spam,' she replied defiantly. She gave a huffy little glance at Bryant now, her former nervousness gone, as if to ask how these men thought they were going to beat the Third Reich if they were not even aware of the existence of sprouts and Spam.

'It's American, I believe,' put in Bryant tentatively.

The first waitress, the woman who had been at the front door, sidled towards the table. 'It's Tang today,' she informed Bryant from the corner of her mouth.

He looked up, embarrassed, and said to the Americans: 'Sorry, it's Tang.'

'What's Tang?' inquired Schorner after a look at the general.

'Same as Spam,' said the woman firmly.

The second waitress nodded like someone whose language was being interpreted. 'It's the same,' she said.

The general said: 'There's no point in coming from America to eat American Spam or Tang. I guess I'll take the sausages.'

Bryant shot a warning glance towards Scarlett. But it was too late. The first waitress said: 'That's all there is. Apart from Tang.'

The second waitress wrote the order laboriously on her pad. 'Everybody?' she said briskly.

The three Americans nodded. Bryant attempted to say something but the woman darted to him challengingly and he miserably acquiesced. 'Four sausages,' she enunciated triumphantly. 'Sprouts and boiled.' Nobody argued. She looked up from her pad brightly. 'Egg?' she suggested. 'We do have egg today.'

'It's dried egg,' said Bryant, desperately shaking his head at the Americans. 'It's not like real egg.'

The waitress regarded him as she might regard a traitor. 'Nothing's like the real thing these days is it, sir?' she puffed. She violently crossed out the word Egg from her pad. 'Dessert?' she said. She paused. 'I suppose nobody wanted the soup, did they?' she said. Even she was against them having the soup. Her unhappy eyes turned down to Bryant, now seeking him as an ally. 'Brown Windsor,' she whispered. She shook her head in warning.

Bryant's eyes went around the puzzled American faces. 'The soup is Brown Windsor,' he announced.

'Sounds like a horse,' said Scarlett jocularly.

'It probably is,' muttered Bryant.

The waitress sniffed fiercely. 'No soup then,' she said. 'Now, dessert.'

'I want Yorkshire pudding,' said General Georgeton decisively. 'I heard all about Yorkshire pudding. Is it on the menu?'

The waitress returned her face to Bryant. 'You tell him,' she suggested.

He nodded. 'Well, sir, Yorkshire pudding is not actually pudding. You eat it with meat.'

'We've got some,' the waitress put in stoutly. 'From yesterday. But we've got no meat to go with it.' She brightened. 'You can still have it, though.'

Bryant rolled his eyes, but the general was pleased with his own show of initiative. 'Okay, okay,' he said enthusiastically. 'I'll take it.' The others nodded. They would too.

'Good,' said the waitress like a schoolteacher getting through at last to a class of backward pupils. 'Now, dessert. How about gooseberries?'

'How about them?' said Schorner. He leaned towards Bryant. 'For Christ's sake, what are gooseberries?'

'They're green,' replied the waitress before Bryant could speak. 'Sometimes a bit hairy. You have them with custard.' She paused and leaned forward confidingly. 'That's yellow.'

'I guess we'll stick with the Yorkshire pudding,' decided the general.

'But . . .' began the waitress.

Bryant leaned heavily towards her. 'Yorkshire pudding,' he said.

156

'For pudding?'

'For pudding,' he confirmed.

She slapped her notepad shut, sniffed and turned. 'As you wish,' she said. 'It's your funeral.'

When she had disappeared through yet another lace-curtained door, this one apparently to the kitchen, for the lace was adhering to the steamed panes of glass, Bryant spread his hands apologetically. 'It's the war . . .' he began.

'I didn't know it was that serious,' mentioned Scarlett. 'Can you get a drink in this hotel?'

'Oh, I should think so.' The first waitress was hovering near the back wall of the dining-room. He motioned her to the table. 'Could we have something to drink,' he asked. Her eyes went to the table but he forestalled her. 'Apart from the water,' he said.

'There's wine,' she said confidingly. 'Norwegian.'

'Norwegian? I didn't know . . .'

'Well, *we* don't know for sure. There was some Norwegians here and they *said* it came from Norway, but I thought it was odd myself. It didn't have a label on it, so I don't know what it is. They were nice boys though, pilots. Two of them got killed over Salcombe . . .' She hesitated guiltily. 'Though we're not supposed to say that, are we.'

'Do you have anything else?'

'Beer,' she said. 'And scrumpy.'

The general, using his initiative again, asked: 'Scrumpy?'

'Cider, sir. Local brew,' said Bryant quickly.

'Okay, let's try that. When in Rome . . .'

'Four half-pints then,' ordered Bryant cautiously. 'Not the rough stuff.'

'It's getting near the bottom of the barrel,' muttered the waitress. 'There's all sorts of muck down there. At the bottom.'

'Four halves,' repeated Bryant firmly.

He was beginning to feel like someone besieged, repelling relays of attacks. No sooner had the first waitress retreated than the second reappeared, new stains on her pinafore, bearing a tray which, from a distance, appeared to be on fire.

'Red hot,' she called cheerfully as she advanced on them. 'Sausages, sprouts and boiled.'

The first waitress brought the four half-pints of cider and put them on the table as the food was being passed around. She stood, with a sort of perverse proprietorial attitude, while the wood-like sausages, the steaming green sprouts and the weeping potatoes were placed in front of the strangers.

'Thank you,' they chorused. 'Thank you.' Bryant looked down through the steam rising to his face from the plate and covered his eyes. Jesus, what a mess.

General Georgeton nodded cheerfully at him through the steam. It had begun to make his eyes water. Scarlett and Schorner examined the food with their forks.

The waitress produced a gravy boat and poured a libation over Scarlett's plate. Schorner watched with silent concern and then raised his hand. 'No soup, thank you,' he said.

The General followed quickly. 'No soup, thanks. I don't want to ruin it.'

Bryant thought it was best to be silent. Resolutely, he kept his eyes down while he began to eat. The wordlessness from the Americans, however, eventually forced him to look up. Schorner had opened a sausage and tasted the sawdust-like filling. He quickly picked up his cider and drank just as suddenly, swallowing the sausage debris and the cider together, a combination that set him coughing. Scarlett was eating something and patently not enjoying it. The general said quietly: 'When we start to bomb this area, let's make sure we hit the sprout fields, okay?'

Annette Barrington had moved her father's herd of Devons into pasture near the tight lane that led to the main Totnes road two miles away. She shouted at the cows as she got them through the gates into the wet meadows. It had been raining for an hour, the flimsy rain of the west, moving in stealthily from the sea, creeping over the fields and low hills, darkening the sky.

The girl, who was seventeen, was wearing a red scarf knotted into a turban. Women who were war workers, especially those in the factories, had adopted the turban almost as a uniform. She wore blue dungarees tucked into an ungainly pair of riding boots. They were splashed with the wet and muck of the farmyard. She looked down to her feet as she moved the herd. Soon she would be moving them for the last time. Thank God.

She knew that her father was businessman enough to get them to sale quickly. There would be no point in waiting until the market was saturated and they would have to be moved to further parts. Prices, as everyone knew, were going to be low. And once they were gone, and the other animals, the farm locked and abandoned, her parents installed somewhere in Wilcoombe or some other town outside the area – then she would be gone too. She was going to volunteer for the ATS on her eighteenth birthday. After working all her life among cow dung she wanted to escape.

One of the contrary red Devons had become entangled with the hedge and was lowing and wheeling. Annette moved in and slapped its hind quarters. 'Get on, you cow!' she shouted, making the last word sound like a curse. God, would she have some life once she had kicked the mud of this place from her boots.

Her father appeared from the house. She knew he was going to a funeral at Telcoombe Magna. Her mother was going also. They came from the door in the worn black they took out on all such regular occasions. They were in their forties but they looked and seemed older.

Barrington called to her but she did not hear because at that moment the large American staff car appeared in the lane and turned into the farm drive. 'The occupation forces,' the farmer muttered to his wife.

'Be reasonable with them, Tom,' said Jean Barrington. 'They're only obeying orders.'

'That's going to be the excuse for all sorts of travesties,' he returned bluntly. She was a woman quiet to the point of being colourless.

The American car drew up and Bryant left it first. 'Ah,' said Barrington, 'it's our cricketing lieutenant. Deserted to the other side, I see.'

Bryant was embarrassed. 'I think we're all in this together, Mr Barrington,' he said. 'This is General

Georgeton who will be commanding the US forces in this area. This is Captain Scarlett. I think you already know Colonel Schorner.'

The Americans saluted and shook hands. Jean Barrington was impressed and, after glancing towards her husband, smiled. Annette began walking up the track from the herd. She wiped the dung from her toe-caps on the legs of her dungarees.

'I understand that you are the chairman of the civic authority in these parts,' said Georgeton politely.

'The parish council,' said Barrington, making it sound like a correction.

'Sure. The parish council. Colonel Schorner has explained to me that you are none too happy about what's going on here.' He held up his hand to forestall any immediate rejoinder. 'And I understand that, Mr Barrington. I can't say I'd like my home taken from me either.' He paused again and looked at the ugly farmhouse. 'But just look at it like this – a lot of guys, like myself and like these three fellows here, have been taken from *our* homes. We didn't go crazy over the idea, but there it was. You'll come back here one day. Quite a lot of us won't be going home.'

Jean Barrington looked sideways at her husband, who had never been a soldier. Annette arrived, standing at the side of the bulky car until her father nodded her forward. She introduced herself to the officers. Bryant remembered seeing her on market days in Totnes, the unhappy face beneath the folded turban. Barrington said: 'It's such a mad waste, that's all. It's typical of the bureaucracy that runs this damned country.' He threw his hand out taking in the fields and the hills. 'This is the best all-round farming country in Britain, and we have to clear out so that you can have a game of soldiers.'

'I wish I could think of it like that,' replied Georgeton evenly. 'A game of soldiers.'

'Christ Almighty, there's the whole of Dartmoor. Miles of it. Empty. Why not that?'

'As far as I'm aware from my reading, Dartmoor has no landing beaches,' said the general. 'We are rehearsing for an invasion from the sea.'

Barrington looked at his watch. 'We have to go to a funeral,' he said. 'So perhaps you'll excuse us.'

He walked by their car and made for the barn. His wife smiled uncertainly at the Americans and then, separately, at Bryant and prepared to follow her husband. 'His whole life's been in this farm,' she said as though making an excuse. She walked towards the barn. To their surprise Barrington emerged at the reins of a pony and trap. His wife climbed in beside him and they went through the thin rain towards the farm gate.

The Americans were left standing awkwardly with Bryant and the girl. As the trap reached the gate and turned into the lane they shuffled around to face her. 'What arrangements has your father made?' asked Schorner. 'Will he go on farming?'

'He's bought a smallholding,' she said. 'Hanna-ford's. The old man was ready to give it up anyway. It's nothing like this, but he'll get used to it, don't worry.' She grinned at them from beneath the wet headscarf. 'As far as I'm concerned,' she said, 'you can blow the whole bloody place to smithereens. And the sooner the better.'

*

General Georgeton was silent-faced when he left the farm. Bryant thought he was angry but, as they moved through the countryside, not only the Americans but the British officer himself realized for the first time the full scope and implications of what was happening. An old traction engine, like something from a museum, its tall trembling funnel topping the hedgerows and snorting black smoke across the land, pulled three rattling wagons loaded with farm implements and uprooted mangolds. The man driving it whirled the wheel of the contraption violently to get it around a bend in the lane. Its great banded iron wheels ground into the surface.

In every village there were trucks and vans being loaded with human chattels. They saw an old man carrying a bag of coal from a shed. 'They're taking everything,' said Scarlett after the long silence. The man had dropped a few lumps and he stopped patiently to retrieve them.

'Coal's rationed,' mentioned Bryant. 'He won't leave that behind.'

At every village, almost every house, there was the puzzled slow activity of people preparing to leave their homes. Bryant recited the name of each settlement as they reached it. On they drove through Burton, Sellow, Normancroft, Mortown and eventually back to the sea at Telcoombe Beach and then inland to the camp at Telcoombe Magna.

At Sellow two British army trucks were squatting under the dripping trees of the small village green. 'Ah, British soldiers,' said Georgeton with a small surprise. For some reason Bryant felt a touch of pique at the way he said it.

'From my unit, sir,' Bryant said. 'They're helping people to move.'

'Hold it here,' said the general to the driver. The staff car pulled up behind the military vehicles under the naked elms. Gilman and Catermole were sitting on the tailboard of the truck, drinking tea. Gilman saw the Americans first. 'Christ, Pussy,' he muttered, 'it's the top brass.'

They almost tumbled to the ground, Catermole spilling the tea on his tunic. 'Give them a good one,' muttered Gilman. With a single movement Catermole swept the tea from his front and brought his arm up into a steely salute.

'Okay, easy,' the general said casually, advancing at the head of his small party.

The British privates remained solid. Gilman rolled his eyes towards Bryant. 'Stand at ease,' said Bryant. They stood at ease.

'How is it all going?' asked the British officer. 'Taking a breather are you? Been pretty hectic, I expect.'

'Yes, sir,' replied Gilman, grateful to the lieutenant for the excuse. 'We've not stopped all day.'

The Americans were looking into the back of the truck, half-loaded with tea chests and boxes, threadbare armchairs and rolls of linoleum pointing out like the barrels of large guns.

'Any trouble, son?' asked Georgeton. 'How are these people taking it?'

Gilman swallowed. Catermole was eyeing the American uniforms and medals. How did they get medals, he wondered, when they had not done any fighting yet? Gilman said: 'We had one old man

164

wouldn't move, sir. Said he wasn't interested in joining.'

Georgeton smiled and the others joined in. 'But you persuaded him,' he said.

'With difficulty, sir. But we talked him round in the end. He didn't seem to be aware of the war.'

Bryant looked at Gilman with interest. He had often thought of him as a man apart the others in the anti-aircraft unit; the soldier who wrote short stories. 'How are the others taking it?' asked Schorner.

'Some are upset, sir,' said Gilman. 'Naturally. They've never moved away from this part of the world before. They don't even have any suitcases. Some big cardboard boxes have arrived, but they're being charged sixpence each for them and they don't take too kindly to that.'

'They know they'll be coming back . . . some time?' added Schorner.

'Yes, sir,' said Gilman awkwardly. 'I expect they do, sir.'

The soldier's eyes went past the American officer. Schorner turned and saw the funeral crawling along the village street. General Georgeton and Scarlett followed their gaze. People in the cottages across the green moved with undisguised eagerness to the low fences at the fore of their gardens. Bryant glanced at Gilman. Somebody had to give the order for the soldiers to come to attention.

The general was well aware and equal to the moment. 'Men,' he ordered gruffly. 'At . . . attention.' The US officers and the British soldiers responded and round Georgeton himself threw up a fat American salute. They stood woodenly while the single funeral car, squeaking with every slow wheel-turn, went by with its elderly crew in threadbare black, looking scarcely healthier than a quartet of corpses, the coffin seeming small and incidental between them. Gilman thought it would never take four to carry that. It was strange how much smaller people became in death. The hearse was followed by an eccentric parade of vehicles; Howard Evans, the doctor, in his little car with Beatrice next to him, a bakery van hung with funeral drapes fashioned from blackout curtains, another boxy little car and then three horse-drawn traps including that driven by Tom Barrington. An old man followed on a staggering bicycle.

Only Evans and his wife, and Jean Barrington, glanced towards the attentive soldiers as the short dumb procession went past. Georgeton remained at the salute. Bryant felt the cold drips from the trees hitting him sharply on the cheek. He moved fractionally away. A curled-up old man in the cottage opposite, one of the ragged line of people who had moved to the fence to watch the funeral, called across the road while the procession was still going by: 'That be Charlie Pendry, sirs. Seventy-three. From Mortown.'

Georgeton dropped his salute and called the others to stand at ease. 'We seem to be getting a good insight into the area,' the general mentioned enigmatically. 'Okay, where next?'

'There's a large house, sir,' said Schorner. 'Telcoombe Manor. It would be the logical place for the officers' mess and administration.'

'Okay, let's take a look at it.'

Schorner half-smiled. 'The lady of the house is er . . . well, formidable, sir.' He turned the matter on Bryant. 'Mrs Mahon-Feavor,' he said. 'You know her.'

They could see he did. He said: 'Yes, I'd say that was a fair description.'

Georgeton shrugged. 'Okay, so she's tough. We've got to face the Third Reich so I don't see how we can back off because of some old lady.'

They turned and made towards the staff car. Bryant called Gilman and Catermole to attention and Georgeton acknowledged them with another salute. 'Yanks,' he heard a woman across in the cottage garden shouting coarsely to a muster of staring children standing in the road. 'They be Yanks. They be coming to live in our 'ouses.'

The four officers sat mutely while the car pulled away. To reach Telcoombe Manor they had to travel along the coastal road once more. The rain had diminished, but the sky still scudded across the untidy waves. Scarlett abruptly reacted to something in the sea. 'Now I've seen everything,' he breathed.

They all saw it now. Close inshore an open fishing boat, crewed by a single man in the stern, voyaged choppily westward towards Wilcoombe, its decks piled high with household furniture. The general instructed the driver to pull up. He turned his field glasses on the boat. 'Chairs, tables, every goddamn thing,' he breathed. 'Even a couple of rabbits in a cage.'

'Maybe he'll just keep going until he gets to New York,' suggested Scarlett.

'He's a friendly guy,' said Georgeton still looking

through the glasses. 'He's seen us looking at him. He's just given us the Victory-V sign. That's real encouraging.' He put the glasses down.

Telcoombe Manor was among lean winter trees, its windows as bleak as old eyes. Not the most elegant of manor houses, it was in need of renovations that should have been carried out the summer the war began. There were signs and remnants of Georgian origins, but there had been a fire in early Victorian times and the building had afterwards been largely reconstructed, with a lack of felicity. Now the brick-work needed repointing and the paint on the door hung like an aged skin.

Bryant went ahead of the party towards the iron bell-pull, but as he did so a gritty howl came from the flank of the house; wild words from a woman and a loud bickering of ducks. Bryant moved slowly around the side, old rose brambles catching his uniform. The Americans followed cautiously.

Before the grid of bare trees was a grey pond upon which a flotilla of ducks was scuttling just out of reach of an irate woman waving a net on the end of a pole, describing arcs and circles like a flag-waving champion.

'Bastards!' Mrs Mahon-Feavor bellowed. 'Bastard ducks! Come here you bastards.' She was wearing a lifeboatman's oilskin, sou'wester and wellington boots.

Her askance eye caught the khaki group as they hesitated among the climbers at the corner of the house. 'Ah!' she shouted. 'You've turned up have you?

You've bloody-well turned up.' She advanced on them fiercely and flung the great net down like a challenge on the sodden lawn at their feet. '*You* catch the bastard ducks!' she cried. 'You want us out, so *you* catch the bastards.'

The Americans had difficulty in confining their smiles. Bryant regarded the lady anxiously and then turned to Georgeton and said nervously, 'General, this is Mrs Mahon-Feavor.' His eyes returned to the lady. 'Mrs Mahon-Feavor, this is General Georgeton.' She shook herself, an action not unlike that of a duck, and water flew from the clefts and recesses of her oilskins.

'We certainly seem to be causing a few problems,' admitted the American general. 'I hadn't thought about situations involving ducks.'

'Well *I* had,' said Mrs Mahon-Feavor still truculently. 'I'm certainly not leaving them here so that you and your riff-raff can blow them to pieces or they end up stuffed with whatever Americans stuff their ducks with.'

'Gooseberries,' put in Schorner softly. He kept a straight face. 'We stuff them with gooseberries, ma'am.'

'I thought you might,' she replied unsurely and less tartly. She turned to see the ducks now congregated with diminished agitation on the pond but muttering among themselves and collectively regarding her with suspicion. 'Bastards,' she swore again. She emitted a damp snort and took off the sou'wester. 'You'd better come in,' she said. 'Take a look at what you're getting.' She moved resolutely towards the front door. 'The bloody dump is falling to bloody pieces anyway,' she added. She pulled a strip of paint from a panel on the door. 'Look at that. If you blow it to kingdom come at least it will finish the job.' She waited, then said: 'As long as the compensation is generous.'

They trooped into the high hallway, wiping their shoes on the worn, wet rug at the door. 'Don't bother about that,' she said. 'If you're going to make holes in the place there's not much sense in wiping your bloody feet on the bloody mat is there.'

Georgeton was conciliatory. 'Well, ma'am,' he said, 'we have an idea we maybe will use this house as our officers' mess and may be an administration centre, so it should be in good condition when you get back here.'

'Officers' mess?' she said, sounding a little interested. 'then how about buying the ducks? Then *you* can catch the bastards. And you can stuff them with bloody gooseberries to your heart's content.'

'Let's make a note of that,' said Georgeton towards Scarlett. Scarlett promised he would remember. Mrs Mahon-Feavor, water still drizzling from her oilskins, led them into another room. It had a vaulted ceiling, its bosses carved like roses. 'Imitation,' she said pointing up. 'Of course. Bloody copied.' The furniture spread about the room was hardly antique, simply old. The chairs and sofas stood about like a herd of faded elephants. She instructed them to sit down. Georgeton, rolling involuntarily into the deep of an armchair, heard a spring echo beneath his bottom. Huge uncared-for portraits of men with warriors' expressions and hands on the hilts of ceremonial swords littered the walls. The afternoon light was dimming.

'You are of a military family, Mrs Mahon-Feavor,' said Georgeton, politely nodding at the paintings.

The Englishwoman sniffed. 'Bloody cowards the lot of them. Cowards or fools,' she informed him. 'We've had more men taken prisoner than any family in England.' She faced Georgeton. 'How many of your chaps are coming here?' she asked bluntly.

'In this house?' inquired the general, a little perplexed.

'No, in the surrounding area,' she corrected impatiently. 'Where all this hoo-ha is going to take place?'

Scarlett interpolated. 'I'm afraid that sort of information is classified – secret, you understand, ma'am.'

'Rubbish,' she snorted fiercely directly at him. 'Bloody rubbish.' She pointed dramatically at the carved ceiling. '*Sub rosa*,' she said. 'Under the rose. Anything that is said under the rose is a secret that is kept honourably.'

'We think about a hundred thousand,' put in Georgeton quickly. 'But not all at once. We'll be moving troops in and out all the time during the special training.'

The staunch lady became suddenly sad. 'The place is going to be very crowded,' was all she said. Then: 'Would you like some tea?' They watched fascinated while she pulled a long embroidered bell-rope. The result appeared to be only silence. 'We are evacuating about three thousand souls,' she went on. 'Seven hundred and ninety-four families, three hundred and ninety-seven old folk. Actually three hundred and ninety-six now because old Pendry died last week. They buried him today. He'll be one who is staying.'

The trio of Americans now grinned at her openly, their first experience of upper-class English eccentricity. She kicked at two starved logs smouldering grudgingly in the huge grate, giving off an almost religious skein of smoke, so thin it had vanished by the time it reached the base of the yawning chimney. Scarlett wondered if wood was also rationed. The chairs were so collapsed and soft that the general felt he was being devoured by his. He looked with comic uncertainty towards the others and saw that they were experiencing similar discomfiture. Mrs Mahon-Feavor sat firmly on an embroidered upright chair and regarded their predicament with some satisfaction. 'Comfortable?' she inquired, and without awaiting their reply: 'Good.'

A woman of incredible age and considerable infirmity brought the tea in. The tray rattled in her knobbly hands, her mouth trembled, her steps were staggered, two short ones followed by a little rush of half a dozen, a stop and then two short steps again. Schorner, getting out of the maw of the chair with difficulty, made to help her, but Mrs Mahon-Feavor waved him aside. 'She's absolutely capable,' she told him briskly. 'Aren't you, Bridget?'

So capable was the crone that she did not trust herself to reply until the tray was tremulously placed on a low table by the fire. Then she straightened slowly and, with a smile like a cobweb, answering a trembling 'Yes.' With some deliberation she then reversed from the area and eventually turned and went out into the darkness of the house.

'Never spoil them,' warned Mrs Mahon-Feavor. 'Remember that while you're here, general. Never spoil the English lower classes. They are quick to take a mean advantage.'

She poured the tea from a beautiful blue and white teapot into cups as delicate as eggshells. The men watched with the fascination of explorers entranced by a native ritual. The Englishwoman handed a cup to each and Bryant was taken aback when he was treated to a smile, a favour revealing a fossil tooth set in the middle of Mrs Mahon-Feavor's upper gum. He realized why he had never seen her smile before.

'Cowards,' she repeated, nodding once more at the portraits adorning the wall. 'This family changed sides three times in the Civil War, you know. Even then the fools ended up with the bloody King. That idiot overhead . . .' She nodded behind her towards the wall, curiously like a footballer back-heading a ball. 'That cretin . . . Major Brindley Mahon-Feavor. He walked out to parley with the Zulu. Fancy trying to talk to the Zulu. Never seen again. And hardly surprising.'

They dutifully looked up to the sad-faced soldier above the fireplace. He seemed, even then, to have some inkling of his African fate. 'Then Charlie over there, see, Captain Charles. A sentimental dolt, he was so carried away by the carol-singing contest between the Hun and the British at Christmas 1914, in the trenches you know, that he stood up to conduct. A sniper got him. The Germans apologized, I understand.'

Bryant saw that when she drank her tea she hooked her solitary tooth over the edge of the cup like a jemmy. He was surprised that the utensil remained undamaged. 'Now I've got two in the blessed Guards, believe it or not, and a daughter made of jelly in the WRAF, scanning the skies or something for the Jerries. The younger dimwit seems to spend his army life playing rugger and the other one . . . well, God knows how he manages. He got to France the week before Dunkirk, in fact I wouldn't be surprised if he wasn't the cause of it.'

Her sharp eyes scanned the walls as if eager to single out another ancestor for abuse. 'My late husband's family, of course,' she explained. 'Mine were clergy. All batty.' She regarded the general challengingly. 'Can your men march correctly?' she inquired to his astonishment. 'I mean swinging their arms and in step and all that baloney?'

'I believe they could try,' replied General Georgeton genially. 'Why do you ask, ma'am?'

'We've got a parade, Sunday after next,' she told him briskly. 'War Weapons Week, National Savings, you know. Parades, displays, all that rubbish, anything to make people part with their money. The war's given them more money than they've ever seen, so they're persuaded to give it back to keep the war going. We're having a parade in Wilcoombe – Home Guard band, the soldiers from that silly gun, the Sea Cadets and the Boy Scouts – they're very smart the Boy Scouts – WVS, Air Raid Wardens, everybody who's got a tin hat in fact. Anyway, if your Yanks are reasonably upright I'd like some of them to join in, perhaps a couple of platoons. But no chewing gum. And no Jews. We're going to church afterwards.'

Georgeton glanced at the others. 'How about negroes?' inquired Scarlett with assumed innocence. 'Are they okay?'

Mrs Mahon-Feavor remained unruffled. 'As long as they're Christian,' she said firmly, 'the hue is immaterial.'

Again the general looked sideways at Schorner. The colonel nodded. 'I guess we could raise enough men to look okay alongside the Boy Scouts,' he said. 'We might even raise a band.'

At once the old lady became interested. 'Oh, that's more like it,' she enthused. 'The Home Guard band is deplorable. They can only play "Blaze Away" and even that doesn't sound like "Blaze Away". And that rude tune, "Colonel Bogey". Then all the children sing to that. It's quite disgusting. They say they can do others, but I've never heard them make anything but a ghastly row. Oh, yes, we could do with a good band.'

They had finished their tea. They looked slightly awkwardly at each other. Bryant rose first. 'I think the general and these other gentlemen have to be on their way, Mrs Mahon-Feavor,' he said politely. 'They still have a lot to do.'

'That's correct,' said Georgeton. 'But first, if it doesn't inconvenience you too much, ma'am, perhaps we could see what accommodation there is in this house. The facilities.'

Immediately Mrs Mahon-Feavor assumed her businesslike expression. 'Are you going to buy my ducks?' she demanded.

Georgeton grinned grimly. 'You win,' he said. 'I guess we buy the ducks.'

In the narrowing dusk of that same January afternoon, Captain Hulton, the United States Army conducting officer, was leading another convoy of American vehicles carrying five hundred new troops south from Avonmouth Docks. They had reached the boundary of the Devon evacuation area and had gone into the incised lanes when they were confronted by a parade of farm vehicles on their way out.

The two formations halted almost nose to nose in the wet and deep cut of the lane. Fresh American faces peered out of the leading vehicles, as anxious as if they feared ambush. Those in the front were astonished to see a monster traction engine, great-wheeled, high chimneyed, like some steam-roller from pre-history. In the dusk it soared above the leading jeeps. Hulton swore, as had become his habit, and left the lead car. His tentative countrymen watched as he straightened his tunic and brusquely advanced on the behemoth. As he did so he saw the extent of the line of vehicles behind it, jamming the narrow lane, their various rickety superstructures standing against the dying sky. From the iron deck of the vanguard traction engine the cheerful West Country face of Doey Bidgood beamed like a spring moon. 'How be then, my old dear?' he greeted the captain amiably. Hulton looked up and thought he recognized the man from the inn on New Year's Eve. Beside him was a plump woman clutching a baby to her bosom, and behind them another character he recalled, Lenny Birch. The American remembered they were the pair who had the donkey.

'You'll have to go back,' said Hulton pompously. 'These are military vehicles and they have priority.'

'There now,' breathed Doey. He leaned over the side of the great iron vehicle. 'It might be, it very loikely is, that you've got what you call priority, my old darlin',' he said confidingly. 'But this incinerator unt got no reverse.'

Stiff-legged, Hulton moved a few paces to the rear and saw that the grotesque machine was towing a farm cart heavy with sacks and with a new lamb wedged below a net at the front. As he watched a small boy's face rose uncertainly alongside that of the lamb. Hulton cursed.

He returned to the front. Lenny Birch had now come to the foreground. Doey said: 'You talk to Lenny, zur. 'Ee got a better tongue than oi.'

'There's nothing to talk about,' insisted Hulton. He realized he was sweating under his tunic despite the chill of the late day. He thought he heard someone laughing from his own convoy of troops. From the tailed-back rustic convoy he was aware of figures moving in the dusk and voices calling, demanding to know why they had stopped. Doey, hearing this, summarily climbed on to the seat of the traction engine and bellowed back into the dusk, 'Us can't get on! 'Tis the Yankee army!'

He sat down and nodded with a kind of rough friendship at Hulton. Lenny said: 'We be moving Mary Lidstone 'ere, zur.' He nodded to the plump woman enfolding the baby. ''Er Ernie be away in Burma, see. A prisoner in the 'ands o' the Japanese.'

Hulton felt the familiar clamminess of defeat creeping across him. 'You've got to reverse,' he tried to insist. 'The military *must* get through.'

'God himself couldn't get through 'ere, darlin',' offered Mary Lidstone benignly. 'Not if this contraption can't go backwards. And it can't, I tell ye that for sod all.'

'Christ,' swore Hulton. He clenched his fists and beat them on some invisible surface. The civilians watched him with some sympathy. 'Christ, Christ, Christ . . .' He repeated the litany as he walked without hope back towards his jeep.

Doey called kindly after him. 'Gaffer! There be a gate back there. Into Blackstone's field. Get your army in there. 'Twill be all right.'

Hulton, still muttering, went to the car immediately behind his own. The officer commanding the unit, a grumpy Texan, was crouched into his overcoat. 'What the hell's going on, captain?' he demanded.

'They can't reverse, sir. There's no reverse on that wagon.'

'Damn it all,' sighed the officer.

'That's what I say, sir. But I guess there's nothing we can do about it. We'll have to reverse along this lane. There's a gate up here. We'll get the vehicles into the field and let these hicks through. It's the only way.'

The Texan sighed. 'I didn't come here to retreat,' he said. 'And now, I'm retreating. Go on, captain, let's get the goddamn thing done.'

Sulkily Hulton saluted and marched along the line of US Army vehicles. Faces turned expectantly on his as the newcomers sought reassurance. 'What is it, sir?' inquired a nervous young voice from the back of one of the trucks.

'A panzer division,' replied Hulton unkindly. 'We got landed in France by mistake.' Silence was the only response to this remark. Hulton realized some of them might believe him. Well, let them suffer; he had to. He saw the farm gate dimly on the right. It was about halfway along the convoy, so that the second half would have to reverse up the lane a short distance before going into the field front-first, then the fore end of the line would have to repeat the process. He pounded his fist on the flank of the car carrying the military police detachment. 'Come on out, you guys,' he bellowed. 'You afraid of the dark or something?'

The snowdrops, their white helmets luminous, tumbled out uncertainly. Hulton explained the manoeuvre. The men kept looking over their shoulders nervously and one sniffed the air. 'He's an Indian,' explained one of the others. 'Well, half. He's sniffing trouble.'

'It's cowshit,' replied Hulton sharply. He went to the gate and pushed it open. There were cows, like a shadow army, at the far end of the field. Their curiosity aroused they began to advance on the gate. Hulton shut it again quickly. He marched the length of the convoy and then on to the traction engine. Doey, Lenny and Mary Lidstone were all eating great slabs of cake and drinking cider from a bottle which they passed familiarly around. Hulton declined the offer to make a fourth at the neck. 'That field,' he said heavily. 'There are cows in it.'

They all nodded. 'Blackstone's cows,' confirmed Mary through her cake and cider.

'They can be Buffalo Bill's for all I care,' snorted Hulton, 'but I can't get the vehicles in the goddamned place if the goddamned cows are going to get out.'

Mary leaned over her shoulder. Hulton saw the tiny revealed face of her baby. 'Davie,' she called towards the cart behind. 'Davie, go and help the soldier with Blackstone's cows, there's a good boy.'

The child that Hulton had seen with the lamb in the

back of the cart appeared obediently. He had the lamb beneath his arm and he handed it to Doey who smiled towards Hulton and said: 'Just borned . . . yesterday.'

'I think I was,' grunted the American. He turned briskly. The boy silently held his hand. Jesus, what sort of people were these? At the car containing the commander he attempted to hide the boy, but the gritty Texan leaned out and said caustically: 'What's the kid, a hostage?'

'He's going to handle the cows,' shrugged Hulton as if it ought to have been obvious. The colonel accepted the answer and, with a sigh of impatience, sat back and lit a cigar. 'I wish I was going home,' he said to no one in particular.

The military policemen were grouped impotently around the gate, half a dozen of them, and on the other side of the gate were the cows. One animal, bolder or more curious than the rest, leaned and licked a snowdrop's helmet. Haughtily the man took it off and wiped it with his handkerchief. They regarded the arrival of the boy with only brief curiosity. Obviously this was a country where the unusual was to be expected. Davie regarded them and their white tops with huge awe, not even aware that Hulton was opening the gate. He continued to stare back when he was inside the field. 'The cows, son, the cows,' Hulton reminded him.

The boy turned on the cattle with much more assurance. He made a clucking noise with his tongue and his gums and waved his small hands once or twice like a conductor bringing out a subdued movement from an orchestra. The cows backed away and then turned and retreated obediently into the darkness at the end of the meadow. 'Okay,' said Hulton, hugely relieved, 'let's get the wagons moving.'

The operation took almost an hour. The military vehicles turned into the field with difficulty, their lights ignoring the blackout regulations and picking out the pale winter grass and the scattered archipelago of cow turds. Eventually the road was clear and, at Hulton's weary wave, the rural convoy started up again, led by the great traction engine. 'Thankee Yank!' shouted Doey as they triumphantly huffed by, the swaying convoy of carts and vans following.

Two of the military vehicles became immersed in the mud of the fields and had to be towed out. Eventually the phalanx was on the tight road again and just about to set off towards Telcoombe and the coast when through the dusk appeared Barrington's horse and trap, followed by the hearse recently utilized in the funeral of Old Pendry. Almost apoplectic, Hulton stamped from his jeep and confronted Barrington. Even recognition did not stem the American's determination.

'You've *got* to go back,' he demanded. 'This is a military convoy. We've wasted an hour already in a goddamned field. You must reverse.'

Surprisingly Barrington regarded the American officer without rancour. 'It's something you have to learn in these parts,' he offered. 'Reversing.'

'Well, reverse, if you please, sir,' said Hulton sulkily. 'This unit needs to get through.'

Barrington glanced at his wife, a worried face beside him in the gloom. 'I don't mind,' he said. 'The horse might, but I don't. And the hearse behind . . . they'll oblige, I'm sure.'

'Then, please, do it,' pleaded Hulton. But he guessed, he *knew*, with his fortune, there had to be something else. There was.

From the greyness behind the hearse emerged a tall man in US uniform. He and Hulton saluted each other awkwardly. 'What's the hold up?' asked the new arrival.

'US Army unit, heading for the evacuation area,' sighed Hulton. 'Disembarked this morning at Avonmouth.' It did not help.

'Unfortunately, captain, I have General Georgeton in the car behind. I'm Scarlett, his ADC. I'm afraid you'll have to let us through.' Hulton knew without looking that Barrington was laughing silently. The British bastard.

'Yes, okay,' surrendered Hulton. 'Sure thing.' He turned wearily. 'Back!' he shouted at his convoy making a motion of the cow-herding boy. 'Back to your field, come on, back to your field.'

At night the dark wind pummelled the sides of the nissen huts set around the anti-aircraft gun. Sometimes it seeped through the seams and whistled into the soldiers' quarters until someone kneaded some mud and blocked the crack. Gilman was writing, scribbling so quickly on an army block pad that he appeared to be sketching. Catermole was languidly polishing a boot. The dog they had acquired was chewing the lace of the other boot. Catermole gave it a push with his stockinged foot.

'We're not going to be able to keep this bugger, you know,' sniffed Catermole. 'Bullivant will soon sniff him out.' He poked his tongue out to see if he could see it reflected in the toe-cap of the boot. He could not, but he did not care. 'Anyway, I like the way *you* got given the dog, but I have to keep it under my bleedin' bed,' he complained. 'I'm the one who's on a charge if it gets found out. Say it does a shit under there. I suppose you want me to say it was me.'

Gilman grinned. On that sort of evening, mid-week, mid-winter, there was a strangely comforting domesticity about the hut. The blackout blinds were fixed over the windows, and Killer Watts had rigged an unofficial circuit of lights to supplement the dim official illumination. The fire enclosed in the iron stove burned amiably. Men sat on their beds reading, writing letters or lay staring at the iron curve of the ceiling as if it were a rainbow. Gilman had asked his other neighbour several times what he was doing as he stared so vacantly. Eventually, the man, Walt Walters, rubbery Midlander, replied dully: 'Considerin', mate, just considerin'.'

Across the corner at the far end of the hut was a radio loudspeaker, connected to the set in the canteen two huts away. It bawbled on throughout most evenings, low in tone for there was no way of increasing the volume, the knob being absent. It was like some constantly mumbling relative relegated to a corner, out of the way. Except on special occasions, like a broadcast by Churchill or an Andrews Sisters show, it was generally left unattended, the noises of regular broadcasts fixing the evening of the week for even those who were only half listening. Tonight it was a programme called *Garrison Theatre*.

The gossiping tones of two women droned from the set. 'Christ,' complained Catermole, 'Elsie and bleedin' Doris Waters. Just like being at 'ome. Nag, nag, nag. Except there's two of them.'

He gave the dog another push because it had begun to suck his sock. 'That bit of stuff that was in the house,' he began. 'The one that said she knew the old bloke what had the dog. Known her long then?'

'New Year's Eve,' answered Gilman, not looking up from his pad.

'Oh, in the pub. Just my bloody luck. I do half your stag so you can go and get a pint and you end up with her. I might have got myself arranged there.'

Gilman turned. 'That dog's sucking your sock,' he pointed out.

Catermole said he knew but he did not mind. 'It's the nearest thing I get to affection,' he shrugged. 'As long as 'ee don't dig 'is teeth in. It's just like my missus. I'm always afraid she'll dig her teeth in.' He returned to the question. ''Ave you got your feet under the table there, then?' he asked. 'With that bit of stuff.'

'Not under the table nor anywhere else,' replied Gilman casually. He studied Catermole's damaged, interested face. 'I went into her house because Bryant was creeping up the hill just as I was going to the pub. She let me in.'

Catermole grinned raggedly. 'Sort of sheltered you?'

Gilman said deliberately: 'Succoured me.'

'That's what I mean, rotten bastard. Didn't tell me, did you?'

'I don't tell you everything, Pussy.'

Catermole sniffed like a boy, leaned over and picked up the *Daily Mirror* from the foot of Walter's bed. He found the comic-strips page expertly. 'That Jane's got some tits,' he commented, running his tongue along his teeth. He looked towards the dopey Walters. 'Even you like Jane, don't you, Walt? Dozy as you are.'

'What's the good of paper tits?' muttered Walters, his expression unchanged.

Catermole let the dog gnaw his toe. He watched it. 'How long's this bloody war going to last, then?' he asked Gilman.

'I don't know.' Gilman was unsurprised. Barrack room conversation was predictable. 'Until we surrender, I expect.'

'The Yanks'll finish for us,' said Walters. 'And I wish they'd get a move on. I've got a lot of things to do.'

Gilman looked at the lumpish form. 'Like what?'

'My pigeons and stuff,' said Walters. They knew he had ended it there. He would say no more. It did not matter.

Killer Watts appeared anxiously through the door of the hut. There was a smear of drizzle on his waterproof cape. He was wearing field service marching order and carrying his rifle with the barrel pointing at his foot. 'Gilman,' he said, 'there's a woman at the gate for you. She came up when I was on guard. I said I'd get you as soon as I came off.'

Gilman eased himself up on the bed. Catermole laughed coarsely. 'There, see, I knew you'd be rogering away there before long.'

Watts said uncertainly: 'She said to bring the dog.'

He looked down and saw the mongrel with Catermole's socked toe in its mouth. 'That one, I s'pose,' he said.

Catermole said: 'We got a million dogs in this 'ut, Killer. Have a gander under the beds.'

'I don't care,' Watts returned solemnly. 'I don't give a fuck. I just said I'd tell Gilman.' He produced a cigarette with a pleased flourish. 'She gave me a fag,' he said.

Gilman was already pulling on his boots. Walters said: 'Bloody Jane ought to be banned. It makes blokes randy.'

Watts hunched out of the hut and Gilman followed him. He picked up the dog as he went. 'You don't mind, do you, Puss?' he said to Catermole. 'We can't keep it here anyway. She's got somewhere for it, I expect.'

'She's got somewhere for it all right,' muttered Catermole. He patted the mongrel heavily. 'Just when I get someone what loves me,' he grumbled.

Gilman pushed the dog under his tunic in case Bullivant or the orderly officer should see him. Outside the rain was enclosed in the wind funnelling in from the sea. It was a pitch night. The dog wriggled against his ribs. He walked with caution towards the gate.

She was standing in a doorway across the road. The sentry, having been primed by Watts, watched him lasciviously. He went smartly across and saw her pale face peering.

'I thought I'd take the dog back,' she said before he could speak. 'The old man's asking about it. I have enough grumbles without that.'

He smiled uneasily. 'That's all right,' he answered. 'Catermole, my pal, was getting fond of it.' He produced the thin mongrel and patted it. 'I'm afraid it wouldn't have been long before somebody found out,' he added. 'And there's all sorts of King's Regulations about livestock in barracks.'

'You'd have thought the King would have had more to think about, wouldn't you,' she said. 'He ought to have my worries.' She held out her slim hands and took the dog from him.

They were standing under the doorway of a small shop. 'I'll walk up with you,' said Gilman. 'Do you want me to carry the dog?'

She handed the animal back to him. 'He should try feeding the thing,' she said. It was as thin as a rabbit. They began to walk up the hill.

'Are you allowed out?' she asked. It was half-mocking.

'Till ten-thirty,' he told her.

She looked at her watch. 'It's just gone nine,' she said.

He grimaced. 'A grown man allowed out till ten-thirty,' he said. 'It's bloody ridiculous.'

'A lot of things are,' she said. 'I've been landed with the old man. He moans and he smells.'

Gilman was conscious of the distance between them. He took her elbow. She did not react. 'There was nowhere else for him to go?' he said.

'Nobody would have him,' she answered. 'And I don't blame them. Not grumbling and smelling like he does. And I'm some sort of relative so there was nothing else for it.' She laughed drily. 'He thinks he's going back tomorrow. Back to his cottage.'

'God, that makes it awkward. What will you do, Mary?'

He was aware that she glanced at him when he used her name. 'I'll have to keep lying to the poor old soul, I suppose,' she said. Then: 'He might drop down dead.'

Her flat tone told him she meant it. They had reached her door, halfway up the hill. The dog was panting as if he had walked all the way. 'Come on in for a minute,' she said casually, turning the key. 'The old boy's probably dozed off now. He'll have to sleep downstairs anyway. There's no room otherwise.'

Gilman followed her into the dark, stuffy hallway, oddly familiar. She waited until the door was closed before she switched on the light in its queasy orange shade. The dog wriggled in his arms. 'He's got a sniff of his master,' said Gilman, putting the animal on the linoleum. It ran towards the back room.

Mary laughed caustically. 'I'm not surprised,' she said. He walked behind her to the sitting-room. The light was on and the fire dawdled low in the grate. Mary stopped and Gilman looked across her shoulder to see the old man, head lolling, asleep in a wooden rocking chair with the youngest child, thumb in mouth, cradled and sleeping in his arms. The dog sat expectantly on the floor. The woman moved forward and took the infant away. It hardly stirred. The dog jumped into the vacant lap and the old man accepted the change, putting his arms around it without opening his eyes. Mary carried the child from the room and went upstairs. He sat in the other armchair and waited. The fire flared for a moment, giving the riven face opposite a brief glow. Mary came back and said without lowering her voice, 'Would you like a cup of tea? Or there's some scotch left.'

'I'll have tea,' he said, just above a whisper.

'Don't keep your voice down,' she told him. 'He'll have to fit in. He won't wake up anyway. When you're that age you sleep deep.'

'A sort of rehearsal for death,' commented Gilman.

She glanced at him sharply. 'Have you been writing anything?' she said. 'You were going to show me some of the things you've written.'

'One day I will,' he replied. He stood up and she suddenly moved forward and stood directly in front of him, her knees touching his. Gilman was looking intently into her face. Her tired eyes were almost closed. Her nose was only inches away. She reached down for his hands and guided them up to her breasts, so that their palms were under the lobes. He could feel the warmth through the wool of her sweater. She held them there; her lids covered her eyes. 'I'm in need of somebody,' she said in a matter-of-fact way.

'Me?' asked Gilman steadily. He wondered if *anyone* would have done.

'Yes, you'll do. I feel like I'm living in a sack.'

He was aware of a moment's hesitation in himself. Then he moved his face and put his cheek alongside hers. He kissed her mouth hard.

The old man by the fire wriggled and set the chair rocking. He half woke but seemed unaware of them although they stood only two feet away. Mary said: 'We could have got down in front of the fire but what with Methuselah here, that's out. The little boy is sleeping in my bed because his cough keeps the other one awake. The only place left is the air-raid shelter,' she said.

'Where your husband put the cuckoo clock,' he remembered with a smile.

She led him towards the door. 'His bit towards the war effort,' she said.

In the confined hallway she turned down a short passage that he guessed led to the back-garden door. Her hand hung back and touched him to a stop for a moment. She opened a cupboard and, to his surprise, handed him a thin, biscuit-like mattress. Then she took out two blankets. 'It's too damp to keep bedding down there,' she explained in her unexcited, conversational voice.

She closed the cupboard and led him towards the door. Everything was as routine. He wondered again how many times she had been through it before. Carefully, more for privacy he realized than because of blackout regulations, she turned off the hall light before releasing the bolt on the side door and opening it. A square of night sky showed beyond the aperture. Wet air touched his face. Mary looked sideways at the house next door before moving stealthily into the garden. Gilman followed.

The corrugated Anderson shelter appeared to fill the garden. His feet squeezed into muddy grass, but quickly they were at the entrance. Taking care she put aside a wooden panel that covered the doorway. The shelter, set half in and half out of the ground, was draped with hanging winter weeds. 'Don't break your neck,' she warned, whispering. 'There's some steps.'

She went first and, awkwardly, he followed her into the hole in the ground. At once he felt the dampness on his skin. There were half a dozen wooden steps before he trod on a firm surface, the texture of coconut matting. Mary remounted the first two steps and groped outside for the wooden frame. He made to help her but she nudged him aside, saying quietly: 'I know how it fits.' She eased it across the door, shutting out the oblong of night, and fastened it with four catches on the inside. Now it was deeply dark. Gilman stood not seeing her, feeling her closeness. He put his hands out and laid them against her waist. 'Let me get some light,' Mary said, briefly pushing herself against him.

He remained standing while she moved about in the tight space. Suddenly the single slight beam of a bicycle lamp appeared. 'There's an oil lantern, but the wick's gone,' she said. She was a few feet away, standing at the foot of a wooden bed with bands of metal criss-crossed to form springs. On the opposite side were two bare wooden bunks. There was a shelf with a couple of china ornaments and a rack of ignored books. The cuckoo clock which had stopped was fixed to the metal wall alongside, the cuckoo quaintly protruding. 'It's all right,' she said, seeing him looking at it. 'He won't watch. Put the mattress on.'

Bemused, Gilman placed the mattress on the rusting metal bands. She patted it in a housewifely way, the first sign of real domesticity he had detected in her, and then spread the blankets on it. 'You don't want a pillow, do you?' she inquired seriously.

Gilman shook his head: 'I think I can do without it,' he mumbled. 'Doesn't it get a bit short of air in here? With the front up?'

'Yes,' she said. 'Stuffy as hell!' Abruptly she sat on the bed and began to pull her jumper from her shoulders. She tugged her head through it. 'That's why the oil lamp's not so good. Suffocation.' She had a vest under the woolly. She unzipped her slacks and began to pull them down. Gilman had remained standing, watching the performance. 'Come on,' she chided. 'You as well. It's not a bloody free show, you know.'

'Sorry,' he apologized. He unbuttoned his battle-dress top and took it off. He sat on the bed to unlace his boots. She had taken off her slacks and she lay back in her drawers and vest, stretching out the whole length of the narrow bed. Her hands went to her hair and she ran it through her fingers. She yawned and then laughed at him.

'Not very romantic, am I?' she said.

'I don't know,' he answered. 'I didn't know what to expect.'

'Well, it's not exactly the place for romance, is it? Not an air-raid shelter.'

His boots were taking some time. He felt he had to make conversation while he untied the knots that he had pulled too tightly in his hurry to go out to her. 'Do you come down here much?' he asked. Then added quickly: 'I mean for air raids.' It was still awkward. 'I meant when the raids were on.'

She did not appear to have sensed any second intent. 'Sometimes,' she said. 'When they were bombing Plymouth and they used to drop whatever they had left around here. Sometimes I don't reckon they used to bother to get as far as Plymouth. They'd just get rid of the bombs and sod off. Can't say I blame them.'

She drew the second blanket up to her shoulders.

'Hurry up with those boots,' she admonished. 'I'm freezing.'

'Sorry,' said Gilman. 'Army boots were not meant for love.'

She gave a small arid laugh. 'I bet you'll make quite a decent writer,' she said. 'You come out with some odd things.'

'Nice of you to say so,' he said. He gave a final heave at the boot. 'There, they're off now.' He took the rest of his clothes off and, shivering, lifted up the blankets and climbed into the bed beside her. There was so little room they were at once forced against each other. He felt her cold skin against his stomach. His arms slid around her shoulders.

'The Germans only came on a few hit-and-run raids, after the real bombing,' she mentioned. 'No sooner they'd got here than they were off again.' She had closed her eyes. She had fine lashes lying long across her tired face. She could have been a beauty. Now she opened her eyes, halfway, and smirked in the timid light of the cycle lamp. 'I hope there's nothing hit-and-run about you,' she said. He kissed her.

Gilman rolled over on top of her, needing to balance so he did not topple from the bunk.

'That's only the second time we've kissed,' said Mary. Her voice was less sharp. She watched his face as though requiring confirmation.

'We seem to be putting the cart before the horse,' he grinned.

'Not one of your better phrases,' she said. Then, almost briskly, 'Come on, my soldier, I'm ready for you.'

They closed against each other. He felt his body

193

warm as she moved strongly beneath his legs and trunk, arching her body and thrusting herself at him. Gilman responded hungrily.

'Wait, wait,' she said breathlessly. 'Go easy, sailor. Please.'

'Soldier,' he corrected. 'I'm a soldier.'

She opened her drowsy eyes and said solemnly: 'So you are. Didn't recognize you without your uniform.' She patted his face. 'Just rest a moment,' she suggested. 'You don't have to be back yet.'

'My ship sails at midnight,' he said.

She managed to shrug. 'You know what I mean.'

Motionless they lay beneath the chaffing blankets, the sweat cooling their bodies. 'I enjoy this,' she said as though speaking to herself. 'It gives me something I need, you know. It makes up for some of the other things.'

'As for me, I didn't even realize,' he confessed with a serious laugh. 'I've not been . . .' He hesitated. 'Well . . . very active.'

'Well put,' she approved. Then, 'Do you mind waiting around like this?'

'No,' he answered. He kissed her. 'If it's what you want to do.'

'I don't often get it like this. My husband does it by numbers – just like a civil servant.'

They lay silently for another minute before she said: 'You can carry on if you like.' She reached above her and, oddly, put out the bicycle lamp.

On the same day as General Dwight D. Eisenhower landed in London to become Supreme Commander of the Allied Forces for the invasion of Occupied Europe, George and Naomi Hicks and Sammy, their son, were evacuated from their shabby shop in Devon, one of the final families to go. It was the third week of January.

George and Sammy put up the shutters on the old windows of the shop at Telcoombe Beach, George defiantly appending a cryptic note: 'Opening again after Hostilities.' Mrs Katlin departed the Telcoombe Beach Hotel in tearful splendour, two taxis being required to carry the old lady and her cobwebbed chattels from the room which had been her small home for twelve years. The taxis were paid for by the authorities because she refused to transport either herself or her possessions in anything less dignified, certainly not an army truck. The Hibberts left their farm. Jake Hibbert looked over his shoulder from the back of the horse-drawn wagon carrying the ultimate cargo of muddy mangolds, mutely, bitterly, over the empty fields and buildings. He had purposely left his front door open and the wind was already blowing it, pushing its way in to occupy the house. They could hear the harsh clatter of its latch even after they had turned the bend in the lane and the house was beyond sight.

Eric Sissons, the vicar of Telcoombe Magna, his stumbling wife and his father were also among the last to go. There was an American tank at the church gate as they left the vicarage and walked with their final hapless suitcases through the unmoved gravestones. Sissons essayed a caustic wave at the soldiers sitting on the tank. 'There was no need to send that thing,' he called with icy jauntiness. 'We were just going.'

The young Americans, themselves hardly knowing what was taking place, laughed hesitantly at what they felt fairly certain must be a joke. It was the slow old man, the vicar's father, who replied to the juvenile grins. 'Let's see you get that thing across the Channel,' he grunted. The soldiers looked puzzled.

'You'll all drown!' shouted Cecily Sissons, who had taken half her morning bottle even at an early hour. Her husband went red and bundled her into his small, clerical Morris. The Americans did not understand.

Before the Morris started off, Sissons, on an afterthought, turned back. He approached the tank stonily. 'Before I leave,' he intoned ecclesiastically at the sergeant, 'I want to inform you that this is a very, very, very ancient church. People in this part of England have been worshipping in this church since long before America was discovered. I am charging you with looking after it.' He let his eyes take in the others. 'Each one of you.'

The sergeant regarded him with initial surprise, replaced swiftly with professional coolness. 'We'll try, sir,' he said. 'We'll certainly try. But me, I ain't in charge of the war. Just this tank.'

Sissons could say nothing more. He could hear Cecily making a fuss with his father in the car. Anxiously he retreated and reached the door. 'Shut up, will you!' he bawled, almost in her face. 'You're showing *us* up in *front* of them.'

Her tantrums dissolved into a jelly of remorse. 'You're ashamed, Eric,' she sobbed into her stained hands. 'You're ashamed of *me*. You, a Christian priest.'

'Shut up, old dear,' said the vicar's father, more

kindly. 'Eric has enough problems as it is. You must realize, girl, that all this has deprived your husband of his living.'

'And his dead,' she sniffed seriously. 'It's the graves I don't like to leave by themselves. They're so defenceless, graves. I hope they don't desecrate them. Are they Christians, do you think?'

Angrily Sissons had started the little car. It bumped and coughed down the lane. He could hear the American soldiers hooting like children at its antics. 'They're heathen!' he shouted back at his wife. His voice fell to a grunt. 'Savage to a man. I don't know what in God's name they're doing on *our* side.'

On their journey towards the coast road, along which they intended to travel to Wilcoombe, they passed lines of US military vehicles. Sombre tanks, hunchbacked transport trucks and jeeps, busily sliding in and out of the convoys. American faces stared out in wonder as the fragile little Morris clattered by them. Then came howls from behind as the new soldiers laughed and cheered, not unkindly, but because they were childish, as soldiers are childish.

Standing at the head of the line of trucks, on a promontory of reeds and sand from which he could see both the landing beach and the brackish water of the inland leys, was Colonel Schorner. He recognized Sissons in the car, his clerical collar like a white grin. He waved. The vicar stopped and, with difficulty, wound down the squeaking window. Schorner loped easily down from the dune and saluted the three people in the car. Sissons had a curiously elderly feeling although he was younger than the soldier. Cecily emitted a little whoop of pleasure. The old man examined the American keenly. 'I see you got rid of the Boy Scouts hats,' he called over his son's shoulder, eager to claim the experience. 'They used to make us laugh in the first war, those hats.'

Schorner smiled agreeably. 'We just did, sir,' he said. He pointed back to the troops standing about the military trucks. 'But see, we still have the gaiters.'

'Ah,' remarked the old man wisely. 'But they're very useful. Very. Keep your legs warm. Stop you bleeding too much when you've been hit.'

The strange logic had never occurred to the American. He laughed unsurely. Sissons gave his father a brief nudge with his shoulder which sent him back into his seat. Sissons sighed: 'How long do you think all this will take?'

Schorner shrugged. 'Wish I knew too,' he said.

Sissons said: 'You can see my church from here.' He remained in the car, but indicated over his shoulder. 'Just over to the left, beyond the higher ground. See the steeple? I would be grateful if you could leave it in one piece . . . Our bishop seems to think it's expendable, but I don't.'

'No church is expendable,' answered Schorner. 'Nor any man.'

'Churches do seem to suffer more than their fair share in this sort of thing,' commented Sissons, still sourly.

'And nuns,' put in the old man in the back seat mischievously. 'Nuns suffer.' Sissons ignored him.

The American colonel nodded. 'Yes, I suppose churches do, reverend. It's because they make good artillery observation posts – and great range-finders for guns shooting the other way.'

'In France,' shouted the vicar's father, 'we always shot at the steeples.'

Sissons regarded the American stonily. 'I must be going,' he said. 'We don't want to be here when you start your pretend war.'

'No, sir,' smiled Schorner coolly. 'It gets noisy.'

He saluted briefly again and Sissons re-started the car. Schorner watched the quaint vehicle wobble along the road, observing the two white faces set in the back window, watching him as they went.

Against the breeze Schorner called orders to the men in the leading trucks and they jumped down and began moving down to the beach, tugging at, clearing the old rusted British barbed wire as they went. Off shore were three Royal Navy landing craft, edging shorewards to land their first cargoes of material for the new American army. It was a firmer, finer day now, the nose of spring, with a clearer sky and a cool sun which coloured Start Bay blue and the land bright green. The long sand of the beach was like settled velvet.

The schoolhouse was set, like a small outpost, on top of the next neck of land and Schorner observed a flash of reflected sunlight as one of the windows was closed. He lifted his field glasses and saw that the young schoolteacher, Dorothy Jenkins, was moving some books from the window sill. Unhurriedly he walked down on to the beach and along the fine sand and then the shingle until he had reached the path leading up to the school. She opened the door as he was approaching. Her smile was uncertain.

'Not breaking curfew, am I?' she said. 'Yet?'

'Not yet,' he smiled. 'It's tomorrow.'

'I don't intend to be here tomorrow,' she replied. He had reached the door now and they walked together into the classroom. Only one of the desks was occupied. Bobby Bewler, the teenage simpleton, was regarding Schorner with wild apprehension.

'This is Bobby,' said Dorothy Jenkins. 'He's keeping me company.'

The lad leapt to his feet, banging the desk seat back like the explosion of a gun, and saluted Schorner dramatically. The surprised officer returned the salute.

'Bobby's a bit different,' mentioned Dorothy. She turned to the boy. 'Sit down, Bobby,' she said. 'That used to be your desk when you came to the school, didn't it.' The youth nodded his head fiercely, an irregular grin severing his vacant, red face. The woman turned to Schorner saying: 'His mother is trying to get her belongings moved from her house today, so I thought Bobby would be better off here. I had to do some clearing up anyway.'

'Does his ma need some help?' asked Schorner seriously. 'I can get some of my boys there.'

She shook her head. 'The WVS, the Women's Voluntary Service, are organizing it,' she smiled. 'I don't think your soldiers would have a hope.'

Schorner looked carefully around the shell of the schoolroom. Everything had been taken away except the desks. 'It's sure a great pity,' he said to her. He watched the boy, whose attention was taken with some insect walking along the wooden floor.

'What, Bobby?' she asked. 'Or the whole business?'

'Both,' he shrugged. 'The whole business, as you call it, and the way it affects kids like him.'

'Less than most, I'd say,' she answered practically. 'Every generation here has had the likes of Bobby. The people are very close, you see.' As they watched Bobby had captured the creature from the floor. It was a small, polished woodlouse. He placed it on the desk in front of him and proceeded to slice it up with an overgrown thumbnail. Schorner grimaced but Dorothy only reacted with embarrassment. 'That's how they are,' she shrugged. 'One day he might become a soldier.'

Schorner regarded the young woman thoughtfully. 'And what will you be doing?' he asked. 'Still teaching school?'

'That's my lot,' she replied simply. 'They're making room for us in the classrooms at Wilcoombe. Everybody's got to squeeze up. They don't like the idea. But we'll manage. You must come and see us there some time. Tell us about American history.'

He could see she was not being caustic. He was accustomed to that now, so he knew the difference. 'Sure,' he said. 'I'd like to do that if I get the opportunity.'

'They enjoyed your poem the other day,' she added. 'The children.'

'Good. I'm very glad somebody's got some good thoughts about us.'

Dorothy went with him to the door. He opened it and the salt air breezed in, catching her dark hair. She laughed and held it down. Peaceful sunlight lay across the sea and the sand. 'I shouldn't worry too much about it,' she said. 'In the end they'll realize that you've come to fight for us.'

'Thanks,' said Schorner sincerely. He half turned

back into the room. "Bye, Bobby,' he called. Only silence came back. He shrugged. 'See how I lose friends and fail to influence people,' he said. They shook hands and he ambled down the path between the short dunes to the beach. The first of the landing craft was approaching in-shore. Schorner turned and saw that the simple boy had joined the schoolteacher at the door of the small building. They waved and, suddenly gladly, he waved back. 'Okay you men,' he called to a group of GIs standing idly on the beach. 'Let's get this thing unloaded. Let's get our feet wet.'

On the next day, the final day allowed for the evacuation of the civilian population, Howard Evans left his surgery in Wilcoombe and got into his car. It was still fine and there was an upstairs window open in his house. Beatrice looked out as he was about to move off. 'Be long?' she called.

'Lunchtime,' he answered. Then: 'I thought I'd just take a last look around.' He nodded eastwards. It was already a different country. 'Over there.'

'Can I come too?'

'All right, if you like.'

She vanished from the window and appeared a few moments later through the cottage front door, pulling on her coat. She had been patching the sleeves on the previous evening and as she got into the car she examined her workmanship with satisfaction. 'Not bad, is it?' she asked her husband. 'A new season, a new design. This one's called "rags and tatters".'

He laughed with her, then said: 'You're sure you want to come?'

Seriously she nodded. 'I think so,' she replied. 'For a last look before it's all altered.'

He accepted the thought. 'It will never be the same again,' he told her. 'Some people will never go back, the look of the land will be all changed. I suppose you could say that today is the end of the century for these parts.'

His words were at once confirmed. They drove out of Wilcoombe and along the coastal road. Within two hundred yards there appeared a military checkpoint, barbed wire and a white-painted barrier. Two American military police stood outside a sentry box. One was black, his face and eyes startling under the domed white helmet. It was the negro who moved forward and stopped the car. He saluted politely. Evans wound down the window.

'I'm the doctor,' he explained. 'Evans. I'm just going to make a final check to see that everything is all right. That nobody's been left.' It sounded a strange explanation even to him.

The snowdrop nodded: 'That's okay, sir,' he slurred 'But tomorrow nobody goes through. That's the orders.'

Evans thanked him and drove on. Beatrice smiled at her husband. 'That's the first time I've ever heard a black man speak,' she said quietly. 'He didn't sound a bit like Scott and Whaley on the radio.'

He said, 'Scott and Whaley? That's just burnt cork.'

She laughed: 'What, for the radio?'

They were driving along by the sea now. The waves were jumping in the sunshine. Two naval vessels were loitering out in Start Bay. 'It's strange, isn't it,' said

Evans. 'Black men have always been *funny* up to now. Acts.'

'Like G. H. Elliott, the Chocolate-Coloured Coon, or the golliwog on the marmalade,' she said. 'Yes. They've always been to amuse us. We're going to have to change our attitudes there.'

'And in a lot of other places.' He nodded out to sea. 'See how the British Navy is mothering the Americans. The ships are ours. That's why they left it to the poor old admiral to tell everybody.'

'Those two don't look very formidable,' Beatrice said, looking out at the vessels.

'Judging by the funnels they're pretty ancient,' said Evans. 'But we probably won't tell the Yanks that.'

They had reached the Telcoombe Beach Hotel. A squad of Americans was digging a trench on the square of lawn that faced the beach. Two other GIs were sitting on the children's swings at the dilapidated edge of the garden. They creaked with rust as the soldiers swung idly. Evans wished the digging party good morning and they stood up and returned the greeting. In the mild sunshine two had stripped themselves to the waist. Their bodies were white, one thin, the other with rolls of fat coiled around his middle. They all studied Beatrice.

'Looking for buried treasure?' joked Evans.

'No, sir,' replied the thin man adroitly. 'We figured maybe we could dig our way out of this place. Escape.'

The doctor and his wife both laughed. The neglected rear door of the hotel was open, moving to and fro in the breeze like a beckoning hand in a shabby glove. They walked across the brief lawn and went in. It felt immediately cold. 'Trying to escape,' echoed Evans. 'It doesn't occur to us that they don't particularly want to be here.'

They fell into silence the moment they began to walk into the hotel, a silence prompted and heightened by their slow and empty footsteps on the bare boards. They walked first into the kitchen, then the guests' lounge, then the dining-room. Each room was naked, its walls and floors marked with the geometry of dust and stains left when curtains and carpets had been removed.

'It's so cold,' muttered Beatrice. 'This place was always so warm.'

Evans nodded sadly. 'Where did Mrs Katlin go?' asked his wife.

'Totnes,' he said. 'They found her a room in a guest house. She'll never come back.' He stopped as they heard a movement. It was already eerie. He touched his wife's arm and walked back towards the kitchen. She heard him laugh. A strange haired dog was sitting looking without understanding around the stripped room. They both recognized it for it had wandered the beach for years. Old Daffy, the fisherman, owned it and its journeys in his boat and its living outdoors in the salty air and sun had turned its coat from black to a gingery brown. They spoke to it and it wagged its sunburned tail, but then turned and went out into the air. 'They'll have a job keeping him out,' forecast Evans.

They followed the dog, called good-bye to the soldiers, three of whom were now sitting on the swings and went out to the car. In silence they drove up to Telcoombe Magna. The road through the village was lined with heavy US Army trucks with men unloading

them, carrying crates and boxes through the churchyard and into the church itself. There was a heavy
machine gun set up in the lychgate. Beatrice had gone
pale. 'That will please Sissons, I don't think,' Evans
said.

There were twenty heavy trucks strung along the
village road. Evans counted them. He stopped the car
just beyond the church but was immediately
approached by a jeep carrying a quartet of military
police. 'This is a military area, sir,' called the man
beside the driver firmly. 'No loitering is permitted.'

Evans swallowed fiercely. Beatrice touched his arm.
'No loitering,' she repeated. 'I think we ought to go.'

Evans growled something within himself as he
started the car. The Americans watched it with the
interest they might give to a foreign insect. Some of
those unloading the trucks whistled at Beatrice. Evans
snorted angrily but she only laughed and said: 'The
women around here are going to find themselves in
demand.'

'While their husbands are fighting overseas,' he
muttered.

His wife laughed again. 'Well, you're not,' she said
soothingly. 'So I'll be quite safe.'

'You'd better be,' he answered.

Her eyebrows went up, good-humouredly. 'I'm not
sure what you mean by that,' she said. 'I hope you
always think I'm safe.'

They drove by the gate of the American camp.
Evans saw that in two weeks it had expanded from the
haphazard settlement of the advance party to a
spreading city of tents and huts. Smoke rose into the
blue spring day, men and vehicles were on the move,

the recorded sound of Glenn Miller's 'American Patrol' sounded over the Devon meadows. 'My God,' breathed Beatrice. 'Look at all that. I would not have believed it possible. Not in a few days.'

Evans had recovered his temper. 'For them,' he said, 'nothing is impossible. They can do anything. Or they believe they can. But it won't be as easy setting up camp in France.'

They continued to drive along the upward-rising coombe, almost enclosed by the banks and hedgerows on either flank. It could almost have been spring for the air was light, the sun slid through the lattice of branches, the old, long stones set into the banks, the ancient shiners as they were called, glowed warmly. They reached the village of Mortown and Evans, almost involuntarily, stopped the car. He and his wife sat, dumbly, looking down on to what had been a living hamlet.

'God, look at it,' she said in a low voice. 'How terrible.'

Even on that bright day a wind was sneaking up the street. It made the sign above the village shop, the tin sign which said 'Lyon's Tea', creak and rattle. Somewhere a door was banging. The patches of sun looked cold as ice floes. Every window was blank, every door stood like a tombstone. Soon weeds and moss would begin to grow in the crevices of the little street. Soon rats and pillaging pigeons would inhabit the small place which had been the home of humans for a thousand years.

Without saying anything Evans got out of the car. Beatrice, as if shying away from closer contact with the visible loneliness, remained where she was. He walked alone down the slope and along the street. There was a brook which ran under a paving stone bridge at the foot of the hamlet and in the new silence he could clearly hear the clatter of the travelling water, something of which he had never before been aware.

Beatrice watched her husband's shoulders hunch as he walked. He paused and pulled his coat collar up about his neck, then continued on the solitary journey. He was almost at the bottom of the single street when he heard a noise coming from a terrace cottage in a tight alley by the Horse and Groom Inn. So deserted was the scene that the sound startled him. He turned cautiously towards it.

From the open doorway appeared the familiarly stealthy figure of Horace Smith, the poacher. He carried his professional bag, an army haversack, slung about his neck. From it protruded the yellow legs of two chickens. He smiled when he saw Evans. ''Ow be you, doctor?' he greeted. Evans grinned with the relief of familiarity.

'Busy, Horace?' he said.

Horace nodded towards the stark yellow legs. 'They'n wouldn't be caught when everybody went,' he explained. 'But I seed no sense in leaving they to be shot by they Yankees.'

'There's not much else left, is there,' said Evans looking about at the newly desolate village. He remembered photographs of ruined settlements in France from the First World War. It was like that except that here every house was intact; only the life had gone.

The poacher shrugged his face. 'Oh, I don' know about that, doctor,' he said. He winked with the eye that was always half closed, his shooting eye. 'I reckon there be a few little hidey-holes with money in them in these cottages. People get old and not trusting anybody you know. They hides away their money and suchlike and then gets even older and forgets all about it. Oh, I bet there's a few quid under these floorboards.'

His eye gymnastically dropped up and down again. 'And there's the bluey . . . the lead from the pipes, and the roofs like of the churches. And the brass door knockers. Ah, there be all sorts of things, doctor.'

'But the whole area is being sealed off,' pointed out Evans. 'I had a job to get past the guards even today.'

'I didn't,' said Horace quietly. 'Nor will I ever. There's plenty of ways in here if you know 'em. And out.'

'There'll be landmines and all sorts of trouble,' warned Evans. 'And the Americans would probably shoot you on sight.'

Horace smiled wearily. 'Now I didn't say it was I comin' back 'ere, now did I, doctor? I'll be making a shilling supplying the Yankees with hare or sometimes I might just come across a stray salmon, you never know. But that's not to say that others won't come in. You just watch, they spivs from Plymouth will be creepin' under the wire to see what they can get.'

'With that sort of risk, they're welcome to it,' said Evans. He looked back up the vacuum of the street to where Beatrice sat in the car. 'I must be going,' he said. 'There's no one left around here as far as you know is there, Horace?'

'Not a soul,' said the poacher surely. ''Cepting me.'

'Well, I wouldn't hang around too long,' advised Evans. 'It wouldn't do for you, of all people, to be caught in a booby trap.'

Horace laughed gummily. 'No danger o' that,' he assured. 'I be goin' anyhow. Just after another call. One o' Lackley's litter ran off when they was clearing out. I think I'll be going to see if I can find any sign of 'im. T'wouldn't do for a little pig to be left all on his own here, would it?'

Evans left him and walked up the steep, bleak, shining street, inhabited only by the sniffing wind. He reached the car and got in. 'Horace,' he said, nodding towards the slow figure at the other end of the hill. 'He seems to think that there's buried treasure under half the floorboards in this area. Not that he's looking for that, not at the moment anyway. He's just collecting mislaid chickens and pigs – out of the kindness of his heart.'

Beatrice laughed drily. 'I bet he is,' she said. 'He could be right about the buried treasure, though. They never did trust the banks. How many times have you been paid with a mildewed pound note?'

'Or with a gold half-sovereign,' he agreed. They had reached the foot of the village hill. Horace had vanished among the yards at the back of the terraced cottages. They began to ascend the opposite side of the valley. Beatrice felt relieved. She looked back at the village and then reached quickly for his shoulder. An American tank was waddling down the opposite hill. Even as she watched, it clumsily slewed in the road and its rump demolished the front wall and windows of the village shop. She told her husband to stop the car and he did so at the apex of the hill.

'They've just knocked down half of Swain's shop,' she said angrily. 'That bloody tank.'

They got out of the car. The tank's end was still wedged in what had been the little window. The Lyon's Tea sign had fallen across the gun. As they watched, four soldiers climbed from the tank and rolled about with merriment in the street. Their torn laughter floated up to the man and his wife on the hill. The tank crew were slapping each other on the back in their hilarity. Fifty yards down the street Horace the poacher appeared, a pig wriggling in the bend of his arm. He watched stolidly.

'Unfeeling blighters,' trembled Beatrice Evans bitterly. 'That was Swain's shop.' Evans turned and saw, to his surprise, that she was crying.

'Soldiers,' said Evans, putting his arm on the back of her neck, 'are rarely known for their finer feelings. It's something they're probably better off without.'

They stood continuing to watch. The soldiers had not noticed either them or Horace. The poacher, confronted with something he knew by instinct he ought to avoid, turned and began to hurry the few yards up the hill towards Evans and Beatrice, the pig still complaining beneath his arms. As he approached he called: 'Did 'ee see that then, doctor? Knocking the bloody place down afore they start.'

He turned in time to see the tank pull away from the building that now leaned on it. With a roaring collapse the entire corner of the terrace fell away, the framework of the shop window hanging on to the tank as though trying to prevent it leaving the scene of the crime. Dust and debris rolled about. The members of the crew who were in the street, still laughing, returned to the tank and climbed into the turret, kicking away bricks and plaster from the steel surface. The vehicle roared throatily and went down the slope to the foot of the village.

'I reckon we better be along our way,' observed Horace wisely. 'Can I come with you, doctor? I bain't havin' any race with that machine.'

All three returned to the car. Beatrice wiped her eyes and muttered finally: 'It's a damned disgrace doing a thing like that.'

In silence they drove along the sunny road. The fields were oddly vacant, no cattle, no horses. They passed the shells of familiar farm houses, no chickens and ducks about the yard now, no dogs lying on doorsteps.

'Are you going to the Barringtons?' asked Beatrice, knowing that her husband would.

'Tom swore he'll be the last to go,' replied Evans. 'I think we ought to make sure he's leaving today.'

'If you don't mind, I'll be leaving 'ee at the cross-roads then,' decided Horace gravely. 'Mr Barrington and me don't often see eye to eye, if you get my understanding.'

Evans nodded knowingly and halted at the crossroads. A farm cart was stopped there and two men were collecting mangolds from a mound at the roadside and throwing them into the back. The horse gnawed the hedgerow. 'Harvesting,' laughed one of the men when he saw Evans. 'Gaffer says 'ee be leavin' nothin' for the occupation forces.'

The doctor knew they were Barrington's men. 'Is he still at the house?' he asked. 'Or have they gone yet?'

The first man looked up from the pile. ''Ee be still there, sir,' he said. 'In fact I don' know that 'ee's going to be gone. 'Ee be wearin' of his Home Guard uniform and 'ee's got 'is gun.'

'Good God,' muttered Evans to his wife. 'I hope he's not gone mad. It won't do for him to start shooting at the Americans.' Horace left the car and disappeared almost magically through the hedge and across the field, the pig still objecting as he carried it at a jog. Evans drove from the crossroads along the lane to Barrington's farm. Anxiously he left the car in the deserted yard and went to the house. Tom Barrington, in his uniform as a captain in the Home Guard, was standing on the doorstep. He had a service revolver at his waist and a double-barrelled shotgun in his right grip.

'God, Tom, you look pretty warlike,' said Evans lightly.

He realized that Beatrice had followed him. 'All ready to move?' she asked brightly. 'Is Jean all packed?'

'Don't worry yourselves,' returned Barrington. 'I'm not going to shoot the first bloody Yank I see. We've still got until midnight, remember. I thought I'd just show them that I've got a uniform too – and I wore it before *them*. While they were still trying to keep *out* of the bloody war. I'd have mounted a ceremonial parade of the Home Guard unit.' He paused a little shamefaced. 'But a lot of the men couldn't get away.'

'We've just seen one of their tanks demolish Swain's shop in Mortown,' put in Beatrice. 'Already. Knocked it right down.' Evans glanced at her, annoyed that she had said it.

'They'll do that to everything, don't worry,' said Barrington. 'This place will be a bloody shambles. I'd like to chuck a few Molotov cocktails at them.'

Evans looked at him with sharp anxiety. 'Now, Tom,' he cautioned, 'don't talk like that.' He turned and looked across the fields. Was there a touch of fresh green on the meadows this spring-like day, or did he just imagine it? 'You'll end up in front of a firing-squad,' he added like a joke. 'And that wouldn't do, would it?'

When he turned again he saw that there were tears shining in Barrington's eyes. He was keeping them back but they were there. 'We would have fought the bastard Germans for every yard,' he said. 'The Home Guard and all of us. Now look what's happening and we're supposed to give up without a protest. Say nothing.'

Beatrice Evans came up the yard and, seeing Barrington's face, touched his sleeve sympathetically. 'Compensation,' laughed the farmer grimly. 'What's bloody compensation?' He threw his hand out wearily. 'How can they give you compensation for this – for your life?'

With no further word he turned towards the house and taking a heavy bunch of keys from his pocket he noisily locked the front door. He banged the palm of his hand against it, as someone might bang the side of a departing truck. 'Right, that's it,' he said.

The three people turned and walked slowly down the yard. The patches of dung were already dry on the stones around the cowshed. Evans thought it was the first time he had seen dung left in his yard. It was getting towards the conclusion of the afternoon, the false first day of spring. The sun was going quickly, almost as if it had regretted its indiscretion, and the air was immediately damp. There was still some gold left on the fields that rose and tumbled on the small hills round about, an afterglow of a day out of season. The sky was without clouds, but the air was dimming. A single bird piped hopefully. Everywhere else, everything else, was silent. They were very aware of it.

'You can just hear the sea,' said Beatrice.

Neither man spoke. They made their way to the lane where the doctor's car stood. 'How are you going?' asked Beatrice.

'Walking,' said Barrington. 'I've left the pony and trap at the police station on the main road. I'll walk up there.'

'Come with us, Tom,' suggested Evans.

'No, I'll walk. I'm in no hurry. The way things are I don't suppose I shall ever come back to this place.

February

By the first week in February there were fifteen thousand American troops encamped in the villages and the fields left by the civilians. From the first primitive outpost which Colonel Schorner and his advance party had established at Telcoombe Magna, the camps had grown across the meadows and up the sides of the easier hills. Trees were hung with wires. Flags and laundry blew in the wind. Lanes were churned with mud, hedgerows flattened, trucks and cranes and tanks were parked in unending lines beneath the metallic winter trees of the villages.

The hamlets and small towns of Devon took most of the people who had been moved from their homes. Wilcoombe, the nearest settlement, absorbed some, others went as far as Exeter, into Somerset and down into Cornwall, the neighbour counties. Some children, who had been evacuated from London during the air raids, and had stayed and become familiar with the West Country, returned as strangers to their original homes, once more evacuated. There was work on the farms for those, and they were the majority, who had made a living in agriculture. Some fishermen went to Newlyn and the Cornish ports with their boats, others went to work in the dockyard at Plymouth. The others, the shopkeepers and small tradesmen, were absorbed into other places. They found some sort of home and job. Many never returned to their roots in Devon for by the time they were allowed to go back they had settled in the new places. They had become different people.

At Newton Abbot and Totnes, to the north, the railway yards were serried with engines and goods wagons. More came in by the hour to be inched forward and unloaded into the waiting US Army vehicles, as if a great industry were hungry for raw material. A railhead company of the American forces had brought in their own engine, a great, gleaming, steaming machine from the Kansas State Railroad, and another was being unloaded at the docks at Southampton. Soon there would be many more, destined to supply the great army once it had established itself in France.

Each day, with more men and materials joining all the time, the soldiers, who had now become the villagers of the region, learned their hard craft. Ten simulated landings in January were followed by four in the first few days of the new month. There was no time to lose or waste.

On the road between Totnes and Newton Abbot a hospital was established almost overnight, using the buildings of a former school on to which were attached long spider-legs of prefabricated huts. It had wards, operating theatres and a substantial mortuary. Doctors and nurses were ready to move in. There were no patients. They would come later, by the hundred.

Dumps of fuel, ammunition and food began to grow along the hedgerows of the quietest places, squared and stepped like small skyscrapers. By the seashore more material was unloaded from barges and boats and the engineers were laying out great areas of concrete, the 'hards' from which the tanks and heavy trucks would embark for the beaches of Europe. In the village hall at Mortown, American Red Cross women served coffee and doughnuts to the troops. They were the only American women in the region at that time and were of such formidable demeanour and proportions that they were considered, rightly, by the US authorities to be safe from molestation, even from the most frustrated and rapacious of soldiers.

These troops of the first weeks were mostly engineers and other work-soldiers set to construct the sites and camps for the infantry who were to be trained in relays along the beaches and the hilly hinterland.

The men of Schorner's advance unit quickly regarded the newcomers with the customary good-natured scorn of veterans. Their camp was now entirely hutted, the tents having been removed to a transit area for the use of incoming units. It had become surrounded by other camps and military areas, like a village swallowed into the suburbs of a growing town. The unit, however, still retained a certain raffishness, a certain confident independence, among all the personnel now occupying the region. They were the pioneers, the first men there. Ballimach said as he watched another company of staring recruits being transported along the tight English lane outside the camp, 'Jeeze, when I see these rookies I feel like Davy Crockett.'

During the first week in February Captain Scarlett visited the unit, driving the well-used route from Mrs Mahon-Feavor's manor house, now become the officers' mess and general administrative centre of the entire evacuation area. The paintings of the old lady's pusillanimous ancestors remained on the walls but all the good furniture had been removed.

At the Telcoombe Magna camp a company of troops was marching and counter-marching across the ground that had been foot-flattened between the huts. Ashes and cinders from the camp's fires and stoves had been thrown on it and stamped in by men wearing combat boots, making it into a primitive parade ground. Schorner, in his doorway, was watching a sergeant putting the men through basic drill routines when Scarlett arrived. The general's ADC saluted. Schorner said: 'We're getting these guys ready for their first battle.'

'They're going to march?' asked Scarlett. Bryant, having seen the car arrive, walked over to the hut and shook hands.

'They're going to march,' confirmed Schorner. 'You remember the old lady, Mrs Mahon-Feavor, said she wanted to put them in a parade. She wasn't kidding. Next Sunday. I guess the British are going to try and march the pants off us. Even the Boy Scouts. It seems like we have to fight everybody.'

Scarlett grinned. They walked into the orderly room. It was now enclosed and comfortable, tables, desks, maps on the walls. 'You've got bigger troubles than that, sir,' Scarlett said. 'Eisenhower's coming down here.'

Schorner grinned. 'You don't say,' he muttered.

'Well, I guessed he would pretty soon. He doesn't worry me as much as Mrs Mahon-Feavor. We've got nothing to hide. We ain't got a lot to show, either.' Bryant was hovering at the door. Schorner glanced at Scarlett who nodded. 'Come on in, lieutenant,' said the colonel good-naturedly. 'We don't want Ike to have to eat those brussel sprouts. That *could* lose us the war.'

'Montgomery is coming too,' said Scarlett as soon as Bryant had shut the door. 'In fact the whole shining circus, as far as I can see. It's on Thursday, so we'd all better be looking sharp.'

Schorner ruminated. 'If it is Thursday, at least they won't see us march with the British Boy Scouts,' he said. 'What do we have to do? I mean, especially?'

'We just get everything right, I guess, sir,' said Scarlett. 'General Georgeton says that Ike's party will only be down here for a few hours. They're busy so it will just be a flying visit. They're coming to Exeter, landing scheduled at ten in the morning, and they'll be gone again by three. We just show them around and show them what's going on. Just make sure all the guys are doing the right things.'

'Okay,' shrugged Schorner. 'As long as they don't hope to see the US Cavalry. We'll be ready for them.'

'All other units are being warned,' said Scarlett. He turned with a short smile on Bryant. 'And he especially wants to see the British troops in the area,' he said. 'Your commanding officer, what's his name . . .?'

'Westerman,' swallowed Bryant. 'Captain Westerman . . . Eisenhower wants to see *our* unit?'

'Sure, you've got it. Eisenhower and Montgomery want to inspect the outfit. Your commanding officer is being told this morning. Monty thinks he'll show Ike what real fighting troops are like, I guess.'

'Our mob?' mumbled Bryant nervously. 'God help us.'

'God help us *all*,' echoed Schorner. 'Maybe they'll tell us how they propose to get this almighty mess across the ocean to France. That's one detail nobody's explained to me yet.'

General Dwight Eisenhower, monkey-mouthed, tall, outwardly bland, and the pencil-faced Montgomery left the US Air Force Dakota on the grass runway at Exeter with a dozen staff officers of both armies, and were met by General Georgeton, Colonel Schorner, Scarlett and Bryant, and were at once taken on a tour of the evacuated region. By now every road was gated and guarded, the perimeter, over its many miles, was lined with barbed wire, and regularly patrolled.

At the road block on the seashore, along the straight stretch between the elongated beach and the inland lagoons, the leys, the party stopped. Eisenhower stood at the wire and looked up over the placid green and red hills, the shadows of Devon clouds roaming across them, to the white and widespread houses.

'I guess these folks must have felt pretty sore about leaving their homes,' he said. 'I know I would.'

It was for Georgeton to answer. 'They didn't jump for joy, sir. But they went along with it in the end because they knew the reason.'

Eisenhower's bald forehead under the forage cap nodded at the houses across the landscape, looking empty as such houses do, even at a distance. 'It can't be too funny to look over this wire and see your own house and you can't get to it and some other guy, some foreigner, can,' he said. 'And that guy, maybe, is going to destroy it. No, that's not a nice thought. Necessary, maybe, but not nice.' He glanced at the military policemen, drawn up stiff as clothes pegs behind the wire. 'I hope you men remember that. Think as if those houses were your own homes. Okay?' The snowdrops nodded stiffly and dumbly. The eyes of the negro policeman dangled under his white helmet. 'When these people go back I want them to find their homes as little disturbed as possible. And that goes for the churches and the bars and everything else. As little as possible.'

Schorner found himself closing his eyes as if in a moment's prayer. The party moved along the road, walking through the raised barrier and along the breeze-touched beach towards the school and the Telcoombe Beach Hotel. After they had gone the sergeant in charge of the military police stood the squad at ease. He marched off towards the police post to telephone the next gate with the news that Eisenhower was on his way. The negro policeman took off his helmet as soon as the sergeant was gone. 'Treat it like *my* house. Jesus, that man just ought to *see* my fuckin' house.'

Montgomery, walking hands behind back, with Eisenhower, sniffed the wind, his pointed nose a touch red at its tip. 'The British are pretty adaptable,' he said, his voice high-pitched even in conversation. 'The inhabitants of these parts will soon get used to things. They're Devonians, you know. It was Devonians who were first called Limeys.'

Eisenhower was becoming accustomed to the English general's little lectures. He was not sure he liked them very much. He smiled indulgently, watching a group of British sailors and American soldiers clumsily unloading a landing craft at the shingle-edge. 'Is that so?' he answered. 'The first Limeys.'

'Devon seamen,' continued Montgomery. 'They used to eat limes in tropical parts because it kept the scurvy away. Foreigners laughed at them and called them Limeys because of it. But they had the last laugh. It was the others who got the scurvy.'

The American general was watching the sea. 'It seems a hell of a long way across there,' he commented. 'Even on a peaceful day like now.'

'Far enough,' agreed Montgomery pensively. He looked at the American. 'Everything has to be right,' he said solidly. 'Weather, machines, men. Everything. The Germans would never have made it, you know.'

'You think that's why they didn't try?' said Eisenhower. 'They knew the score?'

'Oh, Hitler knew well enough. Ample men, plenty of weapons, they were winning everything. My God, if they'd played us at *cricket* just then, I think they would have won. But they couldn't *get* to us. That strip of water was, not for the first time, our salvation. They got together a mad sort of armada, coal barges, tugs, motor boats, paddle steamers.' He snorted: 'Ha! It would have been like Dunkirk in reverse. They even had a sort of concrete submarine, for God's sake. Even if they'd managed to get ashore, which is doubtful, the Royal Navy would have simply cut them off. In the end they realized the thing was a nonstarter.'

'They thought Russia was a better bet,' said Eisenhower.

'It was easier. They didn't have to cross the water. Just rivers. Military men know all about rivers. They don't know how to cross the sea. Never have done.'

'We've got to learn everything new,' cautioned Eisenhower. 'It's okay having the landing craft, if we get enough of them, that is, but getting them ashore in the right places at the right time on the right side, in the right weather conditions. That's going to be the crunch. This length of beach, and the ocean here, are going to be pretty important to us. If we don't get it right here, we're never going to get it right on the other side when the real party begins.' He asked for a map and Scarlett handed one to him. Curiously, instead of looking at it immediately he covered the sea with his field glasses. Montgomery pointed out the headlands at either flank of the horizon, his hand and finger stretching out dramatically. Once more Bryant, standing at the rear of the group, had a mental picture of 'The Boyhood of Raleigh'.

'Start Bay,' muttered Eisenhower eventually, looking down at the map. 'Well, it couldn't have a better name than that.'

A British Army look-out, Private Walt Walters, posted at the apex of the steep street of Wilcoombe and equipped with a lady's bicycle (all that was available and serviceable on the gun-site at that time), spotted the white helmets of the American escort when they were still more than a mile distant. Mounting his machine he clattered down the hill, curling along the quayside at its foot, and eventually arriving with some spectacle into the small camp.

Sergeant Bullivant was waiting. 'They're coming, sarge,' reported Walters, pulling the bicycle from between his legs. 'They'll be here in two wobbles of a duck's arse.'

Bullivant mistook his excitement for panic. 'Calm!' he bellowed with the entire force of his fat voice. 'Keep calm, lad.'

Walters blinked and picked up his bicycle. 'I am calm as calm, sarge,' he complained. A grin began. 'But I reckon you'd better get moving.'

The bulky Bullivant moved. He charged across the small parade ground, picking up his rattling stick as he did so and running it along the corrugated exteriors of the nissen huts. 'Out!' he howled. 'Everybody out! Come on, moooooooove!' His thick khaki thighs now thrust like pistons as he sprinted towards the orderly room. Captain Westerman was already looking from his window with doleful apprehension. Bullivant made signs through the glass. Westerman reacted as he might have reacted had a strong enemy force been sighted, rushing around the orderly room trying to locate his cap, which, having been found, he rammed upon his head like some sort of protective lid. He leaped from the office steps as the soldiers of the sparse unit were forming up on the miniature barrack square. God, he thought again, why weren't there more of them?

Sergeant Bullivant was already bellowing orders, confusing the troops and attracting curious civilian bystanders to the perimeter wire of the small camp. Westerman felt himself break into springs of sweat beneath his battledress. He marched to Bullivant as correctly as he could contrive and whispered, 'Calm, sergeant. Very calm.'

Bullivant looked surprised and annoyed and for a moment Westerman had an unpleasant feeling he was going to make a disparaging reply. He swallowed it, however, with a tight sucking-in of his reddened cheeks. 'Yes, sir,' he said instead. 'Very calm, sir.'

Within himself he thought: 'I hope the bloody gun works, mate, for your sake.' They had been having trouble elevating the gun due to a faulty valve.

Westerman looked distraughtly at Bullivant. 'I hope to God the gun works, sergeant. Just this once.'

'So do I, sir,' replied Bullivant woodenly.

Westerman threw a look at him. 'Oh, come on,' he pleaded. 'Don't let's fall out now. Not you and I. Not with Monty and this blessed Yank coming.' He thought about it, then thrust out his hand. 'Still friends?' he said. Bullivant, surprised, shook it. 'All right, sir. You'll get all the usual co-operation from me, sir.'

The exchange was missed by the troops and the spectators, who, without exception, were now looking expectantly towards the foot of the hill. The growl of the motorcycles became loud, their note changing as they made the steep descent. 'Ready, sergeant?' whispered Westerman, almost pleading. 'Are we ready?'

'Ready as we'll ever be,' answered Bullivant from the edge of his mouth.

'Who be coming?' shouted a woman called Fat Meg from the growing group of spectators at the gate. 'Be it the King?'

'Christ,' muttered Westerman, realizing, not for the

first time, the implications of having a military boundary with a parade ground on one side and a public street on the other. 'I hope *they're* not going to start.' He turned to Bullivant. 'Ask that mob to keep quiet will you, sergeant.' He added: 'I'll watch the men,' as if he thought his troops might at any moment turn and run.

Bullivant saluted, sulkily again. He sighed as he marched towards the gate. 'Now, everybody, move on, if you please,' he said to the crowd which now numbered about thirty. Children were being pushed to the fore so that they could better observe whatever there was to observe. The West Country faces contemplated the sergeant solidly. 'Move on, if you please,' he repeated. 'It's nothing to get excited about. It's not the King, I promise you. It's definitely not the King.'

'I bain't movin',' said the formidable Meg. She was uncouth and grey as an old woman, which she was not, hairs growing from her heavy face. Her cherry red coat was fastened at her throat with a huge safety pin, as a cloak might be. 'I bain't movin' until I seed what I come to see,' she added emphatically.

There was a general grumble of approval from the crowd. 'I'm telling you to move on,' repeated Bullivant, his voice edged with desperation.

'You an' whose army?' demanded the gross woman in the red coat. The simple aptness of the remark brought a collective chortle from the crowd. More people arrived, demanding to know what was going to happen. Bullivant felt like a beleaguered commissionaire. He sensed more than saw Westerman's approach. Breathing patience, the officer, cane fixed like a seat across his backside, strode to the fence. 'They won't move, sir,' muttered the sergeant miserably. He heard the officer's exhaled frustration.

'Now listen you people,' Westerman said patiently. 'We'd really be terribly grateful if you cleared off. This is purely a military matter.'

There was a mildly impressed silence and for a moment Westerman believed he had triumphed. But the motorcycles were sounding as they came down the village hill, their note again changing. 'I be stayin' for one,' announced Meg. 'They throw'd me out of my 'ouse last week, the so-called bloody military. I reckon I got a right to see what be going on.'

'Quite right you 'ave,' bawled a man. 'You got the right, Meg!'

Westerman latched with desperate archness on to the name. 'Meg,' he pleaded. 'Be a good girl and move on.'

She fixed his weak blue eyes with her full hairy stare. 'No,' she said simply. 'I be staying 'ere.' She thought of something funny. 'My feet be 'urting.'

The small crowd collapsed with laughter at this sally. Suddenly, at the turn of the hill, appeared the first formation of four military police, helmets like light bulbs, their legs gripping their muscular motorcycles. With a last, lost look at the assembly, transferred at once as exasperation to Bullivant, Westerman jerked his head and hurried back to the anxious ranks of his soldiers. Bullivant bundled after him. The sentry at the gate was called to attention by the corporal of the guard and another sentry opened the barrier. At once the crowd began to cheer. In the arriving staff car they had recognized Montgomery, and quickly afterwards Eisenhower. Enormous excitement flew through the small group, anticipation mixed with the avid curiosity of remote people who had never seen anyone famous. But the emotions did not include reverence. As the cars paused by the gate the Wilcoombe folk rushed forward. The military police, encumbered by the motorcycles, could do nothing. The British sentry was pushed back against his own box with one forceful hand by the red-coated woman. Devon faces, the faces of a thousand years, were pressed against the car windows at both sides and several at the windscreen.

Earthy hands were waved and disarranged rural teeth grimaced with friendship. From within the car their voices sounded muted but unquestionably demanding. Eisenhower waved feebly back.

Meg, who was now enjoying the status of undisputed mob leader, forced her jellyfish mouth against the window of the car: ''Ow be'ee, Monty?' came her blunted bellow. ''Ow be'ee, boy?'

The inquiry evoked a stiff, unhappy nod from Montgomery, and encouraged a chorus of similar greetings from the people crowding the car. Eisenhower looked perplexed. 'They seem friendly folks,' he observed. 'Maybe we had better just turn the window down.'

'On no account,' replied Montgomery savagely. 'The blighters will be in the car in no time.' He turned to the front. 'Hurry along, driver.'

They were relieved when the vehicle moved forward obediently, pushing aside the faces. Even as it moved Meg tried to keep her mouth against the window, further inquiring as to what Montgomery was doing there. Her lips slid across the glass making a trail like a snail.

The car moved on to the small parade ground and the gate guards, with no little difficulty, closed the barrier on the crowd which re-formed behind the perimeter wire, like prisoners in a barbed compound. They now fell to silence, however, watching the proceedings with hushed fascination. Their eyes and expressions followed every salute and introduction taking place on the camp area. They might even have detected Captain Westerman's trembling as he presented his unit to the polite inspection of the Supreme Commander Europe and the less charitable scrutiny of General Montgomery.

Bryant hovered nervously, making ready to interpolate should he be needed in his function as liaison officer. Westerman looked in more need of liaison than anyone. Eisenhower and Montgomery strolled, the latter sniffing at the place.

'Very small unit, of course,' mentioned Montgomery. 'Almost minuscule.'

'Sure,' agreed Eisenhower amiably. 'We have small units too. No good overmanning anything.'

'Established to pick off any overflying German aircraft from Plymouth. But it's all been a trifle quiet for a while.'

'I liked the flowers at the gate,' said Eisenhower with a quarter of an inch of grin at the right edge of his wide mouth.

'Daffodils,' answered Montgomery not noticing. 'They grow very early down here. Very mild, you know. I think we'd better take a look at the gun. The chaps will be disappointed if we don't.'

'Let's not disappoint them,' answered Eisenhower. They walked towards the recumbent gun and Westerman, fluttering like a nervous wine waiter, approached to discover their wishes.

'The gun, sir?' he said. Oh Jesus Christ, the *gun*. They *would* want to look at the gun. 'Yes, of course, the gun.' The generals wandered ahead like a pair of university dons, hands behind backs in nodding conversation. Captain Westerman caught Bryant's eye. Bryant moved to him. 'I'm not sure the gun's working,' Westerman whispered. 'Valve trouble. It would be awful if we couldn't get it up.'

Bryant swallowed nervously. 'Yes, it would,' he muttered unhappily. 'But when Montgomery wants to see a gun, he wants to see it.'

Westerman closed his eyes as if dispatching a quick prayer. He turned on Bullivant. 'Sergeant,' he said with quivering sternness, 'gun crew to action stations.'

Bullivant nodded wildly. 'It may not ackle, sir,' he whispered.

'It's got to bloody-well ackle,' returned Westerman nastily. 'Get them fallen in.'

Bullivant shrugged, then tightening his fat body like an inflated bladder, he bawled the order: 'Gun crew – to action stations!'

The crew broke ranks and ran towards the gun. This apparently impressed the watchers outside the fence, their numbers now further grown, for there was a rumble of approval and even a slight movement of applause. The visiting generals stood back, benignly observing the drill. The crew took up their positions at the gun. Bullivant, like an actor who knows that the scenery is about to crash down, bellowed the orders.

'Direction – south-west. Range – two thousand feet. Elevation – forty-two degrees.'

The gun swung and the elevation platform wound. Nothing happened. A gunner turned the wheel frantically, like a mad woman at a mangle. Westerman felt as though his mouth was full of sand. The wheel revolved for what seemed like hours. There was no noticeable difference in the elevation of the gun barrel. From the spectators outside the fence there was a restless movement. Then red-mouthed Meg shouted jovially: 'It don't work!' The response was a huge cloud of laughter from the watchers. The gun crew and their officers were red-faced, stiff and sweating. Eisenhower looked abashed. Montgomery's expression became even more like a wedge. Westerman was wondering whether to faint as a diversion when, a gift from God, the barrel began to react. It eased up into the sky to the smiling relief of the soldiers and bright cheers from the watchers. Now the civilians, impressed or contrite, lapsed to quietness again. Bullivant shouted the orders, the gun swerved and reared. 'Load!' bellowed the sergeant. 'Check range. Two thousand. Elevation forty-two. Ready, fire!'

Everyone involuntarily winced for the expected explosion. The crowd at the gate ducked low, fingers in ears. But the only result of the order was a collective shout from all the soldiers on the parade area, and those on the gun itself. 'Bang!' they exclaimed with loud embarrassment.

This anti-climax provoked, at first, a mute astonishment. Then the civilians, led raucously by Meg, collapsed into huge and undignified merriment. They

232

hung on to the wire, almost falling on top of each other in their mirth. 'Bang!' somebody shouted and they all doubled over again with laughter and scorn. Meg's great cheeks were riven with tears.

Montgomery coughed. He looked sideways at Eisenhower who was trying not to laugh. 'Training school,' muttered Montgomery. 'Didn't realize they did it at unit level.' He turned to Bryant. 'Don't you indent for blanks in this unit?' he inquired.

Westerman, a few yards away, eyed Bryant like a frightened horse. Bryant said: 'No, sir, we don't. It's because of the proximity of people's houses, sir. The blanks sound as loud as the real thing.'

The generals turned slowly to leave. As they entered the car after a round of salutes and farewells, Montgomery turned to Westerman and said with a straight expression: 'Jolly well shouted, captain.'

Ballimach sat beside Albie Primrose in a jeep hurrying north out of Wilcoombe; in the rear seat was Pfc Benny Wall, the sentry from Cincinnati. Each different face was crammed with anxiety. Despite the cool day, the fat Ballimach sweated all down the ravines of his cheeks and neck. Primrose's nose was bloodless. The narrow-featured Wall, always nervous, looked like a cornered man.

'For Chrissake, get a move on,' pleaded Ballimach. His great hands cleft the air. 'Hell, how am I expected to get the fucking phone fixed before the big noises get there?'

'I don't know, don't ask me,' answered Albie squeakily. He turned the car violently around the final turn at the summit of Wilcoombe Hall and headed towards the road to Totnes. 'Even Eisenhower can't have miracles. He's got to wait. Maybe even God has to wait sometimes.'

'This is Eisenhower, not just God,' put in Wall pessimistically. 'That's the difference. If it was God, maybe it would be okay.'

Ballimach groaned. 'They can't expect to have a phone where there ain't a phone. Just like some magic. Even me, I'm only human. I ain't Walt Disney. Why didn't they tell us yesterday.'

'They didn't *know* yesterday,' pointed out Albie grimly. He swerved the car into a farm gate. 'Okay, guys, this is it,' he said. 'Get going. I'll tell the man.'

The farm was outside the evacuation perimeter. Ballimach and Wall jumped from the jeep, the fat man paying out a cable from a drum, Wall looking up at the lines attached to a telegraph post at the side of the road. Ballimach followed his skyward glance. 'I ain't going,' he warned. 'I just ain't going. So get that.'

'Me, I'm nervous of heights,' complained Wall.

'You, you're nervous of every fucking thing,' answered Ballimach bluntly. 'But we got you here to climb, so climb, sonny. I ain't falling on my ass and my head any more. How would it look if Ike came by and there was me lying all smashed up again? Get up that goddamned pole, okay?'

Tenuously Wall began to scale the pole using the metal grips at each side. Albie came back. The farmer and his wife, smiling simply, stood at the door of the house, he under a great hat, she behind a clean apron, hurriedly donned at the news of the approaching generals. The man called: 'When you be done, boys, leave it there. Never 'ad a telling-phone in this house. Always thought 'ee might be useful.'

'What's that fucking yokel shouting his mouth about?' asked Ballimach rudely. 'I wish these guys would speak some kind of English.'

Albie did not bother to answer. He checked his watch anxiously. 'You've got another three minutes,' he warned. 'Then we got to make the next place in two minutes. I just don't think we're gonna do it. Not even for Ike. It's supposed to be *forward* planning. And now they think about the phones. Now!'

The sweat was flowing on Ballimach. So much that he could scarcely hold the wires he was twisting into their connections. Wall hung like a monkey on a pole. 'Christ,' he called down as though addressing Jesus. 'They're coming. I can see them on the hill.'

Ballimach bulkily mounted the pole after Wall. Between them they got the wires connected before tumbling down like a pair of circus clowns, Albie jumping up and down with frustration below. The old farming couple began to laugh and applaud as if the performance were especially for them. Albie cursed them again.

'These hicks sure would love to see some blood,' he said loudly as they gathered wires and tools together and hurled them into the back of the jeep.

The earthy rural couple redoubled their clapping. Ballimach shouted, 'Balls!' at them and they roared the jeep out of the farm entrance and into the road.

'The next one is a mile down this highway,' shouted Albie as the jeep hurtled along the empty road. 'And we got five minutes to get it fixed. That's if Ike don't use the one we just put in at the farm.'

'I don't like this army,' grumbled Ballimach. 'Rush, rush, rush.'

'Me neither,' echoed Wall. 'This climbing I don't like.'

Albie grimaced across the jeep's wheel. 'Maybe one day you'll have to fix the telephones under goddamned fire,' he said. 'Panzers all around your ass.'

He swung the jeep dramatically round another bend. There was a straight section beyond, with a high wall on one side and a row of terraced farm cottages on the other. Against the dull, stony colours, a red public telephone box stood like a sentry. It was the border of the cleared area and the cottages had been emptied of people. Barbed wire was fixed across them. As they swiftly rounded the bend a full-grown pig ambled from the verge of the road and, apparently pleased to see them, loped grunting towards the oncoming jeep.

The soldiers howled three separate warnings, but the pig heeded none. It came on. It was impossible for Albie to stop the jeep. The brakes squealed and then the pig did also. It was a shattering crash, with the portly animal bouncing off the front fender and the vehicle slicing across the road, hitting the kerb and ending up slewed across the pavement in front of the vacant houses.

'Christ,' muttered Ballimach looking back at the prostrated animal. 'Look what you done, Albie. You killed the pig.'

'Me! *I* killed it!' bawled the small soldier. 'That fucking pig nearly killed us.' He looked at it. It was humped in the middle of the road, a pile of pink skin.

Its face was towards them displaying a final oafish grin.

'Lousy, stupid pig!' Albie called at it.

'Right, stupid pig!' echoed Ballimach. 'Stupid, Limey pig!'

'Eisenhower will be along in a minute,' mentioned Wall more practically.

The big face of Ballimach and the small face of Albie confronted each other. 'God,' incanted the fat man. 'God, God, God . . .'

The trio moved towards the pig, cautiously at first as though they feared a booby-trap, then abruptly at the run. The great pale body was twitching.

'Maybe it ain't dead,' said Wall hopefully. 'Just kidding.'

Albie Primrose knew death when he saw it, even in a pig. Despite his urgency he had a passing thought that it bore a likeness to Ballimach. 'We got to do something,' he squeaked in the high voice that happened to him in excitement. He tried to bring it down an octave. 'We got to move it.'

'Ike ain't going to like this pig,' forecast Wall dully.

'Get going then for Chrissake!' bellowed Ballimach. He leaned down and pulled at the pig's front trotter. He could hardly move it. 'Come on, get to it!' he shouted at the others. 'We got two minutes.'

'W . . . where?' stammered Albie. '*Think*, you guys, where? It's no use pulling the thing until we know *where*.'

'The houses,' suggested Wall. 'Put it in a house.'

They looked along the terrace. It was no use, they could see that. A dozen strands of barbed wire were strung rigidly across the front of the vacant dwellings.

237

Desperately they looked along the straight street. There were no fields, no trees near enough for concealment.

'Over the wall?' suggested Ballimach. 'Or how about *in* the jeep. We could hide it in the jeep.'

'And say Ike inspects the jeep? How we going to explain the pig?' demanded Albie. 'Let's try the wall. Maybe we can lift him over.'

Hopelessly they dragged the large, dead-weight animal towards the side of the road, Wall and Primrose pulling the front trotters and Ballimach the snout and ears. It moved, slid, across the road. They eased it on to the narrow pavement, beneath the six foot wall. 'Okay,' said Ballimach. 'Let's go. Lift.'

They tried manfully, but although they heaved the heavy animal up to their waists, then almost to their chests, they could not get it further. Sweating and swearing, speared by its prickly hair, they lowered it to the ground.

Ballimach was trembling like a jelly. '*One minute*,' he moaned. 'We only got one minute.'

Albie Primrose looked along the deserted street. 'The phone booth,' he breathed suddenly, joyfully. 'Numbskulls, we are. Put the goddamn thing in the phone booth.'

It was on the other side of the street, at the end of the terrace, but outside the barbed wire. With a final, breathless effort, they dragged the pig across the highway again and, panting, pulled it to the red phone box.

Wall opened the door and between them they heaved the dead pig on to its hind legs and pushed it heavily into the confined, vertical space. Even in their

238

hurry they could not but stand back for a moment to admire their work. The pig, now propped by the glass-panelled wall, was standing almost upright, its snout appearing to rest on the telephone, the flank of its head against the side panes of the box.

Wall roused them. 'I hear them coming,' he warned sharply.

The sound of the motorcycle escort accompanying the generals echoed over the deserted hills and houses. The three ran back towards the jeep, Albie started it and manoeuvred it alongside the terrace. 'Maybe in front of the phone booth,' suggested Ballimach. 'We could hide the pig.'

'Nothing doing,' snapped Albie. 'There ain't time. Anyway, we got nothing to do with that pig in the booth. We don't even know his name. Okay?'

They nodded agreement and stood in an uneven line, the large Ballimach in the middle in front of the jeep. 'Maybe the man will just go by,' said Wall hopefully. 'He's got nothing to stop for here.'

'We ain't put in the other phone,' moaned Ballimach, suddenly remembering.

'Too bad. Too late,' muttered Albie Primrose.

Around the bend curved the white-helmeted out-riders with the staff cars of Eisenhower's party following. The three GIs froze as the escort slowed and the white-starred vehicles pulled up on the opposite side of the road. Private Primrose cautiously swivelled his eyes to the right. God, he could see the pig's head in the phone box thirty-five yards away. Officers seemed to be pouring out of the army vehicles. The three soldiers came to ragged and nervous attention. Eisenhower and then Montgomery emerged from the second car in the convoy. Ballimach thought he was going to faint.

To their minor relief the main knot of senior officers appeared to be interested in the houses and their wire corset. It was Colonel Schorner who approached them, winking easily as he did so. 'Everything okay, men?' he said.

'Pretty good, sir,' replied Albie, swallowing so violently that it hurt. The commanding officer stared at his Adam's apple.

'We didn't get the second field telephone in, sir,' blurted Ballimach. 'We had trouble, sir, and we didn't get time.'

'That's no problem,' acknowledged Schorner. 'General Eisenhower used the first one. At the farm. That was fine, boys, you did a good job, so don't worry. The second was only a precaution.'

He looked sideways and saw Captain Scarlett and Lieutenant Bryant approaching. The American liaison officer said to Schorner: 'I think maybe General Montgomery wants to make a call on the telephone. Is there another field phone rigged, colonel?'

'Er, no,' replied Schorner glancing at his men. 'There wasn't time.'

Bryant said brightly. 'That's all right. Perhaps we could get through on the normal public phone. There's a phone box here. I'll see to it.'

The three GIs paled together. Ballimach was so distressed he believed he might urinate right there in the road. They watched as Bryant marched briskly to Montgomery, saluted and indicated the phone. Albie tried to say some last minute thing to his colonel but no words came out. Wall tightly shut his eyes.

Schorner glanced towards the telephone box. The pig's head stood up quite clearly. 'Oh God,' he muttered. He moved swiftly, marching ahead of Bryant. 'That booth is out of service, lieutenant,' he said. The briskness of tone made Bryant look at him in surprise. He was about to say something when he looked up and saw the pig's profile also. His expression dried. Montgomery was five paces behind. Bryant turned quickly. 'The phone is out of order, sir,' he said. 'I'm sorry.'

'Don't worry, lieutenant,' said Montgomery. 'It will wait a few minutes.' He turned and walked back towards Eisenhower. To the overwhelming relief of the trio of GIs the whole party moved back to their cars, climbed in and set off along the road. For half a minute after they had gone Primrose, Ballimach and Wall remained at stiff attention. Then, all as one, they collapsed sobbing with relief over the bonnet of the jeep. Soon they were hooting and rolling with laughter, great uncontrolled bellows of mirth. 'Christ, what a great guy Schorner is!' said Albie. 'And that cool British guy. Wow!'

Two miles away the official convoy roared along the empty Devon roads. In their car Eisenhower and Montgomery sat, looking at the landscape: 'Strange, strange country this,' murmured Eisenhower. 'Can't say I ever did see a pig in a phone booth before.'

Montgomery yawned. 'Nor me,' he said.

*

Devon church bells rang on Sunday, their airy tunes floating over the already springlike fields from the village churches to the north and to the west of Wilcoombe. Only in the east were they left untolled, sitting dumbly in the towers and belfries of the left countryside.

'They're still quite a novelty, the bells,' said Dorothy Jenkins, the schoolteacher. 'For a long time no bells were allowed, you know. They were going to be rung only if German parachutists were dropping. It always seemed to be a stupid idea to me. Somebody in London must have thought that one up. Surely they could have found some other way. People like to hear the bells.'

Schorner said, with his soldier's logic: 'I guess churches are not connected to the telephone.'

She glanced at him. They were walking down the hill towards the sea where the parade was assembling near the harbour and the gun-site. 'I've never seen a telephone in church,' she admitted.

Schorner looked better than when she had first seen him. Now the tension was gone from his lined face, the awkwardness she had sensed when he had visited the Telcoombe Beach School. He was a countryman who fitted into a countryside. 'Would the parachutists have been able to come down in the dark?' she asked.

The American shrugged. 'Now, it's okay,' he said. 'Our boys make night drops in training. But then, nineteen-forty, I don't know. A few maybe, but putting a whole outfit down at night without radar or the navigation that's available now, well that would be difficult, I'd say.'

'So they would have had to be dropped in daylight

– so that everybody would be able to see them. There would be no need to ring the bells.'

He smiled again. 'It sounds like you might be useful in the war cabinet,' he said. 'Does Mr Churchill know?'

'When you've been an infant schoolteacher,' she replied, 'nothing seems too difficult. But Churchill wouldn't have liked it. He's not a woman's man.' They stopped near the inn. 'I have to go and help with the Oxo and stuff for the children,' she told him. 'I hope the march goes well.'

'So do I,' he replied seriously. 'Our guys don't go overboard for marching. Even the Boy Scouts are going to show us up. And they're out to do it, take it from me. Not to mention the Home Guard and the Air Raid guys, and the Old Uncle Tom . . . what is it?'

'Cobbleigh,' she laughed. 'Old Uncle Tom Cobbleigh and all. Don't worry, it will be all right.' She opened her handbag and took out a folded sheet of paper. 'The children sent you a poem,' she said a little bashfully. 'It's one they learned. Quite a difficult one and I'm not sure they really understand it. Mary Steer wrote it out because she writes without too many blots.'

The American took the folded paper. '"Waiting",' he read. 'That's an appropriate title.'

'Don't read it now,' she said. 'Keep it for later. I must go. Don't let the parade get you down.' Her smile was suddenly warm.

Schorner folded the paper and put it in his tunic pocket. He looked at her with good-humoured slyness. 'We've got a secret weapon,' he whispered. 'A band. A US Army band. All coloured men. You

243

should hear those fellows play. They only just got off the boat. But I'm hoping they're going to get here from Exeter in time.'

'The Wilcoombe band won't like that,' she forecast, still smiling. 'Two bands, playing different things, are going to tangle things up terribly.'

Schorner grinned again. 'That's too bad,' he replied softly. 'You Limeys can't have everything your own way.'

He sauntered down the street. Watching him go she realized again how he fitted into the landscape. Halfway down the slope to the harbour a jeep stopped at the side of the road and a message was handed to him. He read it, returned the salute of the driver, and walked on. Then, he turned, looked back and waved. She felt embarrassed. Her wave was brief.

The village band, a collection of elderly men and young boys, with two large landgirls swinging brass handbells, were cavorting slowly on the cobbled quay, blowing and sucking at their instruments, with disjointed sounds and shuffling feet, like some unpractised saraband. They had no uniforms – although the bell-ringers from the Women's Land Army wore their green jerseys – but most wore a blue cap decently donated by the local Salvation Army who had disbanded because of the war. As Schorner gained the foot of the hill he saw that the rest of the parade was already roughly forming along the road between the gun-site and the row of harbour houses.

Howard Evans and Beatrice were standing at the gate to their cottage, watching Boy Scouts, Girl Guides and Brownies, Civil Defence wardens, Home Guards and the stalwart ladies of the Women's

Voluntary Service mill about attempting to get into some order. Schorner saw that the platoon of US troops had not yet arrived. He greeted the doctor and his wife.

'You're not marching?' asked the American.

'Somebody has to be a spectator,' laughed Beatrice. 'Everybody else is actually *in* something and they're determined to take part.'

Evans said: 'I suppose we could have carried a token stretcher between us, something like that. With a small Red Cross flag. But I think it's just as well that we watch. There's one or two in this extravaganza who are, quite possibly, not going to get to the top of the hill. There's an old man in the band who had a nasty bout of flu last week. If I'd had to bet on him taking part in a procession today, I would have wagered on it being his funeral.' He added with hardly a pause: 'Here comes the Führer.'

Mrs Mahon-Feavor, almost bursting out of the hairy green uniform of the WVS with flesh and enthusiasm, stumped purposefully towards them. ''Morning colonel.'

Schorner came politely to attention and returned the courtesy. 'Good morning, ma'am,' he said.

'Your chaps nearly ready?' she inquired briskly. 'Not a sign of them yet. I see the might of the British army has shifted itself sufficiently to get from its beds.' She glared scornfully across at the anti-aircraft compound where Captain Westerman and Sergeant Bullivant were marshalling their small contingent on the miniature square.

'The US outfit will be here on time,' smiled

Schorner. 'I guess they're just brushing up on their marching.'

'I hope so, from what I've seen,' the old lady rejoined brusquely. 'Have you destroyed my house yet, by the way?'

'It's in fine shape, ma'am,' said Schorner placidly. 'We've just taken out all the electric wiring and replaced it.'

'Good God, why? That wiring's been there years.'

'Yes, ma'am.' He thought it was time to change the subject. 'How long is the march going to be?' he inquired. 'In duration, I mean.'

'I suppose you're worried your chaps won't last out,' she replied loudly.

'I was thinking of the children,' said Schorner. 'The Girl Scouts and those little soldiers and sailors over there.' He nodded along the quay. Mrs Mahon-Feavor frowned and turned. 'Oh, our gallant Army and Naval Cadets,' she said. 'They'll manage, colonel. Three miles. I think.'

'Oh, sure, three miles.'

'Up and down the hill. Six times,' she added emphatically.

Schorner swallowed his astonishment. 'Up and down . . . the hill?'

A dark triumph expanded across the old lady's face. 'Exactly,' she said. 'There's nowhere else to parade is there, colonel? In times past we've marched down the hill, along the coast road to Telcoombe Beach and then to Telcoombe Magna to the church. Unfortunately this is not now possible since you have them barbed-wired, mined and God-knows-what else. There's little point in marching north from Wilcoombe because

246

there are only open fields for about five miles, and this sort of pageantry is rather wasted on cows, don't you think?'

Howard Evans put his hands casually across his mouth, and Beatrice excused herself hurriedly and went into the house. 'You're right, Mrs Mahon-Feavor,' said Schorner carefully. 'You're certainly right. I was just thinking about the old guys in the band and the little soldiers . . . the Cadets.'

Behind the old lady he saw Barrington, in the uniform of a Home Guard officer, approaching. He sighed inwardly. Mrs Mahon-Feavor caught the glance and turned. 'Captain Barrington,' she said, 'Colonel Schorner is worried that marching up and down the hill will be too much for everybody.'

Bluntly Barrington saluted Schorner. The American returned the acknowledgement. 'Our chaps will be fine,' said Barrington, as stiff as his salute. 'I hope you Americans will be.'

'I think they'll be going to try their damnedest,' said Schorner. He was feeling weary of the slow battle by now. 'They're just now marking the toes of their boots.' He smiled at the English puzzlement. 'You know, a letter R on the right and a L on the left. So they don't get mixed up.'

Barrington stepped back a military pace and appeared to be about to make a reply. He thought the better of it and threw up another wooden arm, this time in the direction of Mrs Mahon-Feavor. 'I think we are ready to assemble, madam,' he said. Without glancing at Schorner he added: 'Our side.'

'We'll be off then,' said the lady in Schorner's direction. 'We move away in ten minutes sharp. If your chaps have turned up by then stick them on the end, will you please? After the Brownies.'

Further salutes were flung up and the pair strode back towards the motley, Barrington's backbone so erect it seemed it might fracture, Mrs Mahon-Feavor's rump swinging under the uniform skirt like the back of an overburdened mule. Schorner turned to Evans, grinning sympathetically as he leaned on his fence.

'And I thought we had come to fight the god-damned Germans,' said Schorner.

'They'll change,' forecast Evans. 'They were like that when we arrived and we were only Welsh. In the end they'll come to know the Americans for what they are.'

'Right,' said Schorner turning away. 'Their salvation.'

Waiting to bless the parade, the Reverend Eric Sissons stood in the February breeze, his vestments blowing mildly around and about him like limp white wings. His father, his medals from the First War burnished on his chest, stood stiffly at the side of the road while Cecily, the vicar's wife, slightly and secretly supported herself with a wind-bent tree.

Colonel Schorner stood by Sissons, watching the parade form into its assembly order, the children more composed than the adults. He could hear Mrs Mahon-Feavor shouting at the far end of the quay. The Wilcoombe band were tuning gastrically.

'It's a pity they can't play "The Grand Old Duke of York",' mentioned Sissons, squeezing up his eyes against the sunny wind.

248

'I'm not familiar with that,' said Schorner.

'The band's not actually *familiar* with anything, I'm afraid,' continued Sissons grimly. 'They have a sort of nodding acquaintance with the National Anthem and they play a mangled version of "Blaze Away". They're very tedious I'm afraid.' He looked at Schorner as though he had just heard his previous remark. 'Don't you know it over your side?' he asked. To Schorner's surprise he began to chant. The tone was hollow, ecclesiastical.

> 'The Grand Old Duke of York,
> He had ten thousand men.
> He marched them up to the top of the hill
> And he marched them down again.'

The American officer smiled widely. 'Right, I get it,' he said. 'It certainly does seem a pity we can't hear that. Maybe our band will know it.'

Sissons reacted sharply: 'You have a band, colonel? In this parade?'

Schorner glanced at his watch. 'It's nothing. It's only a little, quiet, US Army band. They just got ashore from a troopship, but I received a message that they had arrived at their post and they'd be right along here. It should add a little . . . well . . . colour, I guess.'

The clergyman appeared visibly brightened by the news. 'Oh, that's good,' he said, but keeping his voice low. 'It will be a change from these miserable puffers and blowers. They've never been able to learn the simplest Christmas carols to play in church. Half of "Away in a Manger" and they run out of technique.'

249

His smile dropped. 'Does Mrs Mahon-Feavor know? About your American band?'

'Not exactly,' admitted Schorner easily. 'I thought it would only complicate matters.'

Sissons frowned so deeply his nose seemed to close over his upper lip. 'If any woman could be described as manic, then it's Mrs Mahon-Feavor,' he confided. 'Hitler in knickers.'

'A tough cookie,' agreed Schorner, stemming his laugh. 'This routine of marching up and down the hill seems pretty oddball to me. Okay, so the coastal road is closed and the villages off limits, and there's nothing but fields to the north, but the road goes west as well. What about the places I've seen on the map? Brinhope and, what is it, Tolling Cove?'

'No good,' Sissons told him firmly. 'Not at all. The inhabitants here in Wilcoombe have had nothing to do with the Brinhope people since before the First World War. Some matter of stolen pigs I think. Things like that tend to rankle in this part of the world. Perhaps it's because, up to now, nothing else has ever happened. If we sent the parade through Brinhope, even if they would agree to go, which they wouldn't, the Brinhope people would turn out and probably pelt us with slops. There was a cricket match once that ended in bloodshed.'

Schorner listened attentively, but he was watching for the arrival of his platoon of troops. The parade was now almost formed and the contingent from the anti-aircraft site were marching bootily from their compound to the front of the procession immediately behind the Wilcoombe band. 'I still have a lot to learn about folks in these parts,' he said eventually.

'Nobody knows them,' said Sissons decisively. 'I doubt if they know themselves.' He heard a small commotion behind him and turned. 'I must go, colonel,' he said without excitement. 'My wife appears to have fallen over.' Schorner followed his look and saw that Cecily Sissons had slid down the trunk of the bent tree. She was sitting bandily on the cobbles holding on to the foot of the tree like a mahout clasping a favourite elephant's leg.

'Oh gee,' said Schorner, 'let me help you.'

The two men, in their respective uniforms, helped the gaping, gasping woman to her feet. She helped them by going hand-over-hand up the curved trunk. 'It's her legs,' explained Sissons desperately.

'Yes, they're full of gin,' put in his father cruelly.

Schorner pretended not to hear. As they got Cecily wedged against the tree again he heard an American voice shouting orders and to his relief saw that his men were rounding the corner to the quay. The platoon was dressed in smooth walking-out uniforms, marching almost languidly, with one separate section of six men in battledress and carrying carbines. As they turned on to the cobbles the colonel saw with annoyance that a group of young girls and women were following them, edging alongside the parade, smiling and pushing hair away from faces, and sticking out breasts. Then they added giggles and began to call the men by their familiar names. 'Hank . . . Harry . . . Sweeney . . .' Schorner's lips thinned.

Sharply he strode towards the platoon which was now moving towards its position next to the Brownies at the rear of the parade, Lieutenant Kenholm, who was at its head, having been briskly directed there by

Mrs Mahon-Feavor. The eyes of the people, participants and spectators alike, followed them as they progressed. Schorner heard remarks and bronchial sniggers from the Home Guard section and saw the indulgent smiles from the British Army contingent. His throat tightened.

Lieutenant Kenholm was blushing to his tight collar by the time the platoon at last reached the tail of the parade. Its contingent of camp-following girls stopped also and stood simpering a few feet away. Even the little girls in the Brownies turned their heads and looked with smiles at the Yanks.

The US soldiers wheeled and halted in their places. Schorner stood quietly at the side, watching them. He moved towards Kenholm. 'These men in battle order,' he said. 'Why haven't they got blackened faces?'

The young lieutenant looked astonished. 'But, sir . . . I didn't think . . . as this is a parade.'

'Get them black,' ordered Schorner. 'I want these people to see what a *fighting* GI looks like. Okay, get to it.'

The armed section were rubbing night-blacking into their cheekbones and on their foreheads below their helmets when Mrs Mahon-Feavor came busying along the long crocodile. 'All ready?' she barked at each section. Everybody was. She pulled up at the tail, surveying the Americans, at first the smoothly uniformed men at the van ranks and then the section who were occupied in blacking their faces. She looked questioningly in Schorner's direction. He saluted and smiled courteously. 'Won't be long, ma'am,' he said. 'The minstrels are getting their make-up on.'

Far at the front the village band struck up, more or less together, into their version of the march 'Blaze Away', and the long, ragged caravan edged forward. Kenholm waited until there was a good gap between his men and the moving-away Brownies in their neat dresses before he gave the Americans orders to march. Collisions were something he could not afford.

The parade presented a curious sight, a strung-out circus eventually turning the corner at the quay and beginning the ascent of Wilcoombe Hill. First, the humphing band, sweat soon sticking grey hairs to the foreheads beneath the blue caps, the well-worn boots striking the cobbles with old, muffled sounds. The brace of Land Army girls swung their handbells, their green-jerseyed chests thrust out like hilly meadows. The whole band played bravely and marched as though they were going to war. Behind them came the Home Guard unit, eyes steady, steps only a little faltering. They had started with nothing on the night in 1940 when they volunteered without a second thought to face an imminent invader; it was not a call to arms, for there were none. Now they had rifles and ammunition and a military air. But now they would never fight a battle; there would be no casualties, no honours, only an elderly, untamed courage. Barrington, his chin elevated exactly to the incline of the hill, strode at their head, the commander who would never know a skirmish.

The three Cadet units followed, lads stepping out, some in uniforms comically too big for them, the battledress tunic dropping in some cases to the baggy trouser knees, the blancoed gaiters flopping like hooves. The Army Cadets were encumbered with webbing which hung to them like a carthorse's harness; the Air Training Corps, their banner *Per Ardua Ad Astra* aloft, trudged gamely, endeavouring to reach not only to the stars, but the top of Wilcoombe Hill; the Naval Cadets, sons of fishermen, many with lanyards and whistles, pulled a two-wheeled milk-cart with long ropes. It represented a ceremonial gun-carriage. Behind them, collectively abashed and led by the beetroot-faced Captain Westerman, stepped out the men of the anti-aircraft unit, some softly singing filthy words to the march.

There followed the Civil Defence team, one pair carrying a symbolic stirrup pump and a bucket, others with gas rattles that had never swung in earnest, others with whistles to warn of incendiary bombs which had been blown shrilly in the days and nights of the bombers. Mrs Mahon-Feavor herself, pigeon-chest bulging, face set like plaster of Paris, led the ladies of the Women's Voluntary Service, and following them were the rosy Land Army girls, the Boy Scouts, the Guides and the Brownies and eventually the men of the US Army.

The hill was liberally lined with spectators and a grubby Union Jack hung over the inn sign of the Bull and Mouth. People leaned from their windows and cheered self-consciously. Schorner, marching at the side of the GIs, felt his temper rising as the girls and women moved along with them, a giggling gaggle, still calling the men's names and making inane jokes. Eventually one girl pushed another and she stumbled into the road just as the Americans were rounding the bend to climb the hill. The young hag fell into the men and the whole contingent piled up and slewed about while she was pulled out by her hysterical friends. 'Halt!' shouted Schorner. The order was as much for the females as for the soldiers. The Americans came to a standstill and the girls fell back against the wall of a house, eyeing him like mares as he strode forward.

Schorner felt his face hot with rage. 'Beat it!' he rasped at the women. 'Get right away. These men are soldiers. Go on, beat it!' The gaggle fell back, watching him with fear and malevolence. He turned to Kenholm. 'Okay, lieutenant,' he grunted. 'Get this outfit moving again.'

They marched off, leaving the females in a clutch by the wall. Schorner heard then, as he knew he must do, the scream of laughter and insolence from behind. The rural raucousness, the shrieking and the shouting. He stared to the front and his men did also. Christ, he thought, roll on the invasion.

Gilman marched in the front rank of the anti-aircraft unit, with Lieutenant Bryant before him and Captain Westerman a further two paces ahead. A strange and unprecedented feeling came over him as he marched; he began to *feel* like a soldier. It was a sensation which came with, was transmitted through, the tight feel of the belt and the harness of webbing, the ammunition pouches, the bayonet scabbard banging regularly against his hip as he marched, the sound of the studs on the cobbled road, the firmness of the beret band around his forehead, and, most of all, from the primitive confidence that issued through his left hand held across the base of his rifle and the warm, wooden barrel of the weapon on his shoulder, touching against his cheek like a familiar. It was so strange. He actually felt *proud*. He almost felt he could march into battle like that, armed, invincible, unhurtable, his jaw tight, his hands steady, his eye fearless. As a million others had.

The band tinkled and rasped ahead of the parade. Gilman glanced sideways at Catermole. He was marching straight and strong, like a warrior also. It was amazing what a few shouted orders, military music and some bystanders could do for a reluctant soldier. What a pity there was no one to take the salute. They should have had someone of importance to take the salute.

As they mounted the hill the pace slowed and towards the top the band became puffing and ragged. Doey and Lenny and Horace Smith, the poacher, were hanging out of the top window of the Bull and Mouth; the landlord and his wife and Minnie Smith and Fat Meg, like two bulging grain sacks, occupied another. Minnie was being wrapped around by the Union Jack flying outside the window and, never being one to let even patriotism get in her way, she tied the flag in a large knot so that she could properly view the parade. Doey, Lenny and Horace, all enthusiastic civilians, were holding pints of cider and they raised them to drink thirstily and audibly as the marchers strode by. As they cheered the cider trickled down their chins.

As they passed the house of Mary Nicholas, Gilman turned his glance sideways, and then up to the bedroom. He could see her standing behind the net curtain, holding one of her children; the forehead, eyes and nose of another infant were at the sill level, clear of the hem of the curtain.

At the summit of Wilcoombe Hill the band had

been reduced to a single melancholy drumbeat, and the tiring bells of the two landgirls. There was just room and time for the head of the procession to turn in the street and begin the cobbled descent. Several of the more ancient bandsmen began to wheeze louder than their instruments. Howard Evans and Beatrice, who had climbed the hill on the flank of the parade, travelled alongside and studied them with anxiety. The middle of the crocodile had reached the turning place, becoming entangled at its edges with those still marching up the hill. Mrs Mahon-Feavor was shouting orders like a commander in a confused battle. The Army Cadets and the Brownies had, by this time, lost step, although the naval lads, pulling their imaginary gun-carriage by its ropes, were trudging gamely.

'I can't see this lot climbing the hill a second time, let alone a third,' said Howard sideways to his wife. 'We'll need to have a casualty clearing station if they do.'

The Women's Voluntary Service contingent were going by, strong shoes on straight legs, plodding the last few cobbles of the uphill climb. Beatrice saw the stockings of several ladies had come adrift and were wrinkling down. A small Brownie was crying and being comforted by a bigger Brownie. The boy carrying the Scout's flag eased it back across his shoulder to rest and caught the Scout behind a glancing blow on the head. There were signs that the parade would end in disaster and tears.

The American unit, also showing signs of heavy breathing, had achieved the summit of the hill. Schorner was thankful they had not included

Ballimach or any of the other overweight soldiers. The colonel's eyes turned left just before the crest and saw what he had been seeking. In a side row of cottages, turning at right-angles to the main hill, had just arrived two US Army trucks. They were unloading negroes holding musical instruments.

As the US troops arrived at the short plateau on the brow of the hill, Schorner called them to halt. The female camp followers were still in attendance, although at a good distance, now halfway up the slope. The rest of the parade was now clattering down the hill, leaving the Americans at the top. Some of the Brownies turned around to see what had happened to their rearguard but nobody else noticed apart from the trailing women who remained in a sniggering knot pointing at the soldiers.

It was a short wait. In the side street the negro band was quickly forming up with animated joy, their brass instruments bright in their hands, the drums and percussion heaved into position, and to the fore the Jingle Johnny, a soldier festooned with bells and streamers, began to flex his tintinnabulating knees and elbows. Once assembled, the band moved out, almost crept out, on to the hill. Schorner felt tempted to put his finger to his lips so that the secret would be kept, but the negroes were soon, and silently, in echelon and at a single sign from the Jingle Johnny they erupted into the 'St Louis Blues March'.

The rousing Southern music burst out over the little English town. Gulls jumped screaming and surprised from the chimney pots. Halfway down the street the rest of the procession faltered and turned round in disbelief. With another trump and a clash, the American band stepped out as one and began the march down the old Devon hill.

The US soldiers, straightened, broadened, strode out behind the swinging band. Lieutenant Kenholm's head went up so high he could see the clouds through half-closed eyes. Schorner grinned within himself. He'd show the bastards!

Down Wilcoombe Hill they played and marched. Their effect on the West Country people was to be seen in the faces. Tom Barrington at the head of his Home Guard stiffened angrily, the Women's Voluntary Service ladies turned, tumbling against each other as they did so. Mrs Mahon-Feavor tried to shout an order but nobody heard. The Wilcoombe band gurgled to a not ungrateful stop. The youth of the town were in no doubt. They broke ranks and cheered and laughed as the foreign coloured men advanced, the Brownies scattering to the roadside, followed by the Cadet soldiers, sailors and airmen. The milk-float gun-carriage broke loose and bumped down the hill before mounting the pavement and colliding with the post box.

There had never been such excitement in that place. Doey Bidgood and Lenny Birch spilled their cider in their efforts to get a better view of the approaching phenomenon. Minnie Smith began to shout hysterically and Fat Meg all but fell dramatically from the window. Everybody was shouting, waving and suddenly singing. The parasite girls who had followed the Yanks began to jitterbug with each other on the pavement.

There was no doubt, the band was wonderful. They clashed and smashed into the jazz rhythms, their march became dance as they came down the slope, syncopation in every step. The Jingle Johnny, a beaming ebony man, jumped and jangled. The landgirls bell-ringers in the band swung their bells hopefully in unison. One shouted sideways to her companion: 'There's no stopping they Yanks, Rosie!'

They reached the broad foot of Wilcoombe Hill with the people avalanching after them. The ragged but sedate parade had, within minutes, become riotous. People were leaping like grasshoppers and clapping their hands; the abandoned girls were still jitterbugging; Doey's cider, tipping sideways as he eagerly hung from the public house window, cascaded on to the entranced Brownies below. Even the Wilcoombe band, overtaken with the excellence and enthusiasm of the playing black men, beamed and bounced modestly as they watched. Only Mrs Mahon-Feavor and Tom Barrington were less than pleased. 'This is what is going to happen, I suppose,' foresaw the lady helplessly. 'They'll just take over everything. And ruin it.'

At the rim of the quay the American band spread into a circle. It was apparent even to Mrs Mahon-Feavor that the parade was at an end. The rustic people pressed around, there were shouts demanding more room for the players, on every face was a smile, a new excitement, something that had not been seen for a long while in that wartime place. The saviours had indeed come. With trumpets.

Then, at the pitch of the rapture, with the band bending, dipping and high-stepping, all in the confines of their circus, a new sound gurgled across the Sunday morning air; the air-raid siren. The English people, used to false alarms or the times when the raiders never came within miles, scarcely noticed it, but the Americans, including, indeed led by, the band, broke ranks and scattered in all directions, up the hill, in between the houses, even under two boats which sat, keels-up, on the quay. One man blew his horn wildly as he ran like the trumpeter of a panic-fraught cavalry. Schorner, amazed and angry, glared around to see his soldiers fleeing in all directions. 'Bombers! It's the goddamn Nazi bombers!' bawled one man as he scuttled past. The colonel grabbed the man by the tunic and tugged him to an abrupt stop. He almost heaved the frightened soldier in front of him. 'Halt!' shouted Schorner, the order meant for any and every man who was scattering. Only the GI he had grasped and held prisoner heard him. The soldier's face was shivering. 'I'm halted, sir,' he replied, his tone vibrant with complaint.

The villagers were rolling across garden walls with laughter. They embraced each other with merriment at the novice fright of their allies. The poacher's wife, Minnie Smith, was hanging her great fat form from the pub window, arms spread out as wings, lips quivering in a grotesque impersonation of engine noise. 'Look out, Yanks!' bawled Doey from the next window. ''Ere be a Jerry comin' for 'ee!'

Even as the words were howled across the sunlit street, a wide cross-shaped shadow flew low across the housetops, its loud engine-noise arriving after it. 'Christ!' howled Doey. ''*Tis* a bloody Jerry.'

Everyone saw the plane within the same moment. Blindly the civilians scattered with as much haste and as little dignity as the American soldiers. The area round the quay cleared in seconds, everyone running outwards to doorways and crannies already occupied by the cowering troops. The bass drummer of the Wilcoombe band fell off the edge of the quay and was only saved from drowning by his buoyant instrument. The bell-ringing landgirls rolled their bulky bodies beneath the turned-up boats, making the GIs hiding there gasp and then take on, even in peril, a grin of pleasure and proprietorship.

Colonel Schorner found himself pressed against the wall of Howard Evans' cottage. The door opened and Evans himself pulled him inside. Beatrice was already in the passage with three of the Air Cadets who were arguing as to the type and firepower of the enemy aircraft. Fat Meg who had left the pub to join the crowd around the band was also here, her great back heaving at the far end of the corridor. Evans opened the door and peered out towards the sea. The black shape of the German plane was easing in a slow threatening circle out over Start Bay. 'He's coming back,' muttered the doctor. 'Get on the floor everybody!'

He tried to shut the cottage door, but two of the Cadets, in their eagerness to get a view of the plane, had advanced too far and, obediently, had now flattened themselves on the coconut matting inside the door, making it impossible to close. Evans cursed. Fat Meg abruptly added to the confusion and danger by tramping over everyone in the narrow passage and charging red-legged out of the door. She stood on the short garden path waving her meaty fists at the advancing plane and bawling hideously: 'Come on, you bastards! Come on then!'

Schorner watched her with astonishment. On his hands and knees he hurried comically forward with Evans just behind him. They swung like a pair of apes, on all fours, down the path, each one grasping one of Meg's swollen purple ankles. She turned and abused them in the same fury that she had expended on the Germans. They pulled strongly at the ankles and Meg, with a monstrous cry, toppled over backwards on top of them in a great cumulus of skirts, petticoats and scarlet drawers.

The bulging buttocks descended full across Schorner's back knocking the breath from him. The bomber came on, steady, enlarging all the time, seeming to head directly for the comic trio grappling on the front path of the quayside cottage. Then Evans, in an odd whisper as though he feared the enemy might hear and be warned, said: 'The gun. Look.'

They remained transfixed in their bundle on the ground. The plane continued on course, its black nose sniffing directly at them. The barrel of the anti-aircraft gun on the quayside swung and Schorner heard orders being shouted above the deep growling of the aircraft's three engines. They watched, transfixed. Beatrice crawled from the doorway and tugged at Howard Evans' sock, urging him to get back under cover. Then, in the open, she too saw what was happening. Mouth and eyes set, she watched the approaching plane, so low now it seemed to be crouching. The gun was swinging around as if it were manipulated by someone with a string. Meg staggered to her knees, then to a squat, and began parading violently up and down like a gigantic chicken. 'Shoot the bastards down, boys!' she howled. 'Shoot their German balls off!'

As though this were the command for which they waited, the crew of the gun fired. The bang shook the houses. The plane was passing slightly to the east at no more altitude than five hundred feet. Even the Wilcoombe gunners could not miss a target so adjacent. The single shot they dispatched sent a great flat section of tailplane flying away, sailing down and then bouncing across the sea like a boy's stone thrown in a game of ducks and drakes. At the same moment, as if in pique, the German bomber jettisoned a single bomb, which struck squarely in the middle of the harbour, sending a fine fountain of water into the air but otherwise causing no disturbance.

The gun crew were dumbfounded. Captain Westerman, relieved beyond dreams that the gun had actually worked, now stood with his hand across his mouth. Sergeant Bullivant's jaw descended. The soldiers all turned with mute astonishment. 'My God,' stumbled Westerman at last. 'Whatever have we done?'

The words cut the tension and the gun crew began jumping up and down, shouting with joy, banging each other on the back. People came running from everywhere, British soldiers, American soldiers, men, women, children, pouring into the army compound and surrounding the jubilant gunners. Bullivant and Captain Westerman embraced each other, until they realized what they were doing. Then, standing back a pace, Westerman, ever doubtful, said: 'I suppose it really *was* one of theirs, sergeant? I mean . . . we are sure?'

Bullivant's enthused, infused cheeks drained to a pulpy white. 'Christ, I hope so, sir,' he said.

But there was no doubt. Doey Bidgood arrived on a wild bicycle and announced that the plane had crashed in a field to the north of Wilcoombe. Westerman, steel-faced, husky, soldierlike, ordered: 'Right, sergeant, let's take the prisoners.'

There was a charge towards the platoon truck, then a second-thoughts rush to get rifles from barrack-rooms. Westerman in his haste strapped his revolver on backwards and scampered towards the truck. Men were piling in. Gilman was already at the wheel and rushing the engine to life. The truck charged through the gate and made for the village hall. People cheered hysterically.

They reached the top of the hill and there, to their dismay, they found themselves in a whole caravan of people on bicycles, on horseback and on hurrying foot, heading towards the crashed plane. Westerman stood up and bellowed in rage at the civilians, but to no avail. Then, as they eventually reached the cross-roads beyond the village the British officer's horror was doubled as he spotted the pennants and helmets of an entire convoy of American vehicles hurrying across the line of the hedgetops, coming at right-angles and due to make the crossroads first.

'Good God, the f-fucking Yanks,' stammered Westerman. He looked around, aghast with guilt. He had never said that word in front of the men before and he prided himself on his clean tongue. 'Beat them to it!' he shouted at Gilman. 'Go on, man, get a damned move on.'

The British platoon truck and the leading American jeep, driven by the determined Albie Primrose, reached the junction simultaneously. Albie, with the greater acceleration and mobility of the jeep, threw it round the corner, almost scraping the bumper of the British vehicle. Four GIs in the back of the jeep jeered and Westerman bellowed back ordering them to stop at once. 'The prisoners are ours!' he bawled. The Americans drove on, Albie pushing the nose of the jeep through the vanguard of the civilians hurrying to the scene, and then gunning the engine down the narrow country lane. Gilman got the snout of the platoon truck inserted after the jeep and before the next US vehicle, sweating and swearing, with Westerman rattling incomprehensible orders in his ear. The officer still had his revolver strapped on the wrong way. Catermole, observing all with his usual benign indolence, said to Bullivant: 'Captain Westerman's going to shoot his own knackers off soon, sarge.'

The field where the bomber had crashed was at the forehead of a slight hill. The plane had landed on the round apex. There had been no fire. It lay there, wings spread, back broken, like a shot crow.

People and soldiers appeared from all directions. Ten American vehicles were quickly there behind Albie's jeep and Gilman's platoon truck. They disgorged troops clutching carbines and tugging with awkward excitement at steel helmets. All would have charged across the field had not Westerman, in a rare commanding moment, shouted, 'Halt!' He attempted to get a grip on his revolver and, after a contortion, pulled the weapon from the webbing holster. 'Everyone lie flat!' he shouted. '*They'll turn the machine guns on you!*'

In a moment the rush was quelled. The GIs, their

expressions transformed, dropped hurriedly into the ditch at the roadside. Westerman, pleased and surprised with his success, shouted at troops in approaching vehicles: 'Spread out, around the perimeter. And keep under cover.'

Lieutenant Kenholm was the first United States officer to approach Westerman. Clumsily he crawled along the ditch as though it were a front-line sap in Flanders. 'Get your boys to keep their heads down, lieutenant,' ordered Westerman dramatically. 'Or you'll be indenting for some coffins.'

Kenholm shouted to left and right. 'You guys – get your dumb heads down. Lie flat. Everybody lie flat.'

Westerman could see soldiers moving all around the perimeter of the large field. 'You'd better tell your chaps across there also. Otherwise they'll be shooting and hitting your chaps over here,' he said loftily. He was enjoying himself. 'And get some bodies back to block the road. All the riff-raff will be here in a moment.'

'The riff-raff?' inquired Kenholm. He thought it might be something to do with the Air Force.

'The hoi-polloi, the civilians,' Westerman told him.

Whistles were being blown everywhere now, but order brought about by prudence had quickly spread around the meadow and no one broke cover. Schorner arrived, threading his way through the vehicles jamming the lane. Behind him came Howard Evans carrying his doctor's bag. 'What's the situation, captain?' asked Schorner. Westerman saluted. 'Junkers. JU 88. Crew two or three. Have to go steady, they may use the machine guns.' His teeth gripped. 'They don't give up easily.'

Looking with care from the cover of the hedge, Schorner surveyed the broken plane. There was no movement. 'You'd think they'd quit as soon as the thing hit the ground,' he said. 'In case of fire.'

'They may be dead,' mentioned Westerman like a veteran.

Schorner acknowledged the remark but added: 'It landed pretty flat.' He looked again, cautiously, and Westerman sensed his reaction. 'There's movement there now,' the American said. He called loudly along the ditch. 'Hold your fire!'

Westerman closed his eyes theatrically. He raised his head and saw the movement at the breast of the plane. An unpleasant thought was growing in his mind that he, as the resident British officer, whose gun had actually hit the aeroplane, might be expected to do something positive, even dramatic. He glanced at Schorner who, by his expression, confirmed the Englishman's fears. Westerman blinked, coughed politely into his hand, and speculatively handled his revolver, as if to warm it. He was saved from having to lead an advance, however, by the arrival of Police Constable Lethbridge of Wilcoombe. He was as thin as the bicycle upon which he creaked up the lane. He patiently dismounted before attaching a padlock and chain to the back wheel of the conveyance, an action accompanied by a distrustful look at the American soldiers in the ditch. He was wearing his police-issue revolver, the weapon grotesquely big around his wasted waist. His eyes were watery but his face and demeanour calmly determined.

'Zur,' he said, addressing Westerman, 'oi think this be a matter for the civil power.'

Westerman could hardly conceal his relief. 'Yes, constable, of course,' he breathed. 'I thought it might be.' He looked sideways at Schorner. 'This is the way we do things in this country,' he explained awkwardly.

Schorner looked doubtful. He glanced over the hedgerow again. A single figure was standing by the wreckage of the plane. 'Okay,' he said. 'If that's how you want to play it.' He glanced at the policeman. 'If there's any shooting, drop flat on the ground.'

Lethbridge returned the look mildly. 'Oi know about that, zur,' he said. 'Oi wuz trained to defeat the invasion.'

Before the grin had fully formed on Schorner's face the pokery policeman opened the gate and walked with stiff authority into the field, the eyes of several hundred hidden soldiers on him. They watched, scarcely believing, as the blue-uniformed figure advanced across the grass towards the crashed bomber.

As he neared it his step slowed, but only momentarily. Then they saw the German airman move forward. Every hidden soldier checked his breath and gripped his rifle more readily. They were astonished when the policeman and the enemy flier merely shook hands.

'Jesus Christ,' muttered Schorner. 'Now I've seen every goddamn thing.'

'Our policemen are wonderful,' echoed Westerman smugly.

They watched as the German led Lethbridge towards the broken fuselage. They saw the Devon man climb with difficulty on to the wing and then peer down into the aircraft. He returned to the ground and, walking like a companion alongside the German, he made towards the gate again.

From every side the American soldiers rose from behind their concealment and stood staring at their first sight of the enemy. The German was young, weary. He looked about him startled when he saw the considerable army materialize. Then a faint smile came across his tired lips and he whispered something to his friend, the policeman.

At the gate Schorner and Westerman waited. The American looked into the young, riven face, and felt his heart fall. The German returned the look with a wry smile. 'There's two others in the aeroplane, zur,' mentioned Police Constable Lethbridge. 'Both dead by the look o' they. Only bits of boys.'

During the second week in February, three days before the infamous St Valentine's Day Dance at Wilcoombe, the United States forces staged the first of their mass pre-invasion exercises along the wide shingle of Telcoombe Beach. Until then it had been confined to individual units.

'The code name is Exercise Eider,' Schorner shouted across the heads of the men assembled on the square at the centre of the Telcoombe Magna Camp. They were standing in rough order, not in ranks, like a crowd listening to an outdoor politician. 'The eider is a kind of duck, the hicks among you will know that.' He ran his eyes along the ranks of attentive, apprehensive faces. 'One thousand GIs are taking part, coming ashore from landing craft or ending up in the ocean, depending how lucky you get or how you shape up as soldiers. There'll be a lot of other war games to follow over the next few weeks. But sometime the games have got to end – and then it's the real thing. So I want this outfit to get it right from the start.'

He frowned down at the written orders bunched in his hand. 'This is a daytime operation,' he said, 'because you guys can't see at night. Not yet. But you're going to have to learn. And soon.' It was a hushed, grey day with no wind. The sky was as flat as paper. The men could hear the calling of the gulls from the inland coombes, gulls looking for the pickings that had, for generations, come from the spring ploughing, the worms from the upturned earth. This year there would be none and the white wings made puzzled circles over fields that were already greening with weeds and rough grass.

'This unit,' said Schorner, 'will come ashore near home. Every man will be familiarized with the details, his own job, where he must be and what he is expected to do. In general, our section will be the area of beach immediately to the east and west of Telcoombe Beach Hotel. That will be nominated a fortified enemy strong point and will have to be taken out as soon as we get ashore. But *no* soldier is to go into that place – the hotel – because it's mined to hell. Okay? It will be our task, once we've got a beachhead, to clear obstacles on the beach, open out the roads and fix communications and construct pontoons across those inland lakes. Those bridges are very important – one day you will understand just how important.'

The Colonel examined their faces. They were

young enough to be his sons. 'Live ammunition will be used in this exercise.' He watched the pinched expressions along the ranks. 'Firing will be overhead, so nobody *ought* to get hurt, but it's going to help you move your asses a little faster than you might do if it was just some picnic. There will also be a bombardment from the British warships at sea. This will be aimed at the hills and the far side of the lakes. Maybe half a mile ahead. So let's hope the Englishmen can shoot straight – and get the range right.'

There was a shuffling among the crowded troops but it stopped as he looked steadily at them as if he had caught each man's eye. 'Okay then,' said Schorner. 'We will move off at eight hundred hours tomorrow. Tonight every man is confined to camp. Briefing by platoon officers will be at twenty-one hundred hours.' He paused. His next sentence, he realized as he said it, came like a plea. 'We've got to get this right because there's going to come a time when practice is going to be too late. Okay? Right. Enjoy yourselves.'

He left the parade to be dismissed and walked back towards his tent. Captain Hulton, the conducting officer, was waiting outside. He saluted. 'Hi,' said Schorner. 'Got any more armies?'

'No, sir,' returned Hulton in his lugubrious manner. 'They've transferred me. I'm not a conducting officer any more. I got a unit lost on Dartmoor. We got lost all night. Jesus it was so cold. I felt like crying, I can tell you, sir.'

Schorner suppressed a grin and he succeeded in looking concerned. 'So what are you doing now, Hulton?'

The doleful officer looked doubtfully at Schorner.

'I'm attached to your unit, sir. This post. Liaison.' He said the final word with descending apology. Then he added: 'I didn't *like* being a conducting officer anyway.'

Schorner breathed: 'Not another liaison officer. I've got them up to my ass, Hulton. There's the English guy, Bryant, and Scarlett from General Georgeton's staff. Soon we'll be having liaison officers for the liaison officers.' Hulton looked as if he might be forced to tears. Schorner shrugged: 'So what are *you* going to do?'

The captain brightened marginally, as if at least he knew one answer. 'Exercise liaison, colonel,' he affirmed. 'I'm attached to this unit to keep in touch with other units during manoeuvres and with the British Navy. That's pretty important.'

'Okay, okay, captain,' said Schorner good-naturedly. 'The navy job sounds impressive. Just get your quarters assigned and your kit moved in. I'll expect you at tonight's final briefing.'

Hulton's face cleared like someone who knows that, at last, they are wanted. He threw up a firm salute. 'Yes, sir.' He marched away across the grey camp, the little, lost officer, who ought to be at home with his mother.

'At least he can't get the navy lost on Dartmoor,' muttered Schorner to himself.

The first of the major seaborne exercises saw the American soldiers moving out in the February half-light, with eerie cockerels sounding across a low, dirty sky. Two hundred men from Schorner's unit climbed

273

aboard trucks outside the camp gate on the night-smeared road. Schorner sat with Hulton and Bryant in his jeep and watched his loaded men creep by like felons.

'In this light they almost look like real soldiers,' thought Schorner. He saw the bulky Ballimach, hung like a camel with his equipment, moving ponderously in the line. 'I wish Ballimach wasn't going,' he sighed.

'Best telephone guy we've got, colonel,' said Albie Primrose at the wheel.

Bryant looked sharply at the driver but Schorner nodded, accepting the American Army tradition that anyone may voice an opinion. 'He'll never drown anyway,' said the American commander. 'That guy could float for years.'

'When the real thing comes he'll be the biggest target on the beachhead,' forecast Hulton lugubriously. 'Like a tank. They could hit him from Paris.' He wrapped his heavy combat jacket closer about him as if it were not only warmth but protection, and looked sideways at Bryant. 'Don't the sun ever come up in this country?' he asked.

The British lieutenant smiled. 'About June,' he answered. 'If you're quick.' He wondered why Hulton had to talk so much.

Schorner finished his coffee and threw the empty mug to a man at the gate. The man caught it like a baseball. Schorner jogged his chin approvingly. 'Okay, let's get this thing moving,' he said to Albie. The driver's nose was outlined, stiff as an icicle in the raw morning. Albie nodded and started the jeep. The heavy trucks snorted behind it. The convoy moved off through the early, empty countryside. Schorner said

274

to Bryant, 'We have a schedule of four landings before the end of the month – then we've got to get the shore drill right. It's no good getting these guys on the beach if they don't know what to do when they're there.'

There were rats sitting in the street at Telcoombe Magna. Bryant saw them with a sick shock. The empty cottages stood like rotting teeth. Pigeons were already inhabiting the thatched roofs and eating themselves gross in the gardens. A window that had been open since the evacuation banged on its hinges like a funeral drum, so insistent that he wanted to get out and go and shut it. All the panes but one were now missing. The soldiers manning the gun in the lychgate of the church watched them go by with shadowy yawns. As they topped the hill, the English Channel came into view, long, flat and blind. 'That ocean looks cold,' muttered Hulton.

'Sure it's cold,' answered Schorner. 'Make sure you keep yourself good and dry, captain.'

Clumsily the convoy descended the road that unrolled towards the sea. By now the sharp sides of the lane had been monstrously carved away, the levels changed, the ancient hedgerows crushed. There was red mud and huge holes and detours into fields; but now a tank could have reached the shoreline from the rising inland. The new landscape, once so nourished and green, depressed Schorner, the farmer. Soon it would be further holed and pitted, the birds that now sang a piping song at morning would be frightened away by the din of battle.

A beach wind shredded through the stanchions of the jeep as they turned west along the coastal road. Short of Wilcoombe widespread areas of white concrete covered the sand and shingle, the first of the hards from which the vehicles of the eventual invasion would be driven to the transporters and landing craft. 'Look at that,' said Hulton suddenly in his complaining voice. 'There's a darned dog on the beach. He ain't supposed to be in this area.'

Bryant and Schorner each grinned privately. The dog, Daffy's dog, the salty mongrel that had for a long time run the Telcoombe Beach, was bounding joyfully along the pebbles parallel with the road, barking and throwing his head up into the travelling wind. Schorner said: 'There's nothing, not even barbed wire, ever going to keep that dog away, I guess. Not even the military police.' He watched the animal carefully, perversely pleased that some creature had managed to remain undirected, free. 'Have we got any cookies?' he asked as Albie obligingly slowed the vehicle. Albie pulled to the side of the road and the trucks behind slowed ponderously. To Bryant's surprise Schorner left the jeep with a ration pack that Primrose had handed to him. The others stayed in the vehicle as if not to intrude on some private moment. The dog came bounding to Schorner and the colonel pulled the wrapping from the packet and held out the cookies. The dog's jaws engulfed the offering and it stood, with cock-eared expectancy, waiting for more. Schorner laughed and cuffed it gently. He turned back towards the jeep and looked up to see the faces of the soldiers hanging out from the backs of the trucks, peering around while hanging on the tarpaulins, all mute, all watching. Bryant saw that Schorner was embarrassed, the first time he had seen that in him. 'Okay, you guys,' shouted the colonel along the stopped convoy. 'Get your heads in. It's only a dog.'

He climbed into the jeep and told Albie to move on. 'That hound,' he said, as if he needed to explain at least something about his diversion, 'that hound's been out in the air and the salt for so long it's darned near changed colour.'

'It belongs to a fisherman they call Old Daffy,' said Bryant. 'He takes it in the pub. It must be impossible to keep it off the beach. I've even seen it swim ashore from his boat. That was in the old days, before . . .'

'Before all this crap got here,' Schorner finished for him. They were moving along the road now, the trucks starting up and grunting after them, like old, heavy men. The colonel eased himself back in the frame seat of the jeep. 'Well, he'll still be running like hell along that beach when we're all gone,' he said.

'Home,' added Hulton nervously as if to dispel any misunderstanding.

'Home,' nodded Schorner. 'Or heaven.' He smiled a little mischievously at the captain's pasty face. 'Or hell. Some place like that.'

The British soldiers at the gun-site stood in a group, like spectators gathered at the halfway line at a village football match. Gilman and Catermole remained apart near the end of the Wilcoombe quay for they had been on overnight guard. Killer Watts was rubbing down the barrel of the anti-aircraft gun with the care of a mother wiping her child's nose. They looked after it with more pride now.

Watts paused, astride the long snout, to watch with

the others as the hunched Americans moved awkwardly into the landing craft rocking in the tight harbour. Moving from the trucks parked on the road at the foot of the village, they trudged in hangdog file to the edge of the quay and down the stone steps to the small, fidgeting vessels. People came from the Wilcoombe houses and others, on their way to work, stopped and stood or sat on their bicycles to watch. It was a muted scene. Occasionally one of the GIs would curse when the landing craft rocked the wrong way as he was boarding it, and a growling admonishment would issue from the sergeant supervising the boarding steps, but little else. Just grunts and vapour from their breaths. Some of the British soldiers were smoking and the wisps curled up into the still, damp air. Several of the Americans looked at them enviously.

'I'm glad it's them, not us,' mentioned Gilman eventually.

'Christ, so am I,' echoed Catermole. 'They're welcome to that game of bleeding soldiers.'

He was unaware of the prophecy in his adjective. 'Getting up in the morning, in the army,' he continued in his awkward way, 'that's bad enough. Bloody cold and grey, with your mouth like a pisspot. But fancy having to get up and know you've got to go and fight the fucking Germans. I wouldn't reckon that.'

Gilman looked at him sharply. 'They're not going *now*,' he said, wondering. 'Surely not. They haven't had enough training. It's only an exercise.'

'Practising,' sniffed Catermole sagely. 'Just practising won't make the real thing any better. Worse.'

They walked, like two pensioners taking a seaside morning stroll, back towards the others of the unit standing on the gun-site. As they approached Bullivant appeared and stood smirking fatly. 'Soldiers,' he grunted, watching the Americans. 'I've shit better.'

'Will you be going, sarge?' asked Gilman with assumed innocence.

'Going?' Bullivant withdrew his big face as if someone had taken a punch at him. He glared at Gilman from his new distance. 'What's that mean, Gilman? Will I be *going*?'

Gilman shrugged. 'On the invasion,' he replied simply. 'You know, charging up the beaches.'

'Don't let's have that from you, sonny,' returned the sergeant nastily. His voice grated like a bad engine. 'You're a bit too clever for the rest of us, but not so clever as you think you are, lad. You'll be finding yourself on a charge before long.'

Gilman regarded him seriously. 'Sorry, Sergeant Bullivant,' he answered with studied politeness. 'I wondered if you would, that's all.' The other men were grinning and Bullivant retreated huffily, turning on his heavy heel and striding towards Watts, still riding on the gun barrel. He shouted for him to get down. 'Fat cunt,' muttered Catermole.

They returned to looking at the embarking Americans. The GIs were huddled under equipment, their rifles and automatic weapons at the trail. Ballimach trundled to the edge of the steps, the wheel of cable sitting on his back like the drum of a one-man band. Gilman recognized the big man and found himself giving a slight, embarrassed, wave. 'Poor

279

bastard,' said Catermole seeing the direction of the salute. 'I'd rather him than me. He'll be shagged out before he gets his feet on dry land.'

The villagers had remained silently eyeing the strange, laden soldiers, as if seeing them in their battle suits, the dun clothes almost covered by belts and equipment, the faces smeared black below the truculent edge of the steel helmets, had made them different men. The medical team unloaded stretchers from the final truck and hung their heavy packs and plasma containers around their bodies. The Devon people noted it grimly. Children on their way to school stopped and looked also, the boys staring at the guns, the girls with a childish but female admiration for the fighting men. Doey, leaning backwards against his muddy bicycle, watching men only as old as he, had to say something, as he usually did. 'Be this the real thing then, zur?' he suddenly asked Captain Hulton who was standing next to the jeep with Bryant. Doey's voice was a considerate whisper. 'You goin' across there now?' He nodded towards the sea as if Hulton might be confused as to the direction of Occupied France.

'They be in their fighting clothes,' put in a woman standing near. Doey's rural brashness was met by Hulton's military pomposity. 'That's classified information,' he said, facing Doey in a manner which made the labourer appear, and feel, important. 'You must know that I can't tell you classified secrets.' Doey, pleased at being noticed even to this extent, nodded agreeably. 'I bain't goin' to tell they Germans, zur,' he said amiably. 'I promise.'

'It's classified,' grunted Hulton before turning away.

Doey glanced about at his neighbours, regarding him with a measure of respect, as if it were he who was giving the final orders. He grinned like a crack in the earth. He called after Hulton. 'I s'pose we got to listen for the bangs, then.'

Bryant looked at his fellow countryman sharply. He moved over. 'Go and dig a ditch somewhere,' he advised quietly. Doey knew the voice and the look. He shuffled away with his bicycle. The crowd grinned at his discomfort. 'Bloody soldiers,' he called over his shoulder, but not too loudly. 'Think they be runnin' the war. T'weren't for the likes o' oi, the country'd be starvin'.'

Most of the GIs had now moved on to the landing craft shrugging uneasily in the confines of the small harbour. Colonel Schorner remained on the stone quayside looking down at the rows of egg-like steel helmets and thinking how strange it was that grown men could be made to stare unerringly ahead. The mist was breaking away from Start Bay, from the enclaves of land where it had clung after the wider water was clear. Bryant pointed out beyond the first ribbon of sea to where a pair of three-funnelled vessels were lying, waiting.

'That looks like the escort, sir,' he said, pointing. Schorner brought his field glasses up. He lowered them at once and looked with a pained earnestness at the young British officer. 'They look very old,' he said.

Hulton was viewing the pair. He confirmed Schorner's observation: 'They look like they ought to have goddamn sails.' He glanced guiltily at Schorner. 'I mean, sails,' he corrected.

Schorner studied the two vessels again. He

breathed: 'They've got three smokestacks each. I didn't think those kind of ships were used anymore.'

Bryant had recognized the shapes. 'HMS *Oregon* and HMS *Florida*,' he recited. 'They've been in Plymouth for the past couple of years.'

'American names,' said Hulton still staring through the glasses.

'They're American ships,' answered Bryant trying not to sound smug. 'Built in the First World War.'

'Two of the fifty we leased to you in 1940,' nodded Schorner.

'That's right. They're very old but they still float. Just about. They roll like mad, so the navy says, and they take miles just to make a turn.'

'But you never look a gift horse in the mouth,' Schorner reminded him quietly. The American colonel continued to look at the ships through the field glasses.

'No, sir,' answered Bryant. 'You don't.'

A heavy US Army staff car slid to a halt on the damp cobbles alongside the quay, causing the assembled civilians to turn as one to see it, like a rehearsed chorus crowd in an opera. Captain Scarlett left the vehicle and walked briskly towards the group of officers, his breath vaporizing. Some of the civilians, now integrated into the scene, wished him a Devonian good morning and he returned the greeting with an involuntary salute. He repeated the movement when he reached Schorner.

'Doing the rounds?' inquired the colonel.

'Yes, sir,' said Scarlett. 'Just trying to figure out if everything's on schedule.'

'Is it?'

'Christ, no. It's okay here because with these limited numbers it's easy, but at Plymouth and Portland and Dartmouth everything's got balled up. One broken down truck and the whole invasion is out of gear. You never saw such jams. And the British police and the mayor and God-knows-who else . . . yes, some people called the Chamber of Commerce, for Christ's sake, all protesting and saying that civilians can't get to work. Get to work! If this doesn't go right they won't have any goddamn work.'

Schorner's mouth wrinkled wryly at the outburst. He turned to Bryant. 'I guess a Chamber of Commerce here is the same as in the States?'

'Businessmen ganging together to protect their businesses,' nodded Bryant. 'Some of them don't know there's a war taking place.' He felt strangely ashamed.

'When the real thing comes along they're going to have to forget their commerce and get off the highways,' put in Hulton grumpily.

'Out there,' said Schorner to Scarlett, 'we have examples of Anglo-American co-operation. Look – dreadnoughts.'

Scarlett pursed his lips. 'I've seen them. There are two more down at Portland. I guess that's what Noah's Ark looked like. Next they'll be wanting everybody to row with oars.'

'When the day comes,' said Schorner, 'maybe we'll have an escort that's a little more up-to-date.' He looked quickly to Bryant.

'I hope so, sir,' said the British officer. 'Those crates will have to get out into the Atlantic to turn around.'

They all laughed, their laughter going up in early

morning vapour. The sound caused the silent soldiers in the barges to look up to the quay with anxiety and envy. Like cattle might look at boisterous slaughter-men. Scarlett said he had to move on down the coast. He shook hands all round and made his way back to the car. The civilians, waiting for him, collectively wished him another solid good morning and he nodded to them. 'That one,' said the knowing Meg solemnly, ''Ee be the one in charge. You can tell by 'is face 'ee's the boss officer.'

One of the schoolboys said it was not true, that the man's insignia of rank was inferior to that of the battledressed colonel on the quay. An argument sparked among the group and Meg cuffed the lad briskly for what she called his dumb insolence. He retreated holding his ear, crying and calling foul names back at her. Meg's everyday truculence had made her accustomed to abuse. Phlegmatically she returned to watching the soldiers.

A blunt-nosed LST – Landing Ship: Tanks – its bow striking the moderate sea like a flat hand, approached the harbour from the leeward of the two escort vessels. 'This one's ours,' guessed Schorner correctly. 'It's the one that bounces best. Okay, let's go.'

With Bryant and Hulton he strode purposefully around to the wet stone jetty, a route which took him directly past the British troops watching from the gun-site. Bullivant, seeing the officers approaching, bundled across the asphalt, and bawled the soldiers to attention before throwing up a rotund and theatrical salute, his hand vibrating against the side of his head like a railway signal. The Americans acknowledged the artillerymen and Bryant returned their smirks with a minor salute of his own. 'Don't get throwing your ring up, sir,' ventured Catermole, nodding towards the boat and the sea. Bryant had gone by. In the background a window opened and Captain Westerman, his chin bubbling with shaving soap, looked out at the scene. For a moment he took it in and then, slowly withdrawing, closed the window and went back to the brush and the mirror.

The large tank landing ship, a blunt and ugly five thousand tonner, had been persuaded alongside the wet jetty. Schorner reached the steep iron ladder, then, at a thought, motioned Hulton and Bryant to climb down to the deck while he remained on the quay. 'Quartermaster,' he called down, 'let me have a loudhailer. Get it up here to me.'

A British sailor brought the trumpet-shaped speaker up the undulating ladder, managing to hand it over, step back a rung and salute. But Schorner was staring out over the little enclosure of the harbour, his eyes narrowing in the salt wind. The small craft were rolling uneasily like cattle in a pen. The lines of rounded helmets remained still, only a few putty faces turned towards him on his elevated place.

'Now hear this,' Schorner called into the loud-hailer. He was too close to it. The blurted shout sent gulls heaving into the mouldy sky. A dog set up a protesting bark in the village street. Schorner saw the doctor's car of Howard Evans pull around to stop before his safe and comfortable house. He noticed Beatrice Evans watching, very still in their cottage window. He felt a tinge of envy. At his shout the GIs had all turned their heads as if they were threaded and linked with wire. On the stone quay the assembled villagers pressed forward, eager to hear. Schorner wished they were not there. He felt like an actor performing an audition before people who had nothing to do with the play.

'You have to shift your mouth back, sir,' called the British sailor helpfully from the deck below. Schorner knew that and his acknowledgement of the advice was brusque.

'Now hear this,' he repeated at the right distance from the funnel. He was very conscious of the civilians, with the mountainous Meg in the centre, like a mother surrounded by children, pushing to the very edge of the harbour on the other side, their ears eager. God, why didn't he have them moved? It was too late now. And too difficult.

'This unit,' he called. Every gull for miles was circling now, a screeching halo over the little town and harbour. 'This outfit will proceed in –' he checked his watch '– in fifteen minutes to the harbour mouth and the open sea. You will be conducted three miles out and there will rendezvous with other assault units aboard vessels from Plymouth, Portland, Brixham and Dartmouth, for the simulated assault on Telcoombe Beach. Each one of you has received individual assignments and orders. You know what you have to do. You know what's expected. So do it.'

He paused and looked along the lines of dumb faces under the small roofs of the helmets that gave protection and, somehow, privacy. 'There are going to be a limited number of opportunities to get it right. Okay? Things may go wrong but I won't have this exercise being loused up by laziness, carelessness or

286

incompetence. What you are going to learn today could save *your* life and the lives of your buddies, when the real thing comes. So let's learn the lessons. Keep to your sections, keep to your orders. There will be a live bombardment from the sea but this will be aimed a half a mile ahead of the most advanced units. If these gunners can shoot straight we shouldn't have any casualties. Okay? Right, let's go.'

He tossed the loudhailer to the sailor on the deck below and climbed down the ladder. The gun-site soldiers watched his head go below the bulwark of the deck. Gilman felt sorry for the Americans. Catermole echoed his thoughts. 'Live bombardment,' he sniffed. 'From the sea. Bollocks to that. I wouldn't like those bloody matelots shooting within *ten* miles of me. Half the time they're pissed on that rum they get for nothing.'

Bullivant moved busily in front of them, his manner like that of a zealous policeman pushing a crowd. 'All right, you lot, back to breakfast,' he said. 'We've got a busy day. Come on, move. Move it.'

Gilman walked towards the mess hut with Catermole. 'What do we have to do today, Pussy?' he asked. He was not sure whether Bullivant could hear him but he did not care. 'Clean our nice gun, I suppose.'

'Got to keep the gun clean,' agreed Catermole loudly. 'Father Christmas wouldn't like it if we let the bang-bang get dirty.'

Bullivant, puce-faced, turned and stamped towards them like a spoilt and angry child. 'You two,' he seethed, still drumming his feet on the ground, on the spot. 'You *bloody* two!'

Gilman and Catermole turned to each other in hastily constructed astonishment. 'What, sarge?' inquired Catermole in a hushed tone. 'Us two? What did we do?'

'What did you *say*, that's more like it,' replied Bullivant still savagely but dropping his voice to a low rattle. He realized they were adjacent to Captain Westerman's window. 'I heard you taking the mickey. That gun –' He pointed dramatically as though he thought they might not know its location. 'That gun has brought down a German aircraft. Killed Germans. That's more than any of those Yanks have done. It's all very well playing games, but we've seen *action*. And no thanks to either of you. *Either*.'

They knew, as they all knew by now, that the Junkers had been hit by gunfire over Plymouth. It was an already-stricken bird.

'Watch it,' incanted Bullivant, his favourite threat. 'Just watch it. Or it will be a two-five-two. I'd love to have you on a charge, Gilman. Love it, I would. Take some of the bullshite out of you. Now get moving. This unit has been assigned air protection duties during the exercise. So let's see if you can be real soldiers.'

They watched him wobble fiercely away. They knew he was romancing again. The gun was not on alert because the valve was playing up again and the barrel could not be elevated. In any case, the Americans now had pockets of anti-aircraft guns and rockets all along the coast and enough fighter planes within minutes to deter or deal with any foolish German raider who ventured from France.

*

Thin sirens were tooting from the harbour as the landing craft pushed out; they sailed one at a time, joining like an ugly necklace behind the Landing Ship Tanks with the commanding officer aboard. Once out to sea they rolled grotesquely under the hulls of the ancient destroyers, the soldiers looking askance at the straight-fingered triple funnels of their naval protectors. The sea was moving moderately in wide, easy, grey waves that slid like vast hands under the flat barges and made the men pale and hold their stomachs. Schorner, now in his flak jacket and helmet, stood on the narrow bridge of the landing ship, its great middle occupied by fifteen clamped down trucks, his own command jeeps and half a dozen motorcycles with their dispatch riders. The motorcyclists sat astride their machines and eased up and down with the ploughing vessel, like riders on a fairground carousel. Hulton was white and cold. Bryant was aware of a tinge of chill sweat on his forehead below his British steel helmet.

'There's the good news,' said Schorner looking back. 'Smokey and Stover are moving.'

The two old destroyers were steaming slowly east, their stacks puffing, signal flags rippling. Even the simple manoeuvre of turning to starboard was necessitating a curve that would take them halfway across Start Bay. 'That's a good name for them, sir,' said Hulton watching them. Bryant asked: 'What does it mean?'

Hulton regarded him as if he ought to have known. 'Smokey Stover is a comic-strip character back home, Stateside,' he said. Bryant nodded as though that explained everything.

As they moved further out into the morning sea they became aware of dark dots strung across the horizon, moving from both east and west, and further out the square, misty forms of large ships. The mock invaders were assembling. A squadron of Mustang fighter planes abruptly arrived overhead and screamed across the proceeding barges at two hundred feet, causing the soldiers to duck, withdrawing their helmeted heads like tortoises. Now the morning was much lighter, the sky spreading a wan grey from along the throat of the Channel. There was the indication of a flat-skied day.

As Schorner's short fleet moved out to the rendezvous point, the two destroyers, having finally accomplished their manoeuvre, overtook the barges and went by only two hundred yards distant with flamboyant wash waves rolling from beneath their bellies. Schorner cursed them as the landing craft, and then the smaller barges, mounted each successive roller and slid sideways down the other flank. It was as if the warships were taking revenge for the soldiers' ridicule.

Now the joining fleets were almost in position, occupying much of the horizon, lying together, Schorner thought, like a herd of cattle waiting to be moved. The naval vessels at the rear and the one large American transport, from which he knew General Georgeton was watching the operation, stood off in the growing light. More fighter planes curled across and there were other reconnaissance aircraft droning high in the vacant air.

'Well, we got this far,' muttered Schorner as the landing craft reached the middle section of the fleet and inelegantly eased round into its assigned position, shepherding its covey of barges with it. Now the whole formation lay, rolling and waiting. A British sailor brought three mugs of coffee from below and the army officers drank gratefully. The captain of the LST, a British naval lieutenant, had not left the side of the wheelsman and had never looked around at his guests. Now the vessel was turned and waiting he walked the few paces across the steel deck, his half-empty coffee mug dangling negligently from one finger. 'Not too bad, hey?' he said through his nose. 'Got her out here. Now got to get her back.'

As always when faced with something British and strange, Schorner glanced at Bryant. Bryant returned a slight shrug. The young man said: 'I'm Young-husband, by the way. Lieutenant RNVR.' Bryant said: 'This is Colonel Schorner, US Army Engineers. And Captain Hulton. I'm Bryant, Royal Artillery.'

'Good,' said Younghusband in a manner which suggested he had been in some doubt about the matter and was glad it was now settled. He looked at the soldiers on the deck and then in the small craft in the sea. 'This is what we call trade,' he said. 'It's the lower end of the navy, you know. Long time since I saw so many brown jobs,' he said. 'Not since Dunkirk.'

He smiled, apparently at the memory, and turned back towards the wheelhouse. Now it was Hulton's turn to ask. 'Brown jobs?' he said. 'What the hell are brown jobs?'

'Soldiers, any sort of soldiers,' said Bryant. 'The Navy calls us brown jobs.'

'I wonder what kind of job he is?' suggested Hulton.

'They call the Navy the Andrew,' Bryant informed him. 'The sea is known as the hoggin, on the upper deck anyway. On the lower deck it's called the 'oggin.'

Schorner looked over the side at the swaying assault barges. 'Everybody okay down there?' he called. Fifty white faces under the lids of helmets looked up. Some smiled tightly, others murmured and others muttered. He pulled his head back. 'The way some of those guys look they'll be glad to be ashore on any beach, even if it's lousy with Germans,' he said.

A hollow siren sounded from the big US transport ship in the rear, followed by a crimson rocket that exploded and fell through the air like a trickle of blood. 'Okay, this is it,' said Schorner. He went quickly to the side again, picking up the loudhailer. 'Let's get it right first time,' he shouted again.

Few faces were upturned this time; most had gone back to staring straight ahead, as though each man was watching a narrow road. The smaller craft began to move forward, a long speckled line stretching a mile each side of the central transport ship.

Lieutenant Younghusband was watching HMS *Oregon*. The signal blinked brightly across the pale morning. He rang for quarter speed ahead and the landing ship rattled and began to move forward. Schorner raised his glasses and, looking across the backs of the assault craft now streaming ahead, he could see the brown seam of the beach and at its centre the white square that was the Telcoombe Beach Hotel, his target.

The blunt prows of the assault craft parted the sea as they travelled shoreward. Their propellers churned the morning surface to dirty cream. The soldiers crouched and waited, each young face already looking old. The cold sea showered over the metal hulls and sprayed them. They wiped the salt away. Each one knew that the pretence of this English morning would be translated, within a few months or even weeks, into a reality from which some of them would never return. They were silent, rolled by the waves; their occasional movements just the blink of the eyes and the regular churning of chewing gum.

Then, from behind and above them, they were shocked by the explosion of the guns from the distant warships. Each man ducked involuntarily as the naval shells howled over their heads, cutting through the empty air and exploding on the green uplands beyond the beach towards which they were journeying. First a salvo, then another, then a new sound, a screech as a flight of rockets rushed through the sky. The soldiers could see nothing because of the high prow of their craft, but they cared nothing either. Every man, at that moment, wanted to be one place. Home in the United States of America.

Schorner steadied his glasses on the surf-line. He was aware that Hulton had gone to the rail, probably to be sick. Bryant, pale, watched the approach carefully, bracing himself as each buck of the landing ship sent its squared nose heaving against the bleak sky. They were both conscious of Younghusband, the naval lieutenant, giving orders so quiet as to be like conversation as the flotilla moved towards the beach.

Shells were bursting like feathers on the expanses of upland green beyond the beach. A quiver of rockets seared above them and danced in a skirted chorus line as they struck the earth. Bryant wondered how much it was costing. Schorner turned and handed the glasses to him. 'That's rich dirt,' was all he said. 'Take a look.'

The young Englishman peered towards the land beyond the beach. Where the explosions had thrown up the fields there were mounds and circles of red Devon soil. It lay like wounds against the bright green of the pastures. His next instinctive movement was to seek out Telcoombe Magna Church. The spire thrust up clearly; smoke moved across it. He wondered how long it would stand. Then his eye caught something else. 'There's something moving on the beach, sir,' he said, pulling the strap of the glasses from his neck and handing them to Schorner.

'On the beach!' snorted Schorner. 'What the hell is it?'

The colonel glared through the glasses. 'It's a man,' he said. 'For God's sake it's a goddamn man. And . . . Jesus, a dog. I don't believe it . . .' As if he couldn't bear the sight he pushed the glasses back towards Bryant. Without looping them about his neck the English officer stared at the figure on the far right of the shingle. He could see a dinghy drawn up beyond the waterline. The man was digging and the dog was running around happily. They seemed serenely unaware of the shells looping across their heads and blowing up in the fields not half a mile beyond.

'He's digging for bait,' reported Bryant solemnly.

'I don't believe it,' breathed the colonel again. 'I just don't believe it.' He took the proffered glasses. 'How did he get by the road blocks?'

'He's got a boat,' pointed out Bryant.

'Sure,' said Schorner with a defeated sigh. 'He's got a boat.'

Hulton, attracted by the concern, lurched away from the rail. He was wiping the back of his hand across his mouth. His eyes were numb. 'Somebody on the beach?' he asked with all the incredulity he could muster.

'Digging for bait,' nodded Bryant.

'These English,' said Hulton. 'The whole country's mad.' He realized that he was standing next to Bryant.

Bryant smiled wanly. 'It must seem like that to an American,' he said enigmatically.

'Lieutenant!' Schorner called towards Young-husband next to the steersman. 'There's somebody on the beach.' Another flight of naval shells screeched over and the British officer had to delay his reply. Eventually he called: 'Yes, I saw him. Fisherman getting bait. Can't do anything now. If he gets blown to bits, that's his jolly fault, wouldn't you say, sir?'

'I sure would,' Schorner grunted. 'He won't be blown to bits, worse luck,' he added sourly. 'Not unless somebody's right off line. But, for God's sake, the bastard's right in the path of our landing.' He turned to Hulton. 'I want that dumb bastard arrested as soon as we hit that beach. Get a couple of heavy police guys to sit on him.'

'Right, sir,' said Hulton. 'I will.' He looked irritably towards the small, recumbent figure on the shingle. 'Fouling everything up,' he complained.

The first wave of troops were nearing the beach to the east now, almost among the surf. Schorner turned the glasses that way and then swept them to the other flank. The landing craft there were almost in line. His own assault group at the centre still had three hundred and fifty yards to go. He looked back at the bait-digger.

'That dog,' he said slowly as he realized. 'That's the dog that was there this morning, right? I fed him with cookies.'

He was conscious of Hulton and Bryant nodding. 'Just make sure I don't act kind to any more dogs,' muttered Schorner. 'I should have known.'

He checked on the distant flank assaults and saw that on the right the landing boats were against the shingle, being pushed and rocked by the moderate rollers coming into the beach. Soldiers were jumping over the sides and running down the ramps into the knee-deep water. He could hear their juvenile war cries coming across the bay even above the vibrant engine of the landing craft. On the left the assault had just made the beach. He could see men balancing on the hulls like clowns waiting until the craft levelled out before jumping. He sighed. Those men, on the real day, would never reach dry land.

Now his attention was taken by his own men, crouched in the boats ahead, bucking over the last waves before the landfall. He heard Younghusband giving orders down a tube; the clumsy craft eased back a hundred yards from the shore. Now the small boats were almost there, jumping among the froth at the sea's edge. He stared up the shingle. The bait-digger was still at his task, taking no note of the commotion of war behind him, above him and on each side. The dog had begun to run up and down barking excitedly. Schorner swore as he watched. The fisherman was in the direct line of the planned attack on the Telcoombe Beach Hotel. One assault boat had already needed to take avoiding action to miss the negligently-moored dinghy and was now twenty yards adrift of the others, sideways on in the short but difficult surf, trying to regain both its equilibrium and its station. A heavier roller pitched it further away. He saw the men jumping haphazardly overboard into the cold sea that engulfed them to the armpits. 'Damn that guy,' the colonel swore, looking towards the boat back on the beach. 'Damn him.'

On shore Schorner's first men, shouting and panting, wet to the waists, ran heavily up the steep shingle that collapsed and slid away under them. The GIs at the front, weapons aloft, reached the flat sandy shelf, there to be confronted by the fisherman and his dog. The dog frisked about with them, barking, its tail flailing. Solidly the man carried on with his bait-digging as though he were the only soul for miles. The bulky Ballimach, pounding up the incline with his coil of cable on his back, ran to the right of the fisherman. He, like the others, reacted with astonishment but, while the first soldiers had rushed on past the bait-digger, Ballimach paused, out of breath, and studied him. The fisherman glanced up, reached out to his bucket and brought it disdainfully closer to him. Then he returned to his digging. Ballimach moved on. The soldiers rushed by.

As the first wave reached the now derelict garden of the Telcoombe Beach Hotel, they flung themselves behind seams in the shingle and two tables of rock and began a stream of fire into the building. Every window went within a minute. A mortar bomb blew in the

297

door. A second wave took the place of the first and they pushed forward to the low wall that separated the garden from the beach. Automatic fire brought down the guttering that had been hanging perilously for years. Only now did the fisherman lift his head. He was surrounded by advancing troops, none of whom now spared him more than a quick and curious glance. His dog was cavorting along the beach, yelping and leaping among the men. 'Silas,' he called gruffly. 'Silas, you come 'ere, boy. You be getting in the way.'

As he spoke he was flattened to the wet sand and pebbles by the assault of two heavy military police-men. They thrust him to the ground and held him there, face down. He managed to move his head to one side; one cheek was pressed deep into the slippery sand. His dog bounced joyously at the game.

''Ee get off, the pair of 'ee,' threatened the Devonian from the corner of his mouth. 'Oi be gettin' damaged.'

Schorner, Hulton and Bryant arrived in a group, Bryant attempting to get to his countryman first. They had disembarked from the landing craft as soon as it had buried its nose into the beach and ran up the incline. Bryant got there first. 'Right,' he said to the snowdrops. 'Let him go.'

They looked doubtfully at the English officer but then saw Schorner and Hulton a few yards away and at once obeyed. The fisherman sat up, rubbing his neck and his shoulders unhurriedly. Bryant saw the whiskery face of Old Daffy. 'That 'urt, that did,' he complained.

'For God's sake, man,' shouted Bryant above the

noise of the firing and explosions all around. 'You shouldn't be here at all. This beach is closed – and you bloody well know it.'

The two Americans were now stopped, looking at him. 'The *roads* be blocked,' pointed out the man with what appeared like patience and logic. 'But there's nothin' to stop oi comin' 'ere in the dinghy. This is where I get my bait. And there's you buggerin' it up with all this.' He waved his arm at the battle.

Schorner was about to say something when he heard orders being shouted from the direction of the hotel. In the immediate area the firing had ceased, although on either flank it was still clattering and the naval shells and rockets flew overhead towards the hinterland. The colonel cursed again as he saw that his men near the hotel were vainly trying to catch the fisherman's sandy dog which was running and curving between them, enjoying the fun as they grabbed and missed and jumped at it and missed again. 'Shoot the goddamn thing!' howled Hulton.

'Don' you go shootin' my dog,' threatened the captive fisherman. 'You shoot 'ee and I'll complain . . .'

All further words were superfluous. The dog made a final dash between the men, leapt the wall of the abandoned hotel and rushed barking through the front door. In a moment there was a huge explosion. The hotel seemed to lift itself from the ground. A blast threw the three officers and the military policemen into a bundle with Old Daffy below them. Debris began to cascade from the sky. Hulton, without raising his head, said peevishly: 'He trod on a mine. Stupid dog.'

Fragments of masonry, wood and shingle fell about

them, and ahead the sandy dust rose like a copse. Their ears were numb and their faces full of grit from the beach. As the debris settled and the dust cloud began to drift away on the breeze the three officers, the military policemen and the fisherman eased up their heads. It was the Devonian who had the first word. 'If you gone and killed my dog, mister, oi goin' to complain,' he said.

Hulton looked as if he might say something, wiping the dust from his mouth, but Schorner was already moving at an anxious run towards the wrecked hotel. Bryant was just behind him. He could see now that a great bite had been taken out of the middle of the building. The dust still swirled and the explosion still sang in his head. Other heads were rising from the shingle. Schorner bawled: 'Everybody stay where they are! Get it – stay where you are.'

'Nobody moves!' shouted Hulton unnecessarily.

The fisherman, trying to follow them, was being restrained firmly by the dust-faced MPs. 'That were a good dog,' he told them miserably.

Now Schorner, Hulton and Bryant had reached what had been the perimeter of the hotel garden. The wall was low and much of the blast had travelled across it. Guns were sounding on both flanks but these abruptly ceased and they walked in an odd silence, broken only by the fall of a window that had been tenuously hanging on to its frame. Its shattering made them jump. Bryant noticed that the children's swing in the garden was moving to and fro.

Then Schorner stopped. In the dip of the garden, where it reached the hotel, were the sprawled figures of three American soldiers. Bryant, looking down at them, realized he had witnessed the first men to die for the invasion.

Gilman was shaving in front of the mirror in the barrack room, so crazed and yellowed that it looked as if an egg had been thrown at it. On a raw February evening the washroom was too cold for human use. There had been noses of ice on the taps that morning. Catermole was already in his marching-out uniform and came to stand behind Gilman, clumsily adjusting the ugly collar of his tunic beneath his ugly face. 'I wonder what lucky big girl is going to have me tonight,' he mused.

Gilman grinned, making a fissure in the lather. 'You and I, friend, will be rolling back here together, drunk as monkeys and telling each other we never cared about women anyway,' he forecast. 'The nearest we'll get to anything warm and slippery is a bag of fish and chips.'

'Get off,' chided Catermole. 'It's Valentine's Night, mate.'

'It's Valentine's Night for the Yanks too,' pointed out Gilman.

'They got their own hop at Newton Abbot,' said Catermole confidently. 'They'll all be there. They won't come to Wilcoombe, will they?'

'Neither will the women,' answered Gilman.

Catermole moved away and ran the toecaps of his boots along the blanketed side of the nearest bed, which was not his. He inspected them carefully. 'You'll get no kudos for clean boots,' Gilman told him.

'You have to kid them you've got a ranch in Texas and money coming out of your bum.'

'Lay off,' grumbled Catermole. 'You're making me feel like I ought to stay here and get into bed with *Health and Efficiency*.' Gilman had finished shaving and was rubbing his face. '*You* ought to be laughing anyway,' said the other man. 'You've got yours all laid on.'

Gilman grimaced. 'I bet,' he said. 'She's not exclusively mine, you know, Pussy. I doubt it anyway.'

Catermole became philosophical. 'Well you 'ave to share things in the war, don't you. Trouble is some other bugger's getting my bit.'

Gilman did up the distasteful collar around his neck, its tight roughness on his Adam's apple. 'God, I'd like just to wear a collar and tie, just bloody once,' he said. 'This is like a rope around your neck.'

He put some Brylcreem on his hair and rubbed it in. Catermole had used water on his. He glanced thoughtfully at the Brylcreem and took a fingerful. He applied that to his scraggy scalp, then combed it down before looking at himself in the mirror. 'Sod it,' he said profoundly. 'I look like one of the Three bleeding Stooges.' They put their boat-shaped caps on in unison, both looked pessimistically in the mirror again, and made for the door.

At the other end of the hut Walt Walters was stretched out on his bed. He called to them, 'Don't wear it out, boys.'

'Who you keeping yours for?' asked Catermole truculently. 'It'll be gone off by the end of the war.'

'Vera Lynn,' answered Walt, holding the iron rail above his head and giving it a gymnastic pull so that

302

his thin body left the mattress as though levitated. 'Vera Lynn will be creeping around 'ere soon. She always does after you lot have cleared out.'

Gilman laughed with Catermole. 'She going to sing for you then?'

'That's right, mucker. She'll be singing "This is Worth Fighting for".'

They left him and went out into the edgy night. The customary wind was blowing off the bay but the sky was clear and the stars looked low and blue. Catermole sighed. 'Bloody 'ell mate, I hope it's not just fish and chips.'

Ballimach knotted his pale khaki tie under the rolling throat and smoothed his tunic over the mound of his stomach. 'Do I look like a general?' he asked at large. 'Or do I look like a general?'

'Sure, like a general store,' said Albie Primrose. 'Listen, even if you get a broad to dance with you she's going to be so far away you ain't going to be able to talk to her. You ought to dump some of that stuff.'

'Okay Pinocchio,' replied Ballimach huffily. 'We all know you'll be clattering around the dance floor on those little wooden legs.' He regarded himself in the billet's full-length mirror. Reality stared at him. 'How can I help it?' he moaned. 'I just got shaped like this.'

'Try eating less chow,' suggested Wall. He was grooming his dark hair with confidence. He showed himself his regular teeth and touched a few of them with the end of his finger.

'Quit counting your goddam piano keys,' snorted Ballimach. 'For Christ's sake, I have to eat, don't I? I got a big space to fill.' He glanced at Primrose, easier game than the handsome Wall. 'Anyway, a dame will know she's got a real guy when I've got her,' he said. 'She'll have to feel around for you, Pinocchio. Even then, maybe she won't even find you. You want to grow up to be a real, live boy.'

Wall was satisfied. He eased his cap carefully on to the extreme side of his head, where it clung daringly. 'You guys better hurry,' he said. 'That love wagon goes in five minutes. You don't want to disappoint all those hungry Limey girls, do you?'

Ballimach glanced at Primrose, and the small man, taking responsibility, said to Wall. 'We didn't figure on going to the big ball. Not at Newton Abbot. That's not for us. We figured we'd go to Wilcoombe. They got a Valentine's Dance there too.'

Wall looked stunned. 'Wilcoombe?' he breathed. 'You're kidding. *Wilcoombe!* God, there'll only be a few hill-billies there.'

'That don't worry us,' answered Ballimach almost shyly. 'We kinda like hill-billies.'

'Aw, come on. You guys just don't care for the competition,' taunted Wall baring his teeth again. 'You know you just don't stand a chance in the big time.'

'Big time? What's big-time about Newton Abbot?' demanded Albie. 'It ain't exactly Broadway.'

'There's going to be negroes,' said Ballimach slowly and archly. His big eyes slowly moved up to meet those of Wall. 'Lots of negroes. Big negroes.'

'So, okay. So they have to take second place.'

Albie said: 'It ain't that we're prejudiced, don't get that idea. It's just that there's going to be a whole lot of fighting in that place. Whites and negroes. There'll be blood on the ground, take it from me.'

Ballimach nodded his support. 'A whole ocean of blood,' he said.

'Drop dead,' replied Wall making for the door. He looked back doubtfully. 'There'll be lots of police,' he added. 'They'll see everything is okay. You guys coming?' He nodded towards the night.

'No, we'll go along and dosey-doe with the hicks,' said Ballimach. 'They don't punch as hard as those niggers.'

From the outside darkness men were whooping and Wall, with a final look from which the doubt had not entirely been erased, went from the billet. Albie looked with equal uncertainty at Ballimach. 'You think maybe we ought to go with them?' he suggested.

'No, to hell,' said Ballimach. 'It'll be okay for you, pal, you're a small target. I got plenty of me for some Joe Louis to hit.'

Gilman and Catermole lounged against the splinter-rough bar of the Wilcoombe village hall, watery beer in their disconsolate tankards, hopelessness in their expressions; the Wilcoombe band supplemented by four retired dance-band musicians who had graced the Imperial Hotel, Torquay, before the war, played with disjointed enthusiasm for the half dozen couples alternately rushing and revolving on the floor.

'Did they say this was a bloody tango?' inquired Catermole before sucking a seam of beer from the glass. 'A bloody tango?'

'That's what they said,' confirmed Gilman. Chalk

from the wooden floor was all over his boots and those of Catermole. Looking down he said: 'We look like Russians, Pussy.'

'Well, this don't look like a tango,' answered Catermole still in the hurt voice. As if to confirm that it was, one of the dancers, the Reverend Sissons, galloped towards them driving a lady in a pre-war wedding dress. Eric Sissons liked to dance and thought he could. He came at the two soldiers with long Groucho Marx steps, sweeping his partner alongside him like an outrigger. Chalk flew from the floor. He bent the lady backwards almost under the ledge of Catermole's beer tankard. The soldier removed it hurriedly and stared down at the pale pan of the woman's face hanging directly below his own. The Reverend Sissons jerked her upright and swooped away.

'An' he calls hisself a vicar,' he grumbled. He wiped the chalk from the toes of his boots, rubbing each one on the opposite leg of his trousers.

'You're only jealous, mate,' commented Gilman mischievously.

Catermole snorted. 'Over that? That bag of rat bones. Looks like he dug her up from 'is graveyard.'

Gilman was, as though casually, watching the door. Every five minutes two or three village people would hustle in out of the rain but Mary Nicholas was not among them. She would be at Newton Abbot, he thought, naturally, where the men were. He drained his beer and taking his tankard and Catermole's he asked the girl behind the bar to refill them. She was a plump landgirl, with, tonight, an unsuitable pink ribbon in her hair and rouge on her cheeks.

Catermole had rudely inquired whether she said Mama and Dadda and moved her arms and legs.

The man who was leading the band, Mr Penningford, had, before the war, been first a cinema pianist and then an organist in Exeter. He conducted with a permanently pained face, every bar another insult. He brought the tango to a premature close like someone trying to put the brakes on a runaway truck. When all the musicians finally reached a standstill he glared at them. 'Oi can understand you not startin' together,' he said loudly across the wooden podium which held his balding music sheets. 'But oi don' know why you can't finish 'un off together. By that time, surely to God, you ought to 'ave caught up with each other.'

The band looked chastened. 'We'll try a waltz,' he said less severely. 'One, two, three, one, two, three. Maybe 'ee won't confuse you so much.'

His teeth had either been measured for someone else or his face had shrunk around them. They projected from his jaw. He faced the sparse dancers and smiled like a trap. ''Tis a waltz next,' he announced. He half turned back to the band before whirling around again with a terrible jokey grin. 'A lady's invitation waltz,' he added devilishly. 'Come on, ladies, now be your chance.'

'I'm going for a piss,' said Catermole briskly. He put his beer down fiercely. 'I'm not letting any old boot in 'ere get her hands on me.'

He was making for the door when three bright landgirls, laughing and rosy, came in. He marched backwards towards Gilman again. Gilman laughed. The be-ribboned girl behind the bar called to the new arrivals and they walked across sturdily, taking their heavy brown coats off as they did so. Underneath they had on their best dresses. Catermole beamed. 'Lady's excuse me,' he said loudly against the ear of the first girl to approach the bar.

She regarded him with wartime confidence. 'Then you'll have to excuse *me*,' she said. 'I've been working with the pigs all day.'

'Poor bloody pigs,' said Catermole loudly, defiantly. Then to the smiling Gilman, 'I *will* go for a piss then.'

'Do that,' advised the girl seriously. 'Enjoy yourself. There's a war on.'

The three had coarsely greeted their friend behind the bar. They ordered beer at the bar and stood drinking it swaggeringly and talking loudly and roughly. Gilman, half-listening, half-watching, thought how women had changed. The war had done that. It was as though a hard covering, a husk, had grown over them. They had put on trousers, despite great controversy, and abandoned the role of softness that had been theirs for hundreds of years. Now, their hands, faces and voices thickened, their hair often concealed by the universal turban, they had become another species. He heard one of the landgirls unselfconsciously say 'fuck'.

Catermole came back. 'Nobody asked you to dance?' he said to Gilman, and nodding at the girls. 'Losing your charm?'

'I told them I was promised,' whispered Gilman. He was still looking at intervals at the door. Mary Nicholas had not arrived and he doubted if she would now. She was probably gone off with somebody else.

As he watched, through the black out hanging at the door came two Americans, Albie and Ballimach. 'The Yanks are here,' he said sideways to Catermole. The landgirls heard and turned. They groaned a collective complaint. They returned to the bar and the beer. Albie and Ballimach, smiling sheepishly, approached the bar but were waylaid by the vicar with extravagant greeting.

'Welcome, welcome to our allies,' he enthused sliding across the chalky floor, a bow-wave of white powder rising over the toe-caps of his patent leather dancing pumps. Nervously Albie and Ballimach backed away. Gilman and Catermole looked on amused. The landgirls had turned and were watching.

'I'm a Catholic,' said Albie hurriedly, as if he felt the confession might save him from something.

'And me, I'm a Jew,' put in Ballimach just as promptly.

'No matter, no matter,' Sissons assured them shaking the small hand of Albie and the big paw of Ballimach at the same time. Gilman heard one of the landgirls sneer: 'Jews.' He turned quickly but she had gone back to giggling with her friends. No one else seemed to hear it except Catermole who turned and grinned stupidly towards the woman as if wanting to share the joke.

For a moment Gilman thought that the vicar was going to buy a drink for the Americans but Sissons saw Doey, Lenny and some of the other villagers coming in the door, struggling their way through the green blackout blanket; he went like a skater across the floor to meet them. Gilman turned to Ballimach and said:

'Would you and your pal like a beer?' Catermole looked surprised but he put on his wide, vacant smile and beamed towards the Americans in a comradely way. He put his tankard on the bar next to Gilman's.

'Gee, thanks. That's very friendly,' responded Ballimach.

'Certainly is,' said Albie. 'Just a little one for me. I have to take this British beer a little at a time.'

None of the soldiers introduced themselves. When the drinks came they lifted their glasses to each other. The landgirls began complaining loudly about men buying drinks for each other before they bought drinks for ladies. Gilman turned slightly: 'I didn't think you counted yourselves as ladies any more,' he said.

'Go and shit,' said the one who had made the remark about the Jews.

'See what I mean,' he said to the other men.

The landgirls began to move away from the bar. 'What a twat,' said one over her shoulder as she went.

Gilman shrugged and smiled at the Americans. 'She should know, I suppose,' he said.

'Who are those girls?' asked Albie. 'They don't seem very friendly.'

'Landgirls,' answered Catermole. 'They get like that through living in dung.'

Gilman said to Ballimach, 'I saw you going on the exercise the other morning, on to the landing craft in the harbour. You're the man carrying the reel of telephone wire on his back.'

Ballimach gave a funny bow. 'That's me,' he said. 'Biggest star of the show.' His mobile face rolled forward. 'And the biggest target, I guess. God, if *you*

310

picked me out so easy, what about the goddamn Germans?'

'Maybe you could carry a white flag or a red cross,' suggested Albie with a sly grin. 'The red cross would be better. Maybe they'd mark you down as a mobile hospital. Then they won't shoot you.'

Ballimach grimaced. 'I don't know about the real thing, pal, but the rehearsal was lousy. I had sand up my ass for days.'

'You lost some men, didn't you?' asked Gilman. 'We heard about it.'

'Sure,' said Ballimach sadly. 'Three guys.' He caught Albie's eye. It was supposed to be secret. 'What the hell,' he said fiercely but not raising his voice. 'I don't see why those guys should just be hushed up. They died didn't they? Just like they was in battle.' He gave a short wave of his fat hand. 'The people around here, they ain't stupid,' he argued. 'They know real shooting from dummy fucking shooting. And that was real shooting and it was a real set of mines that blew up and killed our guys.'

'It was a dog that did it,' put in Albie. He sighed across the top of the beer. 'A crazy dog. He went into that goddamn hotel just as our guys were a couple of yards away. We'd been warned about the mines, to keep away from the building, but I guess that dog wasn't around when the orders went out. He was with some guy, some nut digging for fishing bait on the beach.'

'Digging for bait?' said Gilman. 'A civilian?'

The Americans nodded together, but without emphasis, worried about giving offence.

'Bad enough the Germans killing you,' agreed

311

Catermole solidly. He glanced over his shoulder. The landgirls were sitting in a dogged row, stony wallflowers, glowering challengingly towards the four soldiers. Catermole sniffed. 'I've tormented this lot long enough,' he said. 'I don't want them peeing their drawers.' Gilman smiled and shook his head slowly. Catermole finished his beer with a wet flourish, wiped his mouth with his hand and marched heavily across the floor. With a suggestion of a bow from his thick frame he began at one end of the female line and, having been sulkily refused a dance, went along, being rejected by each of the glowering girls, until the last one, who was smaller, uglier and wore peering spectacles, agreed to dance. The band was playing a quickstep and like many big men Catermole was light on his feet. He spun and fishtailed across the white-clouded floor dragging the slight girl along. She clung on to his neck desperately like a limp albatross.

Gilman and the two Americans looked on with amused expressions. Ballimach rubbed the chalk from his shoes with his army handkerchief. Then from outside the hall came the deep snort of a heavy motor vehicle. The band had come to the end of the quickstep and Catermole sauntered back to the others leaving the stringy landgirl to stagger back to her friends. 'She was real small,' mentioned Albie, who appreciated other small people.

'She's a wet-nurse to the pigs,' said Catermole coarsely. The remark went beyond either Albie or Ballimach. Gilman made a face. In the break between dances, Mr Penningford, the bandleader, dabbed his brow with a red handkerchief, keeping it fixed across his forehead for a moment, an action which gave him the appearance of a wounded man. There came a further cough of the vehicle outside. It stopped and voices sounded. The soldiers looked expectantly towards the blackout blanket. It flurried and in came a confused-looking bus driver, his cap with a grim off-white crown hanging crookedly over his sparse ears, dead cigarette wedged in his mouth.

'How far be it to Newton Abbot?' he demanded of all present. He looked about him like a sparrow. There were random answers, and rudery from the landgirls who were getting drunk. They collapsed against each other in giggles. 'It's twenty-three miles,' said the vicar with certainty. He pointed dramatically like an evangelist in the direction of Newton Abbot.

'Gor, never make it,' sighed the man. 'The old bus won't get up the 'ills. She ought to 'ave been scrap years ago.'

'Can't help you, I'm afraid,' said Sissons positively, thinking that they might be asked to go out into the inclement night and push the vehicle. Voices came from outside. Loud and demanding female voices. Gilman glanced at Catermole. 'Who are your passengers?' inquired the vicar benevolently. 'Perhaps we can accommodate them or be of some help.'

The man removed the defunct cigarette from his tight lips and regarded it quizzically as if wondering where the rest of it had gone. 'Ladies,' he said finally, having thought over the word. 'Ladies from Plymouth, reverend. Going to the Yankees' dance at Newton Abbot. Now they ain't goin' to be getting there.'

Sissons said brightly: 'What a shame. Never mind, bring them in here. We're having quite a jolly time and I think we could make room for a few extra ladies. Might brisk up the dancing a bit. Yes, tell them to come in.'

It appeared that the driver was going to protest. Then, apparently realizing some advantage in the situation, he smiled a cracked smile, replaced the dead butt and nodded: 'That's very Christian of you, vicar,' he said.

Sissons laughed. 'Right you are,' he said.

'Right,' agreed the man sagely. 'I'll send them in, these ladies. Then I'll go empty up the hill and turn the bus around. It'll be pointing downwards then, when they want to go back to Plymouth. If they want to . . .'

He turned and sauntered back towards the blanket-covered door. As he did so the band stumbled into another quickstep and the bus driver did a few deft and jolly steps with an imaginary partner as he went. The vicar approved of this good nature and said, aslant, to Gilman who was standing close by: 'Very good chap. Indomitable, that sort, don't you think?'

Catermole, who thought Sissons was addressing him, became aghast at the word indomitable. He glanced at Gilman like a boy might look towards his father. Gilman nodded towards the vicar. 'Indomitable,' he agreed. 'That sort.'

Taking a consoling swig of his beer Catermole confirmed: 'Indomitable.' He turned in disgust towards the bar. 'Another of them bloody Churchill words,' he muttered. 'Every bugger is walking around saying words like that these days. Just as if they'll win the bleeding war.'

The vicar jollily moved off. Gilman was saying:

'Churchill's got a lot to answer for,' when the black-out blanket wobbled like a fat dancer and was pushed away violently by a painted woman with her hair dyed fiery red; great mouth and black stockings. Behind her came another, blonde, daubed with rouge and powder, bandy as a barrel.

'Bloody hell,' he breathed to Catermole and the Americans. 'It's a whores' outing.'

It was exactly that. A dozen of them came through the curtain, each one making an entrance as though on a stage. A black-haired mystery woman with a twitching eyelid, a curly blonde with a massive nose, a short vicious-looking matron, a rancid-looking girl of about seventeen in a red dress powdered with cigarette ash and a funny buxom lady who lifted her skirt above her swollen knees and performed a brief hornpipe just inside the door. Others followed, thin women, swollen women, women with mouths like caves, skin like leather.

'Welcome,' whispered Sissons, whose expression had disintegrated a fraction more with each entry. He was trembling with confusion. 'Wilcoombe to Welcome.'

His mistake caused great hilarity among the jaunty ladies. The bus driver poked his small wicked face around the curtain and called: 'That be the lot, vicar,' in the manner of a man who had completed a delivery. 'Now you just be careful.'

The prostitutes plunged into a rude hilarity at this. The flabby blonde woman had no roof to her mouth and brayed like a donkey. 'Cheeky little sod,' said the one who had done a dance with her bulging knees. 'I'll give him a kick up the jacksie when he comes back.'

315

She pushed imperiously towards the bar. 'I s'pose we'll have to buy our own bloody drinks,' she said.

The landgirl with the pink ribbon stood transfixed behind the counter, like a doll prize in a shooting gallery. Suddenly the woman from Plymouth was upon her, demanding scotch. The other landgirls had watched with mute amazement and now shifted protectively towards each other like threatened virgins.

No one but the recently arrived whores made any movement, except the ogling band which continued to play, now even more raggedly, Mr Penningford looking beyond his ear to see what was happening. Albie and Ballimach, shuffling sideways, had almost hidden themselves behind Gilman and Catermole. The British soldiers stood transfixed while the Americans peered apprehensively around their allies' khaki shoulders.

They were not long concealed. 'Ooooooh . . . Yanks!' squeaked the yellow seventeen-year-old. She brushed an avalanche of ash from her front and rushed at Albie Primrose. He tried to hurry behind Ballimach, who was behind Catermole. But the ravaged red-head who had entered first now made a target of the fat American. Catermole felt the GI tremble as she came forward. 'Come on, dearie,' she bawled. 'Buy me a drink and I promise you a good one.'

Albie and Ballimach were forcibly pulled into the open, the drinks ordered through the crowd of harlots, and the dollars, nervously produced but quickly grabbed, were swept across the counter. They flung the first consignment of spirits down their throats,

316

coughed and heaved, lit cigarettes and looked around for prey. Under loud threats from the leader of the pack the band had begun to play a foxtrot and Albie Primrose and Ballimach found themselves thrust on to the chalk-strewn floor in the formidable arms of the two women who had selected them.

Gilman, believing there was a threat of a scene if he did not dance with the black-rooted blonde, reluctantly took her heavy hand and projecting shoulder blade and tottered on to the floor. She felt adhesive under her blouse. Catermole, shrinking like a boy, was engulfed by the curly blonde with the gash for a mouth. The Reverend Sissons remained in a corner surveying the scene with an expression of fear. Doey Bidgood stood, cider glass at his chest, by the band. 'Oi reckon these be women of ill repute, vicar,' he announced loudly and with relish. His rural eyes rolled. 'Fornicators.'

'I'm certain it will be all right as long as they behave,' muttered Sissons inadequately. He wondered if he ought to call Police Constable Lethbridge and, as he wondered, so his apprehension increased with an outburst of cat-calling from the landgirls sitting on the cross-wall. They had banded together, like a clutch of hens on a roost, but the effrontery of the invasion and further beer had given them a rude anger.

Ballimach glanced nervously in that direction as he danced with the whore who had selected him. 'Listen, chuck,' she urged in his hair-hung ear, 'for five dollars we can go outside and I'll give you the best time you ever did have. Chuck, I'll destroy you.'

The big American blinked. 'Destroy me?' he questioned.

'Blow you out in bubbles,' she promised.

Albie was similarly entwined with the apprentice. 'Me, I'm fresher,' she boasted. 'See, I'm only seventeen. And I've got more go than any of these shagged out old cows.' She nodded uncharitably at her sisters in sin. 'Give us two dollars now and two after and you won't have the strength to grumble, I promise you. I'll make you feel like a real man.'

'I *am* a real man,' argued Albie plaintively; the memory of Ballimach calling him Pinocchio returned even at this dire moment.

'I'll make you a realer one,' she vowed vehemently. They revolved on the dance floor and he got a draught of her cheap sweet scent. Now he saw that one of her blue eyes had a twist. 'I've got my mac with me,' she urged. 'Two dollars now, two after I done it. We'll go out now and find a place. All right?'

Albie regarded her with proper horror. 'Outside?' he queried, frowning. 'In the open air?'

'We can't do it in 'ere can we,' she said. She was becoming impatient, glancing quickly around to see if there were other possibilities.

'But I take cold so quickly,' defended Albie. 'I really don't think I could . . .'

'Little prick,' she snarled, thrusting her ugly young face into his. 'Go an' screw yourself.'

She let go of him and he backed away towards the bandstand. 'That might be healthier,' he ventured defiantly. The girl had almost got to the bar with illtempered strides. When he called after her she swiftly turned and went at him like a scorpion. Albie backed away, colliding with Doey who was watching mesmerized. Doey's cider spilled over Albie's uniform tunic. The little American turned, apprehensive, apologetic. Doey shouted at him: 'Look ye out there, gaffer!' If Albie did not understand the dialect the urgent tone and pointed finger were enough. He turned to see the young hag only a yard away, a half-full beer glass in one hand, her handbag swinging in her fist on the other side. It burst open at the blow and its contents scattered across the chalky floor.

Albie with instinctive, small town politeness, said: 'Oh my, I'm sorry.' He bent to retrieve a gaudy powder compact, but no sooner had he recovered it and looked up with the thin smile of an anxious-to-please dog, than the beer from the tankard was flung into his button face.

Everyone in the room, the villagers, the soldiers and the visiting whores, had, until then, been transfixed by the developing crisis. The band had wound woefully down and two lines of eyes like quavers were staring from the bandstand. But with the impact of thrown beer on Albie's innocent expression the spell broke. The prostitute screamed with gutter mirth, above which the vicar's pulpit voice cried out for order and common sense. The villagers began shouting.

'Shame! Throw they dirty strumpets out!' bellowed Fat Meg from the bar corner where she was wedged, her meaty forearms on the wood. The presence of women even less prepossessing than her gave her a novel lift.

It was the landgirls who took the first positive action. In a way which suggested they had been only awaiting the signal they charged across the room and pitched with enjoyment and fury into the phalanx of harlots. The undersized girl who had first danced with

Catermole went like a vengeful lizard towards the still screaming teenager who had drenched Albie Primrose. 'Cow!' she howled. 'Rotten dirty cow.' With the instinctive attack of the English schoolgirl she made directly for the eyes and when she could do them only surface damage she grasped the young prostitute's hair and began to swing her around with surprising power.

Everywhere was uproar. Gilman and Catermole, with Ballimach hesitant but then lending his widespread weight to the task, waded into battle, trying to tug the women apart. Gilman was thrown bodily against the bar, colliding with the ribboned landgirl who was clambering across it battle-bent like a soldier going over the top of a trench. Ballimach was kicked brutally on the legs and, while he hopped, received a winding blow in the testicles. He flopped, shocked, against the bandstand, went even more pale and grasped the affronted parts as if taking a count. Catermole had manoeuvred one of the screaming landgirls into a corner and was voluptuously trying to subdue her tantrum by looping his arms about her. The Reverend Sissons scuttled to Mr Penningford and ordered: 'The National Anthem, *quickly*!'

'I 'ope to God these silly buggers know it,' said the bandleader dubiously, turning towards the musicians. He shouted at them: ' "God Save the King".'

The vicar muttered: 'And the rest of us.' He waved his arms helplessly like a random blessing over the mob. Almost everyone had joined in now, the fray becoming more violent and widespread with the distinction between friend and enemy waning. Doey and Lenny were trying to contain a private fight between Fat Meg and the harlot with no roof to her mouth. They had managed to push them into a corner and had corralled them with a village hall bench which they held like a gate across the angle. Lustily, and surprisingly together, or at least adjacent, the band blew into 'God Save the King'. It had not the smallest effect. Amid the mayhem the Reverend Sissons stood at solitary attention singing the brave words.

Legs and suspenders were spread-eagled over the floor. One of the prostitutes had lit a newspaper and was brandishing it like a torch. Horrified, the vicar ploughed through the bedlam and attempted to wrest it from her. 'Fire!' he bellowed. 'Fire!' He found himself felled by the Plymouth fist of the torch-bearer. The band came to a stop, and at the single order, 'Lads!' from their leader they disembarked from the bandstand in a foolish attempt to rescue the vicar. Before the majority had reached the chalky floor Mr Penningford was lying prone, covered in white dust, felled by an accidental blow from Ballimach. Now there were no non-combatants. The main battle was a pile of shouting bodies between the bandstand and the bar with skirmishes occupying several corners. The Plymouth sisters were not without allies. Doey had been struck a fearful blow with a misdirected chair thrown by Meg and he and Lenny were now trying to pin the large, bellowing woman to the floor among the band instruments and music stands.

At the height of the disorder the stringy bus driver, having persuaded his vehicle to turn at the summit of Wilcoombe Hill, entered the hall around the black-out blanket. Confronted with the scene his expression scarcely faltered. He transferred the skeletal cigarette from one edge of his mouth to the other, tightened his eyes, sniffed heavily and quietly withdrew.

Outside in the damp street he was immediately met by Police Constable Lethbridge who was propping his bicycle against the wall of the village hall. ''Evening officer,' said the driver tentatively.

''Ow be you?' returned the constable. He cocked his ear to the noise, enclosed within the corrugated iron of the building. His expression became puzzled.

'Good dance, be it?' he inquired cautiously.

'Oi think you better 'ave a look,' suggested the other man sagely. 'Oi be going to sit quiet in my bus.' He moved away with studied lack of hurry and the constable, asking himself aloud: 'Be it that "Okey Cokey" they be doin'?' went through the door. As he reached the blind side of the curtain it was violently torn from its wooden rings by unseen hands and collapsed like a broken sail across the top of two rolling bodies.

The scene revealed left the policeman sag-mouthed. Exhaustion was forcing most of the contenders to break off their various engagements and they were staggering to the walls and chairs to recover. Several women were still writhing on the boards, their faces patched white from the chalk. Police Constable Lethbridge squinted through the dust and saw the Reverend Sissons sitting, bent almost double, on one of the band stools.

'Somethin' been going on, vicar,' he asked.

'A slight disagreement, officer,' gasped Sissons caustically. 'Nothing you need to worry yourself about. All part of St Valentine's Day.'

322

It was intended as heavy sarcasm. The policeman sniffed deeply, and replied: 'Right you be, sir.' He touched his helmet and left, calling over his shoulder 'Goodnight all.'

An hour later, under a ragged moon, Gilman, Ballimach and Albie Primrose were walking and laughing down Wilcoombe Hill towards the harbour. The wind, coming off the Channel, buffeted their faces and flung their voices. Catermole had gone off smirking with the thin landgirl.

'God Almighty, did you see that poor bloody clergyman when she hit him,' gurgled Gilman. They had spent the past hour helping to clear up the debris in the village hall and drinking what was left of the beer. The whores had been pushed and pummelled into their bus and had clanked off to Plymouth shouting scorn and defiance. Mr Penningford, bruised in body and pride, had told the vicar that he would never conduct in the village again and the Reverend Sissons had replied brusquely that there would be no call for him to do so. One of the cymbals had been stolen and under cover of the fighting someone had put a fresh turd in the bandleader's hat. It had not been the best of evenings.

The three soldiers now stumbled down the cobbled slope, touched with moonlight, recalling each successive disaster and rolling about in their merriment. When they came to Mary Nicholas's house Gilman's smile diminished and he looked to see if there were lights in the window. There were none, but Albie saw him looking. 'Hey, do you know that lady too?' he asked genuinely. 'The one with the great figure and the two kids.'

'What do you mean – too? As well as who?' asked Gilman still looking to the windows. It might just be that she was standing there in the dark, looking into the street.

'All sorts of guys,' said Albie ingenuously. 'Boy, does she have some ass. I've seen her walking along the street, and you better believe it, she has. The guys say she likes company.' He looked at Gilman suddenly, aware all at once that he might be talking out of place. 'Is she a friend of yours?'

Gilman shrugged. 'No, not specially. She's got a husband anyway.'

'Right,' confirmed Albie. 'There's a story, he's some kind of spy. Maybe he ought to do some spying on his own house.'

They had walked beyond now and Gilman pushed it from his mind. After all, he had known. He briefly wondered how many Americans had been on that damp bunk in the air-raid shelter; then he thrust it aside. Christ, he *had* known. He should have known, anyway.

As they approached the harbour they began to sing softly, all three. They sang 'The Quarter-Master's Stores', a song which the English had lustily sung throughout their defeats, and which the GIs had adopted now, in better days:

> 'There were rats, rats,
> Big as tabby cats
> In the stores, in the stores . . .'

All three voices faded. From the darkness at the edge of the harbour there echoed a shouting voice; the words were only echoes as though thrown up from a deep pit.

The trio ran down towards the harbour. As they approached they could hear the resounding almost eerie calls from below. 'That's our guy Wall,' panted Ballimach to Gilman. 'He's in our outfit.'

They reached the edge of the harbour and, looking down, saw a scene of pure melodrama. On the stone boat slipway a man was trying to pull a bulky figure clear of the water. It was like a fisherman trying to land a porpoise. With gasping, hysterical curses, he was tugging from below the arms, slipping forward, once sliding right across the form, because of the seaweeded stones. When he became aware of them he released her and Gilman heard the wet, heavy flop as she hit the slipway. 'Come on, come on, for Chrissake!' the man sobbed. 'She's too heavy. I can't get her up there.'

Gilman said sharply to Albie, 'Get the doctor. He only lives over there.' He pointed fiercely. 'His name is Doctor Evans. Then go across to our camp and get a stretcher. There's a guard at the gate. Make him understand. And run.'

Albie went, his thin legs parting like sticks across the cobbles. Gilman followed Ballimach who was already halfway down the slope of the slipway. In other circumstances it would have been hilarious. The big American, hurrying, was suddenly upended on his bottom, slithering down the seaweeded incline; as he tried to get up he fell again, forward on to his hands, like a clown. Wall was shouting abuse at him, the words rebounding from the old harbour wall. Gilman descended more cautiously, digging the sides of his boots into the cracks of the stones, holding his arms straight out like a man who believes he might be able to fly. He still felt drunk but he had pushed the sensation fiercely away from him. He realized that Ballimach had done the same, had forced himself to rationality.

Gilman reached Wall just as Ballimach slipped again; again forward; the English soldier ended the journey crawling on all fours across the slimy stones. Wall was sitting on the cobbles, panting, still trying to pull; the big woman was sprawled on her face like a side of beef. Wall was shivering violently. Gilman looked to see if the woman were shivering. Did people shiver after they were dead?

'Turn her over,' he said to Wall. He got his arms under the fat, slippery body.

'Those bastards took off,' complained Wall strangely. 'They just took off, for God's sake. I had to go in and get her.'

'Quit,' said Ballimach savagely. 'Stop blabbermouthing. Turn her over like the man says. Let's get her up this goddamn slope.'

As soon as they turned her Gilman saw who it was. Fat Meg. He had thought so, even in the dark and though she was face down. Her features looked blue even in the scanty moonlight. 'It's Meg,' he said unnecessarily. 'She was at the dance.'

'I know, I saw her,' said Ballimach. Fat people notice other fat people.

'Quit talking will you,' pleaded Wall. 'Give her respiration for Chrissake. *You* Ballimach. You're the biggest.'

Ballimach did not know how. Neither did the others. Their invasion training had not reached that chapter. 'Turn her over again,' he said decisively. 'You got to do it from the other side.'

They pushed her halfway over and she flopped the rest. Ballimach, on his knees, hovered above her hesitantly, like someone beginning a new sport. He then pressed down hard with his great flat hands on the base of the woman's lungs. He pulled back and tried again. Then a third time. The others watched anxiously. Wall had his hand across his mouth. Suddenly he turned away and was sick on the stones, throwing up all the beer he had drunk. 'Jesus, that stinking water,' he sobbed. Ballimach continued his attempts. Gilman leaned over and, tenderly, shifted the woman's mouth so it was more to the side. Wall bent down and stared closely at the mouth. 'Faster,' he whispered to Ballimach. 'For God's sake faster. There's nothing coming out. There's supposed to be goddamn water coming out.' He waited, then shouted plaintively, 'You ain't doin' it right!' He staggered to his feet, slipped, but recovered and tried to push Ballimach aside.

Ballimach resisted him easily. 'Take it easy, pal,' he said angrily. 'She ain't your mother is she? I'm doing the best I know how.'

They heard voices above and looked up to see Albie Primrose with Evans, the doctor. Beatrice Evans wrapped in an army greatcoat was just behind as they peered down at the scene. Boots sounded on the cobbles and four of the guard at the camp came running. They had brought their rifles but no stretcher.

Albie took an incautious step on to the slipway and slid down like a man on skis, only being prevented from going into the darkened water by colliding with the prone body of Meg. Fiercely Wall pushed him away. Evans caught hold of the chains along the wall and eased himself down more carefully. Beatrice followed him. They got level with the group and then balanced across the intervening couple of yards. The doctor listened for the woman's breath, tested her pulse and then leaned down to her heart. Finally, with his wife shining a torch, he leaned forward and looked into her blank eyes.

He straightened up. 'There's nothing left to do,' he shrugged. 'She's dead. Poor old Meg.'

Wall was shivering with the cold. 'I tried to get her out,' he said with a hushed voice. 'Jesus, it was freezing in there. She was so heavy. I kept losing her. It took me goddamn hours.'

'There's an ambulance on its way,' said Evans. 'You'd better go too.' He glanced around at Beatrice. She took off the greatcoat and handed it across the dead body to the trembling GI.

'Gee, thanks,' he moaned. He wrapped it around himself. Gilman took his tunic off and handed it to Beatrice. She smiled briefly at him as she accepted it.

'How did she come to be in there?' asked Evans.

Even in the darkness they saw that Wall was startled and afraid. 'She fell in,' he said. 'She just fell right in. Honest to God, sir.'

March

Spring caused some surprise. St David's Day had widespread sunshine, the first day of what was to be the driest and sunniest March in the memory of anyone in the West Country. General Eisenhower had called a strategic conference in Bushy Park, just outside London, for the following day. Colonel Schorner left the camp at mid-morning with Bryant.

Schorner sniffed. 'I can't believe today,' he said. 'Look at that sky.'

Bryant laughed: 'The locals will be dancing around the maypole soon.'

'And cricket?' suggested Schorner. 'There's cricket?'

'Yes, sir,' said Bryant. 'You're going to really enjoy cricket.'

They were to meet General Georgeton and his ADC, Captain Scarlett, in Exeter at lunchtime, before driving to London. From Telcoombe Magna Albie Primrose took the coastal road to Wilcoombe. The direct route, through the north-leading lanes, was now so damaged and congested with US military traffic that it was quicker and less uncomfortable by the longer road.

The concrete hards were now spread like wide white aprons along the coast; only yards inland were the batteries of rockets and anti-aircraft guns, pointing at a sky from which no enemy had yet appeared. 'If the Germans cared to send one reconnaissance aircraft, for only a couple of minutes, and he managed to make home base, they'd know just about everything,' commented Schorner. 'Nobody can disguise this sort of parade.'

'It must be the same throughout the south of England,' answered Bryant. 'Every inch of beach, every single harbour.' Then he nodded solemnly towards the concise horizon. 'And it's the same over there. Germans dug in everywhere.'

Schorner gave a dry cackle. 'There you have the difference,' he observed. 'All they have to do is wait. We have the problem of getting our asses over there.'

Bryant felt disturbed. 'Do you think we'll do it, sir?' he asked.

'Sure. Sure, we'll do it, son. But it's never been done yet, remember. Nobody has ever landed a real army on a heavily-fortified coast and got away with it. I'm not talking about raids or picnics. I'm talking about *invasion*. Jesus, look at what just happened at Anzio, and years ago at Gallipoli. Put them on the beach – and leave the poor bastards there. That's not going to be clever enough.'

'And if we don't manage it?' said Bryant.

Schorner was looking out to the placid spring sea. 'We fail,' he shrugged. 'We high-tail out, as best we can. Get back here and lick our wounds for a long time, I guess, a few years even. Then we try again, or the politicians get a negotiated peace, or somebody internally overthrows Hitler.'

Bryant felt an oddly childish disappointment. 'It's *got* to go right,' he muttered.

'Sure, lieutenant, and when I see Ike tomorrow I'll tell him you said so.'

They had driven the length of the beach and gone out through the barbed-wire barrier. At the bottom of Wilcoombe Hill, where the road turned right and upwards by the harbour, they saw Evans standing beside his small car outside the cottage gate. Schorner told Primrose to drive the car the few yards off the road. Affably Evans greeted them and Beatrice came from the door and up the path. She was wearing a faded, summery dress. The American thought they were two people who would never be changed; by wars or even time.

'It's spring,' smiled the American. He got out of the car. In their enclosed garden there were daffodils hiding behind the old walls.

'I told you it came here too,' laughed Beatrice. The light dress made her slim and jaunty. For a moment Schorner remembered how much he wanted to go home. Bryant left the car and looked across the road to the British gun, now outmoded by the neighbouring rocket batteries. He wondered if it would remain there until the end of the war. Soldiers were moving without hurrying in the compound and a finger of light smoke came from the cookhouse.

'St David's Day,' said Evans. He patted the head of a daffodil with affection, as though it were a pet. 'Our patron saint in Wales, you see.'

'Now that's something we don't seem to have caught up on in the States,' said Schorner admiring the clean and vivid daffodils. 'We ought to have a patron saint. We have Columbia, but I don't think about her as a saint.'

'Dewi Sant, they call him – Saint David,' said Evans as though speaking of someone he knew personally. 'This is his flower, the daffodil. His father was a saint also and his mother was a nun.'

'Sounds like a strong cast,' said Schorner. He looked casually at Evans. 'You know I asked for the inquest to be adjourned?' he said.

'Of course,' replied the doctor just as calmly. He saw Albie Primrose lean forward to listen. 'I have to give evidence,' he added.

'And I have to be there,' said Schorner. 'We will also have a US Army lawyer present. That's normal where GIs are involved.'

Evans thought it sounded like an apology. 'You can't have everybody being a saint,' he said. 'Not soldiers.'

'I guess not.' His brows furrowed. 'Who's the patron saint of soldiers anyhow?'

Evans smiled. 'I don't know. Better ask the vicar.'

'Just now the Church is not looking too charitably in my direction,' shrugged Schorner. 'We're getting flak because of the trouble at the dance also.'

The doctor nodded. 'Yes, I heard. It might come as a relief when you only have to face the Germans.'

'That could be,' agreed Schorner. He smiled at Beatrice. 'You look like the spirit of spring today, lady,' he said.

'Nothing like an hour of warm Devon sun to start them springing around like fawns,' laughed Evans. 'Your boys will be feeling the sap rising.'

Schorner regarded him with genuine concern.

'*Don't*, for God's sake,' he pleaded. 'Don't I have enough troubles?' He and Bryant were getting back into the car.

They said good-byes and drove from the harbour apron and up the steep Wilcoombe Hill. Schorner was silent for several miles as they manoeuvred their route along lanes and roads, piled with war material, cases of ammunition, food, pyramids of gasoline, drums and cans. Soldiers moved about like a thousand storekeepers, convoys pressed along the road, military police waved them on when they saw the stars on the car. There was scarcely a sign of civilian life.

'That daffodil sure is a pretty flower,' said Schorner eventually.

'The Welsh also have the leek,' mentioned Bryant. 'And that's ugly.'

Schorner closed his eyes and lay back against the cushioned seat. 'Bryant,' he said, 'do you think those GIs pushed that woman into the harbour?'

Bryant said evenly, 'No, sir. I think she fell. She was drunk, and she often was. I think she fell in. Just as they said.'

'I hope you're right,' muttered the colonel. 'I sure hope you're right.'

They met General Georgeton and Captain Scarlett in Exeter, the bombed old city bathed in optimistic new sunshine. People were out in the ruined streets, a sense of lightness in the way they walked. The destroyed buildings had been tidied as if a houseproud woman had been at work with a broom. There were even wild flowers growing on some of the gaunt gaps. There were daffodils in window boxes and cut into bunches on the pavements outside shops, among baskets of vegetables. Worn-out buses, a few cars, bicycles and horse-drawn carts moved in the centre of the city; uniforms and military vehicles were everywhere. Outside the fine, damaged cathedral, two jeeps were pulled to the side and American soldiers, hands in pockets, caps on the backs of their greased heads, were fooling for the benefit of half-a-dozen shopgirls, sitting out for their lunch hour. Two of the GIs were wrestling, bringing raucous laughter from the girls and wild jeers from their comrades.

'They don't look like killers, do they?' sighed General Georgeton. He and Schorner were travelling together. Scarlett and Bryant were following in Schorner's staff car. Georgeton's driver gave a double touch on the horn and laughed to himself as the Americans sprang to attention on the sidewalk and saluted the passing car. One of the brash girls stood up too, imitating them, at attention, her arm raised in a mocking salute. 'Few killers do, sir,' replied Schorner. 'They'll find out soon enough.'

'You're having trouble with the civilian population,' said Georgeton casually. 'I got a report. A woman got drowned and some of our men were involved.'

'She was a well-known drunk,' replied Schorner defensively. 'She fell into the harbour and some of my men tried to get her out. One guy was in hospital with exposure for three days. But some dumbheads ran away. We don't even known who they were. They weren't from my unit. My guys didn't even know them. But they panicked and they beat it and, naturally, the rumours started.'

334

'Doesn't sound too good,' said Georgeton. 'Sooner it's cleared up the better.'

'There's an inquest on Friday.'

'And you'll be there. What are the other problems? With the local people.'

Schorner sighed. 'We have plenty. We're in a spot. Every other place in this country you have the troops and you have the civilians together. They have to get by somehow. There's no other place where the civilians have been dispossessed, moved out of their homes and their farms, so that the troops can blow them to hell. It doesn't help good relations. Most people are okay, they understand or they say they understand, but there's a real undercurrent of bitterness. All the time I feel it.'

'You'll have to learn to live with it,' said Georgeton.

'I'm learning,' replied Schorner. 'Every day.'

The car braked and they watched a long-barrelled gun being moved along the road, a monster with army outriders. They were in the suburbs of Exeter now and the civilians scarcely did more than pause to see the giant move along. It was like a dragon in a carnival. 'How are we going to get that thing over the sea?' said Georgeton. 'You're the engineer.'

'It sure won't float,' smiled Schorner. 'We'll get it over okay. Our problem will be what to do with it on the other side. We've got a railhead company arriving at the end of the month. They've got to get railroad trains and wagons across there.'

'Sure,' said Georgeton. 'I'm afraid you're going to get a lot of oddball units.' He paused, then said: 'I've assigned a Grave Registration Company to you for the actual assault.'

Schorner swallowed. 'A Grave Registration Company?' he repeated. 'Oh, boy, that's great news.'

'Don't thank me, colonel,' said Georgeton. 'Maybe they're not the most popular travelling companions, but they've got to live somewhere, just like every other outfit, and they've got to get across real quick after the first invasion wave. Folks back home want to know *where* and *when* their boys got killed.' He hardly paused this time. 'What other troubles do you have? Locally.'

'Fights,' answered Schorner simply. 'We had one at a Valentine Dance. It wasn't our guys' fault but they got the blame.'

The general shrugged. 'We have fights all over,' he commented. 'Real bloody fights some of them. Knives and all that stuff. We have whites fighting negroes, and Americans fighting British, and the infantry fighting the paratroopers. We'll have the goddamn doctors fighting the nurses yet.'

'I guess we brought them over to fight and it's taking a long time to fix the real thing,' said Schorner. 'Exercises, war games are okay – we've had a total of twenty-four simulated invasions by now – but everybody knows they're just pretending. They think that everything is just another exercise. They probably won't believe it's the real thing until they've shot their first German.' He thought about the doctors and nurses. 'The hospital is nearly ready, I hear, general.'

'Sure, another couple of weeks. I've seen it. Jesus Christ, it's frightening, Schorner. God, it really is. A million miles of empty beds, wards, operating theatres, a morgue like a football field. If we have that many dead they're not going to get them into heaven or hell on the same day.'

336

'What's the feeling at the top?' asked Schorner. He glanced at the window between them and the driver to make sure it was closed. Georgeton saw his look and nodded that it was.

'We'll hear the latest tomorrow, I guess,' he said. 'From the big chiefs. But everybody is worried as hell. They ought to be. It's okay piling up all these tanks, guns, railroad trains and God-knows-what else on this side, but anything could go wrong and screw up the whole operation. Weather, especially the weather, logistics, heavy resistance, the chance of a panzer corps just sitting on the beach as we go ashore. Gee, you know as well as anybody.'

'Sure,' agreed Schorner. 'That stretch of water could lose us an army.'

'A war,' corrected Georgeton. 'If we get a storm we could be finished before we've started.'

'These old warships give me bad dreams,' put in the colonel. 'Those two broken down hulks. What sort of protection are they going to be?'

'Ask Eisenhower. Or some guy who knows God,' said Georgeton. 'Maybe you'll get a chance at the briefing.'

'Who do the British think? After all, it's their Channel.'

'Montgomery is not somebody you would want to take home to your mother,' answered Georgeton. 'I wouldn't take him home to mine. He's an arrogant bastard, but he's no fool. He's damned shrewd. He, and all the other high echelon, are putting great faith in Hitler drawing the wrong card. They believe he'll be convinced that the landings will be in the Pas de Calais. It's the shortest crossing and it would make

337

historical sense. Hitler thinks the British would love to go back the way they got themselves thrown out. Just for the sake of history. Poetic justice. That's what they think he thinks, anyway. Let's hope he's doing that.'

Schorner said: 'I don't believe Hitler is that crazy. Not with all this material piling up here in the west. I don't believe it.'

'Nor do I,' said the general. 'I think he'll guess right, and he'll be sitting waiting for us with his panzers. It's going to be fucking murder, colonel. Fucking murder.'

The great gun held up Scarlett and Bryant in the second car. They waited with three other vehicles and a group of almost indifferent pedestrians as the giant, its barrel seeming to point the way, was manoeuvred around a difficult corner. The owner of the butcher's shop at the junction came out, a stout man wearing a threadbare traditional striped apron, and stood on the pavement shouting instructions to the driver and crew and illustrating them by waving a blood-stained cleaver.

'Butchers never look hungry,' observed Bryant.

'He'd be crazy if he did,' said Scarlett. 'When the butcher starves there's no hope for anybody.'

They watched as anxiety creased the man's sausage-like face, while the barrel of the weapon turned a fraction at a time. The butcher began using the cleaver like a threat. Eventually the gun just cleared the upper storey of the shop. A pale face appeared at the window above and the butcher began shouting and gesticulating upwards.

'Somebody's sick in the room,' suggested Scarlett.

'He missed anyway,' said Bryant. 'Maybe they'll send in a claim for disturbance.'

'They do,' nodded Scarlett. 'We have claims from people whose dogs get scared.'

One of the American soldiers manoeuvring the gun was undersized, smaller than Albie Primrose, who sat at the wheel of their car. The divisional flash on his little arm bore the words: 'Hell on Wheels'.

'Are you married?' asked Scarlett. They knew little about each other.

'Yes,' said Bryant. He added: 'I'm hoping that my wife will be coming to London. She's trying to get down by train from Manchester so we can spend some time together. I've almost forgotten what she looks like.'

'I know how you feel,' agreed Scarlett. 'Jesus, what I'd give just to see my wife's little butt.' His face became sad.

Bryant said: 'I'm not sure mine will be coming, yet. She's going to try, that's all. She is on war work and it's difficult.' He sounded as if he were trying to convince himself.

'How long since you saw her?' asked Scarlett.

'Four months. Last leave,' said Bryant. 'I haven't had any leave since before Christmas, and with this present job I can't see much chance of getting any. Not unless they give us a quick forty-eight hours before the invasion.'

Scarlett said seriously: 'I sure hope she comes.'

'So do I,' said Bryant. He wondered if she had better things to do.

*

Bushy Park on the western outskirts of London is bordered by the River Thames and Henry the Eighth's magnificent red palace of Hampton Court. General Eisenhower had called a briefing for six in the evening in a prefabricated building used as an officers' mess and set on one flank of what had become an American military city.

Now, the park's lofty walls were embroidered with skeins of barbed wire, the gates restricted, the paths broadened into roads. On occasion civilian gardeners were permitted to enter to attend to the seasonal wants of some of the rarer plants and shrubs in the gardens. Outside the tall heraldic gates and the guards, children waited for gifts of gum and women waited for dates.

Early in the evening, before the fine March day had fully died, the camp followers were removed from the entrance and soon US Army staff vehicles converged on the park, with the occasional British Army, Air Force or Navy car, and the transport of various officers of the allied armies, including the French, the Canadians, the Dutch and the Poles.

Senior officers, a hundred and twenty of them, sat on rows of wooden chairs, curiously like pupils in a big classroom, murmuring among themselves as children do, but watching the doors through which the Supreme Commander would enter. When he came in, with his immediate staff officers, and with the stiff-striding General Montgomery, the assembly clattered to its feet.

Eisenhower, his impish head nodding a greeting, took the middle chair of those arranged on a platform at one end. His grin was grim. Montgomery took off his beret with the two badges fixed to it, hung it on a chair back and sat down tiredly. Other staff officers, from all the services, took the other chairs. It was as formal as a group photograph. A balding captain on Eisenhower's staff, who spoke more like a padre, stood and outlined the areas to be covered by the briefing. 'Questions and comments after the briefing,' he said primly.

Dwight D. Eisenhower stood. His face was waxed and weary, but the voice was convincing. 'Our weather experts,' he began, 'are the people we need to give our attention to.' It sounded strange, as if he had, by error, begun in the middle of his speech. 'It's not one damned bit of use trying to float this operation even across that ditch between England and France if we're going to get shipwrecked on the way. History is stuffed full of men who came to grief in the Channel, ask the admiral who commanded the Spanish Armada.'

There was a polite acknowledgement of the small joke. His voice was lowered. He sounded like a man speaking poetry. 'We need the moon,' he said. 'We need the tides. We need the darkness for cover, we need moonlight to identify the dropping zones for the paratroops. We need daylight for our engineers to clear obstacles on the beaches, we need the night to get close enough to those beaches undetected by the guns of the enemy. We need the currents and the weather. In short we need, more than anything else, good fortune.'

'Some dates in May and early June commend themselves on these counts. Any of them, or all, may be confounded by the weather. If we miss these days then we might as well forget it until the fall – and that's too late. It's got to be soon, gentlemen, or not at all.'

Schorner, ten rows back, sitting next to General Georgeton, leaned forward listening as intently as every other man but, quietly, insisting in the bottom of his mind, he kept getting thoughts about his home. He thought of the trees and the fields that swept to the Blue Ridge Mountains, the spring, the wind, his dogs barking at night, people coming over on Sundays; his wife. When would all this game, this charade be finished? Ever?

The room was darkened and a map of the Channel coast, both sides, England and France, was projected on to a back screen. Schorner, in his mood, had a brief memory of sitting in the picture house when he was a boy; the moment when the beam from the projector cut through the shabby place and made a white square on the screen.

General Montgomery had appeared, standing like a schoolmaster with his baton, pointing out the areas of Britain where the great army was now building, in the south east the British and Canadians, the Americans in the south west. Ports of embarkation were pointed out with the precision of a pedagogue; he embarked into a grumble about the shortage of landing craft due to the demands of the United States Armies in the Pacific. Schorner glanced at Georgeton. Georgeton whispered: 'Ike's agreeing with him.' Eisenhower was nodding his domed head.

'It is thus imperative,' said Montgomery with his narrow bark, 'that mishaps, accidents, casualties to any type of landing craft must be kept to a minimum. Tell your chaps to be careful.' The stage lights went up and he stood there, lean as a tree, his sharp face pushed aggressively towards them. 'We will get across the Channel,' he said slowly, almost mischievously, as if he had some hidden plan they knew nothing of. 'My father was a great jumper,' he added suddenly and to their surprise. 'When he was at Cambridge he jumped the hall steps at King's College at one bound. Mind you, he had God on his side. He was afterwards a bishop.' He paused again. 'That was in 1866,' he added curiously.

Schorner said: 'My God,' under his breath.

Georgeton glanced at him. 'Sure,' he whispered. 'Mine too.'

There had been a slight breeze of laughter at Montgomery's remarks, almost entirely from the British officers. Now he stalked off to his seat and sat down holding his cane between his legs. The officer like a clergyman then stood and invited questions. They were slow, hesitant, at first, but once the first few had been put, they thickened. 'Ask about those goddamn escort ships,' whispered Georgeton. Schorner glanced at him but the general said: 'You're worried about them, colonel. *You'll* have to tell your boys.'

Schorner waited and when a pause appeared in the questions, he stood. He announced his name and rank and unit. Then he added: 'Sir, on a recently-conducted exercise, I was surprised, so were my men, when we saw that our escorting naval vessels were two very old destroyers, First War vintage. They had three smoke stacks and were slow and difficult to manoeuvre. Are these escort vessels just temporary or can we expect them during the invasion of France?'

A British naval officer, a vice-admiral, stood to answer. 'They're jolly good ships,' he said bluntly. 'American I might say, acquired by us in 1940, together with some old aeroplanes and some rifles that looked as if they'd come from the Civil War.' A puff of laughter quickly died. 'They may be slow, but they have guns pointing in the right direction. They will add firepower to the naval bombardment which will precede the invasion. The answer, sir, is yes, they will be used.'

'Thank you,' said Schorner, sitting down. 'I'll tell my boys.' Several men in the rows before turned about and looked towards him. The vice-admiral had another thought. He stood again. 'During the assault stage of the invasion there will, of course, be a screen of modern ships, and since the Germans have only a few small warships, E-boats and the like, in the Channel area, we don't anticipate any trouble from them on D-Day. In 1940 the Germans thought twice about invading this country because we had our Navy, almost intact, and we were jolly well waiting for them. An army is no match for a navy at sea. Never was.'

Bryant went to Euston Station on the underground. He stood all the way, at the end of the shabby compartment, surrounded by silent, weary people. He remembered, in 1940, he had seen, on a tube train like this, an advertisement for Bovril, the beef drink, which showed a family happily taking it down to the shelter in preparation for a night of bombs. There was a certain uppish humour about that; in those times, despite the nightly terror, people had been fighting, buoyant. On that day, he recalled, the tube train had gone through stations where hundreds were already lying beneath their blankets, like corpses on the platforms. They had staked their pitch for the night. Whole communities below the ground. Later, while the Junkers dropped their death, they would be singing Cockney songs deep down in the protecting earth.

But now the war had gone on too long. Even in those days they had been fresh. There were now few air raids, only the long grind of another bleak day, waiting for it all to finish. It had become pitted in the faces of the people, in their skin, like the grime of miners. There were painted slogans on London walls demanding a 'Second Front Now!' They were put there at night by Communists and others. The Russians had been fighting alone. But even these slogans had lost their eagerness now. There had been no second front; not unless you thought of the invasion of North Africa or Italy as a second front, and no one did. Even now – while politicians planned for after the war – many people did not think the invasion of Europe was imminent. It had become a time of apathy and disbelief.

Bryant, as he travelled in the underground train, wondered if he would survive the invasion. His life was so changed that he could hardly remember being anything else but a soldier. He wondered about his wife, Margaret. There was a woman about her age and wearing a wedding ring standing a few feet away talking earnestly to an American airman. They were the only people conversing. She held his arm, just below the elbow, firmly.

Now he even found it difficult to imagine what his wife was like. It was only months but it seemed years. Her face, her shape, seemed to have become indistinct, as if she were drifting off into a mist across a field.

The train trembled into Euston. All the escalators were out of order so he joined the patient, trudging people going up the stairs to ground level, people in old humped coats, with scarves and balaclava hats and gloves made in wool of khaki, air-force blue or navy. Thousands of woman hours had gone into knitting for the forces only for the comforts to unerringly find their way back to civilians. Perhaps it was a just law, a proper redistribution. There was very little for the comfort of the common man. Only bread, vegetables, fish and rabbits were not rationed, and it was difficult to get fish and rabbits.

There were posters at Euston calling for yet another effort with National Savings. 'Lend to Defend His Right to be Free', it said over the picture of a child. 'Salute the Soldier', 'Careless Talk Costs Lives', 'Potato Pete Says Potatoes are Good For You', 'Coughs and Sneezes Spread Diseases', 'Watch Out in the Black Out', the incantations were everywhere and everyone knew them. Every pane of glass in the great station roof had been blown out during the bombing and had not been replaced. The evening had turned to a March chill and the cold air fell down on the people waiting dumbly to go home.

Bryant found that the train from Manchester would be an hour late, not an unreasonable delay. He went into the buffet and bought the *Evening Standard*. He avoided the war news and turned inside. There was to be some cricket in the coming summer. Lord's would be used. The Oval was still a prisoner-of-war camp with German soldiers walking about the sacred place. Did they ever wonder what the Oval was *for*?

Middlesex County Council were to start thatching classes, at night school, said a small paragraph. He smiled and wondered how long it took to learn to be a thatcher; years he imagined. Someone must be confident about the outcome of the war. A Dutch soldier was standing a few yards along the buffet, a cup of thin tea before him, a meat pie cold as clay in his hand. His face was without expression. His eyes scarcely blinked. He merely stared from the grimy window, out into the dark, moving, station. Bryant wondered whether he would ever get home to Holland again. Or if he cared now. It must have been a long time.

The hour stretched on. With ten minutes to go, an excitement tightening his chest, he left the buffet and went across the darkened concourse to platform three where the train was due to arrive. He remembered feeling like this when his mother met him from school at the end of term. The steam of the train and the warmth of his mother's arms. The ticket collector, in his little box, which, Bryant imagined, gave him some private comfort, said that he had no idea whether the train would be only an hour late. He said it, poking his head from his box and with a mean sort of glee. 'Could be hours, sir,' he hummed. 'Hours and hours.' The man prepared to pull his head back.

Bryant tried to be good-humoured. 'I hope not,' he replied. 'My wife's on it.' He wondered why he had to tell the man that. It had a faint touch of boasting. The ticket collector would be there, looking out like a nosy neighbour, when Margaret came down the platform, through the wafting steam, slim and confident, smiling her stage smile, and she would come forward and they would embrace while the man began to collect tickets all around.

'Your wife?' said the collector, pretending to be incredulous. 'I wouldn't wait for my wife. Blimey, I'd be glad if the bloody train never got here at all.'

Bryant's face fell boyishly. The man looked momentarily sorry. 'That's what being in the army does for you,' he advised. 'Keeps you separate, don't it. Nothing like being miles away to keep marriage going, I say.' He leaned confidentially. 'I was in myself, of course. Time of Dunkirk. Invalided out. Feet. My feet are two of the horrors of this war.'

He shifted his boots backwards slightly, guiltily, as if he thought the officer might want to inspect them. Bryant grinned and then the grin tightened as he looked up and saw the train, like a fussy ghost coming through its own steam, shuddering into the platform. 'You're all right now,' said the ticket collector. 'Here she is. Must have heard you.'

Bryant pulled his tunic down and felt the edge of his cap was straight across his forehead. At once he thought he saw her coming through the steam, even among all the other ghostly forms. But he was wrong. The first passengers bundled by, the ticket collector taking their tickets and, curiously, watching Bryant from one side of his eye. There were a lot of passengers on the train, as there always were in wartime, and many of them stumbled because they had stood in the corridors, throughout the journey. Bryant was conscious of a cry, a greeting, an embrace from others waiting outside the barrier, but he continued to peer through the steam. She did not come.

He waited, his heart getting colder and more sad, as the seconds went by. The crowd of passengers thinned. He still hoped, thinking she might be having trouble with her suitcase, or she was in the toilet, trapped in there, perhaps. It was the sort of thing she would have had happen to her. The final passenger was a woman, a shape materializing from the vapour. But it was an ATS girl in uniform. She went by, giving him a half-salute which he automatically returned, and walked into the embrace of a man, a civilian, standing behind.

'Looks like that's the lot,' said the ticket collector. He regarded Bryant with something like sympathy. 'You can never tell with women,' he said. 'They always get lost, or something happens, or they change their minds. They're always bloody changing their minds. Believe me, I know better than most.'

'There's nobody else, is there?' asked Bryant miserably. He realized the ambiguity of the question. 'Nobody's likely to be left on the train? Perhaps she fell asleep.'

'The guard's checking it,' said the man. A train guard swinging a torch advanced down the platform. 'Anybody left, Bertie?' asked the ticket man.

'Nobody,' the man called back. 'They all got off, no drunks, nothing. Just somebody left a gas mask. Army one. He'll be in trouble, won't he.' He swung the khaki bag from his other hand.

'Sorry, sir,' said the ticket collector genuinely. He

realized he was watching a small tragedy. 'Maybe she missed it. Accidentally, I mean.'

'When is the next one?' asked Bryant.

'Five hours, at least, even if it's not late, which it will be because it always is,' said the man. He took a timetable from his pocket. 'Not that this is much to go by,' he sniffed. He read it carefully in the light of his torch. 'Midnight,' he said. 'Supposed to be. Sometimes that don't get here until the early hours. Three or four.'

Slowly Bryant turned away and walked back towards the entrance to the underground. He felt chilled with disappointment. His throat and his eyes were salty. Just before the underground stairs there was a rank of telephone boxes. They were all occupied but, all at once resolved, he waited, pacing along the line like a sentry. A woman in a straggling fur coat finished at the end box. She came out crying. Bryant had an odd temptation to put a hand on her shoulder but she hurried away. He replaced her in the box. It took ten minutes to get the operator. Nothing was easy in wartime and so many things were sad. He waited. The phone began to ring at the other end. It was soon picked up. Margaret was laughing before she spoke the number. She stopped when she heard him, said: 'Oh, excuse me,' but not to him, and left the phone to return a moment later. Bryant was desperately counting out coins on to the flat black surface of the coinbox.

'I'm at Euston,' he said. 'You didn't come.' It was half hurt, half accusation.

'I wouldn't be speaking to you on the phone if I had, would I, silly?' she said lightly. Her voice dropped to a surface, anyway, of seriousness. 'Honestly, darling, I couldn't. They can't spare me. There's a social tonight and they want me to help. I have to.'

'But Margaret,' he said abruptly. 'I'm damned well waiting here. Christ Almighty, don't you care . . . ?'

'Don't go crazy,' she said roughly. 'I only said I would *try* and get there. I didn't promise. I thought I *could* until this morning. And there was no chance of getting in touch with you then. I'm sorry.'

'So am I,' he blurted. 'Very bloody sorry.' Crazy was a word she would never have used before.

'You'll get some leave soon, won't you?' she said petulantly. 'You always seem to be the last to get leave. You're too much of a dogsbody, darling.'

'Perhaps I am,' he agreed. 'In all sorts of ways.'

At once she sounded sorry. 'I would have, if I could,' she said. 'Look, I'll come down tomorrow. How about that? Promise, honest injun.'

'I don't think I'll be here tomorrow,' said Bryant. 'Not in London.'

Margaret paused. Then she said: 'In that case I would have been coming all that terrible journey just for a couple of hours.'

'At least it would have been a couple of hours,' muttered Bryant. There was a silence at both ends. Then Bryant said, 'How is Elizabeth?'

'Oh, Lizzie's fine,' she replied with sharp brightness. 'Growing up. Changing, like all of us.'

It was enough. He wanted to get out of the phone box. 'The money is running out,' he said.

'Like it always used to,' she said with a strange laugh. 'In the old days.'

He ignored it. 'I'll telephone next week,' he said. 'Wednesday, as usual.'

'All right, darling, Wednesday. I'm always in on Wednesday.'

He returned to the Officers' Club by taxi, perplexed and angry. As he walked into the foyer Scarlett came out of the windowed bar and called: 'Where's the lady?'

Bryant laughed wryly. 'Find the lady, more like it,' he said.

Scarlett's expression dropped. 'You couldn't *find* her? How so?'

'She didn't come,' shrugged Bryant. 'She wasn't on the damned train and I phoned her and she had never even left. She's busy with the war.' He paused and said bitterly: 'Her particular war.'

'Gee, she didn't show. I'm sorry. Like hell, I'm sorry. Come on, I'll buy you a drink.'

Bryant smiled briefly at his concern. 'Right you are,' he said. 'That's the next best thing, I suppose.'

They walked into the bar. It was not crowded at that time of the evening. A group of American Air Force officers were reliving a raid they had made over Germany, their hands moving around like bombers and puffing noises to imitate anti-aircraft fire. The barman was bald and wise-looking. His braided uniform was dim and baggy, his face thin but bright. They climbed against the bar and Scarlett ordered two double scotches. The barman smiled enthusiastically as if trying to live some memory.

'So what do you do now?' asked the American eventually. 'Sit down and read a good book?'

'I suppose so. I've left it that I'll telephone on Wednesday.' He took the first heavy sip of scotch. 'God, she sounded miles away, and not just in distance. She's just completely changed. The bloody war does that to people. It makes lives so different. It's me too, I've changed as well.'

Scarlett grimaced. 'Nobody is going to come out of this the same as they went in,' he philosophized. One of the Air Force men was demonstrating a crashing plane, tipping his flat hand one way and another until the fingers struck the bar and he made a sound like an explosion. He picked up a scotch and drained it, then put it down for a refill. 'Me, I have to go back and look my wife in the eye,' continued Scarlett. 'And she's got to grit her teeth and get on with life with me. After that first Hollywood hug and kiss at the bottom of the gangplank – then the problems are going to start for one hell of a lot of people. No man can get up out of a chair, go away for years, she thinks maybe for ever, and then come back and just sit down in the same goddamn chair like nothing's happened.'

He leaned suddenly confidingly, and with a short smile, towards Bryant. 'Listen, why don't you take a trip with me tonight?'

'Where?'

'Aw, it's just a place. Real nice. It's for US officers, but I can take a guest. It's not too far and it's okay, nice and pleasant, sophisticated I guess you could say. And there's an English girl I know there. I met her the first night I was in London.' He shook his head slightly in disbelief. 'Straight off the plane from the States.'

Bryant grinned drily. 'The first night?' he queried. 'You chaps don't waste any time.'

'That's the reputation we get. But this wasn't intentional. I was just trying to catch a breath of air, but walking around with no lights in town at all . . . well, I got good and lost. And then I saw this door and in I went. It was great, believe me, and she was great. A real smart girl. So I went along with it. I didn't need the excuse of being lonesome. I tried it but it wouldn't wash.' He glanced at Bryant. 'How about it?'

The Englishman drained his drink and called to the barman for two more. 'It sounds like just the thing I need,' he said.

There was a moon that night over London, the sky flat and pale behind it and floating there in front of the stars a shoal of barrage balloons, silent as fish moving in a clear sea. The city did not seem so dark to Scarlett as it had done on that first night for now he had grown used to the blackness of the countryside. Vehicles and people moved about like confident phantoms.

'Those balloons,' asked Scarlett as they walked from the officers' hotel, 'did they ever get any Nazi planes down?'

'A few, not many,' said Bryant looking up at the dotted sky. 'They kept the bombers at a height, which didn't do a lot of good because they just dropped their load from there. It would be difficult to miss something as big as London.'

'I guess the idea is that they couldn't pick out special targets,' said Scarlett.

Bryant laughed. 'That's what everybody thought when they believed that the war was going to be sporting. At the beginning. You know, military objectives only. Some hope of that. They just stayed higher and let the bombs go at random.' He quoted: ' "German bombs dropped at random." Did you see that film "Random Harvest"?'

'Sure. Greer Garson. There's that great last scene when she calls, "Smithy," and Ronald Coleman turns around. What a movie.'

'We went to see that after we got married. It was a sort of honeymoon,' recalled Bryant wistfully. He realized he was feeling a little drunk. He wondered if Scarlett was also. The American was regarding the balloons again.

'So they're just up there to look pretty,' he said. He began to count them approvingly. 'And they sure do look pretty.'

'You're right,' said Bryant. 'I've thought about it like that. They gave everybody some sort of enjoyment, like Christmas decorations all year round, and just when people needed something to make them look *up*.'

'We go down,' said Scarlett. They had reached the steps leading down to the basement where the club was located. 'There's something satisfying about going below the ground too, don't you know. It's cosy and exciting at the same time. You could always get laid in a place like this. And in comfort.'

'Laid?' asked Bryant. 'You mean buried?' The American laughed.

They reached the door and Scarlett rang the bell. There was a brass plate on the door. Bryant tried to read it in the dimness. 'It's got a high-sounding name, which I don't recall,' said Scarlett. 'But the guys call it The Wishbone Club.'

The door opened and the emaciated young man that Scarlett recognized from his previous visit hovered patronizingly. 'Members?' he enquired.

Scarlett answered: 'Sure we're members.' He walked in, not quite brushing the man aside. 'Is Mrs Manifold around?'

The man's thin nose was red on his stark face, as if he had collided with something. 'Sign please,' he sighed impatiently. He went behind his gilt table and pushed a book towards them. Scarlett signed 'Dwight D. Eisenhower' and 'General Montgomery' for Bryant. The young man did not bother to look. 'Mrs Manifold is in the lounge, sir,' he said starchily. 'I'll call her if you wish.'

'Don't worry, I'll know her when I see her,' said Scarlett easily. He moved into the comforting lounge, with its sofas, its tables and its velvet bar. 'What a goddamn bug that guy is,' he said quietly to Bryant. 'Somebody should spray him.'

The Englishman was about to reply when Jean Manifold came casually towards them. She wore a long black dress, her shoulders creamy against the material. She held a glass in slim fingers and she was smiling gently. Bryant had not seen a woman like that since before the war.

Confidently Scarlett stepped forward and embraced her, but the Englishman saw at once that she was unsure of his identity. She laughed briefly and stepped back to regard him. She glanced at his rank insignia. His hands remained on her waist. She took hers from his shoulders. 'Captain,' she said with a slight falter, 'how terrific to see you again.' She said the 'terrific' in pseudo-American.

356

'Captain, the hell,' complained Scarlett. '*Oscar* . . . Oscar Scarlett. Don't say you don't remember.'

'Of course I remember,' she protested with another laugh. She embraced him theatrically, pressing herself against him. 'Captain Scarlett. Sounds like Errol Flynn.' She eased herself slightly away and looked towards Bryant. 'And you have a friend. Somebody on *our* side.'

'Okay, he's British,' smiled Scarlett. 'But the poor guy can't help that.' He turned to Bryant and then abruptly realized he did not know his first name. Bryant had never heard him called Oscar before either. Bryant held out his hand. 'I'm Alan Bryant,' he said politely.

'I'm Jean Manifold,' said the woman.

'And *I'm* lost,' said Scarlett. 'Jesus, I just knew I shouldn't have brought this smooth Englishman along. We just haven't got the style.'

'You haven't got a drink either,' laughed Jean. She raised one crimson-nailed finger towards the barman. He nodded and came round to the table where they were placing themselves. 'The first round is on the house,' said Jean. She glanced at Scarlett, still unsurely. 'Remember?'

'I'm not the one who forgets,' he corrected good-humouredly. They sat back comfortably. Bryant's despair and disappointment were still heavy within him. God, how could she have just not *troubled*? How could she be so casual about their marriage. What had happened to women? He glanced up at Jean Manifold, now laughing with her arm lying casually across the back of Scarlett's neck, and saw his answer.

There were not many people in the place. Jean said

it was early yet. But officers were away on duty for longer periods now. Soon, as she said, there would be none to go there at all. They would be busy with the fighting. A small pout of sadness touched her cheek.

Half a dozen American officers with attendant girls came in. The men were lively and loud; the women quiet, nervous. Just as the drinks arrived, Scarlett exclaimed: 'Hey, that guy. I know that guy. He was at Camp Blanding, Florida, with me. He said they'd never send him overseas! Ha!' he turned apologetically. 'I'd like to ask him how come they did,' he said. He rose with slight unsteadiness. 'I won't be long.' He glanced at Jean and added, 'Keep . . . Alan . . . keep him happy, will you?'

With a suspicion of a stagger he went across the floor where there was a back-slapping reunion with the other American. Drinks were placed on the bar. Scarlett seemed quickly to forget he had left them sitting at the table.

'You don't remember him do you,' said Bryant with a smile.

Jean Manifold shrugged. 'Sure, I remember him,' she said irritatingly, again trying to sound American. 'But you meet a lot of guys . . .' She glanced up with a sort of guilt and amended it. '. . . a lot of men here. Mostly Americans. It's not difficult to get their names mixed up.'

'No, I suppose not. Names are something which go by the board in wartime, don't they? Like a lot of things. We've been working together for weeks now, not all the time but off and on, and he didn't know I was called Alan, and I didn't know he was Oscar.'

'Perhaps it's just as well,' she said moodily. She

twisted the stem of the glass in her fingers so it turned like a roundabout. 'You don't want to get too close to people these days. It doesn't pay. What's your story?'

'I'm what I look,' he said. 'I work with the Americans, that's all. I'm a sort of go-between.'

She looked at him as though she were really interested, which he knew she was not. 'No, I mean what are you doing here? This is okay . . . all right for those who haven't got anywhere else to go. No home, nothing like that.'

'Oh, I see. Well my home is in the north.'

'You don't sound like that. Have you changed your accent because you're an officer or something. Officers really don't sound right with northern accents.'

Bryant shook his head. 'Not at all. My family are from down here originally, but I went to the north when I was married, just before the war.'

'Oh, you're married.'

'Yes, I've got a little girl. She's called Elizabeth.' He wondered why he wanted to tell her.

'Where is your wife?' asked Jean.

He frowned into his drink. 'Well, if you'd asked me that a few hours ago I would have said she was coming to London on the train so that we could spend some time together.'

Jean Manifold nodded: 'But she didn't show . . . turn up.'

'She didn't turn up,' he confirmed.

'It happens to everybody,' she said. 'Believe me, I've heard it so many times. My husband's in a prison camp. I dread the day we'll have to meet again. Dread it.'

'And he's counting every moment,' said Bryant seriously. 'It must be terrible when you're stuck behind wire and you don't know when it's all going to end.'

'Don't tell me, please,' she sighed. 'I feel guilty as hell about it. But I can hardly remember him, you know, that's the awful part. Any more than I can remember your friend Oscar over there. Now, after all this time, I just don't seem to be able to keep my mind on his face. I've got pictures of our wedding day. But every time I look he seems to fade away a bit more. Soon he'll be gone altogether, just a stranger.' She pouted and gave a brief, hard laugh. 'I can't even recognize myself holding that bouquet,' she said. 'Bloody fool that I was. Still am for that matter.'

Bryant said: 'Will you have a drink?'

'Why not? I'll probably get plastered tonight. I do sometimes. Quite often.'

'You look very good on it,' said Bryant genuinely. 'It must suit you.'

'Thanks. Up to now, all right. But I'm going to look bloody raddled by the end of the war.'

'I think most of us will,' he pointed out. The waiter approached and she ordered the same again, a Vodka Collins. Bryant did not know what that was. He had a scotch and he ordered another for Scarlett who was laughing, leaning over the bar with the other group. 'I think he's forgotten us,' smiled Bryant. A small band clambered without enthusiasm on to a draped rostrum.

'He's just getting his own back because I'd forgotten him,' shrugged Jean.

They were in the club until one in the morning. By that time it had grown crowded and curtained with smoke, with the band playing without inspiration above the voices. Then Americans began to leave, some with women; others, most of them staggering, without. Bryant had drunk a lot but he was surprised to find himself still calm. Jean Manifold was outwardly the same, as she had been the whole evening. Scarlett was sitting at their table again with his buddy from Camp Blanding, bemoaning the idiocies of the US Army and the war. Bryant sized him up. He would have to get him back without attracting a lot of attention at the officers' club, although he imagined that they were not unused to drunks there.

'What fouls me up,' Scarlett was saying loudly. His collar was undone and his hair had fallen damply across his forehead. 'Is that after all this goddamn time, years, we still have to have these old, old fucking destroyers as escorts. This is supposed to be *modern* war, for Chrissake. And we get these things that should have been on the scrapheap since the first fucking war . . .'

He paused and saw Bryant and Jean Manifold regarding him across the table. 'So what?' he said defiantly but with some guilt. 'So goddamn what? Listen, pals, the GIs don't feel so crazy about being out there in that cold English water, with those old English ships. Garbage, just garbage.'

'They're old American ships,' put in Bryant, realizing as he said it that he was adding to the error.

'I don't care whose old ships they are, they're still *old*. If our boys got attacked by the Germans they'd have no chance. No shit chance at all. So there. Those things can just about crawl in the water . . .'

Bryant said: 'Oscar, we'd better go.'

361

Scarlett looked around guiltily. 'Come on. We're all friends in here,' he said as an excuse. 'It don't matter what I say in here.'

'Even so, we're leaving,' said Bryant.

'I'm just going,' added Jean Manifold.

'Okay, we're leaving,' said Scarlett. 'If you say so, we are.'

He stood heavily, swayed, but straightened himself with exaggerated care and began to make for the door. 'I'd better get him back to the club,' said Bryant. Jean smiled, a little tightly he thought, then went to get her coat. He helped her on with it when she returned. It was a fur, well looked after. He helped Scarlett who was struggling with his greatcoat, pulling up the trapped collar for him.

'You're very patient,' said Jean Manifold without great interest. She was peering into her handbag. 'He'll have to learn to look after himself someday, you know.'

'I realize that,' said Bryant. He suddenly appreciated why she was offhand. 'Oh, I'm sorry,' he said hurriedly. 'I'll get you a taxi, if I can find one.'

'Don't worry, I'm only round the corner. Just walk me to the corner. Can we get Andy Hardy that far, do you think?' He was astonished at the scorn in her voice.

'Between us I think we'll manage. We'll soon find out when the fresh air hits him.'

They were among the last people in the place. The starved-looking young man and one of the elderly waiters were waiting to close the door behind the two. They had been hovering near the table a few minutes before.

362

Once they had climbed the steps, assisting Scarlett, who had begun to sing moodily, and gained the street, the American stood more firmly and began to walk with reasonable steadiness. He walked next to Bryant with Jean Manifold walking on the inside, near some walls which at one time had been embellished with iron railings.

'Look at that,' said Jean waving her hand airily above the low wall that remained. 'Took the lovely railings away. This war takes everything away, even the railings.'

Out in the air she had become a little fey. She performed a slightly girlish hopscotch between the indistinct paving stones. 'They were always useful to lean on, the railings,' she said. 'They'd be very useful just now.'

She stopped Bryant by holding his arm. Scarlett wandered on a few steps and then, realizing his supporters had been left behind, he sauntered back. He said nothing but stood swaying dumbly as if trying to work out what was taking place. Bryant was conscious of the woman's well-formed face in the dimness. She stared up into the buttoned night and said, 'The stars look nice don't they. Nothing's gone wrong with the stars.'

Bryant smiled. 'A lot of people never noticed the stars before the black out,' he said.

'You're right, you know,' she nodded, beginning to walk again. Scarlett was again momentarily caught adrift but he quickly shambled after them, like a dull child not wishing to be left behind.

There were no other people in the street. The wind seeped around the tall corners of the Victorian houses.

A policeman appeared wearing a steel helmet, a clumsy revolver, and riding a bicycle. He shone his torch on them and wished them a steady goodnight. They returned the wish and arrived outside the house where she lived.

'I'll be safe from here.' She smiled slightly at Bryant.

He felt disappointed. 'Oh, yes, good,' he hesitated. He returned the smile. 'I'd better go and get Andy Hardy back.'

Scarlett had begun singing another song. He sang softly and sentimentally:

'I'm gonna buy a paper doll that I can call
    my own,
A doll that other fellas cannot steal.'

'We'd better go,' laughed Bryant. He moved forward and kissed her calmly on the cheek. He felt her face move in a smile as he did so. They parted and he attempted to lead Scarlett along the pavement. The American began to stagger again.

Her voice came from behind. 'Alan,' she said, 'I don't think you're going to make it.' That pseudo-American again. 'I guess you'd better bring him in. I'll get some coffee.'

Bryant turned and looked back at her, bulky in her coat, standing in the dark. A small, tight sensation grew in his chest. He turned Scarlett and walked back to the house. 'That's if you want to,' she said.

'Thanks,' he said looking towards the American. 'I think it might be a good idea.'

Scarlett was singing without tune as they mounted the cracked steps in front of the house; he seemed to need something more substantial on which to lean. As she opened the door he all but fell into the front hall. He spread his hands with drunken extravagance. 'Home again,' he said.

Jean guided them into the close sitting-room. A lamp was glowing in a corner, she switched on two others; kneeling in her evening dress and fur coat, she put a small shovelful of dusty coal, with a curious touch of domestic pride, on the dying embers of a fire. 'Every night I time it perfectly,' she said. 'If I make it up before I go out it's just right when I get back.' She put the shovel down and wiped her hands against each other. 'I'm sorry about your wife,' she said strangely. 'Perhaps it will be all right. You never know with these things.'

'Yes, perhaps,' said Bryant. 'How does the coal ration last?'

'Not too badly.' She moved towards a door which he guessed led to the kitchen, on the way taking her coat from her shoulders and throwing it with care across the back of the deep sofa, where Scarlett was already stretched, his eyes dropped, his lips moving but silent. 'Gone, I'm afraid,' she decided. 'Bye bye, baby.'

She went into the kitchen and Bryant wandered to the door after her. He remained leaning against the jamb, watching her. 'I stay in bed nearly all day, especially now, at this time of the year,' she said. 'Sometimes I go out shopping or to the pictures with friends. But I don't need the fire all day, so that saves the coal ration.'

Briskly she took cups and saucers from a cupboard. The kitchen was handsome, a whole room converted, with cupboards and gadgets and modern-looking taps over the sink. The kettle was electric also, a rounded shape. On the wall were two country pictures, prints in cheap wood frames. 'The Yanks can't help out with the coal,' she continued. She spooned the coffee from an American jar. 'That's the only thing they can't do,' she said. 'Anything else, booze, cigarettes, butter, steak. Rationing doesn't worry me. And, of course, nylons.' She eased up her long dress to the knee. 'But no coal. I suppose it would be too much to expect presents of coal. Maybe one day I could try it. Some guy who's really sweet on me.' She laughed aridly and let the hem drop. 'I sound like an American sometimes, don't I,' she said. 'I can't help it. It rubs off.'

The kettle boiled with a whistle. 'Every modern convenience,' he smiled.

She made the coffee in a pot and put it on a polished wooden tray with the cups, sugar and milk. He offered to carry it but she took it past him into the sitting-room. Scarlett was slumped over, half on the floor, as if he had been shot. 'I don't think Oscar is going to have any coffee,' said Jean. Together they eased him back on the sofa. He grunted and made a brief face without opening his eyes.

They sat on the high-winged chairs on either side of the small glowing fire. 'How about a drink to go with the coffee,' she suggested, abruptly bright. Without waiting for a reply she stood and went to a cocktail cabinet at the back of the room. It lit up when she lifted the lid and a bell-like tune played. 'Should Auld Acquaintance'. 'Anything, just about anything,' she invited. 'Brandy. I've got some genuine French brandy.'

'That's wonderful,' nodded Bryant. He had made up his mind now; he stood up and walked over to her. They were touching at the shoulders, looking down into the garish light of the cocktail cabinet as though it held some secret. She glanced sideways at him. 'It doesn't do much for your complexion, Alan,' she murmured. 'It's ghastly, isn't it? Another present.'

He held out his hands and revolved her slowly towards him. Willingly she turned. The points of her breasts were snubbed against his tunic, her face only an inch lower than his. His forefinger touched her chin. 'Pink isn't my colour,' he smiled seriously. 'And you are very beautiful without it.'

'All right,' she said softly. It was as if they had come to an agreement. 'Yes, it's all right, darling.' She moved against him and their mouths touched, her hands sliding up to the back of his collar. The sensation of her body ran through him. He kissed her again on the mouth and then on the neck, feeling her thick hair cascading over both their faces.

She said: 'Perhaps I can make you forget waiting for the train, and her not being on it. I couldn't let anyone down like that. When my husband comes back I'll be there.'

Bryant kissed her once again, enjoying the engrossing but casual lips. 'It's in here,' she murmured as they pulled apart. It was as if she were showing him the bathroom. In a gentle but businesslike way she disengaged herself from his hold and began to walk towards the bedroom. Then, returning as if she had almost forgotten his presence, she gave a facile smile

367

and looped her arm around his waist. Like lovers taking a walk they went to the bedroom. There they stood looking at the bed, linked together still, like newly-weds in a furniture store.

'One thing about the last few years,' she said. 'It's taught people how to put their arms around a stranger's waist.' She moved forward and carefully pulled down the counterpane. The room was quietly lit by one lamp on a table near the wall. 'It's also taught people to sleep together,' she continued almost tonelessly, her hands at the back of the neck of her dress. Bryant remained near the door, motionless, his eyes on her. He made to move forward, but she shook her head. 'Don't,' she said. 'I like to get undressed without help.'

He remained still. She smiled a little doggedly at him and said: 'No need to stand to attention.'

Bryant felt himself flush. He went to the other side of the bed and undressed. As when they were sitting in the winged chairs at the fireside, it was curiously sedate.

'Do you undress your wife?' she asked.

He shrugged. 'One upon a time.'

'I'm sorry,' she said, looking up. 'I just do it to tease.'

She had pulled her dress off her shoulders. He was standing in his army shirt and his tie still knotted. With only a glance across the bed, she unfastened the American brassière and pulled it away. She rubbed her hands on her breasts and looked up to see him staring at them. They were full and dull, resting against the whiteness of her ribs. Bryant went on his knees and began to move across the bed towards her like a boy. She laughed, blithely for once, and tugged at his khaki tie. 'Wait for it,' she warned playfully.

She began to pull the dress away from her hips and stomach. Bryant crouched, watching the white skin of her stomach appear; she was wearing a suspender belt and white knickers. 'With or without?' she asked jokingly. 'The garters, I mean.' Looking up, she saw his boyish expression in the pale lamp and she reached across to him with kindness. 'I'll take everything off,' she offered. 'It's more comfortable.'

Quickly, now, as if she had finally no further reason to act a part, she took off the stockings, the knickers and the suspender belt. Bryant rolled on to his side on the bed. He looked at the shadows of her naked body as she leaned over to pull the sheets and blankets back. Shadows under her arms, under her breasts, between her thighs. 'Let's get in,' she suggested. 'In case what's-his-name walks through. Some fool broke the lock of the door.'

In those few words he could see the life she had allowed to happen. Some fool breaking the lock of her bedroom door. He eased away from the covers on his side of the bed and rolled into the composed sheets. Stamped in heavy letters on the corner of the top sheet was the inscription 'US Army'. The distraction was momentary for at that moment she was in there with him, against him; rehearsed, rolling and rubbing; her mouth gasping easy endearments. Her breasts lay heavily against his face, warm as cheeks, and he turned his mouth and suckled at one of them. He eased himself gently above her and put his hands between her slim, warm thighs. Did they have US Army stamped on them?

They made love, and then rested, on their backs, looking at the indistinct ceiling. Jean turned and whispered, teasingly close to his face, 'Was that any help?'

'A great deal,' he said.

'I'm sorry about your wife,' she mumbled.

'To hell with my wife,' muttered Bryant. He felt her breasts move as she laughed quietly.

'That's what I say,' she answered. 'All the bloody time. To hell with everybody.'

They looked quickly towards the door as it was clumsily but slowly pushed open. Scarlett staggered in. He stumbled unhurriedly towards the bed and lay down, above the covers, on the other side of Jean Manifold. 'That goes for me too,' he mumbled drunkenly. 'Fuck them all, I say. Every goddamn one.'

Hands in pockets, Albie Primrose walked like a lost, bespectacled child among the moving, shadowed crowds of the West End of London. The pavements were full of men in uniform, many drunk, and women who bellowed at them from doorways and corners. He had been to the Rainbow Corner Club in Piccadilly, and had three sarsaparillas and two cream doughnuts. Everything was in Rainbow Corner; all-American, the band playing 'Moonlight Serenade', the intimate dancing. He had gone to the dance floor and asked a broad American WAAC to dance. She refused rudely but he did not care. He thanked her politely for nothing, finished his doughnut. He bought a packet of US Government popcorn and walked into the London street.

He remembered Ballimach's jibe about his ambition to grow to be a real live boy. God, he really did feel like Pinocchio sometimes. As if to confirm the sensation there was the little wooden fellow, on his strings, with old Geppetto, his father (a carpenter like the father of Jesus), pictured on stills outside a cinema.

He realized he had never seen the movie. It was cold in the street; all the movement and the voices, the bold shouting from one side to the other as drunken soldiers and dirty women taunted each other, all that only made it seem more chill. The words came from skulls in the dark. He felt suddenly homesick. For America, for the wholesome things of life.

Abashed, he made a quick entry into the darkened foyer of the cinema. There were some heavy-skirted curtains. He found the opening at the third attempt and blinked in the lights on the other side. A dusty attendant with a drooping shoulder loitered in the area before the paybox. He had a dilapidated uniform, epaulettes flying out like wings, and torn peaked cap like some campaigner from somewhere far-off and forgotten. 'Half-crowns only,' he grunted when he saw Albie.

'Sure,' said Albie, moving towards the paybox, although momentarily surprised at the popularity of the children's cartoon film at nine in the evening. He paid his half-crown and the deteriorated attendant ripped the ticket in half, an action of surprising venom. 'Bloody disgrace, that's what I call it,' he muttered. 'Bloody filth.'

Albie, not yet familiar with the ways of the British and certainly not with those of the Londoner, nodded agreeably. The man jerked his head towards a double door at the end of the lobby. 'That's the way, Yank,' he said ominously. 'As if you didn't know.'

The small American did not know. He wandered uncertainly into the large dark cave of the cinema. Pinocchio and Jiminy Cricket were singing on the screen. Albie smiled recognition. It was warm in the darkness, almost fetid. The audience appeared to be in some numbers, but restive, moving vaguely, whispering and laughing among themselves. In the absence of an usherette, he sat one from the end of a row that was occupied by a huddle of patrons at the far end. With a peaceful pleasure he turned his face to the screen and settled back with the US Government popcorn.

Interested as he was, he could not help feeling that the other patrons, or most of them, were restive. The sniggering laughter continued, out of sequence with the doings of Pinocchio on the screen, and there were outbreaks of squeals and hushed curses. Albie was puzzled. Then a white, thin woman appeared in the aisle almost at his elbow. She waited with some impatience, indicating that she wanted to get to one of the seats the other side of his. He could see how white she was even in the dimness. She stood like a ghost.

Albie politely stood to let her pass. She brushed against him, spilling the popcorn from the bag held tightly to his chest. He apologized.

'It's quite all right, dearie,' she assured him in a nasal whine. Even by the altering light from the screen he could see she was scraggy and poor. She sat down wheezily and began to scratch her stomach. Hurriedly Albie returned to Pinocchio. To his amazement the woman casually leaned across and took some popcorn from his opened bag. Involuntarily he moved it away. Several corns fell into his lap with the sudden movement. Almost absently she picked these morsels up and put them in her slit mouth. She was so thin her cheeks bulged. He could almost see the popcorn through the skin. Her eyes were on the screen.

'I 'aven't got my fare 'ome,' said the woman after swallowing the popcorn. She still had her ghostly face away from him.

'Pardon, ma'am?' asked Albie. He felt afraid.

She breathed impatiently, her bosom sighing against the bones of her chest. 'Do you fancy something?' she asked. Then, with a grotesque impersonation of culture, she amended: 'What would be your preference?'

'Me?' replied Albie. 'Ma'am, I just want to watch "Pinocchio".'

'Fuck Pinocchio,' she said as if that might be the answer. Leaning confidingly towards him she whispered in her Cockney croak, 'Look, I'm very cheap, mate . . . buddy. It's ten bob if you want me on the floor. A quid if I get down between your knees.' She nudged him to ensure his attention, smiled a hellish smile and made a pumping action with her fist. 'And a hand job is seven-and-a-tanner.'

Albie stared at the deathly face. Jiminy Cricket was singing: 'When you get in trouble and you don't know right from wrong, give a little whistle.' The prostitute, half watching the film muttered: 'Whistle up my arse.'

She could see Albie was about to get up from the seat. She tugged him back desperately. ''Ang on,' she pleaded. 'Five bob.' There was a pleading in the lined face and cracked voice. 'I ain't even got the bus fare 'ome,' she repeated. 'It costs me a fortune to get in this fucking fleapit.'

Somehow Albie trembled to his feet. His shaking hand went to his pocket and found a sixpence. Blindly he pushed it towards her. She took it, held it in her palm and screwed up her eyes. 'You ain't getting anyfing for a tanner,' she protested loudly. 'Wot you want for a tanner?'

'Beat it,' begged Albie. 'It's your bus fare.'

The woman sent out a dog-like call. 'I ain't getting on my knees for a measly tanner,' she howled. Laughter and scorn erupted from all parts of the cinema. Shakily Albie got up and made for the exit. The whore followed him. 'Come on, Yank, it's more than a tanner!' she shouted. Screams of mirth came from women in the rows of seats. Men shouted banal advice. Albie's glasses tipped sideways across his face. The skinny woman grabbed his arm viciously. 'Trying to diddle me!' she cried, 'Fucking cheating Yank.'

An arm shot out of a seat immediately beside the aisle and Albie found himself held by a big American. 'Listen, pal, pay up,' grunted his compatriot. 'And quick. We don't want any goddamn snowdrops in here.' The vile hand squeezed him, making him start with pain. The woman was sobbing realistically and stamping her foot. On the screen old Geppetto had lost Pinocchio and was setting out to find him.

'I didn't *do* anything,' protested Albie in a loud whisper. 'Not a thing.'

''Ee *couldn't* do anyfing!' bawled a female voice from the dimness. Ribald squeals of laughter blew up.

There was some activity by the curtains at the rear of the cinema. The threadbare attendant was shouting something incoherent down the gangway. 'Pay up, I said,' demanded the big American at the end of the arm. Almost in tears Albie plunged his free hand into his pocket and took out a pound. He thrust it towards the woman who grabbed it like a starving fish grabbing a morsel. She turned haughtily and strode towards the screen waving her prize and shouting. The arm let Albie free. He rushed, sobbing, towards the exit, through the foyer, watched by the phlegmatic attendant, and went into the street. 'Never 'ad it before, I s'pose,' mentioned the attendant to the girl behind the cash desk. She nodded without interest and licked the end of her nose.

In the street Albie found he had exchanged one nightmare for another. Two women were fighting on the pavement, fists and nails and handbags flailing. One caught the other's jet hair and swung her round like a club. They were being urged on by fifty servicemen in the uniforms of half a dozen allied countries and by a gaggle of their fellow strumpets. As Albie stumbled away, trying to avoid the scene, the handbag, drawn back by one of the brawlers, caught him on the side of the face. He shouted a blasphemy and rushed away, running madly, head down along the street, with no one taking notice of him. Realizing suddenly that his rushing might make him the target for any military police patrol, he pulled up. Sweating he began to walk aimlessly, muttering to himself over his foolishness.

Jesus Christ, wasn't anything *good* in the world any more? Did no one do proper, ordinary things? A woman was on her knees in front of a sailor in a doorway. Albie shied away. Who were these nightmare people? God, why wasn't he home in clean America?

Colonel Schorner had been sitting for an hour in his room at the Officers' Club, writing to his wife. He was not a man given to long letters and since his arrival on New Year's Day in England, although he had written regularly, twice a week, he had rarely stretched beyond two pages. Now he had written twelve.

The telephone rang and he picked it up. It was General Georgeton. 'Feel like hitting the town, colonel?'

'Wow,' smiled Schorner. 'Don't say you got tickets for the Windmill.'

'Sorry, Carl,' said Georgeton, genuinely rueful. 'Sometimes I wish I were a buck private. I figure they have more fun.'

'Sometimes,' said Schorner. 'It can be lousy.'

'Right. No, it's just that there are these people, English family, who take pity on American officers and ask them over to their house for a meal. I met the guy before, he's an English gentleman. Yeah, that's about it. You know, the way we figured they all used to speak. Like in the movies.'

'I do,' agreed Schorner. 'And they've invited *me* too?'

'I called them up,' said Georgeton. 'And they said come over and bring a guest. So if you want to be a guest?'

'Fine, I'm not doing anything,' answered Schorner. 'When, sir?'

'In an hour. I'll meet you in the lobby.'

'Right, general. I'm just finishing a letter home.'

He heard Georgeton pause. 'How many pages do you write, Carl?'

'This time, twelve,' Schorner told him with what he realized was an odd pride.

'That's good. That's very good,' said Georgeton. 'By the time I've thrown out the things the censor wouldn't pass anyway, I can't think of more than a darned page to say. What is there to write about, for God's sake? Apart from the army and we're not permitted to do that.'

'As a rule,' admitted Schorner, 'I have the same difficulty. I guess social gossip is not our line.'

'Maybe we'll get some tonight,' said Georgeton. He hung up.

Schorner finished the letter and signed it formally, 'Your loving husband'. He looked at what he had done, just looked at it, he did not read it through, and sighed. If it had not been for this lousy war he would be there now, spring ploughing, watching the high snow melt, going home when it was getting dark to his own house, his wife, his dogs, his comfort. Love and ambition had already mellowed to satisfaction when his life was disturbed. How would everything be now? How would it survive? Would it? He took his diary from his tunic pocket and on the bottom of the letter copied a poem he had written down. It was the one given to him by Dorothy Jenkins, the schoolteacher, and her children: an exchange for the verses from his Robert Frost he had recited to them.

Every day you do not come,
A little bit of summer dies,
A rose leaf flutters from a rose,
With less expectant eyes.

Every day you do not come,
A blackbird from some lofty spray,
Watches another sunset fade
And sings his heart away.

At the foot he wrote, 'I was given this as a present by some children. I hope you like it. It's called "Waiting" and was written by a lady called Helen Holland.'

Schorner folded the letter carefully and put it in a US Army envelope. He hoped the censor would not think the poetry was a code. Soldiers devised all sorts of cryptics to send private, often salacious messages home to their wives and girls. The military censor office had a lurid collection pasted on its wall.

He had a bath and smoked a cigar in the bath. He realized that, like many others, he felt a sense of growing impatience now. When was the game going to stop, the clowning, the pretence of war, the build-up, the tanks, the materials? The dumps at the sides of the roads, the railway engines, the readily-equipped hospitals with their waiting doctors, nurses, blood bottles and morgues. He thought of the mountainous gun being pulled through Exeter that day and blew a cloud of smoke as though it were coming from the barrel of the weapon. He did it again, several times, firing salvoes towards the horizon of the bath water.

He shaved and dressed unhurriedly, picked up his

letter and went down to the lobby. General Georgeton arrived after five minutes and they went into the bar and had a drink. They watched the group of air force officers re-enacting their bombing raid on Germany. 'Reliving it,' nodded Schorner, smiling over his gin. The general watched. A plane, represented by a flattened hand, was crashing. 'Re-dying it,' corrected Georgeton.

The general's driver took them to the house in Kensington. 'Hickson,' Georgeton reminded Schorner as they approached. 'Major-General Henry Hickson. His wife's name is Ursula. They're okay though.'

Schorner looked from the car window. Even in the dimness of the black out he could sense that they were in an elegant area. The houses were old, built with grace and space around a square in tall terraces, and there was a treed garden at the centre. The lesserdark of the sky filled up a gap in the middle of the terrace along which they were driving, a space left by a bomb. Trees were lined regularly along the pavement and the branches showed like tributaries against the sky. The drive eventually found the house and halted.

Before they left the car a brief snatch of light showed from the doorway of the house, so shadowy it was almost like the entrance to the unknown. By the time they had reached the step the silhouette of a man was standing to greet them, waving a small torch to illuminate the step. They gained the warmth of the hall and the man, wearing a faded butler's jacket and trousers, placed the torch on the hatstand and sprang to iron attention. Georgeton and Schorner swiftly

379

glanced at each other in embarrassment and both came to a token stance in acknowledgement.

'Burgess, sir,' said the man sharply. 'Ex-Fourteenth Hussars. I was General Hickson's batman.'

'Wish you were in this war, Burgess?' asked Georgeton conversationally as the man took his coat.

'Never served in a war, sir,' Burgess replied sedately. He took Schorner's greatcoat. 'Joined up in nineteen-twenty-two, invalided out thirty-six. Never heard a single shot fired in anger, sir.'

Schorner smiled: 'That goes for a lot of us,' he said. 'Including me.'

'Soon alter that,' said the man cryptically. Then, with a drop of his voice, 'I expect sir.' Changing his conversational voice to a formal tone he said: 'This way, sir.' He led them through a heavy blackout curtain hung across the hall and into the pleasant light of a square lobby, marbled floor, with expensive walls and a rank of framed portraits of military men. Schorner moved sideways towards one. It drew him. It was a young, diffidently, smiling officer, in modern field dress. It looked out of place among all the scarlet and gold braid of the other uniforms.

Burgess saw the glance. 'Captain Willie Hickson, sir. The general's son.' His tone was odd, as if he were making an announcement. As he led the way two people came from a room on the left and welcomed them. Henry Hickson was a thin, grey man, with a deep expression. His wife was a tiny woman with a dark face and sharp eyes. Schorner thought she had been crying.

Burgess, the butler, snapped to attention and

marched stiffly away. Georgeton and Schorner were again uncertain of what they should do.

'He always does that, I'm afraid,' said General Hickson. 'Can't break him of it. When he's wearing a hat the bloody fool keeps saluting. Never seen a day's fighting, either.'

They laughed and said that Burgess had told them that. They followed the general and his wife into the room. There was a modest fire in the grate. Two glasses of sherry were already on a tray by the fireplace. The Americans agreed they would have the same.

'I hope you didn't mind me telephoning, sir,' said Georgeton. 'I remembered your kind invitation and . . . well, we don't get too many chances of being in a house, somebody's home, these days.'

'You are both very welcome,' said Mrs Hickson. She was like a small, dark bird, thought Schorner. She moved with brief movements. Her dress was old but cared for. Her hands were delicate and she had a slim wedding-ring and a small diamond ring next to it. A string of pearls looped from her neck where the skin folded. A younger woman came into the room, her face a striking likeness to the old man's.

'This is my daughter, Celia,' said Hickson. He introduced Schorner and Georgeton.

The girl was tense. She took a drink and said briskly: 'Up for the big war conference?'

Georgeton looked embarrassed. Hickson said, 'Celia,' reprovingly.

'Oh, sorry,' sighed the girl. 'I thought everybody knew.' She smiled but only shortly. 'You can always tell by all the top brass in London. In the restaurants and theatres and suchlike.' She looked challengingly at Georgeton: 'When's it going to be, general?'

'Celia,' said her father again. Her mother laughed and said: 'Celia would never make a spy, would she? She's too blunt.'

'My guess,' said the girl confidently, 'is the last week in April. And the war over by Christmas.'

'You'd better tell General Eisenhower,' suggested Schorner mildly. 'Because nobody's told *him* yet.'

After dinner, at eleven o'clock, they were seated again in the room, drinking coffee and port which Burgess, the manservant, had brought in a decanter on a tray. Schorner had sensed an unease throughout the evening. He would have been happier had there been more light in the room. Major-General Hickson said, leaning forward as though about to divulge some tight secret, 'Montgomery's father was a bishop, you know. A famous jumper in his day.'

Georgeton glanced at Schorner. 'He had mentioned it. The jumping,' said the American general. 'He mentioned it only today.'

'Ah,' said Hickson with understanding. 'He must have been reminded by a letter in *The Times* today.' He stood and went to a library table in the corner, returning with a half-folded copy of the newspaper. He opened it in a careful, elderly manner. His wife was staring into the low fire.

Celia said quite suddenly to Schorner, 'I decided to be the one who did *not* join up.' She looked at him directly, as though challenging. 'Everybody else, women I mean, couldn't wait to get into uniform to have a good time. Or into munitions and earn massive amounts of money. There are women going home with six or seven pounds a week in their pockets and they feel the war's the most wonderful thing that's ever happened.'

'I don't think that what you have said is entirely correct, dear,' put in her mother. She did not look up from the fire. Schorner remained puzzled. 'The girls of this country are doing a wonderful task.'

'If you say so, mother,' acknowledged Celia quietly. She was still tense. Turning to Schorner she went on, 'I felt that by keeping on with my job, more or less running a large office with most of the men away, I was doing just as much for the war effort, as they call it, as putting on fancy clothes and sitting, smoking twenty a day, in some ATS orderly room. That's all many of them do, you know. There *is* nothing else for them to do.'

Schorner nodded: 'Most of the armed services are doing nothing very much right now,' he observed. 'It's just waiting.' He thought briefly of the poem he had sent that day in his letter.

'There is fighting in Burma,' said the girl firmly. 'Remember that.'

'Sure, sure, and all over the Pacific. And Italy but I don't feel that I, personally, am contributing very much right now.' Schorner was being kind. He thought her expression eased. Her father had opened *The Times* and read the letter through to himself. 'Here it is,' he said with an old smile. 'All about Montgomery's father jumping up the steps to King's College, Cambridge.' He slowly read the letter to them.

When he had finished, Georgeton and Schorner laughed politely. The Englishman regarded them and then the newspaper wryly. 'I suppose it must be a mystery to you gentlemen how people in the midst of a war can take up time and space in *The Times* writing of such trivial things. I suppose it comes under the general heading of light relief. I remember in the Great War, as we called it, a professor writing to *The Time*, in nineteen-fifteen or sixteen, when the boys of this country were being slaughtered in mud; he wrote an amusing letter complaining about the shortage of *leeches* in London. Yes, leeches. Those that were obtainable were, he said, usually second-hand.' He rolled his head and laughed silently. 'Leeches,' he repeated to himself.

The two Americans again responded politely and Georgeton said: 'That seems very British, sir.'

Hickson seemed to have descended into a private reverie. 'We are fortunate in this war to have senior officers who were just subalterns in the first show,' he said, looking up sharply. 'They saw the terrible way that war was conducted; the mud, the blind indifference to the killing of troops. They would not be likely to make the same mistake themselves. Thank God for that, I say.'

It was almost midnight. Burgess brought their coats and they went to the door. The car was in the empty street. The elderly couple said good-bye in the hall but their daughter came through the heavy blackout drape and walked with them down the stone steps. She took a coat from the hatstand and held it around her shoulders.

'Please don't come out, young lady,' said

Georgeton. 'I guess we're used to the darkness now.'

She said: 'It's perfectly all right. It's not cold.'

Schorner guessed she was doing it for a reason. As they reached the pavement and were saying good-bye she said suddenly, 'I'm sorry it was a little sombre tonight.' She stood awkwardly and pulled the coat around her neck. 'After you telephoned today,' she said deliberately, 'my father had another telephone call from a friend at the War Office. My brother was wounded two months ago in Burma. He was in hospital at Chittagong.' She smiled wryly. 'Sounds like some sort of musical instrument, doesn't it,' she said. 'Or a game.' She lifted her face, full of grief, and said, 'He died there yesterday. I came home and found the pair of them weeping in the arms of Burgess.'

The inquest on Fat Meg Pender was to take place in the village hall where Meg herself had been fighting at the St Valentine's Ball only an hour before she drowned in Wilcoombe harbour. On the day the seating was arranged as it was for concerts and winter talks, with extra seats brought from the vestry of the church and from the school.

An hour before the coroner was due to arrive, and before the caretaker had pulled the bolts on the door, the South Devon people were waiting to be let in. Some, who had been among those evacuated, had returned from other parts of the country. Once the door was opened every available public seat was claimed. The coroner's officer, Constable Burridge, a cheerful balloon of a man from Totnes, had to clear half a dozen prospective spectators from the two benches reserved for the jury.

''Ee'll be wanting the county coroner's place next,' he said amiably as he ushered them out. The fortunate ones who had gained seats sat doggedly hushed, their eyes fixed ahead, their backsides tentatively occupying the chairs, their manner indicating that they feared that the slightest misdemeanour might result in their being ejected. Mrs Bewler, who had the crazy son, sat with him, both impassive as wood, until, on the thought she bent close to his ear and whispered: 'Us don't want any of youm mad fits this morning. 'Tis goin' to be worthwhile seein', this is.'

An American Army legal officer stayed overnight at the camp at Telcoombe Magna and travelled in Schorner's car to the court. He was a slight, unimpressive man, with cloudy fair hair that sprouted in patches on his domed head. His pink face, his demeanour and his conversation were without humour. Schorner did not like him.

'I still can't figure why we had to give the advantage to them and let the inquest take place here,' he protested, not for the first time, to the colonel as they drove along the beach road. It was a mild, blowy day. Clouds puffed over the sea.

Schorner said: 'I guess it was just politics. If the court had been some place else the folks here wouldn't feel they'd be getting a fair deal. They figure that this woman Meg was one of theirs so they should be there when the verdict was given.'

The legal officer's name was Parker, Captain Alvin R. Parker. 'Sure, I'm aware of that, colonel. But we don't have to do *every*thing the natives want.

There's a proper and correct coroner's court in Exeter and inquests are traditionally held there. An official inquiry into somebody's death should not be concerned with giving a bunch of hicks their pint of blood. In any case, what about our boys? I'd say they were at a disadvantage down here. They're going to be objects of hostility.'

Schorner smiled privately but said only: 'I'm sure the matter has been talked about plenty between the US Army and the British. And right here is where they've fixed it's going to be.' He glanced out of the window. They were running along the last section of the road before the harbour. 'This is Wilcoombe,' said Schorner. 'You wanted to take a look at the place where it happened.'

Parker nodded. 'Sure thing. It's going to be more than useful.' He glanced with something like worry at Schorner. 'Not that there's going to be any difficulty, colonel,' he said firmly. 'Your boys are in the clear. It's an open and shut case. She got drunk, she fell in, she drowned.'

Albie pulled the car into the side and Parker got busily out. He could have been only five foot two inches in height. Albie smiled to himself because he always did when he saw anyone smaller. The army certainly did not reward tallness with rank.

Schorner followed the legal officer and together, against the stiff breeze coming in salt gusts across the harbour, they walked to the old stone wall and looked down at the seaweeded slipway. Parker squeezed up his small eyes as if trying to visualize the deposition of evidence. With it apparently recalled and arranged he gazed down the slipway. 'Right, I've got it,' he said to

Schorner confidently. He glanced up. 'What's that?' he asked, looking towards the anti-aircraft gun.

'A British AA gun,' answered Schorner, slightly surprised that an army officer should not know.

'You don't say,' breathed Parker. 'That's a real relic, colonel. What junk.'

Schorner, to his own slight surprise, felt a puff of annoyance. 'It's a good gun,' he said stoutly. 'Brought down several Nazi planes. They're dead shots those gunners.'

'It's still old,' muttered Parker. 'Very old.'

The colonel spotted a movement at the front of the cottage by the harbour and paused until he confirmed that it was Howard and Beatrice Evans leaving their gate. 'We'll give these folks a ride,' he mentioned to Parker, taking in Albie Primrose with the remark. He said to Parker: 'This is the doctor, a nice guy, Evans.'

A sharp worry split Parker's small face. 'Wait a minute, though, sir,' he said. It was the first time since his arrival on the previous evening that he had called his superior officer 'sir'. Schorner put it down to his being in the legal branch and not a genuine soldier. 'Why?' he asked.

'This guy is a witness, right?' Parker said. 'He may be a hostile witness. I don't think it's a good idea we should be seen with him. You understand, it could lead to difficulties.'

Schorner sighed and privately confirmed his dislike of his countryman. 'Is it okay to wave to him?' he asked with no change in his voice.

'I'm sorry, colonel, in these things you can't take too much care.'

'Okay,' nodded Schorner, just concealing his

impatience. But Howard and Beatrice had seen them and were approaching smiling. Schorner introduced them to Parker. Parker said bluntly, 'I have just been advising Colonel Schorner that it would not look good if we had a long conversation just now. It's a matter of procedure, if you understand.'

Howard Evans blinked and Beatrice smiled straight at the man's face. Howard said: 'You are quite right, of course, sir. That wouldn't do at all.' He waved his hand gallantly: 'Would you like to proceed first? We'll stay here, count to a hundred and then follow.'

Parker became sullen. 'There won't be any need for that. We have the car here.' A dead smile crossed his face. 'We won't detain you.'

Schorner pedantically shook hands with Howard and Beatrice while Parker scowled. He gave a stiff little salute and turned towards the car. The colonel followed, making a face. He called over his shoulder as he reached the car, 'How are the daffodils, Howard?'

'Fine,' replied Evans, laughing. 'Blooming.'

The car drew away with Albie, wearing a private grin, at the wheel. The English couple watched. Schorner waved from the window. Parker stared straight and aloof to the front. Howard Evans said: 'What a poisonous little bastard.'

'Yes,' nodded Beatrice. 'Poor Colonel Schorner. He didn't seem very happy about the company did he.'

They began to walk up to the village hall. They could see a clutch of people grouped outside. 'Meg would have been pleased,' murmured Howard. 'Getting all this attention.'

'What do you think will happen?' she said, taking his arm comfortably.

'Did she fall or was she pushed?' mused Howard. 'I must say I'd like to see our legal beagle fall on his face.' He grinned wryly. 'Meg would have been tickled,' he said again. 'God, she's probably put the bloody invasion back by three weeks.'

There were times, in that place that spring day, when Schorner felt that he was enmeshed in some rustic dream. Sitting in the Wilcoombe Hall, surrounded by those earthy faces and observed by those ancient eyes, he wondered once again how even a war could have brought him from his familiar home to that foreign land. The room was high and tatty, cream-painted walls and tall dusty windows. Some of the panes, broken since the outbreak of hostilities, had been replaced by board or even slate, so that the light came through in chequered patterns. The floor was grimy and, he thought, was probably always so. In one corner was an obese but moribund stove, above which, browned at the edges by some previous heat, was a picture of Christ, a print of Holman-Hunt's 'The Light Of The World'. It was askew, and from its surrounding dust it was apparent that it had been for some time. Next to Christ was a dart-board.

But, as always, it was the people in this rough room that drew his eyes. The woman with the mad son who now was patting his head to keep him hushed; the labourer, Doey, whose ruby face he saw first on New Year's Eve when they came to that place. The blank-looking vicar, whose name he had forgotten. Evans and his wife sitting together, seriously but with a short smile for the people who nodded to them or greeted them with a wave. Barrington, the farmer, Schorner's unsought, unwanted adversary, solidly staring ahead, his huge head apparently built on to the collar of his coat, his wife meekly touching her fingertips together as if verging on prayer. He wondered where their daughter had gone. If she had escaped as she had vowed. A stirring at the door announced the arrival of Mrs Mahon-Feavor, with the escort of one of her military sons; the old lady flushed and feathered, the boy as blank as a dummy cartridge. She advanced towards the front of the public seats, authoritatively tapped Mrs Bewler and the mad boy on the shoulders and ushered them to the rear of the room. They made no protest. Schorner watched and saw that Burridge, the coroner's officer, allowed them to stand in a corner to see the show. Burridge patted the idiot boy on the head. Mrs Mahon-Feavor sat ceremoniously in her seat and her army son, after standing to ritual attention, eventually sat beside her, arranging his mother's heavy cape warmly around her.

The performance, fascinating as it was to Schorner, had no visible appreciation from the stranger, Captain Parker. His sulky expression remained on Private Wall, sitting apprehensively among the group of United States soldiers at the front on a long and polished new pew brought from the church. Ballimach, whom Parker watched with disdain, as if by his bulk he gave the US Army a bad name, sat next to Wall; Albie Primrose sat beside him, in stature like his son. Behind sat Gilman, the English soldier, studied closely by Parker as a potential enemy.

A rod of spring sun pierced the patched and dirty windows, striking by chance the sparse hair of Captain Parker, causing his cloudy curls to shine like a halo. He found the sun's attention uncomfortable and moved irritably sideways. It was eleven o'clock; time for the inquest to begin.

As the church clock up the hill began to drum the hour, the bulbous Constable Burridge, the court officer, in his shiny police uniform, stood in front of the seated people and opened his mouth immensely wide, as though he was going to sing.

'Oyez! Oyez! Oyez!' he bellowed. The Americans, and many of the English who had never attended an inquest before, were taken aback by the ancient words of the opening. The Americans blinked with embarrassment, the English rustics smirked. Having called the words, each one distinct and loud, he closed his mouth with a plop of satisfaction. His fat chest heaved and he called: 'All you good people of this land draw near and give due attention to the matters arising from the death of Margaret Victoria Pender –' A low howl and a sniffle interrupted his words, coming from the seats behind, and many people turned to see a potato-faced man trembling there, his eyes afire with tears. He wore a rough jacket and a black tie circling a bare neck, since his shirt had no collar.

The coroner's officer silenced the intrusion with a wide glare. The man dropped his face into scuffed hands. Then, as if he had lost his place because of the interruption, Burridge began again: 'Oyez! Oyez! Oyez!' Parker glanced caustically at Schorner, his eyes shrugging. The door at the rear, next to the lopsided Jesus and the dart-board, was rattled.

'Everybody rise!' bellowed the officer. 'Everybody rise for His Majesty's Coroner for this county . . .'

Obediently they rose but it was immediately apparent that His Majesty's Coroner for the county could not get in. The door handle was again strongly rattled. Burridge turned like an actor who has missed a cue. He advanced with official strides on the door. He was one of those heavy men who somehow walk in silence. His boots made only padding sounds. Grasping the door handle he tugged. It refused to open. 'You'll 'ave to be goin' round, zur,' he shouted through the panel. ''Er won't budge.' The homely language after the official intonation caused Schorner to smile. Comments were whispered. Even the man in the black tie and no collar slowly looked up with curiosity from the sanctuary of his hands. Schorner glanced towards Evans and returned a scarcely less than broad grin.

Doey Bidgood stood at the front. 'Be you wantin' an 'and, Ernie?' he inquired of the official. ''Tis allus a right sod, that door.'

He moved forward and added his efforts jogging the brass door knob up and down with the same energy as he might use to milk a stubborn cow. 'Stuck,' he announced eventually. 'Bluddy stuck. Oi reckon that bluddy caretaker been and left it locked. 'Ee's a no-good bugger at the best o' times.'

The incident was concluded by the coroner's confused face appearing at the street door to the rear of the hall. 'I'm coming in this way, Ernie,' he called firmly over the heads which immediately turned.

'Yes, sir,' responded Burridge. 'So be you, sir.' He turned and bellowed again at the bemused spectators,

'Oyez! Oyez! Oyez!' The coroner, a stout, grey man in a black frock coat and benign countenance proceeded down the central aisle like a schoolmaster entering a waiting class.

The court official pulled the chair away from the scratched table and the coroner sat down. Everyone else did so too. A cardboard folio of papers was brought and placed at his elbow, next to a carafe of grey water and a glass. He looked up and smiled genuinely. 'My apologies for the entrance,' he said. 'Not the best start for the proceedings. Perhaps, since we have present many who will be strangers to inquest proceedings in Great Britain, I may be allowed to introduce myself. My name is Doctor Eustace Wood and I have the title of His Majesty's Coroner for the South Hams district of the County of Devon.'

Captain Parker immediately stood. 'I am Captain Alvin Parker, sir, legal officer for the US Army Fourth Division.'

'Thank you,' said Dr Wood. 'I am pleased to make your acquaintance. Today perhaps we may both learn something.'

The coroner turned his attention to the differing faces, the rustic expectancy of the local people, the thrust out chins and noses of the jury, the bemused calm of the American military men; the nervous eyes of the witnesses.

'Before we proceed,' he continued, 'I must point out that the function of this inquest is to inquire into the death of Margaret Pender of this parish on 15 February 1944, and to ask the jury –' he nodded in an encouraging manner to the eight men and four women on the cross benches '– to ask the jury to bring in a verdict.' The people in the jury fidgeted impatiently. The foreman was Jenks, the undertaker who had buried Meg Pender. A frown touched Dr Wood's disarming face. 'I must warn you at the start to listen to the evidence and the evidence alone. And also I have to remind you that this is not a court of law in the sense of a magistrates' court or an assize court. We cannot undertake their function here, even if it were desirable. That is for others.'

Parker bit his slim lip. 'Prejudice,' he hissed at Schorner. 'Even the suggestion of criminal court proceedings is prejudice. We're going to take a rough ride here, colonel.'

Dr Wood glanced inquiringly at the sound of the American legal officer's whisper but Parker dropped his eyes to the papers in his hand. 'Right,' said the coroner. 'Let us proceed. Call the first witness.'

'Daniel Arthur Pender,' called the court officer and the shaggy man with the black tie and no collar stood up, his expression as awry as his dress. 'That be oi,' he said defensively.

'Take the stand then,' returned Burridge as if talking to a dull child. He padded across the room with a Bible held reverently.

'Where be it?'

'This chair,' the coroner called to him, pointing at a separate chair. 'We don't have anything resembling a stand.' He smiled a little impatiently, but kindly, and Daniel Arthur Pender shuffled forward to give his evidence. He took the oath melodramatically, spat unnecessarily on the black binding of the Bible to seal the act, and stood to military attention facing the coroner.

'You are Daniel Arthur Pender, the husband of the deceased?'

'The dead lady, sir. Yes.'

An audible excitement brewed in the courtroom. Whispers shuffled along the lines of seats. 'Silence please,' called the officer.

Daniel looked belligerently at the spectators. 'There might be them that don't think I am, but I am,' he said. 'An 'ave been this many a year.'

'When did you last see the deceased?'

'You mean alive, sir, or dead and all stiff?'

'Alive, please.'

Daniel put his rugged hands to his tie and pulled at it as a condemned man might try to get a moment's relief from the hangman's rope. 'Now, that be a puzzler,' he said conversationally. 'Oi reckon it was just afore the war begun.' He stared at the coroner and, as though the matter needed elucidating, added: 'Against Hitler.'

'Not since then?' asked the coroner.

'No, sir. Oi been away helping with the war.'

Dr Wood said hurriedly: 'But you recognized her body.'

A thin sniffle, gradually transforming to a whine, came from the witness. 'Aye, sir. Terrible that 'er was. I'd know my Meg anywhere. It was 'er all right.' His face shivered and his eyes glazed. 'There wadn't nobody like my Meg.'

The coroner glanced at the court officer. 'I think that is all,' he said to the ragged, standing figure. 'We only need evidence of identification from you. Please accept our sincere sympathy.'

The man gave a truncated sob, hardly more than a

sniff. 'Somebody pushed 'er,' he said suddenly. He hung on to the back of the chair as though daring them to dislodge him. The coroner held up a warning hand, but Daniel Pender bravely ignored it. 'They bloody Yanks!' he cried. 'They pushed my Meg. 'Twas them buggers what drowned 'er.'

Captain Parker was on his feet with such force that Schorner backed quickly away from him. 'Objection, sir!' he demanded. 'This kind of thing —'

'I know, I know,' said the coroner pacifyingly. He turned to Pender. 'I didn't hear a single word of that,' he said.

'Then oi'll be telling you again —' started the man. The sentence was arrested by Burridge who, moving bulkily but silently forward, put his arms like a hoop around Pender and guided him towards the back of the court. The scraggy man was still protesting. 'Oi be telling the God's truth —'

The officer placed a broad hand firmly over his mouth, like a boy silencing the school sneak. 'You b'aint allowed to say it,' he whispered fiercely, close to the grubby ear. 'Somebody else 'ull say that, Dan'l Pender.'

Parker had sat down again. At the constable's words he made to leap to his feet but then sank back hopelessly. He said to Schorner: 'This gets worse.'

'Not one bit of what has been said will go down in the record,' said the coroner easing forward and talking directly to the American. Parker nodded stiffly. 'Next witness,' called Dr Wood.

'That's all very fine,' whispered Parker to Schorner. 'It still remains that it has *been* said. Everybody in this room heard it.'

397

'Dr Edward Burt,' called Burridge, reading the name from a piece of paper. 'Dr Burt, please.'

A puzzled whisper gathered in the room as a tall, tight-skinned man who had appeared at the back walked forward with brisk importance. He carried a folder. 'You are Dr Edward Burt?' said the coroner. 'Home office pathologist?'

'Yes, sir, I am.' He did not look up but continued to rifle through the papers in his file as if uncertain which dead body to select.

An impressed buzz continued through the spectators. Doey leaned forward and said loudly to those immediately in front, 'I saw 'is drawin',' he said. ''Ee scribbles on his papers. All guts, you know, loike livers and lungs and intesterines.'

'Silence,' demanded the court officer.

Doey acknowledged the rebuke with a stiff little bow and sat back smirking. He darted forward momentarily to whisper in Lenny Birch's ear, 'You take a look when 'ee comes by us.' Then, looking slyly up to see the constable observing him sourly, he put his finger to his own lips, as if admonishing the officer, and settled in his chair.

'The deceased,' intoned the pathologist, 'was a healthy, well nourished woman . . .' There was a murmur of general agreement throughout the room. Schorner smiled into his hand. '. . . of thirty-five.' A general expression of amazement, like a dozen seepages of gas, came from the people of Wilcoombe. Women whispered together and men raised their eyebrows.

But their attention was soon back to the witness. 'My post-mortem examination revealed three pints of salt water in the lungs –'

A terrible howl came from the rear of the court. It was Pender again. ''Ee cut up my Meg!' he accused, his face crumpling into a dozen bags. 'My lovely Meg!' He let his head fall once more into his wooden hands and rocked sorrowfully to and fro. Mrs Bewler and her son looked around sympathetically. Mary Lidstone put her thick comforting arm about Pender's collarless neck.

Looking only mildly irritated, the coroner explained: 'The pathologist *has* to perform a post-mortem to determine the cause of death, Mr Pender. It is his duty.'

'Oi could 'ave told ye that she drowned without cutting 'er up,' shouted Pender truculently. 'She were pushed in the dock by they Yanks, that be 'ow.'

Captain Parker, his young, puffy face suffused and blotchy, sprang up and said: 'I protest, sir, at the conduct of this inquest. That man must be removed at once. He should have been removed before.'

The coroner sighed. He whispered to the court officer, 'Get him outside, Ernie, will you? Give him a shilling for a pint.' Burridge moved forward with his great, soft footsteps and easing Pender from his seat, led him sobbing to the door.

'Shame,' muttered one of the women. 'Jus' for telling the truth.'

Parker clenched his pale fist. 'I told you, sir,' he said to Schorner. 'We should never have let it be held here.' He glared along the engrossed expressions of the jury. Jenks, the foreman, saw him looking and importantly wrote something down.

The coroner was leaning, confidingly, towards the American officer. 'I must tell you, sir,' he said mildly, 'that such interruptions are not unknown to me. In these rural places passions run very deeply. Deaths are felt more keenly than perhaps in your country with its gangsters and cowboys and suchlike. Or taken more to heart than perhaps in the army where death is an everyday matter. Here people have known each other for a long time, for generations, and the sudden demise of anyone is of great interest and importance, it's a loss to the whole, and is liable to give way to unofficial passions.'

As he finished he smiled encouragingly towards Parker who, baffled, stood: 'Can I assure you, sir,' he muttered, 'that no death – no matter whose it is – is taken lightly by the United States Government. That is why we want the truth in this unfortunate case. The truth is not helped by the kind of scenes we have witnessed here in this courtroom.' He looked about him as if seeking support. Only Wall looked at him with any hope or sympathy. The pathologist drummed his fingers.

'Quite so,' answered the coroner quietly. 'I want to assure you that I have heard nothing out of place, nothing that I will remember.' He smiled at the jury who turned their faces to him like disciples.

'No, sir,' Jenks the foreman affirmed dramatically. 'We 'eard it all right, but we didn't take one bit o' notice.' He turned to the others: 'Din we?' They mumbled and nodded agreement.

The coroner's smile towards Parker indicated that he felt sure that the reassurance would be accepted. Parker bowed sulkily, hardly taking his backside from the seat as he rose. 'Gangsters,' he whispered icily to Schorner when he had fully sat again. '*Cowboys.*'

The pathologist finished his evidence stiffly, like a

notable dramatic actor taking part in an inferior repertory company farce. He nodded with some sympathy at Parker and left the witness chair stiffly, walking down the centre aisle and, as he passed Doey, deliberately covering the doodlings on the cover of his case file. Doey smiled and commented loudly: 'There's a nice suit 'ee was wearin' w'ant it? Wonder 'ow many coupons 'ee gave for that 'un?'

At the back of the room the Home Office man climbed into his overcoat. But at the exit door he hesitated. Burridge quickly sensed his dilemma. He padded to him, touched him aside and put his head out of the door, like a lookout. 'No, zur,' he assured the pathologist. 'Dan'l Pender be gone. I 'spect he's over at the pub. They be open early today, on account of the inquest.' He had a second look, his head turning both ways. 'If you loike I'll walk you to your car.'

'That will not be necessary, thank you,' said the pathologist rigidly. 'It was merely that I did not want trouble from that unbalanced person.' He went out.

''Fraid old Pender's going to bash 'im up and spoil 'is suit, I 'spect,' whispered Doey loudly to those around. There were sniggers. Constable Burridge, passing on his return to the front of the court, wagged a finger. The people creased their lips and put their hands in their laps.

Howard Evans was the next witness. They listened to him attentively in a manner which suggested that the Wilcoombe people knew they could get sense and fairness from him. 'I was called from my house by an American soldier,' he said. He looked around and pointed at Albie. 'That gentleman there,' he said.

Albie blushed and nodded acknowledgement like one greeting a tentative acquaintance. 'It was one-ten a.m.,' said Evans. 'With my wife I hurried down to the slipway where I saw two other Americans and a British soldier trying to pull Mrs Pender up the stones. They were having a difficult job because of the seaweed and the slime. I managed to reach them. But when I examined the woman I formed the opinion that she was dead.'

'What sort of things were the soldiers saying?' asked the coroner.

Evans looked slightly surprised. 'That is difficult to answer, sir,' he said. 'It was a very confused business. But I remember one man kept shouting something about the others going and leaving him and that Mrs Pender, Meg, had fallen in accidentally.'

'Do you see that soldier in court?'

'Yes, sir. That gentleman.' He pointed at Pfc Wall. The GI quickly looked down at his shoes and rubbed the toes together. 'He was very upset, almost incoherent, but repeating that she had fallen in.'

The coroner said he had no further questions. He eyed Parker. The American was already on his feet. 'Doctor, if Wall was so excited, upset you say, as to be incoherent, are you sure that's what he said? That she had fallen in?'

'Yes, sir. I recall him saying that several times.'

'Don't you think that it was reasonable that he was upset, in the circumstances?'

'Yes, sir. It was very unpleasant altogether.'

'And was it not reasonable that he would say that this woman had fallen into the water, since that is just what she had done?'

'Yes, I suppose it's reasonable. I didn't form any opinion as to why he said it, only that he said it, very excitedly, and kept repeating it. Even after we had managed to get her up the slipway he said it.'

'And you don't have any opinion now as to why he said it, other than he was trying to describe truthfully what had happened?'

'No, sir, I don't.'

Gilman, sitting, waiting, watching Evans and trying to fix the scene of the tragedy, suddenly saw Mary Nicholas come into the back of the room. She was wearing a light brown shawl, like some peasant woman. It was wrapped loosely around her shoulders. She held the front in her pale hands just below her stomach. Her hair was tight around her head. She looked white and tired, but beautiful.

He heard his name called while he was still looking at her, wondering where she had been lately. The voice startled him and he upset his chair in his hurry. 'Yes, sir,' he answered the constable and heard his own army boots clump on the wooden floor. He took the Bible, swore the oath and gave his name and rank.

The coroner leaned affably towards him. 'And what did you see of this unhappy incident?' he said.

'I was walking down the street, Wilcoombe Hill, that is,' began Gilman slowly. 'It was about one o'clock and I had been to a dance in this room, sir, where we are now.'

'Were you with anyone else?'

Gilman answered: 'I was with two American soldiers, sir.'

'Are they in court?'

'Yes, sir, the small chap there –' he nodded at Albie Primrose '– and the larger chap there.' There was some muffled laughter as he indicated Ballimach. 'I don't remember their names, sir.'

'And what happened when you reached the quay at the foot of the hill?'

'We heard shouting and we ran down there and saw this other American soldier – the one pointed out by Dr Evans, sir – trying to pull this lady up the slipway. He couldn't manage it and he shouted to us to go and help him. I told the little fellow to go for the doctor and the big chap and I went down to give a hand. It was very slippery and it took us by surprise and we slid all over the place. The woman looked in a very bad state, terrible, and although we tried our best there trying to revive her with artificial respiration, there was not much we could do.'

'Yes, you are to be commended for your efforts, Private Gilman. Do you remember anything that the first American soldier, Pfc Wall, that is, was saying? The soldier who was already there when you arrived?'

'Not a word, sir. He had been drinking, like all of us. It was Valentine's night, so he wasn't very clear. He kept on about somebody running away and that the lady had fallen in by accident.'

'You don't recall his actual words?'

'Only at the end, sir, when the doctor had arrived. Then I remember him saying: "She fell in, she fell in. Honest."'

'Honest. He said that?' asked the coroner quietly.

'Yes, sir, I remember him saying that.'

Parker stood and slowly, menacingly it seemed to

Gilman, faced him. The English soldier swallowed heavily.

'How long have you been in the British Army, Private Gilman?' he asked.

Gilman, caught unawares, had to calculate. Parker interrupted. 'If you can't count the time, what month and year did you join?'

'November, thirty-nine, sir. Three months after the war started.'

'You've never been promoted?'

'No, sir.'

'Why is that, do you think?'

'I don't know, sir.'

'Is it because you're not very capable?'

Gilman paused. 'I'm not very ambitious, sir.'

There was an approving murmur at the reply. The US captain sniffed. 'You had been drinking heavily that night?'

'A few pints.'

'You were drunk?'

'Yes, sir, I would say I was drunk.'

'Incapable?'

'No, sir, I wouldn't say that. I could walk straight. We were just, well, we call it merry.'

'But despite being drunk – merry – and, on your own evidence, being very confused about the events of that night, despite that, you recall clearly Pfc Wall saying the words, "She fell in – *honest*"?'

'Yes, I remember that, sir.'

'Honest? You remember that one word. Honest?'

'Yes.'

'I would liked to put it to you, Private Gilman, that Pfc Wall said nothing of the kind. And that you, in your drunken state that night, were in no condition to remember it.' Gilman was silent.

'Would you like to answer that?' invited the coroner.

'There's nothing more I can say, sir,' said Gilman.

'That's the best thing you've said yet,' retorted Parker.

He sat down angrily. The coroner looked towards him. 'Nothing further, I take it?'

'Nothing further,' snapped Parker.

'Thank you, Private Gilman. Call the next witness.'

'Private First Class John Wall.' The constable's shout was unnecessary since Wall was sitting almost under his chin. Schorner could see the GI's hands shaking as he went to the stand. They still trembled as he took the Bible and the oath.

As Wall stood, ashen-faced, waiting for the first question he saw a rat walk unhurriedly from the opposite side of the room where the small kitchen attached to the hall was located. He watched it with fascination and loathing and only just recovered to answer his name and rank.

'Please tell the court what happened on the early morning of February fifteenth this year,' requested the coroner. 'Carefully. In your own words.'

Wall watched the rat. He heard himself speaking. 'I had been at Totnes, sir, at a US Services dance for St Valentine's night and I had come back on the bus to Wilcoombe where I was going to pick up a liberty truck to go back to camp, sir.' The rat was sitting quietly by the wall apparently listening to the evidence. No one else had noticed it. He was the only person in the room looking directly at it. Everyone else was watching him.

The coroner was mildly impatient with his preoccupation, his hesitancy. 'Yes, yes,' he prompted.

'There were some other guys, not from my outfit, who were there and we were horsing about by the quay. Everybody was a little drunk, I guess. Then along came this lady . . .' He glanced around as if fearing to give offence. 'Very large,' he compromised. 'And she was pretty, well . . . jolly, I guess you would say. She shouted to us and kind of staggered towards us and we were fooling around with her.'

'What form did this fooling take?'

'Well, dancing with her. That kind of crazy thing. She was very fat and she was dancing with three of us at a time. Then . . . then somehow . . . God, I don't know . . . how . . .' That shit rat was staring at him. He could see it. It began to advance across the floor, close to the feet of the people in the front row of chairs.

'Yes, go on. Please go on.'

'Then . . . she fell into the harbour . . .' He could stand it no more. The rat was on the toe of Mrs Mahon-Feavor's shoe. She did not feel it. 'Sir . . .' yelled Wall desperately. 'There's a goddamn great rat . . . just there . . . down there . . . Look!'

Those in the front row jumped to their feet, some shouting, some screeching. Mrs Mahon-Feavor fell backwards spectacularly into the row behind. The other people stood pointing out the rat to each other.

There was uproar everywhere. The coroner was on his feet pointing directions for the capture or killing of the creature. Constable Burridge had miraculously produced a lavatory plunger and was striking vainly under the chairs trying to stun it. The weapon bounced on its rubber cup. Cries rose from all places.

'Here it is!'

'Here be the bugger!'

''Ee be over here! Kill 'un! Kill 'un 'fore 'ee bites!'

In front of the turmoil sat Captain Parker like an apparition, a sheen of sweat on his face, looking stiffly ahead, his papers held firmly under his clenched pale fist. Schorner was watching the tumult with fascination. Wall was standing at the witness chair yellow to the neck, sweat dripping down his brow, his eyes wide like a man in a fever.

The rat had wriggled through the room and eventually escaped untouched through the door into the street. 'Order, order!' shouted Constable Burridge. 'Everybody be seated please.'

'I shall adjourn the proceedings for ten minutes,' said the coroner decisively. 'It will enable us all to collect our wits.'

He stood. 'Everybody rise!' bawled the court officer. They all stood and Dr Wood, with a little bow, marched first to the rear door, which, at one pull, he remembered was locked. He turned and, with decent dignity, walked down the aisle and out into the street. He went round to the rear of the building and sat in the small room there. He had trouble in not laughing aloud and alone.

In the courtroom Parker stood like a blade of grass, bleached and dead. He stared at the wall ahead, not acknowledging anyone, not even Schorner. Eventually the colonel said: 'Life's never short of little items of interest down here, captain.'

'I can see that,' said Parker bitterly.

Gilman stood and walked a few paces into the room towards Mary Nicholas. She saw him and stood, a tight smile on her slim face. 'Where have you been hiding?' she asked before he could speak.

'Nowhere. I just thought you were busy.'

'Who told you that?'

'I heard, that's all.'

'It's a lie. I haven't been out with anybody else.'

'I didn't say you had. I said I heard you were busy.'

'That's what you meant.' Her voice, which in the crowd she had kept low, now became sharp. 'You shouldn't listen to the dirt that goes around.'

Gilman was astonished. 'I'm sorry,' was all he could say. He glanced about them. Nobody seemed to have heard, but two women were looking directly at them.

'Don't mention it. I know my reputation,' she said sullenly. 'If you'd been with me that night you wouldn't be mixed up in this.'

'I'm not mixed up in it. I was there, that's all.'

'She was pushed into the harbour.' She descended to a knowing whisper but said it casually, then held out a hand to silence his protest. 'Pushed,' she said firmly. 'I saw it.'

'Oyez! Oyez! Oyez!' The yell of Constable Burridge terminated that and all the other conversations in the room. 'Everybody take their places.' From the door at the rear the coroner entered at a gait, the people parting to let him through. He regained his seat and performed his truncated bow. He sat and everybody sat, except Private Wall. He stood, limp now, at the witness chair.

'Now where were we?' said the coroner amiably. 'Yes. Mrs Pender had just fallen . . . gone . . . into the water. Private Wall, how did that happen, do you think?'

'I don't know. I didn't see,' said Wall quickly. 'I was pretty drunk, sir, and we were singing and horsing about and suddenly I heard one of the other guys shout that the fat woman was in the harbour. I thought they were kidding. Then I ran over and saw her in the water.'

'And how did you react?'

'Sir?'

'How did you feel when you saw that she was in the water?'

'I was scared, sir. Really scared. I started shouting out. And then I saw that the other guys had gone. They just went. I don't know where. But they cleared.'

'And you still don't know who they were?'

'No sir. I figured they rode in on the bus but I don't know for sure. I was full of booze . . . drink. I've never seen them before. I can't even remember their faces. There are a lot of American troops in this area, sir.'

'The police have tried to trace them but failed. You've tried to remember.'

'Yes, sir, I've tried hard. But I don't know. There are thousands of guys . . .'

Wall's face was the colour of sour cheese. The coroner persisted. 'So you are telling this inquest that at the moment this unfortunate woman fell . . . went . . . into the water to be drowned, you were looking the other way.'

'Yes, that's the truth. It was all confused. I don't remember anything real clear.'

'However, you remember clearly that you had turned away then and you did not see what happened? Remember you are on oath, won't you?'

Schorner felt Parker straighten at his side. The

410

legal officer made to stand up but the coroner had been expecting it. Without giving him anything more than a swift glance from the edge of his eye, not so much a flap of the hand, he said: 'Yes, Captain Parker, I know. You will have your opportunity in a moment.'

His lined face beamed in a fatherly way at Wall, the very smile making his wrinkles change their courses and patterns. 'And what happened afterwards?'

The relief on Wall's face that the moment was over was evident. 'After the others had gone, sir, I ran down the slipway. As soon as I hit the seaweed down there my feet went from under me and I slid down into the water. The lady was not very far away and I managed to grab hold of her and kind of tow her in. I pulled her up on to the stones and tried to bring her round. Then the other guys, Ballimach and the English soldier, arrived and then the doctor.' He stopped. The coroner waited, saying nothing. The vacuum resounded in the dusty room. Wall had to fill it. 'She fell in, sir, I'm sure. Nobody pushed her, sir.'

While the jury was in the adjoining room, having trooped out into the street to get there, the remainder of the people stood and talked in confined voices. Gilman went out into the street where Mary Nicholas had gone. It was a clean spring day, windy now, with gulls screaming on the chimney pots.

'What did you see, then?' he asked her. She was standing on the pavement smoking a cigarette.

'Not now. I'll tell you sometime.'

411

'Don't you think you ought to tell somebody, the coroner or the police?'

She smiled grimly. 'And stand up there and have my private business questioned? What were you doing down by the harbour at night? Who were you with? No bloody fear. There's enough poison put around about me as it is. What good would it do, anyway?'

'It might do some good for the American, Wall.'

She looked at him bitterly. 'You always think the best of people. You're a real innocent, aren't you?' She turned abruptly and walked down the hill, the smoke from the cigarette drifting over her slight shoulder.

Gilman swore to himself and turned angrily back into the hall. On the steps outside Colonel Schorner was standing with Lieutenant Bryant, Captain Parker and Tom Barrington. As Gilman saluted, Barrington was saying: 'I think you have to realize the resentment that has built up. It was bound to happen and it has. I'm not even talking about this case.'

'I hope you are not, sir,' said Parker sharply. 'Here is a case of an American boy risking his life to save a drunken woman and getting a lousy deal for it.'

Barrington was nonplussed. 'Yes, all right,' he said. 'But there is a general feeling of resentment . . .'

Schorner said suddenly but quietly: 'Unfortunately for us – as well as you – we are here until we are ordered to leave, resentment or not. You'd better get that straight. On the other hand, I want to make life as easy as possible for everybody, including myself. If it's okay with my superiors, and I'll have to check with them, I'm willing to have a meeting with yourself and anybody else you like, your council or whoever, to try and straighten a few things out.'

'There are plenty of those,' said Barrington but less forcefully. 'That might be useful.'

'Bryant here is my liaison officer. He'll call you and fix a date.'

'Yes, sir,' said Bryant.

Barrington said: 'I'll wait to hear then. Good morning.' He walked back into the courtroom.

Parker muttered, 'Don't they just think they're so superior, these British.' Schorner realized Parker never swore.

'Hold it,' smiled Schorner. He nodded towards the grinning Bryant. 'You have one here.'

'I mean the civilians,' amended Parker. 'They milk the US Army of every last cent, everything from the price of a cup of their lousy tea to compensation for land. Land for training men who are fighting a goddamn war. And then they belly-ache. How they belly-ache. You should see the cases I get to deal with. Women screaming rape when they're so ugly they ought to grab anything they get and be grateful.'

Bryant said: 'I'll see if I can do something about fixing that date, sir. The old lady, Mrs Mahon-Feavor, and Mr Barrington ought to be able to work it out right away.'

'Make it in the next couple of weeks,' said Schorner. 'We're getting busy.'

Bryant left. Parker was still angry. 'You'd blow through the roof, colonel, if you knew the things about the British that I know. Give me our niggers any day.'

The jury appeared selfconsciously from the kitchen at the side of the hall and led by Jenks, at an undertaker's pace, they trooped back into their benches. Everyone else followed. As Schorner went in Howard Evans approached. 'Am I allowed to speak to you now?' he whispered. Schorner grinned and eyed Parker who was making for his seat. 'I guess so,' he said. 'Now the big boss is out of earshot.'

'Will you come to supper on Saturday?' said Evans. 'We've been promised a fresh chicken.'

'Sure. I'd love to.'

'We're inviting Dorothy Jenkins from the school as well. You've met before. Is that all right?'

'It's fine. Thanks. I'll be there.'

'Eight o'clock,' said Evans.

They returned to their places. Constable Burridge eyed the door for the coroner's return. At the moment he saw what he took for his shadow he bellowed: 'Oyez! Oyez! . . .' He faltered. Through the door, as the people obediently rose, sauntered Daniel Pender.

He gave a diffident smile and called down the court, 'Oi'm back. Oi'll just stand by 'ere and say nothing.' The Wilcoombe people laughed and sat down.

'You mind you do then.' The warning came from the coroner who entered while attention was on Daniel. Burridge shouted, 'Oyez, Oyez, Oyez,' again and spectators, witnesses and jury jumped to their feet again.

When all was finally settled the coroner said: 'Have the jury reached a verdict?'

Jenks stood importantly and said: 'We have, sir.'

'What is your verdict?'

''Tis an open verdict, sir. We don't know what happened – and we thinks that nobody ever will.'

*

414

Each day Schorner's men were on the assault craft, on the long beach, or advancing hopefully over the lakes by pontoon and into the rising hinterland. Another day, another drill. Gradually they were becoming soldiers but it was taking a long time.

As the days in March grew longer, the weather became dry and fair. The great invasion build up increased, until it seemed that every field and road in the south and west of England had become a storehouse or a supply route for the great army waiting to move. These preparations had a codename – Bolero – for, like Ravel's music, they increased in volume as time went on.

The clocks of England had been adjusted to permanent summer time, a matter which had given rise to caustic comment from troops camped in deep mud during the winter. The device was said to assist the farmer and the production of war materials by providing more daylight hours. In March double summer time, a two-hour adjustment, came into being.

Each day now the pretended battle raged and rumbled across the western countryside. Plumes of smoke rose into the springtime sky like black trees. Thousands of men lay in holes and trenches while shells from their own guns fell close, sometimes too close. Eight infantrymen died in two separate accidents of misdirected gunfire in the course of a three-day exercise. Thirty others received wounds, some were taken to the new hospital prepared for the invasion where they provided useful practice for the military doctors and nurses.

The civilian population could only watch from afar,

although each day they heard the rumble and crump of heavy guns, although the sound of small arms fire hushed the birds, and aircraft breaking low across the trees scattered cattle. A mis-aimed shell struck near a hen house a mile outside the evacuation area and there were stories of feathers floating as far away as Salcombe. A donkey in the next meadow to the hens was never seen again.

Rumours ran wild in the small towns and hamlets: a mad pilot had deliberately dropped a bomb on Eisenhower during a tour of inspection; the GIs were dying like flies of cholera; there had been a mutiny and many officers had been butchered. The truth they saw was in the blackened faces and fatigued eyes of the men in the jeeps, trucks and tanks which daily used Wilcoombe Hill.

At Wilcoombe the Home Guard company had, with official sanction from its divisional headquarters and a long, patient, sigh from the Americans, under-taken patrols around the perimeter of the 30,000 acres of occupied area. It had become another country of different people with barbed frontiers and armed squads patrolling both sides of the wire.

Colonel Schorner had been to supper at Howard and Beatrice Evans' house, with Dorothy Jenkins, the schoolteacher, as the other guest. He had driven himself and, having delivered Dorothy to her door, he drove back along the coast road to the checkpoint.

It was eleven o'clock and a seasonal moon was hanging low over the Channel, spreading its neutral light on the soldiers on both shores. For the first time since he had been in England he felt a sureness, an expectation amounting almost to happiness. Things would be all right soon, the battle would start, they would win for certain and the war would be over. He could go home. He ought to go home. In an odd way he was actually getting to like this alien place.

As he approached the barricade he could see there was something happening there. Lamps and torches were dipping and dancing and in the general moonlight he could see two distinct groups of figures. He drove closer and saw that his military police, their white helmets bright as mushrooms in the moon, were confronting and bring confronted by a haphazard section of soldiers which he realized at once were members of the Wilcoombe Home Guard.

He stopped the jeep and unhurriedly clambered out. His men were relieved to see him. 'What's the trouble?' he asked, walking casually. He saw that Tom Barrington and the vicar, Eric Sissons, were in the short British contingent. There were half a dozen others, oddments of men, wearing battledress, woollen commando hats, and with black spots on the highlights of their cheeks. They looked curiously like a group of travelling players.

Barrington, a sten gun lodged below his arm like the top bar of a gate, and with a revolver on his webbing belt, stepped forward and saluted stiffly. Schorner returned it. 'We are carrying out assigned duties, colonel,' said Barrington. 'I am in command of this patrol and we have our orders to check the perimeter of the occupation area. Your men in the white bonnets don't seem to want to let us carry out these duties.'

'Sergeant,' called Schorner. The military police sergeant, as wide-fronted as a truck, a westerner with

417

a stony face, emerged from the guard hut.

'Sir,' he said, saluting, 'I've just called the British civil police. Standard orders, sir. These people have been trespassing.'

A clamour of argument rose from the Home Guard patrol, all speaking at once like boys at a football match. Barrington, embarrassed when he saw Schorner's quick grin, ordered silence. The vicar looked sulky and kept tugging at his woollen hat. Instead of a gun he carried a wooden club.

'Okay,' said Schorner patiently, 'what exactly is the trouble?'

'One of these men was under the wire,' said the sergeant quickly before the other side could speak. He nodded. 'The little guy there. The one holding the raccoon.'

Horace Smith, the poacher, parcelled in a large uniform, the belt and webbing ringed around him like string, crammed his face with enormous anger. 'Raccoon!' he exploded. 'Rac – fucking – coon! Oi'll 'ave you know this be the best bloody ferret in Devon.'

'It got under the wire,' explained Sissons, wanting the matter over. He made a wriggling motion with his hand. Barrington glared belligerently at the vicar. 'And he went to retrieve it,' finished Sissons bravely.

'In that case,' said Schorner firmly, 'he was off limits.'

'I didn't know he had the ferret with him,' grumbled Barrington. He glowered towards the flickering-eyed Smith. 'He won't come again.'

'Sure. If he'd stepped on an anti-personnel mine he wouldn't be in a position to come again,' pointed out Schorner. He looked at Barrington. 'Is it really

418

necessary, Mr Barrington, to patrol this boundary? We do it pretty thoroughly from the inside.'

'I know you do, colonel. So *we* do it outside. Our duty is to check that everything is all right. Those are our orders.'

'Great,' sighed Schorner feeling his anger rising. 'Then make sure that your Home Guard obeys orders. If your men have to bring pets on patrol see they keep control of them. Goodnight, Mr Barrington. I apologize – *Captain* Barrington.'

The Devon farmer tightened his mouth. Then he bawled an order for the patrol to fall into line, followed by a shout to bring them to attention. The first order was so accentuated that it startled not only the Americans but his own men as well. They clattered to a disorderly line and then to attention. They lumbered off into the moonlight, Horace Smith wrestling with the ferret under his battledress blouse.

The Americans watched them move silently away. Schorner said: 'Okay, get the gate up. I want my bed.' He drove through not looking at the guards. But he had scarcely gone a hundred yards when he heard their whoops of laughter. He grinned and, shaking his head, muttered to himself in what he could summon of a Devon accent: 'Raccoon. Rac – fucking – coon.'

The Home Guard were by then beyond the first rise and fall of the sloping ground so they heard the laughter only faintly. Barrington grunted: 'They're kids. You wait, the Germans will have a field day.'

They marched up a defile going north from the moonshone sea. At one point they could see a segment of Telcoombe Magna village. Sissons automatically looked towards his church. He stopped abruptly, causing the man behind to collide with him. 'Hark,' he said, raising his wooden club. They all stopped and listened.

'Somebody is playing the church organ,' he whispered. 'I can hear it clearly.' They stood and they could all hear it.

'My God,' breathed Sissons. 'What is it?'

Horace Smith, clutching his ferret, made a tentative answer. 'Sounds like that "Twelfth Street Rag" to me,' he said.

Mrs Cecily Sissons had listened to the start of the news, as she always did, and smiled her fond, daft smile as a greeting to the voice of Alvar Liddell. 'Good evening, Alvar,' she said with exaggerated softness and a little bow of the head. It was, 'Good evening, John,' if the announcer were John Snagge, or 'Bruce, how are you?' for Bruce Belfrage. At times she felt they were her only reliable friends. She spoke to each one with the same gushing familiarity except Wilfred Pickles, a late-comer. She liked neither his accent, which was northern, nor his common-sounding name. By the end of the news, however, it never mattered for she had invariably abandoned both her devotion and her attention to the warring world that day, and had slumped forwards or backwards in her chair, the emptied bottle and rimed glass brushed by her limp hand. If she went to sleep hanging forward either Sissons or his father would give her a push so that she toppled back into the deep chair because she had been known to tip out of the seat and had once brought the bulky radio set crashing from its bamboo table, a catastrophe that had scarcely roused her. Sissons had found her sprawled with her arms about it as though she had found a wooden lover.

The wireless set and the bamboo table were theirs, but most of the things in the house were not. 'I don't think we'll ever go back,' he had forecast to his father. 'The place will be ravaged, wrecked; church and vicarage. Nothing will ever be the same again in these parts.'

The older his father got the less he cared. 'I don't see that it makes any difference where we are,' he pointed out. 'Life's no different. Every day another bit falls off me, a bit of my ear fell off today; she gets her bottleful down her gullet, and you prance around like a woman in your cassock and bray at those tomfool services of yours. What difference is there?'

Sissons stemmed his bitter reply. Each day he found less point in communication with both his wife and his father. He spent lonely hours in his emergency study, much of the time reading through the books he had loved in boyhood and had kept, but had only redis-covered during their enforced move from Telcoombe Magna. Henty's *Wulf the Saxon*, Percy F. Westerman's brave adventures and the Biggles books by the renowned Captain W. E. Johns kept him occupied if not enthralled. There were ecclesiastical matters to be dealt with but far fewer now he had lost his own parish. He thought of volunteering for one of the services but he believed the war would be finished by Christmas. Sometimes he read the Bible, but not often because he had read it before.

That night he was waiting for Horace Smith, the

poacher, and occupying the time with Henty, although he had little mind for reading. It was nine-fifteen so Cecily would be well slumped by now, although he would need to check before he went out; his father also dozed readily about this time. That was to the good. The less people knew about his movements for the next few hours the better.

A soft but assured tap came on the window, and although he was expecting it, the sound caused him to start guiltily. Like a spy he crept to the casement and, turning the oil lamp as low as it would go without going out, pulled the curtain. He could only see Horace Smith's face as a pale patch but the sabre-toothed grin was close against the glass. A spectral finger beckoned against the pane. Sissons felt his courage slide, but after a brief thought he pulled himself together and went stealthily round to the front door.

'Wait here a moment,' he ordered in a whisper before Horace could speak. He did not want the poacher in the house, even as an accomplice. The thin man nodded cagily. He looked like an elf standing in the darkness, guile folded into every crease of his face, his clothing purloined from the Wilcoombe Civil Defence storeroom. His rubber boots had been intended for use following a poison gas attack.

Sissons was clad in a blue siren suit, a thick one-piece overall with a line of odd buttons from the fly to the throat. He turned into the house and glanced into the dim sitting-room. They were both lolling in sleep. Cecily was hanging forward; he pushed her back softly, not through any late-occurring tenderness but because this might be the one time in her sad and soaked life that she could wake and spoil everything.

Alvar Liddell was saying that the Russian Army was advancing on four fronts. Sissons made to switch him off but then changed his mind. Instead he turned the volume down, went to the front door and out into the Devon darkness.

Horace was awaiting him mischievously. 'Now you're certain about this, Smith, aren't you?' said the vicar. 'I mean, you're sure of getting through the wire and finding our way to the church?'

'Sure as I be about anythin',' replied Horace. He looked straight at the vicar, a challenge. 'Surer than I be about a lot o' things, reverend. Like Jesus.'

'All right, all right,' sighed Sissons petulantly. 'This is not the place to discuss theology. As long as you *do* have a way. It's not just one of your fancies.'

'If 'tis a fancy you can have your ten bob back,' said Horace sincerely. 'But oi reckon it ought to be five bob now and five bob when 'tis done. You might step on one o' they mines.'

'Oh, wonderful. I thought you knew the way.'

'Aye, but I b'aint been right to the church these last weeks. There be no call for me to go to the church now, be there? But I been through the wire and right to Telcoombe Magna, tons of times. There's a lot o' trade over there now, rabbits, hares, pheasant, partridge, even a few hens what people ha' left behind. I done better since they Yanks been 'ere than ever afore in my life.'

'I'm not here to hear your confession,' said Sissons rudely. 'I just want to know what's going on in my church. And I want to make sure that you know what you're about. Get me in and get me out again and ten shillings is yours. It can come from the organ fund. Ten bob's not going to make that much difference now.'

They were walking from the house, through the garden, untidy even in the darkness. 'Most people is countin' on the insurance, reverend,' said Horace conversationally. 'They reckons they Yanks are going to pay out so much there's everybody in these parts is goin' to be millionaires. They'll have to pay a few hundred quid for the likes of the Telcoombe Beach Hotel, I 'spect. Not a brick left on top of another brick. I reckon your church must be worth near as much.'

Sissons contained his wrath at the man's idiocy. 'Come on,' he ordered. 'Let's get a move on. There's a moon tonight.'

'Eleven, seven, first quarter,' recited Horace. He grinned with grotesque pride. 'I knows about the moon.'

They moved along the lanes, in a curious, short, indian file. Horace took a sack from inside his blouse and carried it in his hand. 'Listen, Smith,' said the vicar. 'You're not going poaching tonight, are you?'

'Why not, reverend? I do near every night, 'cepting Sundays. I listens to the hymn-singing on the wireless on Sunday nights.'

Sissons, ignoring the remark, caught the little man's shoulder. 'But *I* can't be found with you with stolen game in the sack. How would that look? What would I say to the bishop?'

Horace stared at him in the darkness as though trying to detect some secret in his face. 'You say the same to the bishop as you say if they catch you and shoot you up agin a wall for a spy, I s'pose,' he answered logically. 'What's a bit of poachin' alongside spyin', if you don't mind me askin'?'

The clergyman acknowledged the point with a grunt. They continued to move along the low darkness of the lane. Although he had spent ten years in the region Sissons quickly found himself confused, then lost. Eventually they crossed a sloping field and went through a lofty wood, which he recognized as being on the fringe of Barrington's farm. They were approaching Telcoombe Magna from the north-west.

'There be the wire, just there, see,' said Horace quietly but not whispering. 'The bottom strand is cut just by that hawthorn. I know that 'cause I cut it.'

'What about the patrols?' asked Sissons.

'They're along two or three hours a'tween them,' assured Horace. 'And you can hear they comin' a mile away. They smoke and you can see the red ends. They're always talking and swearin' though they don't seem to have as many swear-words as us. I'm always on the other side of the hill afore they get anywhere near. Nobody's ever seen the wire's been cut either. They be a bit dopey like that, these Yanks.'

They advanced on the wire, then, as if to give the lie to Horace's confidence, a line of figures, irregular and dark, abruptly appeared on the near skyline and began moving downhill along the perimeter. There were no cigarettes and little noise. The poacher and the vicar lay flat against the dew-damp grass and waited until the soldiers had passed only a dozen yards ahead.

'So much for your knowledge,' said Sissons bitterly.

''Twas all right. Maybe they be tightenin' things up. But they be gone now. They won't be back for a couple of hours, any road.'

'We could easily have been caught,' grumbled Sissons. His knees and his hands were wet and all four were shaking.

'We was outside the wire,' pointed out Horace. 'If they'd asked we could ha' said we was 'aving a quiet prayer loike.'

The clergyman glared at him in the dimness. He stemmed his retort and asked tersely: 'How long before we can go on?'

'Better give 'em five minutes,' Horace assessed casually. He sat back against the bole of a tree. Sissons squatted moodily in the shadow. 'Many a night oi spent out like this, reverend,' said the poacher slowly after a while. 'Just sittin', waitin' for some trade, a li'l ol' rabbit or a long hare.' His voice seemed to drift in the dark.

'Don't expect me to approve of your poaching, Horace,' said Sissons, though not unkindly.

'Now oi wouldn't that,' replied Horace sportingly. His voice quietened again. 'But 'tis strange sittin' by yourself at night, when you can't tell the difference between a field and the sky. Not sometimes anyway. Then you get nights with good stars and the moon. They used to call the moon the parish lantern in Devon in the old days, vicar, you know, when my ol' dad was a boy.'

'Yes, I've heard it.'

'Just sittin' 'ere at night sometimes I wonder maybe what I might ha' done. Loike, maybe, if I been learned, it could be that I might be loike one o' they generals, or a reverend same as you. But here I be catching rabbits and pheasants for trade. 'Tis a funny twist is life.'

Sissons was wondering if his wife had fallen off the chair yet. Horace seemed to read the thought. 'Mind, I got a lot to be thankful for. Not bein' fit for the army, so I could stay at 'ome, and my missus, fat as a sow though she be, she's a good old maid.'

The vicar put his face close to his watch. It was a quarter to ten. 'Why wouldn't they have you in the army?' he asked.

'Legs,' answered Horace mysteriously. 'They said the legs wasn't no good. I weren't goin' to argue, so I went 'ome again.' He added: 'They didn't like my eye either.' As though he did not wish to pursue the subject, he stood and said, 'We better be goin' on.'

He stood easily, Sissons stiffly, and they took up their curious indian file again and moved ahead. They were within two yards of the wire before Sissons saw it.

'In by the back door.' Horace gave a subdued guffaw. He went directly to one section and efficiently pulled the bottom two strands apart. A gap about ten inches high was exposed under the coil. 'Right, vicar,' said the poacher, holding the next strand up politely. 'Under you go.'

'Under there?' muttered Sissons doubtfully. 'I doubt if I can.'

'Either that or we dig a burrow,' smirked Horace. 'Can't cut any more wire. They Yanks b'aint that mazed.' He lifted the strand to its tightest extent and Sissons, flat on his stomach, prepared to crawl under.

'There aren't any mines here, are there?' he said.

'Not that 'as ever bothered me,' said Horace ambiguously.

'I hope not. Here goes.' Sissons shuffled and scraped forward before rolling quite athletically beneath the wire and out on the forbidden side. He cleared the coils and remained at a crouch.

Horace squirmed under like a ferret. 'That wadn't too bad, vicar,' he said, grinning encouragement. 'You b'aint so soft as you look sometimes.'

Sissons grunted and said: 'Let's get a move on.'

Horace led the way across open country now, fields that Sissons recognized, down towards a group of farm buildings. 'We ha' got to get along in the ditch now, boy,' said Horace. 'They got one o' they bazooka guns in the yard there and they be just as loikly to shoot it at us. They be jumpy as bloody frogs. Come along a 'ere.'

His heart thundering against his siren suit, Sissons dropped obediently into the deep Devon ditch and followed the poacher. It was wet, thick and smeary. The mud soaked through the baggy knees of the trousers, smothered his hands. For the first time his nerve began to seep away. Horace froze like an animal just ahead and Sissons pushing forward felt the top of his head collide with the man's bony backside. Someone was emptying a bucket into the ditch ahead. The smell of human sewage filled the enclosed space. The water from the bucket drifted down the ditch running first between the knees of Horace and then those of the vicar.

'I emptied the honeybucket!' shouted an American voice. 'Nobody else would.'

428

'Wow!' another exclaimed. 'Now maybe I can have a clean shit.'

The two Englishmen remained stiff and still in the stench of the ditch. After several minutes Horace eased his head above ground level, only to see the American soldier astride the honeybucket less than two yards away. The GI began to sing idly:

> 'The stars at night
> Are big and bright,
> Deep in the heart of Texas.'

Sissons winced as he lay among the deposit of excreta. Eventually the man was heard to move and the bucket clanked metallically. 'Georgie,' he called, 'I can't wipe my ass. Pass over the *Stars and Stripes*, will you? You've read it all by now, surely.'

'Okay, okay,' answered another voice amiably. 'But don't put your ass on Yvonne De Carlo. I'm sleeping with her tonight.'

Cramp and the nausea caused by the smell were causing Sissons double agony. He knew he would have to move soon. God, if they got up now they'd probably be shot without anyone thinking twice. He wondered how much damage a bazooka did. To his great relief he heard the soldier move. Then, new horror, as another deluge of urine and turds was flung and descended between him and Horace, trickling only inches in front of his nose. The American soldier, clanking the bucket, went away still singing 'Deep in the Heart of Texas'. Sissons gagged in the stench.

Horace moved forward as soon as prudence

allowed. Fifty yards of crawling and he emerged from the defile and crawled warily to the shelter of a hawthorn hedge. ''Ow be you, vicar?' he whispered. He did not appear concerned.

'Covered in filth,' said Sissons through clenched teeth.

'Makes your 'air grow nice, they say,' replied Horace.

He turned away and began to go downhill, under the shadow of the hedge, until they reached the wall on the eastern end of the church. Beyond was the area of the graveyard where the village victims of the Black Death, almost the entire population, were buried in a mass grave.

'There be your church,' announced Horace as if the vicar might be in doubt. 'Now, can oi be havin' my ten bob?'

'God,' breathed the vicar, 'can't you wait until we get back?'

'I only said I was goin' to *bring* you 'ere,' pointed out the poacher. 'For myself, oi'll be going along now. It may be that you mayn't get back at all, or it may be months afore they let you out. I'd be glad of the favour now.'

From his sodden pocket, Sissons pulled a wet ten shilling note. 'Take it,' he said.

'I was,' replied Horace. He looked craftily around, spying his retreat. 'Don't be forgettin', they got a sentry post around the front.'

'I know that,' said Sissons.

'Right. 'Tis away for me, then. Good luck, vicar. 'As been a pleasure, 't'as.'

With that he was gone like a shade merging with

darkness. Sissons felt so alone, and so immediately apprehensive, that he almost called him back. He crouched, half lay, against the churchyard wall and gradually levered himself to his feet until he could look over the creepered coping.

At first it seemed that all was silent and dark. Then he noticed streaks of light coming from the windows at the western end of the church, low, shining from below badly fitted screens or curtains. His nose travelled along the rough stone, ivy and damp lichen of the wall. As he reached the limit of the movement the organ sounded, a blunt blast from within the building. Sissons felt his stomach clench and his anger ignite. The tune bellowed out, a blatant, jumping jazz tune. His face tightened.

Then the door opened and a passage of yellow light ran out. Three Americans, drunk as apes, stumbled along the ragged gravestones. He watched as one leap-frogged over a tottering cross. Another began to urinate, a silver bow in the moonlight, against an ancient angel.

He was tempted to leap the wall and frighten the skins from them, but he could hear the metallic touches of their weapons. He desisted. One of the men went back and closed the church door with his foot. They turned and rolled away, talking and sniggering, towards the lychgate at the front.

Sissons scraped himself up on to the wall and dropped noisily into the churchyard. Then, with a growing anger overcoming his fear, he advanced on the door of his ancient church.

Still fixed to the outer door was the notice issued by the bishop appealing for the protection of the churches and the burial grounds. Someone had appended a Star of David in thick ink or boot polish. He opened the door by the old iron handle, once more feeling it familiarly warming to his hand. The organ had temporarily stopped its raucous progress but as he entered the porch, as if the player were awaiting him, it struck up yet another frantic, fanatic fanfare. Sissons was staring at what had been the inner door of the church. Once it had been covered with green baize, smooth as a billiard table, and upon it the church notices used to be pinned.

Now it had been carved, shaped, sawn, into two swinging flaps, tops and bottoms missing, like the doors of a western saloon. Across both halves in rough and gaudy paint were the words 'Diamond Lil's'. From the spot where he had been abruptly brought to a halt by this second intimation of sacrilege, Sissons could only see the upper part of the nave over the swing-doors. Lights were burning, church lights augmented by large arcs slung on wires, but even the illumination of these was diffused by a loitering layer of smoke. Voices came too, mostly in conversation but with outbursts of laughter and cursing. Determinedly he took another pace.

What he saw over the door caused his whole being to boil. He was not a man totally convinced by his calling, but he felt deeply for the church which was, and had been for centuries, the very focal point and symbol of the village, its life and its uncomplicated faith. Now, his face hot, his eyes burning with astonishment and anger, he saw what the Americans had done.

Pews were on end, stacked against the precious

432

windows and the family memorial tablets on the wall; others were arranged in squares with tables at the centres. Men were sitting, sprawling, sleeping with their boots on, drinking from tins which they pitched, as he watched, into the raised pulpit or the medieval font. The exceptionally fine brass lectern, in the shape of an eagle, was, not inappropriately, hung with the Stars and Stripes. The organ was pounding, and through the mist from Camels and Lucky Strike he could see two khaki figures on the organ stool pounding like marionettes as they thumped out their banal melody. From there his eyes went to the altar, even for him, a doubter, the symbol and centrepiece of this place. He could hardly focus it through the smoke. An inch at a time, as though walking into a dream, he pushed the swing doors open and walked down the aisle.

At first the men were so preoccupied with their recreation that no one saw him. There were a dozen poker schools operating and a group of recumbent men were facing, in an attitude of worship, the altar and the cross of Jesus. They were playing dice. They rolled the bones up the marble chancel shouting and cursing about their fortunes. Beneath his feet as he slowly walked there was a thick carpet of cigarette and cigar butts. In the side chapel dedicated to St Mary Magdelene he saw two men playing table tennis; the communion rail had become a bar with a busy barman passing over tins of beer and Coca Cola. The cans, many of which had missed the receptacles provided by the pulpit and the font, were littering the floor. The place was heavy with a dozen smells. He had never known it so warm.

433

He was three-quarters of the way down the aisle, the path covered by the brides and the carried dead of Telcoombe Magna for many generations, and had reached the point where the choir normally halted and bowed to the cross, when a GI, sitting with three kings in his hand, glanced up from the poker table, with its hundred-dollar kitty, and saw the gaunt, blackclothed, angry and avenging figure creeping forward. 'Gee, guys,' he breathed. 'We got a fucking ghost.'

The words were enough for Sissons. He had reached a point where his vision took in the altar and he saw that the cross had been removed (he had prudently taken the candlesticks himself but had thought that no one, if only through superstition, would take the cross) and that the altar table had become the base for a line of coffee urns and soft-drink containers, with a heated, glass-fronted receptacle for hot dogs at one end and a vat fronted with the words 'Miss Tutti-Fruiti Ice Cream' at the other. The sight of this abomination was enough, but the blasphemy of the poker player triggered off a violence, a storm of fury, a breaking vengeance, such as few of them had ever seen.

Sissons rushed, shouting, screaming, at the immediate poker school, the one to which the GI who had spotted him belonged. The men turned and their faces altered. Their hands made to grab the money from the table and clutching this and their cards, they tried to get out of the way. But Sissons, bellowing the name of Jesus Christ, charged at them. From all parts of the church soldiers hurried, beer, table tennis bats, cigars in their hands. The organ players tumbled from their stool and hurried to look around the angels at the foot of the pulpit. Nothing could prevent Sissons' headlong rush. Men who could escape climbed over pews with all the agility gained in battle training. Others fell backwards and the vengeful vicar lifted the card table and flung it at them. They managed to fend it away with their dollar-filled hands. He then picked up a small chair, one he recognized, even at this moment, as having come from the vestry, a gift from a tiny man called Mulcoombe who had used it to sit in the aisle during services because he could not otherwise see. Now he grasped Mulcoombe's chair like a club and began to lay about the soldiers who were within range. They shouted and protested and flailed their hands ineffectually, like women. One podgy man, cornered by the junction of two pews, crossed himself repeatedly in the face of the Church of England man's onslaught.

Surprise and wrath were, however, the vicar's only weapons. He was abruptly grabbed from behind and then his legs were caught and he was boisterously hoisted head-first into the pit of his own pulpit. He crashed face-down on to a lining of refuse; beer tins, bottles and newspapers and tobacco ash. He sobbed with surprise, pain and frustration, aware that his clerical legs were wriggling above him, provoking an outcry of mirth from the Americans. His echoing protests and curses only added to the wild laughter. With some athleticism he managed to curl his trunk sideways so that his legs fell into the open entrance of the pulpit. He fell heavily on to his knees on the steps; his fury even more fierce. The howls of the soldier mob were sounding all around. His hand, still in the rubbish, came into contact with something odd and he realized he had grasped a French letter. With another thrust he stood upright, his face livid, blood under his nose and on his forehead.

They went wild with delight as he reappeared in the pulpit like a jack-in-the-box. He spat at them and then, realizing he still held the condom, he threw it in the face of the man immediately underneath. The soldier held it and whooped as he whirled it around his head like a prize.

Sissons ducked below the top level of his position and picked up two beer tins and a bottle. Standing up again he threw them directly at the Americans who retreated hurriedly before this more serious bombardment. He went down again for more ammunition, bringing up a handful of tins which he flung one after the other, shouting: 'Swine! Heathen swine! This is a Church of God! Take that! And that! You uncivilized bastards!'

Once again he found himself grasped from behind. This time the grip was assured and unbreakable. 'Okay, okay,' a voice said coolly, close to his ear. 'You've had your fun.'

'Fun! Fun!' Sissons exploded. He tried to swivel but the man held him without effort. He forced him down the garbage-strewn steps of the pulpit and then eased him into a seat at the corner of one of the pews. Even in his agony he recognized it by the carving on its upright of an angel with a fishtail, like a mermaid.

'Poncho and Williams,' called the man who had grabbed him. He had authority. 'Hold this man.' Through his streaming eyes Sissons could see it was a young officer.

He was sobbing. 'Swine, blasphemy . . . swine . . .'

'Okay,' said the officer, unruffled. 'We heard.' He pushed his hard, young face close to Sissons. The men were holding Sissons enough to prevent him moving. 'You are in a military area,' said the man slowly and succinctly. 'This area is prohibited to civilians.'

Sissons could feel the very flesh of his face trembling. His eyes streamed. 'I am,' he gasped, 'I am the incumbent of this church . . . this . . .'

'You are off limits,' said the man firmly. His tone rose a fraction. 'I don't care who you are, sir, you're off limits.'

'You're heathen,' replied Sissons bitterly. He looked around at the desecration and the faces of the young soldiers who had perpetrated it. They were grinning but puzzled. 'How do you think you can win a war when you do this sort of thing?'

The officer took the question calmly. 'We're going to try,' he said. 'This is a designated recreational centre for men on battle exercises in this region.'

'Our Lord Jesus . . .' muttered Sissons with hesitation, as though he suspected they might not know the name. 'Jesus threw the usurers and gamblers from the temple. This is just the same . . . There were men throwing dice!'

'We don't have a requirement for religion right now,' said the officer. 'You're under arrest for being off limits.'

'This church has been used for thousands of years to worship God,' persisted Sissons, slowing his voice. His glare had reduced to a plea. 'Didn't you read the notice on the door? Long before you or your country were heard of, people were coming here with dignity

. . . with . . . piety. I don't suppose you even know the meaning of that.'

The officer's face became firm. His mouth thinned. 'Is that so?' he said. 'Okay, since you know all about these things, let me show *you* something, mister.' He nodded at the two men who held Sissons. 'Okay, leave him.' They released the vicar, who looked up, puzzled. 'Take a look at this,' said the officer. 'Take a look at what we found.'

Stiff, bruised, hurt, Sissons stood up and followed the youth. The other soldiers followed mutely, with their cigars and cigarettes and beer, with their cards and dollars. They trooped along the chancel towards the altar. There, like some ritual procession, they stopped.

'Get rid of the coffee,' said the American. Men moved forward and lifted the urns and hot dogs from the altar table. Sissons saw that the cross had been parked in a corner. He felt his legs trembling.

'Move it,' said the officer. The same men eased the altar table away. Sissons opened his mouth but said nothing. The altar table was clear of the east wall of the church. In all his years there it had never been moved. The officer went smartly forward and pulled away a regular block of stone set among the irregular granite. Sissons felt his throat drying. The stone came away easily. It had obviously been moved frequently and recently. 'Shell-blast dislodged it,' explained the young man casually like a guide. 'And see what we found underneath?'

A square aperture was revealed and the officer produced a torch and shone it sharply into the darkness. Sissons almost cried out. There, carved in stone, was a great penis and testicles.

438

'Phallic worship,' said the American with a shrug. 'Somebody used this place before you Christians got here. Maybe they had more fun. So, sir, don't tell me about dignity and piety. Sometimes they just don't fit.' The words came out like a sneer. The young man was steely, angry. 'And,' he said tightly, 'you're still in a prohibited area.

In all his life Sissons had never been drunk; but now a sudden madness like drunkenness took him. The stone penis and the balls behind the altar made him sick and strangely frightened. Around him were youthful, grinning, foreign soldiers, their faces like lanterns. He cried out and pushed the lieutenant backwards, the action of a violent child. It took the Americans by surprise and there was a quick opportunity for the vicar to run for the vestry door. It was unlocked but, even as he turned the handle and pushed, one of the soldiers lifted a carbine and would have easily shot him between the shoulders had not the officer shouted for him to drop it. The clergyman threw open the door and stumbled in.

Panting, eyes streaming, he switched on the single light and pushed the great old bolts home on the door. The ancient key was missing, a triviality but he cursed about it. Thieving louts. The room was full of boxes, Coca Cola, beer and behind them he could see, forlornly peeping out like a hiding fugitive, the linen banner of the Church Lads Brigade.

He turned out the light and took three steps across the flagstones to the outer door. It opened at once and he rushed into the cold, wide night. The stars were out. The moon grinned mockingly at a man running away from his own church.

The churchyard wall was only fifty feet away, beyond a few gravestones and crosses; he stumbled across them like a hurried ghoul and flung himself over the wall. As he gained the road he was confronted by a crowd of American soldiers, waiting and watching for him. They raised a cheer as he appeared across the wall. He crouched, cornered, and then challenging: 'Go on, shoot me then! Shoot me!' he scampered down the road swerving from left to right, this tactic causing further riotous howls from the men.

Ahead he could see further men, the guards from the lychgate. There was a gap in the hedge on his right and a familiar stile. Sissons wriggled twice, like a frantic footballer, and then turned off and jumped across the stile. He knew the field well. Sometimes the Sunday School had been held there on hot afternoons and on light evenings the village children had used it for games.

Now it stretched blackly before him, a great hole. Without easing his momentum he charged wildly across the stunted grass, his arms flapping, his long legs bounding comically. He was almost at the centre of the meadow when he was picked out by searchlights, one coming from each flank of the field and one from directly ahead. The violent beams dazzled him. He threw his hands across his eyes, caught his foot in a knoll of grass and pitched forward on to his chest. He lay there sobbing and grasping the grass in exhausted frustration at the centre of the blazing light.

From immediately behind came a frightening explosion. The earth shook and clods of grass and mud fell around. For a moment he thought they were *shelling* him. Then across the beams came a voice through a loudhailer. Even with the distortion he knew it was the lieutenant from the church. 'Okay, sir,' it blared. 'You are now in a mined area. I repeat – *a mined area.* Stay where you are. Repeat – *stay where you are. Do not move.'*

All the breath wheezed from Sissons' body. An inch at a time he looked up across the tufted horizon of the field. The lights glared and spread in large pools around him, like a three-ringed circus. He tried to stop the shaking of his wet and damaged body. He clutched at the grass in an attempt to keep himself still; to prevent himself running.

'Okay, sir,' came the echoing voice from the void. 'That's good. That's excellent. Stay in that position please, sir. We will send some help. But, I repeat, you are in a mined area. Do not move.'

Two of the long beams went out and the Devon vicar lay there like the last actor in a tragedy, the spotlight pinning him to the stage.

Nothing happened for fifteen minutes. The cold seeped through his clothes and his raw knees were wet and aching. He hardly shifted an inch. He wondered if a prayer might assist him, but decided it was unlikely. If there were a God, He must understand and be a party to these situations. He seemed to have a special glee in bringing malice to His clergy. Sissons shivered and waited.

After fifteen minutes the voice came over the loudhailer again. 'Sir, are you okay, sir? Wave your arms if you're okay.' Sissons waved achingly. 'Hold it!' bellowed the voice, frighteningly. 'Not too much

441

waving. And make sure your arm stays as close to your body as possible.'

'What's happening?' called Sissons woefully across the low grass of the field. 'What are you doing about this situation?'

'I'm sorry,' came the relayed voice, 'we don't hear you well and we can't get any closer until the engineers arrive. They know the way through, we *think*. We've sent for them but they're asleep, I guess.'

'God,' muttered Sissons, his face in the field. 'God, God, God.' It was a curse more than a prayer. His teeth accidentally bit into the ground and he spat the earth out angrily. Then the searchlight went out, plunging him into a bottomless, lonely darkness. He turned his head to look behind him. Perhaps he could crawl the way he had come. That was where the explosion had been. He decided not.

'Sir, we're sorry about the light. We have orders to keep them to a minimum,' blared the night voice. 'The engineers are on their way, I hope.'

'Do something! Do something!' shouted Sissons angrily.

'Sir?'

'Bollocks,' said the vicar, a word he had never before used. He laid his face across his cold and muddy hands. 'Bollocks,' he repeated to himself with a sniffle.

The light abruptly stabbed across the field again, making a bright yellow-green path across the grass. 'How you doin', sir?' came the voice cheerfully.

Sissons heaved himself up on to his elbows, then his wrists, his body concave, the attitude of a walrus. 'Do something!' he bellowed with all his strength. He flopped forward dismally. The cold and damp of the night had enveloped him now and soaked through his skin. He felt like a corpse.

'The guys are coming right now,' the loudhailer called. He thought he heard vehicles. The light went out and he realized how much he missed it.

'Put the light on, please,' he said in a whisper. As though they had heard all three beams suddenly appeared and began to circle, apparently looking for him. 'Over here!' he called. 'Over here, you fools!' They swam around the field and eventually the original beam, the one he thought of as his own, picked him out and after a quick, worrying jerk away, came back and settled on him with the incandescence of an angel. The others wandered across the field and he saw to his relief and joy that there were two or three men, on their hands and knees, moving cautiously as hunting animals in the illuminated channels.

'Here!' he shouted, holding up one arm but replacing it prudently as close to his body as possible. Then, pitifully: 'Here I am.' The men called something back and moved, but very slowly, towards him. It took twenty minutes, it seemed like hours. As, at last, they approached he saw that the leading man had a long probe in front of him with which he was gingerly scratching the ground ahead. The others were probing likewise on each side. Inch by inch. His neck ached from watching them. Surely to God they knew where they'd put their own mines.

They were only ten yards away and he could see their features, when the leading man called to him: 'When I push this stick out to you, sir, come towards me, on your gut. Right along the line of the stick, okay? Don't roll or shift either side. If you do we could all go together. Check?'

'Check.' The strange word came out like the croak of a heron. Then, the strangest thing, as he twisted to move towards the prone man, a tingling, almost a thrill, went through his blood. He could hardly breathe, his heart drummed, his legs and arms quivered. With a tremendous effort he stilled them all. He regulated his breath, he calmed his heart, he controlled his limbs. Then he began to move, fraction after fraction, towards the American soldier.

'Right,' encouraged the man, whispering. Sissons wondered why he had to whisper. 'Right sir, that's great. Take it easy now. That's fine. That's really fine . . . We'll make an engineer of you yet, sir. Take it easy, not too fast now.'

'I don't want anybody hurt,' answered Sissons halfway towards the man. He rested briefly, the probe now directly below his chest and stomach.

'Nobody gets hurt with mines,' drawled the man. 'They say you don't feel a thing. Just a little moment of regret.'

'Thanks,' said Sissons, not indicating whether it was for the philosophy or for the help. He began to edge forward again, held out his arms on the instructions of the engineer and felt himself grasped by the hands.

'That's okay,' breathed the man. 'Open your arms like you love me.'

'I think I do,' returned Sissons gratefully. He wanted to laugh. It was going to be all right now. They were going to get him out. The soldier pulled him forward in the way of a fisherman easing in a cumbersome catch. Now he had the Englishman by the shoulders, now under the armpits.

'Okay,' said the soldier when they were literally face to face. 'When I turn you just give me a little time to manoeuvre and then you make it along behind me. Just don't get up and run or anything.'

'I promise,' said Sissons with feeling.

'Great. Keep the soles of my boots in front of your nose, at a regular distance. We got to give these other guys behind me the opportunity to move off first. Then I'll turn over and go back towards the perimeter, and you follow, taking it real easy all the way.'

They had to lie facing each other, bathed in the vivid beam of the searchlight, while the soldier's comrades performed a careful and complicated turn, so that they faced the direction of their journey back. 'How d'you get out here anyway,' inquired the American. He had produced a chunk of gum and was revolving it around his mouth only an inch from Sissons' lips. The soldier inquired if he would like some but the vicar shook his head. The American, almost absently, blew a bubble of gum from his mouth. Sissons watched it grow in front of his face. His eyes squinted.

'After a buck rabbit, maybe?' suggested the man.

'No,' replied Sissons with weary dignity. 'I'm the vicar of that church.'

'Is that so?' There was no overwhelming curiosity in the voice, no wonderment at the English clergyman lying in the middle of an American minefield in the middle of the night. 'That's a nice church,' said the man. 'Pity it's so old. In the States, see, we keep building *new* places. All the time. We wouldn't let a building get as old as that.'

Sissons was beyond caring. He nodded dumbly and the man, blowing another balloon of gum, acknowledged a signal from his comrades, did a slow and complicated turn-about, like a slow circus tumbler, and ended the movement with his face to the perimeter. He began to crawl forward on his stomach and Sissons gratefully followed, keeping the muddy soles of the American's combat boots an inch in front of his nose.

It took twenty minutes. Then he felt the soldier rise to his knees and then his feet. After another six feet, with enormous relief, he did the same. There were a hundred or more Americans standing in the road, waiting for them. As he stood up they raised a cheer. Sissons, cold and stiff as he was, smiled. In a way, and whatever might follow afterwards, at that moment he almost felt he was one of them.

The postman who delivered the mail on his bicycle, descending adventurously down Wilcoombe Hill with one foot scuffing the kerb, called, characteristically, last at the anti-aircraft gun-site. Despite Captain Westerman's protests that there might be some message of importance to the war effort, the routine had gone on imperturbably throughout the years since the gun was first established there.

'A message?' repeated the postman loftily as he once delivered the letters after nine o'clock. He had a wet moustache and dingy eyes. He blinked them at

Captain Westerman, who had personally queried his tardiness. 'And what sort of message would you be expecting to get in this place?' His glance swam around disparagingly at the last phrase, taking in the sad huts and the dumb gun. 'We might get all sorts of things,' objected Westerman uncertainly. 'Movements, assignments. All sorts of things. Orders.'

'Tidings,' returned the postman mournfully. 'I think you'd be more likely to be getting tidings here. Not messages.' He thrust the corded package of letters into the captain's hurt hands and rode away with shaky grandeur.

Thus it had gone throughout the entire war, even when the postman died and gave way to another. The army mail was always last. One morning Bryant arrived in the orderly room after the arrival of the post and saw Captain Westerman looking with hurt bewilderment at a letter he had just opened.

'Ah, there you are, lieutenant,' said the captain morosely. 'Wondered when you'd show up. How are our allies?'

'They seem to be busy, sir,' said Bryant easily. 'Getting things ready for the big day.'

'We've got our own big day,' returned Westerman with drama in the raising of his eyebrows. 'We've got *orders.*' He stared at Bryant. 'You won't believe this, but they're going to take our gun away. Our bloody gun.'

Bryant was genuinely surprised. 'What for?' he asked. 'What's the unit going to do without a gun?'

'They say the thing is obsolete,' grumbled Westerman. 'And they point out that it doesn't work properly anyway, something I've been telling them for

447

ages. An anti-aircraft gun ought to be able to elevate to more than twenty-five degrees, don't you agree? Unless it's meant exclusively for the dive bombers. You know how damned difficult it is to get the thing up when it's needed.'

'And they're not replacing it?'

'No intention of doing so, by all accounts. The important thing is that they're breaking up the unit as well.'

'The War Office probably thinks that if you haven't got a gun then you won't need any gunners,' pointed out Bryant reasonably.

'No need to be funny, lieutenant.'

'I'm sorry, sir. What's going to happen?'

'Well, I thought at least they'd replace the gun with something a bit more like it. We still need to protect this bit of coast, and especially now with the invasion threatening actually to start at long last. God, if the whole show was bombed and obliterated before it actually set sail everybody would end up with egg on their faces, wouldn't they? But the powers that be say that the area is now adequately covered by the Yanks and their rockets and whatnot. We're not needed, Bryant.'

'The unit is being dispersed.'

'More or less. Some of the men are going to Woolwich, to the depot, where I suppose they'll spend the rest of the war cleaning their boots. I've been posted to Ross and Cromarty, would you believe. God, it's difficult enough getting home from here, but *Ross and Cromarty*. I've looked on the map and it's bloody miles. I'd be better off in Germany.'

'And what about the remainder?' asked Bryant.

'Well, you're fixed, you're already seconded to your Yanks, so that's that for the duration. A dozen men have to go to Plymouth for . . . guess what, Bryant? You'll never credit it . . . a refresher course on the *Bofors* gun. Christ, the Bofors! They'll be going back to those bloody things the Romans had next, you know to sling rocks.'

Bryant said: 'The Bofors is still a good utility weapon, sir. Did they say why?' he asked.

'Not a thing. They never do,' replied Westerman. 'They'd tell the bloody Germans before they'd tell me.'

As he drove the fifteen hundredweight lorry up the sharp Wilcoombe Hill, Gilman saw Mary Nicholas standing outside her house, on the sloping pavement, as if she had been expecting him. He pulled up. She looked gaunt and pale, but the fine eyes came at him from under the shelter of a functional scarf about her head. Some of her hair had escaped and was blowing across her forehead. 'Want a lift?' Gilman called out. He noticed she was smoking an American cigarette. She still had the packet in her hand. She smiled and climbed into the cab.

'Where are you going?' she asked.

'Plymouth. Where is it you want to go?'

'Anywhere. Plymouth will do.' She said it airily.

His eyes went sideways to her. He started the rough engine and the small truck began to climb the hill. 'We're shifting,' he said. 'Moving out. Next week. Shouldn't be talking about it really. It's under the heading of Careless Talk, I suppose.'

She laughed easily and he felt surprise at his own annoyance. 'I know already,' she answered. Her head shook. 'I never thought we'd be rid of you. I thought that gun had taken root down there, like the geraniums.'

'We're being posted to Plymouth,' he said, trying not to show his offence. 'About a dozen of us. The rest are being shoved around to various units.' He gave a faint sneer. 'Old Bullivant, you know, the fat sergeant, he's being left in charge. He'll be in charge of nothing – nobody. Should just suit him. You watch, he'll be stuck there till the end of the war.'

'Clever Sergeant Bullivant,' she said unexpectedly. They had mounted the hill and were into the country of fields and soft spring hills, all sun-bright, the ploughed fields, raw and red, spread with white gulls.

'Where did the old man go, by the way?' he asked. 'The old chap with the dog who they foisted on you.'

'Oh, he died,' she said simply. 'They moved him to Totnes and he died. He was getting on anyway. The dog's dead too.' She waited and then said, 'It'll be a nice change for you anyway, Plymouth.'

'God knows what they've got in store for us,' said Gilman, his eyes watching ahead. 'It's supposed to be training on the Bofors gun, which must be somebody's joke.' Then, but with the realization that she would be unimpressed, he added: 'Or it's security cover for something else.'

Mary said confidently, without turning her head, apparently studying the curling road between the meadows and coombes: 'I bet it's the Bofors, just like they said.' A small rabbit ran into the road and, terror-stricken, off again. 'The rabbits are moving about,' she said. 'Soon be summer.'

'How do you know that?' he asked. She sounded very certain. He had meant to ask her about what she had seen on St Valentine's Night and how she had seen it. 'How do you know about the Bofors?'

A thoughtful grin touched her pale face. 'I'd make a good German spy, wouldn't I?' she said. 'I just get to hear things. You'd be surprised at what I know.'

'Like what happened to Meg Pender,' he put in quietly.

'Yes, that as well. I'll tell you if you like. I'm easy.'

He pulled the short truck into the open gateway to a field. The sea, blue with white creases, was moving just beyond the fresh green of the rising ground. It was about two hundred yards away. 'Yes, I would like,' said Gilman. He turned his face to her, but she remained looking straight forward beyond the windscreen to the sea. She looked as if she might be searching for a boat. 'I went down there for a walk, to the quay,' she began; she was picking her words. 'I had to get out. I thought you might have even poked your head in the door, but you didn't come. So that's what I did.'

Gilman said: 'Sorry. I would have done, but I thought you might be occupied that night, busy.'

'Oh, did you? Well, all I was occupied with was my bloody kids, that's why I had to get away from them for half an hour. You can't believe what it's like. It's sickening, boring, miserable.'

'What have you done with them today?' he asked.

'Why should you worry, I'm not. I've left them with the old woman next door. She's boiling today and she's glad to do it for a packet of fags.'

'Sorry. I interrupted,' said Gilman. 'So you went down to the quay.'

'Yes. I just wandered down there, just to get out of the four walls, like I said. I was standing in a doorway, that one that used to be a shop, that's been closed since the war. I was trying to light a cigarette, but it was breezy. Then these Americans came along, plastered all of them, and Meg, the drunken great lump, came the other way. She started shouting at them, and you know what a mouth she had. And they began fooling about and one of them gave her a shove. In she went. I buggered off.'

'So did they apparently,' muttered Gilman. 'Was it that GI – the man Wall who pushed her?'

'No,' she said firmly. 'It wasn't him. I was only a few yards away and he was separate from the others, just like he said at the inquest. One of the other men gave her the shove. One of them who ran away.'

'And you decided against telling the police,' he said.

'What good would that have done? They've tried to find those Yanks, anyway, and they haven't found them. Half the time I don't think they even tried all that much. They're going to need every soldier they've got when it comes to the invasion. What's one fat, drunken old cow compared to that?'

She turned quite softly to him: 'Listen, whoever did it has got his punishment coming, don't you worry. You're a real blue eyes, you are.' She shut off the conversation. 'Do you feel like walking over there?' she suggested, nodding towards the curving field and the bright wrinkled sea. She smiled at him mischievously. 'We could pick some bluebells.'

'It's too early in the year for bluebells,' said Gilman,

taking the key out of the truck and pulling his army greatcoat from the space behind the seat.

'Buttercups, then,' she laughed, already getting out of the cab. 'Or dandelions. I don't care what we pick.'

She really did not care, he thought; about anything. He followed her across the springy grass. Airily, she walked ahead, smoking another Lucky Strike and letting the puffs fly in the breeze. She swung her backside provocatively and turning round laughed at him. 'What's the matter?' she called. 'Frightened?'

'Scared stiff,' he replied. She took off the plain scarf and her hair swiftly jumped into the breeze, flying back beautifully. Her hands ran through it and she laughed again. 'It's lovely, isn't it?' she said pointing out at the sea and the pale sky. 'Better than being stuck in a house with two moaning kids. Mind, anything's better than that.'

Gilman caught up with her and looping his arms around her brought her to him. Playfully she pushed at him, pretending to protest. He leaned towards her to kiss her and she smirked and avoided his mouth. 'I said pick buttercups,' she said childishly.

'Afterwards,' he said. He wanted her now. Her bony thighs pressed up to him; the contrast of her white neck arched from the dull woollen dress. She playfully pulled her head away like a pony and her breasts hardened against his tunic. It did something to her for, at once, she finished playing and eased herself against him, the body relinquishing its tautness, her arms sliding about his neck; her lips were no longer thin, as if the same signal had softened them.

They kissed with enjoyment, trying to work up passion. Archly she peeped up at his eyes and putting

453

her lips next to his ear muttered, 'I'm not stripping. It's too early in the year.'

Laughing, he caught her around her narrow waist and, clung together, they walked down the easily sloping grass towards the sea. Where the meadow ended there were outcrops of Devon rock, edging the cliffs which they could now see dropping to the beach on each flank. The Channel groaned far below. 'No nearer,' she said. 'I'm no good on heights. I'd hate for us to tumble over there still copulating.'

Until then he still had a small doubt as to what she would allow him to do. Now, kissing against her neck, he pulled her firmly to a natural couch of rock with thick grass cosseted in it. They sat down, facing away from the wind and the sea, protected by the back of the frayed stone. It was secluded, enclosed, the grass cushioning their backsides. 'It's better than our air-raid shelter,' she said, pressing the ground.

Gently Gilman pushed her back. She went willingly and lay staring at the clouds and the sky, as if she were surprised at their presence. A blank look closed over her face, she dropped her eyelids and began to breathe deeply and peacefully.

Studying her features like that, expressionless in the windy sun, Gilman realized what he already knew, that for her anyone would do; he could have been almost any soldier from any army. She opened her eyes and smiled at him along her body. 'Don't start getting too romantic about it,' she said, looking at his expression. 'You'll be writing me poems next. And I haven't got time. I'm waiting.'

'Sorry,' mumbled Gilman stupidly. 'I'll put the coat over us.'

'Keep it on,' she answered practically. 'Then it won't slip all over the place.' She saw the doubt in his face. 'You can do it with your coat on, can't you?'

'Yes, of course I can.' He eased himself above her and began to lift her skirt. She was wearing nylon stockings, something he had never seen before. He pushed his hands up them to the top.

'You ought to be able to do it wearing your pack, as well.' The joke was soft. 'And your gas mask for that matter. Careful with the nylons, love.'

'I wasn't sure that was what these stockings were,' admitted Gilman. 'They feel terrific. Right to the top.' He pushed the palms of his hands up the sheen until his thumbs touched the cool, slack, naked flesh of her legs. The corset suspenders which held the nylons were rigid against her skin. He was beginning to sweat in his overcoat. How could he pull her knickers down? They were trapped in the cage of elastic supports for her stockings. He touched her on the triangle of material between her thighs. 'Excuse me,' he asked. 'How am I supposed to get through this lot?'

To his relief she laughed outright. 'You're not so bad after all, darling,' she said. 'You can't get them down without undoing all the fastenings. And I can't get this corset off, that's for sure. Just pull them aside. There's plenty of room.'

'You seem to think of everything,' he murmured.

'It would never have occurred to you,' she teased. She had closed her eyes once more, this time with an attitude of finality, and lay in the breeze, her pale face painted like a watercolour by the mild sun. Clumsily Gilman undid his fly buttons with one hand, the other supporting him on the ground, the position taught in basic training when firing a bren from the prone position and observing the target. It was difficult. One of the buttons came off in his hand. Prudently he put it in his overcoat pocket.

Such was his uncomfortable position, with the weight of the coat on top of his battledress tunic and coarse army shirt, the toughness of the military trousers, and all in a confined area, that he feared he might fail her. He felt as if he were clad in cardboard. Everything seemed stiff except that which he wanted to be stiff. He pulled out his penis, wan and loose. It seemed to blink in the sun. He shuffled forward on his knees.

His anxiety was premature. She put her hand out as she felt his advance and caught the poor pale sausage in her fingers, coddling it and stroking it, still with an air of being somewhere else. Her fingers went below him and he moved so she could stroke him until he grew quickly erect. 'Thanks very much,' he breathed gratefully.

His own left hand now found the cloth of her knickers again, the cushion over her pubic swelling, and he tapped at it gently with the tips of his fingers, like someone carefully knocking on a door. He knew he had done the correct thing for he felt her react at once, a groan creasing her blank face, her legs twitching. With an ease that surprised him he hooked his index finger into the cloth and persuaded it aside. He felt she was warm, pliable. 'Don't hang about,' she suggested matily from the other side of the rock. 'I don't take long to get ready.'

Neither did Gilman now. He moved closer, up the isthmus of her legs, and plunged himself into the accommodation of her body. Luxury engulfed his whole being. He hardly moved at first, as if he could scarcely believe his luck and didn't want to spoil it; as if it were possible she might not even be aware what was going on. Mary had more immediate needs. 'Move then,' she admonished him quietly. She pushed her thighs urgently up at him and, pausing to get the timing, he responded. Each time he waited or rested, for the great weight of clothing was not only inhibiting but wearying, she urged him on like a driver poking a donkey. Rolling with sweat, his thighs running, his hands sliding against her buttocks, he made the final effort and then lay there, panting and perspiring above her.

'Again,' she said casually. 'I want it again.'

'Christ, darling, give me a minute. All this gear. Everything's piled on top of me. I feel like an old clothes shop. And these brass bloody fly-buttons are cutting into me.'

'I can feel them too,' she mentioned. 'But I don't mind. It doesn't matter to hurt a bit. Come on, son, surely you can do it again.'

'Just give me a breather,' pleaded Gilman. 'I'm out of condition for this sort of thing. Let's have a break.'

She sulked all over her body. He could see her face, he could feel the rest. She moved her hands to her bag and fumbled. 'Get my lighter, will you?' she said, holding a packet of cigarettes. 'I can't reach.' He found the lighter, made from the case of a machine-gun bullet, the sort that many people had, made unofficially in spare moments in the munitions factories. She took it from him and lit the cigarette herself, still lying on her back with him crouched over her and the overcoat like the shell of an armadillo. She took a petulant puff at the cigarette and blew the smoke towards the sky, just missing his chin as he contemplated her and thought about her oddness. 'You don't, do you?' she said, nodding towards the Lucky Strike packet.

'No,' confirmed Gilman. 'Never have.'

'Bad habit,' she said seriously. The fact that their sexual parts were still lying adjacent to each other had apparently been temporarily dismissed or forgotten. 'I seem to have them all. Although I don't drink that much, not really.'

'Perhaps I ought to start now,' he suggested.

She glanced up. 'It was you wanted to rest,' she said.

'Smoking,' he corrected. 'I meant smoking. I could start now. There doesn't seem much else for me to do at the moment.'

She smiled and with abrupt tenderness touched his cheek with one finger. 'You're keeping me warm,' she said. 'That's worth doing, now isn't it? You don't want to start dragging. It'll only make you cough.' She shut her eyes and added practically: 'Anyway, I've only got a couple left.'

Blowing another cloud of smoke, like a signal, she said sympathetically: 'You can carry on if you like. You'll be getting a cold.' She took a deep draw. 'I'll just finish this.' She sucked at it again and tossed it away. It disappeared over the rock.

'That's how fires are started,' said Gilman, attempting to play the same sort of casual game.

'Let's see if you can start one,' she replied. 'It went

over the cliff anyway,' she added curiously. 'Probably went right down to the beach. I gave it a good flick.'

Gilman by now realized that it was no use expecting anything to be usual with her. His penis had retired again but the minute it touched her its head began to move like an inquisitive caterpillar. He was surprised for he had no great experience and had never done it twice in succession.

They moved close and locked into each other and she began to cry small cries and then changed to pig-like groans. He wondered, as he worked, if she really felt it like that or whether it was merely her act, for the benefit of herself, the moment and the man. Now a worry was beginning to niggle; about the army and the lorry. What time would he get to Plymouth? What excuse could he make for being late? To his surprise, in the middle of the conundrum, Mary began to gasp and thrash below him, like a fish on a gaff. Then she relaxed, almost collapsed, and opened her stirring eyes to smile up at him.

They lounged against each other, the wind wriggling under the coat chilling his buttocks and her thighs. 'We ought to be going, darling,' he said in what he hoped sounded like a caring whisper. Her eyes had shut again.

'More,' she said. 'Go on, just once more.'

Gilman pulled himself away from her, up on his hands in the instructed position for grenade throwing from the prone position. 'More?' he asked aghast. 'But, God, I can't, love. I'm not a machine.'

She grinned happily at him. 'I didn't say you were,' she answered. 'But you could try, just one tiny one.'

'What about the lorry?' he said plaintively. 'I've got

to get that stuff to Plymouth. They're expecting it. They have papers and time-sheets and all that. What can I tell them if I'm so late? It's only twenty-odd miles.'

'Tell them you had a blow-out,' she suggested slyly. Her hands went to his neck and tugged at him. 'Come on, that was smashing last time. I really felt it. I want some more.'

'Mary, I can't.' He took one hand away and balancing on the other held his limp member for her to examine. 'Look at that. I couldn't get that into a cave.'

He suddenly saw that she had got the keys to the fifteen hundredweight. She was dangling them teasingly. At first he did not appreciate what she was going to do. Her face had taken on an impudent pose, much younger and freer than her strained looks earlier. It was as though she had been released from some private confinement. 'More,' she repeated girlishly, 'or over the cliff they go.'

Gilman could not believe it. She was only playing. She *had* to be playing. Her hand bent, ready to fling the keys. 'You're mad,' he breathed. 'You're barmy. You wouldn't do that.'

Mary laughed slightly. 'I would. I've done worse things than that. A lot worse.' She was challenging him now. Threatening him. 'Come on, soldier,' she taunted. 'Once more, or whoosh, over they go.'

Gilman said: 'All right, Mary. I'll try. But I can't do what I can't.'

'Good lad,' she said sweetly. 'Come on, I'll help.' Her hands went to his member. 'I'd help you a bit more,' she said conversationally, 'but it makes my lips sore out of doors.'

He made a sudden lunge for the keys, flinging himself across her with such force that she screamed and threw herself sideways as far as she could, even though trapped by his body. He grabbed at the keys. 'Stop it!' she screamed. 'You bastard, swine.'

'Give me,' he said grimly. 'Give me them.'

He thought he had won for she suddenly collapsed beneath him and he believed she was crying. 'All right, tough guy. Here they are,' she shivered. He relaxed his hold on her wrist. As soon as it was free she drew back her hand and flung the keys with all her strength. The glint of the sun caught them. They went in a curve over the rock and grass, in the same path as her cigarette stub had done, disappearing over the immediate horizon.

'Bleeding hell!' howled Gilman. He clambered up from her, wet and tacky, and stumbled, pulling up his trousers as he went, towards the edge of the cliff. The keys had gone, that was certain. They were somewhere far below among the brown pebbles and the soapy tide. He looked back hurriedly for he had a sudden idea she might push him after the keys. She was standing by the rock, laughing.

He stumbled towards her angrily, his stupid trousers dropping around his knees. 'You're mad,' he shouted in her face. 'Stark raving bloody mad.'

She stopped laughing and backed away, attempting to look contrite, but the grin kept breaking out. 'I didn't know they would go over the edge,' she protested. 'Honestly.' She sat petulantly on the grass, put her hands under her dress and began to fiddle with her knickers.

'Listen,' said Gilman grimly, 'what the hell am I going to do without the keys?'

'My husband always says that,' she said moodily, sitting on the rock. 'The very same words, come to think of it. *Stark raving bloody mad.*' She looked up at him with pleading. 'It's just I do things on impulse,' she said. 'I can't seem to help it. The idea comes and I just do it.'

'So I've bloody noticed,' returned Gilman nastily.

'We could go down and look for them,' she suggested. 'That would be like a film wouldn't it, searching around on the sand and the pebbles for the keys, and the waves coming in and all that. I could even have a wash in the sea. I feel horrible.'

He regarded her wearily. 'That's nothing to how I'm going to feel,' he forecast. 'I'll be doing jankers for a month. Come on, get up. I'll have to think of something.'

She stood up. He offered her a hand but she ignored it. She strode off towards the road, a few feet in front of him, tossing her hair and strutting as if she might be a film star. 'Anyway,' she called over her shoulder, 'if they put you inside for a month you'll miss the training.' She stopped, turned and faced him dramatically. 'I might even have saved your life.'

He was so accustomed to her inconsequences now that he did not bother to query what she had said. It was just gabble. Catching up with her he walked alongside, wearily, defeated, towards the road and the parked fifteen hundredweight.

'What am I going to say to bloody Bullivant?' he grumbled.

'Say you just somehow lost the keys. After all, you

did. It wasn't your fault. Well, not altogether your fault.'

'He's going to believe that like a shot, I don't think. But it's the only thing I can do, get a lift back and go and tell him. Christ, you've put me in for the high jump.'

They were nearing the gate now, walking up the last sloping grass. The sun had gone and the breeze was less friendly. 'I told you,' she said. 'I might have saved your life.'

Now they were at the lorry. He leaned on the door and said: 'What in God's name are you talking about?'

'If you get a month in the glasshouse or . . .'

'I won't go in the glasshouse. It's not that bad.'

'Whatever it is, then you won't go to Plymouth for the Bofors gun training. Then you won't have to go on the landing ships. No invasion for you, my lad.'

Astonished, Gilman stared at her. She smiled with coltish pleasure. 'Landing ships? How . . . how do you know that?' he demanded. 'How could you know?'

'I just know,' she said. 'I have friends. The guns are going on the landing ships.'

The truth of the information got to him. 'Christ,' he said. 'If that's right, we'll be chucked into the invasion after all. That's not going to be very funny.' He was almost talking to himself. 'But Bofors, why Bofors? They're so old. What about all these rockets they've got? It can't be . . .'

A Royal Air Force truck came along the road and pulled up. 'Wilcoombe, mate?' asked the driver. He had bright ginger hair and a storm of freckles. 'Straight on,' said Gilman. 'You can't miss it. Unless you go into the sea.' He jerked himself to reality. 'Hey, hang on. You could take us back there.'

'Right,' said the airman. 'Jump in.' He glanced at the woman. 'Nice day for an outing,' he said. Then to Gilman: 'Are you leaving the truck?'

'I haven't got any choice,' said Gilman. 'I've lost the keys.'

The youth laughed. 'Blimey, I've done that before now. Why don't you start it up with your badge?'

Gilman said, with slow hope: 'What d'you mean?'

The airman laughed again and got down from the cab. 'Blimey, don't they teach you brown jobs anything?' he said. 'Your cap badge. Use that. Come here, I'll show you.'

He took his own RAF cap badge and climbing into the cab of the fifteen hundredweight pushed the topmost metal point into the ignition key slot. He turned it without difficulty and the engine sounded obediently. Gilman was overjoyed. He slapped the airman on the shoulder. 'Thanks very much, chum,' he enthused. 'Let's hope it works with mine.'

'You've got to have brains in the Cream, mate,' smirked the airman. He took Gilman's cap badge and easily started the engine with it.

'That's terrific,' said Gilman. 'I'll soon fiddle another set of keys. Thanks a lot.'

'You won't be wanting a lift then,' said the airman, patently disappointed as he eyed the smiling Mary.

'I won't,' confirmed Gilman. 'I'm supposed to be going to Plymouth.' He nodded at the woman. 'But you can take her back, if you like.'

The ginger man grinned broadly. 'If I like? I'll say I like.' He strode towards Mary who was already standing by the blue vehicle. 'I'm taking you off his hands, love,' he said cheerfully.

'Not just my hands,' muttered Gilman to himself. He watched her climb into the RAF truck. The wind blew her skirt and he had a further moment to admire her legs. Then, composed and affable, she sat down and the driver got in and, with a split grin, started his own engine. Gilman waved a little lamely. They both waved back.

'And watch her,' he called as the truck moved away. He couldn't tell whether they heard or not. He doubted it. 'She's stark raving bloody mad.'

Scarlett found Colonel Schorner standing on the rising ground behind the leys, the inland lakes across the coastal road from Telcoombe Beach. He was alone, watching a flotilla of small landing craft moving irresolutely towards the steep, pebbled shore.

'How're they doing, sir?' asked Scarlett from below. He climbed the sandy mound.

'Just great,' grunted Schorner unconvincingly. 'It's like trying to get a consignment of goddamn camels ashore. Every time it gets worse. We had so many men in the water last week, it looked like a mass baptism.'

'You mean there's room for improvement?'

Schorner lowered the glasses. 'Room for it? I think they've given me every dumb guy who's never seen the sea. They're from Dakota and Oklahoma. They've never seen it except in the movies or books in school. Take a look will you.'

Scarlett took the glasses. He swept them across the

sea, focusing as he did so. 'They seem to be getting off the craft okay,' he commented.

'Sure, sure, they get over the side. But see *where* they get over the side. Over the *wrong* side. Twenty yards too soon. They're above their dumb heads in water before they start. You don't have to believe this, but they use their rifles to feel for the bottom.'

'How is it when they get to the beach?' Scarlett sighed and returned the glasses.

'*When* they get to the beach, *if* they get to the beach, they're so played out all they can do is lie there. Last week I found three of them asleep down behind a ridge of pebbles over there. You can't make them believe that one day it won't be for fun. They've still got to get across these lakes after they make the beach.'

'We got the protection for the LSTs then. The anti-aircraft guns we asked for.' Scarlett's tone was ironic. He knew what had happened.

'Oh sure, sure,' nodded Schorner sardonically. 'Bofors guns. Bofors! What in God's name are we doing with Bofors guns?'

'With British gunners,' added Scarlett. 'Maybe they can handle them okay.'

'Poor stooges, that's all I can say. If we get a concerted air attack on the invasion fleet I don't think a couple more Bofors guns are going to help the guys in the LSTs and LCTs. According to the Supreme HQ it's Hobson's choice because we don't have anything else we can spare either for troop landing ships nor the tank landing ships. And it's only *now* that anybody even *thinks* of it.'

Scarlett said, 'According to Supreme HQ, we asked

for some rockets from the Pacific, but they didn't show. Anyway there was some doubt about whether they could be used from the platforms of the LSTs.'

'I know, I know,' said Schorner unconvinced. 'They pat us on the back and say, "Don't worry, boys, everything is just going to be hunky dory." '

'The Bofors is adaptable,' said Scarlett with pessimistic optimism. 'It can be used as a surface weapon.'

'In case we meet a German pocket battleship,' grunted Schorner. He began to walk down the hill towards his jeep standing with Scarlett's on the road. Albie and the captain's driver were talking and smoking. 'What else is new?' asked the colonel. 'Go on, make me feel good.' He stopped and frowned at Scarlett. 'You know what I've got to do today? I've got to go and get the third degree from the leading citizens of this area – they've got complaints up to their asses. One of them is that priest who got through the goddamn wire.'

Scarlett laughed. 'We heard the news. Your boys kidded him he was in a minefield, right?'

Schorner grinned at the memory. 'Gee, was that guy grateful to get away. They exploded a dummy charge in the field, just to make him think it was the real thing, and they had him lying there for an hour before they got him to crawl out.'

'It was a great idea,' laughed Scarlett. 'He won't be back.'

'I hear he was so grateful to be rescued, he's changed his tune about the Yanks,' said Schorner. 'What else do we have that's new and exciting?'

'Well, we've got a film star coming to sing to the guys.'

'Not Eddie Cantor?' groaned Schorner. 'Please don't let it be him. I read in *Stars and Stripes* he was threatening to entertain us.'

'No,' said Scarlett, 'Sherree Ann Lorner. Maybe Cantor's got the big eyes, but she's got everything else. Bigger. She's a lousy singer but who cares?'

'And she's scheduled to give a show here?' said Schorner, pleased. 'The guys will go for that.'

'Right here. End of next month, it looks like.'

'Great. That ought to send the troops to France in the right patriotic frame of mind. A nice bold pair of all-American tits is better than "Old Glory" any time.'

Captain Scarlett looked at him curiously. Then he said: 'Sure, I know what you mean, sir. I guess it's the best they can do. It's a shame each guy can't have a Sherree Ann Lorner all to himself. But there's not enough to go around.'

Schorner poked a face and said: 'There never is. Of anything. Well, at least it isn't Eddie Cantor.'

An obese landing craft was approaching the beach almost directly ahead, it's maw open like a feeding fish. The flap clattered on its chains as the hull scraped the bottom and three jeeps followed by a truck, all loaded with men, the truck towing a field gun, ran efficiently on to the beach and began to drive carefully over the metal square that formed the emergency road over the pebbles.

'That looked okay, sir,' commented Scarlett. He liked Cantor himself and he wondered why the colonel did not. Maybe he just did not amuse him; or maybe Schorner was anti-Jewish. A lot of people with German names were still anti-Jewish.

'Sure, they got it right at last,' said Schorner

nodding approvingly at the vehicles. 'And my outfit is hot at getting the grids down across the beach. Cantor, he just can't make me laugh. My wife thinks he's terrific. But I don't go for the voice and the goo-goo eyes.'

'No shelling today?' said Scarlett. He looked down in time to see Bryant pull up in his jeep. The British officer walked towards them.

Schorner said to Scarlett: 'You should be getting a report at headquarters about yesterday's shelling. They took the weather-cock off a church.'

'That's what weather-cocks are for,' grinned Scarlett.

'This was half a mile outside the evacuated area. They're checking their range finders today.'

Scarlett and Bryant laughed. 'We don't seem to be endearing ourselves to the clergy,' said Bryant. 'They'll start praying for the other side soon.'

'Some already are going that way,' said Schorner. 'You know, gravitating towards neutrality. Christians never understand war, anyway. That's why they end up on different sides, each making a claim on God. Right over there are Germans with some crazy idea that *our* God's going to save *them*.'

They began to walk back towards the vehicles, crossing the coastal road and standing on the levelled area of what had been the Telcoombe Beach Hotel. Now all the debris had been moved and the rooms were marked out only by the foundations, like a full-scale architectural plan. Bryant wondered if the hotel would ever be rebuilt, whether people would doze on that beach again in peaceful, uncertain, English summer sun; whether children would again play on the garden swing, curiously still in position, although petrified with rust? Would there come a time again when the deck-chairs would be out, people would blandly eat ice-cream wafers, and laughter echo from the sea?

The big landing craft had discharged its vehicles and men and was now backing hesitantly away from the shingle like a slow but sensitive man who has just realized he has been offended. Scarlett said: 'They're going to try and get a railroad train on one of those LSTs. They're trying it in Plymouth right now. They figure, I guess, that the Germans won't leave too many docking facilities for us to use. So they'll get it across on a landing ship.'

'As long as they don't put it on the assault phase,' smiled Bryant. 'A railway engine would look wonderful going up the beach right behind the US Rangers.'

'They'll be stranger sights,' forecast Schorner confidently. 'Maybe there'll be some guy digging for bait. Or maybe the French will be out sunning themselves and drinking wine.' He went back, hunch-shouldered, towards the jeep and slowly climbed in. Albie Primrose started the engine.

'This afternoon at three, colonel,' Bryant reminded Schorner apologetically. 'The village elders.'

'How could I forget?' groaned Schorner. He tapped Albie on the shoulder and said, 'Let's go, soldier.' They drove away.

'He hates it,' said Scarlett, nodding after the jeep. 'Every goddamn minute of it. And he's going to hate it more and more when the shit starts to fly. But he'll see it through to the last dead German – or *they* get him.'

470

'His family must have come from Germany at some time,' suggested Bryant.

'Four generations, I bet,' said Scarlett. 'It must make things even tougher. He's a good guy.' He suddenly put an arm on Bryant's shoulder and grinned boyishly. 'Take a wild guess who's going up to London with General Georgeton,' he said. 'I aim to take a week's leave before we get too busy with this war. Any messages for anybody.'

'Tell her she's wonderful in bed,' answered Bryant genuinely. He smiled. 'And you're a rotten bastard.'

'She knows all that,' returned Scarlett. His smile widened mischievously. 'Why don't I tell her you got a dose of clap?'

'That's something else she knows,' retorted Bryant. They both laughed.

Then Scarlett said: 'I know this seems a bit crazy asking, but I'm a gentleman in disguise. You don't mind do you?'

'Good God, no,' exclaimed Bryant. 'You saw her first. And if you hadn't got so pissed I wouldn't have been involved with her at all. I was just a poor substitute, Yank.'

'You're just a modest fucking Britisher,' replied Scarlett. He became solemn. 'She's anybody's, I know,' he added. 'But I like her. She gives me something to look forward to. If it came to a choice between climbing in the sack with her and getting an ever-loving letter from home, I'd vote for the sack, any time. That's levelling with you.' He waited. 'Did you get to hear from your wife?'

'Of course,' said Bryant. 'She writes very jolly notes mostly telling me all about the new friends she keeps

471

making. From the sound of it they're predominantly from New Jersey, Maryland and Virginia.' He shrugged. 'I've decided not to think about it until the war's over. Give Jean my love and tell her I'm sorry I had to send you in my place.'

They shook hands genuinely. 'Okay, I will,' said Scarlett. 'I guess we'll have to share her.' He thought. 'And she'll have to share us.'

'And . . .' said Bryant. 'Mind how you go.'

Scarlett knew what he meant. He looked worried. 'You mean about last time. You mean, "watch what I say",' he returned. 'Sure, I'll keep sober and keep my big mouth shut. It could be *my* life I'm saving.'

The evening the previous week that Schorner had spent having supper at the house of Howard and Beatrice Evans had been one of the happiest times since his arrival in England. With wartime politeness he had taken with him from the camp a two-pound can of US Army ham, preserved fruit, ice cream and a tin of coffee. It was received with embarrassment, joy and thanks. Food rationing was tighter then than it had been through the entire war and it was to get worse. Bread and potatoes, but little else, remained free of rationing. The news that a shop had a few rabbits for sale brought people flocking to queue at its door. The normal meat ration had descended miserably to six ounces a week.

Howard had opened the final bottle of good sherry, and some red wine given to him by a French naval officer stationed in Plymouth.

To have a home, four real walls about him, and to

472

eat with these decent people, was a balm after months of the soldier's life. Schorner told them about West Virginia and his farm and family. Dorothy Jenkins, her dark face touched by the light of the lamps and the fire, watched and listened. Schorner was glad she was there. After the meal, while Howard and his wife went into the adjoining kitchen, he asked her: 'How are my kids at the school?'

'Irrepressible as ever,' she said. He could see she loved them. 'They enjoyed moving to Wilcoombe, of course, the novelty of it, the time-wasting. Anything but lessons. But we've settled down. You must poke your head around the door some day.'

Schorner said: 'I will. It's great to see faces with no problems on them.'

'How is our old school faring under your artillery bombardment? Has it still got a roof?'

'Yes,' he said cautiously. 'It did yesterday. I asked the British Navy to resist using it as a sitting target, and I told my boys not to shoot through the windows. The last time I checked inside it looked in good shape, although some bright GI has been chalking messages on the blackboard.'

'Nice messages, I hope.'

'Interesting messages, but not the sort the children ought to read.'

'Have you had men killed?' she asked suddenly, hurriedly. 'Perhaps I shouldn't ask.'

His eyes and mouth became grim. 'You shouldn't. But I guess everybody knows. They certainly know about the casualties at the hotel, when the whole building blew up. That was the fisherman's dog.'

'I saw he was fined ten shillings for trespassing,' she

said. 'Old Daffy, the fisherman. It was in the local paper.'

He sighed. 'That was how it worked out. Those guys were plain unlucky. There have been others. When you set out to create battle conditions you're going to have accidents.'

Dorothy said sadly: 'I see them in the street, when they drive through, poor fellows. They look so exhausted, worn to the bone.'

'And they haven't started yet,' he answered gravely. 'They get so bewildered, I guess you could say. They don't know which way the sun comes up. They get dirty and deaf and scared. And they know this is not even the real thing, they're just playing.'

'You look tired yourself,' she told him quietly. 'You must have lost a stone in weight since I first saw you.'

He grinned hurriedly. 'How much is a stone?' he asked. 'Is it like a guinea or a rod, pole or perch? I thought one of the few things we have in common was weights and measures.'

'It's fourteen pounds, one stone,' she said, her voice at once that of the schoolteacher. 'And you've lost it.'

'I'll put it back when I get home to the Shenandoah Valley,' he said. 'In a couple of months, I'll be the fat farmer again. It suits me better than soldiering.'

She smiled at him: 'You look forward to that, don't you? That's a silly question. Of course you do.'

Howard Evans came in with the coffee cups. 'Real coffee,' he said cheerfully. 'Courtesy of the United States Armed Forces.'

'That's why we came to England,' returned Schorner laughing. Evans went out again. 'It's all there is to look forward to,' he told her. 'Except times like this. War is no business for any man. It's a beast's game. This is the first time in weeks I've felt civilized, human.'

Looking down into her cup she said: 'I think you're very human, and civilized.' Her eyes came up to his face. 'And so do the children, except they wouldn't phrase it like that. To them you're the nice Yank officer.' Her smile became a quick laugh. 'They're very impressed with your rank. After your visit I had to get a wall chart from the US Information Service showing all the ranks and badges and so forth. Billy Steer noticed that little silver castle you have.' She moved her hand and touched the badge in his lapel. 'We found it on the chart, the engineer officers' badge.'

'Next to the colonel's insignia they have written, "Colonel Schorner, US Army". They spelt it themselves too. They think you're in charge of the whole world.'

'Sometimes I do too.' He laughed, then said: 'That poem they gave me, "Waiting" by Helen Holland.'

She nodded and recited thoughtfully:

> 'Every day you do not come,
> A little bit of summer dies.'

She said: 'It's a nice poem but they gabble it like all kids do, and when Devon kids gabble, they gabble.'

'I put it in a letter to my wife,' he mentioned.

Dorothy regarded him seriously. 'It says a lot of things,' she said.

'I told her it was a gift from some English schoolchildren and their pretty schoolma'am.'

'Oh, that will have given her a lot to think about, I'm sure,' she said mischievously. 'I certainly know how I'd feel, thousands of miles away, left to look after the house and the chickens, and to get a letter about an allegedly pretty English schoolma'am, even if I suspected she might be something less than that. And a romantic poem, too.'

'I said it was from the children too,' he pointed out. 'In exchange for Robert Frost's poem. It was, remember. Sarah won't be upset. She's good at keeping her emotions under control. Ten minutes after I get home I'll be clearing out the cowshed, you just see.'

'How old are your sons?' asked Beatrice Evans. She had come in with Howard and they sat down.

Evans poured out a glass of port for each of them and lifted it in a toast. 'To us all, and those we love,' he said, looking serious. 'May it all be all right in the end.' He saw his wife's expression. 'Sorry, Beatrice.'

'That's all right,' answered his wife. 'You will have your dramatic moments. I don't want to deny you that.' She turned to Schorner. 'Your boys, how old are they?'

'Tom is sixteen and Cliff is about to go into the Air Force any day now,' answered Schorner. 'That's one personal reason I'd like to get the war finished. I don't see the Air Force and Cliff getting along. He's okay on a four-legged mustang but I don't see him flying one.'

They talked for another hour. Evans said cautiously: 'When you have to go before the inquisition, Tom Barrington and company, would you like me to be there?' He looked embarrassed. 'To see fair play. Or am I being clumsy?'

'You're being clumsy,' confirmed his wife. 'He does things for the best,' she shrugged at Schorner.

'It's a kind thought,' said the American. 'But you don't have to get involved, Howard. You've got to live and work here long after we've gone. I can handle it. Mrs Mahon-Feavor is going to be pleased that we've given her house a renovation. It looks like a million dollars.'

'Which is more than she does,' grinned Beatrice. 'She's a tough old bird, but she can be kind and generous.'

'She just didn't like being thrown out,' shrugged Schorner. 'Nor did Tom Barrington, nor did a lot of the others. It's Barrington I'm sorry about. I think he's a good man and maybe we could have been friendly.'

Dorothy said: 'The other afternoon Mrs Mahon-Feavor was threatening to go down and occupy her usual piece of beach this summer. She's always had the same spot, every year. That chauffeur of hers, that man who looks like a ghost, used to drive her down, take an armchair out of the Rolls-Royce and set it on the pebbles. She would sit for a couple of hours staring out to sea. When she was fed up she would whistle him and he'd carry the armchair back and take her home.'

Schorner groaned. 'Please don't say that lady is going to be sitting there next time we have a practice landing. That's more than I could take. I'd rather face a panzer division than Mrs Mahon-Feavor in an armchair.'

It was time to go. Schorner was driving his jeep and he took Dorothy to her house at the top of Wilcoombe. At her door they shook hands and she said: 'Please promise to come and see us again, at school.'

'Yes, teacher,' he promised. As he turned to go she leaned forward and put her lips on his cheek. He did the same for her. They said goodnight and he drove down the hill, singing like a boy against the exhilarating wind.

Now, a week later, on his way to Wilcoombe for the meeting with Barrington and the other civilians, Schorner found himself thinking of Dorothy and the children in her school. 'Hold it, Albie,' he said, touching the driver's shoulder. Private Primrose slowed the jeep.

'Where's the Wilcoombe school, do you know?' he asked.

Albie did not know but he pulled the vehicle over to the kerb, got out and asked a man polishing the apples outside his greengrocer's shop. The shopkeeper gave him brief directions.

'I know now, sir,' said Albie climbing back behind the wheel. 'You want to go there?'

'Why not. I think I'm going to need a little hope.'

If Primrose understood he made no indication but drove quickly up the steep hill of Wilcoombe and turned the car just as steeply down into a coombe. The school, a locket of smoke wisping from its red chimney, was at the pit of the road. The colonel said: 'You come as well, son. Maybe you'll go for this.' Puzzled, the bespectacled driver stopped the car and followed his commanding officer into the low-doored schoolhouse. A baggy woman with folds up her neck met them one step inside, her arms untidy with exercise books. She also held a wooden blackboard cleaner which she dropped to the floor at seeing the two Americans, sending clouds of chalk dust puffing up as from an explosion. Schorner glanced dolefully down at the brown toecaps of his shoes, now coated with chalk. Primrose picked up the cleaner.

'Good morning, ma'am,' said Schorner taking off his cap.

Primrose hurriedly did likewise. He handed the wooden duster to her. She took it with only a nod.

'Was it Miss Jenkins you were wanting?' she inquired, indicating she knew anyway. Schorner swallowed guiltily. 'Well, I thought I'd look in and see the boys and girls,' he said lamely. 'I haven't visited them since they were evacuated.'

'I see.' She gave a cold sniff. She looked down at his chalky toe-caps as if he had arrived like that. 'They are excellent, thank you. Everything is being done that can possibly be done – in the very difficult circumstances.'

Schorner hesitated. 'Would it be convenient to . . .'

Her reaction was that it would not be convenient if left to her. 'Wait here,' she said brusquely and then, to demonstrate she could see no difference in their ranks or appearances, she added: 'Both of you.'

Albie eyed Schorner and the colonel grinned ruefully. The baggy woman jerked through a door. Somewhere children were reciting multiplication tables. 'Schools always smell the same, sir, don't they?' said Albie. 'Goddamn chalk.' He sneezed spectacularly. He had been trying to hold it back. Now Schorner turned and saw that the young man's eyes were watering.

'That's why I was never any good in school,' said Albie genuinely. 'The chalk got into everything.'

'I hope the Germans don't get around to using gas,' said Schorner, keeping a straight face.

'Oh boy, I hope so too. That stuff really is bad for people like me with allergies.'

The woman returned and immediately behind her, as though she had followed surreptitiously, came Dorothy Jenkins. She poked a small face at the other woman's back and shook Schorner's hand. The colonel introduced Albie.

She ushered them through the door and the baggy woman went sternly down the opposite corridor, her heavy soles sounding like a policeman's boots on the floorboards. After the door had closed Schorner heard her shout, 'Yanks!' over her shoulder. He pretended he had not.

Dorothy put her hand to her mouth. 'I'm afraid Miss Parsons does not approve.'

'Of Americans,' sighed Schorner. They had walked to the outside of the classroom and he could see the children looking eagerly towards the panes of glass in the door.

'Of anything,' amended Dorothy. 'I'm afraid she resents most things. Men, Americans and especially me and the fact that my children have been pushed into her school.' Her voice dropped to an enjoyable whisper. 'She used to call herself the headmistress, you see, and sign her letters "Headmistress". A lot of people did not realize she was the *only* teacher in the school. Now there are two of us she can't do it. Anyway, come in.'

She pushed the door and it squeaked as it opened.

The children suddenly sat straight-backed, arms folded in front, clear of the desks, with smirks irrepressibly splitting their small clear faces.

'Children, you all remember Colonel Schorner.'

'Yes, miss,' they chorused almost together.

Schorner, quickly feeling both embarrassed and pleased, gave a brief bow. 'Hi, children,' he said. 'This is a very important man I've brought to see you.' He indicated Albie.

'He drives the jeep,' called a squeaky voice.

Albie blushed and Schorner looked at the little girl. 'That's Mary Steer, I know,' he said.

'And I'm Billy Steer,' rushed the red-faced boy next to her.

'I know, I remember from last time. How come you two are sitting together?'

There were knowing giggles from the class. 'It's the only way I can be sure they will *not* look at anyone else's work,' Dorothy told him. 'If they sit anywhere else they start peeping over somebody's shoulder.'

'And they don't if they sit together?'

'Being brother and sister, they won't *let* each other,' she added with pretended firmness. The class erupted with juvenile approval. The two children sat with identical scarlet country faces, their cheeks puffed with trying not to laugh.

'Albie here,' said Schorner, 'says he didn't like school because of that duster you use for cleaning the blackboard.' He picked one up from Dorothy's desk. 'The chalk used to get up his nose.'

The children wagged with laughter. Albie put in firmly, surprising Schorner: 'No sir, it wasn't the *chalk*.

But that thing sure hurts when the teacher throws it at you!'

The class erupted again. Schorner thought he saw the folded face of Miss Parsons pause for a spying moment at the windowed door, and then vanish.

'Sir, where do you come from?' The question was directed at Albie from Billy Steer.

'Sir, from the United States of America,' returned Albie promptly. He was quick to realize it was not just a futile question. 'From Pennsylvania,' he added. 'Town called Pottsville.'

The children thought that funny too. Albie glanced slightly at Schorner, as if worried he might be either upstaging his superior or giving away classified information. Schorner put his head on one side approvingly.

'We have a map,' said Dorothy quickly. 'We have been trying to imagine what sort of places the American soldiers come from.' She pinned a coloured map of the US on the blackboard and smiled shyly at Albie. 'Could you show us, please?' she asked.

'Right,' said Albie affably. 'If I can find it.' He went to the board and made an exaggerated pantomime of trying to detect his home state. The children giggled and, encouraged, he took off his rimless glasses and wiped them strenuously. That made them shout with enjoyment. 'There,' he said at last, pointing, 'I thought maybe somebody had moved it since I've been away. It's the best state in the Union and, take it from me, there are certain folks who would like to steal it away.' He became serious and Schorner stood and watched in growing surprise as he walked quietly forward and said: 'It was founded by an Englishman, you know, William Penn, that's why it's called Pennsylvania. I guess he maybe even came from these parts. I don't know. He was a Quaker.' He looked challengingly at the children. He appeared to have forgotten the existence of Schorner and the teacher. 'Anybody know what a Quaker is?' asked Albie, peering through his glasses earnestly.

'A man who eats Quaker Oats,' tried Billy Steer.

The children did not laugh but looked seriously to see if that was the answer. The colonel and Dorothy composed their faces. 'No, not quite,' said Albie. 'We have Quaker Oats too, for breakfast. And there's sure a picture of a Quaker on the front. He's the guy in the funny flat hat.' As though he had remembered his senior officer, he turned and inquired seriously: 'Am I doing okay, colonel?'

'Never heard better,' encouraged Schorner. Albie returned to the class.

'No,' he said, 'the Quakers are people who believe in goodness and peace. They don't believe in hurting nobody. My folks were Quakers. They don't even like me being in the army.' The class had become quiet. Albie grinned infectiously: 'Come to think of it, neither do I.'

Everyone laughed again at that. Schorner said: 'I guess we must leave. I have to go and answer a few questions myself.'

Dorothy glanced at him sympathetically. 'Is it today, the Inquisition?'

'It sure is,' he sighed. 'I hope it's half as easy as coming here.'

Albie said good-bye to the children and they chorused in return. He went out towards the jeep.

There was a vacant moment before Schorner followed him. Dorothy filled it.

'Would I be terribly forward if I asked if you'd like to come to my house to supper?' she said, her voice low.

Schorner smiled gratefully. 'Name the night,' he said. 'Only the invasion will stop me.'

'Saturday then,' she suggested. 'But, please, don't bring anything. I don't want you to think I've just invited you for ice cream.'

'I won't think that,' he said, touching her wrist lightly. 'But I'll bring something anyway. See you then.'

'You can tell me about the Inquisition,' she said.

'I feel a whole lot better about it already,' he smiled. He walked towards the jeep as Albie started the engine. The faces of the children filled the lower classroom window. In the next classroom there was only one face, that of Miss Parsons. As he finally turned to go Schorner saw the word form on her puffy lips. 'Yanks.'

Lieutenant Bryant met Schorner at the village hall. There were some local people standing idly outside, curious to see the colonel's arrival. Everyone in Wilcoombe knew that the meeting was taking place; it was impossible to hide anything like that. The rural rumour-mongers had been working vigorously, their normal industriousness given new encouragement by the thrills and uncertainties of war.

Stories sneaking around the town and the adjoining countryside were of uneven sensationalism. Some had it that Eisenhower himself was to arrive in Wilcoombe to explain the American point of view, although most realistically discounted this. Others said that a huge amount of money – all in dollar bills – was being brought into the village hall under armed escort, to pay out additional compensation to the people dispossessed by the occupation; another was that the Americans were seeking permission to use the cricket field outside the small town to bury their increasing number of dead following inaccurate artillery fire during manoeuvres.

There was some disappointment, therefore, when Schorner, familiar to many, and his bespectacled driver arrived without additional echelons, to be greeted by the everyday British lieutenant who had been having a half of cider in the pub at lunchtime. Tom Barrington, the chairman of the parish council, the Reverend Eric Sissons, still with discoloured forehead and bruised hands from his minefield adventure, and Mrs Mahon-Feavor, staring as if imprisoned by the net of her own hat, were counted into the hall, with some spasmodic applause from the street spectators, and the small crowd lingered until Schorner arrived, to be greeted with a stiff salute from Bryant.

A rumble of approval rolled from the soldiers and would-be soldiers in the audience at the smartness of the British greeting. Schorner's comparatively easy American acknowledgement was greeted with frowns. They would never make soldiers. 'Our'n were the best, don' you think,' a man said loudly from the pavement. 'That durn Yank looked loike 'ee was squeezing 'is boils.'

Bryant led the way into the hall. Some flags had been draped around the walls, covering Holman-Hunt's doorstep Jesus, in preparation for an Aid-to-Russia Whist Drive to be held that evening. An enormous Russian hammer and sickle banner was strung across the centre of the back wall and beneath this, like the downcast committee of a workers' collective, sat the three leading residents of Wilcoombe.

They were arranged around the scarred table which Schorner had last seen used by the coroner at the inquest of Meg Pender. By their side was a lady with a grey bun of hair surmounting an angular frame, giving her the aspect of a ball of wool impaled on the end of a knitting needle. She alone smiled nervously as the soldiers entered, although Tom Barrington and Eric Sissons stood with polite grimness. There was a seat placed centrally, facing the committee, for Schorner, but Bryant stood carefully aside. There were English handshakes and unnecessary introductions and Schorner sat down.

'Perhaps there might be a seat available for Lieutenant Bryant, Royal Artillery,' he suggested. 'He is my liaison officer. He is my source of information and helps me out with things British.' He allowed a minor smile to edge his lips. Faces went left and right like doors but no one made any comment. Bryant pulled a chair over and sat discreetly at the side. Then the knitting-needle lady took out a great fold-over pad and a long pencil, the point of which she licked with deep thought.

'Is this lady intending to take notes?' asked Schorner, his expression lifting.

'Miss Benning is the clerk to the council,' said Mrs

Mahon-Feavor, leaning across the table. She had lifted her hat veil but it was about to descend again over her eyes. 'She will keep the record.'

'I'm afraid,' said Schorner quietly, 'there will be no record.'

'But we always have minutes . . .' began Sissons.

'This is one time there will be no minutes,' put in Schorner firmly. 'No notes can be taken. This meeting, ladies and gentlemen, is entirely unofficial, off the record, private or whatever you like. If you insist on it being otherwise, there will be no meeting. I have very firm orders on this.'

'Oh dear,' said Miss Benning. She made as if to lick her pencil again but then resisted and looked around lost and sorry. 'Do I have to go?' she asked Tom Barrington. 'Or can I listen?' She leaned confidingly towards him. 'I can remember most of it,' she whispered. 'And write it down after they be gone.'

'I think,' said Schorner, his firm smile directly on her, causing a flustered blush, 'it would be appreciated if you left the room, ma'am.'

Miss Benning dragged her spinster's eyes from Schorner and looked back at Barrington. The farmer nodded for her to leave. She snapped her pad together, snapped her handbag after stowing the pencil, sniffed out and snapped the door.

'Right,' said Tom Barrington, adopting a similar businesslike air to Schorner. 'No record it is. Now, can we ask some questions?'

'That's why I'm here. I'll do my best.'

Barrington glanced sideways at his colleagues and said: 'When will we be getting our land back?'

'I think you know, Mr Barrington,' said Schorner

slowly, 'that I can't answer that in any way. It will come back to you when we move out. I guess after the invasion of Europe. And I don't know when that will be.'

'You're a farmer,' pursued Barrington. 'So am I. I'm stuck in a muck-heap of a smallholding. I feel as though I'm in a hole in the bloody ground.'

'I am very sorry, as I've told you before. I farm about twenty thousand acres in West Virginia.' He paused. 'I know what you're driving at and the answer is that, okay, as a farmer, I certainly wouldn't like to be in doubt as to the day I could next work my land. The seasons don't wait around for anybody. You need to order seed and plan your year. Believe me, sir, you have my sympathy but there's nothing I can do and nothing I can tell you. As you know there is provision for compensation.'

Barrington sighed at the word. 'A fat lot that's going to be,' he said.

Mrs Mahon-Feavor said briskly, 'None of the people, the tradesmen, the shopkeepers, have had any compensation for loss of goodwill.'

'That's a difficult thing to judge,' said Schorner, thinking that neither had he. 'As you know, all compensation is being assessed by the British Government. It has nothing to do with us.'

'How much damage has been done to the houses?' asked Barrington. 'We've heard the gunfire. People say the whole area has been ravaged.'

'About twenty per cent of the homesteads and other buildings have had some damage,' admitted Schorner. 'About two or three per cent have been badly hit. But we're going to put everything back

488

eventually. We photographed every house. In a couple of years you won't know we came by here at all.'

Sissons had been silent, his chin studiously in his hands; now he stirred. 'My church at Telcoombe Magna has been desecrated,' he said, but not confidently. 'I saw it myself.'

'So I heard,' said Schorner, keeping his mouth straight. 'You were in a prohibited area, sir. You risked your own life, and the lives of the men who had to get you out of that jam.' He waited.

Sissons looked down at the table. 'The organ was playing jazz,' he protested lamely. 'They were gambling, dice and cards . . . There was beer. The pews are marked with cigarette burns.' There returned a painful memory. 'The pulpit is full of rubbish.'

'It's not the first time,' put in Mrs Mahon-Feavor hastily and unexpectedly.

'The church,' said Schorner evenly, 'is the only building large enough to use as a rest and recreation centre for men who have been undergoing training under rigorous and dangerous battle conditions. We asked for, and got, permission from the bishop for its utilization. He thought it was a worthwhile Christian use, considering the war situation, the circumstances.'

'The bishop?' queried Sissons with quiet shock. 'He did not inform me.'

'He informed us,' said Schorner. 'That was all we figured we needed.'

'He never did like the parish,' retorted Sissons sadly. He looked up with new challenge: 'In any case – *recreation*. He couldn't have meant *that* sort of

489

recreation. Choral singing or quiet reading perhaps.'

'Most of these guys don't go in for choral singing,' replied Schorner, his voice dropping. 'And some of them can hardly read. They look at the funnies. You know – King Kong, L'il Abner, that sort of literature. But as long as they're sharp enough to pull a trigger or lob a grenade, we take them. We even grab them. And when we've got them, as far as we can, we try to give them some comfort, some place to go. Pretty soon home for those boys is going to be a lousy hole in the ground.'

He felt his voice hardening. Mrs Mahon-Feavor said with exaggerated sweetness, 'We are worried about the women situation.'

Schorner said solidly: 'So am I.' He looked directly back at them.

'It has various manifestations,' she went on when the expressions of the others had subsided. She was deliberate now. 'There was that unfortunate business in this very room on St Valentine's Night. Hardly a night of love, I think you'd agree. Prostitutes from Plymouth by the busload – fighting. Here.' She pointed dramatically at the floor.

Barrington put in carefully: 'The night poor Meg Pender ended up in the harbour.'

Schorner's look was as careful as the Englishman's words. 'Right,' he confirmed. 'I recall it. The night poor Meg Pender fell into the harbour.' He returned to the old lady. 'The outbreak of fighting, as it was reported to me, ma'am, concerned these ladies from Plymouth and some English girls of the Land Army. We don't have any control over either.'

Mrs Mahon-Feavor became haughty, which she

did easily. 'Those wretches from Plymouth would never have been here if they hadn't come hunting for American soldiers,' she sniffed. 'At every street corner, on most evenings, there are your soldiers hanging around with local girls of the lower sort. And there are a number of silly girls in trouble, you know. Pregnancies.' She managed to drop her voice and make the word rumble at the same time.

'I understand that a situation like that requires two,' replied Schorner. 'I have to tell you now, ma'am, that I have received a directive on this matter which says, pretty bluntly I'm afraid, that these mothers will have no standing whatever if they try to take legal steps to involve American servicemen in paternity cases. That's not my order, that comes from the US Army legal department.' He looked with some sympathy at them. 'And, there is nothing to say that they would ever be accepted even as wives into the United States either. They could end up on Ellis Island as all foreigners do and then be deported.'

'What is your advice then, colonel?' said Sissons suddenly leaning forward into the shocked silence.

'Tell the girls to say no,' said Schorner simply.

There was a further hush. 'Anything more?' asked Barrington, looking at the others. He was prompting Sissons.

The vicar was reluctant, but could not avoid it. 'It has been rumoured,' he began, 'that American soldiers who have been killed in these mock battles have been buried wholesale in a field down by Telcoombe Beach. Is this true?'

A dull bristling redness came to the American's face. 'Sir,' he said, taking difficult control of himself.

His eyes went to slits. 'We do not bury our dead soldiers *wholesale*, nor do we bury them in any field. Nor, for that matter, do we bury them in your churchyard. The bodies of US servicemen killed on active service are returned to their homes in America for burial, if that is at all practical. In this theatre of war, at present, it is practical. We have a great many planes returning to the United States every day. They take our dead back where they belong.' He stood abruptly. 'I think that is all the time I can spare,' he said stiffly.

They also stood, automatically and without saying anything else. Schorner said, 'Thank you,' turned and marched out. The three people remained grouped oddly under the hammer and sickle.

'I think you really upset him then,' said Mrs Mahon-Feavor glaring at Sissons. 'You always were a bit of a bloody fool.'

April

By the first week in April the whole of southern England had become like a vast freight yard; crates and boxes and pyramids of fuel, jerry-cans piled on roadsides and in fields, with tanks, guns, trucks and jeeps creeping unsurely among them. The soldiers who were to fight the approaching battle seemed almost insignificant as they moved in slow lines and with increasing bewilderment along the tight roads among the towers of war material.

After the driest March for a century, the first April days brought traditional rain and soon the firm ground was awash with mud. Apart from the British divisions, the Canadians, and those from France, the Empire and the occupied countries, which spread their dun tents across the green of the springtime land, there were a million and a half Americans training and waiting. Two of these were Privates First Class Ballimach and Primrose. They were lying in a shallow depression in Wilcoombe Beach. Men were moving across the shingle in the morning sun. It was yet another exercise.

'Shit, that's all we see,' complained Ballimach. 'Shit and exercises. Who was the first guys here? Go on, tell me, who was the first?'

'You and me,' nodded Albie. He rolled into the

shingle to give Ballimach more room with his cable drum.

'And how, buddy. We had this place all on our own-i-o, right? And what happens, we get pushed and squeezed up, further and further into the mud. And *still* they come. How they can get all these guys in this one little country I don't know.' His fat eyes squeezed in thought. 'Shit and exercises,' he repeated.

'And you have to get in line for the shit,' confirmed Albie. 'You get in a line half a mile long for chow and then you get in line for the honeybucket.'

Ballimach looked at him with serious concern. 'I don't like to hear you mouthing like that, Albie. That bad language. It's not like you.'

'My folks were Quakers,' agreed Albie. 'It's the army done this for me. All the shit and exercises.'

'I guess we'll all be Quakers soon,' said Ballimach dolefully but pleased at the pun. He snapped a wire with his pinchers and clipped it to a junction. He laughed and Albie looked at him without understanding. The long beach was spread with two hundred engineers, laying lines, fixing the metal trackways up the shore, digging illogical trenches that refilled with the shingle as fast as they were dug. 'That's a joke,' explained Ballimach. 'Quakers, see? Like quaking . . .' He stood and wobbled his great girth extravagantly. 'Shivering. Shivering with goddamn fright.'

'You ain't got any slimmer since you been in England,' mentioned Albie examining the mountainous man. 'It's that cider you drink. On the level. If anything, I figure you're fatter, Ballimach.'

'Thanks a million, pal. Why don't you swim over

right now and tell the Nazis. Go on, tell 'em that Fatso Ballimach is coming and they just can't miss him. Listen, when they start letting off with those twenty-two millimetre bang-bangs, it don't matter how big you are.' He looked down at the slight soldier sprawled against the shingle. 'You, you'll be blown hell of a longer distance than me.'

Albie looked thoughtful. 'I'll level with you, Ballimach,' he said eventually. 'I don't want to go.'

'Me neither, pal,' agreed Ballimach pathetically. 'I thought I'd be smart. If I was marked down as a meathead in these war games they'd replace me. You know what I mean, if I was too fat and too slow. Then they'd put some other poor bastard in the invasion. So I slowed down even more and I do more things wrong. I even *tell* them I'm doing things wrong. I report *myself* for incompetence. Nobody even notices. They want *me* on that beach.'

'There's so many dum-dums around,' philosophized Albie, 'that even a fat dum-dum like you don't show up too bad.' He glanced quizzically at his friend. 'Is that why you fell out of that tree?' he asked. 'Like you did, the very first day when we first got here. Remember, you fell out of the tree? Did you work that out?'

'How can I forget I fell out of the fucking tree?' asked Ballimach resentfully. 'Is falling out of a tree something you forget – even when it's three months ago? The answer is no. It was genuine incompetence. But even that didn't get me taken off the invasion.' He rested his great face on his meaty fists. 'You know, if every other goddamn GI chickened out or got sick, I'd still be there, trying to run up that beach. All on my ownsome.'

495

Albie said: 'I'll tell you something for nothing, Ballimach, I think those guys who just arrived in that small outfit they put in the hut the other side of the church – I think those guys are weird. You know, nobody knows what they do, and they don't tell anybody. They're real quiet about things. And they keep to themselves. It ain't natural for soldiers to keep to themselves, now is it? Somebody said those guys said they're Intelligence.'

Ballimach shrugged hugely: 'So they're Intelligence,' he said. 'So they keep to themselves like they got the plague. So that's what happens when you're in Intelligence – nobody talks to you.'

Albie glanced at his big watch, like the face of a doll on his thin wrist. 'I don't know why I've got to be on the beach, anyway,' he complained. 'I'm supposed to be Colonel Schorner's driver. There ain't going to be many places to drive that first day.' He sighed. 'I'm just a lucky guy to have an officer who wants to be right at the front.'

'Maybe, Albie, you'll be the first to drive into Paris,' suggested Ballimach, his eyebrows rising optimistically. He had finished the connection and they now sat together in the pebble hollow waiting for the ships spread grey across the bay to start the bombardment. 'Two minutes,' said Albie, looking at the watch again. 'Then cover your ears.'

'Maybe we could get deaf,' said Ballimach without real hope. 'You can't even get drafted if you're deaf. The racket on this beach every day could make you deaf.'

'Too late,' dismissed Albie. 'Now, they'd think you was real lucky to be deaf.' He became thoughtful. 'I sure wouldn't mind being the first to drive into Paris. All those señoritas.'

A single loud explosion came from the left marker of the naval vessels crouching out on the sea. It was a coloured tracer and they watched the shell go over with practical interest. 'Shorter than ever,' grumbled Ballimach. 'Every day those Limey guys are trying to kill us. They sit out there on their safe goddamn ships and try to see how they can kill us.'

Further protest was engulfed by the successive thundering which broke out from the horizon, explosions, flashes, crackling along the strung line of ships, the shells whistling like scimitars through the air above them and descending with explosions shuddering but unseen, just inland. A cloth of smoke soon drifted across the beach. They lay beneath it, regarding it moodily.

'Here they come,' yawned Ballimach. Another salvo roared overhead but his reference was to the landing craft which were now grunting shorewards through the smoke. The sea was bucking after rain and wind in the night and the two Americans knew that half their sea-sick comrades coming in to land would end up to their waists, or even shoulders, in the chill water.

This time there was an additional diversion. Two of the landing craft collided metallically as they approached the beach, the nose of one swerving and burying itself into the hull of the second. 'Boy oh boy,' breathed Ballimach. 'Now we got a shipwreck.'

The two blunt vessels, locked together like ugly lovers, careered towards the steep shelf of shingle. They lost way and began to wallow haphazardly in the surf, as though struggling out of their depth. The decks were coped with the helmeted heads of the soldiers, the heads crammed on one deck shouting and cursing and waving disconnected fists at the troops on the other. As the two vessels struck the beach some men toppled overboard into the shallow, churning water.

Ballimach and Primrose rolled over with hilarity. Their laughter became dumb mouthing as another salvo cleft the air and exploded inland. The GIs were struggling ashore from the two craft, still bawling abuse at each other. On the decks the crews of the craft had joined in the curses and the waving of fists. Albie Primrose looked at his friend and, before the next shells, said soberly: 'Pal, I don't know why *we're* laughing. What's so funny?'

Fatigue details had cleared the church at Telcoombe Magna of rubbish. The pulpit had been emptied of cans and so had the font, the cigar and cigarette stumps had been swept from the aisle and the chancel. Bare, frigid, bereft even of the ecclesiastical colours of altar cloth and flowers, it presented a suitably sombre place for the unscheduled conference hastily summoned by General Georgeton.

By the time the general arrived every comfortless pew was occupied by silent and apprehensive Army, Navy and Air Force officers, mostly Americans but with a few British uniforms sitting among them. As the general came in through the old arch of the church door every man stood. He was in no mood for formalities and after a stiff wave of his hand, half a

498

salute, half a sign for them to sit down, he strode straight to the brass eagle lectern. The Stars and Stripes remained about the eagle's neck. The general appeared not to notice it.

'This is no damned good,' he grumbled as soon as he stood there. 'I want to see everybody's face and I want everybody to see mine.' He looked sideways. 'I'll use that – the pulpit,' he decided. 'If God strikes me dead then He strikes me dead. Maybe I'll be glad.'

These remarks were addressed to Captain Scarlett, summoned back from his leave in London. Scarlett agreed nervously and, without necessity, formally pointed the way to the pulpit. Georgeton grunted and strode heavily past him; Scarlett could hear the short gusts of his breath. He stumped up the wooden steps and turned to confront the ranks of officer faces.

'All right,' he began sternly. 'Let's not waste time. Every man here knows why I've called a conference this afternoon. It's too bad that it turns out to be in church because what I have to say is not easy to say in church.'

There were some polite smiles but he did not care or notice. His voice remained sharp: 'The fact is that we have come to a point in our preparations for the invasion where if we do not get off our asses and do something radical, *and* soon, we might as well forget the whole thing – tell Hitler he's a good guy, and go home. And Eisenhower won't like doing that – not at all. So a lot of things have got to be straightened out.'

Isolated in the incongruous pulpit he ran his eyes despondently along the dim length of the church. 'Every officer here today is aware, or should be – if he isn't, he has no right to his rank – that training in this area is getting like a comedy show. Except it's not funny. And the closer we come to the real thing – and take it from me it's getting closer all the time – the worse it's getting. Every exercise seems to be a bigger mess than the one before. Last week we had Exercise Buck. *Buck!* If I wasn't in a church I'd call it something else.'

Schorner was sitting with Bryant. A mangy black cat walked casually in from the churchyard; a cat abandoned during the civilian evacuation and living wild since. It began to purr loudly and wiped its wet and ragged back across the colonel's shins. He gave it a firm push. It edged beneath Bryant's feet and began to mew loudly and plaintively. Its cries seeped through the silent church.

General Georgeton was saying, 'Everything that could go wrong has gone wrong, and not just once . . .' when he heard the cat. Its thin mews rose insistently. Faces began to turn. Georgeton looked up icily.

Schorner turned to Bryant. 'Get rid of it, for God's sake,' he muttered. 'Get it *out!*'

Bravely Bryant caught hold of the cat around its scraggy waist and with a stupid and uncertain smile backed towards the west door of the church. The cat complained painfully as he carried it. He pushed it out into the rainy day and then shut the door on its tail. It howled violently and he had to quickly open the door again to release it.

'My God,' breathed Georgeton from the loft of the pulpit. 'My Almighty God.'

The general looked gaunt while the young officer sat, pink cheeked, in his pew. 'That's what I mean,' he said eventually. 'That just about typifies the way things are getting fouled up.' He picked up a sheet of paper. 'Every day I get reports and each day seems more crazy than the one before. We have landing craft colliding – six incidents in two months – we have men taking thirty-five minutes to get ashore after the landing craft have grounded. Thirty-five minutes! The Nazis would have time to go home, have breakfast and then come back to finish us off.'

His growing glare circled. 'I have a report here of medical teams getting on to the beach and their equipment arriving nine hours, *nine whole hours*, after. What are they supposed to do for the wounded? Tell them to rub it better? Sing them a lullaby? We have guns at one end of the landing area and their ammunition at the other. We have reports of men *sleeping* on the beach because they can't keep awake long enough for the order to go forward.' Even from where he sat Schorner could see the general's hands were shaking. He gripped the top of the pulpit to still them.

'Embarkation has been terrible. Every road jammed, every junction messed up. The hards that were laid down for the loading when the *real* thing happens have been so damaged by ill-use that we've had to call off using them. So now everybody gets bogged down in the fields. The way the military police try to get the traffic unsnarled, they might as well be on Fifth Avenue, New York City. There's no order to anything.'

He paused and through the pause, over the shocked heads of the officers, came the plaintive and insistent mewing of the cat outside the church door. Georgeton took three deep breaths. 'Lieutenant,' he called down the church. 'You, the British officer who took that cat out before.'

Bryant, hot-faced, stood. 'Yes, sir.'

The general said evenly, 'Get that cat *out*. Shoot it, drop it under the track of a tank, lock it in a tomb, do whatever you like, but get rid of it. Okay?'

'Sir,' said Bryant, coming to attention as smartly as he could from the confinement of the pew. He went out of the door. The sly cat was waiting for him and shot past him into the church. It ran unswervingly down the aisle and into the chancel. Someone threw a hymn book at it and missed. The book lay open on the floor. Bryant ran after the cat, excusing himself loudly as he went, chasing it through the choir stalls until it eventually turned and – to his relief – dashed out through the door again. Bryant went out after it, closing the door prudently behind him.

'But,' Georgeton started again. He had waited and watched the pursuit. 'If embarkation has been lousy, and it has, then disembarkation has been terrible, a shambles. The timing, the handling of landing craft and vehicles and beach discipline – all terrible. We've had casualties, we've suffered losses, men killed, through sheer goddamn ineptitude. And it's got to stop right *now*.'

He paused. 'At the beginning of next month,' he said, slowing, 'we are going to undertake the final exercise. Exercise Lion. Somebody had the idea to call it Exercise Lulu, but the whole thing has become plenty enough of a laughing matter. I don't want a hundred widows hearing that their husbands were killed during Exercise Lulu. So it's Exercise Lion.

'It will be the biggest and the last before the real

thing. We've run out of time. Briefings will commence next week in Exeter and Plymouth. Everybody has got to get it into their heads that this time it's *got to go right*. The plan will be to land three separate forces on Telcoombe Beach, the convoys coming from different directions, and at night. Every man under my command earmarked for the initial assault on D-Day and engineer and back-up units will be part of this. There will be airdrop landings, fighter and bomber strafings and a major bombardment from the sea.'

He waited and then said: 'There has got to be a risk that the Germans will use this exercise to mount a sudden attack on our ships. They'll soon pick it up through increased radio activity. This attack could come from the air or by submarine, or surface raiders. And they'll lay mines like ants lay eggs. We must always have this in our minds and we must be prepared for such an attack and repel it.' He looked sardonic. 'It might be good practice for us.

'I don't have to tell you that not one word I have said is to go beyond this room. At this stage of the war it should be unnecessary to repeat this. But the fact is, and this is another and a most serious aspect of the general mess that has built up over the past few weeks; the fact is that security is disgraceful. Every two-bit civilian for miles around knows exactly what is happening and when. We might as well put it out on the radio and in the newspapers. It's just great when some lousy cowhand can tell you what time your troops are scheduled on the beach.

'This time, Exercise Lion is going to be right. General Eisenhower and General Montgomery will be coming down to sit in the stand.' He stared at them stonily. 'I want it to go well, to be right. It had better be.'

Abruptly he turned and walked down the pulpit steps. The assembled officers stood and came to attention as he left the church. He threw up a wry salute and went out into the churchyard rain. The cat was sitting under his staff car and as he approached it jumped lightly on to the roof of the vehicle. Bryant, who had been lurking under the lychgate, turned to grab it. It moved out of his reach but remained on the roof.

Captain Scarlett who was walking a pace behind the general said quietly: 'It's a black cat, sir. Maybe it'll be lucky.'

'Scarlett,' said General Georgeton, 'you're a goddamn fool.'

The anti-aircraft gun was moved on the first Monday of April, a huge, impersonal army vehicle with a towing crane arriving to take it away. It was dragged from the site where it had been for four familiar years with no regard or respect from the aggressively cheerful and strange soldiers who came for it. They pulled it off like a noble bull being dragged dead and ignominiously from the bullring.

'That's a good gun that is, mate,' said Catermole stoutly to one of the soldiers who came to take it away. He jabbed a stubby finger at the piece. They were all laughing and swearing as they shackled it up. 'There's not many guns like that left,' he insisted close to the man's ear.

The soldier did not care and looked annoyed. 'All

right, all right, I 'eard you,' he answered. 'But it's about as much use now as a wank on a Saturday night.'

Catermole bridled. 'Listen mucker, it's all right for the likes of you, charging around picking up other people's guns, but we shot down a bomber with that.' He pointed furiously. 'Crashed just over the 'ill there. We got it right in the guts.'

The stranger sighed. He was a man with a tarnished smile, wearied as if with many battles. 'Listen, I don't want to 'ear your war 'istory,' he told Catermole. 'All we got to do is get this wreck on the back of our lorry and drag it off.'

Catermole sniffed truculently. 'Bloody 'ell, all you blokes are is scrap merchants, just scav . . . scav . . . what you call 'em.'

'Scavengers,' provided the other soldier almost politely. He had been called that before. Even clearing up bomb damage. Scavengers.

'Right,' affirmed Catermole. 'Dead right. I s'pose you'll be goin' over to France, won't you, fifty miles behind the bloody action, picking up the bits.'

The man was not annoyed. They were just moving the gun from its position, its unaccustomed wheels turning unhappily. 'It's got a squeak,' said the removal soldier. 'You blokes 'aven't overdone it with the oil can, 'ave you?'

Catermole's blasphemous reply was truncated by a fat bellow from Sergeant Bullivant; it was his special shout that began with an order and curled up into a whine. 'Battery! Baaaa – ter – eee. On parade!' Catermole put two fingers up to the outsider and turned towards the broken tarmac at the centre of the nissen huts. Bullivant was standing so stiff and sticking his stomach out so far and so tight that it seemed he might split up his middle seam. 'Come on! Come on! Let's have you!'

Gilman was trying to write a poem in the latrine, on the wall but unerotic. He hurried out and joined the oddments of men who were now falling into something resembling ranks on the parade area. Captain Westerman, ramming his cap over his eyes as though he might want to shadow tears, stumped down the steps from the orderly room, followed by Bryant.

The little unit came to attention and they stood thus while the gun that had been their companion, their daily work and their reason for being, was drawn squeakily away. Bullivant brought them upright and the captain threw up a theatrical salute. The soldiers of the removal squad watched with scarcely hidden amusement. 'Blimey,' said the man Catermole had been upbraiding. 'You'd fink it was Churchill's funeral.' He made a deep sound approximating to the Funeral March and grinned at the standing ranks. 'What a mob,' he said to one of his comrades. 'Rough as a badger's arse.' He glanced behind, to the place where the gun had rested. There was a small collection of rubbish; papers, a forlorn boot and a dead seagull. 'I s'pose they reckon they shot that bugger down as well,' he muttered.

For some time after the gun had creaked out of the gate, watched now by a thunderstruck section of the Wilcoombe inhabitants, the soldiers in the camp remained at attention. Doey Bidgood, standing close to the fence, called over: 'What you goin' to do now, boys, throw stones?'

They all heard, eyes swivelled nastily. Westerman seethed: 'God, I'd like to have that big mouth under my command.'

Bullivant called the parade to ease, back to attention and then lachrymosely dismissed them. He knew it was for the last time. 'Catermole,' said Bullivant softly. 'Be a good lad and get a dustpan and brush. Sweep up that seagull, will you?' Catermole nodded uncomplainingly and went off at his ungainly gait. 'This time tomorrow they'll all be gone, sir,' Bullivant ventured to Westerman. 'End of the story.'

'True, sergeant, true,' said the officer giving his thigh a quick slap with his cane. He glanced at the swollen sergeant. 'Except you and I, Bullivant. And I'll be off to Ross and Cromarty on Wednesday. Then you'll be here by yourself. You'll be a one-man unit, commander, NCO and gunner, all in one.'

Bullivant looked as if it had not occurred to him. 'I suppose that's right, sir. There'll be a lot to do, though. Tidying up and suchlike.'

'Looking after the geraniums,' mentioned Bryant who had been standing silently with them. 'Mind you keep them watered.'

A blush edged across Bullivant's face. 'I don't expect I'll be here all that long, sir,' he said gruffly. 'They'll find a posting for me soon enough, I expect.'

'Ross and Cromarty,' repeated Westerman slowly as if to himself. 'I've looked it up, Bryant. Have you seen where it is?'

Bullivant threw up his best salute, which always resulted in his webbing belt riding up his stomach. 'Shall I carry on, sir?'

'Yes, do, sergeant,' answered Westerman. 'And make sure that seagull gets cleared up.'

'I've given orders, sir,' swallowed Bullivant. He saluted again and wheeled like a carousel before stamping off.

'They'll have a job to find somewhere for him, sir,' said Bryant.

'Gross, isn't he,' agreed Westerman. 'Just as long as he doesn't follow me to Ross and Cromarty.' He looked at Bryant as if he thought the lieutenant might know the whole strategy. 'Whatever are we doing with a unit up there?' he asked. 'Are we afraid of aggression from the Icelandics?'

Thankfully Bryant saw a jeep back in at the gate. Scarlett climbed out and strolled to them. 'Never march, these Americans, do they?' commented Westerman under his breath. 'They slump. Their arms would fall off if they swung them.'

Bryant introduced the American officer. 'Must be off,' said Westerman immediately. 'A million things to do before I go.'

'Like pack his shaving kit,' mentioned Bryant with a wry grin as his CO marched away. 'And take his poker-work mottoes off the wall.'

'They've taken your gun,' noticed Scarlett. 'Was it the Germans?'

'Quick raid across the Channel,' laughed Bryant. 'Looks strange, gone, doesn't it. Everyone had grown quite attached to it. There wasn't a dry eye in the place.' They watched Catermole march, quite smartly for him, across the open area, carrying a brush and a dustpan. He circled the dead feathers uncertainly before sweeping up the seagull. 'How was London?'

asked Bryant mischievously. They began to walk towards the jeep.

'I wanted to tell you about it,' said Scarlett.

'They got you back soon enough.'

'For the general's blow-up,' nodded Scarlett.

'What's known in our army as a good bollocking,' said Bryant.

They climbed into the jeep but Scarlett did not start the engine. 'Listen,' he said. 'I got worried. I still am.'

'Not the clap,' said Bryant. '*Not* Jean Manifold.' He saw the American was not joking.

'Not Jean,' the American shrugged. 'That was no dice. When I got there she was being nice to a goddamn US Ranger, and you know the size of those guys. She just nodded to me, that's all. I'm not too sure she recognized me again.'

'That's how she has to be, I suppose,' said Bryant. 'But what's the worry?'

Scarlett looked around. A few people were still staring through the wire at the novelty of the absent gun. He started the engine of the jeep and drove along the coastal road towards the checkpoint. He drove slowly. It was a mild day, the beach busy with noisy birds. In the bay idled half a dozen small craft and farther out the pair of old destroyers.

'About them,' said Scarlett, nodding at them.

'Smokey and Stover? What about them?'

'You remember that night I got drunk, in the club in London, and I opened my big mouth. What exactly did I say?'

'A lot of things. The sort of rubbish anybody talks when they're pissed.'

'But about those *ships*? Level with me, I did go on

509

about them, didn't I? That's why you warned me this time.'

Bryant nodded: 'You did. But it was nothing. You complained about them being old and slow. The sort of thing anybody might say.'

Scarlett tightened his lips. 'But is it? Jesus, why couldn't I keep my great mouth shut. That's information that could be picked up by anybody – by the Germans.'

'What's the worry now? You did it and that's all there is to it. I won't tell. We all talk too much sometimes.'

'It's not as simple as that. You know that guy who was at the desk in that place, the thin one with the pinky eyes – and the older guy, the waiter. They were *right there* when I said it, right? Even I remember them, standing there listening.'

'Yes, I think so. What about them?'

'They vanished, that's what about them. They were a couple of queers, living together, and the old guy had been in prison. All sorts of stuff has come out. The police and secret service guys have been looking for them.' Woefully he looked at Bryant. 'They could have been spies.'

It was a night of deepest dark along the coastal road, with a clumsy wind buffeting across the low land. The wind came from the very hole of the night, somewhere far over the sea. Off-shore Schorner knew there were thirty-three ships ranging from a US heavy cruiser to a wallowing water-carrier, lying there now, only pricked with light, waiting for tomorrow's resumption of the everlasting rehearsal.

The colonel was going to Dorothy's house. Lying on the seat at his side in the jeep were two bottles of wine, tinned fruit and ice cream. As he reached the beach checkpoint and the military policeman approached, his torch bouncing, the Californian burgundy rolled across the seat. The snowdrop spotted it and looked up and saw it was Schorner.

'Okay, sir,' he said saluting casually. He grinned towards the wine. 'Have a good night, sir.' The man stood back and waved him on as the barrier went up. Schorner cursed quietly as he drove. Cocksure young bastard. But he found himself grinning. For once he felt youthful again.

The wind had Wilcoombe to itself although there was the customary Saturday night singing drifting from the blocked windows of the Bull and Mouth. His men, despite their initial disgust at the British beer, now treated the pub as their regular haunt. Of native institutions only the Totnes fish and chip shop was as popular. At the Bull and Mouth they had taken to cider. They had told the landlord that the beer ought to be left in the donkey.

Beyond Dorothy's small, square house at the summit of the hill was an enclosed yard facing an old and dark barn. He had previously noted its strategic possibilities and now he turned the jeep over the gapped cobbles and left it in the shadow of the brooding building. Putting the wine and food in a US Army canvas bag he sidled to the front of the street, to the corner house, and knocked carefully on the door.

To his dismay it was opened by an elderly, pear-faced woman. For a moment he thought he had mistaken the house, but she smiled a long smile like a slack rope, and beckoned him in. 'Dorothy's through there,' she said. 'I'm her auntie. I thought I'd come round and take a look at you.'

'Oh fine,' said Schorner, still uncertain. 'And how do I look?'

The old lady laughed. Her mouth dipped; her teeth were spaced like posts in a valley. 'All right. All you boys look all right. Better than our scruffy lot, all beer and swearing like they are. And your boys are lovely dancers. I've watched them at Totnes. Doing that buggering.'

'Jitterbugging, dear,' corrected Dorothy. She arrived, smiling at Schorner's confusion. She and Schorner shook hands formally.

'Give him a kiss, if you like,' said auntie. 'I'll shut my eyes. And I won't take a squint, promise.'

Dorothy regarded her sternly. 'Now, you promised, didn't you?'

'I did too,' admitted the old lady. 'No messing of things up.' Her elongated face descended even further but then she looked up and beamed at Schorner. 'That's what I promised.'

They went into the small room with a table already set. There were three places on the white tablecloth. It had a neat mend at one corner. 'I didn't think you'd mind auntie being here for a while,' said Dorothy near his ear. 'She's a dear and she did so want to meet you, Carl.' She looked up at the old lady. 'She had a boyfriend from America, a soldier, in the First World War, didn't you auntie?'

'Oh, he was a devil,' smiled the aunt. Dorothy had poured three glasses of sherry and the aunt had already drained her glass before she finished the brief sentence. She held it out for more.

'Now, you, steady on,' suggested Dorothy good-humouredly. She turned to Schorner who was regarding the old lady quizzically. 'She doesn't agree with the war,' she explained. 'So she's having no part of it, only when it's forced on her. They've arrested her twice for contravening the blackout regulations – at the beginning of the war her windows were blazing like a lighthouse when everything else was pitch black. People accused her of signalling to the Germans. Since then I've taken all her lightbulbs out except two and I have to go into her house and pull the blinds across. She doesn't agree with the shortage of sherry, either. As you can see.' She wagged her finger at the pleased-looking woman and half filled her sherry glass. 'That's all there is, auntie,' she warned.

'The American soldier,' said Schorner. 'Did you ever see him again?'

'No!' she said with a puff of her cheeks. 'Mind you, never expected to.' She wandered off into memory for a moment, but then returned briskly. 'I was just a young maid. Had his way with me and then off he went. Never heard another dickie-bird of him. He was a cowboy he said, I think. Or was it an Indian? One of them. He wore a funny hat, I know.'

Schorner was laughing. Dorothy had gone into the kitchen and she called from there: 'Whatever tale is she telling you?'

''Tis the truth,' objected the aunt. She displayed her teeth like flags. 'Same as I always told you. He wore a funny hat.'

'Feathers?' suggested Schorner playfully. 'You can tell Indians, they wear *feathers*.'

'No, it was pointed, like the Boy Scouts wear. He said they wear their hats in bed in America. Is that true? It seemed a very funny idea to me.' To Schorner's relief she did not want an answer. 'But he was nice, you know. Real romantic. Like in the fillums, although we didn't have pictures in those days, of course. Not heard of in these parts. But I often wondered if I'd see him on the fillums. When they opened the picture palace in Totnes, before the war, I used to go and see if I could spot him, even if it was just in the crowd. I went to all the cowboy films. Tom Mix, and the one with the white horse that sings.'

'Roy Rogers,' suggested Schorner.

She appeared astonished. 'You *know*!' she exclaimed. Then: 'But I s'pose you would do, coming from there. I 'spect you see them every day on their horses.' She went into another reverie. Then she said: 'I've wondered if his son might be one of your boys over here now. I mean, 'tis possible. I've thought of that when I've seen them and I've thought, "I hope Charlie's son don't go and get 'isself killed." His name was definitely Charlie, but I can't rightly remember his other. I fancy it was one of those difficult names.'

As Schorner said: 'We have plenty of difficult names in the United States,' Dorothy came in with a steaming soup tureen.

'It's only vegetable,' she said. 'But I made it fresh from the garden.' She glanced at him and grinned. 'And no sprouts,' she said. 'I've heard how you all hate sprouts.'

Schorner nodded: 'Little cabbages,' he said.

514

They sat at the table and Dorothy asked him to pour the wine. The old aunt sucked her glass dry in a moment, the wine sizzling through her teeth. 'Hmmm,' she said. 'That's nice. I knew he'd bring something, Dotty. I *said*, didn't I? Did he bring some ice cream?'

'Auntie,' said Dorothy patiently. 'Yes, Colonel Schorner did bring some ice cream.'

'Oh good,' said the old lady happily. 'I never agreed with them doing away with ice cream. Just because of the war. And rationing eggs. The hens still lay eggs even if there is a war. The hens don't know. I've heard that the Germans eat butter instead of ice cream. We can't even get the butter and we're the ones who's reckoned to be winning.' She looked at Schorner for confirmation. ''Tis right, we are?'

'I think we're about halfway there,' said Schorner cautiously. Dorothy said: 'Auntie, could you keep quiet for a few moments, do you think?'

'If you like, dear,' nodded the old lady affably. She finished her soup spectacularly, spooning up the final dampness from the plate and pursuing a fugitive carrot around the rim. She swallowed it with a gulp of satisfaction. 'That Charlie,' she said. 'Oh, he was romantic. Wore his hat in bed.'

When they had finished the meal, monopolized, despite Dorothy's efforts, by the old lady's reminiscences and philosophy, she suddenly announced that she was tired and wanted to go home.

'All that chatting,' said Dorothy kindly. 'People wearing their hats in bed!'

'That was Charlie, the American. God's honour,' said the aunt quietly. Dorothy helped her on with her coat. Schorner offered to take her home but Dorothy said: 'She's only three doors away. I'll take her. Just make yourself at home.'

After elaborate good-byes and a pledge extracted from Schorner that he would try to discover Charlie, or at least the son of Charlie, the two women went out into the windy street. Dorothy had taken a coat down from a peg in the hall and, in the darkness, while the old lady was at the front door, the American helped the English girl to put it around her shoulders. His hand touched the top of her arm and he left it there for a moment. Her hand came up and lay gently across it. Then she said: 'I won't be a moment.'

He touched the door against the jamb, so that it did not close. Then, with an odd, hopeless feeling, almost a sensation of surrender, he went back into the close room. There was a small, lively fire in the grate. The lamps would have barely provided light to read. The armchair was worn down to comfort. He sat in it gratefully. Not for the first time he wondered at the circumstances which had brought him, a man nearing middle life, far from his house, his family and his land, to this strange, puzzling, comfortable place; in the house of this woman twenty years younger who, within a few minutes, would be returning to him.

She was quickly back, giving a loud shiver as she entered the door. 'The wind's very cold,' she said from the darkness. She came into the room and smiled with genuine pleasure at the sight of him in the armchair. 'You look very settled there,' she said. 'It fits you.'

'It's not your special chair is it?' he asked, rising.

'It's for you,' she said. She was clearing the dishes from the table. He moved to help, but she waved him back. 'Help with the washing-up, if you like,' she told him. 'But we'll have some coffee first. American coffee. Beatrice Evans, bless her, gave me half her tin.'

She balanced the dishes and took them past him. The edge of her dress rolled across his arm as she went through the door. 'I hope you didn't mind auntie,' she called from the kitchen.

'She was a surprise – *that's* for sure,' he acknowledged, laughing.

'Her and Charlie,' she giggled. She appeared at the door. 'I wonder what really happened.'

'A story,' he shrugged. 'Another story. They happen all the time.'

'It's a natural occurrence, I suppose,' she said. 'Wars and soldiers, people meeting.' She halted abruptly and, as if fearing she had said too much, she went back into the kitchen. The dishes sounded. He sat smiling in the orange light of the fire. He could feel his limbs resting.

'How is it you got to be a colonel?' she called from the kitchen. 'I mean, if everybody joins the army more or less at once, which is what happened isn't it, how do they choose who is going to be what? Do they pick you if you're bigger than the others or do they think you've got the eye of a leader?'

'There have been times when I've thought that way,' he answered.

She appeared at the door again. 'I've put the kettle on,' she said. She sat on the arm of the chair and, naturally and quietly, they held hands.

He looked into the fire. 'Do you still want to know, about how they select officers?' he said.

'Yes, I'm very interested,' she replied. 'I'll sit here until the kettle boils. If it goes over the top it puts the gas out. How did you?'

'In my case I joined the National Guard, that's like your Territorial Army. In 1939. Not many people in America wanted any part of *any* war then, against Hitler or anybody else. Some guys went over the border and joined the Canadian Air Force because they weren't blind as to what was going to happen anyway. But the rest, well they were happy to let the world bleed, just as long as the blood didn't run on America. I didn't see it like that but I had a farm and everything and I couldn't take off for Canada and, in any case, I was too old to fly operationally. So I enlisted in the National Guard in West Virginia.'

'And they made you an officer.'

He laughed. 'Sure. I had my own gun.'

'Get off,' she giggled. She let go of his hand and went into the kitchen. He stood up and walked in after her. She made the coffee and he poured the milk into the cups. 'Somebody told me you are forty-seven,' she said conversationally. 'That's young for a colonel, isn't it?'

'Not at all. It's just like being a schoolteacher, I guess. The classes tend to be bigger, that's all.'

She took his coffee from him and they went into the other room. The wind hooted like a hooligan past the window. She sat him down in the armchair again and sat herself on the arm.

'This,' said Schorner patting the side of the chair, 'is very nice.'

518

'Yes, I suppose it is. I thought you would like it. You put the jeep around the corner, didn't you? I saw it wasn't in the street.'

'Yes. I didn't want to shock the neighbours.'

'The rats will chew the tyres,' she said. 'They come out of the barn at night.' Without a pause she said: 'You've got grey eyes, haven't you?'

'They reflect the colour of my hair,' he grinned. The grin quietened on his face as she leaned across from the arm of the chair and kissed him on the mouth. They kissed a second time, each holding a half-full coffee cup in one hand, each searching for the table to set the cups down.

'Silly,' she said. She eased away from him and took both cups, setting them on the table. Then she turned and knelt on the fireside rug, her face forward, her hair covering his lap.

'Could you spare an hour for a lonely girl?' she said.

'Could you spare an hour for a lonely soldier?'

She looked up, her eyes moist, warmth in her face. 'I took the liberty of putting two hot water bottles in the bed,' she said. 'It ought to be warmed through by now.' He put his face down to hers and kissed her again.

Before the first ten days of April were finished, the plans for the Allied assault on the coast of Europe were all but final: as close as they could ever be. Now the factors were of the same family – the tides, the moon and the weather. There were days in May when they might simultaneously be right, the tide full early in the morning, the moon rising late; only the imponderable weather being in doubt. There were three days in early June, one later that month and another in July. After that the chance would have gone. Perhaps for ever.

An anxiety to get on with the battle now spread throughout all the troops along the southern coast. The weeks of work and training now resolved themselves into the soldier's enemy – the waiting. At Telcoombe Beach, on 12 April, a squadron of the latest amphibious tanks arrived and stood impressively on the concrete hards, their rockets pointing with token belligerence towards Normandy. Out to sea loitered the old former American destroyers, HMS *Oregon* and HMS *Florida*, and the large, unsteady Tank Landing Ships and Troop Landing Craft – the LSTs and the LCTs – two now armed at the stern with the spiky but elderly Bofors guns. On the same day as the amphibious tanks arrived, so did Miss Sherree Ann Lorner. She was taken to the US officers' mess at the Manor House and allotted an escort of an officer and six men. Captain Scarlett, the general's ADC, was given the task of appointing the officer. He appointed himself.

'Me? I don't even want to hear about it,' said Pfc Ballimach on receiving the news of the star's arrival. 'What's the use of showing a guy something like that, something he can't even touch? I don't want to hear the dame sing. I heard her sing and she sings lousy. So, you tell me, what's in it for me?'

'You'd never get near her with that stomach anyway,' mentioned Albie. They were in the bar of the Bull and Mouth at six o'clock. Miss Lorner's appearance was scheduled for nine o'clock in the Victoria Rooms, Totnes.

520

Gilman and Catermole were standing against the bar, smiling. 'With her big bangers, mate, and your big gut, you'd just have to send messages,' suggested Catermole.

'Okay, okay,' shrugged Ballimach. 'Now I get it from everybody's goddamn army. But, I ask you, buddy, what good is this dame to me? Is she going to help me die with a smile on my face? Is she hell. I ain't even gonna check her out.'

Gilman said: 'At least you get some glamour. We get Vera Lynn.'

'What's the matter with Vera Lynn?' demanded Catermole aggressively. 'Maybe she don't have the big bangers, mate, but she can sing like fuck. She makes me cry.'

Gilman nodded: 'That's the bloody trouble. She makes everybody cry. "White Cliffs of Dover" and "We'll Meet Again". Christ, when I'm out there on that tin tub with that Bofors going off in my ears, I want to remember something funny.'

Catermole nodded. He stared almost challengingly at the Americans. 'You blokes don't get anything like the bloody liberties what they take with us,' he asserted. 'Jesus, we say we want something to make us laugh, you know, like proper entertainment, and they send down a bleeding Punch and Judy Show. Punch and Judy, for fuck's sake! And a ballet dancer, some old cow who creaked like a shithouse door every time she opened her legs. That's what we get.'

'Which of the LSTs are you on?' Albie asked Gilman.

Gilman said: 'It's the one that goes up and down like a lift.'

'Those guns, those Bofors guns, are they very smart? We're going to be hoping they are.'

Gilman shrugged. 'Depends what comes at you. They're fast and noisy, but they're not exactly the latest craze. I thought they were going to go in with rockets.' He leaned closer to Albie because they talked together more easily than with Catermole and Ballimach. 'Do you realize we used rockets at the battle of Waterloo?' he said.

Albie appeared only a little puzzled. 'Did you win?' he asked. Gilman grinned. 'We only talk about the battles we win,' he said. He drained his beer. 'Are you on to this stuff yet?'

Albie sighed: 'I'm sorry. It gives me dysentery. I'll have a Coca Cola if that's okay.'

Ballimach said: 'I don't get dysentery. Jeeze, I wish I did sometimes. It takes the pounds off so quick you can hear them falling. I guess I'll have some cider.'

Catermole put his tankard down silently and Gilman ordered a pint. 'Let me pick up this tab,' said Ballimach. 'I want you guys to shoot straight with that crazy-looking gun and especially for me. I'm keeping in good with you.'

The bar was crowded from end to end now. Smoke moped a foot off the ceiling and Horace Smith the poacher began to bang on the corner piano with his small knotty hands. He was a poor player, so poor that the songs frequently emerged as totally changed. Minnie, his wife, supported him powerfully, standing at the upright, holding her great fist around the brass candlestick holder and moaning grotesquely along the approximate theme, every now and then bursting into words when she recognized something.

522

'Sweetheart, sweetheart, sweetheart,
Will you love me, evaaah.'

'Bloody 'ell,' grumbled Catermole. 'Hitler's secret weapon is on the go again.'

Ballimach and Albie looked at each other. 'Maybe,' said Ballimach, 'we'll go and see Sherree Ann Lorner after all.'

'Minnie is real,' pointed out Gilman wryly. 'You can touch her.'

'And how,' answered Albie. 'I think maybe Sherree Ann wins by a short vote.'

'Go and see 'er,' suggested Catermole. 'Get 'er fixed in your 'ead and then go back, get into your pit and close your eyes tight. It ain't too bad like that.'

'Why is it,' asked Ballimach, 'that all the things I *hate* are real? And all the things I *like* I have to pretend?'

Minnie, attempting to reach an impossible pitch, choked noisily over the piano, spitting all over Horace's balding head. He stopped and wiped his pate with his hand. She took a monstrous swig of beer and choked even more spectacularly.

'Oh boy,' said Albie. 'That Sherree Ann Lorner seems more lovely all the time.' He said to Ballimach, 'Let's go.' They went.

The Victoria Rooms, Totnes, was a staunch grey building, one hundred and twenty-three years old, which had received visits from famous men. Gladstone, the fading Wellington, Livingstone, Robert Scott, raising money to go to his death in the

Antarctic, Le Petomane, the famous theatrical farter of Paris, Asquith, Lloyd George, Elgar and Lewis Carroll had appeared on its wide stage.

Sherree Ann Lorner was, in her way, staunch also. She was blonde and younger than the Victoria Rooms by a century. In her shorter history, however, she had received even more visits from outstanding men. She was naturally sensual; a young woman gifted with breath-taking breasts and lovely lips; she had been married three times, although, as she, with sweet banality, pointed out to newspaper and radio interviewers, any girl is allowed three mistakes.

Her tour of Britain in the spring of 1944 had been a trail of triumph. The all-American blonde had not stinted in this simple service to her young countrymen committed to one of the most dangerous missions in history. She stood bravely in camps, cinemas and concert halls and sang loudly, if not very well, the spotlights for ever nosing her famous creamy cleavage. Her dresses always shimmered, her hair waved goldenly, her lips had a lovely red sheen. When she gave them 'The Star Spangled Banner' at the conclusion of her performance, standing erect and beautiful in the splashing lights, her chest wonderfully extended towards the khaki audience, there was not a man who would have not gladly gone at once from there to die in battle. She was not, as some commentators attempted to represent, the cosy woman these men had left behind. She *was* America and they were fighting for her, tits and all. Many a young soldier, as he watched, had a lump in his throat and another in his pants.

Captain Scarlett, the lady's officer escort and the six

GIs detailed as her euphemistic guard of honour watched from the wings of the old hall in Totnes, enjoying the profile view of that famous bust, expanding and contracting like a beautiful bellows, as she sang her songs. The place was full of faces, each one a small, longing reflection of the lights upon the stage. One section of the auditorium was allocated to, as distinct from reserved for, black troops. No faces could be seen from there; instead, two hundred eyes glittered like a colony of fireflies.

Miss Lorner did her sincere best. She sang songs of home and Hollywood, she told a few cosy stories, two naughty, and danced with a hapless soldier brought at random on to the stage to perform as her stooge. She dragged the gangling boy across the boards, plastered against her, in an exotic and exaggerated tango until the place was uproarious with the howls of soldiers in frustration. The callow rookie, pressed against those breasts and that shimmering stomach, could only lie there, eyes shut tight, like a child against its mother.

Scarlett witnessed the performance with respect and some admiration. He had to take her back to the officers' mess at Telcoombe Manor after the last riotous applause had gone, the hall was empty and the soldiers had wandered to their tents. He sat between her in the back of the roomy staff car, a padded armrest between them.

'I think they liked me?' said Sherree Ann, provoking a compliment.

'Oh sure, they loved every minute,' said Scarlett. He touched the driver on the shoulder and directed him towards the mess. 'How couldn't they? You were wonderful, Miss Lorner.'

'It's all I can do,' she said surprisingly. He half glanced her way in the dark. 'I feel just terrible when so many of those poor boys are going to die.'

At first Scarlett felt a gob of anger rising in his chest. He thought she was reciting the sentiment like some weary Hollywood war script. Her voice sounded like that, as though she were mouthing the words on the screen; but then he realized it was the way she always spoke. She had been taught and conditioned to it. He looked sideways at her and saw that her face was fixed and full of sadness.

'We have some other guys,' he said cautiously, 'who couldn't get there tonight because they have a duty assignment, or they've been on exercise all day and they have to remain within the security perimeter.'

'Oh,' she sighed. 'That's a real pity.'

'It is,' said Scarlett. 'They have to be out at dawn again. In this area we use live ammunition to simulate real battle conditions.'

She remained looking ahead. She had a mink coat wrapped around her fine body. Even in profile he detected her pout of surprise and dismay. 'You mean, our soldiers are *shooting at each other*? They get wounded and killed?'

Scarlett said: 'Not shooting *at* each other, although it happens. But we've had some dead and wounded over the past few months.'

'What a *waste*, captain,' she said, her already low voice going to a whisper. 'That's the most terrible thing I ever heard. They're not even using up their lives on the goddamn Germans.'

'That's how it is,' shrugged Scarlett.

526

'Can I go and see these guys?' she asked. 'I mean, I have to go some other place tomorrow, I don't know where, they're all the same to me in this country. But I could go right now. I could see them and sing to them tonight.'

'It's an idea,' admitted Scarlett. 'Will you have to clear it with somebody? You know, your producer or somebody?'

'Herbie?' she said scornfully. 'He's with the band – full of booze by now. I should check it's okay, but I don't feel like it. I don't see why I should have to ask every time I want to do something. I'll have to put my hand up to go to the bathroom next.'

She turned to half face him. Again Scarlett realized how beautiful in her full, fleshy way she was; a real dish, all eyes and lips and bosom. 'Do you know, captain,' she said huskily. Scarlett swallowed. 'I think I'm going to ask you to take me right to those soldiers – and now. Can I get to see them?'

Scarlett grinned at her in the dimness. He decided he liked her, as well. 'Maybe that could be arranged,' he said. 'Even at short notice.'

'Terrific,' said Sherree Ann. She had an idea and her face lit with excitement. It was the first time he had seen her animated off the stage. Her pale soft hand flapped towards him and he felt its frank, brief and unmeaning touch on his face. 'Let's make it a party,' she suggested breathlessly. 'I've got a crate of bourbon in the back of that car we left here, at the old house. It's Herbie's, but he's had enough for one year. I can borrow that.'

'Are you sure?' he grinned cautiously. 'It will probably foul all sorts of things up. For me too. No

527

unauthorized civilians are permitted in the combat area.'

'*I'm* not an unauthorized civilian,' she said stoutly. 'I'm Sherree Ann Lorner. I could go tell Eisenhower to go take a jump at himself and he'd have to do it quick. Anyway . . .' Her voice dropped. 'Anyway, I feel like a party myself. All I've had in this country is driving and getting up there, and sticking my chest out, and singing, and meeting goddamn ancient boring officers who hand me nice glasses of lousy sherry. I feel like kicking the can around tonight.'

Scarlett sniffed in the dark. 'I think it's my duty to arrange that,' he said solemnly.

He drove her into the prohibited area through one of the isolated northern checkpoints, where there were only two dozy sentries. He had taken over the car himself now and the six GIs of the escort were following, puzzled, in a jeep. Scarlett had told them they could slope off quietly if they liked, but to a man they requested to remain in the company of Sherree Ann Lorner.

As they approached the checkpoint Scarlett suggested that she might think about concealing herself below his gas-cape, so as not to alert the guard, but she refused indignantly. 'Listen, soldier,' she said, the conditioned Hollywood voice unknowingly dipping into an accentless dreamy, 'if I go anywhere, I go as me. Keep your gas-cape for the gas.'

The sentry's eyes opened to wakefulness when he saw the passenger. She smiled like the moon at him and he called his buddy from the guardhouse to take a look. The second man came out scratching and his face fell, then rose in delight when he recognized the captain's passenger. Sherree Ann leaned from the car and blew a kiss to both. One lifted the barrier dopily, the other went at once to the back of the guardhouse to relieve himself.

'Where did all the people go?' asked Sherree Ann as they drove through Burton and Mortown, black shadows at the roadside, with the pale light of the night sky showing in patches through roofs and gutted windows.

'They left,' said Scarlett briefly.

'I don't blame them,' she muttered, staring out at the rubble. 'When you play games in this army you sure play games. The real thing won't come as such a surprise, I guess.'

'A shock,' he corrected. 'That's the general idea. The place we're going is a church, by the way.'

'Oh, I just love churches,' she said, Hollywood taking over again. 'I'm crazy about those priests' dresses and the way they swing that smoking bucket around. I've been married in three different sorts of churches, you know. Not that any of them made any difference.'

'Are you married right now?' asked Scarlett. He explained: 'I don't have a chance to keep up with the movie gossip.'

'Sure, I think so, Charles Damare. But he's a lush. I mean, how could any guy get hitched to somebody with a body like this and prefer a slug of whisky?'

'It takes some believing,' he said honestly.

'I'll say. The studio thought it would be a great idea. The studio is a bum.'

'We use the church as a recreation centre because we don't have any building big enough inside the combat area,' he said. 'There were some village halls but they were made of wood and stuff and they tended to collapse easily, catch fire, you know during the exercises.'

There was a silence until she said, as if seeking reassurance, 'What do you think about me? Do you think I'm dumb, captain?'

'No,' he said, embarrassed. 'I think you have a great act.'

'That, as they say, is the story of Sherree Ann Lorner's life.' She peered from the window of the car. 'It's such a dark place, England,' she murmured. 'I can never see it properly. Even in the day it seems dark. Just look out there. It's like looking up Trigger's ass.'

He blinked at the expression but confined himself to a shrug. 'We've had some real nice weather,' he said defensively. 'Down in this area, that is. Maybe it's been different other places where you've been.'

'It's after California,' she shrugged. 'I think I'd go blind, if I lived in this country. Have you noticed how people don't look up? They walk around looking at the kerb.'

'I guess they'll look up again one day,' he said. He thought how odd it was that he should resent her comments about the British. 'Okay,' he went on, driving up the last hill. 'Here it is. St Peter and St Paul, Telcoombe Magna.'

'Double billing,' she said. 'St Peter and St Paul. That's cute.'

He pulled up at the lychgate with its gun emplacement, opened the car door and she stepped to the dewed grass. One of the gunners in the lychgate saw who had arrived and ran into the church with the news. The others, two young, pale soldiers, stood in panic to attention.

Scarlett escorted her down the churchyard path, the six-man escort had climbed from their vehicles and were following. 'All these dead people,' she sighed, looking at the dark teeth of the graves. 'And what's that?' She stopped and pointed. 'That little house with a roof and a door.'

'It's a vault,' said Scarlett. 'They put whole families in there.'

'Gee,' she sighed. 'It's a wonder they can breathe.'

He found it difficult to tell when she was joking. He led her into the porch and pushed open the saloon bar doors. Fifty GIs, warned by the man from the gate, stood staring; weary, dirty, white-faced, grown urchins. 'Hi, fellas,' said Sherree Ann Lorner with her famous smile. She let her mink drop away from her front. To a man they shouted with appreciation and moved hurriedly to her.

'Steady. Hold it,' warned Scarlett. The soldiers skidded to a collective stop. 'Okay, guys, give Miss Lorner a little room. Come on, fellows, move back. Take it easy, now.'

Obediently they shuffled back but with no man taking his eyes from the vision.

Her smile tightened and a young sadness came to her face. 'Hi,' she repeated but softly. 'I just thought I'd come and see you boys.' She pushed forward. 'You got any music here? Maybe we could have a song.' She looked at Scarlett. 'And don't forget the bourbon. I think we all need a drink.'

The officer in Scarlett faltered for a moment. 'It's . . . well, it's only beer and soft drinks allowed here,' he said. 'No spirits. Not on operations, you see . . .'

Her eyes tightened into spikes. 'Bourbon,' she said threateningly. 'Let's have the bourbon. Beer? Who d'you think I am, Marjorie Main?'

Scarlett grinned involuntarily and the GIs burst into cheering. Sherree Ann moved forward down the aisle with the soldiers around her, following her like an excited Sunday School. As she swayed towards the east window with its Jesus and attendant saints, she slowly took off her mink and revealed the shimmering dress and the splendid form it clothed.

Albie Primrose and Ballimach appeared at the door at the head of another contingent of soldiers from the tents. The news had rapidly spread. More were on their way, running in oddments of clothing across the cold camp. The little eyes of Albie and the large creased orbs of Ballimach took in the momentous scene. Sherree Ann Lorner at the heart of the khaki rabble, but with a decent space left for her to walk untouched down the aisle. At the chancel steps she curiously stopped and bowed to the altar. 'I've been in church before,' she said airily to the soldiers. 'Plenty.'

Scarlett had been left at the distant door. He pointed to Primrose and Ballimach. 'You two men, get the crate of bourbon from the car. Okay?'

'Sure, yes, sir,' answered Albie, still looking at the film star now in front of the altar table. She turned, arms outstretched, like a beautiful priestess.

'I never thought I would be this slow going to get bourbon,' said Ballimach still in the doorway. 'Jeeze, see what I see?'

The throng of men had parted and she had revolved again and, slender back to the nave of the church, was performing an impersonation of Carmen Miranda, swaying her delicious bottom to imaginary music. 'I – eye – eye – I like you veery much . . .'

'Gee,' acknowledged Albie, still lingering. 'That sort of thing makes you feel like it's all worth it.'

'The bourbon,' Scarlett reminded them from the other side of the aisle. 'She'll still be here when you get back.'

'I sure hope so, sir,' replied Albie fervently. He and Ballimach, with a final look at the vision in the sparkling red dress, went out into the dewy Devon night.

The two GIs who played the organ had now arrived in the church and together mounted the long stool. One was in wildly patterned pyjamas with an overcoat over them and ammunition boots on his feet. His partner wore a combat jacket and an English fisherman's sou'wester hat. They played 'I Danced With The Dolly With The Hole In Her Stocking' while Sherree Ann Lorner swayed and bawled it to the rafters of the nave. The men began to jolt, bumping their feet on the slabbed tombstones and brass memorials set into the time-worn floor; the jolting became jumping. Beer cans were passed from hand to hand and tossed to friends. Then Albie and Ballimach arrived with the bourbon and pushed their way through the growing crowd of soldiers inside the church door, and outside in the porch, their heads poking over the top of the saloon doors.

Captain Scarlett quickly took charge of the crate. He took two cardboard cups and a bottle and pushed the rest of the crate with his foot towards Ballimach. 'Okay, big fella. You see everybody gets fair shares, I don't want any fighting.'

He need not have worried. The attraction of alcohol was easily eclipsed by that of the woman. Soldiers could always drink. Ballimach, his eyes irresistibly drifting down the church, and Albie Primrose, pushing around bigger men to get his share of the view, dispensed the bourbon. It was swiftly passed around. Scarlett poured a measure for Sherree Ann. She stopped her song and watched critically. 'Hey, more than that!' she called at him. 'I'm a thirsty girl!' There was a huge roar of approval and Scarlett, grinning wryly, trebled the measure and passed it to her, with five or six pairs of hands touching the cardboard cup with as much care as would have been afforded to the Holy Grail. Sherree Ann took it and emptied it briskly, provoking more delighted cheers. The cup was passed back by the same route and Scarlett dubiously refilled it. He took a drink of his own and watched her as she commenced her dance once more. She was like some wonderful Salome in that ancient church, her sparkling body lighting it like a flame, her face glowing with an earnest honest happiness, her long and lovely arms held up and out to the men, her breasts bursting, her backside waving towards the shadowed altar place.

Although they swayed with her and smiled towards her with boyish gratitude for what she was, and what she was doing, the GIs kept shyly at a decent distance until one, braver, shuffled forward, a cardboard cup of whisky in his hand, and began to dance with her. Scarlett, watching carefully over the lip of his own

534

container, moved momentarily forward but relaxed when he saw it was unnecessary. The soldier kept a yard away from the star, dancing before her, duplicating her movements, his gritty grin matching her red and white smile.

'Hey, Randy, me next!' demanded one of the swaying, watching soldiers. He edged forward trying to ease his comrade to the side. The first soldier showed no sign of moving over. Scarlett lowered the bourbon and called briskly down the church, 'Soldier, move over. Let everybody have a little.' Sherree Ann looked towards him and extended her fruity tongue.

The first GI turned and glared at Scarlett, standing against one of the stone columns, beneath the little wooden frame that had once displayed the hymn numbers but now displayed a drawing of a naked Snow White and seven erotic dwarfs. The officer allowed the cup to drop six inches lower than his face and stared back. Still dancing, the GI moved sideways. His replacement was now swaying with equal extravagance in front of the rolling breasts of Sherree Ann. More soldiers were pushing and agitating on the periphery of the dance. Scarlett glanced around for a sergeant. There was none in his vicinity, only Albie Primrose, thoughtfully drinking a Coca Cola and watching the strange, sacrificial display.

'Soldier,' said Scarlett, 'you're the colonel's driver, right?'

'That's right, sir. Pfc Primrose.'

Scarlett remembered the name. 'Okay, Primrose, I'm putting you in charge of this entertainment.'

'Sir?'

'Get those guys organized in a line, a proper line. If

they want to dance with the lady they've got to take their turn. Get them to line up.'

The diminutive Albie looked towards the men clamouring for the next dance with Sherree Ann. 'What if they won't line up, sir?' he queried.

'Tell them it's an order,' Scarlett told him. 'I'll be right here. I'm not going anywhere yet.'

'Yes, sir,' said Albie, still doubtfully. He moved towards the crowd, but then glanced back. 'About thirty seconds each?' he inquired. He counted quickly along the khaki backs at the chancel steps. 'That makes seventeen minutes of dancing even with just those guys. The lady's going to be tired.'

'Thirty seconds,' agreed Scarlett, marvelling at the soldier's logic. 'No, wait, maybe twenty-five.'

Busily Albie went down the aisle of the church and began pushing the men into a line. 'Come on, you guys. A fair deal for all.' There were protests and return pushes but he turned with a pointed finger and referred the grumblers to the observing captain lounging against the Norman column. Soon there was a distinct and not disorderly rank passing in front of the pulpit. The soldiers continued to jog on the spot to the music, their heads and arms jerking, jumping, like the moving parts of a long engine. Sherree Ann laughed when she realized what was being organized. Then she burst into louder hilarity, stopping and bending forward with the mink, giving the men the gift of a sudden and glorious view into the dark and delicious cleft between her breasts; her outburst caused by the sight of the bespectacled Albie standing at the front of the line, like an official starter in a race, checking his watch and ushering in a new partner every twenty-five seconds, calling away the bemused man already gyrating before the star.

One solider, his face alight with delight, moved in for his turn but, instead of keeping his distance, moved into close contact with Sherree Ann, his arms going around her neck, his jawbone against hers, the huge softness of her bosom laid against his shirt. 'Slower,' he pleaded loudly to the organists. 'Slower, slower . . .'

Albie glanced awkwardly towards Scarlett. The officer, smelling trouble, shook his head slowly. Albie gave the soldier a prod with his finger. 'Break it up,' he said. 'Break it up. You're tiring the lady.'

The man took no notice. Then Albie yelled close to the sweating, joined faces: 'Okay, guy, time's up. Let's keep the game moving.' Other soldiers began to protest from the frustration of the line. Sherree Ann, smiling and hot, pushed the soldier gently away. He broke off with a drugged grin and stumbled away to the front pews where he sat with his face held pathetically in his hands.

An amazing scene had formed. The music continued its loud and insistent beat, the twin organists jumping like puppets along the long stool. At the centre was the beautiful girl, her face sheened with sweat, her breasts damp, her mouth held open, dancing with her quickly-changing partners. What astounded Scarlett was that, unwilling to surrender the moment, the men who came away from the girl began, by instinct, to dance with each other. They spilt into jitterbugging couples, swinging and twisting and even throwing each other over their backs in the side chapels as the tempo of the music increased. A soldier with two drumsticks established himself behind the church lectern and began to beat out the rhythm on the bald brass head of the holy eagle.

As Scarlett watched the dancing soldiers a lump climbed into his throat. 'You poor bastards,' he muttered, in pity. 'You poor dumb bastards.'

At two o'clock in the morning they reached the Manor House again.

'You have a small cottage to yourself,' mentioned Scarlett eventually. 'It's nice. It used to be the gardener's place but we've renovated it as a kind of guest house. You won't be disturbed by all the early rising in the morning. Some officers have to be out tomorrow by five.'

They had reached the sturdy gates and the high wall of the old house. There was a sentry on each side and they checked the car as it went in. They grinned with realization when they saw the officer and the Hollywood woman in the back.

'The guys who have been with us all night,' said Scarlett, 'are temporarily billeted here. You know, the lucky escort.' He remembered Albie, whom he had told to drive them back, and leaned over. 'I'll fix it so you can get a bed here, soldier,' he said. 'I need this car in the morning. I'll check first thing with Colonel Schorner.'

'It's okay, sir,' said Albie easily. 'There's a truck going from here every day at five a.m. I can get back before the colonel's going to need me.'

'Good. Thanks.' Scarlett turned to Sherree Ann. 'You don't have to worry about a thing,' he said.

'Each of the escort guys will take an hour on duty outside the cottage. Just in case you feel nervous.'

'They don't have to do that . . .' she began.

'We'd be happier if they did,' said Scarlett. 'And they'll think it's a privilege.'

'Okay,' she said. 'So will I.'

They left the car. 'I'll show you around,' suggested Scarlett.

She kissed him lightly on the cheek. 'I'll find my way,' she said. 'It's only small. Goodnight.'

Scarlett looked seriously at her. 'That's the plainest brush-off I've ever had,' he said.

'That's what it is.' She smiled. 'Goodnight, captain.'

He turned the key in the lock of the front door and gave it to her. She thanked him and went in, leaving him on the step. Scarlett, a little drunk, gave a theatrical salute, turned and walked away.

The cottage had been warmed by a wood fire in the tight sitting-room and another in the bedroom. Sherree Ann Lorner smiled to herself as she looked around when she was alone, walking from one room to the other, her luxury robe over her slip, another bourbon in her fingers.

Although the cottage was small it was not so strange to her. Before Hollywood, before the space and cleanliness and luxury, she had come from a small, threadbare house in Blanco County, Texas. Her people were part of an impoverished community, agricultural workers who existed in dusty settlements on sparse work, for those were hard days in Texas. All they had was a beautiful daughter.

Now, warmed more by the look of the two fires than their meeting heat, she wandered about touching the pale plaster walls, the paint flaking in some corners where hasty decoration had not reached. Someone had put a vase of new daffodils on the tray that held the drinks bottles. She picked two and putting one yellow bloom in her ear and the other to her mouth played at telephones, imagining she was calling her mother at home. She smiled as she saw that the curtains had been pinned to the window frames, obviously transferred in a hurry from some other place. The cottage was on one floor, the sitting-room, a kitchen hardly the size of her Hollywood refrigerator, a newly-installed but basic bathroom, with a set of army towels over the bath, but with a cake of exclusive Parisian soap there also. She wondered where they had obtained that. The box of tissues was American. The painstaking embroidery on the bathmat said: 'Beach Hotel, Telcoombe Beach.'

She turned into the bedroom. Her teddy bear was already sitting between the sheets, propped against the white pillows. He was always the first thing she unpacked once she was alone. 'You look pretty sharp there,' she told him and stepped back a pace for further admiration. Teddy looked almost kingly, sitting in the voluminous bed, six foot across and supported by brass columns with finials, with a brass rail running across top and foot.

Her glass was empty. It took her by surprise but she went without worry to the sitting-room and poured herself a heavy bourbon. Walking back towards the bedroom she saw that there was a cupboard under what may have at one time been a staircase. It had been painted roughly and it opened with one tug of the handle. 'Just bugs in there,' she said to herself, peering into the dark cavity. As a country girl she was not apprehensive. An elderly spider appeared and walked sedately from the cupboard and then returned, as if she had courteously opened the door for him. As her eyes became accustomed to the darkness she saw that, pushed to the far end of the low cupboard, was a carton the size of a shoe box. Leaning down she reached into the dust and took it out. It was coated with dirt. She blew at it and then opened the lid. Inside, almost shocking her, was a china doll. It was broken and scarred, one of its eyes was blank, and mice had been chewing its aged yellow dress and its hair.

'Oh, you poor darling,' sighed Sherree Ann. 'Here, have a drink.' She put the bourbon glass to the doll's mouth and pretended to pour. It was like being a child again in Blanco County.

Cradling the doll in her free arm, she carried it to the bathroom and, taking its dress and its linen pants off, she washed it carefully in the basin, wiping both its good and its malefic eye, and getting a nail brush from her vanity case to brush and arrange its hair. 'You can't wear those dusty old things any more,' she said.

She carried the doll back to the bedroom and went to her portmanteau. Eventually she decided on a pair of silk panties which she manipulated, folding them over, so that both leg holes became one. She slipped this over the doll's head. 'Just fine,' she said in her softly drunken tone. She realized she had drained another glass of bourbon but she did not care. She wasn't going anywhere. 'Now I want you to meet my teddy bear. His name is Darryl Eff. I named him after Mr Zanuck.'

She sighed. 'Except he don't give me so much trouble as Mr Zanuck.' Tucking the doll into the bed next to the bear, she said: 'Darryl Eff, this is . . . Now, I wonder what your name could be? I guess you're a Limey doll, so I had better call you a Limey name.' She tried to think of one and finally, with inspiration that pleased her immensely, decided. 'Queen Mary,' she announced. 'Darryl Eff, this is Queen Mary. Don't you think she's cute?'

She puffed her creamy cheeks into the pretence of a pout because the bear failed to answer. Sadly she filled the glass with bourbon for what she promised herself would be the last time before she went to bed.

She sat on the side of the bed, lonely and disconsolate. Her dressing-gown slipped from around her breasts and she looked down at them; her famous breasts, cradled in the expensive silk bodice of her slip. 'Tits,' she said addressing them. 'Tits, you may be big and you may be pretty, but you're no goddamn use to me.'

Outside, beyond the bedroom door and the small entrance hall, was the front porch of the cottage. She had heard the delegated sentry moving about several times, reassuringly because, despite her self-possession, she was often deeply afraid at night. Now it came again. The movement of feet and a night cough. Inside her the bourbon seemed to wriggle in her stomach. She giggled privately, went to the small side window and spied out on the man guarding her. The six soldiers of the escort had been in the group throughout the afternoon, when she had arrived at Exeter air base, and during the evening, but she had hardly noticed them as individuals. There were so many men around.

Now she manoeuvred herself close to the window and the wall so that she could view the sentry. But the angle was too tight. There was a shadow and a dark movement within the shadow but that was all. Sherree Ann tiptoed mischievously back into the bedroom.

The plan came quickly, as it often did when she was drinking. She went into the small hall and once more opened the low cupboard. 'Bider,' she called softly. 'Where are you, Bider?'

With obedience that pleased but did not surprise her, the spider appeared and came once more out of the door as she held it open. 'Hello there,' she greeted it. 'I just knew you'd be waiting. Come on, Bider, this girl needs you.'

Without qualms she picked up the creature in her cupped hands. It struggled momentarily but then gave up, curled its legs into its body and crouched against her skin. 'Okay, let's go,' she grinned.

Carrying the spider back towards the bed she lifted the eiderdown, blankets and sheets and dropped it into the middle before folding over the covers once more. 'Now don't you suffocate,' she warned. She sat on the side of the bed again and counted another minute, before drawing in a lovely breath and emitting a controlled cry. She had counselled herself against making it too loud. She did not want to wake the whole of the complement of the officers' mess, nor even the whole of the guard. Jumping up and pulling her robe close about her she hurried towards the front door, sobbing wonderfully.

She reached the door and unlocked it to a rattle of

questioning knocks from the outside. It was opened and the small, worried and white face of Albie Primrose poked in. Half his thin body followed. 'A spider!' Miss Lorner was already crying. The words collapsed on her lips as she saw who had answered the call. 'A spider,' she repeated, deflated. Jesus Christ, didn't she get some luck.

'Where, ma'am?' blustered the little man as he came into the hall. He had a huge revolver with a great webbing holster and a lanyard around his neck that looked, on him, like a hangman's rope. As he rushed into the cottage he drew the revolver which seemed half as long as the arm that held it. His eyes were blinking and bright behind the rimless glasses.

'No!' cried Sherree Ann. She hurried and closed the door. She hardly knew why. 'It's only a spider. Put that gun away.'

Albie looked down at the revolver in amazement. 'Gee,' he breathed, ashen-faced. 'I didn't know I'd pulled it out. I'm not used to one of these. I borrowed it from the other guy.'

'The other guy?' she said. Her act had gone now. She looked at him, almost relieved that she had somebody else to pity.

'He was supposed to be on duty outside the door,' explained Albie. He looked abruptly concerned. 'Don't . . . don't, please, Miss Lorner, don't tell anyone that. Not Captain Scarlett. There'll be a whole·lot of trouble.'

She walked into the bedroom and sat on the end of the bed. He remained outside in the hall. From there he said: 'Those guys, they been on duty all day, like getting ready for you to arrive and follow you around, and they were all pooped out, you know. So I don't sleep any good out of my own bed, so I told the guy I'd do his guard.' He added shyly: 'He gave me two bucks.'

'You were the driver,' she said, pointing at him standing in the hall. 'I remember you.'

'It's because I'm smaller than the rest of the army,' he nodded philosophically. 'I kinda stand out in reverse.'

She smiled. He smiled sheepishly. 'Where's the location of the spider?' he inquired.

Sherree Ann had forgotten the spider. 'Oh, God, yes, he'll suffocate!' she exclaimed. To his astonishment she began frantically to pull the bedclothes away. Albie stepped halfway into the room. 'Come and help,' she said breathlessly. 'He's trapped in the bed.'

Astonished, Albie moved in to help. 'Okay, ma'am, Miss Lorner, don't worry, I'll catch him. I'm real good at catching insects. It's being small . . .'

'Don't,' she admonished suddenly. She turned and sat upright on the bed. Her robe had fallen open and Albie felt pink points of embarrassment and fascination glow on his cheeks. Her bosom was undulating in its silk hammock. He made his eyes crawl away. 'Don't you hurt him,' she said. 'Not a hair on his l'il head.'

'Oh, okay,' he said. He took off his glasses and wiped them with his handkerchief. The situation was going mad. 'I'll be gentle with him. But you still want to find him?'

'Yes, he's all lost in there.' She leaned over and Albie was almost sick as the lovely breasts rolled forward. They both began to search the warm sheets. Albie looked up and saw that the teddy bear which had been propped up against the headboard on the opposite side of the bed had toppled out. The doll was leaning like a one-eyed drunk. 'Your teddy has fallen out of bed,' said Albie.

She sprang from beneath the covers. 'Darryl Eff!' she exclaimed. 'Oh poor Darryl Eff!'

'I'll get him,' offered Albie. He was surprised at the sweat running from his neck. It must be the weighty and unaccustomed gun. He went round the bed and lifted the teddy bear into the sheets again.

'Is he okay?' Sherree Ann asked anxiously.

'I think so,' said the bemused Albie. She crawled across the bed, those wonderful udders swinging. She pulled the teddy bear close to them and ran her hand across the bear's brow.

'I hope he's okay,' she said. 'He's my oldest friend.' She regarded Albie like a co-conspirator. 'Don't you have a teddy?' she asked.

Albie felt himself blush. 'It's difficult in the army to have a teddy bear,' he explained honestly. 'The other guys would laugh.'

She sighed. 'I guess you're right,' she said. 'I don't know why soldiers have to be so tough.'

Albie said: 'I'm not tough. I'm not going to find it easy to kill anybody. I hope I don't have to. Even a German.'

A pointed look entered her fine eyes. 'Will *you* have to go?' she inquired. 'I mean, across *there*. To France or wherever the place is? When we land?'

'I guess so. On the very first day.'

'That's not fair,' she said stoutly. 'You're not big

enough. And you wear glasses. I'm going to tell General Eisenhower . . .'

Albie held out a hand and accidentally touched hers. 'Please don't,' he pleaded. 'I don't think he would listen and it would get me into a scrape. I *have* to go because I'm Colonel Schorner's driver and he's the kind of commander who is going to be right at the front of the fighting.' He sighed. 'I'm the guy who's got to drive him there.'

'You poor kid,' she said. 'Here. Sit down. I'm going to get you a drink. I need one myself.'

'I don't drink,' started Albie. He touched her hand, again by chance, and muttered: 'Very much . . .'

Her eyes widened. 'That's exactly how it is with me,' she said as if they shared some rare ailment. 'I don't drink very much – at a time.' She got up and rolled towards the sitting-room. 'But there seem to be more times . . . all the time.' He heard her pouring the drinks. He looked around full of wonder.

Sherree Ann returned. She had pulled the robe decently about her again. She carried two glasses and her smile was serene. Albie blinked when he saw the amount of liquid in his and backed away as the power of the bourbon got to his nostrils. 'I'm supposed to be on duty,' he said, taking the glass.

'Since your duty is guarding me, I've taken you off duty,' she said firmly. 'What's your name?'

'Oh, gee, I'm so sorry. I'm Pfc Primrose. Albert . . . well, Albie.'

'Primrose?' she said. 'That's a beautiful name, Albie.'

'Sometimes I don't think so,' he said dolefully. He regarded her longingly through his lenses. 'I have a lot of trouble sometimes with the guys. We got guys with uglier names, plenty, but nobody with a more embarrassing name.' He looked into his glass and was amazed to discover it empty.

'I'll get another,' she said, seeing his look. 'Just one more.'

'Take it easy,' he called as she went out to the other room. He was amazed at the firmness of his voice. It even seemed deeper than usual.

'Don't worry, Albie,' she called back. 'The US Government thinks I run on bourbon.' She returned to the room. The gown was open again. Desperately he tried not to look at the tops of her legs moving under the silken slip. 'Maybe they're right,' she said. She gave him the glass and they touched the rims.

'How about the spider?' he heard himself say.

'Oh, sure, the spider,' she said seriously. 'He's in there somewhere. Do you think he'll be able to breathe?'

'He'll be okay,' replied Albie adopting the air of one who knows about spiders. 'As long as we're not sitting directly on top of him. There may not seem a lot of air under there to us humans, but there's plenty to a spider. Let's see where he's hiding out.'

Confidence such as he had never known, or even known about, was sprouting within Albie. Things like this *did* happen after all.

'Take that silly gun off,' she suggested. 'You could frighten him to death.'

'Don't I know it,' agreed Albie. 'It has the same effect on me.' He began to struggle out of the harness, the lanyard and the holster. She leaned forward and helped him, the warm smell of her body wafting to him. His fingers got in each other's way as he tried to undo the buckles. 'I never thought I would ever have a chance to be with you like this, Miss Lorner,' he blurted. 'I mean, looking for spiders and everything.'

She smiled like a sunrise. 'Albie,' she admonished, 'my name is Sherree Ann.'

'I know.'

'Then *call* me Sherree Ann. Now let's locate this spider. I know he's got in there somewhere.' Determinedly she pulled the covers of the bed fully back and began to search the crevices of the sheets. 'Come on out, Bider,' she said softly. 'We know you're in there.'

'Bider?' said Albie, moving across the bed from the other side. He could not believe he was doing this. Was this what drinking bourbon did for a man?

Suddenly, shockingly, she eased herself across the sheet and slid her fine soft arms about his thin neck. They travelled around him like white snakes. Had they been snakes Albie would scarcely have reacted differently. He froze, stiffened, solidified and then, when he felt he could move his face, he looked up and straight into her blissful and beautiful countenance. The neck was pale, swinging away to the revealed shoulders and the turbulent bosom. Her mouth moved to him again and he managed to frame his dry lips sufficiently to receive the kiss. 'Albie,' said Sherree Ann Lorner. 'I'm so lonely.'

'But *me*?' he croaked. Jesus, he could still blow the chance. Jesus, don't let him blow it. 'I mean, yes, sure, of course.' He forced himself to crawl across the bed towards her, like an invalid, deliberately getting his knees up to the mattress and using them to propel himself forward.

'*You*, Albie,' she confirmed as if she had waited for him for her entire life. 'And *me*.' She slid around the bed, bringing her legs beneath her in a graceful and athletic circle like a gymnast. Her arms remained circling his neck as though she feared he might want to escape. She used them to pull him to her and then, once he was horizontal, rolled luxuriously on top of him. Albie choked and coughed. 'Gee, sorry baby,' she crooned next to his head. She kissed him with soft passion.

Albie still didn't believe it. 'Will I be able to tell the boys about this?' he pleaded.

Each morning when Dorothy left her hill house at Wilcoombe the sound that first she heard outside her door was that of the children shouting in the playground of the school. It never failed to make her smile, a smile of recognition, familiarity and pleasure. She had always taught small children; the school for the older pupils was at Totnes and sometimes she had idly wondered at what age they stopped shouting.

The everyday sensation was always heightened as she turned the corner from the hill to the brief, dipping road into the coombe, for into her view at once came the enclosed playground with its running children, the voices louder because she was clear of the houses. It was fully spring now, the coombe clothed in fresh leaves with poplars fingering the sky on the upper slope, and the vale hawthorn and ash growing greener with the lengthening days. Daffodils ribboned the sides of the valley and the air had warmth. She was happier than she could ever remember. Even Miss Parsons, the other teacher, would not worry her today.

The little school was grey stone, built before the 1914 war. Generations of villagers had learned their lessons there, chanting their multiplication out into the air of summer afternoons, watching the first mysterious curves of the written word on the blackboard, making their first stammering attempts to read, singing lustily to the off-key piano. The playground was small and surrounded by a fence of chicken wire. In one corner were the red-brick lavatories.

Village children were very punctual, few of them having far to travel and mothers taking a pride in ensuring they were on time. As she neared the gate she, of habit, ran her eye over the small, busy figures in the yard. No Mary Steer or Billy this morning.

Miss Parsons came to the single step and waved the bell violently. She wished Dorothy a businesslike good morning and turned into the building.

The pupils, irrepressible, jumping, skipping, chattering, formed two lines in the playground. 'Quiet now!' called Dorothy standing on the step. 'All quiet.'

Obediently the noise ceased; they still shuffled and fidgeted, but calmed quickly. 'Right,' said Dorothy. 'Miss Parsons' class, march in.' The first crocodile, the original children of the school, tramped in their sandals, boots and plimsolls into the building. Dorothy scanned the line of her own class which she had brought from Telcoombe Beach. She knew each bright face intimately. 'Where is Mary Steer?' she asked. 'And Billy Steer?'

'Don't know, Miss Jenkins,' chorused the voices.

'They was with Bobby Bewler,' piped a voice.

'Bobby Bewler?' said Dorothy.

'Yes, miss, 'im that's mazed.'

The observation brought a furrow of giggles. Briskly she told them to be quiet and marched them into the classroom. A worry was already growing in her. Bobby Bewler was a simpleton, harmless but no companion for a seven-year-old boy and his younger sister. Before reading out the names in the register she went back out into the sunshine of the playground and, going further to the road outside the gate, searched both ways. The road was empty. Now the children had gone inside, clear birds sounded in the trees about the school. She decided to give Billy ten minutes and then do something about it; organize a search or call the constable.

Returning to the desk she began reciting the names in the register. 'John Billman, Josie Billman, Edgar Cornford, Billy Durley, Mary Dandridge . . . Sylvia Dandridge . . .'

Her voice slowed as she saw the top of a head at the windowed door. The door was pushed hesitantly open and Mary Steer walked into the class. Her face was pink with guilt. She sidled towards her small desk.

'Mary Steer,' said Dorothy sharply. 'You're late. Where have you been? Where is your brother?'

'Billy be just comin', Miss Jenkins.'

'Sit down, then.' Dorothy returned to the register. '. . . Georgie Farthing, Brian Harrington, Nancy Jennings . . .' There was a heavy metal bump from the desks. Dorothy glanced up. Mary Steer had reached her desk and was bending trying to retrieve something which had fallen on the floor. As Dorothy watched, it rolled out into the aisle. A hand grenade.

The little girl started forward as though to pick it up like a runaway ball.

'Don't!' Dorothy screamed at her. The child, immediately shaking with fright, jumped back to her desk. The ugly metal pineapple stopped rolling and lay against the leg of the desk of Georgie Farthing, who stared down at it. The other children were trying to see what it was.

'Sit down,' ordered Dorothy, forcing control into her voice. She felt her whole body shaking and was amazed that the words sounded firm. She knew enough about hand grenades to see that the ringed detonation pin was still in position.

'Children,' she said, reducing her tone to a cold calm. '*Without running*, everybody must leave the classroom. Wait! Leave your desks by the *outside*, keep away from the middle. Now, all stand.'

The pupils stood stiffly, the small faces and fear-filled eyes looked towards the centre aisle and at Mary Steer. Georgie Farthing began to sob softly. 'Don't cry, Georgie,' said Dorothy. 'It won't hurt you.' Nancy Jennings, a fat ginger girl who sat next to Georgie, put her freckled arm about him. He pushed it away. 'Right,' said Dorothy. 'Leave the classroom, very quietly.'

The children obeyed, going out in two tiptoeing lines that curved away from the spot where the hateful weapon lay on the wooden floor, like a round rat, its head against the iron stanchion of the miniature desk. A nausea consumed the teacher.

Still watching the object she backed from the room and then turned into the other classroom. The sturdy

Miss Parsons revolved an ill-pleased face from the blackboard. 'Why have you let your class out?' she asked.

'Miss Parsons,' said Dorothy, still fighting to keep her voice level, 'can you just come outside for a moment? In the corridor.'

The other teacher frowned, the face setting into ready grooves; she put down the chalk and moved towards the door. 'No talking,' she warned her class. Some of them looked out of the window as soon as she had gone and saw the other children, huddled in a group near the gate. They were looking back at the window, except for Mary Steer whose small blue eyes were fixed on the lavatories at the corner of the playground.

In the corridor Dorothy faced Miss Parsons. 'There's . . . there's a hand grenade in the classroom,' she said. At last her voice croaked. 'Mary Steer brought it in.'

The other teacher looked annoyed, as if she did not believe her. She stared through the panes. 'Where?' she demanded. 'This isn't some sort of fun, is it?'

'It's by the second desk on the aisle,' pointed Dorothy, now whispering as if she feared her voice might set the thing off. 'It still has the pin fixed in it, so it shouldn't go off. You'd better get your class out into the playground. I'll telephone the police.' Suddenly, with horror she thought of Billy Steer.

With a strange snort, the other teacher was already hurrying back to the other room. Dorothy said after her: 'Billy Steer is somewhere. He didn't turn up . . .'

'Billy Steer is *your* responsibility,' snapped the other woman. As she reached the door of her classroom she bellowed: 'Out! Out! Everybody leave the school!' The children came tumbling out, running into the sun-splashed playground with cries of 'What's up?', 'What's goin' on?' to their playmates already there. Dorothy was ahead of them. She reached Mary Steer and grasped her arm firmly. 'Where is your brother?' she demanded. 'You *must* tell me, Mary. Did he have any more of those things?'

Mary looked around, her eyes awash with frightened tears. 'Billy be in the lavs, Miss. 'Im and Bobby Bewler. 'Twas 'ee found them bombs. They got another, miss.'

Dorothy's whole body tightened. Miss Parsons was strutting from the schoolhouse. Her question: 'Did you phone?' was stopped before it was half out.

'They've got another one,' Dorothy trembled. 'In the lavatories. Billy Steer and Bobby Bewler.'

'Bewler? Oh God, he's off his head!' cried Miss Parsons.

'Get them all away,' muttered Dorothy. Her eyes had not left the brick lavatories. 'Please, get the children away.'

She began to walk across the tarmac playground. Behind her the senior teacher drove the children from the gates. People were looking from the windows of the cottages across the lane. 'Billy Steer,' called Dorothy. 'Billy . . . Bobby Bewler . . . I know you're in there. Don't touch that thing, Billy. Don't touch it. Come on out.'

Halfway across the playground she thought it had worked because the slyly smiling Bobby Bewler appeared. He was pale and fatty, his eyes permanently crossed, his face always idiotic. 'Where's Billy Steer?'

Dorothy demanded. She rushed forward. 'Has he got that thing in there?'

She was answered at once. A terrible explosion blew the glass roof off the lavatories. The bricks toppled from the top of the walls and smoke spat from the entrance and through the opened top. The bang and the blast sent her stumbling backwards. The simpleton boy stood gaping at the dreadful thing and burst into huge bawling tears. Dorothy lifted her hand and smacked it across his white face, streaked now with brick dust. 'Shut up!' she shouted.

She walked slowly towards the lavatory door, smoke still clouding from the roof and door. 'Billy!' she called. 'Billy Steer . . . Billy?'

Colonel Schorner picked up his telephone. A voice babbled from the other end. His whole body seemed to dry. 'Oh, God,' he muttered. 'Jesus.' Then firmly: 'I'll get an ambulance there right away.'

He put the phone down and bawled, 'Albie!' He picked the receiver up again. Albie appeared at the door of the hut. Schorner was already speaking into the phone. 'This is the commanding officer. Get an ambulance to the school in Wilcoombe, and at the double. A child has been injured by a grenade. Get there quick. Take him to the US Military Hospital at Newton Abbot. Got me? Okay, move!' He banged the phone down.

'That's terrible,' said Albie at the door. 'You want to go there, sir?'

'Yes, get me to the school,' said Schorner. The telephone rang again; he almost left it but after a moment's hesitation picked it up. 'Schorner.'

'Sir,' said the voice. 'It's the medics here. Lieutenant Browning. That incident . . .'

'What about it? Get the goddamn ambulance there!'

'Sir,' persisted the officer, 'we have orders that no civilian personnel can be taken to the Newton Abbot base hospital, sir. Only severe cases of military personnel, sir. No civilians . . .'

'Get him to that hospital,' Schorner grated down the phone. 'Get the kid to the hospital, lieutenant, or I'll have my hands around your goddamn throat! Do it!'

'Bastard,' he swore, slamming down the phone. 'Stupid bastard.' He picked it up again. 'Give me the US Hospital at Newton Abbot and I mean quick,' he rasped. He was through quickly.

'Get me the commanding officer,' he told the switchboard operator. Albie watched his face suffuse as the man replied. 'Get me *somebody* then,' he ordered. 'And move your ass, soldier. This is Colonel Schorner, Engineers, at Telcoombe. I've got a casualty on the way and I want to make sure it's treated right. Don't argue, son. Get me an officer.'

He waited. Albie had gone and the car was already waiting, its engine running, before a voice came on the other end. 'Captain Millbach here,' it said. 'Is there some trouble, colonel?'

'I've got an ambulance on its way to you right now,' said Schorner tersely. 'An English child –'

'No civilians,' the other officer broke in. 'That's a strict order, sir.'

'My ass, strict orders!' Schorner shouted. 'Listen,

557

captain that kid is on his way. It was a US grenade, okay? I'm taking full responsibility . . .'

'There is an order, sir –'

'Fuck the order,' bellowed Schorner. 'I repeat, that kid is coming there on *my* orders. Do something about it, Captain Millbach, d'you hear? Do something. I'm going to call General Georgeton right away. If you don't help that kid I'll come and shoot your goddamn balls off. Got it?'

He thrust the phone down, then picked it up again. 'Get me General Headquarters, Exeter,' he ordered. 'I want General Georgeton, right away.'

He waited, drumming his fist against the desk. Albie pushed away an orderly who was coming into the hut with a fistful of mail. 'Later, later,' he warned.

The soldier's eyebrows went up when he saw Schorner's face. 'We lost the war?' he asked Albie.

'Beat it,' said Albie.

Schorner got a connection. 'General Georgeton, yes. And hurry, if you don't mind, it's urgent. What? Jesus Christ . . . Right, okay, put Captain Scarlett on.'

Scarlett spoke briefly from the other end. 'Okay, colonel,' he said when he had heard. 'They *do* have an order, but I'll clear it. They're just dumb doctors. If I get busted I'm going to need you. I'll see you at the hospital.'

Schorner picked up his cap and ran for the door. Albie was ready in the car. The colonel jumped into the back and they started fast across the camp towards the gate. 'The hospital, sir?' asked Albie.

'The school, Albie. We'd better take in the school on the way.'

'In case those meathead medic guys don't get

558

there,' guessed Albie aloud. 'That sounds like a good idea.'

The little soldier drove at speed down the long and narrow hill to the sea, then roared along the coastal road almost crashing the boundary barrier. 'Emergency!' he shouted at the confused military policeman on the gate. Schorner leaned forward to add his order but it was unnecessary. The snowdrop raised the barrier and whistled softly as the car shot on. 'I guess the big day is here,' he called to his colleague at the guardhouse door watching the car disappear to the west.

They speeded up Wilcoombe Hill and then immediately down into the coombe towards the school. A crowd of villagers were standing solidly outside the railings in the placid sunshine. They turned as they heard the car and parted to allow it through. Even then Schorner could see their hostile faces. A civilian ambulance was standing at the gate and in the playground the village policeman was saying something to Miss Parsons who was sobbing into a pink handkerchief. In the corner the brick lavatory was blackened around its top and glass was lying across the ground. Schorner got out of the car and pushed his way into the schoolyard. 'Did the military ambulance get here?' he said to the constable.

'It got here all right, sir,' said the policeman saluting, an action which brought a murmur of disdain from the villagers. 'They took Billy Steer off in it.'

'It was one of your damned, hateful bombs,' Miss Parsons wailed. 'You're all just killers . . . all of you.' She turned away and hurried to the gate.

'How bad was Billy?' Schorner said to the constable.

'Bad, sir,' said the man calmly. 'They bain't meant to cause pinpricks, be they?'

Schorner started to glare at him but he ceased when he realized it was a statement, not an accusation. 'Where's Miss Jenkins?' he asked.

'She went in your ambulance, sir. With the boy's mother.'

'Was he alive?'

'I couldn't rightly say. I got here just as your medical blokes was lifting him in. He didn't look very lively to me. Both 'is arms was off.'

A sickness gripped Schorner's chest. 'Jesus,' he muttered.

'That won't help, sir,' returned the policeman with the merest touch of censure. 'The mischief's been done.'

He turned away and made a token movement to send the people back from the school gate. Schorner wheeled and hurried towards the car. The crowd fell into sulky silence as he reached them and went between them, then, as he got in the car, an old woman up in a cottage window began to bawl abuse. It took only a moment for the crowd to join in. The swear words were mingled and confusing but the raised fists were plain enough and the word 'Yanks' repeated with hate from all around.

'Let's get out of this,' Schorner ordered Albie. 'The hospital.'

As the car moved, the rural fists began to beat on its roof. Albie accelerated and they were soon out of reach. Schorner cursed to himself. He did not turn round.

560

They reached Newton Abbot after a flying journey through the military traffic clogging the roads. Just outside Wilcoombe, Schorner had told Albie to stop at a military police control point and had ordered one of the white-helmeted motor cyclists to ride before them clearing the way.

At the hospital, a clean and widespread pattern of low buildings, they saw Scarlett coming down the steps from the main casualty area. He hurried forward, clay-faced. 'They couldn't do a thing for him, colonel,' he said heavily.

Schorner stood staring at the hospital. 'Not even with all the stuff they've got here,' he said. It was a comment, not a question.

'No, sir. He was dead on arrival.'

The American colonel looked behind Scarlett and saw Dorothy Jenkins walking, almost staggering towards the steps, her arms about a bent and weeping woman. He felt himself pale as he walked towards the pair. He reached them at the foot of the steps. Dorothy looked straight ahead, a terrible stare, as if she did not see him. Little grunts of sorrow were coming from the other woman.

'I have a car,' he muttered as they walked past him. Neither answered.

Drained, he stood and watched them go. 'Get a car for those people will you, captain,' he said to Scarlett. Scarlett saluted and ran up the hospital steps. Schorner was still standing watching the women. Albie stared after them also, his face puckered.

Then the pair stopped and slowly turned. It was the hunched crying woman who led the way back. Dorothy followed a pace behind, her expression like ice. Schorner moved towards them. 'This is Mrs Steer,' said Dorothy when they had reached each other. 'Billy's mother.'

Schorner was speechless. The woman looked up with a wet ingrained face. ''T'wadn't your fault,' she said with ghostly quietness. 'You couldn't 'elp 'un. 'Twas just the war.'

May

On an evening when the Devon air was as light as cotton, soldiers in vehicles moved from the camp and made for the embarkation area. All along the inlets and harbours of the south-western coast ships, boats and strange craft were readying.

The soldiers were in thousands, appearing from many directions, assault troops, tankmen, artillery units, infantry, engineers and a dozen other trades of war. As they moved on Wilcoombe and the other embarkation harbours they stared at each other in surprise and an odd resentment, as suspicious strangers might in such a crowd. They were not comrades, they were just going to the same fight. Under their low helmets and trailing their many weapons they made for the ships, the long steel landing ships, deep as valleys, each five thousand tons and carrying five hundred men and their vehicles to battle. At Plymouth, where a French battleship with a huge and inexplicable clock on its superstructure had lain in the Sound since 1940, there were strange sights. A company of Rangers, the commandos of the US Army, went aboard a landing craft in the full regalia of Red Indians, heads shaved, warpaint on their cheeks, stamping their feet and brandishing tomahawks along with their sub-machine guns. It was to be a full dress rehearsal, in every sense, for the invasion.

The conventional soldiers under Colonel Schorner's command had only the short drive to the boarding point, the harbour at Wilcoombe. Others who boarded at that point came from widespread units and camps, three and a half thousand of them, embarking in eight landing ships. They were watched by the Devon people, fallen to silence, as if they had begun to understand. Doey Bidgood shouted to the easily recognizable Ballimach as the GIs left the trucks at the harbour, 'Be this the real thing then, Yank?'

The camel's hump of cable drum on Ballimach's back shrugged. 'Don't ask me, Mac. Ike don't tell me a single thing.'

It raised a few ready smiles with the people and among his fellow soldiers. Most realized that it was to be one more exercise; one more, but the last before the genuine day. Colonel Schorner stood on the harbour wall, checking the men as they trooped by, almost as if he were counting them in case any were missing. They were hung with bandoliers of ammunition and grenades; weapons, rifles, machine guns; the now famous bazookas and flame-throwers were carried down the worn sea steps and on to small craft. The soldiers were black-painted and quiet. Their equipment as assault force engineers was already loaded on the eight five-thousand-ton landing ships lying like logs out on the evening-shadowed sea. The sun had backed away almost to the Atlantic, its low light silvering the bay and giving the land a rosy hue. Gulls cried, their voices alarmed, as they flew around the boats leaving the tight harbour.

Schorner watched the whole of his unit embark – two hundred men – and then boarded the last of the barges with Scarlett, Bryant and Hulton. 'Nice to see Smokey and Stover again,' the colonel commented wryly as they rounded the high harbour entrance and saw the two elderly destroyers puffing away from their stacks like contented old men out fishing.

Hulton said: 'Are they kidding or are we really going to be stuck with those museum pieces?'

'I think you can count on it,' said Schorner. He tried to make it sound as if he were satisfied. 'We've got to use everything, captain. I wouldn't be surprised to find a Louisiana paddleboat out here.'

Scarlett said bitterly and quietly to Bryant, 'They used eighty-seven LSTs on some peewee league landing in the Pacific last month. Eight-seven for some lousy island with a handful of scared-as-shit Japs to defend it. We could do with some of those. The guys out there don't mean to take risks.'

'Maybe they've already taken too many,' said Schorner. Scarlett looked embarrassed because he had not realized the colonel would hear. 'Maybe they figure that they'd like to stay alive now that the war is about to shift to this theatre.' He put his field glasses up and scanned the assembled ships on the aluminium sea. After some minutes, he added: 'But that don't make it any easier for us.'

As they progressed south then west through the easy evening swell, the horizon became built up with basking ships. The soldiers felt encouraged to see so many. They pointed them out to each other. The arms of the two headlands of Start Bay opened away from them. Schorner looked back reflectively at the

565

comfortable land behind, retreating now from clear sight in the dusk. The hills and coombes, the white patches that were people's houses, the places of trees, the long straight beach.

They all watched the bulky herd of ships. 'Jesus Christ,' said Scarlett abruptly. 'That's a locomotive. Now I've seen everything. A railroad train at sea.'

Bryant and Schorner looked out towards the flotilla of craft that were lying ahead, large, cumbersome, blunt-nosed landing ships and landing craft wallowing among smaller vessels and the two destroyers, HMS *Oregon* and HMS *Florida*. On the deck of one of the large, boxy landing craft next in the convoy line could clearly be seen the outline of a steam locomotive.

It was time for the barge to put into the side of the LST, five thousand tons unladen, capable of taking twenty-five tanks aboard and unloading them directly on to a beach through an opening bow and a lowered ramp. Each was as slow and awkward as a hippopotamus. Schorner watched his men climb aboard, up the landing nets and nodded with satisfaction as he saw the heavily-laden soldiers reach the higher deck. They had learned.

He went aboard the same way, followed by Bryant and Scarlett. Hulton followed, ivory-faced under the streaks of black across his cheekbones, his eyes moving with apprehension under the steel helmet. Schorner watched him clamber aboard. 'Still wish you were back in Georgia?' he joked encouragingly.

'With my mother,' completed Hulton. 'With all my heart, sir.'

They climbed along the deck, above the well in which the vehicles of the unit were already sitting. An advanced amphibian tank, scheduled to go first on to the beach to provide fire cover for the assault troops, was immediately behind the bow doors; followed by four dukws, the amphibious troop carriers, known as ducks; then came the trucks carrying the immediate supplies, fuel and ammunition, that would be needed once space had been gained for them to move. The metal treads to be spread along the beach, beneath the tracks and wheels of the vehicles, the explosives for detonating obstacles, the first ambulance, were all aboard. Four hundred soldiers also.

As they moved along the narrow catwalk towards the stern of the ship Schorner said: 'We got our gun. And our gun crew.'

Lieutenant Bryant saw the Bofors had been seated on the rear platform of the LST, its crew, the men of his own unit, sitting around it. The horned barrel of the gun rested on its cradle. 'May I go and have a word with our chaps, colonel?' asked Bryant.

'Sure, lieutenant,' said the American amiably. 'Tell them if they have to shoot to shoot straight, okay?' He was going towards the bridge where the young naval commander, Younghusband, was already waving enthusiastically like the captain of a shrimping boat sailing on the evening tide. Bryant thanked the colonel and clambered over the Bofors' own ammunition boxes towards the gun. There was a sergeant in charge, a man new to Bryant. He was short, solid, his flat British helmet giving him the appearance of a fire hydrant. Briskly he ordered the crew to attention. Bryant recognized Gilman, Catermole and Killer Watts.

'Sergeant Spence, sir,' said the NCO introducing himself. 'Joined in Plymouth.'

'I wondered who was going to remind them to use this thing,' smiled Bryant. He greeted the men he knew. They looked different now, in their battle order; soldiers suddenly born out of the domestic ninnies he had known less than a month ago at the Wilcoombe gun-site.

'Finest gun in the world, sir,' said the sergeant, poking a stubby finger at the Bofors. 'Don't care who says otherwise. Never was one like it, never be one again. Rapid fire, anti-aircraft, anti-tank, anti-personnel. Anti-anything, sir.'

Bryant grinned at the enthusiasm. 'What's it like against submarines?' he joked.

'Be lovely, sir, if the elevation was right. That gun can do anything but have a baby.'

Bryant touched him on the shoulder. 'There'll be enough people having babies,' he forecast, 'before this lot is through.'

Gilman said: 'May I ask a question, sir?'

Bryant peered from beneath his helmet rim. 'Fire away, Gilman,' he said. Gilman, he saw, noticed the aptness of the phrase. Sergeant Spence was regarding Gilman with an edge of hostility.

'Is this *it*, sir?' asked Gilman steadily.

Catermole nodded: 'The real thing, sir?'

'The invasion?' said Gilman.

Watts said: 'Yes, sir. That.'

'They'll tell us,' said Bryant. 'As soon as this Noah's Ark gets under way. But I don't think you need to say your prayers too heavily tonight.'

Gilman smiled at the officer's friendship. 'Thank you, sir,' he said. 'It's got to happen sometime, but we just wanted to know.'

'I don't have to write out my will after all,' said Catermole.

'You should have done that anyway, Pussy,' said Bryant with affection. 'It's a soldier's duty.'

'I got so much, sir, I'm letting my lawyers sort it out,' chatted Catermole.

Sergeant Spence said: 'So we won't be needing Betty tonight.' He patted the stock of the Bofors.

'I didn't say that,' said Bryant, keeping his voice low. 'With an armada this size floating about in the English Channel, the Jerries may well decide to have a go. They've got planes, they've got submarines, they haven't got any big ships but they've got some torpedo boats along the French coast. I don't think we can afford to count that out, sergeant.'

It was almost dark now, the last edge of daylight like a bad join along the western horizon. As Bryant turned to walk forward again, Catermole said: 'Is that a puffer train over there, sir? On that LST? Or is it a secret weapon?'

Bryant said: 'Looks strange, doesn't it? A railway engine at sea. They're trying it for size, I expect. This is the last chance to get it right, the same as everything else.'

Watts said: 'Can't see that chuffing up the beach.'

Bryant agreed. He turned in the dusk. 'All right, chaps. Keep warm and, more important, for God's sake keep awake. I'll see you get some cocoa or whatever's going once we get moving.'

'It's Yankee rations, is it, sir?' asked Spence.

'I imagine so. Being out here all night is going to be bad enough without having *our* hard tack. The Americans wouldn't eat it anyway.'

He left them and returned towards the super-structure of the vessel, like a collection of huts four-fifths of the way back towards its stern. Often he felt very strange being in charge of men who, in the main, were older than himself. Catermole was two or three years his senior, Gilman perhaps a year, Watts the same, and the sergeant ten years. It was something to which he had never become accustomed.

He reached the island superstructure and was beckoned up by Scarlett. A naval rating handed him a mug of coffee. 'Your boys will be getting some soon, sir,' the sailor said, nodding towards the Bofors. 'Got to look after our own lads, haven't we?'

There were ten officers in a group near the bridge, plus Younghusband, the naval reserve captain of the LST. Schorner had a torch on a sea chart. 'Your gunners okay back there, lieutenant?' he asked Bryant.

'Yes, fine thank you, sir.' Bryant realized they had been waiting for him. 'Sorry.'

'And that gun is ready for anything,' added Schorner good-humouredly.

'They can't wait to start,' said Bryant. 'The sergeant says it would sink a pocket battleship.'

'Great,' said Schorner. 'Personally, I can do without a battleship.' His eyes moved around the darkened faces. 'I aim to give you a general briefing,' he said. 'After that I want you to go to your own men and fill in the spaces for them. We've got just about four hundred GIs on this ship. I want each guy to know where he's going and at what time. That's the least we can do for them. I don't want them to think we're holding out on them, not on anything.'

570

He waited. Whistles and hooters began to sound like endearments across the dim and flat water. Signals were sparking from the bridges of the two destroyers. 'I think you will all know by now, and if you don't you don't keep your ears open – this is *not* the real thing. It is an exercise with the codename Lion – the final exercise. Tonight it's all got to go right because we've run out of time.

'The schedule is to sail due east out of Start Bay and across Lyme Bay, towards Portland, to turn and come back on the same course until we are in approximately the same position as we are at this moment. A not untypical piece of planning. Another force, much larger, is coming east from Plymouth, sailing in about three hours. A third convoy is coming from Dartmouth. In all we will have maybe three hundred vessels of various types and up to twenty thousand men, most of which we want on that beach by daybreak.

'Our own particular convoy, H2, consists of eight Landing Ships Tanks, with a bridge pontoon carried by LST33, and a railroad train by LST22.' He looked up and grinned in the dark. 'These little technicalities have to be figured out sometime,' he said.

'I don't have to tell you what the landing procedures are. Each of you has his orders, his priorities and his beach drill. But I need to add one thing here – the considerable danger of German intervention in this exercise.'

The lugubrious Hulton, at a finger signal from Schorner, handed over a single sheet of paper. It was caught by the ocean breeze and fluttered fiercely in his hand like a captured white bird. The colonel said: 'We would be living with Judy Garland over the rainbow if we believed that an exercise of this magnitude would be overlooked by the enemy. Increased signal traffic alone, the volume of it, never mind what the heck it is saying, is enough to put the Germans on the alert. They also have various other ways of breaching our security. Information passed to them. People talking too much and too loud.'

By the merest fraction of a glance Bryant caught Scarlett's eye. Quickly both turned to Schorner again. 'This report I have been handed,' said the colonel, 'is a general survey of potential enemy forces in this immediate area.' He smiled his grey smile, hardly to be seen in the darkness. 'These guys, these Intelligence eggheads, they think of everything,' he said as he read. His illumination was the single narrow torchlight. Its parameter made his lined face more deeply incised, his eyes metallic. Bryant remembered that he was not yet fifty. Schorner read aloud: 'It says here, "Attention is invited to the fact that this portion of the Intelligence annexe concerns enemy forces which may be met in *actual* combat – and does not concern enemy forces *assumed* for the purpose of the exercise."' He looked up. 'In other words, it's not cardboard dummies we're talking about. So get that straight.'

A bleep came from the small shed-like bridge of the LST and the British officer, Younghusband, with a glance at the American colonel, excused himself. He went to the bridge and they heard him giving orders into a mouthpiece. Almost at once the craft began to move. The lieutenant leaned matily from the upper rail and said: 'Can I listen from up here, sir? We're under way. I'm afraid the timing of the exercise is up the spout already.'

Schorner looked up and smiled the smile he kept for people he really liked. 'Sure. Just like Tugboat Annie,' he said. He returned to the document. 'Okay, this is the score, then. These are the enemy forces available in this area. First, submarines. In the past three years there have been only two reports of German submarines operating in the English Channel. But one of these was last month. So maybe this guy will be nosing around tonight. These clever people' – he tapped the vibrating paper – 'they say so.'

He returned to the document. 'Surface vessels,' he said. 'I read here that within striking distance of Start Bay – right here – on 11 April, less than a month ago, there were six Moewe class torpedo boats and four Elbing class destroyers, with four others not too far away. That's plenty. There is also the fact that this convoy is twenty minutes flying time from the Luftwaffe, if they're not scared of the dark.'

Even in the easy evening sea they could feel the clumsy LST begin to wallow as it began its journey towards Portland Bill. The two old destroyers were making little hooting sounds, as though in encouragement, as they turned and followed. The convoy, like a slow herd of cows, was edging eastwards. Other ships were spreading far out, soon to be lost in the anonymous night. Even the destroyers and the other landing ships, almost devoid of lights, were soon only wraiths.

'Now – the primary danger,' continued Schorner. An orderly was passing around mugs of coffee. Scarlett could see Schorner was annoyed, although he did not comment on the intrusion but took the mug in one hand. He then looked up towards Younghusband still leaning chummily over the bridge. 'Do you think, lieutenant, that we could keep this meeting private for a few more minutes?'

Younghusband's face arched in surprise; then he realized. 'Oh, the steward. Yes, sorry, sir. I expect he was afraid the coffee would go cold.'

It was said in concise British cheerfulness. Schorner said: 'If we don't get this right then the coffee won't be the only thing. Okay, just keep this deck clear.'

Younghusband looked hurt. His head disappeared on to the bridge and they could hear him giving sharp but indistinct orders. When he came back he looked chastened and quiet, no longer holding his coffee mug.

'Okay,' said the colonel, 'the primary danger – German E-boats. I think I'd better just go over what this Intelligence annexe says. It reads: "A flotilla of sixteen E-boats, thirteen known to be operational, are based at Cherbourg. These boats have been operating in the Start Bay area and attacks can be expected *nightly*, at any time after dark until approximately two hours before sunrise."'

Collectively, involuntarily, the officers in the group looked around at the gathered night. The sea sounded against the hull with regular slaps.

' "Attacks from these craft in the current exercise is a possibility that cannot be over-emphasized. The last recorded E-boat sortie was in March."'

The colonel said: 'And, just so we really get the message about the kind of troubles we've got, they've added a few personal details. The newest and largest

E-boats are operating in this area. They are one hundred and six feet long and have a displacement of ninety-five tons. And get this. They have speeds of thirty-eight knots and the newest type are believed to be capable of forty-eight knots. They can cut this to below twelve knots by using only one engine.' He looked wryly up to Younghusband. 'What speed are we making right now, lieutenant?' he inquired.

Younghusband said: 'Three, going on to four knots, sir.' He judged Schorner's expression and ducked back into the bridge canopy. His face emerged again. It was like a one-man performance in a miniature theatre. 'Three point four, sir,' he said. 'The set speed is four but not many of these can make it fully laden.'

'That's walking speed,' said Schorner, adding: 'so the escorting destroyers have to cut down their speed?' Younghusband looked out to where he knew the ancient *Oregon* and *Florida* were ploughing. 'They can manage about fifteen knots,' he said apologetically. 'That old couple.'

The American officer turned again to the black-cheeked, helmeted group. Their life jackets gave them the appearance of a collection of fat men. 'So there you have it. Our only defence, if these E-boats come for us, is that we'll be going too slow for them to catch us.'

There was a dim laugh from the officers. Schorner continued: 'According to this, these E-boats are armed with two twenty-millimetre guns, one fore, one aft, and on this year's model these have been upgraded to forty-millimetre cannons. Their main armament, however, is better than this. They carry four torpedoes, probably of the latest homing-in type,

575

and these they fire at full speed at ranges less than six hundred yards.'

From the catwalks around the side and from the deep vehicle deck, soldiers were staring up at the small congregation. They could hear nothing, only see the serious fattened shapes. The men squatted and lay where they could, their equipment loosened, their weapons laid down, the dumb vehicles set among them.

'E-boat tactics I won't bore you with,' continued Schorner. 'I guess we won't see them in the dark anyway. This intelligence study says that they cruise in groups of three or four searching for shipping. Well, they won't have to search much for this circus.' He read some more of the directive. ' "Attack is made after the first escort vessel of the convoy" – in our case one of those two old smokers out there – "has passed the last group of E-boats." Having attacked they beat it in a cloud of smoke, which is about the only good news in the entire document.'

He folded the paper and thrust it into his battledress pocket. 'Okay, you've got it. It may not happen, I certainly hope to God it doesn't. But we need to be prepared. I want you all to make sure that your men wear their life vests at all times.

'That's all,' he said. 'Each of you make sure that your men are informed and alert. If it all goes okay and we get ashore on schedule, we'll all have time for a game of baseball tomorrow afternoon.'

The officers left and as they did he called Scarlett, Hulton and Bryant to closer consultation. 'Sorry about the depressing forecast,' he said. 'Maybe it won't happen. But the fact is we're out here wearing no pants if those E-boats do come after us. It's not an exaggeration.' He studied their worried faces. 'I know, I know. You thought like me that we were winning the war. You thought all that war material we saw piling up all over England was going to be enough. We had enough guns and enough ships and planes coming out of our ears. So did I. But here we are holding the wooden spoons, out in the ocean with two old destroyers and outmoded guns, with a fleet of E-boats licking their chops like big bad wolves just over the horizon. Well, that's how it is. And there's nothing we can do about it.

'I have a particular order for you three officers. If we get into action I want all three of you to stay *real* close to me. This is an instruction from way up. It's my luck that I'm one of a group of officers who know enough about the details of our projected landing in France – Overlord – to make us a great catch for the enemy. I've never felt so wanted before. I must not be allowed to fall into German hands, got it?'

They nodded dumbly. 'My group has the uncomplimentary codename of BIGOT,' he continued. He spelled it out. 'I understand it was the code for the top-secret echelon in the Torch landings in North Africa, but reversed. It was then called TO GIB, *to Gibraltar*, which was a cover for all top security documents during that operation. They've turned it around to make it BIGOT – and I'm a BIGOT. On no account must I be made a prisoner, in case I start to holler. Okay? If there is any danger of that, each of you must take a collective and individual responsibility to kill me. Got it? If I'm floating around in the ocean and those E-boat guys look likely to pull me out – shoot me. And that's a strict order.' They said they would and then dispersed. Bryant, walking towards the gun, looked back over his shoulder and saw Schorner's solitary outline. He felt overwhelmingly sorry for the man.

At midnight there was some loitering fog in Lyme Bay. It crept in silent fingers over the side of the LST, chilling the huddled men among the vehicles. Those down below were warmer but scarcely more comfortable, lying on the trooping decks in random positions like dead men when a battle is done.

'There's four hundred GIs on this tugboat,' complained Ballimach, who, because of his size, was less comfortable than most. 'Four hundred, and I get the lousiest place to put my ass. And this iron goddamn coffin keeps going up and down like the Atlantic City roller coaster.'

'The ocean is pretty calm tonight,' pointed out Albie. He had wedged himself between Ballimach's drum of cable and the wheel of a truck. He ate alternately from a tin of army pressed beef and a half pound bar of chocolate. 'When there *is* a storm then you'll think you want to get ashore even though the Nazis are there.'

'They ought to give us seats,' grumbled Ballimach. 'Real seats like on a train or a bus or the movies. If you're going to war, surely they can give you comfortable seats.'

Wall had been looking over the side of the ship at the misty sea; his eyes tightened each time he imagined he saw or heard something. He was damp with nervousness. Albie said to him: 'What's with you all the time? You, getting up and looking over. There ain't a thing to see out there, Wall.'

'I'm scared,' admitted Wall. 'I'm so scared I feel like jumping into the ocean.'

Ballimach laughed, a strange sound that rattled in the fog. Some men trying to sleep on the metal deck nearby rolled over and complained. 'There's no future in it, son,' he said. 'There's not a whole lot of future in what we're doing right now, but there's even less in jumping over the side.'

Wall sat down miserably. 'There's *some* guys got seats,' he complained. 'Those special guys who were in camp. That outfit we couldn't figure out.'

'They got seats?' asked Albie. 'How come they got seats?'

'Don't ask me, buddy. But they're right up that front end of this tin can, sitting on seats. What's so special about those guys? They keep them separate from the rest of us and now they got seats.'

Albie said: 'Go and ask them, Wall. Go right over and ask them. Ask them why they got seats, why they're so special.' He knew Wall would not. 'I'll take a walk and see for myself,' decided Albie. He rose and stretched his short legs. He could have slept in the seat of the colonel's jeep, but he preferred to remain on the deck. 'Ballimach would only bellyache,' he explained. 'And there's a whole lot of belly to ache.'

He moved towards the front of the LST, stepping over and between the huddled soldiers. When he was a child his father had taken him to see the National Guard parade on Washington's Birthday and now, quite suddenly, after the years, he remembered it. It was strange how then he had thought of soldiers as upright and shining. Now look at them.

He saw the men of the mysterious unit sitting in a

small encampment beyond the nose of the amphibious tank that was to be first on the beach at the assault. There were ten men and they not only had portable seats but a table with coffee and the remains of a meal on it. Albie studied them. They looked no different from other soldiers, maybe a little more studious, for they sat in attitudes of thought.

'Hi,' he said cheerfully, approaching them. Some of the men were dozing but the two sitting nearest looked up. He was not certain in the difficult light but he thought they were glad to see him.

'Hi, soldier,' said the nearest. 'What are you doing here?'

'I'm just in the war,' shrugged Albie. The man offered him some coffee.

'Thanks,' said Albie genuinely. The issue coffee had been bitter and cold by the time it reached his corner. He poured a cup and stood against the snout of the amphibian to drink it.

'Here, kid,' said one of the men kindly, 'take a seat. It's better to drink sitting down.'

Albie sat, still wondering at their mystery. Were they older than other soldiers? They seemed of no particular rank or uniform, although it was difficult to see now, everyone looked much the same in battledress and life vests, every man a blot. He took the stranger's seat and the man stood where he had been standing. Gratefully he drank the coffee. 'Eighteen before midnight,' he mentioned conversationally, checking his watch.

'And all's well,' added the soldier sitting next to him.

'I just hope it goes on that way,' said Albie, not

comfortable. 'I don't go a whole lot on this floating around. I like to have the earth under me.' He thought the remark brought a dry chuckle from someone at the other end of the group. 'They say we got to look out for E-boats,' he continued nervously. 'Me? I wouldn't know an E-boat from an A- B- or C-boat. Even if I could see it I wouldn't know.'

The man next to him casually but quite suddenly leaned out of his cape and put his hand to Albie's throat, causing the small soldier to jump in apprehension. The coffee spilled and the man apologized. His hand remained however and he said: 'I just wanted to see your dog tags.'

'Dog tags?' said Albie. 'Sure, I got dog tags.' He fumbled for the identity discs and pulled them free of his shirt and battledress. The man tightened his eyes to the light of a tiny torch he produced and read: 'Albert C. Primrose. 2288456. That's a nice name,' he said. He put the tags back inside Albie's shirt in a disquietingly professional movement.

'You guys go around checking that GIs are wearing dog tags,' decided Albie. 'Am I right?'

'You're right,' said the man who had given him the coffee and now stood against the tank. 'We check dog tags all the time.'

It was dawning on Albie. He looked from one to another. The standing man told him anyway. 'We're what they call a Grave Registration Company. We get around checking on dead guys and making sure their graves are marked.'

Albie almost bit through the coffee mug. 'That's why we got a table and chairs,' went on the second man conversationally, almost with eagerness. 'This is our office, see. Once we get ashore we scurry around making sure that every guy who dies is properly registered.'

The small soldier looked at the faces. 'That,' he hesitated, 'is a great service . . . a very necessary service.'

'Sure,' said the seated man. 'We know that. If you get killed you want to know that your folks know where you are buried, don't you?'

'Oh, sure I would. I'd be much happier then.' He rose. 'Well, I must get back to my buddies. It's been real nice meeting guys with . . . with an . . . unusual job like you guys have. Thanks for the coffee. It was good.' He tried not to hurry away too quickly but still he fell over a sleeping man and backed away from a flurry of curses. He picked himself up and waved his fingers at the grave men. Then he hurtled over the prostrate forms and between the vehicles until he reached Ballimach and Wall again.

'Okay, so you found out,' said Ballimach.

'Didn't they have seats, just like I said?' demanded Wall.

Clay-faced under his black paint, looking like a boy on Hallowe'en, his eyes dilated behind his glasses, Albie said simply, hoarsely, 'They're a Grave Registration Company.' The mouths dropped like twin traps. 'They tell you when you're dead – I mean they tell your folks when you're dead.' Albie shook. 'One of them took out my dog tags!'

'Jesus,' muttered Ballimach. 'Didn't I just *know* it? Those guys, when we was back in camp, those guys was always looking sideways at me, kinda measuring me. I knew it. I goddamn knew it.'

'I said I like to have the earth under me,' remembered Albie in a whisper. 'And they all agreed.'

'That outfit put it about that they were Intelligence,' said Wall indignantly. 'Back at Telcoombe. Other guys asked them. They said their outfit was a special Intelligence unit. Gathering information, that's what they said.'

Ballimach pointed out lugubriously, 'I guess that's what they do. They just didn't mention what kind of information.'

'Who can blame them?' asked Albie more reasonably. 'That's terrible, lousy work. Checking on corpses.' A shiver trickled down his small frame. 'It gets colder,' he said. 'I hope I don't meet up with those guys again.'

Fifteen miles away, to the south-west, a flotilla of German E-boats of the latest class were rendezvousing at sea, having left their base in Cherbourg half an hour earlier.

They lay prone about the base of the Bofors gun, a tableau of men such as had been much represented in memorial stones to the fallen of the First World War, and would later be carved again. They were not asleep, for on the hard, damp deck, with the wind-pushed mist moving around, the grunting of men and of engines, sleep was all but impossible. In addition, they were on the gun platform at the blunt stern of the unstable craft and the rise and fall and pitch were most felt there. Landing ships were meant for facility of landing, not voyaging.

Killer Watts eventually sat up, aching and cold, and

leaning back against the metal bulkhead began to grumble. He sat, legs out, head and shoulders sagging forward, arms hanging limp, like some beggar on an eastern street. 'I don't know what I'm doing here, on this fucking thing,' he moaned. The complaint was quiet enough to have been addressed to himself. It was Catermole who answered, lying flat, a tarpaulin from the gun across him like a shroud. 'When you find out, Killer,' he observed, 'ask for me, will you, mate?'

'You're here because your country needs you,' said Sergeant Spence. It was defiant but strangely shy. 'I know you lot think I'm some bullshitting old regular, and so I am. But at least I know what's what. I was there in nineteen-forty when you lot got orange juice in your rations.'

Gilman lay depressed, his eyes and mind stuffed with aches, his mouth full of cold. 'What is what then, sarge?' he said. 'You tell us. Go on.'

'I mean,' continued Watts, as if no one else had said anything, 'I get in the army and they say that I've got to be a sparks, so it's not my trade. We had gas in our house. But I said all right, because that's all I could say, because you can't argue, can you?'

'What was your trade, then?' asked Spence. He eased himself up now and so did the others, surrendering to the fact that sleep and any kind of comfort were unattainable.

'Unemployed,' said Watts casually, not lifting his face. Spence let it go. Watts said: 'So I have to learn about all this electricity bollocks. And then, after all that, they stick me out here on the sea and tell me I got to fire this bleeding gun. It don't make sense.'

'Not a lot does,' put in Gilman.

'I reckon the safest way to get to be a cook is to volunteer for the paratroops,' put in Catermole.

Spence regarded them in the dark. 'You're a lot of soft moaners,' he said. 'I've been in twenty years now.'

None of them had realized. It was like admitting you were mad. Even Watts brought his chin up from his chest. 'Christ,' breathed Catermole. 'Twenty years. It feels like a hundred I've been in and it's only two. What you been doing for twenty years, sarge?'

'Being a soldier,' said Spence. He said it with a little arrogance. Gilman realized he meant it. 'I was one of those who got taken off at Dunkirk and I'm bloody *glad* we're going back. I hate those bastards. They're the enemies of our King and Country.'

It came out so unselfconsciously now that only Catermole could offer a remark. 'But it's no sort of bloody life is it, the army?'

'It's the best job there is,' asserted Spence. He looked down at the huddled Watts. 'A job for life. I've been all over, I have. India, Egypt . . .'

'They reckon there's a shortage of crumpet in India and all the crumpet in Egypt is poxed up to the armpits,' said Catermole predictably. 'Is that true, sarge?'

Gilman said craftily: 'You'll be unemployed soon, sarge . . . Once all this is over.'

Spence said: 'There'll always be war, you can bet on that, son. When this lot's all done, give it a year or so and the balloon will go up again. With Russia this time. I've got a job for life.'

'Until you get killed,' put in Gilman.

'Same thing,' shrugged Spence. 'What do you do, Gilman?'

Watts interrupted. 'My old man reckoned that all the women in France was poxed in the First World War,' he said. 'He reckoned you could get it just by dancing with them in those French cabarets. But he got hisself gassed in the end, not like fatal because I wouldn't be 'ere, would I? But he got hisself gassed which 'as got to be worse than getting pox, and not so much pleasure in it.'

'My old man was unemployed,' said Catermole reflectively. 'Ten-and-a-half years. He was a bloody good footballer, my old man. Through being on the dole that was, see. He 'ad a 'ell of a kick. Sometimes he used to take me with 'im when he was trying to get a job, you know to see the bosses, and he always used to give me a kick to make me cry so that they'd feel sorry for us.'

Gilman said: 'Did he ever get the jobs, Pussy?'

'Nah, they didn't want the poor old bloke. He'd got arthritis in his hands, couldn't use them some days, so he didn't get the jobs, or if he got them they soon gave him the shove.'

Spence said again to Gilman: 'What did you do in civvy street?'

'In a bank,' said Gilman. 'But I'd had enough of that. I'm not going back there.'

'What are you going to do then after?'

'I'm trying to get on with writing,' said Gilman. 'I've been doing a correspondence course. I don't know what I can do, but if I could get a job on a newspaper or in advertising or something like that . . .'

Spence sniffed as if testing the Lyme Bay mist. 'Writers,' he said scornfully. ''Cause of half the trouble in the world, writers. Wars, everything.' He nodded out towards France and then at the crowded troops forward of them. 'All this,' he said, then amended, 'half of this lot is caused by writers. Shouting the odds and the next thing you know there's a war.'

'I thought you approved of wars,' said Gilman. 'They keep you employed.'

'I didn't say any different, son,' said Spence. 'I just said that writers caused half of it. The stuff they put in the papers.'

'What I reckon,' said Watts doggedly, 'is, that when you get out of the mob and get married like, it's no good having a fuck *every* night with the missus, is it? Walt Walters says you more or less have to. I don't reckon that at all. Not every night. I was thinking about it yesterday, no, I tell a lie, on Friday. That's the night I ring the girlfriend. But I couldn't fancy going home from work and having it every night. Saturdays, yes. Few pints, get home and get on the job. That makes sense, don't it?'

'Russia's definitely next,' said Spence confidentially and confidently. 'You can just see it happening can't you? They hate the Yanks and the Yanks hate their guts, no matter what they make out. And we're stuck with the Yanks, so it makes sense. I think that when we've got the Germans on their arses, all that will happen is the Ruskies will keep advancing one way and us and the Yanks will be going the other, and the balloon will go up again. You see.'

'Why do they always say about the balloon going up?' asked Watts curiously. 'I reckon balloons are bleedin' good. Like when you're a kid and you've got a balloon.'

Catermole said: 'You know that bird what you was

giving it to?' Gilman realized he was talking to him. He said nothing. 'She's been giving it to the Yanks. There's always Yanks going to 'er 'ouse.'

'So what?' said Gilman. 'She can do what she likes. She's nothing to do with me.'

Watts began to light a cigarette but the sergeant moved forward sharply and almost knocked it from his hand. 'You know the orders, Watts,' he rasped. 'That could be seen for miles.'

'Bloody 'ell, sarge,' complained Watts. 'Who's going to see me having a drag. The fishes?' Carefully he folded the cigarette and put it in his tunic pocket. He settled back against the bulkhead and began to sing in a soft whine:

'Kiss me goodnight, sergeant-major,
Tuck me in my little wooden bed . . .'

Five miles away, just beyond the lip of the night horizon, the formation of E-boats was fanning out.

At fourteen minutes past midnight, already half an hour behind its schedule, the torpid convoy turned off Portland Bill and began to retrace its course across the wide night of Lyme Bay. Wispy moonlight now alternated with fields of fog across the dim sea. At twelve-fifty the ungainly turn-about had been accomplished; eight long and bulky landing craft – crowded with soldiers and machines – and the two escorts were rolling west again. Ten minutes later HMS *Florida* began to signal.

On the bridge of the LST, Lieutenant Younghusband took the message from the signaller. He sent for Colonel Schorner who was sitting awake, his eyes staring at darkness, in the front seat of his jeep. Bryant and Scarlett were sitting propped against the bulkhead. They stood and followed their senior officer up the steel ladder. Hulton came from below and saw them on the bridge. He climbed awkwardly after them.

Younghusband said to Schorner: '*Florida* is having to break off, sir. She's got trouble with her boilers, poor old dear. She's going into Portland.'

Schorner said: 'That's not good news.'

'It's not very, is it, sir,' agreed Younghusband. 'But she'll never be able to keep up. Not even at our rate of knots.'

'That leaves us with only one lame duck to look after us,' sighed Schorner. 'Not that it makes a hell of a lot of difference.'

'It's crazy when you think about it,' put in Hulton sulkily. 'That we have to sail all this way, just to sail back. Right under the noses of the Germans and with inadequate protection. Those intelligence warnings about E-boats certainly didn't sound like bedtime stories to me.' He caught Schorner's critical eye. 'Sir,' he added lamely.

'Soldiers have always been told not to ask too many questions,' the colonel said. 'Just do it.'

'More or less the same goes for the Navy,' put in Younghusband cheerfully. He looked around the dark horizon. 'Mind, you are apt to wonder sometimes where everybody else has gone. Ah, there goes *Florida* now. Cheerio, *Florida*. She'll be home and in bed in an hour.'

'Lucky girl,' commented Scarlett.

Schorner put in: 'Are your men okay, Bryant? Awake?'

'Yes, sir. I've checked on them every fifteen minutes. They're sitting around the gun.'

'I'll double look-outs, sir,' said Younghusband without being asked.

Schorner thanked him and said: 'Let's double-check that everyone is wearing life vests.' He went down to the deck. Scarlett followed him. Bryant went back to the Bofors crew at the stern. Hulton remained on the bridge trying to stare through the night. Only the shadow-shape of the LST directly ahead was visible.

'What difference look-outs will make I don't know,' confessed Younghusband with a shrug. 'When something is coming at you at forty-plus knots there's no real advantage in seeing it any sooner.'

Hulton was frightened and looked it. He did not like the sea and the darkness. 'It beats me,' he complained in a whisper. 'What sort of a war is this anyway? By this time we're supposed to have every goddamn thing we need to conquer the world. And here we are, thousands of guys, vehicles, tanks, ships, cruising up and down like dummies saying to the goddamn Nazis, "Here we are, come and get us." And that old hulk of a destroyer is going to do nothing quick.' He looked at Younghusband with forlorn hope. 'What do you think she'll be able to do?' he asked.

'Call for help,' suggested Younghusband with a touch of mischief. 'These decisions, old boy, are made by people way up high with yards of experience and gold braid, you know.'

'Yeah,' said Hulton. It was not much short of a snarl. 'But I bet those bums who made them are not out here on this fucking sea in this fucking boat tonight. They're warm in their fucking beds.' The curses were like sobs.

'Very likely,' said Younghusband mildly. He looked up hurriedly as the signaller came to the cramped bridge.

'Signal from *Oregon*, sir.'

Younghusband took the signal form. 'She's got something on her radar,' he said. Hulton's helmet jerked upwards, his eyes bright points of anxiety. The British officer shrugged. 'Probably something of ours,' he said. 'Part of one of the other convoys, off course.'

'I'll tell Colonel Schorner,' offered Hulton hurriedly. He almost fell down the iron ladder to the deck and went like a disjointed hurdler over the prone forms of the dozing soldiers. Schorner and Scarlett went back with him to the bridge. Bryant returned from the gun platform and joined them.

'Could be nothing,' Younghusband was saying. 'These things often turn out like that. Just sea ghosts.'

'We don't have radar?' asked Scarlett.

'Not on this ship,' confirmed Younghusband lightly, giving the impression that he did not believe in it. 'The leading LST has it, and number five, after the pontoon. One radar in Red Beach convoy. One radar in Green Beach, that's us. That's our ration.' The signaller returned to the bridge. They were like men in a lift now, close together. Bryant, at his own suggestion, went back to the gun platform. He waited long enough on the ladder to hear Younghusband say:

'They've lost the blips now. Probably nothing more than a shoal of porpoises.'

Schorner had just said: 'Great, I like the idea of the porpoises,' when the big landing ship, three hundred yards ahead, was abruptly outlined by a great flash and an explosion that cracked across the water.

'Torpedo,' snapped Younghusband. 'It's the bloody E-boats.'

He pulled a toggle and a honking klaxon sounded over the ship. There was no need for it, for every man who could be was at the side, hundreds of apprehensive eyes, looking at the high flame that caressed the clumsy craft ahead. They could see men jumping like frogs into the water.

Schorner grabbed the loudhailer. 'Get your heads down!' he shouted. 'Everybody take cover! Do not panic. Repeat – do not panic.'

His first order was obeyed, his second ignored. The men scrambling from the sides of the ship fell on top of those among the vehicles in the open hold. Other soldiers began pouring out of the companion hatches from the decks below. Schorner bellowed again, his voice monstrous over the dark deck. 'Order. Every man stay just where he is. That is an order.'

'Stand by to pick up survivors,' Younghusband ordered. 'There they are, the E-boats,' he added, pointing calmly. 'Four of them. See, to starboard. In the searchlight – now.'

A light had probed out from the destroyer, wallowing as she tried to turn like some obese and ancient sheepdog turning to face wolves.

'I bet Jerry can hardly believe his luck,' breathed Younghusband. His eyes closed, as if he were suddenly weary of it, then he opened them, straightened up and looked firmly out to sea.

At the fringe of the beam, low on the oily sea, were the slight shapes of the E-boats. They appeared to be voyaging unhurriedly, like a herring fleet. Bryant, on the gun platform, picked them out at the same time. He shouted for the gun to be brought around to bear on the targets. Sergeant Spence repeated the order and Gilman and Catermole and Watts swung with the weapon as it turned towards the E-boats. Young-husband raised a casual, almost languid, signalling arm from the bridge. 'Fire!' ordered Bryant.

The noise of the gun was shattering. It loosed off a stream of shells towards the low-lying craft, sending up a fence of spray. 'Short!' bellowed Bryant. He had never been in action before. He was soaked with the sweat of excitement and fear but his voice and body remained steady. 'Range six hundred,' he called firmly. 'Fire!' Another staggering burst of shells streamed towards the enemy flotilla. Spray and smoke clouded the targets. When it had cleared they saw one of the E-boats tearing at them, cleaving the night sea at tremendous speed, its machine guns and cannon firing as it came.

'Fucking 'ell,' muttered Catermole, looking around the shield of the Bofors. 'Now we've gone and upset them.'

Machine-gun fire rattled along the hull of the LST. The direction was low. The attacker curled off only two hundred yards away while Bryant was still frantically trying to reduce the trajectory of the Bofors. But now the shells were screaming clear above the German vessel, ploughing the sea two hundred yards in its wake. The E-boat curved with vicious grace. It loosed a torpedo, straight at the easy target. The weapon cut through the darkened sea leaving a phosphorescent trail.

'Down!' bellowed Younghusband from the bridge. He hung on to the rail like a child on the branch of a tree. Schorner and Scarlett were spreadeagled on the platform below, their eyes stark in their smeared faces. Men were crouched along the decks between the vehicles and crammed bent down on the catwalks twenty feet above them.

Only Younghusband and the British gun crew on their respective elevations could see the torpedo. Its twinkling track snaked towards them. Bryant had a strangely sedate memory of fishing as a boy and seeing the line cutting through a pond. He felt himself grasped by Sergeant Spence who pulled him forcefully to the metal deck. 'Sorry, sir,' said Spence.

They heard the torpedo strike the metal of the hull with a clank, an almost funny anti-climax. Bryant took his hands from his ears and looked up at the bridge. The other LST was burning so fiercely now that he could clearly see Younghusband laughing. 'It didn't go off,' Bryant said unnecessarily to Spence.

The crew picked themselves up from the plating. Watts said with hopeless hope: 'Maybe it's just a practice, sir. All part of the exercise.'

Bryant had a grim grin. 'Do you think that's a practice, Watts?' he said, pointing to the LST burning half a mile away now, drifting and blazing, explosions rending the interior as ammunition ignited.

'Here he comes again,' muttered Spence. 'Christ, sir, let's get the fucker this time.'

Bryant had been watching too. The gun was swung and they let off a long burst of shell fire at the E-boat, streaking through the reddened darkness at them. The sound of the gunfire made some of the American soldiers look up as if it encouraged them. But the attacker, untouched, protected by its speed, banked in on the same course and loosed the torpedo from impudent close range. Younghusband shouted from the bridge again and the men in the guts of the long cavernous vessel flung themselves flat. Spence, cursing like a hooligan, kept the gun firing at the E-boat but once more the trajectory was too high, the target too swift. The torpedo came at the landing ship and once again struck amidships. Another metallic clunk. Nothing more.

'Good God,' bawled Younghusband to Colonel Schorner. 'This lot are worse than we are.' As he shouted the E-boat did a tight curve and fired its machine guns and cannon over the deck.

The fusillade was frightening, cutting along the metal deck like a terrible saw. Schorner, flat on his face in front of the bridge, screwed his head sideways and prayed hurriedly as the bullets cut across him. So this is what it was like. God help them all. But he knew the burst would be quick, for the attacker would have to turn away. It was like being strafed by an airplane. The firing ceased as he thought the thought. He looked upwards to the bridge. 'Lieutenant!' he shouted. 'Younghusband, are you okay?'

Younghusband's face appeared over the rail. Everything; colour, texture, flesh, seemed to have been dragged down out of his features. But he was laughing in a boyish way. 'The bastard's shot my hand off, sir,' he said, pushing a stump gushing blood over the rail for Schorner to see. Schorner fought down his sick. 'Medic!' he bellowed over the loudhailer. 'Medics to the bridge. At once!'

'They've got a lot of clients,' mentioned Younghusband, still attempting to sustain the casual. He leaned on the rail like a man leaning on a fence to talk with a neighbour.

'You've got to sail the ship,' grunted Schorner. 'Good, we got some.' Two medical auxiliaries and a doctor bustled over the deck. The smoke was easing now and Schorner saw the hurrying attendants were stepping across prone men, men who would never move again. The doctor got there first. 'See to the Englishman,' ordered Schorner. 'He's got to handle this thing.'

Younghusband's face had vanished and they mounted the ladder to find him sprawled on the bridge. He was still conscious. 'Sorry,' he said as they got there. 'Felt I had to sit down for a moment.' The helmsman steering the LST stared straight ahead. There was a fire burning on the forepart of the deck and the smoke was obscuring his view. 'Trifle starboard,' Younghusband called up to him. 'Wind will take it away then.'

'Starboard,' answered the British sailor. He looked backwards for a moment, over his shoulder. 'You going to be all right, sir?'

'He'll be fine,' answered the American doctor twisting a tourniquet around Younghusband's forearm.

Younghusband said: 'It doesn't need three, does it, doc?' He nodded at the hovering medics. 'It's not a bloody traffic accident.'

The doctor sent the other men back to the troop deck. Screams and cries were coming from there. Oily smoke palled across the vessel. Schorner wished to God that the daylight would come. He looked at his watch. Ten to three. Not yet. He looked down at Younghusband. The Englishman said: 'It's going to handicap my bowling something dreadful, colonel.'

A dulled explosion, like the striking of a deep gong, reverberated across the water. It seemed to start far down in the sea's cellar and then rose and broke the surface with a vast roar. Scarlett got to the bridge just as it sounded. He and Schorner looked across the fire-red horizon. The other LST was sinking at the base of a hideous pyre. On its deck the American railway engine stood out like an iron ghost. Orange, ruby, cherry-coloured, lights flared all around it. Clouds of dusty smoke rolled over the black Channel. The LST lurched as they watched and turned like a tired cow on to its side.

'Jesus Christ,' muttered Scarlett. 'I never thought I'd see a railroad train sink at sea.'

'How many casualties do we have?' asked Schorner, forcing his attention from the sight.

'I've checked the rear, the stern,' reported Scarlett. 'Eight dead, fourteen wounded, six very bad. Hulton's checking the front end. Here he is.' He suddenly saw Younghusband on the floor almost hidden by the doctor. 'Is he okay?' he asked.

As if to answer, the doctor helped the youthful Englishman to his feet. Propped against the rail of the bridge the lieutenant spoke conversationally to the steersman. The ship veered. Schorner saw men in the water. 'Stand by to pick up survivors,' said

Younghusband weakly into his loudhailer. He glanced at Schorner. 'We're not going anywhere,' he grinned tightly. 'There's no point in scarpering. They'll catch us anyway.' He gave an order and Schorner heard the engines change. The vessel was so slow, however, that there was little noticeable difference in their progress.

Hulton, sweating with terror, had reached the platform below the bridge. 'Are you all right, sir?' he squeaked at Schorner.

'Fine, just a slight headache,' answered Schorner. 'What's the casualty report, captain, that's what I want to know?'

'Front part of the ship, sir,' stammered Hulton. 'Fourteen dead and twenty-three wounded. That part got it first.' He looked around. 'We're slowing down,' he said in a hurt tone.

'We're picking up survivors from the other LST,' Scarlett answered him as the colonel clattered down from the bridge.

Hulton looked amazed. 'But, we're a sitting duck . . .' he said, but keeping his voice low towards Scarlett.

'The sailorman is not holding out on us. He says so too,' said Scarlett. 'And I guess he's right.' He thought Hulton was going to say something to Younghusband. 'Drop it,' he said tersely. 'He's driving with one hand.'

Bryant came to the platform below the bridge. Scarlett stared directly at him. 'It happened,' he muttered. 'Like I said.'

'Bloody rubbish,' answered Bryant brusquely.

Younghusband was giving orders to his crew. The LST had stopped and the nets were going over the side to men crying out in the water. 'Where's the destroyer?' demanded Hulton. 'Where's the goddamn escort, for Chrissake?'

'Here's the Jerry again,' said Younghusband. It was hardly more than a mention. The E-boat was slewing through the red haze. Another followed it, then a third. 'God in fucking heaven,' said the young naval officer. 'They're out to nail us this time.'

All three German vessels came abreast, searchlights rippling along the decks of the LST. Bryant rolled headlong across the steel plating and toppled over on to the lower deck. He almost collided with Schorner trying to scramble up. 'I'm going to the gun, sir,' he said.

'Do that, son. Get the bastards!' shouted Schorner. He gave what was almost a wild laugh. Then the whole vessel was swept once more with a vicious cannon- and machine-gun fire. On all fours Bryant scampered like a monkey to the gun platform at the rear. He could see the Bofors was firing, coughing shells at its tremendous rate towards the disappearing E-boats.

'Killer's been killed, sir,' said Gilman unaware of the wordplay. Watts was lying against the bulkhead, holding his stomach as if with an ache.

The gun stopped firing. 'We can't hit the swines,' complained Spence. 'Not at the speed they're shifting.'

Bryant bent down and looked at Watts. He was the first man to die under his command. Gilman looked at the dead soldier. His teeth began to chatter.

'I'd like to get those bleeders in my pub,' threatened Catermole with his own logic. Bryant looked back towards the bridge. He could see Schorner looking through field glasses. The fire in the forward part of the ship was still burning, giving an illuminated backcloth to everything aboard.

Younghusband was watching the men coming over the side from the water, being helped by his sailors and the American soldiers; rolling over the rail, oil and blood covered like wounded porpoises, lying on the deck, sobbing or silent. He looked up. 'Here he comes again,' he said quietly to Schorner. 'He'll probably get us this time.'

A single E-boat emerged through the draped smoke, speeding directly at them. The Bofors began to stutter again. One of the shells caught the stern of the German vessel and even above the din Younghusband heard the British crew cheer like madmen. But the attacker was unfaltering. It flipped like a seal and ran broadside on. The torpedo was released just before the moment of turn. The men on the bridge, Schorner now, Younghusband and Scarlett watched it come through the water. They were merely spectators; there was nothing to be done.

'The incompetent fool's going to duff it again,' muttered Younghusband wonderingly. 'He'll miss by twenty feet.'

Bryant had turned the gun on to the torpedo, the shells splitting the water. But the angle was again inadequate and the crew were left cursing and impotent.

Younghusband began to laugh weakly. 'Silly duffers, sir,' he said to Schorner. The bandages on his arm were soaked with blood. 'Two duds and now they're going to miss.'

Soldiers on the upper deck began to peer over the side at the torpedo. 'It's a miss!' called one voice. Others rose and cheered as the weapon sped towards the grey water behind the stern. The cheering was at its highest when the track turned and headed straight towards the hull.

'Homing,' muttered Younghusband. 'It's got a homing device. Rotten cheats.'

'Scatter!' bellowed Schorner through the loud-hailer. 'Down!'

The torpedo struck the LST ten feet from the stern. It exploded vividly, throwing a thick column of water, fire and metal up over the rail. The Bofors gun and its crew were blown backwards, Catermole and Spence being killed at once. Bryant was saved by an open steel door and Gilman was merely thrown sideways and down the ladder, landing on the men lying below. 'Pussy,' he called when he picked himself up. 'Pussy! Where are you?'

'Gee,' complained one of the huddling GIs. 'He's worried about his goddamn cat.'

Gilman reached the gun platform. The gun was hanging over the side like a dead stork. Acrid smoke hung in the air. A fire had started below. Bryant was leaning over Catermole. He turned and saw Gilman's aghast face. 'He's gone,' said Bryant. 'So's Spence.'

'Oh Christ almighty,' trembled Gilman. 'Not Pussy. Not him.'

Bryant caught his arm. 'Let's get forward,' he said. 'This thing's not going to be afloat for long.' Like a parent with a wet-eyed child he led Gilman away from the gun platform. Men were rushing away in a mass. There were shouts and orders, cries from wounded men, curses from others. Bryant saw men in panic jumping over the side of the ship.

Above the tumult, the shouts, the rush, the explosions and fiery smoke, he could hear Colonel Schorner calling orders over the loudhailer. Then another ear-cracking explosion rocked the LST on the port side. A second E-boat had come in through the smoke and fired another torpedo. Machine-gun and cannon fire sliced across the deck. Men spilled over on every side. Others screaming, some on fire, jumped over the side. A cliff of flame was enveloping the landing craft on the opposite side to Bryant. He and Gilman reached the bridge superstructure in time to see men, shouting, fighting, burned, bloody men, rushing from the hatches. Red smoke poured out with them.

Bryant, bawling to be let through, finally got to the bridge platform; Gilman was just behind him. He looked around for Scarlett and saw him lying on the platform below, half propped against the bulkhead. He saw Bryant and croaked at him. The British officer got to his side. 'I told you, Alan,' he said. 'I goddamn told you. It was my big mouth.'

'You're talking balls,' said Bryant fiercely. 'Where are you hurt?'

'Something's got me in the back,' muttered Scarlett. 'There's a hole you could crap through. One of the medics had just plugged it.'

Bryant heard Schorner shouting at him. He ran to the bridge leaving Gilman on the lower platform with the wounded American. Schorner was blackened, with blood all down his battledress. 'Are you hurt, sir?' asked Bryant.

'Very hurt,' returned Schorner. 'But not physically,

son. What a stinking disgrace. Look at those men.' He put the loudhailer to his lips and bawled through it again. The men he shouted to took only a brief look before scrambling for the side and jumping over. 'Half the poor bastards don't have their life vests fixed,' muttered Schorner. He turned to Younghusband. 'Lieutenant, how are we doing? How long before this thing sinks?'

Younghusband replied: 'I'll give her half an hour, if she gets no more torpedoes.' He was weak and shaking now. He heaved himself upright. 'Hear that?' he said suddenly. 'Listen. You can hear their engines. There must be a whole flotilla. They're either coming in for a last bite or they're pissing off. Sorry about the language.'

They all tried to hear over the shouts and rabble aboard the LST. Smoke was obscuring most of the vessel now, men running in and out of it like rushing ghosts. Younghusband listened again. They could hear the loud E-boat engines now, like motorcycles revving on a track. The sound increased and then, miraculously, moved away. 'They're going,' said Younghusband, wryly smiling. 'They're going home.'

'And we're sinking,' said Schorner. He turned and looked through the smoke towards the bow of the landing craft. There was less noise on board now, less shouting coming through the blackness. Voices came from the water instead. 'Can we get the gate down?' asked Schorner. 'The sea's pretty calm.'

'You want to get the ducks in the water,' guessed Younghusband. 'Not a bad idea.'

'Sure, and that amphibious tank,' said Schorner. 'Might as well use them as lifeboats.'

'We could try,' said the British officer. He sank down to the slanting plates of the deck. The dressings on the stump of his arm were dripping blood.

'Bryant,' said Schorner, 'get as many men together as you need and have them man the amphibians. Get the wounded, as many as you can, aboard them. As soon as the gate is lowered we'll get them into the sea. Okay?'

'Right, sir.' Bryant saluted and climbed down from the bridge. Gilman was still standing by Scarlett. 'How is it, Oscar?' asked Bryant. Scarlett nodded. The English officer looked around, trying to see through the confusion. 'Where's Captain Hulton?' he asked.

'Maybe he's gone to see his mother in Georgia,' suggested Scarlett. He laughed extravagantly and then coughed, bringing half a pint of blood cascading from his mouth. Bryant glanced at Gilman. 'Stay with him, Gilman,' he said. 'We're going to try and launch the ducks. He's got to be on one of them.'

'Yes, sir,' said Gilman. 'Have they gone, sir? The Jerries?'

'I think so,' said Bryant. 'I bloody well hope so.' He turned and went through the smoke. He could feel the craft rolling around with the currents and the wind. Men were lying all over the deck, many of them with the stillness of death on them. Among them he saw Hulton, lying with a suitably outraged expression, his eyes closed. There was blood all around his neck. Bryant went and touched him. He toppled to one side, his face remaining vexed. Bryant began to pick out soldiers who were still on their feet.

'Colonel Schorner is going to try and get the

amphibians launched,' he shouted. 'You men get to them and get the wounded aboard.' He suddenly saw Albie Primrose. 'Primrose,' he called. 'We've got to get these ducks launched. You drive one.'

'Right, sir,' said Albie quietly. He added: 'You seen Ballimach, sir? The big guy?'

'No,' replied Bryant. 'Come on, Primrose. This thing will be turning over.'

Albie moved to the nearest duck. He did so without hurry, as if he did not care greatly. 'Usually,' he muttered, looking through the smoke again, 'you can't miss Ballimach. You look and there he is.' He pushed back his helmet and putting his small hands to his mouth yelled: 'Ballimach! Where the hell are you?' Ballimach did not answer.

The gate of the LST began to move then, the bow opening like pincers, the ramp creaking down as it was intended to do when the vessel was close inshore. It was sinking now but without drama or hurry; the ship behaving better than the men. The list had evened out, the breach made by the second torpedo poetically balancing the first on the opposite side. Schorner was calling orders to the men from the bridge. There were fewer than a hundred left aboard now. The bows were fully open and the gate was almost down. 'Great,' he said over his shoulder to Younghusband trying to keep the vessel straight with the current. 'You've done a great job, sailor.'

'Thanks, sir,' said Younghusband. He was hanging against the rail, giving orders in almost a whisper to the helmsman. 'Perhaps you'll tell my mother.'

Schorner looked at him. 'We'll get you aboard the

first duck to get off, son,' he said. He could see the Englishman was losing blood heavily again.

'Don't worry yourself about that,' said Younghusband. 'I'll be all right here. I'll have to stay aboard for a while anyway.'

Schorner said: 'Stay aboard? Why?'

Younghusband tried a laugh. It did not work well. 'Captain and his ship, you know. That stuff.'

'This isn't a goddamn ship,' said Schorner savagely. 'This is a sardine can.'

'It's a ship to me,' argued the young officer mildly. 'There, we've got the gate down now. I should get your vehicles off as quickly as possible, sir.'

With another astonished look at the youth, Schorner turned and went down to the deck. The engines of the ducks were already revving, water wriggling through the gate ahead. Men were clearing away debris that would prevent them driving off. Now the E-boats had gone there was order once more. 'Okay,' Schorner shouted. 'Tell that tank to go.'

Bryant at the forepart of the ship, up to his knees in water, beckoned the tank on. It rumbled forward and dropped into the sea, wallowing, but then, a curious sight, paddling away as its marine screws took over the propulsion. The ducks followed, running down the ramp and into the water. Daybreak had begun to crack across the sky and in the first grey light came the strange sight of the vehicles driving from the stricken vessel as if from a garage.

Schorner was on the last duck. Bryant moved towards the rear of the emptying LST. Its great deck opened like a smoke-filled cave before him, a primitive place, dark and full of shadows and death. 'I'm going to get Scarlett, sir,' he said.

'He's aboard already,' said Schorner. 'And that English soldier of yours.' He looked backwards towards the wrecked superstructure. 'Go get that madman off the bridge,' he said. 'You talk to him. He won't listen to me. We'll wait – but hurry.'

Bryant climbed to the bridge platform once more. The smell of burned flesh was like roast beef. He saw Younghusband leaning, apparently nonchalantly, on the rail watching the smoking world. 'You've got to go,' he said briskly. 'Orders from Colonel Schorner.'

'Sorry, chum,' said Younghusband. 'I'm not going yet. Get that floating Cadillac off.'

'I'm ordering you to leave,' said Bryant briskly. 'Who do you think you are, the fucking boy on the burning deck? The wounded have been cleared as far as we know.'

'Some of my crew are below,' said Younghusband. 'Can't be moved.' He smiled. 'Listen, I'm not trying to get a medal. Now all that junk is off she'll probably float a while longer anyway. Christ, half the navy must be on its way now. We're only six miles off-shore. Surely somebody must know. The destroyer may come back from chasing the E-boats. They've got no chance of catching them. You go on. Save yourself for D-Day.'

Bryant realized he was adamant. 'You're mad,' he said. 'This thing is going to turn over at any minute.'

Younghusband grinned. 'If you think that, I should piss off fairly quickly, old son. Cheers.' He turned his back and went to the rear of the bridge section. He had his arm inside his tunic now and the front was wet and red. 'Bryant,' called Schorner hoarsely from below, 'get that officer down here.'

'He refuses, sir,' he called as he clambered down. 'He says he'll stay,' he said when he reached the amphibian. 'He doesn't seem to think it will sink. But he wants as little weight as possible. He says the sooner we get off the better.'

Schorner hesitated. Then he said to Albie, 'All right, Primrose, get this thing moving.' He covered his face with his hands. 'Crazy young bastard,' he said. 'If I was that age I'd want to live, like hell I would.'

Seagulls came with the daylight, cruising and crying as if distressed by the wreckage, human and material, that was spread across the flat, dawn waters of the Channel. They dropped and picked morsels from the surface. From the amphibian Colonel Schorner looked out on the sad and astonishing scene. The English coast seemed so near it looked touchable; they could see smoke rising from houses. And yet all about them were the bobbing reminders and remains of the night of death. The LST, as Younghusband had prophesied, remained floating a mile away, the port side of the nose down, starboard stern up, like a flotsam orange box.

On the far spread of the horizon, as a sun full of mocking promise rose into an innocent sky, were ships, many ships, apparently unconcerned that the enemy had penetrated them and made such a victory for himself. Schorner's heart was bitter. He looked out at the stoic vessels. 'Where were you when I needed you?' he muttered. He and Bryant crouched coldly on the deck of the vehicle. Scarlett had died an hour before, convinced to the last that the disaster was caused through his careless tongue. Bryant had argued all through his last minutes that it was not so, that many factors could have brought out the E-boats, the most likely being the observation of the fleet from an evening reconnaissance aircraft or the great increase in signal traffic which the Germans would have detected easily. Schorner asked Bryant what Scarlett had worried about. 'He had a mad idea that all this was his fault,' answered Bryant hopelessly. Then he realized what he had said. 'He was just wandering, delirious, sir. He died arguing about it.'

'Nice of him to take the blame,' muttered Schorner. 'Somebody has to.'

Among all the floating wreckage and the bodies of men who had died before they ever saw a German appeared one strange humped object, jolting gently on the petrol-coloured sea. Albie Primrose watched it idly, then with growing grief and realization. 'Sir,' he whispered to Schorner. 'Sir, that looks like Ballimach, sir. Those things are his cable drums.' The amphibian was making a little way, waiting with the others spread around over a square mile to be picked up. The large body of Ballimach, with its ridiculous twin drums on the back, came conveniently to the side as if the dead man had recognized his friends. 'It is,' trembled Albie. 'That's him all right. You couldn't miss Ballimach any place. Not even in the ocean.'

Schorner touched his arm. 'Take it easy, son,' he said. 'A lot of guys have lost their pals.'

'I guess there's no room to bring him aboard?' asked Albie, looking around and knowing that there wasn't. The craft was crammed with soldiers, weary, wounded, dying and dead. 'There isn't,' Bryant said softly to the American. 'Not for someone as big as that.'

Albie was still staring at the floating face-down figure. It looked like a man studying the seabed. The pants had ballooned clownishly. 'No, there never was a lot of room for Ballimach,' said Albie.

He put his arm over the side and caught the stray end of one of the field telephone cables. Thus he held on, towing the big dead man alongside the boat, carefully watching, steering like a boy with a big toy boat.

The cumbersome HMS *Oregon* had now moved alongside the amphibian in the distance. Schorner could see lines being thrown from the destroyer to the hulk. There was no movement on the askew deck. He wondered whether Younghusband had lived and thought again how much someone like that had to live for. Bodies still floated among the debris in the sea but there were no further signs of living men. The sun rose higher, beaming strongly, ironically and cruelly on the placid aftermath of disaster.

'Two other ships, sir,' said Bryant suddenly pointing landward. 'They're just coming out.'

'Maybe they had to finish breakfast,' commented Schorner sourly. The men in the duck watched, faces like stones, while the two vessels, small minesweepers, made their way across the limp water. One curved off towards the more distant amphibians, now drifting more than a mile away, and the second lost way two or three cables' distance from the amphibian. They were British ships. The clean crew hurried on to the rail and stood staring at the ravaged soldiers crouched in the odd boat.

Gradually the minesweeper manoeuvred alongside. Ropes were thrown to the amphibian and the two craft brushed. 'Wounded first,' ordered Schorner quietly to the men on his boat. 'Tell them, in case they don't know we've got wounded,' he said to Bryant. It was as though he delegated the task to him because he spoke the language.

'We've got a dozen wounded men,' shouted Bryant to the white-faced sailors above. 'They'll be coming off first, all right?'

'Right you are, soldier,' called a cheerful voice from the bridge of the minesweeper. Bryant felt Schorner look up sharply. It was the captain of the small vessel, another Royal Naval Reserve lieutenant. 'Bit early for fishing,' he called, to them.

'Tell that bum to clamp up,' muttered Schorner angrily.

Bryant felt his own anger rising also. 'Would you mind getting on with the job, lieutenant,' he called. 'We're not in the mood for jokes.'

'Bit touchy this morning, eh?' returned the officer indomitably. 'Soon get everything moving.'

'Why,' asked Schorner quietly in Bryant's ear, 'do the British cover everything – even a fuck-up like this – with a fusillade of funnies?'

'I wonder myself. The stiff upper lip's all right in its place, I suppose, but to hell with the red nose and squeaker.'

They began to raise the wounded to the deck of the minesweeper, dozens of hands reaching to help. The lieutenant wandered conversationally down to the rail as it was happening. He leaned down and Schorner and Bryant saw a face haggard far beyond its years. 'Bastards those E-boats,' he said. 'They got at us in March, you know, sir. Only just finished patching this thing up. Eight of my chaps killed. They're totting up quite a nice old score one way and another.'

After the wounded they passed up the body of Scarlett and three others who had died. Albie was still towing Ballimach. 'Could you help get my friend out of the water, please,' he called to the sailors on the deck. 'He's kinda heavy.'

They clambered across the amphibian and hauled the dead man with his idiotic cable drums from the sea. Albie turned away as they brought him out and stared towards the summery Devon hills.

Schorner was last on board. He climbed to the deck and wearily acknowledged the salute of the mine-sweeper's commander. 'Shankill, sir,' said the young lieutenant. 'Glad to have you aboard.'

'Not as glad as I am,' muttered Schorner. He leaned against the bulkhead.

'Tell your chaps to make themselves at home,' suggested Shankill amiably. 'We don't have a lot of room for passengers. The mess boys are getting tea. Or would you prefer coffee?'

'Anything,' said Schorner patiently. He jerked up, as did all the others, at the close sound of gunfire. Some of the soldiers dropped on to the deck 'It's all right, chaps,' Shankill called to them. 'It's only *Oregon*. She's putting the LST out of her misery.'

They watched as the old destroyer, backing away, having taken off the last bodies from the LST, fired three deliberate shells into the drunken hull of the landing craft. As though affronted the ugly vessel jumped on end and then turned over like a dead elephant and quickly sank. Bubbles and debris rose.

'Danger to navigation,' Shankill informed them before they asked. 'Might do all sorts of damage.'

Schorner thought he was speechless by now. But he looked broken and said to Bryant, 'I'm glad that destroyer managed to sink *something*.'

The American colonel and the British lieutenant went below for their coffee. The wounded were laid out on beds and mess tables, a naval surgeon moving among them with two assistants. Plasma bottles hung like gourds from the ceiling. The two officers walked into the wardroom. Silently they sat drinking the coffee. 'What a mess,' sighed Schorner eventually. 'I still can't believe it happened.'

'Nor me, sir,' said Bryant. 'Or how.' They felt the minesweeper begin to move.

'I'll be *one* who wants to know the answer to that,' promised Schorner. 'How?' He leaned back against the wall. His eyelids dropped. 'Scarlett,' he said, as if trying to remember someone from long ago. 'He didn't have to come. He just came for the ride.'

'He wanted to,' shrugged Bryant.

'Not one of them ever saw a real German,' sighed Schorner. 'They came all those thousands of miles, went through all that training, and then they die without seeing the enemy. It doesn't seem fair.'

Schorner did sleep then. He slumped against the wardroom wall. A naval steward came and eased him sideways, his head against a cushion. Bryant studied him and reflected again that he was a man at the point of middle age. The Englishman felt stiff and empty.

613

Getting up from the seat he went in through the mess-room where the wounded were stretched. One man was chanting softly to himself, '. . . a doll that other fellas cannot steal. Those flirty floody guys, with their flirty floody eyes . . .' Bryant staggered out into the beautiful day. On such days as this, he remembered as a boy running early to the beach to be there before anyone else, to see the new waves on the morning sand, to make the day's first footprints, to find flotsam by the shore. Christ, there should be a lot of flotsam after this. From the rail, standing among the dumb, defeated men, he looked back on the sea strewn with bobbing bodies and wreckage. Full of sadness he turned and faced towards the land. Devon looked like paradise, early misty, summer green the slopes, white the houses. He saw they were heading directly for Telcoombe.

They reached the harbour ten minutes later, sidling in among the small safe craft. Bryant looked up and saw that the quay was lined with faces, soldiers and sailors, and there were ambulances lined on the road.

The minesweeper docked at the foot of the same steps from which they had embarked only fifteen hours earlier. First the wounded were gently taken off, then the dead, then the men who had survived the night of tragedy and mistakes. As Albie Primrose began to climb the stone flight he began to weep. Gilman who had not spoken to him during the time in the amphibian or on the minesweeper, preferring to leave him alone, now moved ahead of the men in front and put his arm around the small American's shoulder. 'Come on, mate,' said Gilman kindly. 'Don't let them see you cry.'

Albie looked at him gratefully. His face was smeared like an urchin's. 'No,' he agreed. 'I can't do that.' They began to mount the steps together.

'Are you okay?' Albie sniffed quietly.

'Fine,' said Gilman. 'Pussy bought it, though. My pal, Catermole, you remember him.'

'Sure,' nodded Albie miserably. 'That's terrible. Lots of guys too.'

'It puts you off the invasion,' said Gilman oddly. Albie nodded. They had reached the top of the steps and came to the familiar view of Wilcoombe. Almost automatically Gilman looked across to the deserted gun-site. Standing there, at a stiff and seemingly permanently salute, like a fat khaki statue, was Sergeant Bullivant. Gilman turned away.

At the top of the steps on the quay were all the military personnel, fussing and shepherding. There was a lipsticked WAAC handing out coffee. With Albie, Gilman walked by, shaking his head. They abruptly found themselves on the familiar quay, behind a barrier but with, it seemed, all the population of Wilcoombe staring at their blackened, bloodied and defeated faces. PC Lethbridge, wearing his bicycle clips, kept a token arm out to prevent the watchers moving forward. Ambulances were moving. Gilman saw Mary Nicholas at once; she smiled at him as if they were at a dance. Then he saw tears on her white face. Howard and Beatrice Evans were moving among the wounded. As the American and the British soldiers reached the point where their own trucks were waiting to return them to camp, Albie looked up into the stark questioning eyes of the civilians. The unmasked questions were not difficult to imagine.

Had they tried the invasion? Had it been ignominiously repulsed? Was all lost?

'It's okay,' Albie sobbed loudly at them. 'We was just practising.'

Late in the afternoon General Georgeton drove down to Telcoombe Manor, to the US officers' mess. Colonel Schorner was in the main room, beneath the paintings of Mrs Mahon-Feavor's defeated ancestors, writing letters to the wives and mothers of the men of his unit who had died. He stood up when Georgeton came in and the general said: 'Sit down, Carl.' He nodded at the task. 'Doing the painful duty, eh.'

Schorner, his eyes black rimmed, nodded. 'I want to get it over with, sir,' he said. 'The hard thing is trying to say something that sounds convincing to a wife in Lincoln, Nebraska.'

Georgeton sat down heavily. A steward came over but after asking Schorner if he needed a drink he was sent away. 'Thank God it wasn't called Exercise Lulu after all,' he breathed.

'That's about all there is to thank God for,' commented Schorner. He looked up. 'How many?' he asked.

'Between six and seven hundred,' Georgeton told him.

'Oh, hell.'

'Everyone went bananas,' said Georgeton. 'From Ike downwards. There's a security clamp on the whole thing. Damage to morale and that kind of thing. The bodies washed up on the beaches are being blamed on a storm.'

616

'Some storm,' commented Schorner bitterly.

'The top brass were afraid that the BIGOTS might be picked up by the Germans,' continued the general. 'There were stories of the E-boats pulling men out of the water. Everyone was scared to hell that the whole works was going to be given away. They've had squads collecting name tags from bodies everywhere, along the beaches, in the morgues, even sending divers and frogmen down to the first LST. But I think they've checked them all now. No BIGOT is unaccounted for.'

'BIGOT,' muttered Schorner. 'I know a different meaning to that word, general. Not just their god-damn code. I'd like to know who let that foul-up happen? I lost half my men. They came to fight, not get drowned, picked off like that. Who was it?'

'Blame God if you like,' muttered Georgeton. He looked grey and fat and old. 'Or Roosevelt or Churchill or Eisenhower. Blame who you like, Carl.'

'I'd like to know,' returned Schorner. 'Maybe he'd like to write these letters.' Then he said, 'I'm sorry about Scarlett.'

'So am I. A good guy. He made sure he went. Said it was necessary for experience.'

'He had that all right, poor man.' He looked almost pleadingly at Georgeton. 'How,' he asked, 'can any-one who's supposed to be sane send a convoy of eight slow transports on a voyage to nowhere – back to where they started – and with two, crappy old war-ships, later reduced to one, to protect them? How many navy ships do we have for the invasion – three, four, five hundred?'

Georgeton sighed. 'I know, I know, Carl. They're

yelling the same questions at each other in Supreme Headquarters right now. There were warships operational, but they were spread out over such an area that your convoy got left short. There was also a mix-up in timed sailings because of fog at Plymouth. But in any case there's nothing any large ship can do against those E-boats. The Germans took them overland, by railroad, to Cherbourg, would you believe. They can still teach us a lot about war. We've got to have them eliminated by air attack or they'll cripple the invasion too. They could have done it last night.'

'I hope that sounds convincing to my boys,' said Schorner. 'Some of them don't want to fight any more, and I don't blame them. They're blind goddamn furious at the way they were left exposed like that.'

'The shipping situation is not good,' sighed Georgeton. 'Admiral King – sitting on his ass in Washington – is the dumb bastard who's screwing it up. You think *your* soldiers never heard of Europe before they got here, well here's an admiral who never heard of it either. It was only two weeks ago he released anything like the US naval forces we'll need for the invasion. Half of them haven't even gotten here yet. And when you realize at the last count there were available more than *thirty thousand* landing craft of various types, all over the world – thirty thousand – and we're going to have to mount the invasion of Europe with less than ten per cent of that total. Some have been sent to the Pacific from the *Mediterranean*, goddamn it.'

He paused and glanced at Schorner as though he hoped he was convincing him. 'If the Germans had carried on with their work last night,' he confided, 'instead of high-tailing it out. If they'd sunk all eight of the LSTs in that convoy, which they could have done with ease, Carl, I doubt very much if the invasion would have been able to go ahead. The transport situation is that tight. Everything is tight.'

Schorner was regarding him steadily, almost sorry for him. 'And we think we're going to win,' he sighed at last.

'That seems to be the idea that's being put around,' said Georgeton. 'But we've got to do better than we did last night.'

'I'll go along with that,' sighed Schorner miserably. 'We'll never get a single GI above the high water mark otherwise.'

Georgeton sat hunched and heavy. He looked down at the letters on the low table before Schorner. They made him remember, and he reached to his tunic pocket. 'I had a letter,' he said. 'From the old guy, Major-General Hickson. Remember we went to his home?'

'Sure,' said Schorner. 'The night after his son died, and we didn't know.'

'Right. He wrote me, wishing us well and that sort of thing, from himself and his wife. And he enclosed a letter for you.' The general handed over the envelope. 'It's a little curious,' he added. 'See it says it must not be opened until the eve of the invasion.'

Schorner smiled a trifle. 'Just like Christmas,' he said. He put the envelope away. 'I'll need something to read just then. As long as it's not the old guy's plan of battle.'

'There's a debriefing tonight,' said Georgeton.

'After Exercise Lion. At Exeter. I'll send a car for you.'

'Right, sir,' agreed Schorner. 'My driver is pooped. And he lost his buddy. I'll be there.'

Georgeton felt in his briefcase. 'I have a casualty manifest,' he said reluctantly. He handed it to Schorner. 'You'll probably want to see it.'

Wearily Schorner took the typed pages. His eye went down the lists, his own unit first. He turned over. 'The Grave Registration unit is no more,' he said.

'Strange isn't it,' agreed Georgeton. 'And the British lost a lot of sailors.'

'Including Lieutenant Clive Younghusband, RNVR,' said Schorner sadly reading the name. He put the list on the table.

Georgeton rose to go. 'Everything's going to be okay, Carl,' he said quietly. 'It's got to be.'

Schorner stood up tiredly. 'Maybe I could put that in the letters,' he said.

June

The long, clear and serene days of May changed with June to low and rainy weather. Over the Atlantic the meteorologists saw a trough advancing on Europe. The generals in England looked at the collecting skies and wondered if they had missed the chance. Only two early June days were left when the tides and the moon would be right.

At Wilcoombe, the cool summer rain wandered from the sea, in a way thoroughly familiar to the Devon people, but causing affront with the Americans. Bryant moodily drove along soaking lanes to the camp at Telcoombe Magna on 2 June and found Schorner squatted in his hutted office. He smiled, however, when he saw Bryant and they shook hands. It was the first time they had met since the night of the E-boats.

'So you've volunteered for glory, I hear,' mentioned Schorner.

The British lieutenant pulled a face. 'I don't know about glory. After the other night I shall do my best to keep my head very close to the ground, sir.'

'We'll be glad to have you, Bryant,' continued the American. 'It's the best news I had all week.'

'Thank you, sir. It was a choice . . .' continued Bryant. He was staring at a map on the desk. Embarrassed he took his eyes from it. 'It was a choice,' he repeated. 'Between glory, as you call it, and Ross and Cromarty.'

Colonel Schorner was puzzled. 'That sounds like a department store,' he suggested.

'If it were I might have considered it,' laughed Bryant. 'It's way up in the north-west of Scotland. Very wild. It's not that I mind, I'd probably enjoy it. But Captain Westerman, well . . .'

Schorner understood. 'Ah, I got you. Your former CO. He's gone there?'

'Right, sir. I couldn't see us spending the rest of the war together, like a couple of old biddies, so I volunteered to continue the liaison job. Once your chaps link up with the British force there'll be plenty for me to do. And my French isn't too bad.'

'Great.' Schorner picked up the map from the desk. 'You might as well see where we're headed,' he said. 'Recognize that?'

Bryant studied the map, a long straight beach, wide bay, a road also, immediately along the shore and, within the road, the amoebic shapes of lakes.

'If I didn't know differently, sir, I'd say it was Telcoombe Beach. Apart from the outcrops of rock, just offshore, and the disposition of these houses, which are different to Wilcoombe, it looks the same.'

'Utah Beach,' said Schorner. 'Our landing beach.'

'That's why this area was picked,' realized Bryant. 'It looks the same.'

'It was. It was difficult not being able to explain to all those folks who wanted to know why we didn't go some other place,' nodded Schorner. 'It's almost identical, even to the lakes, for which, incidentally, the Germans are responsible. They're artificially flooded areas. But the beach, even to its camber, the road, the rising land just inland, the general compass directions, just about north to south in both cases, and even the sea currents, are very approximate.'

Bryant said: 'Where is Utah Beach, sir? Is that still secret?'

'Until tomorrow,' said Schorner. 'There'll be a briefing then. Anyway, I'm glad you're going to be along, son. My French is worse than my English.'

In a strange way the great army now withdrew within itself. Movement, anyway, was strictly limited by security, but the hundreds of thousands of soldiers, mainly American, British and Canadian, in their camps throughout the south voluntarily stayed within their rain-soaked tents and waited. Soldiers plodded in mile-long queues through the dripping lines, standing in mud, eyeing at the dark June skies, waiting to be served with food. They talked in the rain-hung tents, played cards and dice, wrote their letters home; if they felt like it they prayed in private or in services held along the length of the military region by padres and rabbis. It would not be long now.

On the evening of 3 June, Schorner trudged through the cloying mud of his own camp, the first hamlet of what had become over the months a vast army city; a land of guns and men, of piled supplies, of waiting vehicles. Off-shore and in the many harbours, the ships of the invasion force fretted in the uncomfortable sea. There was no sign of the weather abating. Another day gone. Only two remained.

After the night of the sea action there had been

many replacements in Schorner's engineering unit. The tents and huts were full of strange, young, questioning faces. Nobody went out. They stayed and occupied themselves, checking over their weapons equipment minutely many times. Sometimes the tension provoked a quarrel among the enclosed men, but not often. There was more singing than shouting.

The colonel was grateful to find Albie in charge of one situation at least. In the small soldier's hut there had been an outbreak of minor dysentery, particularly among the replacement troops, but Schorner found that Albie had organized activities adapted to their needs. Four men played cards in a sheltered outside area while astride chemical toilets, and several others wrote letters seated on the same devices. Albie, who had been promoted to corporal and now walked with a strangely pushed-out arm so that no one would miss the stripes, introduced the commanding officer to the new men. Colonel Schorner shook hands all round, advising the men on the latrines not to bother to rise, and then went back into the hut and towards the hut door with a mixture of remorse and hope in his heart. At the door Albie threw up a rigid salute, as befitting his stripes, in seeing the colonel away. 'Keep going, Albie,' sighed Schorner, standing in the rain at the door.

'Sure, sir,' said Albie. They were like old campaigners now. 'And you, sir. Just keep going.'

The little soldier returned into the hut. He went to the annexe, to the men in their strange sitting places. '*Now*, they crap,' he muttered to himself.

Schorner's walk through the rain was desultory. He felt the drizzle thickening and tugged up the collar of his combat jacket. He stood undecided in the vehicle park and then, after the hesitation, he climbed in his jeep and drove towards Wilcoombe.

Over the Channel was a grey evening light, winter in summer. It would not be dark before ten but there was nothing of June in the prospect that spread as he drove along the coastal road. The sea was morose and heavy, bullying the shoreline, rocking the fleet of dark ships set out in the bay. Clouds scurried like raiders from the west, fat, full of rain and wind. The vivid green land, the fields and the trees lining the inland lanes were thick and dolefully dripping. Water gurgled in the desolate streets of the abandoned villages. The rats sheltered in the houses. Now there would be no more shelling, no more tanks, no more soldiers. It was too late for all that now. Soon, in a season, the land would have almost recovered from their depredations, the ground would be turned, the crops would grow and be harvested, animals would be in the meadows again and people in the houses and farms. He wondered where he would be.

All along the shore, the concrete hards were lined with war vehicles; tanks awaiting loading, trucks and strange machines; bulldozers and cranes; jeeps nose to rear like flocks of dun sheep. Soldiers moved among them, slow, wet, hunched soldiers. Schorner shook his head. At the military police barrier the sentry approached, his helmet shining wet, his oilskins like dead leaves. 'Hope the sun shines for the big game, sir,' said the man.

'So do I, son,' said Schorner. 'I'd hate it to be spoiled now.'

He drove along the smeared evening road towards Wilcoombe. There it was, cluttered on its ancient hill, its feet in the sullen sea. He realized what a familiarity and affection he had for this foreign place. He was uncertain what he was going to do now. Only with the feeling that there were those he needed to see.

He drove first to the harbour front, mist and rain mixing, cobbles wet, the sea banging dumbly against the unyielding walls. He pulled up outside the Evans' house and saw the curtain flick as he stopped the jeep's engine. Beatrice was at the door before he had walked the length of the garden path. Howard stood just behind her, smiling in his serious way over her shoulder.

'You should have been here in March,' Beatrice called, attempting lightness. 'The weather was beautiful.'

'I was,' he reminded them as they let him in. The house was so familiar now, the low ceiling, the home-feeling of it. He automatically turned into the sitting-room. Beatrice had put a vase of early summer flowers in the vacant fireplace. Howard asked him if he was cold but he said not. 'I find this place really warm,' he said as he sat down.

'You arrived in time to drain the last bottle of sherry,' said Howard, walking into the kitchen. 'I was just going to get it.'

'I thought that was for victory,' suggested Schorner.

'We'll drink it now. No time like the present.' He came back with the glasses. They raised them silently and with sadness.

Eventually it was Beatrice who framed the words. 'God go with you, Carl. And with your men.'

Schorner stared down into the sherry to hide his embarrassment. 'Thanks,' he said. 'I've known real friendship from you both.' He laughed grittily. 'I was a stranger in a strange land,' he said. 'And looking out at that weather I realize I still don't know anything about it. I mean, is this June or is it June?'

'It will clear tomorrow,' forecast Evans. 'Wilcoombe play Totting in the afternoon. They always have that match on a Sunday and it's always fine.'

'Cricket?' asked Schorner.

Howard looked abashed. 'Yes, cricket,' he said.

'Maybe I'll come over and watch,' said Schorner. 'I've got to find out about this game sometime.'

'I won't be playing,' said Howard. 'Not just now.' He went to the window and looked out on the stormy Channel.

It was Beatrice who said: 'It's going to be quite soon, isn't it, Carl?'

The American shrugged good-humouredly. 'Any time in the next six months,' he answered. 'Nobody seems to be able to get a free afternoon. I hope it's soon. My boys are going to start fighting among themselves before too long.'

He rose. His face composed, he said: 'I just called by to say thanks for everything – being so civilized to a foreigner.' They were speechless. They stood shaking their heads and then they both embraced him together. Beatrice had to turn away and go into the kitchen where she said something was boiling over. Schorner went out soon after. Out into the rain.

After he had gone Howard stood staring out of the window for a long time. 'He makes me feel like half a man,' he grunted eventually. 'I feel ashamed to be here, staying safe, when he is going like this.'

'You'd be a liability,' she said with careful cheer-

627

fulness. 'With your poor old lungs you'd be carried off before they'd even landed.' She put her arms about his shoulders and they stood like that, facing the miserable sea, for several minutes.

Schorner had just driven the jeep to the point where the hill began to rise into Wilcoombe when an old, pristine Rolls-Royce drew up on the other side of the street and he saw Mrs Mahon-Feavor waving violently from the rear seat. He stopped and was about to leave the jeep when the old lady's spectral chauffeur left his seat and opened the rear door so that Mrs Mahon-Feavor could get out. She motioned Schorner back towards the jeep and then climbed rheumatically into his back seat. 'Rest, colonel,' she advised. 'Have plenty of rest. You'll probably find you will need it at some time.'

He grinned at her affectionately. 'Now, listen,' she said. 'I wanted to ask you if I could take my armchair down to the beach. I'd like to see the boats go off.' She looked directly into his amused but ambivalent face. Her large eye winked with theatrical exaggeration. '*You* know what I mean,' she said. Not needing a response, she went on. 'I used to like to go and sit on the beach in the summer but I find those silly striped deckchairs intolerable. So I get that old fool driving the car over there, I get him to bring down an armchair to the sands. Now, I don't suppose there is a spot left where I can sit?'

He knew it was a question. 'Mrs Mahon-Feavor,' he said, 'as you know the whole length of Telcoombe Beach is a restricted area . . .' Her face continued grave. 'But . . . there is a short stretch, about thirty yards, of shingle, I guess, just to the east of the harbour down there, almost under the wall, which has never been wired off and is clear of dangerous obstacles.' A smile was already cracking the old lady's face powder.

'Yes, colonel,' she encouraged. 'Do go on . . .'

'If you took your chair down there and restricted yourself to that little piece, I don't think anybody is going to bother you. I'll tell the military police you're not a spy.'

'Oh, thank you,' she said sincerely. 'I want to see the boats go off and to wish them God's speed, you know. When exactly will that be, colonel? I won't tell anyone, honestly.'

Schorner grinned at her again. 'You'll only want to sit there when the weather is fine, won't you,' he said. 'There's no point in sitting out in the rain.'

'Ah, no indeed,' she agreed sagely. 'Thank you, thank you enormously.' Her expression calmed. Her gloved hand touched him on the shoulder. 'I want to tell you how very sorry I was about the men you lost,' she said. It was the first time he had ever heard her say anything in other than a forthright voice.

'Yes, thank you.'

She pursed her wrinkled lips. 'Sounds the sort of idiocy that my family might have perpetrated. Whose fault was it?' The tone was of one who had always demanded to be told and invariably was.

'I think it was the Germans',' said Schorner serious-faced.

'Ah, I see. Yes, they would.' She began to clamber from the back of the jeep. 'Good luck, colonel,' she said briskly. 'Our prayers will go with you.' She suddenly leaned and kissed him on the cheek. He sat transfixed, the smell of violets wafting about him while she stumped across the road back to her car. 'Come on, you old dolt,' she bawled to the chauffeur. 'Let's get a move on.' She waved royally as she drove away and Schorner waved back.

He had not intended to go into the Bull and Mouth but as he was driving up the hill he saw the creaking sign and it recalled the first night, New Year's Eve, when he had gone in there. He stopped the jeep and walked through the door, pushing his path through the old thick curtain, now hanging in holes and threads. The bar had only half a dozen drinkers. Tom Barrington was one. Gilman, sitting moodily on the far side, a pint between his elbows, was another.

'Colonel Schorner,' said Barrington. 'Can I buy you a drink?'

'It needs to be a small one, thanks,' said Schorner. 'This is getting like Christmas.'

'People saying good-bye,' suggested Barrington. He smiled. 'You can't answer that, I know.'

Schorner said he would have a beer although he was not sure how it would mix with sherry. He vaguely recognized Gilman. 'You were on the gun, on the LST, one of Lieutenant Bryant's boys,' he said.

'That's right, sir,' said Gilman, standing up.

'Take it easy,' said Schorner. Barrington told the landlord to put another pint in front of Gilman and the soldier thanked him.

Horace Smith, sitting in mid-bar, watched the beer go along the counter under his eyes. ''Evening, colonel, sir,' he said. Schorner wished him good evening. Horace knew a poacher could never expect a drink from a farmer, even if they were in the same Home Guard unit. 'When they started the Home Guard 'ere,' he said conversationally to Gilman on his other side, eight feet away, so he spoke loudly, 'they only had one bloke as was a stretcher bearer. *One* stretcher bearer. T'was a good job they Jerries never came, oi'll tell you . . .'

Privately Barrington said to Schorner, 'I was wrong, and I'm sorry.' His face was rueful. 'I think that's the first apology I've ever made in my life,' he said.

'I know how you felt,' acknowledged Schorner. 'As a farmer I would have felt the same.' He lifted his glass and Barrington did also. 'Soon it will be all yours again,' he said. 'They'll start clearing the area as soon as we've moved out. That daughter of yours will be herding those nice Devons across the meadow again.'

Barrington laughed shortly. 'I doubt it,' he said. 'She went off to join the ATS and now she's engaged to one of your Air Force chaps in Norfolk. Nice lad he seems. It might last, it might not.'

'You never can tell,' nodded Schorner. Gilman got up to leave. 'Excuse me,' said the American to the farmer. He turned to the British soldier. 'You okay now, son?'

Gilman was surprised. 'Yes, sir, thanks. I wasn't hurt. It was just my pal. He was killed.'

'Right,' said Schorner. 'I'm glad you came out of it all right.' He looked thoughtful. 'Lieutenant Bryant,' he said, 'do you get along with him?'

Gilman looked puzzled. 'Yes, sir. He's a very good officer.'

'He's staying with us, on attachment. I guess he's going to need a driver.'

Gilman looked nothing less than shocked. 'Oh, sir. I see. Well I'm being sent on a course, sir. Next week. I've already been posted, sir.' He threw up a quick and unnecessary salute and made for the door.

Schorner laughed. 'I don't blame you, soldier,' he said. 'I wish to God they'd send me on a course.' Gilman went out hurriedly.

Schorner glanced back to see Barrington regarding him solidly. Horace Smith said: 'Be you wanting any rabbits, colonel? How be you off for hares?'

Schorner politely refused the offer. He said to Barrington, 'I hear you have a big cricket match tomorrow?'

Barrington shook his head. 'No cricket match in these parts is ever big. If this weather continues the ground will be soaked anyway. I suppose we could get the vicar to pray.'

'How does the reverend feel about you playing on a Sunday?' asked Schorner. 'Does he think it will bring the wrath of God down?'

'He's umpiring,' shrugged Barrington. 'I don't think he's worrying about God so much these days. He's joining the RAF, you know. Volunteered. Not even as a padre. Just an ordinary aircraftman. He ought to be trained in time for the next war.' With only a quick pause, he said: 'I couldn't believe my eyes when I saw you and your men coming ashore at the quay that morning. Somehow war had never seemed so terrible to me before. You've taught a lot of people a lesson in these parts, me not the least. I'm proud to have known you.'

632

Once more Schorner went out into the dusky rain. He was climbing into the jeep when he saw Doey Bidgood and Lenny Birch sauntering downhill towards the inn, string around their trousers at the knees, hands in pockets, ragged faces wide with smiles. 'Best o' luck, zur,' said Doey. He took on much the same confiding expression as Mrs Mahon-Feavor had assumed, as if the secret was held by only them. 'Over there, I mean,' said Doey, nodding his head towards the growling Channel.

'Thanks, boys,' replied Schorner. He had often wondered how old this pair were. Lenny touched the jeep. 'Do you reckon that these jeeps will be sold off to anybody once the war is over, loike?' he asked. 'Oi wouldn't mind 'aving one o' they myself.'

'I'll save this one for you,' said Schorner with a laugh. They joined in unsurely. He started the engine and drove up the hill.

''Ee be a real gentleman,' decided Doey. 'Makes you feel you wouldn't even mind being in the army with an officer like 'ee.'

They went into the inn and were gone from view by the time Schorner slowed the jeep at the summit of the rise. He turned it in by the mouldy barn and left it there. Then he walked around to Dorothy's door and knocked. She answered at once. Her face lightened when she saw him. 'Thank God you've come, Carl,' she whispered. 'I was so afraid you'd go without saying good-bye.'

She opened the door and he stepped into the small hallway and then into the room where they had sat before the fire that night. Dorothy turned and rushed against him, holding her arms about his body, hugging and crying at the same time. He lifted her wet face and kissed her on both cheeks. Then they kissed closely. 'I'm sorry, Carl,' she stumbled, needing to say it quickly. 'How could I ever blame you for Billy Steer? As though you could help it.'

'We're all contributing,' he shrugged. 'It was the most terrible thing I can ever remember.'

'Please sit down,' she said, still flustered. 'I'll get some tea, or would you like a drink? I've got some wine.' Schorner sat in the fireside chair. The room was chill. A strange sense of formality had come between them.

'No, Dorothy,' he said. 'I won't have anything. I need to get back.' Aware of the awkwardness, she sat in the opposite chair, hands in her lap.

'You won't be coming back to this country I suppose,' she said.

'I don't know about that. Once things get going, once we've pushed on a little, I'll probably need to come back for briefings or conferences. They'll always think up excuses for them.'

'But that would be in London.'

'Yes, I figure it would be London.'

He put his fingers into his breast pocket and took out a military envelope. 'I wrote you a poem,' he smiled. 'It's not Robert Frost or even Helen Holland, but I wrote it for you. Read it sometime when you have a moment.'

Her hand trembled as she took it. Schorner rose and said: 'I've got to get back, Dorothy.'

She was trying not to cry. She went to the door with him and they kissed gently for the last time, hardly brushing each other with their bodies, their hands just touching arms. 'Remember me to the kids,' he said when he was outside the door. 'And take care.'

He turned quickly and walked up the few yards of hill before turning the corner. She did not watch him go but closed the door slowly and with sadness. Taking the envelope she sat down by the cheerless fireplace and stared at the chair he had just vacated. Suddenly with a cry that filled the small house she stood and ran to the door. She looked down the hill and saw the jeep was almost at the harbour, its brake lights bright red in the grey rain. It was too late. Everything was. She returned to the house.

Stiffly she went back to the chair. She felt frail and cold, like an old woman. Sitting there she opened the army envelope and, tears dropping on the paper, she read the poem he had composed. It was called 'For Dorothy'.

Sometimes I will think about this town
Of seagulls,
Singing in its streets.
The doorstep sea, the shingle sound.

When the war is done and gone,
When the dust of battle and of men,
Is stilled,
And we that are left, if we are left,
Have left for home.

Then, in my inland place,
I will taste again the salt,
See a star above a wave,
And listen to the narrow wind about your house.

Damp June evenings made for cold houses. People did not light summer fires and after two or three days of Devon rain the interiors of their rooms became comfortless. Mary Nicholas was sitting eating bread and jam reading the *Daily Mirror* at her table, with the two small children bickering unheeded on the floor. There was a double knock at the street door. She looked up and then to the late clock.

She went down the passage and opened it. Private First Class Wall was standing in the drizzle, a stretched expression on his face. 'What do you want?' she asked brusquely.

'I got to talk to you,' he said. 'Just for a couple of minutes.'

After hesitating, she opened the door and allowed him into the narrow hall. 'Here,' she said. 'This will do, won't it. The children are making a noise in there.'

'Okay,' he said. Rain and sweat smeared his face. He looked as if he had been running. 'I came to tell you that I'm going to the British police,' he said. 'I'm going to tell them I pushed her in the harbour.'

She laughed outright, but quickly stifled it. 'Why do that? You didn't push her anyway, she slipped. I'm a witness.'

'Right, lady. You stay a witness. If the police ask you, say you *saw* me do it. Say we were together down there like it was, and she came along and saw us and started making trouble. Tell them about what happened. Except you say I pushed her.'

The woman's face creased, then cleared with realization. 'I understand,' she said. 'You're no hero are you. You prefer a safe police station cell to being shot at by the Germans.'

Wall's face was a white disc in the dark passage. 'I ain't going,' he said. 'Jesus, on that goddamn landing ship . . . That was plenty. I'm not going through that again, for Uncle fucking Sam or anybody. I'm going to give myself up – tell them I pushed her in and let them take it from there. Anything's better than that shit beach over there. I'll tell them you're a witness.'

She smiled grimly. 'So, you save your skin, then when it comes to court you change the story and say it was an accident after all. You were just confused.'

'That's about the width of it,' he answered. 'Stay with it, okay?'

Mary Nicholas said laconically: 'The things I do for the Yanks.'

'Yes, sure you do. What about Hulton, Captain Hulton? I heard about him, too.'

'He's dead,' she said. 'At least he didn't run away.'

'Call it what you like, honey. I just want to stay alive. I've got a lot of reasons for living.'

She pushed him towards the door. 'Tell them to the police.'

On Sunday morning the rain eased across the West Country, although the sky was cold and scudding and the sea lumpy. At noon Schorner, in battledress, was sitting in his hut watching the telephone, waiting, like so many others, for the order. On the desk, across the blotter, lay his sub-machine gun and his field glasses. He had written his soldiers' letters and now there was nothing to do but wait. For the twentieth time he went through the orders, maps and documents in his case.

He knew they were complete but it occupied the time. In the camp the men – their equipment piled around them – were still playing cards and dice under the drying tents.

At that moment Schorner remembered the letter that General Georgeton had passed to him; the envelope from the old English officer, Hickson, with the caution that it was not to be opened until the eve of the invasion. He took it from the map case where he had put it among his personal effects. If anything was the eve, this was it. He opened it carefully. It contained a short letter and another, smaller envelope. The letter was dated 1 May 1944. It read:

Dear Colonel Schorner,

My wife and I were talking last evening about the course of the war and of your forthright campaign. We wished to make some gesture which we felt might encourage and assist you and we decided it would be appropriate to ask you to accept the enclosed medal ribbon. It is the ribbon of the Military Cross awarded posthumously to our son, William, who won it in Burma. We hope you will carry it with you as you go, and that it may remind you, from time to time, that you carry our hopes, our prayers and the honourable tradition of all men who have fought for freedom and right.

> Yours sincerely,
> Henry Hickson
> Maj.-Gen. (Retd)

Schorner choked with emotion. His fingers clumsily opened the small envelope and he drew out the silver ribbon with the single blue stripe. He held it in the palm of his hand and closed the hand over it. The telephone jangled. He picked it up, listened, and replied: 'Yes, sir. We're all ready.' It was time to go.

All along the grey southern coasts of Britain that day, from Falmouth in the far west to the Thames, troops began moving from their camps and heading for the transports and landing ships in the ports. The assault forces first, the British from Kent and Hampshire, the Canadians from Sussex, the Americans from Dorset, Devon and Cornwall. Tanks and trucks and guns were already loaded in the holds of the LSTs. Now the men filed aboard and took their stations. The sea remained heavy. Seasickness pills were handed out like small gifts as the soldiers went aboard the craft, together with packets marked: 'Bags; Vomit'.

In Devon, trucks carrying Americans moved along dripping lanes towards the small ports in sheltered estuaries. Schorner's unit began moving out in the early afternoon. By three o'clock the Telcoombe Magna camp was emptied. Colonel Schorner returned there in his jeep once the column was on the road, awaiting loading at Wilcoombe. Albie Primrose drove him back and Schorner left him in the vehicle while he went alone along the vacant lines of tents and huts. The dull June wind blew among the buildings and made the khaki tents shudder, like the wind that had riddled the deserted villages.

On the far side of the camp he halted, staring at a line of trash pits which had been filled over. The red earth lay on them like freshly dug graves. He turned quickly and walked back towards the jeep. Albie watched him affectionately. As the colonel walked he saw the wing of a tent half hidden among the lines, and walked along the row for a clearer view. Across the canvas was painted: 'Good-bye Doris, Good-bye Phyllis, Good-bye Jane'.

'Right, Albie, let's get going,' sighed Schorner, returning to the jeep. 'Let's get the show on the road, as they say.' Albie grinned and turned the jeep for the last time out of the field and into the lane.

They had to take the northern route to Wilcoombe because of the pre-arranged traffic pattern. The roads were full of troop-carriers but they overtook the slow trucks and were soon approaching the town from the top of the hill. The slope was jammed with vehicles. Albie said: 'Lieutenant Bryant is just here, sir.' The English officer was standing in his stationary jeep peering over a farm gate and into a field. As they edged nearer he turned, saw it was Schorner and pointed wryly at what was happening in the field. It was the cricket match. Wilcoombe were batting, the opposing players, in whites, in their fielding positions, the bowler making his run to the wicket. Schorner saw that Barrington was one of the two batsmen. He played the ball towards a fielder who picked it up, then stood and Barrington stared towards Schorner who now stood also taking in the pastoral scene. The Reverend Sissons, who was an umpire, white-coated and wearing a straw hat, also turned and saw the American officer.

Barrington waved his bat in farewell and Sissons waved his hat. Schorner waved back. 'God be with you!' called Sissons. The cricket players stood staring.

Bryant walked back and said, 'You wouldn't have liked the game, sir.'

'I don't know,' grinned Schorner. 'It has a certain air of peace about it.' He nodded towards the port. 'Everything going okay with the embarkation?'

'It seems so,' said Bryant. He grimaced. 'The old lady, Mrs Mahon-Feavor, is sitting on a chair on the shingle. All fur-coated. She's waving to the craft going out.'

The colonel laughed and sat down again as the jeep began to drive forward through the military traffic. Bryant returned to his vehicle and it moved ahead also. From the top of the hill the harbour came into view; dark lines of soldiers moving aboard the waiting craft. Out in Start Bay was spread a fleet of grey ships. A formation of bombers sounded overhead. Schorner took a deep breath as he watched. This was it. For many miles, in many harbours, the scene would be the same. Men and weapons moving forward, hearts sounding, eyes hard; going on the final adventure of the war. The Magic Army was moving to battle.

Author's Note

Although *The Magic Army* is a work of fiction, the main events therein – the evacuation of a large area of South Devon for use as a US Army battle-training region, and the sinking by E-boats of ships in the American troop convoy off Portland Bill – are widely based on fact. The characters in this novel are, however, fictional and are not based on real people, now living, or who were living at the time.

I would like to acknowledge the help given to me in researching these episodes by the staff of the National Archives and Records Service, Washington, DC; the Public Record Office, Kew, London; the Editor and Publisher of *The Kingsbridge Gazette*, Kingsbridge, Devon; and many individuals both in Britain and in the United States.

Grateful acknowledgement is also made to: Jonathan Cape Ltd for permission to quote from 'Ghost House', from *The Poetry of Robert Frost* edited by Edward Connery Latham; Faber and Faber Ltd for permission to quote from 'O What is that Sound', from *Collected Poems* by W. H. Auden; Southern Music Publishing Co. Ltd, 8 Denmark St, London WC2H 8LT for permission to quote from 'Deep In The Heart of Texas' by Don Swander and June Hershey; Chappell Music Ltd for permission to quote from

'Blues In The Night', music by Harold Arlen, words by Johnny Mercer, © 1941 Harms Inc. (Warner Bros), British Publishers Chappell Music Ltd.

I would also like to acknowledge the following books:

The Land That Changed Its Face by Grace Bradbeer
The Struggle for Europe by Chester Wilmot
The Longest Day by Cornelius Ryan
The GIs by Norman Longmate
How We Lived Then by Norman Longmate
The People's War by Angus Calder
US Army Handbook 1939–45 by George Forty.

Leslie Thomas
Somerton, Somerset
June 1981

Available now in Arrow Books,
Leslie Thomas's acclaimed novel

WAITING FOR THE DAY

Midwinter, 1943. Britain is gripped by intense cold and in the darkest days of the war. It is six months before D-Day and the battle to liberate Nazi-occupied Europe.

RAF officer Paget is heading home for Christmas, back to the resurrection of a passion he thought was long over.

In a freezing hut on Salisbury Plain, Sergeant Harris is training his troops for landing on the shores of Normandy, but his mind is occupied with thoughts of just how his young wife is coping with his absence.

Lieutenant Miller has arrived at an all-but-derelict mansion in Somerset where his American division has set up its headquarters. His affair with an English-woman is both bittersweet and potentially dangerous.

Cook Sergeant Fred Weber is enjoying fishing off the coast of occupied Jersey. His calm is soon to be shattered as his war takes on a violent twist.

Each man is heading inexorably towards the beaches of France, where the great battle will commence...

'Warm characters, immaculate period detail and dialogue that neatly evokes the wartime sense of humour as part of a story that packs a surprising emotional punch' *Daily Mail*

Buy *Leslie Thomas*

Order further *Leslie Thomas* titles from your local bookshop, or have them delivered direct to your door by Bookpost

☐ Waiting for the Day   0 09 945719 9   £6.99
☐ Dangerous Davies:
    The Last Detective   0 09 943617 5   £5.99
☐ Dangerous in Love   0 09 947423 9   £6.99
☐ Dangerous by
    Moonlight   0 09 942170 4   £6.99
☐ Dangerous Davies and
    the Lonely Heart   0 09 943677 9   £5.99
☐ Other Times   0 09 941523 2   £5.99

FREE POST AND PACKING

Overseas customers allow £2 for paperback

PHONE: 01624 677237

POST: Random House Books
c/o Bookpost, PO Box 29, Douglas,
Isle of Man, IM99 1BQ

FAX: 01624 670923

EMAIL: bookshop@enterprise.net

Cheques (payable to Bookpost) and credit cards accepted

Prices and availability subject to change with notice
Allow 28 days for delivery
When placing your order, please state if you do not wish to receive any additional information

www.randomhouse.co.uk

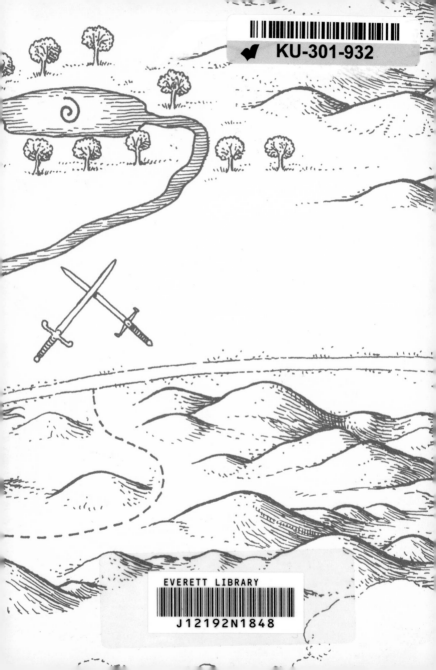

CROWN
OF
DREAMS

PENDRAGON LEGACY
≈ BOOK 3 ≈

CROWN OF DREAMS

KATHERINE ROBERTS

templar

A TEMPLAR BOOK

First published in the UK in 2013 by Templar Publishing,
an imprint of The Templar Company Limited,
Deepdene Lodge, Deepdene Avenue,
Dorking, Surrey, RH5 4AT, UK
www.templarco.co.uk

Copyright © 2013 by Katherine Roberts
Cover illustration by Scott Altmann

First UK edition

1 3 5 7 9 10 8 6 4 2

ISBN 978-1-84877-852-8

Printed and bound in Italy by Grafica Veneta S.p.A.

For my father

Contents

Characters

ALBA – Rhianna's mist horse, a white mare from Avalon.

ARIANRHOD – Rhianna's maid, ex-maid of Morgan Le Fay. Her cheek bears a scar in the shape of a pentacle.

CAI – young squire at Camelot who becomes Rhianna's champion.

CHIEF CYNRIC – leader of the Saxons.

ELPHIN – Prince of Avalon and only son of Lord Avallach.

EVENSTAR – Elphin's mist horse, a white stallion from Avalon.

GARETH – older squire, Cai's rival.

KING ARTHUR – king of Britain. His ghost appears to Rhianna while his body sleeps in Avalon awaiting rebirth.

LADY ISABEL – lady in charge of the damsels at Camelot.

LORD AVALLACH – Lord of Avalon and Elphin's father. Leader of the Wild Hunt.

MERLIN – King Arthur's druid. Morgan Le Fay drowned his man's body but his spirit lives in the body of a merlin falcon. He can still work magic.

MORDRED – Rhianna's cousin and rival for the throne; the son of Morgan Le Fay.

MORGAN LE FAY – Mordred's mother, and Arthur's sister, a witch. Now dead, her spirit advises Mordred from Annwn.

NIMUE – the Lady of the Lake, who took King Arthur's sword Excalibur after Arthur's death and gave it to Rhianna.

QUEEN GUINEVERE – Rhianna's mother.

RHIANNA PENDRAGON – daughter of King
    Arthur, raised in Avalon.

SANDY – Cai's pony, rescued from the Saxons.

SIR AGRAVAINE – grumpy older knight.

SIR BEDIVERE – a young knight, also known as
    'Soft Hands' because of his gentle
    nature.

SIR BORS – leader of King Arthur's knights.

SIR LANCELOT – Arthur's champion knight,
    whose love for Queen Guinevere
    caused him to break the Lance of
    Truth when he fought against his king.

THE SHADRAKE – a dragon from Annwn,
    breathes ice instead of fire and hunts
    between worlds.

UTHER PENDRAGON – father of King Arthur
    and Morgan Le Fay. Now dead, his
    spirit lives in Annwn.

To Dragonland

Druid
Beacon

SUMMER SEA

Lonely Tor
[Glastonbury]

Marshes

Stone
Circle

To Mines of
Lyonesse

Four lights stand against the dark:
The Sword Excalibur that was
forged in Avalon,
The Lance of Truth made by the
hands of men,
The Crown of Dreams, which hides
the jewel of Annwn,
And the Grail said to hold all the
stars in heaven.

The Dragon's Lair

Mordred reined in his horse and eyed the cave behind the waterfall. A strange green glow came out of it, lighting up the valley. Water dripped from the trees, from his cloak and off the end of his nose. Why did dragons have to make their lairs in a land where it rained all the time?

"So what are you waiting for?" he snapped. "This must be it. Go in there and bring me King Arthur's crown."

His bloodbeards looked at each other uneasily. Seeing Mordred clench his fist, their captain drew his sword and rode reluctantly towards the wall of green water. His horse rolled its eyes and dug in its hooves.

"I think the horses can smell the dr-dragon, Master," he stammered.

"Nonsense!" Mordred said. "The shadrake's forgotten we were supposed to be following it. You all saw it fly off. If it had stuck around, we might have found this godforsaken place sooner."

"Horses sense more than men, Master," the captain pointed out, glancing nervously at the sky.

"Go in on foot, then!" Mordred used his good leg to kick the bloodbeard off his horse. "You can still run if you need to, unlike me. We'll wait out here in case the shadrake comes back."

The captain shuddered. But he knew

better than to argue with his master. Gripping his sword, he vanished into the hillside. Shortly afterwards they heard a muffled yell, followed by the rattle of falling debris. The water glittered eerily green, spooking the horses again. The men paled and crossed themselves.

"Oh, for Annwn's sake!" Mordred snapped. "Do I have to do everything myself? Leave your horses out here and follow me."

His stallion snorted at the water, but stopped playing up when Mordred growled at it. He ducked over the horse's neck to avoid the spray. Its hooves echoed inside the rocky tunnel, which sloped downwards and burrowed deep into the hillside. At every turn, the eerie green glow brightened.

Sweat bathed Mordred as he remembered

his underground sickbed, where he'd almost died after his uncle, Arthur Pendragon, wounded him with Excalibur during their final battle. But that had been a whole year ago. King Arthur was dead. The Sword of Light was in the hands of Arthur's daughter, who was afraid to blood the blade in case it stopped her taking the sword back to Avalon, where it would help bring her father back to life. Mordred had no such worries. As soon as he got hold of his uncle's crown, he'd ride to Camelot and blood his blade as many times as was necessary to claim the throne.

They emerged in a vast cavern, which stank of dragon. Jewelled daggers, rusty swords and dented shields were piled around the walls, along with what looked suspiciously like human bones. One of the piles had avalanched, and his bloodbeard captain lay groaning underneath it. His men hurried over to help.

"Leave him," Mordred snapped, seeing that the man was still breathing. "Find the crown, you fools! Quickly, before the shadrake comes back."

While his men searched through the dragon's hoard, Mordred rode his horse slowly around the cavern, prodding at the treasure with his spear. "Where is it, Mother?" he whispered.

"Here, my son," whispered a woman's voice from the shadows.

Mordred froze. His mother's spirit lived in the underworld of Annwn now, and until today he'd always needed her dark mirror to speak to her. "Where?" he said warily.

"Right under your feet, you foolish boy," the witch hissed. "What do you think is making the light in here?"

Mordred's horse stopped dead and threw up its head, banging him on the nose. He looked down and sucked in his breath.

His mother's body lay half buried under the treasure, her dress torn and stained. A crown encircled her dark hair, glittering with coloured jewels. As his horse's hooves dislodged the pile, he saw that one of these – a large green stone at her forehead – was glowing eerily. There wasn't a mark on her, and for a wild moment he thought she wasn't dead.

Then he saw her spirit rippling in the green light. *Dark magic.*

His gaze fastened greedily on the crown.

He slid clumsily out of his saddle and fell to his knees beside her. He tugged at her dress with his left hand, pushing the dragon's treasure off her body with the stump of his right wrist. "Help me, then!" he yelled at his bloodbeards.

They came running.

"Morgan Le Fay!" the captain breathed, still looking a bit dazed. "So this is where she ended up. I always wondered how she died."

"That dragon must've killed her," said one of the others, looking nervously at the tunnel behind them.

"Don't be stupid," Mordred snapped. "My mother's a powerful enchantress. She controlled the shadrake. It led us here, didn't it?"

Before his bloodbeards could point

out that the creature had abandoned them halfway to Dragonland, he reached for the crown. It was stuck, so he had to brace his good leg against the rock and pull. The crown came free with a sudden jerk, leaving a line of charred blisters across his mother's forehead, and rolled across the cave.

Mordred scrambled after it, picked it up and examined it carefully. Some of the jewels were missing, but it was definitely the same crown his Uncle Arthur had worn in their final battle. Triumph filled him. He ran a finger over the dent his axe had made when he'd split the king's helmet from his head, and smiled at the memory.

"Behold the Crown of Dreams!" he announced, showing it to his men. "You see before you one of the four ancient Lights, with more power than Excalibur, and twice as much magic as that useless Lance my cousin stupidly gave to her squire friend! This crown belonged to my Uncle Arthur and gave him the power to command men and dragons, and now it's *mine*..." He lifted the glowing circlet above his head.

"Careful, my son!" said his mother in a tone that sent a chill down his spine. "Don't put it on yet."

Mordred scowled as his triumph evaporated. "Why not? I thought that was the whole idea. I've got Pendragon blood, so it won't harm me."

"I've got Pendragon blood too, foolish boy, and it *killed* me."

He lowered the crown and glanced uneasily at his mother's body, which had begun to blacken and shrivel. "How?" he whispered. "How did it kill you?"

"I was careless. There's a jewel missing. I assumed it was a minor one, knocked out during the battle. But it's one of the magic stones, the one Arthur stored his secrets inside when he sat on the throne of Camelot. You've got to find that jewel and destroy it before the Crown of Dreams will accept you as the next Pendragon."

Mordred looked at the piles of treasure in despair. Find a single jewel among this lot? Worse, what if the stupid dragon had lost the stone on its way here, carrying the crown from the battlefield? It could be lying at the bottom of the Summer Sea.

"We'll be searching all year!"

"No you won't," the witch said. "Because

the stone's not lost. If my ex-maid's information is right, it's still at Camelot. Arthur must have taken it out before the battle as a precaution. He left it with Guinevere, and now your cousin has it."

"*Rhianna!*" Mordred clenched his fist in rage. He might have known King Arthur's daughter would stand in his way again. "We have to get it from her," he growled. "I need to raise another army."

"You don't need an army to catch a fly." His mother smiled. "Not even one that stings like your cousin. My ex-maid still has my mirror, so I can control her. This is what we'll do…"

◀ 1 ▶

Witch Maid

A year long in Avalon Arthur slept
While his queen in fairest Camelot wept,
And a damsel with the Sword of Light
Fought shadows summoned by
the evil knight.

Rhianna fidgeted on the hard bench, fiddling with the ugly black pendant her mother had insisted she wear today in honour of her father's memory.

As princess of Camelot, she'd been given

a seat at the front, below the round window with its dragon design where Queen Guinevere had been kneeling for ages in a pool of red and gold autumn sunlight. The chapel was full, and in the hush she could hear people shifting their feet and coughing behind her.

She scowled at her mother's back, wishing she could go riding in the woods instead. It was exactly one year since her cousin Mordred had killed her father on the battlefield at Camlann and Merlin had brought the king's body through the mists to Avalon.

A *whole year* since she'd learned she was King Arthur's daughter, and she still hadn't completed her quest!

She swung her feet in their embroidered slippers in an effort to keep warm and wished she'd worn her boots instead. Her father wouldn't care if they looked silly with her dress.

The queen wore a simple blue gown with no jewellery. Copper hair, the same colour as Rhianna's, flowed loose around her shoulders. She was sobbing softly, which did strange things to Rhianna's insides. She felt embarrassed that her mother could cry before all these people. Then she felt guilty because she couldn't find any tears herself.

"My father's *not* dead," she muttered, touching his sword, Excalibur, which was lying on the bench beside her. "I've told you a hundred times! He's going to return to Camelot, just as soon as you let me out of here so I can look for the last two Lights and complete my quest..."

A touch on her shoulder made her jump. At first she thought it was her father's ghost, since he often appeared when she got upset. But it was just her friend Elphin, who had ridden through the mists with her from Avalon last year.

The Avalonian prince's eyes glowed violet as he leaned forward to whisper in her ear. "Let your mother pray for him if it makes her feel better," he said. "Then she'll be all the happier when we wake King Arthur and bring him back from Avalon, won't she?"

"*If* we ever manage to wake him! It's been a year, Elphin… a whole year!"

"A year in which you've won the Sword of Light from the Lady of the Lake, fought off a shadrake from Annwn, mended the Lance of Truth, rescued your mother from Mordred's dark tower, and been named heiress of Camelot." Elphin's lips twitched. "Father's right, you humans are much too impatient sometimes."

"That's because we haven't got as long to

live as you Avalonians," Rhianna said. But she smiled, too. Her friend was right. Though things at Camelot weren't as good as they might have been if Mordred hadn't killed her father, they were a lot better now than before she and Elphin had ridden through the mists.

"Don't worry," Elphin whispered, still teasing her. "I won't let Mordred kill you before you finish your quest."

"*I* won't let him kill me, you mean," Rhianna said. "I've got Excalibur, remember? But it'll be winter again soon, and the knights are hardly going to let us ride out on a quest to Dragonland in the middle of a snowstorm, are they? You saw how much snow there was last year. I think they're delaying so they'll have an excuse to stop me going."

Her voice had risen. "Shh!" Elphin said,

giving her shoulder a warning squeeze. "Your mother's looking at us."

The queen had finally stopped praying and turned to face the congregation. She frowned as she waited for Rhianna and Elphin to stop talking.

She cleared her throat and said, "Today we remember my lord Arthur Pendragon, who was slain by the traitor Prince Mordred on this day one year ago. Since the king cannot be with us in body, we'll honour his spirit, which still lives in his sword, Excalibur." She beckoned to Rhianna.

"Here we go," Rhianna muttered.

With a resigned sigh, she drew the Sword of Light from its red scabbard, which she wore at her left hip these days so she could draw the sword right-handed according to knightly code.

Feeling a bit self conscious, she went to stand beside her mother. She rested the point of the blade in the circle on the floor, where the squires would kneel to do their vigil before they became knights, and laid her hands on the white jewel set into Excalibur's hilt. The jewel warmed under her touch and began to shine faintly.

One by one, the knights walked up the aisle to kneel before Excalibur and renew their vows to their Pendragon. Sir Lancelot led them, his silver hair splashed with colour from the dragon window. He glanced up at the queen as he kissed the sword's hilt, and Rhianna saw her mother blush. "May King Arthur's spirit live forever!" he said loudly, before returning to his seat.

Sir Bors and Sir Agravaine were next, followed by the young knight, Sir Bedivere, whom everyone called 'Soft Hands'. Sir Bedivere winked at her and smiled in sympathy. "Soon be over, Damsel Rhianna," he whispered.

The ceremony went on and on. Rhianna's feet turned into little blocks of ice, and her arms ached with holding the blade still so that it wouldn't cut anyone. In battle, Excalibur's magic always made her feel stronger. But today, she could feel something working against the power of the sword.

She remembered feeling like this when she'd held its blade to Mordred's throat in the summer, and had a sudden sense of being watched. She peered suspiciously into the shadows at the back of the chapel and thought she saw a dark figure standing by the door.

"Come on, child," the priest said gently. "There are still a lot of people waiting."

Rhianna blinked and the figure vanished. She was being silly. Mordred would not dare come into Camelot's chapel alone, not after being captured and thrown into the dungeon the last time he was here.

Cai, the squire who had been with the knights sent to meet her when she rode through the mists from Avalon, was next in line. He had grown taller over the past few months, which made him seem less plump. Since she'd knighted him in the summer so he could be her champion and carry the Lance of Truth, Cai should really have come up first with Sir Lancelot, not last with the squires. But she was glad to see her friend's cheeky grin.

As the boy knelt, a draught flattened the candle flames and the air chilled. Before he could kiss Excalibur's jewel, the doors of the chapel suddenly blew open with a crash, making everyone jump.

Some of the damsels sitting at the back screamed. As people looked round to see who had interrupted the service, a girl with wild black hair covering her face came running up the aisle and launched herself at Rhianna.

Startled, Rhianna took a step back and lifted Excalibur. Then she recognised her maid Arianrhod and quickly lowered the sword, confused.

"Oi, witch's maid, watch it!" Before Arianrhod could attack Rhianna again, an older squire called Gareth grabbed the girl's hair and pushed her into the crowd. Arianrhod stumbled over a bench and fell to the floor beneath it, writhing and whimpering.

People crossed themselves. Cai tried to help

the girl. But everyone had crowded round to see what was wrong, and he couldn't get through.

The knights pushed through the crowd and picked the fallen bench off Arianrhod. "Get back!" Sir Bors bellowed. "Give the poor girl some air."

"Never mind air," a woman muttered. "It's fire that one wants. I always said you can't trust an ex-maid of Morgan Le Fay's. Keep her away from our princess, that's what I say!"

"Yeah," another agreed. "She just tried to kill Princess Rhianna."

"Nonsense," Sir Bedivere said, kneeling beside Arianrhod and catching her flailing wrists. "The noise scared her and she tripped, that's all. I think she's ill. Someone fetch Lady Isabel from the Damsel Tower."

"She was perfectly all right this morning," the first woman pointed out. "That wind wasn't natural, if you ask me – did you see that shadow flee out the door?"

People nodded and began to mutter about witchcraft.

Rhianna had heard enough.

She jumped on to the front bench. "Don't be so STUPID!" she shouted. Her voice, loud enough to be heard across a battlefield, echoed around the chapel. Excalibur's white jewel blazed in response.

Everyone stared at her, startled into silence.

"Arianrhod won't hurt me," Rhianna continued. "She's my friend! Let me through."

The queen frowned at her. "Get down from there, darling. This isn't the time or the place for battle stunts…"

Seeing that it would be the fastest way through the crowd, Rhianna had already kicked off her slippers and was leaping barefoot from bench to bench. She dropped beside Sir Bedivere, laid Excalibur down and knelt to comfort her friend.

Arianrhod clutched at Rhianna's dress, struggling to free herself from Sir Bedivere's grip.

The knight gave her a worried smile. "I daren't let go of her while she's like this, or she'll hurt herself," he said softly. "I think she might have hit her head when she tripped. We have to get her out of the chapel. There are too many people here."

"Maybe the priest can calm her down?" Sir Agravaine suggested.

Rhianna tried to catch Arianrhod's ankles,

but her friend's foot thumped into her cheek.

"Leave her to the knights, darling!" called the queen. "You'll get hurt."

Just as Rhianna wondered if she would get more bruises from her maid than she'd had from her enemies, otherworldly music tinkled around the chapel, making everyone smile. Elphin stood in the doorway, haloed by golden autumn sunshine. He had fetched his Avalonian harp, which he continued to play as he clambered over the benches to join them.

He looked down at Arianrhod. "*Sleep now,*" he sang, magic in his voice. "*Sleep.*"

The girl's eyes closed, and she sank back to the floor. Sir Bedivere picked her up. The crowd sighed in relief.

Rhianna smoothed her dress and retrieved

Excalibur. "Take her up to my room," she ordered in a shaky voice.

Sir Bors shook his head. "I'm not sure that's the best idea, Damsel Rhianna."

"What's wrong? She's my maid. She's always in there, anyway. What's she going to do? Put a spell on me?"

The knights looked doubtfully at Arianrhod, who hung limply now in Sir Bedivere's arms, her dark hair trailing to the floor. The squires and damsels whispered uneasily. The priest looked uneasy, too. The queen didn't seem to know what to do.

"Oh, for goodness' sake!" Rhianna said. "Sir Bedivere can carry her up there. I give him permission. You're not going to attack any of the damsels, are you Sir Bedivere?"

The girls giggled as 'Soft Hands' blushed.

"No, Princess Rhianna," he said.

"Well then, that's settled. Put her in my bed. I'll be up to check on her as soon as we've finished my father's prayers."

This seemed to do the trick. People stopped muttering about witchcraft and remembered they were supposed to be praying for their king's soul.

The queen pulled herself together. "Rhianna's right. We can't let an attention-seeking maid disrupt my husband's service. Let's put this unfortunate interruption behind us. Who's next?"

The knights righted the benches, and everyone returned to their seats so the priest could bless them. Rhianna barely heard a word he said. She kept thinking of that dark figure she'd seen, before the doors had crashed open and Arianrhod attacked her.

Behind her, Elphin cradled his harp in his lap, a six-fingered hand resting across the strings to keep them quiet. He touched her shoulder. "Are you all right, Rhia?"

She nodded. "I think so." She raised a hand to feel her cheek where Arianrhod had kicked her, and realised that sometime during the struggle she'd lost her father's black pendant.

✤❀✤

After the service, people gathered in the courtyard. Stalls had been set up serving roast boar and mead to those who couldn't fit inside the dining hall. Squires and servants hung about in groups in the autumn sunshine, discussing Arianrhod's strange behaviour and whether the maid could really be a witch like her first mistress. One of the older knights muttered about a trial by fire. The squires, overhearing this, began to gather sticks and bits of straw to build a bonfire so they could 'test' the other damsels, who screamed and fled towards the dining hall with the laughing boys in pursuit.

Rhianna elbowed through them all, chilled by their teasing. "Grow up!" she snapped at Gareth as she passed the squire. "How can you joke about burning someone? You know it's not Arianrhod's fault she had to serve Morgan Le Fay while the witch lived at Camelot."

She hadn't found her pendant in the short time she'd stayed behind in the chapel to look for it. One of the knights must have picked it up. She'd get it back later. Her friend was more important. She hurried to the Damsel Tower with Elphin at her heels.

Lady Isabel, the tall golden-haired woman who looked after the damsels, tried to stop the Avalonian boy at the door. But Rhianna seized his hand and pulled him inside. "I need him to play his harp to help Arianrhod get better," she explained breathlessly.

Lady Isabel shook her head. "First Sir Bedivere, and now a fairy prince! I don't know what Camelot is coming to since you arrived, Damsel Rhianna." She grabbed the back of Cai's tunic as the boy tried to follow them in. "Not you as well, young squire! I draw the line at two boys in Rhianna's room at once."

"But she needs my help, too," Cai protested. "I'm the Pendragon's champion. *And* I'm a knight now."

"All the more reason why I'm not letting you up there." Lady Isabel turned the boy around and marched him firmly back into the courtyard. "You go off to lunch, young knight. It's not like you to miss the chance of a good meal."

Cai pulled a face and looked up at the high windows of the tower in frustration. "Elphin's a lot more dangerous than me," he grumbled. "He might charm all the girls away to Avalon with his harp."

Rhianna smiled as she led the way up the stairs. "Just don't charm Arianrhod away until we find out what's wrong with her, will you?" she told her friend, pausing at the door to her chambers.

Elphin did not reply. He was looking past her, his eyes whirling purple. "That explains what happened to your father's pendant," he said in a wary tone.

They stared at the sleeping maid. Sir

Bedivere had put her on the bed and pulled a cover over her, but Arianrhod was trying to kick it off. She seemed to be having some kind of nightmare. Rhianna's missing pendant dangled from her hand, its chain wrapped about one slender wrist.

"It must have got tangled round her arm when I tried to help her in the chapel," she said in relief, rescuing the pendant. "She's having another bad dream, poor thing. Can you play your harp for her again?"

Ever since the guards had found the maid unconscious in the dungeon after Mordred's escape during the midsummer feast, Arianrhod had suffered from nightmares. No one knew exactly how she'd come to be down there. She claimed not to remember a thing.

Elphin ran his fingers over the strings, and

Arianrhod's back arched. She cried out in her sleep and mumbled something. They caught the words 'crown' and 'jewel' and 'Annwn'.

He lowered his harp and shook his head. "Sorry, Rhia. Something's working against my magic. I think she's under a spell."

"Morgan Le Fay again?" Mordred's mother had used the poor girl for a spell once before, cutting her cheek with a dagger and leaving a pentacle scar. Lady Morgan's spirit was in Annwn now, but the witch could still use her magic to reach the world of men.

"I don't know," Elphin said, still wary. "But your pendant's not black any more. Something's happening to the stone, look."

2

Arthur's Jewel

A single jewel Arthur left with his queen
When he rode to battle on Camlann's green.
Mordred's axe cut the fearless king down
The day a dragon stole Camelot's crown.

Rhianna hurried to the window and dangled the pendant against the sun. Although still dark, the stone no longer seemed ugly. A dim red light now flickered at its heart. Wondering if it had been damaged during the struggle in the chapel, she touched it and felt a slight heat.

"Careful, Rhia," Elphin warned. "We don't know where it came from yet."

Crown... jewel... Annwn... Arianrhod's words suddenly made sense.

"The Crown of Dreams, which hides the Jewel of Annwn!" She stared at Elphin, shivering with a mixture of excitement and terror. "That's what the song says, isn't it? The one Merlin sang for us in Avalon, when he brought my father's body through the mists? I should have realised before! My father gave this jewel to my mother the night before his last battle. She told me it turned black when he died, and you sensed an echo of magic in it the first time I showed it to you... Oh Elphin, I know it's only small but what if this is the *Jewel of Annwn*!"

She held the dark jewel at arm's length by its broken chain and looked at it with fresh eyes. Thank goodness she had kept it, and hadn't thrown it into Lady Nimue's lake as an offering as she had thought of doing at first.

But Elphin shook his head and said quietly, "If that were a thing of Annwn, I would not be able to touch it without pain, Rhia."

"But you didn't touch it, did you?"

"I touched it when you wore it at the Midsummer Feast, remember?"

"I'd forgotten that. But it was still black then, so maybe its magic wasn't working properly. We have to show it to Merlin!"

They went through to Rhianna's sitting room, where a small, grey-blue falcon was leashed to a perch under the window. No one had cleaned in here this morning, and feathers spiralled up from the floor. Rhianna pulled off the bird's hood and rested her hand on Excalibur's hilt so she could talk to Merlin. The druid's spirit had been trapped inside the little merlin falcon since Morgan Le Fay drowned his man's body on their way over from Avalon last year.

The bird fluffed its feathers, making Rhianna sneeze. "Have you brought my breakfast?" he grumbled. "No one's fed me this morning. Where is everyone?"

"The damsels will be back soon, Merlin," Elphin said with a smile. "I expect they'll bring you some meat from the feast." He ran a slender finger down the speckled breast. The merlin shivered in pleasure and nibbled at his knuckle.

Rhianna sighed. "When you two have quite finished grooming each other, we've got something to show you, Merlin."

She opened her hand to reveal the pendant. Merlin gave it a keen stare. She felt sure he recognised the stone. But as she tried to decide if it had changed colour again, the bird turned its back on her and returned to his grooming. "Put that thing away, Rhianna Pendragon," he grumbled. "I'm not interested in your baubles. Go and show it to the damsels, foolish girl."

She checked the door to make sure they were alone, and lowered her voice. "You might be interested in this one. We think this is the Jewel of Annwn."

"Whatever gave you that idea?" The merlin stretched a wing and eyed Elphin in amusement. "The Jewel of Annwn, she says...

as if such a thing could be worn around her neck without stealing the breath from her throat, or lie against a mortal heart without stopping it stone dead. Even set into the Crown, Annwn's jewel is dangerous enough, but there at least, the rightful heir to the throne can wear it without fear of dying."

Rhianna felt faintly disappointed. She frowned at the stone and scrunched up the chain to put it back into her pocket. "Then it's just some old pendant my mother gave me, after all. I thought when it changed colour like it did—"

"It *what*?" Merlin turned round so quickly he almost fell off his perch. "Let me see."

"You wanted me to put it away just now," Rhianna said, irritated. "Make up your mind."

"Hold Excalibur closer," the druid instructed.

"That's better. Now then, let's have a proper look." He twisted his head to examine the stone with each eye in turn. "Hmm, mmm... ah yes, I see now. This isn't Annwn's jewel, you silly girl – it's Arthur's. Seems your father's secrets did not die with him, after all."

"What secrets?" she asked.

The bird fluffed its feathers again, grumpily. "If I knew that, they wouldn't be secrets, would they? Only another Pendragon can look into the king's jewel and see the secrets he stored inside."

Rhianna frowned. "So why can't I see them? I've got Pendragon blood."

"Because, Rhianna Pendragon, its magic won't work by itself. You'll have to put it back into your father's crown before you understand."

"So Rhianna's right – this stone *did* come

from the Crown of Dreams," Elphin said. "I sensed its power before, but never thought it might have come from one of the four Lights! Why didn't the queen tell us what it was? Didn't she know?"

"Of course not," the merlin said. "If she'd known what it really was, she'd have been too scared to accept it. I told Arthur to take it out of the Crown before the battle in case things went badly – and a good thing I did! As far as Guinevere was concerned, it was a parting gift from her loving husband. I counted on its ugliness to keep it safe from any light-fingered maids. While Arthur's jewel is here with us, no impostor can use its magic to take the throne. But that light you can see inside means the Crown has been found… Hmm. This changes things."

Rhianna had been thinking of Arianrhod's fingers on the pendant. But when Merlin said the Crown had been found, she instantly forgot her friend's strange behaviour. "Who's found it?" she said. "If it's Mordred, we've failed! I need all four Lights to bring my father back from Avalon…"

"You're not listening, as usual." Merlin pecked at her hand again, almost making her drop the pendant. "I never said you needed all four Lights to bring Arthur back to the world of men – but it's true he'll need as many of them as possible if he's to defeat the dark knight and restore Camelot to its former glory when he does return. I'd hoped the Sword and the Lance might be enough to lure his soul back into his body. Arthur never possessed the Grail anyway, and while the Crown was buried in a dragon's lair, it was safe enough from enemy hands until he came back to reclaim it. But now the Crown has been found, which changes things. Without your father's jewel in place, it won't work properly and it's dangerous to wear. But it's the Pendragon crown and it contains the secrets of the old Dragonlords, so Mordred might be able to use it against us if he gets hold of it. You need to go to Dragonland and get it back as soon as possible."

"That's what I've been telling my mother and the knights for months!" Rhianna said in frustration. "But they won't listen to me. They keep saying they can't leave Camelot unprotected to ride out on another quest, in case Mordred's planning to attack the castle with a new army. They don't seem to understand I need to find the Crown before he does.

Will you fly in to the Round Table meeting again, Merlin, and talk to them all again like you did in the spring? If you tell them what you just told us, they'll have to let me go and look for it!"

"Let *us* go," Elphin corrected. "You're not going anywhere without me and Cai."

Rhianna grinned. "All right, us." She pulled a face at the little hawk. "I suppose we'll have to take Merlin as well to show us the way..."

Shouts in the courtyard below the window distracted them. Merlin fluttered up and down his perch. "What's going on out there?" he grumbled. "Rather a lot of noise for a memorial service, if you ask me."

"They've been drinking mead," Elphin said, his eyes purple with disapproval. "It's probably another fight."

Then they heard feet pounding up the stairs and Lady Isabel's angry shout. Rhianna drew Excalibur as Gareth, the squire who had called Arianrhod a witch in the chapel, burst into the room.

"Damsel Rhianna, you got to come quick!" he puffed. "There's a man in black armour outside who says he's come for Arianrhod, and Cai's challenged him to a duel!"

A chill went down Rhianna's back as she remembered the shadowy figure she'd seen in the chapel before Arianrhod had attacked her.

"Mordred!" she breathed, staring at Elphin.

Her friend shook his head. "He wouldn't dare come alone, not after what happened at midsummer. And anyway, Cai's got more sense than to challenge Prince Mordred to a duel."

"I'm not so sure." She thought of how proud

Cai had been when she knighted him last year.

"Young Sir Cai, the shortest knight who ever lived, duelling?" The merlin let out a screech that sounded suspiciously like a bird-laugh. "That'll be something to see! Take me outside."

"It's not *funny*!" Rhianna said, rushing to the window. "Cai's going to get himself killed out there."

"Cai's going to get hurt," Gareth agreed. "That's a real war lance the challenger's carrying, not a wooden jousting spear."

Rhianna leaned out to see the jousting field where, in the spring, the squires had tilted for fun. Today, the autumn sun cast long shadows across the course from the wall, and at first she couldn't see anyone. Then she saw Cai's pony, Sandy, gallop out of the gates with his mane glowing like fire.

The boy still wore his squire's uniform, but he carried the Lance of Truth, which left a trail of glitter through the air. After him ran a crowd of eager squires, cheering him on, followed by the adults from the courtyard shouting at them to stop. At the far end of the field, a shaggy black horse reared as the stranger raised his lance to answer Cai's challenge.

Rhianna tried to see if the man had a crippled leg and one hand like her cousin, but he was too far away.

Gareth jostled behind her, trying to see as well. "I'd say the maid's as good as his," he said.

"Oh stop it, Gareth!" Rhianna said, wondering why he'd run all the way up the Damsel Tower to warn them if he disliked her friends so much. She sheathed Excalibur and scowled at the boy. "If you want to make yourself useful, go and saddle Alba for me. I've got to get changed, and I'm not doing it with you in here."

Gareth looked alarmed. "Saddle your fairy horse? Not me!"

"I'll do it, Rhia," Elphin said, slinging his harp over one shoulder and pulling Gareth out of the room. "Better be quick changing, though. They're not hanging about out there."

Rhianna saw the knights' big horses gallop out of the gates and set out across the field after Cai's pony. She relaxed slightly as she recognised Sir Bedivere's chestnut, Sir Agravaine's black, and Sir Lancelot's white stallion.

"A knight who carries the Lance of Truth cannot be killed," Merlin said. "Where are you going, Rhianna Pendragon? Let the lad take care of it—"

His words ended in another screech as she fixed the hood back over the druid's head.

Rhianna hurried back to her bedroom and found Arianrhod at the window, woken by the noise. Her friend swung round with frightened eyes. "Who's that man out there?" she asked. "Why is Gareth saying he wants me? I had a horrible dream about my old mistress Lady Morgan… she didn't send him, did she?"

"Don't worry, we won't let him touch you, whoever he is," she told the maid, opening her clothing chest and pulling out her armour. "And Lady Morgan's dead now, you know that. Stay here."

Lady Isabel had reached the top of the stairs. She pressed a hand to her side and frowned at Rhianna and Arianrhod. "I don't know what's been going on up here…" she began.

Then she noticed what was happening outside the window. "Is that young Sir Cai on his pony? What does he think he's doing? The queen specifically said no jousting today."

"Don't worry, Lady Isabel, Cai's not going to joust," Rhianna said, already out of her dress. She pulled on her riding leggings and slipped her Avalonian armour over the top. The silvery material fell to just above her knees, light enough to dance in, yet strong enough to stop an arrow. Finally, she buckled Excalibur around her waist. Feeling much more comfortable than she had done in the chapel, she hurried down the stairs after the boys.

"Damsel Rhianna!" Lady Isabel said, losing patience. "Where do you think you're going dressed like that? Your mother's expecting you at lunch."

"I'll have lunch later!" Rhianna called back over her shoulder. "I've got a duel to stop."

3

The Challenge

A stranger came on Arthur's Day
To claim the maid of Morgan Le Fay.
So Camelot's champion rode out to fight
One boy and his lance against a knight.

On her way down the stairs, Rhianna wondered what she'd do if the challenger under that battered helm did turn out to be her cousin Mordred. But Elphin was right. Mordred wouldn't come to Camelot alone, not after the last time, when he'd been captured and thrown in the dungeon.

She clenched her fist on Excalibur's hilt. Whoever it was out there, she wouldn't let him hurt Arianrhod or Cai.

Her beloved mist horse, Alba, waited for her in the courtyard, saddled and bridled. Elphin was already mounted on Evenstar. The two Avalonian horses shone in the shadows, their white manes rippling almost to their knees, and their silver-shod hooves pawing the castle yard.

Are we going home now? Alba said, whinnying when she saw Rhianna.

"Soon, my beautiful one." She gave the mare's nose a quick stroke before springing into the saddle. She felt bad every time Alba asked that, because she knew the little horse meant home to Avalon. It had been a whole year since either of them had tasted apples from Lord Avallach's orchard. "We're going racing instead," she said. "You'll enjoy that, won't you?"

Alba shook her mane in excitement. *I will win today. I am very fast.*

Rhianna smiled.

"Rhia," Elphin said, nodding at the gates, which had begun to close. "We'd better hurry if we're going to get out."

Men came running out of the dining hall to man the walls. She saw bows and arrows in their hands as well as half-eaten pies, and her stomach clenched. What if Mordred had come with his army, after all? She drew Excalibur and trotted Alba towards the gates. Elphin followed with his harp on his back.

"Sorry, Princess Rhianna," one of the guards said, stepping into her path and raising his spear. "We've orders to keep you inside until we find out who that stranger is."

"Out of my way, you fool!" Rhianna said impatiently. "Cai's out there. You can't let him tilt against a grown man. He'll be killed!"

"The boy carries the magic lance, and that stranger doesn't look like much of a knight," the guard said with a glance at his friend. "We think young Sir Cai'll be all right."

"Then you're idiots!" Rhianna gathered up her reins and headed Alba towards the shrinking gap between the gates. She closed her eyes as they loomed closer.

"Mist, Alba," she whispered. "Mist."

The guards yelled in alarm when they realised she was not going to stop, and jumped out of her way. She heard Elphin's harp tinkle across the courtyard, and something solid brushed her shoulder. Her skin prickled. She opened her eyes to see Excalibur's jewel shining brightly. Then Alba was through the gates and galloping down the slope towards the jousting field, with Evenstar close on her heels. She glanced back over her shoulder and saw Gareth squeeze through the gap and run after them. The gates shut behind the squire with a dull boom.

"You're crazy, Rhia!" Elphin called. "You can't mist through the closed gates of Camelot! If they'd shut them all the way, you and Alba would both have broken necks by now, and I'd be taking your body back to the crystal caverns to lie with your father's."

She grimaced. "They didn't shut them, did they? They knew they'd be in more trouble with my mother if they hurt me than if they let me out. Is that man one of Mordred's bloodbeards, do you think?"

The challenger didn't look crippled like her cousin, but Mordred might have used magic to make himself appear whole. His helm was closed so nobody could see his face.

Elphin frowned. "I can't tell from here. Surely the knights aren't going to let Cai go through with this?"

Despite the closed gates, a surprising number of people had managed to get out of Camelot to watch. They climbed on to the stands beside the jousting field, where, normally, pavilions would be set up and seats draped with flags and banners. Today, there were no colourful flags and no cheers. The crowd watched in silence as Cai trotted his pony to one end of the field, and the challenger trotted his horse to the other.

The boy looked scared, but gripped his lance in a determined fashion. The stranger laughed.

At first Rhianna wondered if the knights planned to teach Cai a lesson, as they had done with her at the spring joust when she'd tilted against Sir Bedivere. Were they counting on the boy to pull out and let a grown knight take his place? Then she saw Sir Bors and Sir Agravaine quietly trotting their horses up behind the stands, out of view of the stranger. Sir Lancelot waited at the other side of the course with more knights.

"Clever. They're going to trap him when he's made his run before he can recover his balance," Elphin said. "Cai's just got to duck. He'll be all right, Rhia, don't worry – I'll help him, like I did before." He balanced his harp on Evenstar's withers and readied his fingers over the strings.

Sir Bedivere mounted the stand with a trumpet. He announced, "The stranger claims Princess Rhianna's maid Arianrhod belongs to him. The Pendragon's champion says the stranger's wrong. This tilt will decide the matter, according to Camelot's law." He checked the positions of the knights creeping up behind the stands and noticed the two mist horses standing in the shadows. He shook his head urgently at Rhianna as he lifted the trumpet to his lips.

"He means don't interfere," Elphin whispered.

Rhianna gripped Excalibur tighter. "I know, but I'm not going to let that man kill Cai!" she hissed.

A blast rang out, and the black horse sprang into a gallop. Sandy was only a few heartbeats behind. The stranger lowered his lance. After a bit of a fumble, Cai managed to lower the Lance of Truth, which sparkled brighter as Elphin played his harp. Sir Bors and Sir Agravaine fixed their eyes on the challenger and drew their swords as he galloped closer.

"Duck, Cai!" Sir Bedivere called.

But Cai didn't seem to hear. He gripped the Lance of Truth as if it were his only friend in the world. He was getting too big for his pony, Rhianna noticed – and too big to duck a lowered lance easily.

"Race Sandy for me, Alba!" she shouted, urging the mare down the course after Cai's pony. The crowd gasped as she galloped out into the sun with Excalibur shining in her right hand. Sir Bedivere shouted something she didn't hear above the pounding hooves.

"Cai!" she yelled. "Pull up, you idiot!"

Sunlight flashed into her eyes, half blinding her. Cai didn't hear her any more than he'd heard Sir Bedivere. Squinting from behind him, she could see he had the Lance of Truth aimed straight at his opponent's shield. She had to admire her friend's bravery. But if he didn't pull up, he would die.

Elphin's harp sang out louder across the field. Excalibur warmed in her hand. Its jewel glowed brighter and its blade left a trail of light through the air. The Lance of Truth brightened, too, maybe sensing the Sword nearby. In front of them, the black horse loomed larger against the setting sun with every stride.

"Faster, Alba!" she yelled.

I will win this race, the mare snorted.

The mist horse's nose caught up with Sandy's tail, then Cai's knee. Finally, the boy noticed Alba. He gave Rhianna a startled look.

"Damsel Rhianna!" he gasped, as she leaned across and grabbed his rein to pull the pony out of the other horse's path. "Don't—"

Too late.

There was a blinding flash as the Lance of Truth clashed with the challenger's lance. Somehow Excalibur got caught between them, and went spinning out of her grip. The crowd gasped in horror as Alba misted under her to avoid the weapons. Sandy, being a sensible sort of pony, shied out of the way too, unseating Cai, whose saddle slipped sideways. Then the challenger was past them. Splinters of his lance showered around them as the ground rushed up to meet Rhianna.

Cai fell on top of her with a grunt and they rolled together in the mud. Rhianna closed her eyes, feeling sick. They ended up in a tangle of limbs against the central barrier and lay still, catching their breath.

"Are you hurt, Damsel Rhianna?" Cai asked in a shaky voice.

"I'm still alive, no thanks to you," she muttered, sitting up and rubbing her shoulder.

She looked anxiously for Excalibur. The sword stuck out of the mud nearby, thankfully undamaged. She got shakily to her feet, wiped the blade clean on her leg and sheathed it. Sandy and Alba came trotting back together. Both horses looked sheepish.

I am sorry I misted, Alba said. *I thought you held the shining sword, so you would stay on me.*

"I did, until my so-called champion here knocked it out of my hand with the Lance of Truth," Rhianna said.

Cai flushed, rubbing his wrist. "I wouldn't have done, if you hadn't put Excalibur in the way," he said. "I'd have knocked that dirty spy off his horse instead! He wasn't even a proper knight. Why did you stop me?"

"He'd have skewered you first, more like. You are an idiot Cai! Why didn't you let Sir Lancelot challenge him?"

"I'm supposed to be your champion now! Any rate, Sir Lancelot's still angry with Arianrhod for letting Mordred out of the dungeon in the summer, so he wouldn't have jousted to save her from that man."

"He wouldn't have let an untrained squire joust in his place."

"I'm not untrained!" Cai's flush deepened. "I've been practising every day since you knighted me. If you hadn't stopped me just then, the Lance's magic would have worked, I'm sure of it."

At the other end of the barrier, the stranger had been surrounded by angry knights. Sir Agravaine and Sir Bors dragged him off his horse and quickly disarmed him. They pulled off his helm, none too gently. Everyone went quiet as they looked at the challenger's face.

Rhianna clenched her fist on Excalibur. To her relief, it wasn't her cousin. But she'd recognise that horrible scar anywhere. It was Mordred's bloodbeard captain, who had almost killed her twice now, and tortured Sir Bors last winter in the Saxon camp. A dragon had clawed his face during the battle that followed, but he hadn't died. His mouth twisted into a sneer when he saw Rhianna staring, and he spat into the mud.

"Is that who I think it is, Rhia?" Elphin asked, trotting Evenstar across to join them.

She nodded, chilled.

Sir Bors obviously recognised him too, because he clouted the bloodbeard on the ear, knocking him into the mud. "That's for what you did to me last year," the big knight growled, putting his boot on the captive's neck. "Where's Prince Mordred and your blood-drinking friends?"

The bloodbeard bared his teeth. "W-wouldn't you like to know?"

"What do you want with Princess Rhianna's maid?"

"She served my master's mother, Lady

Morgan Le Fay. Mordred wants a word with her. You all saw me unseat the Pendragon's champion – according to Camelot's law, I believe that means you must hand the maid over to me."

The crowd began to mutter.

"Bloody cheek, him coming here invoking King Arthur's laws!"

"The maid *did* let the dark knight escape at midsummer, though."

"We don't want Mordred's lot coming down here again. Maybe it'd be easiest to let him take the girl?"

"Nobody's taking Arianrhod anywhere," Rhianna said firmly, leading Alba across to the knights and their prisoner. "Least of all that man!"

She appealed to Sir Bors. "Can't you see,

Mordred sent his bloodbeard here to stir up trouble? You can't possibly believe him! Elphin thinks Arianrhod's under a spell."

"Ha, so you'd believe a *fairy* now? Since when have Lord Avallach's people cared about men's affairs?" The bloodbeard sneered at the Avalonian boy, who watched silently from a distance, clutching his harp.

Sir Bedivere took her by the elbow. "Don't get too close, Damsel Rhianna," he warned. "He seems to have come alone, but it might be a trick."

"It's a trick, all right! Arianrhod's innocent."

"Seems the witch-maid's put a spell on your princess, too," said the bloodbeard in a sly tone. "What's happened to King Arthur's famous laws? Does every man who comes to Camelot in good faith get challenged to a duel, and then

– when he wins in a fair tilt – get dragged off his horse and arrested by Camelot's knights?"

The crowd muttered again.

"He does, when he's the same man who commanded the traitor's army," Sir Bors grunted. He wrenched their captive's arms behind his back and hauled him to his feet. "Come on, scum. Maybe we'll get some answers out of you after you've spent a night in the dungeon."

"This proves King Arthur's dreams for Camelot are dead!" the bloodbeard shouted as he was marched away. The crowd watched him go, still muttering uneasily.

Sir Bedivere sighed. He gave Rhianna's shoulder a squeeze as they followed the knights. "We'll get to the bottom of this, Damsel Rhianna, don't worry. That was a brave thing you did out there. I thought young Cai was going to get himself skewered, as well. Don't know what's got into the boy lately – he seems to think a magic lance can turn a squire into a champion knight without all the hard work in-between. In fact, he's rather like a damsel I know, who thinks a magic sword can turn a girl into a Pendragon…"

He eyed Excalibur's muddy blade in amusement and lowered his voice. "Next time, use your left hand if you're in trouble. Staying alive is more important than knightly codes."

Rhianna flushed. "I've fought more battles than Cai has."

Sir Bedivere stared after their prisoner and sighed. "I know you have, Damsel Rhianna. And I've a feeling there will be a few more to fight before Camelot's safe from the dark knight. Prince Mordred obviously hasn't given up yet."

4

Round Table Meeting

In Dragonland the crown lies hidden
Where Mordred and his men have ridden,
And druids of old breathed their last
Keeping the secrets of Pendragons past.

After the excitement of the challenge and the capture of Mordred's captain, Camelot was in uproar. Some people said that the duel was a disgrace on Arthur's Day, while others blamed Arianrhod for bringing the bloodbeard into their midst in the first place. The knights were jumpy about security and doubled the guard on the gates.

As they rode back into the castle, Rhianna tried to tell Sir Bedivere what Merlin had said about her father's crown. But the knight they called 'Soft Hands' wouldn't listen to her. "We've more important things to think about now, Damsel Rhianna," he told her. "Your poor mother's upset enough, what with that bloodbeard ruining Arthur's Day and you flinging yourself on the end of his lance like you did, without worrying her about jewels and crowns."

"But it's not just any crown!" Rhianna said. "Don't you understand? It's the Crown of Dreams, the third *Light*!"

"And if you want to keep the first two Lights, you'll let us deal with this new threat from Mordred before we do anything else," Sir Bedivere said with uncharacteristic firmness. "Go see to your horse, and leave the fighting to us men, for once." He shook his head at her and went off to supervise the squires, who were excitedly discussing the duel instead of getting on with their work.

As a last resort, she tried to find her mother to tell her that the jewel in her pendant had come out of King Arthur's crown. But the queen had retired to her rooms with Sir Lancelot and would not answer the door.

"She's not very pleased with you for missing King Arthur's special lunch," Lady Isabel said, giving Rhianna's muddy armour a disapproving look. "Probably best to let her calm down a bit before you see her."

Rhianna retreated to her room in frustration, where she found Arianrhod sobbing on the bed. She spent the rest of that afternoon reassuring her friend that the bloodbeard had been taken to the dungeons and couldn't hurt her, then giving Merlin a blow by blow account of the duel, by which time it was too late to do anything except fall asleep with her hair still full of mud from the jousting field.

Rhianna woke with a stiff neck to find the Damsel Tower buzzing with fresh gossip. It turned out the knights had spent the night questioning their prisoner, and Queen Guinevere had called a meeting of the

Round Table straight after breakfast.

"I haven't time to eat all that now," she said, pushing away the laden tray Arianrhod had brought her and leaping out of bed. "I mustn't be late for the meeting!"

Arianrhod immediately started fussing about the state of Rhianna's dress, which had been flung into a corner yesterday when Rhianna had changed into her armour to help Cai.

"Leave it!" Rhianna snapped as Arianrhod tried to drag a brush through her tangled hair. "It doesn't matter what I look like. I want to hear what they found out from that bloodbeard, and why he wanted you."

A herald in the courtyard below her window announced the meeting was about to start.

"I've got to go," she said, snatching an apple from the tray. "You stay up here, all right? Then you'll be safe. Lady Isabel won't let any strange men into the Damsel Tower – you know what she's like."

Arianrhod managed a little smile. "I'm sorry, Rhia," she sniffed.

"What for?"

"For attacking you in the chapel."

"That wasn't your fault." Rhianna buckled her sword belt over her dress, distracted by the knights hurrying across the yard towards the Great Hall. "Elphin says you were under a spell. We'll talk about this later, when the meeting's finished. You can get a bath ready for me."

Arianrhod brightened up immediately. "Shall I bring up lunch from the kitchens, too?" she said. "So we can eat while we talk?"

"Whatever you like." Impatient with the

domestic details, Rhianna hurried down the spiral stair, munching the apple.

She paused before the big doors of the Great Hall to get rid of the apple core, smooth her skirt and run her fingers through her hair. A pile of swords waited outside the door. The knights were already inside, taking their seats around the circular slab of blue stone marked with druid-spirals, but the queen had not arrived yet. She straightened Excalibur – the only sword allowed into a Round Table meeting – and took a deep breath before she entered.

Sir Bors, Sir Agravaine and Sir Lancelot stood at one side of the hall in the shadows, arguing. She caught the words *Dragonland* and *Mordred*. Then Sir Lancelot said, "Shh!" and turned his strange pale gaze upon her. Seeing her, the other two lowered their voices.

Rhianna marched past them with her head held high. She took her usual place at the Round Table, next to her mother's seat.

Sir Bedivere picked a grass seed out of her hair as he took the seat on her other side. "The queen's still at breakfast," he said quietly. "You've time to snatch a few bites, if you're hungry."

"I've already had breakfast," Rhianna said, thinking of the apple. "What are Sir Lancelot and the others talking about? Is it to do with that bloodbeard? Arianrhod said you questioned him last night. Did he talk?"

Sir Bedivere grimaced at the three older knights. "I wasn't involved, but I expect we'll find out soon enough. Ah, here she is."

Queen Guinevere swept through the doors, wearing a green silk gown trimmed with gold. A tiara twinkled in her hair as she walked through a sunbeam that was slanting through the hole in the roof above the Round Table. She'd regained her beauty since her imprisonment in Mordred's dark tower, and all the men's eyes followed her.

Rhianna wished her mother would move faster so they could start. But just before the big doors swung shut, a plump figure squeezed through with a half-eaten honey-cake in his hand, distracting everyone.

"Cai!" she said with a flush of pleasure. This was the first meeting of the Round Table since she'd knighted her friend up at the lake. She'd forgotten he could join them now.

The knights blinked at the boy as he hesitated near the doors. It seemed they had forgotten, too.

"Well, come in then, young Sir Cai," Sir

Bedivere said, smiling. "Take a seat. We've got a few vacancies, thanks to Mordred's lot up at the North Wall."

"The boy's too young!" protested Sir Agravaine. "We've got important matters to discuss this morning."

The queen had been frowning at the state of Rhianna's hair. She turned her frown on Cai as he began to slide into one of the big chairs. "What's that squire doing in here?" she asked in a confused tone.

"Cai's a knight now, Mother," Rhianna reminded her.

Sir Bors cleared his throat and said, "Cai, I know that you've been knighted, but the next meeting might be more suitable for your first time with us. Agravaine's right. We'll be discussing the things we've learned from that bloodbeard we caught yesterday, and they're not pretty."

"If I'm old enough to hear it, then Cai's old enough," Rhianna said firmly. "Without him and the Lance of Truth, you wouldn't have caught that bloodbeard in the first place. He'd still be creeping about Camelot, spying on us all."

"I know what you're going to talk about, any rate," Cai said, glancing at her. "You tortured the prisoner last night, didn't you? All the squires are saying so. We heard his screams."

Some of the knights frowned.

"Now, you know very well King Arthur forbade the use of torture at Camelot, Cai," Sir Lancelot said. "Just squires' gossip," he reassured the queen. "You know what they're like."

Guinevere frowned too. But then she sighed and said, "I suppose what we've got to discuss today is no worse than squires' gossip. He can stay, if he promises not to tell all his friends what goes on in here. You understand, young Cai? What is spoken of at the Round Table is for the ears of Camelot's knights and those of Pendragon blood only."

Cai nodded solemnly.

Sir Bors gave him a doubtful look. "Right," he said. "We've wasted enough time. Sit over there and keep quiet, Cai. If you open your mouth just once, I'll throw you out myself, get it?"

Cai nodded again. He grinned at Rhianna and quickly stuffed the rest of his breakfast into his mouth before anyone could tell him off for eating at the Round Table.

Rhianna had hoped to learn what the bloodbeard wanted with Arianrhod, but the knights seemed more interested in the information he'd given them about Mordred. Sir Lancelot stood up and gave an account of the interrogation, interrupted now and again by Sir Agravaine.

When they'd finished, the men muttered uneasily.

"So it seems Mordred's holed up in Dragonland," Sir Lancelot said. "I wondered where he'd got to after he escaped from our dungeon at midsummer. He's probably avoiding the roads and working his way back north. I propose we go after him and cut him off before he reaches the North Wall. If we can trap him in Dragonland without his army, we should be able to finish off the traitor once and for all."

The older knights nodded in agreement.

"I agree. Let's put an end to all this stupid wrangling over the throne," Sir Agravaine said. "We don't need Mordred now we've got Rhianna. I say we kill the dark knight and have done with it."

Queen Guinevere frowned. "And leave Camelot unprotected?"

"Mordred's hiding like a frightened rabbit in Dragonland," Lancelot continued. "We routed his army in the north, and we're at peace with the Saxons now, thanks to our princess here, so there should be no threat to Camelot while we're gone. If you need us, my lady, light the druid beacons and we'll return at once. We shouldn't be long. The prisoner will soon tell us where his master's hiding now we've loosened his tongue."

But Sir Bedivere said, "I don't like it. What if the bloodbeard's lying? That nonsense about Damsel Rhianna's maid could be just a smokescreen. What if he came here to lead us into a trap? And what about the dragons?"

This set off more grumbling. A grizzled old knight said, "The maid's probably part of it. We should question her, too."

"No!" Rhianna said, her stomach doing strange things. If Mordred was in Dragonland, then that would be the perfect excuse for the third part of her quest. All she had to do was make sure the knights didn't leave her behind. "Arianrhod's got nothing to do with this. I think I know what Mordred wants…"

"We never found out who her parents were, did we?" continued the old knight. "Mighty convenient, how we found her abandoned on that hillside as a baby. The witch planned for the long term, we know that now. What if she planted the girl in Camelot as a spy to be brought up here among us hearing all our secrets, and now his mother's dead, Mordred wants the maid back so she can tell him everything she's learned about us?"

"Don't be silly!" Rhianna said, but she couldn't help thinking of her friend being found senseless in the dungeon after Mordred escaped. And Arianrhod herself had told her how she'd been found as a baby, abandoned outside Camelot's gates. She couldn't believe her friend would betray them, though.

"The maid's not important," Sir Lancelot said firmly. "Mordred's man didn't even get to see her, so let's not get distracted. If we take all our knights, we should be able to deal with the traitor, even if it is a trap. We know Mordred hasn't had time to raise another army. At most he'll have a few bloodbeards with him, and if there's enough of us we'll be able to handle them and any dragons that might show up. I doubt there's many of the creatures left these days, anyway."

"There's at least one," Rhianna said, thinking of the shadrake that had attacked them last year. "And I think I know why Mordred's gone there – my father's crown is in Dragonland too."

The knights stared at her.

"The Crown of Dreams is in Dragonland?" Sir Lancelot said. "How do you know?"

"A little bird told me." Rhianna smiled sweetly at them, enjoying herself now she had their attention.

Cai grinned, seeing the joke.

"She means Merlin," Sir Bedivere explained for the benefit of those who did not know how the druid had escaped Morgan Le Fay's ambush. "His spirit lives in the body of a hawk now."

"So *that's* why Mordred went to Dragonland!" Sir Bors said. "The little devil's cleverer than we thought. A dragon stole the crown from the battlefield after Arthur died – where else would it have taken its treasure? It's probably got a lair somewhere in the hills."

"Yes," Rhianna said. She fumbled in her pocket for the black pendant and started to explain about King Arthur's jewel, but the men weren't interested in the dull-looking stone.

"The prisoner didn't say nothing about a crown," Sir Agravaine said, scowling.

"Good," Sir Bors grunted. "Then at least we know Mordred hasn't found it yet."

"That bloodbeard's lying through his rotten teeth, more like," growled Agravaine. "He talked too quickly for my liking. I said we should have used more persuasive methods to loosen his tongue."

The knights began to argue about the best way of doing this. Cai listened eagerly, but Rhianna felt a bit sick.

She was glad when the queen leaned across and touched the pendant. "This jewel came from Arthur's crown?" her mother whispered. "I never knew... why didn't he tell me? I just thought it was a magic stone that changed colour when he died."

"Maybe he wanted you to keep his secrets safe?" she said, too embarrassed to tell

Guinevere the real reason her father had been sparing with the truth. "I have to go with them, Mother! I have to get the Crown of Dreams back. It's one of the four Lights my father will need to defeat Mordred when he returns to Camelot."

"Oh no, darling." The queen shook her head. "This is a war party. There might be fighting."

"I can fight! I've been training to use Excalibur in my right hand like a proper knight." Rhianna stood on her chair so she could draw her sword to demonstrate. The blade glimmered faintly as it sensed the magic of the Round Table. This got the knights' full attention, and she announced, "I'm coming with you! I've got Pendragon blood – I can speak to the dragons if you need me to."

She expected another argument. But Sir Bors merely sighed and said, "Sit down, Damsel Rhianna. Don't worry, we're not leaving you behind – you and your friends will only ride after us like you did last time, and then Mordred will just pick you off one by one. I'm taking you with me, where I can keep an eye on you. If we see a dragon, we might need Excalibur's magic. But you'll stay out of the fighting this time, even if I have to tie you to a tree to keep you out of it."

Rhianna grinned.

"Does that mean I can come, too?" Cai asked, his eyes shining. "I'm the Pendragon's champion now, and I've got the magic lance."

"Cai, shut it," Sir Agravaine warned. "Of course you're coming. We'll need someone to groom our horses."

The queen shook her head again. "Take the squire and the Lance of Truth with you if you must, but you're *not* taking my daughter into those wilds everyone knows are crawling with druids and dragons – and now, it seems, Mordred's bloodbeards as well! I forbid it."

"You can't keep me here, Mother," Rhianna said, her blood rising. "Sir Bors is right. I'll just ask Elphin to help me with his magic again, and we'll ride across the Summer Sea after them. Besides, you said I could go and look for my father's crown, didn't you?"

"That was when Mordred was safely locked up in Camelot's dungeon, not loose in Dragonland with God knows what riff-raff he's persuaded to help him this time," the queen said. "Be sensible, Rhianna darling. The knights can easily look for Arthur's crown on their way to get Mordred. After all, they know what it looks like, and you don't."

Before Rhianna could explain about the song pictures in Avalon, and how Merlin had shown them the first three Lights in the crystal walls of Lord Avallach's palace, Sir Lancelot put a hand on Guinevere's arm and whispered something into her ear. The queen gave Rhianna an exasperated look.

The silver-haired knight slammed his hand down on the table for attention.

"We've discussed this long enough," Sir Lancelot said. "If Princess Rhianna's right about Arthur's crown being in Dragonland too, then we can't delay. We have to go after Mordred before he finds it, because if he discovers how to use its magic to control dragons like the old Pendragons used to do, then having an army won't help us very much. I thought we'd have more time to get the information we needed out of the prisoner. Now it looks as if we'll have to take the bloodbeard along with us. We'll leave the older squires and enough men here to hold Camelot. Cynric and his Saxons should be able to deal with any threat to our boundaries in the meantime. Use the rest of today to polish your swords and say your goodbyes. We ride out tomorrow at first light."

The hall filled with noise as the knights began to discuss the campaign in excited voices.

Guinevere still looked worried. Sir Lancelot reached across to squeeze the queen's hand and told her not to open the gates until he got back. Cai was grinning from ear to ear. Rhianna smiled and slipped the black jewel back into her pocket.

Dragonland, she thought. *We're going to Dragonland tomorrow!*

❊

The meeting broke up soon after that. Cai slid out of his chair and rushed around the table to Rhianna, his eyes shining with excitement.

"That was great!" he said. "It's going to be a proper war party, just like in King Arthur's day! Do you think they'll let me have a bigger horse to ride? Sandy's getting too small, really, now I've got a lance to carry. Will you ask the stablemaster to find a new mount for me? He'll listen to you…"

While the boy chattered on, a guard came in and muttered something to Sir Bors. The big knight exchanged a dark glance with Sir

Agravaine, and the pair of them hurried from the hall.

"Come on," Rhianna said. "I want to see what they're up to."

Her mother broke off her conversation with Sir Lancelot. "Darling, where are you going? I want to talk to you before you leave. I thought we could have lunch together…"

"Later, Mother! " she called back. "I've got to have a bath first."

The queen frowned after her as she and Cai escaped the hall.

Giggling, they ran down the long corridors after the two knights. "You shouldn't lie to your mother," Cai said. "A bath? That's a good one."

"Actually, I do have a bath waiting for me." Rhianna thought guiltily of Arianrhod, waiting up in the royal bathroom with the scented soaps, and lunch.

"Yeah, you do stink a bit," Cai said.

"So do you, *Sir* Cai!" She pushed him into the wall, and he gave her another grin.

"Watch it, Pendragon!" he teased. "Don't forget I carry the Lance of Truth now."

"Don't forget *I* carry the Sword of Light and can call on your knightly spirit to die for me any time I like." She rested her hand on the sword's hilt, but did not call on the magic. Excalibur was too powerful to use in play.

Cai sobered. "Is it true what you said about that pendant you wear being one of the jewels from King Arthur's crown?"

"Merlin says so. It hides my father's secrets, apparently. He doesn't know what they are, though."

The boy pulled a face. "More trouble, I expect. And now we're going to Dragonland, which is supposed to hide the gate to Annwn. I just hope Mordred's not found that! His bloodbeards are bad enough, without having the dead on his side as well."

Rhianna frowned, thinking uneasily of Mordred's witch-mother. "I thought the dead couldn't come back from Annwn? I thought only dead heroes who are taken to Avalon can return to the land of men, like the ones who ride with the Wild Hunt?" *Like my father will, when I take him the four Lights and his soul returns to his body*, she added silently.

"I dunno, Damsel Rhianna. The squires say the dead haunt the abandoned dragon lairs, and that's why it's so wild there. Nobody really knows what lives in Dragonland. Sir Lancelot said all the dragons were dead, and we know *that's* not true…"

"Shh!" Rhianna said. "Hear that?"

Sir Bors and Sir Agravaine had turned down the steps leading into the dungeons. Torchlight flickered below, and they heard a faint scream. The sound was swallowed by stone and darkness, but the back of Rhianna's neck prickled.

She drew Excalibur and crept down the steps after the knights. Cai followed, his dagger clutched in his fist, treading on her skirt. The door at the bottom stood open. Beyond it lay darkness.

As they hesitated, a shadow loomed up the wall. A slender figure appeared in the doorway below, struggling to free her arm from Sir Agravaine's grip.

Rhianna's heart jumped in recognition. "It's

Arianrhod!" she said. "What's she doing down here? I told her to stay in my room. Come on!"

She leaped down the rest of the steps with Cai clattering at her heels and ran smack into Sir Bors, who stood guard at the bottom.

He whirled, his sword half out of its scabbard. "Damsel Rhianna!" he growled in exasperation. "Haven't I taught you never to creep up on an armed man like that? I might've killed you!"

"Where's Sir Agravaine taking Arianrhod?" Rhianna demanded. "She's innocent! She shouldn't be down here with the prisoners."

"Too right she shouldn't," Sir Bors said. "Bring her over here, Agravaine."

The dark-haired knight dragged the weeping Arianrhod across to them. The maid's eyes lit up in relief when she saw Rhianna.

She raised her tear-streaked face and said, "My lady, please tell them! I dozed off while I was waiting for you and had another dream, and when I woke up I was down here…"

"She brought food for that bloodbeard scum," Sir Agravaine growled. "I told the guards nothing to eat till I said, so they stopped her at the door and sent for us."

"It's cruel not to feed him," Arianrhod whispered.

"Are you crazy?" Cai said to her. "That man almost killed me out there yesterday, and now you're *feeding* him? Maybe you really are a spy for Prince Mordred, like everyone says you are."

"That's enough, Cai," Sir Bors grunted.

Arianrhod shook her head miserably. "No! I'm not a spy, I promise! Lady Rhianna, tell them, please."

Rhianna frowned at the maid, who cast nervous glances at something in Sir Agravaine's other hand that reflected the torchlight. With a chill, she recognised the dark mirror she'd stolen from Mordred in the summer – the one that worked as a spirit channel and they'd all assumed Mordred took with him when he escaped. Morgan Le Fay used it for her enchantments. Now she knew why her friend had been acting so strangely.

Mocking laughter came from the cells. "Throw the girl in here with me!" shouted the bloodbeard. "I'll soon teach her a lesson."

The guards went off to silence him.

"Why did you hide this mirror, Arianrhod?" Rhianna asked, taking the thing from Sir Agravaine and warily turning the glass to the wall.

The girl hung her head and whispered, "Lady Morgan came to me in a dream and told me to... I think I must have sleepwalked, as I don't remember hiding it."

"Did she tell you to take my pendant in the chapel, too?"

Arianrhod flushed. "I... don't remember."

Sir Bors sighed. "We haven't time to get to the bottom of this now. We've got work to do." He opened an empty cell door and checked inside. "Lock the maid in here for now. That'll keep her out of mischief till we're gone. We can't afford to lose the bloodbeard like we lost Mordred. We need him to lead us to his master."

"No!" Arianrhod gasped, and began to struggle afresh. "Please, my lady! Please don't let them put me in there!"

Rhianna stiffened. "It's not Arianrhod's

fault. She's under an enchantment."

"All the more reason to lock her up for her own safety," Sir Bors said gruffly. But his expression softened when Arianrhod started to cry. He called to one of the hovering guards. "Get the girl a proper bed down here, and whatever else she needs. She's to be treated well, but she's to be kept under guard till we're back from Dragonland."

The big knight frowned at Rhianna's blade. "Damsel Rhianna, be sensible and put that sword away before you hurt someone. I don't want a stupid fight over this. If you want to ride with us tomorrow, you'll let us deal with your maid the way we think best. Otherwise, we'll have to waste time sorting out the matter before we leave, and then Mordred might get hold of this crown that you and Merlin seem to want so much. So which is it to be?"

Rhianna clenched her fist, but slid Excalibur back into its scabbard. Sir Agravaine gave her friend a gentle push into the cell.

Arianrhod stared at them, tears running down both cheeks. "I got your bath ready before I fell asleep, my lady," she whispered. "But who's going to wash your hair for you?"

"I'll manage," Rhianna said brightly. "It doesn't have to be perfect. We're riding to war tomorrow, not a feast."

Cai drew himself up and said, "Yeah, Dragonland's no place for a damsel! You'll be much safer in here, Arianrhod."

The men glanced at Rhianna. She didn't know whether to laugh, or thump Cai for suggesting she wasn't a proper damsel.

"Cai," Sir Agravaine growled, propelling

the boy back up the steps. "I said, shut it."

Before the door closed on her friend's tearful face, Rhianna tightened her grip on the dark mirror. "No one will hurt you in here, Arianrhod," she promised. "I'll come and see you before we go tomorrow."

It was actually a relief not to have Arianrhod fussing over every little thing. After she'd bathed and eaten, Rhianna packed her own clothes, leaving out the tiaras and spare dresses her maid would have tried to include for her. Then she barred the door and propped the dark mirror on the windowsill.

She rummaged in her clothing chest and found another chain for the pendant – a stronger one than last time. She hung it around her neck and changed her slippers for her boots. Finally she drew Excalibur and stared into the black glass.

"Mordred!" she called. "I know you can hear me! The knights have got your bloodbeard spy locked in the dungeons. Arianrhod's safe. You'll never hurt her again."

At first, all she could see was her own reflection with Excalibur's blade glimmering in her hand. But as she peered closer, a shadow stirred in the glass. Quickly, she reversed Excalibur and brought the hilt of the sword down hard on the mirror.

There was a loud CRACK, and the glass shattered with an unexpected flash of green light.

Rhianna jumped out of range as the pieces tinkled to the floor. She smiled grimly and stamped on the broken glass to make sure all the magic was destroyed. It crunched satisfyingly under her boots, and the green light died.

She checked Excalibur, a bit worried the sword might have been harmed by the blow. But the Sword of Light had been forged in Avalon and seemed fine.

She laughed. "That scared you, didn't it, cousin?" she said to the empty room. "That's what happens when you come after my friends! You'd better start running, because we know where you are now, and we're coming after *you*!"

Dark Plans

Mordred woke in the shadrake's lair, bathed in sweat. What a nightmare! His cousin Rhianna had been standing over him with Excalibur, wearing the missing jewel from the Crown of Dreams around her neck. He'd woken up just as she brought the sword down to crush his skull.

He checked the crown was safe and scowled about the cave. His men had stabled the horses in one of the tunnels behind the waterfall and built a fire at the entrance. They had furnished this alcove for him from the dragon's treasure, but his captain should have been back by now. How long did it take to ride to Camelot and get a jewel off a silly maid? It would be winter soon, and then the rain would turn to snow. He shuddered at the thought of being trapped in such a godforsaken place until spring.

The crown glittered in the candlelight, mocking him. So pretty, and yet so useless – its jewels hiding magic he dared not use. He snatched it up, limped over to his mother's body and prodded her blackened bones with a spear.

"Well?" he snapped. "What's happened to my captain? Did he get into Camelot? Why's he taking so long?"

The witch's spirit did not appear immediately. Mordred ground his teeth in frustration and raised the crown over his head.

"Mother!" he hissed. "If you don't answer me, I'll ride to Camelot right now and use this thing to claim the throne—"

"Not until you've taken care of Arthur's jewel, foolish boy!" the witch said, rippling into view at last and frowning at him. "Yes, your man is inside Camelot, but he seems to have got himself arrested. That interfering squire who carries the Lance of Truth saw through his disguise and challeged him to a duel. Unfortunately, my ex-maid wasn't able to get hold of the stone in time, and now it looks as if she won't be able to."

"What do you mean, woman? I thought you said you could control her?"

"I did what I could, but the girl was careless, and Rhianna smashed my mirror. Your cousin wears the jewel around her neck, and now it seems she's riding to Dragonland with the knights on a quest for the Crown. The bloodbeard must have talked."

Mordred frowned, thinking of his nightmare. "My men never talk under interrogation. They've all sworn to die first."

The witch gave a dark smile. "I'm sure they have. But a dead captain is no help to anyone. Alive, he might still be of some use to us. Don't worry, my son, all is not lost. Since we've failed to get the jewel out of Camelot, we'll let our eager Rhianna bring it to us."

"How many men are coming with her?" Mordred asked, getting worried now.

"I'm not sure. I've lost contact with my maid now. But I doubt all the knights will come. Lancelot will be too worried about leaving the queen unprotected, after we captured her up in the North last year. We just need to make sure our brave princess is separated from her friends so your man can get hold of the stone."

He smiled, feeling a bit better. "I'll make her give me the Sword of Light and the Lance of Truth as well," he said. "She's bound to bring them on her quest, isn't she?"

"That's my boy," the witch said. "But don't underestimate her this time! She almost got you killed in the summer. I'll do what I can to help, but I can't work miracles if you find yourself at the wrong end of her blade again. I think it's time you had a few lessons in using that crown of yours."

Mordred grinned, then remembered how she'd told him the crown had killed her. He eyed her blackened body. "I thought you said it was dangerous?"

"All magic is dangerous!" his mother snapped. "But your men won't stand a chance against two of the Lights unless you help them. A dragon attack should do it, and the Jewel of Annwn is strong in this place. I'll teach you all I know."

◄❙ 5 ❙►
The Road to Dragonland

Arthur's knights rode out at first light
With Sword and Lance both shining bright,
To hunt the traitor who killed their king
In valleys shadowed by the dragon's wing.

Rhianna thought she'd never sleep. Pieces of the broken mirror flashed darkly at her from the floor every time she tried to close her eyes, reminding her of the way Morgan Le Fay had enchanted her friend. When she eventually dozed off, she dreamed of her cousin Mordred sitting in her father's place at the Round Table wearing the Crown of Dreams, and spent the rest of the night tossing and turning in a nightmare where the dark knight ruled Camelot.

She woke before dawn, dragged on her armour over her Avalonian leggings and laced up her boots. The yard was already full of horses and squires making ready for the journey. Shaking away the echoes of her dream, she buckled Excalibur around her waist with cold fingers. She reached for her father's black jewel and held it up to the light. Was it her imagination, or had it turned paler overnight?

She tucked the pendant under her armour and hurried downstairs to keep her promise to her friend.

The knights had already hauled their prisoner out of the dungeons. The bloodbeard stood shivering in the dawn, leashed by his wrists to the back of a wagon and watched by two armed guards. He looked tired and beaten. But when he spotted Rhianna crossing the yard, he raised his head and bared his teeth at her.

She glared back at him and hoped the knights would make him walk all the way to Dragonland.

The dungeons were deserted apart from Squire Gareth, who had been given the job of looking after Arianrhod. Her friend seemed to be the only one in the cells, which made her glad. At least the place wouldn't smell.

Gareth scowled when he saw her. "What are you doing down here? I thought you were riding to Dragonland with your *champion*, playing at knights."

"I want to see Arianrhod," she said.

The boy hesitated and glanced up the steps.

"Oh come on!" Rhianna snapped. "She's my friend. You know she's only locked down here for her own safety."

"She's a witch," Gareth muttered. "Sir Lancelot says she might put a spell on you."

"You don't really believe that! Let me in and I'll make sure you get guard duty on the walls instead of down here while we're gone."

He gave her a quick, hopeful look, then shrugged. "Don't matter to me. Won't be much excitement around these parts while you're away, any rate. Waste of time you all going after Mordred, if you ask me... you'll never find him if he doesn't want to be found."

"We're not just going to look for Mordred. I'm going to look for my father's crown, the one the dragon stole from the battlefield. The one that makes its wearer into the Pendragon."

That shut the boy up. He stared at her then shook his head. "So you fancy yourself as queen? Your mother might have something to say about that."

Rhianna sighed. "My mother knows why I'm going. Just let me in."

She waited until Gareth had closed the cell door behind her. Then she fumbled under her armour for the pendant. "Listen, Arianrhod..."

"Oh Lady Rhia!" The girl flung herself at her and held on tight. "My lady, please, you have to listen to me. You can't trust that bloodbeard! Last night, after you'd gone, there was a sharp pain in my head and I suddenly started remembering things. I know now why Lady Morgan made me come down here with her dark mirror – the bloodbeard used it to speak to her spirit! You've got to warn the knights. I think he's up to something."

Rhianna frowned. "I must have broken the enchantment when I smashed the mirror…"

"You smashed it?" Arianrhod blinked at her. "Then that must be why I remembered!"

Rhianna nodded grimly. "I didn't realise breaking it would cause you pain. Don't worry, nobody will be using that mirror to enchant anyone ever again. Listen, Arianrhod, this is more important. I want you to do something for me while we're away."

"I'll do anything for you, my lady, you know that!" the girl sniffed. "But how can I, if I'm locked up down here? I can't even clean your room for you. I'm not much use as a maid, am I?"

"You can do this."

Rhianna peeped through the door to check Gareth was not listening. She drew Arianrhod to the back of the cell and pulled the black jewel over her head. She hung it around the girl's slender neck. "I want you to look after this while I'm away," she whispered. "Try not to let anybody see it. If they do, just say it's an old pendant I gave to you because I didn't like it, all right?"

Arianrhod's eyes widened as she touched the stone. "My lady! But this is your father's jewel—"

"Yes, and I think it'll be safer with you in here until we get back. Just in case that bloodbeard is up to something, as you say.

Nobody must know you've got it."

The girl smiled. "Don't you worry, Lady Rhia. I'll guard it with my life!"

Rhianna smiled too. "You won't need to do that. Gareth is supposed to guard you with *his* life. As long as none of Mordred's bloodbeards get down here while we're gone, it should be safe enough. If Lady Isabel comes to see you, just tell her what I told you. With all the knights gone to Dragonland, my mother's the only one who's likely to recognise the pendant, and I doubt she'll come down to the cells."

Arianrhod sighed. "No, the queen never visits the dungeons. She's been afraid of the dark ever since Mordred captured her and locked her up in his tower." She glanced uneasily at the shadows.

Rhianna hadn't known that. Her mother hid it well.

"Have you got everything you need in here?" she asked.

Now that it had a proper bed and rugs on the floor, the cell looked much more comfortable than yesterday. Arianrhod had taken one of the bedcovers and fixed it to the hooks on the wall, so it hung like a tapestry. She had been allowed some candles too, spare dresses, and her trinket box full of Rhianna's unwanted jewellery.

Arianrhod nodded. "I've enough, my lady."

"Good." Rhianna gave her an awkward hug and knocked on the door. When Gareth let her out, she looked back at her friend and hesitated. "Will you be all right?"

Arianrhod sat on the edge of the bed and gave Rhianna a brave smile. "It's not for long, is it?

You'll soon be back with the Crown of Dreams."

Rhianna smiled too. "As soon as I can, I promise."

"And then the knights will kill Mordred, so we can all be safe."

"Yes," Rhianna said, trying not to think too much about her cousin. "And when I've found the Crown, we can all go and look for the Grail of Stars and bring King Arthur back from Avalon. Then nobody will hurt you or lock you up in a dungeon ever again, I promise."

Gareth rolled his eyes.

Arianrhod bit her lip. She started to say something else, but Cai's voice yelled from above, "Damsel Rhianna? Are you still down there? Sir Bors says if you're not up here in two shakes of a horse's tail, we're leaving without you!"

"Go, my lady!" her friend said. "And don't forget your hairbrush…"

"It's already packed!" Rhianna lied, grinning as she sprang up the steps.

❁

They took the Roman road the knights had used when they rode to the North Wall in the spring to rescue the queen and bring back Sir Lancelot. As they crossed the bridge, Rhianna looked back at Camelot's white towers and remembered how she had watched the knights ride out that day, as much a prisoner in her room as Arianrhod was now, in the dungeon. But she'd got out with a bit of help from her friends.

She patted Alba's shining neck. "The knights know that even if they locked me in the dungeon, I'd find a way to escape and follow them," she told the mare.

Alba tossed her head. *I want to gallop*, she complained. *These big horses are very slow.*

Rhianna smiled. "I know they are, my darling," she said. "But at least we're going with them this time. That's more fun than using the druid path to catch up with them, isn't it?"

Elphin glanced at her and shook his head. No doubt he'd have preferred to use the magical path Merlin had shown them, which allowed them to travel quickly between stone circles using the spiral pathfinder Elphin wore around his neck to open the mists. But she always found riding with the knights exciting.

The men were in high spirits because Sir Lancelot led them again. The big horses pranced, the knights' lances glittered in the sun, and her father's red and gold dragon banner flapped proudly in the breeze. People ran out of the villages and towns to wave and cheer as they trotted past. Rhianna didn't even mind that they wouldn't let her ride at the front. Here, in the middle of the party with her friends, she could keep an eye on the bloodbeard, who stumbled along behind the wagon. He seemed docile enough, but she didn't want him behind her where he might get up to mischief.

She checked the sky for Merlin, but couldn't see the little falcon. Before leaving the castle, the knights had sent messages by hawk to the volunteers who manned the druid beacons which formed a line of sight across the Summer Sea, from Camelot to an old fortress on the far shore. Merlin had flown off with the hawks to check the fire magic would still work if the volunteers needed it. He'd promised to meet them in Dragonland. She just hoped he wouldn't get distracted by a rabbit and forget.

As they rode further north, Elphin gazed across the marshes beside the road, humming a sad song in his throat. The raised banks and stretches of misty water suddenly seemed familiar.

"Isn't that the way to Avalon?" she said, remembering how they had ridden in the opposite direction with Sir Bors and Sir Agravaine last year, after losing Merlin in the mists between worlds. So long ago, it seemed now.

Her friend nodded. "I think so, yes."

"Then aren't we going the wrong way? I thought Dragonland was back that way. Oh, Arianrhod *said* that bloodbeard was up to something! We've got to warn the knights."

"We can't cross the Summer Sea with all these horses, Damsel Rhianna," Cai said. "They don't have magic shoes like your mist horses do. We got to keep going north on this road till we get to Corinium, and then head west across the river to Dragonland."

"How long will that take?" Rhianna looked longingly at the narrow tracks leading off into the mist. "Elphin, you don't think we could…?"

He put a hand on her rein. "No, Rhia," he said firmly. "Let's find out where Mordred's hiding first."

They camped that night on a hill near a town with public baths built by the Romans. Rhianna wanted to visit them, but Sir Bors wouldn't hear of it. "This isn't a sightseeing trip, Damsel Rhianna," he reminded her, tweaking her braid. "Besides, you had a bath last night, didn't you? Two baths in two days is a bit much for someone who grew up in Avalon. I thought you'd at least want to roll in some mud first."

Rhianna flushed as the other knights chuckled. She caught the bloodbeard looking at her again and scowled at him.

They passed through Corinium without stopping and headed west. This road was more overgrown and showed fewer prints. They trotted past some blackened, smoking huts and then came to a town beside a river, where the people did not cheer them. When they saw the Pendragon banner, they complained about a dragon swooping out of the hills and setting fire to their homes.

Sir Agravaine went to question them and came back looking grave.

"It can't be the shadrake that attacked us last year," he said uneasily. "Unless it's learned to breathe fire as well as ice. We're getting close to the border. If this is Mordred's doing, we'll have to keep a good lookout from here on in."

Sir Bors rode his horse across to the bloodbeard and seized his hair in one fist. "You know anything about this?" he growled.

The prisoner bared his teeth. "Ask the damsel," he said. "She's a Pendragon, isn't she? Meant to be able to control dragons, I've heard. Maybe she sent the beast?"

"You know that's a lie!" Rhianna clenched her hand on Excalibur's hilt and glared at the bloodbeard.

"Don't, Rhia," Elphin whispered, putting

his hand over hers. "He's only trying to upset you. Stay away from him."

She was glad when they left the burning town behind. She felt sorry for its people, but the knights didn't have time to stop and help them. The road got rougher as they rode. The mist horses delicately picked their way over the stones and puddles, but the bigger horses stumbled, and the wagon wheels kept getting stuck in the mud. Wooded valleys dripping with wet ferns led off between the hills. They went slower and slower as the road became little more than a sheep track. Rhianna divided her attention between the hills and the trees, keeping an eye out for dragons and worrying about Merlin.

As she was wondering how they would ever find her cousin or the Crown of Dreams in such a wild land, shouts came from the front of the party, and the wagon carrying their supplies jerked to yet another stop.

"It's that bloodbeard again," Elphin said.

Cai stood in his stirrups to see, and almost dropped his lance when Sandy put a hoof down a pothole.

"He's sat down in the mud," Cai reported. "Sir Bors is trying to make him get up. Dunno why he's bothering. They should just drag him if he refuses to walk."

Rhianna frowned. "Cai, stop showing off," she said. "Don't forget that's the Lance of Truth you're carrying, not a squire's spear."

Cai pulled a face. "It might as well be! The knights still treat me like a squire. They seem to have forgotten I was the one who challenged that spy to a duel and lured him into their trap so they could catch him."

"They haven't forgotten you fell off, though," Elphin said, winking at Rhianna.

"I wouldn't have done if Damsel Rhia hadn't got in the way," Cai grumbled. "I'd have unhorsed that bloodbeard. I'm supposed to be her champion. She should have let me take care of it. Tell her, Elphin."

"I tried," Elphin said, still teasing. "You know she never listens when she's got a sword in her hand."

Before Rhianna could argue, Sir Bedivere came trotting back down the column. "Cai, get down off that pony," he called. "We need something for the prisoner to ride that won't get him very far if he makes a run for it. This road's not made for carts. We're going to leave the wagon here and carry the supplies between us."

Cai frowned at the bloodbeard. "But what about me?"

Rhianna saw the men unhitch the horses from the wagon and smiled in understanding. "You wanted a bigger horse, didn't you Cai?"

"You can take one of the carthorses, Cai," Sir Bedivere confirmed. "That grey mare's quiet enough."

Cai's face broke into a grin. He patted the pony apologetically. "I'm sorry, Sandy. I'll come and groom you tonight."

While Cai struggled on to the back of the tall dappled mare, the knights hauled the bloodbeard into Sandy's saddle and linked his ankles under the pony's belly with the rope. They passed Sandy's reins to Sir Bors. The bloodbeard sat silently and sulked.

"He hoped they'd untie him so he could

make a break for the hills," Elphin said.

Rhianna watched the unloading of the wagon impatiently, itching to make a break for the hills herself. Then Cai barged between them on his big mare. Alba shook her mane and made a comment about human boys who could not control their horses.

They made better progress after that, though still too slow for Rhianna's liking. In the afternoon, it started to rain. She pulled her cloak over her head and thought how pointless a hairbrush would have been.

❦

That night, they camped in a wooded valley with a loud stream rushing down a gully. The bloodbeard was hauled off his pony and leashed to a tree as usual. Cai went to comfort

Sandy, while Elphin took Evenstar for a drink. As Rhianna unsaddled Alba, she felt the bloodbeard watching her again. She scowled at him.

"You," he hissed. "Yes, you, Pendragon girl! Come over here. I've got something to tell you."

She glanced around. Nobody else had heard. His guards were struggling to erect a shelter in the rain and wind. The knights were still seeing to their horses and trying to light a fire so they could cook supper. Sentries patrolled the edges of the camp, keeping a lookout for enemies in the dark.

"Don't be scared," the bloodbeard said, raising his bound wrists. "What can I do, trussed up like this? I've been trying to talk to you for ages. But them knights of yours keep you wrapped up like a soft damsel who's afraid of getting a twig stuck in her hair."

This got Rhianna's blood up. Clenching her fist on Excalibur, she strode across. But even though he seemed docile enough, she remembered Arianrhod's warning and stood carefully out of reach. "What do you want?" she said.

He glanced at his guards, who cursed the shelter as a sudden gust of wind ripped it from its ties to collapse on their heads. "Come closer, Pendragon girl," he whispered.

She wasn't going to fall for that trick. "I can hear you just fine from here."

The bloodbeard pulled a face. "Please yourself. But my information isn't for anybody else's ears. It concerns your father's crown."

Rhianna's skin prickled. She glanced back at Elphin and Cai, who were still grooming the horses. "What do you know about King Arthur's crown?" she said. "Have you seen it?"

"Oh, I've seen it all right." The bloodbeard grimaced. "Want to know where, don't you Pendragon maid? Got your eye on it yourself, no doubt? Mighty pretty it is too, with all those jewels. Suit you very well, I'd say."

She saw one of the knights glance in their direction, and crouched behind a bush so her bright hair wouldn't give her away. "If you tell me where you saw it, I'll see if I can get you something hot to eat tonight," she whispered.

The bloodbeard's face twisted a bit, and she knew she'd touched a nerve. "I'm not hungry," he grunted. "We northerners are used to fighting on empty bellies, unlike you soft summer landers."

"Please yourself," Rhianna said. She eyed

his leash. It looked too short to allow him much movement. She crept behind his tree and quietly drew Excalibur. With a quick leap, she put the blade to the bloodbeard's throat. "Now tell!" she said.

He grinned at her. "Nice move. But I think you're bluffing, Pendragon maid. I've heard you can't blood that sword of yours if you want to take it back to Avalon for your father."

"Maybe I don't want to give it to my father. Maybe I want to keep it for myself. So tell me where you saw the Crown of Dreams! Quick, before the knights come back. I'll count to three. One… two…" She pushed the sword a little harder against his throat.

He pressed his head back against the tree and laughed softly. "All right, all right! You'd do a better job of interrogation than your knights, I'm thinking. But if you cut my throat, you'll never find your father's crown, because I'm the only one who can lead you to it. It's in a dragon's lair quite close to here. If you release me, I'll take you there."

"Why are you helping me?" Rhianna asked, suspicious.

"Prince Mordred abandoned me. He sent me to Camelot alone to punish me for letting him get captured in the summer, knowing I'd be caught and tortured. If I help you gain the crown, you'll keep Mordred off the throne and I'll be safe from his revenge. If you want to kill me afterwards that's up to you, but I prefer to put my trust in Arthur's daughter than in Morgan Le Fay's witch-brat."

She stepped towards him, lowering Excalibur. "Where?" she demanded. "Where is this dragon's lair? Is Mordred there, too?"

"Funnily enough, that's just what your bullies of knights want to know."

He suddenly lunged forward and grabbed her ankle. She stumbled in surprise as the leash uncoiled from where he'd been hiding it under some leaves and looped around her arm. He slammed her wrist against the tree, sending the sword flying. His hands grabbed her hair, catching in the tangles, and she felt his filthy fingers fumbling at her throat.

It was a trick, after all.

"You're lying!" she choked, trying to free herself but only getting more tangled in the rope. "You've no idea where the Crown is. You just want to escape… so you can run… back to your master… let me *go*!"

6

Ambush

Arthur's great army fought on the plain
But their horses stumbled in the rain.
Attacked by dragons, their blood ran red
In mist-bound valley their captive fled.

The sound of their struggle alerted the knights. Help came in a confusion of shouts and running feet. Cai, who was closest, charged across the clearing with the Lance of Truth and launched it at Rhianna's attacker with a furious yell.

She fought to free her hair from the bloodbeard's grasp as he hauled her in front of him to make a human shield. "No, Cai!" she gasped.

Fortunately, the boy missed his target in the dark. The lance sparkled past Rhianna's ear and got stuck in the tree. While Cai struggled to free it, Elphin's harp tinkled out into the night, distracting the bloodbeard. Sir Bors and Sir Agravaine came running with Sir Bedivere hot on their heels, shouting at the prisoner's guards to help.

The men struggled out of their collapsed shelter. They grabbed the bloodbeard and hauled him back against the trunk, wrapping his leash around his neck until he half choked.

Sir Bedivere helped Rhianna up, while

Sir Bors thumped the prisoner on the nose. The bloodbeard grinned and spat blood into the big knight's face, so Sir Bors thumped him again.

Sir Lancelot arrived and took charge with a furious glare. "What's going on here? Get the princess away from that man! I promised Queen Guinevere I wouldn't let him get within spitting distance of her!" He scowled at the two guards. "How did this happen? What were you two doing while the prisoner was attacking our princess?"

The men flushed and mumbled something about the shelter falling on them.

Sir Bedivere took Rhianna's elbow and tried to lead her away. She pulled free of him and picked up Excalibur. She looked down at the bloodbeard, panting, and gripped the hilt of her sword. She wanted to punish him for tricking her but couldn't get past Sir Bors, who seemed intent on beating the prisoner to death.

Then Elphin's music *changed*, and she began to think more clearly. She raised Excalibur until its blade gleamed in the firelight and shouted, "Stop!"

The big knight stepped back. Cai, who had finally managed to free the Lance of Truth from the tree, came to stand beside her. He pointed the lance at the bloodbeard.

"Don't kill him," Rhianna said. "He didn't hurt me, not really. It was my fault. I was stupid, I got too close."

Sir Lancelot frowned at her. "You sure you're all right, Princess?"

"Yes. I didn't see him down there in the dark, and he… er… caught my ankle as

I went past." She saw the bloodbeard's eyes flicker to her face and dared him to say more. "We need him to show us where Mordred's hiding, don't we?" she said. "He won't be able to do that if you strangle him."

At this, the guards loosened the rope from the prisoner's throat. The bloodbeard coughed and sagged in relief, gasping for air.

Sir Lancelot sighed. "Princess Rhianna's right," he said. "Secure that man so he can't move, and don't take your eyes off him from now on. If you know what's good for you, you'll not try that again!" he added to the prisoner. "You've just said goodbye to your supper. We don't feed scum like you who think it's funny to attack defenceless damsels in the dark."

"I'm not a defenceless damsel," Rhianna pointed out.

But the knights were not listening.

"Serves you jolly well right if you starve to death!" Cai said, giving the bloodbeard a jab with the Lance of Truth before they left him to his guards.

Rhianna discovered she was shaking. It took her three attempts to sheathe Excalibur. She clenched her teeth, still angry with herself for being fooled by the bloodbeard's lies.

§

"Why did you go over to talk to him?" Elphin whispered later, as they sat beside the fire sharing some nuts and berries, while the men chewed strips of salty journey meat.

"She didn't," Cai said with his mouth full. "You heard her. He tripped her up in the dark, the sneak. Probably been looking for a chance to get his greasy hands on her ever since we left Camelot. Are you *sure* you're not hurt, Damsel Rhianna? He looked like he was trying to strangle you! Good thing we stopped him in time."

She rubbed her throat and frowned. "I don't think he wanted to kill me. I think he was looking for something."

Elphin's gaze flew to her neck. "King Arthur's jewel? Is it still safe?"

"I hope so," Rhianna said, thinking of Arianrhod locked in Camelot's dungeon.

Cai frowned. "What do you mean, you hope so? Can't you check?"

"She can't check, because she hasn't brought it with her," Elphin said quietly. "Have you, Rhia?"

Her friend's violet eyes held hers, full of the magic of Avalon. She couldn't lie to him, even if she wanted to. "No," she admitted with a sigh. "I left the jewel with Arianrhod."

"You did *what*?" Cai jumped to his feet. "But that's no good! I thought we're supposed to put it back into the crown when we find it, so that its magic will work properly?"

"Sit down, Cai," Elphin said, still quietly. "Don't tell the whole world." He glanced across at the prisoner's tree to check the bloodbeard wasn't listening. "So now he knows you haven't got the jewel."

"He knows I'm not wearing it. He doesn't know we haven't brought it with us in one of our packs."

Elphin nodded. "Good point. You might be right about it being safer where it is, if Mordred's lurking around these parts as well. I don't like the sound of those dragons burning towns. But you still haven't told us why you went to talk to that bloodbeard captain in the first place."

"She didn't—" Cai began.

"I wanted to find out more about King Arthur's crown," Rhianna admitted. She told the others how the bloodbeard claimed to have seen it. "But he's lying, isn't he? He obviously only said that to lure me close enough for him to grab me so he could steal the jewel and take it to his master."

"Yeah," said Cai. "He must be lying, because whoever wears that crown becomes the next king of Camelot, and we all know that's not going to be Prince Mordred."

Elphin said nothing. They looked at the tree again, where the prisoner was slumped in his tight bonds. He'd have a stiff neck in the morning. Rhianna wished she'd had time to ask him more questions before he'd grabbed her. Could she creep over there when the others were asleep?

"Don't even think about it, Rhia," Elphin whispered, guessing her thoughts. "I played the sleeping magic for him. He'll be dead to the world until we're ready to ride in the morning."

Morning dawned grey and damp. While she saddled Alba, Rhianna fretted about Merlin. How would the druid ever find them in these foggy valleys? He was such a small hawk. What if he'd got lost or eaten by a dragon on his way across the Summer Sea? Then she fretted about the bloodbeard and his claim to have seen the Crown of Dreams. What if he hadn't been lying? What if he really did want to betray Mordred and help her? She needed to ask Merlin what to do, but as usual the druid was never around when she needed him.

Alba had to nudge her for attention. *You are very distracted this morning*, the mare snorted. *You put my bridle on backwards. It is hurting my ears.*

Rhianna stopped looking for the little hawk and patted her mist horse. "Oh! I'm sorry, my darling!"

She sorted out the bridle. Then she helped Cai mount his big grey mare and passed him the Lance of Truth, before vaulting into her own saddle. Elphin was already mounted on Evenstar. She watched the bloodbeard as the men hauled him on to the pony. In the daylight, she could see his new bruises.

One eye was swollen shut, and he seemed woozy, almost falling out of his saddle. His guards had to walk alongside to hold him on.

Elphin's enchantment must still be working, she supposed. She'd have to wait until later to get any sense out of him.

The track wound steeply upwards, and soon they were surrounded by thick mist. The knights had to ride in single file, and they lost sight of the front and the back of their party. Rhianna gave up hoping for the merlin to appear. If the druid was flying in this, then he could look after himself. Alba tucked her head to her chest in misery.

Just as she wondered if they had lost the road entirely, she glimpsed green lights in the mist. She squinted uneasily at them. The jewel on Excalibur's hilt began to glow.

"I don't like this, Rhia," Elpin whispered, reaching for his harp. "There's magic at work here…"

Even as he spoke, an unearthly shriek came out of the fog. They heard the flap of large wings overhead.

"Look out!" Cai yelled. "Dragons!"

Rhianna ducked as a monstrous, winged creature dived out of the clouds to strike the knight riding in front of them. He fell from his saddle with a grunt, and the dragon snatched up his dropped sword to add to its treasure pouch. The other knights spun their horses on the narrow path, drawing their swords as a second dragon swooped down on them.

Alba reared in terror, and Rhianna had to grab the mare's mane to stay on. She fumbled desperately for Excalibur and drew the shining blade, trying to see where the first creature had gone. Yells of alarm sounded ahead, and a riderless horse galloped past them.

Shouts and curses came from the back of the party as the loose horse reached them.

"What's happening?"

"Who fell off?"

"Is Merlin back?"

"That's no hawk, stupid! Don't you know a dragon when you see one?"

"One? There's hundreds of 'em up there! Look out…"

Rhianna tensed. She could only see two of the creatures. Then Sir Lancelot yelled back down the path, "Protect the princess!" and several big horses pressed close to Alba, blocking her view.

The second dragon made another dive at

the column, causing yet more panic and confusion. Seeing the shadow of its wings in the mist, she thought at first it was the shadrake that had attacked them in the summer. But then it opened its mouth and belched out flame, rather than ice, and she realised it must be one of the dragons that had burned the border town.

Elphin pulled out his harp. Avalonian music tinkled across the hillside, and the dragon-fire soon fizzled out. But the horses were terrified now, bucking and plunging and neighing. The knights had a hard time staying in their saddles.

The first dragon swooped back out of the smoke. Rhianna swung Excalibur at the creature as it passed overhead. It was so close she could feel the heat of its fiery breath on her cheek. Flames licked her hair. She beat them out with her shield and held on grimly to the sword, its blade shining in the mist.

"Leave us alone!" she yelled. "I am Rhianna Pendragon, and I order you to go home!"

Her voice sounded small compared to the dragons' shrieks, but they heard her.

"WE KNOW YOU ARE THE PENDRAGON MAID," boomed one.

"WE MUST NOT HARM YOU."

"BUT WE CAN TAKE ALL YOUR PRETTY WEAPONS."

"You won't take mine!" Cai yelled, raising the Lance of Truth. "This here's a magic lance, so you'd better watch out. Stay away from Damsel Rhianna, or I'll skewer you with it and roast you over your own fire." His new horse did not look so quiet any more, but he clung bravely to the reins as the grey mare pranced like a warhorse.

Alba pranced too, not to be outdone. *Do you want me to race Sandy again?* the mare asked.

Rhianna's head hurt with the booming dragon voices, and her right arm ached from swinging Excalibur over her head. For a moment she thought her mare was confused and had forgotten Cai no longer rode the pony. Then she saw Sandy's tail disappearing into the mist with their prisoner. In the confusion of the dragons' attack, the bloodbeard had somehow taken control of the reins with his bound hands.

"Sandy!" Cai wailed, noticing the escaped prisoner too.

Rhianna stared after the pony in frustration. "The bloodbeard's getting away!" she shouted at the knights. "I'll be all right – go after him!"

As the knights hesitated, the dragons dived again one from each side. Fire lit up the hillside, showing wild-eyed horses, confused men, and frightened squires clutching their weapons, not sure whether to fight or flee.

Cai's mare reared, and as he flung his arms around his horse's neck the Lance of Truth came whistling down across Alba's nose. The little horse misted to avoid it. Rhianna gave up trying to fight right-handed according to the knightly code, and swapped Excalibur back to her left hand. As she did so, a large claw appeared out of the smoke and struck her arm. The sword went spinning out of her grasp.

With a cry of triumph, the second dragon back-winged and snatched Excalibur out of the air. Weakness washed over Rhianna as the sword vanished into the dragon's pouch.

"THANK YOU, PENDRAGON MAID, THIS IS A VERY SHINY WEAPON. WE WILL GO NOW."

"It's taking the Sword of Light!" she shouted, dragging Alba's head around. She stood in her stirrups in a futile attempt to regain the sword. "Elphin, *do something*!"

Her friend raised his harp again, but the music did not have much effect on the dragon, which shrieked a final farewell as it flapped away into the mist. The other dragon swooped one last time and snatched up a few more dropped weapons before flying after its friend.

Elphin's fingers moved faster and faster as he tried to put out all the fires the creatures had started. Cai had somehow kept hold of the Lance, but had lost control of his reins. None of the knights were chasing the bloodbeard. They had scattered across the hillside, still fighting invisible dragons. She heard Lancelot's voice shouting orders from the mist, faint and far away.

"Over here!" Rhianna shouted. "They went that way! Can't you see?"

But the knights obviously couldn't see. And without Excalibur to light up the mist, she couldn't see very much, either. Was that shadow another dragon? Maybe the knights were right, and there were more of the creatures than she thought?

She hesitated a moment longer. The dragons would be weighed down by the weapons they had stolen from the knights, but they could still fly faster than any horse could gallop.

"Race that dragon, Alba!" She dug her heels into the little horse's sides.

The mare barged past the nearest knight's horse, almost knocking Rhianna out of the saddle. She saw the man's wide-eyed look. Then they were plunging off the path and down the rocky hillside after the dragon that had stolen her sword.

Dark Trap

Mordred ripped the Crown from his head with a shaking hand. It burned his forehead every time he put it on. He dared not wear it for long periods.

Dragon wings still flapped in his ears, and he could hear the echo of their booming voices. He stared around the shadrake's lair in alarm. The knights had escaped the ambush and were coming this way! At the sight of his men dozing around the fire instead of keeping watch at the tunnel, his alarm turned to panic.

"Mother!" he yelled. "Mother, help me!"

The witch glimmered into view, looking

serene and beautiful in the glow of the green
jewel. She frowned at his trembling hand.
"Pull yourself together, boy!" she snapped.
"Don't drop that crown. What's wrong
this time?" Her voice turned sickly sweet,
taunting him. "Your cousin send you another
nightmare?"

"Worse," he reported, clutching the crown.
"She's coming down here!"

Woken by his yell, two breathless
bloodbeards appeared at his alcove, weapons
drawn. He waved them away with a scowl.
"I thought I told you to keep watch! Get
back to your posts. Can't you see I'm busy?"
The men took one look at his mother's spirit
and backed out again.

He lowered his voice. "I sent the dragons
to ambush the knights like you said, but

the stupid creatures won't obey me. They abandoned the attack, and now Rhianna's bringing Arthur's entire army to murder me! I thought you said they wouldn't all leave Camelot? Sir Lancelot's leading them and that bully Sir Bors is with them too. I'm sure I spotted Sir Agravaine and Bedivere as well... If they trap me down here, I'm dead."

The witch sighed. "Arthur was never such a coward, even before he wore the Crown. I suppose you've lost contact with the dragons?"

"Stupid things flew off with the Sword!"

"Excalibur?" the witch said, eyebrows raised.

"Of course Excalibur," Mordred said, rubbing his temples. "I wouldn't have given myself a splitting headache getting them to steal some ordinary sword. I've plenty of useless old blades down here already." He cast a scathing look around the piles of treasure.

His mother sighed again. "Didn't I warn you not to try anything tricky with that Crown until you've dealt with Arthur's jewel? Dragons are difficult enough to control, as it is."

"They were meant to bring the sword to me, not fly off with the thing," he muttered.

To his surprise, she chuckled. "Still, it was a good try. Without Excalibur, the girl will be vulnerable. She's coming this way, you say? Is she alone?"

Mordred calmed down a bit and started to think more clearly. "She was when I last saw her. But the knights won't be far behind."

The witch smiled. "Leave the knights to me. You concentrate on the damsel. Do you think you can handle her on your own, or do you need my help for that, too?"

Mordred brightened up at the thought of his cousin trapped in here with him. He put the crown back on and went to rouse his men. "Make yourselves useful and find a strong chain!" he told them. "Fix it to the wall over there. We're making this place ready for a princess."

7

Captive

The thief lured Rhianna from the hill
Through valleys where ancient
stones stand still
And enemies lurk in shadowed wood
To catch a damsel with their muffling hood.

Rhianna galloped blind into the mist. She could not see much past her mare's white ears and soon lost sight of the dragons. She heard someone call her name and glanced back to see Elphin urging Evenstar after her. Cai's horse followed him, the Lance of Truth swinging wildly.

Too embarrassed about losing her sword to face her friends yet, she urged Alba faster. They crossed a river, galloping over the surface of the water in a sparkle of Avalonian magic, raced up the hill on the other side and plunged into the next valley. Now she couldn't hear the dragons ahead or her friends behind.

Alba's neck foamed with sweat as she dodged through the trees. Rocks flashed under the mare's dainty hooves. Then a mossy stone loomed out of the mist right in front of them. Rhianna had been watching the sky, so did not see it in time to swerve. Alba threw up her head at the last moment and *misted*.

She grabbed desperately for the disappearing

mane, knowing she was going to fall off, just as she used to before she carried Excalibur. She prayed it would be a soft landing, and her head would not hit a rock. Trees and sky whirled around her as she rolled in wet leaves and came to a stop against another stone.

Still a bit shaky, she picked herself up and caught Alba's rein. She was furious with herself for losing Excalibur. Her friends could easily have been hurt by those dragons. Now she couldn't even protect them if the creatures attacked again, because she had lost the Sword of Light.

I am sorry I misted, Alba snorted. *Please do not be angry.*

"I'm not angry with you, silly," she said, patting the tired mare. "I should never have tried to swap sword hands back there, and

I didn't look where I was going again, did I? Who put that thing in such a stupid place, anyway?"

She scowled at the stone that had caused her fall. More mossy stones loomed out of the mist nearby, reminding her of the stone circle where they'd taken the magical spiral path north to catch up with the knights in the summer. But some of them leaned at strange angles, and others lay broken in the ferns.

She started to worry about her friends. What if they'd been hurt trying to keep up with her? Cai had the Lance of Truth to carry, and he wasn't that good a rider yet.

"Don't worry, my darling," she said to Alba, trying not to think about the dragons. "I expect they've stopped at that river. Cai's horse can't gallop across water."

Evenstar can gallop over the river, Alba reminded her.

"Elphin would stay to help Cai. We'll go back and find them, and then we'll look for that dragon together."

She began to lead the mare back the way they had come then stopped, her neck prickling. Ahead, a rider waited in the mist between the trunks. The horse looked about the right size for Cai's new mount, but its rider did not carry a lance. Had he dropped it?

"Cai?" she called, leading Alba towards the horse.

The rider turned his mount and trotted away into the trees.

"Cai, you idiot – it's me!"

She caught movement out of the corner of her eye and stopped again. Another horse trotted through the trees nearby.

"Elphin…?" she said, less sure now.

It is not Evenstar, her mare said.

Rhianna's stomach clenched. The knights looking for her, maybe? "Sir Bors?" she whispered. "Sir Bedivere? Is that you?"

The second rider raised a bow, and a black-feathered arrow thudded into the tree beside her.

Heart pounding, she vaulted back into her saddle and urged Alba into a gallop, ducking branches and swerving around trees. Her neck prickled as more arrows zipped past her ears. *I'm wearing my Avalonian armour*, she reminded herself. Then she remembered how the last time she'd been hit by a bloodbeard's arrow, before she'd got Excalibur out of the lake, she had fallen off. She fumbled for the

Pendragon shield that was strapped to her saddle and raised it over her head.

This meant she could not gallop so fast, but fortunately her attackers could not get a good aim through the trees, either. Then the air around her shimmered green, and the stones loomed back out of the trees – she must have ridden in a circle! As she slowed Alba, confused, the bushes in front of her erupted with dark shapes. Alba misted again, and she grabbed for the mane in desperation. She almost stayed on this time, but she still felt dizzy from her earlier fall and lost her balance.

She rolled at the feet of her assailants, while her mare galloped off. A sack went over her head. She struggled and kicked, but it did no good. There were at least four of them, and they were grown men, stronger than her. They took the shield, pinned her arms to her sides, and wound a rope around the outside of the sack.

"Damn little wildcat!" one said, sitting on her legs. "Near had my eye out. Get hold of that white pony of hers, before her friends come down here looking for her."

"Nah, they're too busy with those dragons."

"I only saw two of the beasts, and last I saw they was flapping off home. Prince Mordred's obviously not as in control of them as he thinks he is."

"Stop chattering and take her boots," snapped a new voice. With sinking heart, she recognised it as belonging to the bloodbeard captain who had escaped earlier. He bent down to whisper through the sack. "Time you found out what it feels like to be alone among enemies, Princess."

"Let me go!" she said, angry with herself for riding straight into his trap. "I'm King Arthur's daughter! His knights will hunt you down, and this time they'll kill you for sure. My friends are right behind me, they'll be here any moment... they've got the Lance of Truth... and Elphin's a prince of Avalon... he can do magic..."

She got a mouthful of sack as the bloodbeard pushed her head down into the leaves. He chuckled. "Then we'd better get you somewhere safe where they can't find you, hadn't we?"

Rhianna felt them tug off her boots. As the rope went around her ankles, she sucked in a final breath. "Find Evenstar, Alba!" she called through the muffling sack. She heard the thud of small hooves fading and went limp with relief. At least they hadn't caught her mist horse.

"Sorry, sir," one of the men muttered. "Crazy animal nearly trampled me."

"Let it go," grunted Rhianna's captor, hauling her up. "We can't waste time chasing it now. Nice and quiet, I said. You made enough noise to wake the dead."

"The dead *are* awake, sir," said one of the men in a nervous tone. "I'm sure I saw Mordred's witch-mother back in that lair."

"They're on our side, don't worry."

The captain chuckled and lifted Rhianna across a saddle. She started to kick again, then felt a pony's muzzle sniff her bare feet and realised it must be Sandy. She lay more quietly, glad of his familiar bulk beneath her.

"That's right, Princess," the bloodbeard said, mistaking her limpness for fear. "You lie nice and still and you won't get hurt. Prince

Mordred wants to talk to you about a jewel."

✣

Prince Mordred wants to talk to you about a jewel.

All through that jolting, smothering ride, the bloodbeard's words churned in Rhianna's head. Did that mean Mordred had found the crown? If he had got hold of it, he would use it to attack Camelot, and without Excalibur she'd not be able to stop him.

At first she hung limply over Sandy's back, sick with worry for her friends, unable to think straight. Then she realised that if Mordred *had* found out how to use the crown's magic, he wouldn't need to talk to her. He'd simply have told his men to kill her. She remembered Merlin saying no impostor could take the throne while Arthur's jewel was safe, and breathed again inside the sack. Thank goodness she hadn't brought the pendant with her to Dragonland.

She tested the ropes again. But they were not going to come off in a hurry, and the bloodbeards had taken her boots so she would not get very far running in the woods. They were trotting fast, and she didn't want to fall from Sandy's back trussed up like this. She lay still, saving her energy for when she met her cousin.

Eventually, the pony slowed to a walk. They went downhill. She heard hooves splashing in water, and the roar of a waterfall. The pony lurched up and over what sounded like some rocks, and freezing spray drenched her feet. Then things went dark on the other side of the sack.

The horses' hooves echoed, so she knew

they had gone underground. There was a strong smell, noticeable even through the filthy sack. A chill went through her – dragon stink.

Finally the horses stopped, their snorts loud in the cave. The bloodbeards, who had grumbled and cursed most of the journey, went quiet.

"What took you so long?" a voice called.

Rhianna tensed as she recognised her cousin's sly tone.

"Had a bit of trouble," said the captain. "Her horse kept disappearing in the mist."

"Avalonian tricks," Mordred hissed. "Where's the animal now?"

"I don't know, Master," said the bloodbeard. "It ran off. You told me to grab the girl, not the horse. We got the Pendragon shield too."

"So I see. I'm glad you managed at least one

of the tasks I sent you to do." He paused at her feet, and Rhianna's skin prickled. "I hope you haven't damaged her? She's remarkably quiet."

Rhianna's breath came faster. She heard the tap of a crutch as her cousin limped nearer.

When she judged he was close enough, she jerked out her legs. She was rewarded by a grunt of pain. The bloodbeard captain chuckled.

"What are you laughing at?" Mordred yelled. "You almost ruined the whole operation, bringing Camelot's knights with you to Dragonland! What were you thinking of? If I hadn't sent those dragons to ambush them, you'd still be snivelling in their clutches now. All right, get the girl down off that pony and take her inside. The men know where to put her. I've got something to take care of out here. Then, my brave cousin..." He limped round to the other side of the pony and touched her cheek through the sack, making her shudder. "You and I are going to have a nice little chat, and you are going to tell me what you've done with that jewel your father took out of the Crown of Dreams."

"I'm not telling you anything!" Rhianna shouted through the sack, and he laughed.

"I see you know what I'm talking about. Good, that's a start." He limped away before she could swing her legs around to kick him again.

The bloodbeards handled her with extra care after that, as if they were being watched. Two of them carried her through an echoing space to somewhere more muffled, where they set her down on something soft. Then they loosened the rope about her ankles.

Rhianna tensed, listening for clues. Where had her cousin got to? How many men were guarding her? She thought only two, but there might more out in the cave. She'd have to be ready to run fast.

As she gathered her courage, she heard the clank of a chain and felt something cold click shut around her ankle. She kicked frantically, but too late. They loosened the ropes about her sack and quickly stepped back.

By the time she'd fought her way out of the filthy thing, the bloodbeards had retreated down the tunnel, leaving her chained in a small alcove. Rhianna tugged at the chain, but it had been hammered into the rock and held firm. She flung the ropes after them with a furious shout. "Take this thing off me!" she yelled. "I'm King Arthur's daughter! You can't treat me like this! You'll be sorry…"

She tried to see where they had gone, but from her position she couldn't even see the waterfall that hid the entrance to the cave, though she could still hear its roar. With such a loud noise, nobody outside would hear her scream.

She hugged her knees, fighting tears. She wouldn't give Mordred the satisfaction of seeing her cry. She took a deep breath and looked around for something to use as a weapon. Her alcove was lit by a single candle, but it had been placed out of her reach. Bones were piled in the corners. She sat on a red cloak with a bloodstain on one corner. She touched the blood and turned cold.

A chuckle made her tense. "Not so tough

without your magic sword, are you, cousin?"

Her skin prickled as Mordred's crippled body filled the entrance to her prison. He leaned on a spear, and something glittered about his head.

"You haven't got Excalibur, either," Rhianna pointed out, trying to decide if the chain was long enough for her to kick him again. But he stayed out of reach in the shadows of the tunnel.

Mordred smiled. "Ah, but one of my dragons has. Don't worry, it'll keep the Sword of Light safe for me until I'm ready to ride to Camelot and claim my throne."

"They're not your dragons," she said, gritting her teeth. "And it's not your throne. It's King Arthur's, and when he returns from Avalon he's not going to be very pleased when he hears how you chained me up like a slave."

Mordred sighed. "We've already had this conversation. Your dear father is not going to return to the world of men for a very long time, if at all. Only the Grail of Stars has the power to command an unwilling soul back into its body before it is ready, and you'll never find the Grail without the knowledge stored in the Crown of Dreams. You didn't even take him the Sword of Light when you had the chance last year. You wanted to keep it for yourself, and look what happened… still, what can you expect when you give damsel a sword? Anyway, you're wrong, cousin. They *are* my dragons."

He limped forward into the candlelight, tossed back his cloak and smiled at her. He had washed and curled his hair so it hung across his scar, making him look quite handsome. He wore a black gauntlet over his stump, and silver and black tunic embroidered with his double-headed eagle. On his head sat a glittering crown with a green jewel glowing at his forehead – the same crown she had seen in her dream, and in Merlin's song pictures back in Avalon at the start of her quest.

He smiled triumphantly at her. "Suits me, doesn't it, cousin? This is the crown of the ancient Dragonlords, passed down through the Pendragon bloodline to the true heir. Whoever wears this crown can control dragons and command the forces of Annwn. So you see, the Sword of Light will soon be mine as well as your father's throne. An army of dragons and ghosts should take care of Camelot's walls, I think."

Rhianna's heart sank. All the strength ran

out of her. That bloodbeard had been telling the truth, after all.

"The Crown of Dreams," she whispered.

◄▌ 8 ▐►

Dragon Riding

Dragon riders of great renown
Were those who wore the Pendragon crown.
The Jewel of Annwn shines far and wide
Yet its smallest stones do secrets hide.

At first, Rhianna felt like bursting into tears. Mordred leaned on his spear, watching her with his dark smile. The crown glittered on his head as if it had been made for him. Did it really give him control over dragons? If so, she'd as good as handed him Excalibur.

Then she saw the tense look in his eye and remembered the bloodbeards who had captured her saying: *Prince Mordred's obviously not as in control of them as he thinks he is.* A flicker of hope returned.

"But the Crown doesn't work for you, does it?" she said sweetly. "Not without King Arthur's jewel. That's why you haven't killed me – you need all the jewels before you can use its magic."

"It works well enough," he said through gritted teeth. He took a step closer, his fist tight on the spear.

She pressed back against the rock, acting scared. He might wear her father's crown, but he was still a cripple. If he came just a step or two closer, she might be able to kick that spear out from under him and turn it against him. Then she would make the bloodbeards let her go.

But Mordred stayed just out of reach of her chain. He laughed at her frustrated expression.

"Give it up, cousin. You're no shrinking damsel – I know your tricks. You're right, though, in a way. I need that jewel so I can destroy it and everything Arthur stood for before I can claim the Pendragon throne. I was informed you wore the stone around your neck, but it seems not. Tell me where it is, and maybe I'll let you live to see me crowned King of Camelot."

"Never!" Rhianna said.

Destroy her father's jewel? All his secrets would be lost.

He nodded, as if he'd expected her to say

as much. "Then it seems I'm going to have to persuade you to help me another way. If you're not worried about your own life, maybe you'll be slightly more worried about your little friends out there in the hills. They're all alone, you know, looking for you. I'm guessing, since you don't have it, that one of them has the jewel. Rather than waste any more time, I'll simply send my shadrake after them. The creature might have to kill your friends to get hold of the stone, but that'll save me the bother. So if they don't have it, now's the time to say."

He waited, a little smile playing on his lips.

She turned cold at the thought of the shadrake hunting Elphin and Cai. But if her cousin couldn't control ordinary dragons properly, how would he control the shadrake from Annwn?

"The shadrake can't hurt them," she said, hoping this was true. "Cai carries the Lance of Truth, and Elphin's got his harp."

"Ah yes. The second Light made by the hands of men, and the magic of Avalon... one useless in a squire's hands, the other useless against a creature of Annwn. Well, cousin, you'll find my power is stronger than you think. Watch and learn."

He closed his eyes, and the green jewel at the front of the crown began to glow. The air in the cave turned colder. "Come, shadrake!" Mordred called. "I wear the crown of the ancient Dragonlords who once rode you through the skies. I command you to return to the lair where you were born!"

At first nothing happened. Rhianna breathed again. He must be bluffing, trying to scare her. She quietly unbuckled Excalibur's empty scabbard. While he was distracted, maybe she could use it to hook the spear towards her?

But even as she coiled the belt ready to swing, a green flash lit up the tunnel behind Mordred, dazzling her. A dull boom echoed deep within the hillside, followed by scrabbling claws out in the cave. Frightened neighs came from the horses.

"I COME, PENDRAGON!" bellowed a familiar dragon voice.

An icy wind rushed up the tunnel, blowing out some of the candles. Small stones fell from the roof and a trickle of dust landed in her hair. Rhianna brushed it off, sweating a little. What if the stupid creature brought the whole hillside down on them?

"Not in here!" Mordred looked round in alarm. "Get after the Avalonian prince and that useless squire who carries the Lance of Truth, and kill them for me. Bring me any jewels you find on them. And while you're at it, bring me the Lance as well."

"WILL YOU RIDE WITH ME, PENDRAGON?"

Mordred's face twisted in sudden pain, and Rhianna saw her chance. She spun the scabbard across the floor, aiming for the spear he'd been using as a crutch.

The buckle end of her belt whipped around its shaft, jerking the dark knight off balance. He fell to his knees, and the green glow from the jewel faded. The Crown of Dreams slipped off his head and rolled across the floor.

Rhianna dived after it at the same time as

Mordred. The chain tugged at her ankle, but not before her fingers closed about the crown. It was unexpectedly hot, and she almost let go again. Mordred grabbed it too, having abandoned his spear when he realised the trick.

They were evenly matched. His crippled leg handicapped him, just like her chained ankle. But he only had one hand, and he needed that to grip the crown. She reached for his spear with her free hand and brought it down as hard as she could across his knuckles. He let go with a yell of rage and called for his men to help him.

Fending off the dark knight with the spear, Rhianna retreated against the wall and did the only thing she could think of. She took a deep breath and jammed the Crown of Dreams on to her own head.

༄༅

Her heart pounded with a mixture of excitement and terror. She had no idea what to expect. Would its magic work for her, or would it kill her?

At first the crown felt too big, and she thought it would slip over her eyes and make her look stupid. Then it tightened, and she felt little spots of heat from the jewels, warmest on her forehead where the green stone still glowed faintly. There was a cold patch near the back – was it where her father's missing jewel belonged?

A great hush surrounded her. Then the whispers started inside her head.

"*Who is she?*"

"*A damsel…*"

"*Another witch like Le Fay?*"

"*No, a warrior maid of the blood… but a girl cannot inherit the throne.*"

"*Best get rid of her so the crown can pass to the prince…*"

She almost snatched the thing off again. But she knew she wouldn't get another chance to help her friends. She closed her eyes like Mordred had done and thought of the dragon.

"Shadrake!" she called. "Shadrake, can you hear me? I wear the Crown of Dreams now. I'll ride with you. *I'm* not afraid."

Dark wings flapped inside her head, banishing the whispers. Something pressed between her eyes. She felt the dragon's surprise… then suddenly the pressure eased, and her spirit was flying above the clouds through a red and gold sunset.

It was so beautiful, she forgot her body was chained in the dragon's lair at the mercy of her cousin and his bloodbeards. It felt like a dream, only better, because she could feel the wind on her cheeks and smell the ice in the air. She was spirit-riding the shadrake, just as Merlin had done before he found his falcon body!

Through rags of mist far below, she saw a wooded valley and a river with two white horses standing on the bank. A small figure dressed in Avalonian green knelt beside the water, studying some prints in the mud. His back was turned to the dragon as it shrieked in recognition and dived, carrying Rhianna's spirit helplessly towards him.

"Elphin!" she yelled, forgetting he couldn't possibly hear her. "Elphin, look behind you!"

Her viewpoint swerved back towards the

wood as a grey horse came galloping out of the trees, ridden by a plump squire clinging to a lance. The dragon's eye focused on the glittering weapon, and she felt its desire for the shiny thing. The boy pointed the lance determinedly at her and shouted a challenge.

"Cai!" she gasped. "Don't! It's me—"

The shadrake back-winged in confusion. She saw Elphin spring to his feet and run for his harp, which he'd left tied to Evenstar's saddle. The shadrake breathed a long plume of ice, freezing the surface of the river. Evenstar misted one way to avoid it, and Alba – the second horse – misted the other.

Glad to see her mare had escaped the bloodbeards, and forgetting she was in the body of a dragon, she chased the little horse. Alba fled over the river, cracking the ice and misting again. The shadrake shook its head in annoyance.

Elphin went down on one knee, looking very small and alone. His harp shimmered in the sunset, and his thin face was raised towards her. She heard a faint ripple of Avalonian music. For a heartbeat his violet eyes met hers, and she heard his voice singing in her head.

"Four Lights stand against the dark... The Sword Excalibur that was forged in Avalon..."

"Leave my friends alone!" she commanded the shadrake, suddenly seeing how to distract it. "You don't have to take their treasure. I know where there's a beautiful, shiny sword!" She summoned a memory of the red dragon carrying off Excalibur, and the shadrake shrieked again and abandoned its attack.

With strong wing beats, they flew over

the wood and up into the mountains. She looked down and saw the old stone circle where she'd been captured flash beneath them. The shadrake crossed the road where the dragons had ambushed their party, but she could see no sign of the knights. A chill went through her. Where had they got to? She hoped they weren't dead.

Then she saw a rock shaped like a finger on a mountain top, and glimpsed the entrance to a cave. Smoke curled out of the hillside. As the shadrake flapped closer, her heart beat faster and she knew it had brought her to the right place. The red dragon that had taken her sword launched itself out of the cave, screaming a challenge and belching out flame. The shadrake breathed ice in answer, and the two dragons met in a shower of icy rain.

"No," she gasped. "No, don't fight—"

Laughter broke the spell, and something snapped in Rhianna's head as her spirit whirled back to the shadrake's lair.

She opened her eyes, expecting to see Mordred and his bloodbeards. But Morgan Le Fay's ghost sat on a pile of blackened bones, blocking the way into the alcove and stopping Rhianna's spirit from returning to her body. The witch's ghost looked more solid than she had at the North Wall in the spring. Her hair glimmered with green light.

"So, Rhianna Pendragon," she said with another laugh. "You managed to get the Crown of Dreams off my idiot of a son and spirit-ride the shadrake. Enjoying the experience, were you?"

Rhianna scowled at the ghost in frustration.

"Go away. I'm not scared of you. You're dead. You can't hurt me."

The witch chuckled. "Clearly you've no idea what wearing that crown really means. This is one of the gates to Annwn, where the dead can pass into the world of the living. You heard them when you put the crown on, didn't you? The voices of the old Pendragon lords? So tell me what I want to know, and maybe I'll let your spirit return to your body. I believe my son asked what you did with your father's jewel. You haven't brought it with you, so where did you leave it?"

"Think I'm going to tell *you*?" Rhianna said, trying to slip past the ghost.

"Yes, I think you are," said the witch. "Because I wore that Crown too, you know, and I've had more practice in using it than you have."

Rhianna felt dizzy. To her alarm, a vision of Arianrhod sitting in Camelot's dungeon flashed unbidden through her head.

Her friend's eyes widened. "Lady Rhia!" she said, springing to her feet and staring about her in confusion. "What are *you* doing here? Are you a dream…?"

"Oh, how very clever of you!" Morgan Le Fay smiled at Arianrhod and clapped her ghostly hands. "The missing jewel's still at Camelot, isn't it? In the one place nobody will think to look, locked in the dungeon with my poor little ex-maid – who is accused of witchcraft when, for the first time in her miserable life, she's actually free of me. How delicious! I think Mordred's going to enjoy this."

"Except I smashed your mirror so you can't tell him, can you?" Rhianna said.

But the witch was still laughing. She waved her hand through Arianrhod's shadow, making it fade away. "You're forgetting the Crown of Dreams, my dear. It records the secrets of every Pendragon who wears it, including yours."

"No…" she whispered, realising the mistake she'd made in putting on the crown before she fully understood the magic.

Morgan Le Fay chuckled. "Oh yes, as soon as my son wears the Crown again he'll see where you left your pathetic jewel. And that's not all. Merlin probably forgot to tell you, but that pretty green jewel at the front contains the secrets of the first Dragonlords, back in the days when Pendragons were not concerned with boring things such as Round Tables and knightly codes. They rode dragons, flying with the storm, taking what they wanted, when they wanted it."

The witch's eyes flashed.

"Then the Romans came with their roads and their hot baths, and Arthur built Camelot in their image. My brother preferred dragons carved into his throne and woven on his tapestries rather than living in his hills. So he sent his knights to kill them. But they didn't find them all, and there are still some breeding pairs in Dragonland. When my son takes the throne, we'll get rid of Arthur's silly dreams of chivalry and restore the old ways."

Rhianna was starting to feel panicky. If she didn't get back into her body soon, Mordred might do something horrible to it. "But Mordred can't take the throne until he's destroyed my father's jewel, can he? That's why he wants it so badly – while it's still safe, he can't destroy King Arthur's dreams for Camelot."

"Oh, aren't you the clever one," said Morgan Le Fay. "I almost wish you'd been my daughter. Maybe we should make you into Mordred's queen. He'll need someone to bear his heirs when he takes Camelot's throne."

"I'd rather die!" Rhianna said, reaching with her spirit for the green jewel that held the secret of dragon riding. Could she persuade the shadrake to help her escape? The witch's ghost wavered as a wing flapped inside her head.

Morgan Le Fay pursed her lips. "Still fighting, my dear? What a stubborn damsel you are. On second thoughts, I don't think my son will be able to handle you. You're rather more of a threat than we anticipated. So now we're sure you haven't brought the stone with you, I think it's best if we just bury you in here. It's a pity you have to die, but you give people hope, and hope is a dangerous thing. I'd love to talk longer, but I have to go and help my son open the Gate now. Have a good death, Rhianna Pendragon. I'll see you on the other side very soon."

The witch disappeared as someone snatched the crown from Rhianna's head. She jolted back into her body to find the rock shaking around her and showers of stones rattling down from the tunnel roof.

Mordred scowled down at her, holding the crown and breathing heavily. She must have dropped the spear. His bloodbeard captain held the point to her throat. More bloodbeards crowded into the alcove, staring nervously at the cracks appearing in the roof.

Mordred waved them back. "Get out of here, you fools! Wait for me outside. I'll take care of this."

He shook his head at her. "That was stupid, cousin! What did you think you were trying to do? I've spent weeks learning how to use this crown! It killed my mother, you know. It's dangerous if you don't know what you're doing, and now you seem to have brought the entire mountain down on our heads."

"That wasn't me – it was your crazy mother. She's going to open the Gate of Annwn! You've got to stop her."

"Really? And why would I want to do that?" He glanced up in alarm as more grit fell from the roof into his hair. "I'm afraid I can't stay to chat any longer. I'd run if I were you, cousin… oh, but I forgot, someone seems to have chained you to the rock. Suppose you think I'm going to release you so you can escape? You should have tried that trick before we found out you don't have your father's jewel."

"You can't destroy it!" she said desperately. "You don't know what secrets it might contain."

He paused, and she thought he might unchain her. Then another shower of stones fell between them, and he smiled. "Good try, cousin. But you don't know either, and I don't need you to discover them now I've got the Crown. I doubt my uncle's secrets are of much interest, anyway." He limped back down the tunnel gripping his bloodbeard's shoulder.

Rhianna blinked after him through the clouds of dust. She heard the horses leave the cave, then a loud rumble deep inside the mountain. A chill went down her spine as she remembered the witch's words. *We'll just bury you in here.* She tugged at the chain in terror and opened her mouth to call him back.

The tunnel roof collapsed in a rush of rock and billowing clouds of foul-smelling dust. Ghostly warriors howled out of the depths of the mountain and poured past her in a glowing green river. She huddled against the rock, pulled the bloodstained cloak over her head and made herself as small as possible to avoid the falling stones.

"When I get out of here, you'll be sorry!" she yelled.

The air that had come up the tunnel suddenly cut off as the alcove crumbled around her, and her world went dark.

DARK ARMY

Mordred clung to his horse's neck as it galloped through the waterfall after his fleeing men. Boulders splashed down around him, and the river roared and foamed underfoot. They were halfway down the valley before he dared pull up. He looked back at the pile of rocks that blocked the cave mouth and shook his head in exasperation.

"It's your own fault, cousin," he muttered. "I gave you a chance! Why couldn't you bring the stupid jewel with you, like a normal damsel would have done?"

"That was close, Master," said his

bloodbeard captain, drawing rein beside him. He frowned at the cave, too. "Do you want us to dig her out?"

Mordred pulled himself together. "No! She's done us a favour, burying herself in there. We should be able to get into Camelot while the knights and her friends are still looking for her here in Dragonland."

"She might not be dead," the bloodbeard pointed out.

"If she isn't, then she'll soon wish she was," Mordred growled. "I'll be sitting on Arthur's throne by the time she digs her way out of there with her bare hands. Now stand back – my mother promised me an army."

He jammed the Crown of Dreams on his head. The bloodbeards drew back warily as the green jewel began to glow.

A wind howled along the valley, whipping up the river. Then a ghostly green horse leaped out of the hill through the curtain of water, ridden by a warrior wearing a winged helm and wielding a large axe. Behind him poured a stream of other ghostly horses and riders. The waterfall glimmered green as they passed through it and entered the world of men. All were armed, and all had fierce expressions with death in their eyes.

The bloodbeards' horses plunged and snorted. The pony the captain had used to bring the girl here broke free and galloped off, plunging into the flood up to its belly. The captain turned his horse to give chase.

"Let the stupid animal go," Mordred snapped. "It can drown for all I care."

His stallion laid back its ears as the warrior

in the winged helm rode closer. He gripped his reins tightly for courage and faced the ghost.

"So the new Pendragon calls us out of Annwn to fight again," growled the warrior, casting a glance at the bloodbeards and their trembling horses. "Not much of an army. I expected more from a grandson of mine."

"King Uther!" whispered one of the older bloodbeards. "It's Uther Pendragon, back from the dead!"

The other men muttered uneasily and drew closer together.

"My Saxon allies will be waiting for us at Camelot," Mordred said, more confidently than he felt. "My cousin made a treaty with them last year, but they'll soon change sides again when they see the way things are going.

We've got boats waiting to take us across the
Summer Sea. I assume your – er, men – can
ride across water?"

He tried to count the ghostly warriors.
But they kept fading and then reappearing
again in the green light cast by the jewel,
making him feel queasy. The Crown burned
his forehead. It didn't fit as well as it had
before his cousin wore it – curse the girl,
who'd have thought she would dare snatch
it off him and try to use it herself?

"Water is no barrier to spirits," said Uther
with a harsh laugh. "Let's get going! I'm keen
to see this great castle my son is supposed
to have built after my death. Oh, and your
mother sent this for you."

Mordred had been about to remove the
crown before he made a fool of himself.

He barely caught the black gauntlet the ghost threw at him. Cold shivered through him – *a thing of Annwn!* Then the stump of his right arm began to itch, and he realised the gauntlet still contained a human hand – his own right hand, which Arthur had chopped off with Excalibur at the battle of Camlann, and the shadrake had carried into Annwn when Rhianna banished it last year.

His captain's expression grew fearful. The man had reason to be wary of it, since he'd helped Mordred use its dark magic to torture prisoners during the hunt for Excalibur. Mordred tucked the severed fist into his belt with a smile.

Uther's gaze followed it. "Morgan said you used to be a pretty boy," he said with another chuckle. "Shame Arthur cut you up so badly in the battle. But when you join us in Annwn, your wounds will not matter. You'll be able to ride with us, whole and strong again, without pain."

Mordred scowled at his grandfather. "I'm not going to join you in Annwn, old man," he snapped. "When Camelot's throne is mine and I've learned all the secrets of this Crown, I'm going to send out every man who can ride a horse to look for the Grail of Stars. I'll make myself whole that way."

"Did you hear that? My grandson thinks he's going to escape death." Uther's ghost laughed. All the other ghosts laughed too, rippling green across the river.

Mordred shuddered. It was getting dark in the valley, and Annwn's chill had worked its way into his bones. He could hear his mother trying to tell him something, but it would have to wait until his head stopped hurting. He snatched off the crown and hung it from his belt beside his dark fist. To his relief, as the green glow died, the ghosts faded to vague glimmers in the night.

"We're wasting time," he yelled at his bloodbeards. "To Camelot! My throne awaits."

9

Gate of Annwn

Darkness was Rhianna's fate
Buried at Annwn's ancient gate,
Where ghosts and shadows haunt the hills
And river of death from the rockface spills.

Rhianna opened her eyes to darkness and silence. She felt bruised all over. She uncurled, threw off the cloak in a shower of small stones and shook the dust from her hair. She could see nothing at all. Was she dead?

She crawled warily towards where she remembered her cousin standing, and something behind her clanked... the stupid chain. She felt around in the dark until she found the sword belt she'd thrown at Mordred and spent some time trying to open the manacle with the point of the buckle. But she couldn't see what she was doing and kept stabbing her fingers in the dark. She wished she had listened to Arianrhod and put some pins in her hair. She might have picked the lock with them.

Tears came when she thought of how the witch had tricked her into putting her friend in danger. Then she thought of her cousin's smile as he'd limped away down the tunnel and tightened her fist on her empty scabbard.

He'd left her in here to die!

"You won't take the throne," she said

through gritted teeth. "It's my father's, and I'm going to get out of here and stop you."

"*That's my brave girl*," said a voice.

Rhianna's stomach jumped. She spun round, clutching the buckle like a weapon, and stared into the dark. Had one of Mordred's bloodbeards got trapped down here with her? But it didn't sound like something a bloodbeard would say.

Then her Avalonian armour began to glimmer, showing her King Arthur's ghost looking very pale and thin against a slab of rock. It seemed the roof had collapsed, by some miracle missing her on the way down and creating a pocket of air.

"Father!" she gasped. "What are you doing here? This is the Gate to Annwn! You mustn't go there, or I'll never get your soul back into your body in Avalon... how did you get in?"

"*Rock is no barrier to a spirit,*" the ghost said with a smile. "*The magic of the Crown shines brightly. You were not hard to find, daughter. But you must get out of here before the rest of the roof falls.*"

"What do you think I'm trying to do?" she muttered, eyeing the cracks in the rock above her head.

"*Try the other end.*" The ghost pointed to the place where her chain had been staked to the wall, and she realised a crack ran right through the fastening.

Her heart leaped in hope. She groped her way back along the chain and poked the buckle into the crack. After a bit of work and a broken nail, the stake dropped into her lap.

She gathered up the hateful chain in relief,

wrapped it around her waist and fastened her sword belt over the top to keep it out of the way. Grinning, she sprang to her feet and hit her head on the roof. "Ow!" she muttered, seeing stars.

"*Keep your head low*," her father's ghost advised. "*The tunnel is not blocked, but you'll need to move some stones.*"

Rhianna rubbed her head, dropped back to her knees and crawled over to the tunnel. She heaved a large stone out of the way and scraped at the rubble, enlarging the hole. It still looked very small. She'd hoped to see daylight, but more darkness waited ahead. She thought of the underwater tunnel she'd swum through to find Nimue's cave and Excalibur. This was no worse, not really.

She took a deep breath and wormed her

way through the foul-smelling dark. She had to stop several times to move more rubble out of the way, squeezing the stones past her and pushing them back along the tunnel with her feet. By the time she tasted fresher air ahead, her fingers and toes were bruised and bleeding.

With a final rattle of stones, she crawled out of the tunnel into the larger cave the bloodbeards had carried her through. Then, she'd had a sack over her head. Now, the glimmer of her armour showed her piles of treasure and pale bones.

She stood up warily and picked her way across the lair. There were sharp things underfoot, and no sign of her boots. She found a rusty dagger among the dragon's treasure and used it to cut up an old cloak that had been lying near the bones. She tied the strips around her sore feet. Then she studied her prison.

A great wall of rubble blocked the entrance to the lair. Boulders the size of horses reached all the way up to the roof. Her heart sank. She'd never shift those on her own. Could she dig another tunnel between them? She carefully began to remove the smaller stones that filled the gaps between the larger rocks, using the dagger to lever them out.

Meanwhile, her father's ghost sat down on a pile of the dragon's treasure and stared at a heap of rags and charred bones lying at his feet. He frowned slightly, as if searching for a memory, then touched the body.

"*Sister,*" he said sadly. "*Why did you have to oppose me?*"

A chill went through Rhianna as she recognised the blackened bones as those

Morgan Le Fay's spirit had been sitting on earlier.

She glanced uneasily at her father. He kept fading and then shimmering back into view with a start, like someone trying not to doze off. His ghost looked even paler and thinner than it had the first time she'd seen him. Was the witch's spirit trying to lure him through the Gate to Annwn?

"Tell me more about the Crown of Dreams," she said to distract him. "Merlin told me its jewels contain secrets, which can only be passed on to another Pendragon. You gave one of those jewels to my mother and told her to give it to me, didn't you? What secret does it contain?"

The ghost frowned at her. "*Something to do with the Grail, I think… things are hazy now* my spirit's out of my body, but Mordred must not wear that crown with my jewel restored."

"No chance of that!" she said, snatching up a broken spear to use as a lever on the boulders. "He wants to destroy it, not restore it." She had to get out of here before her cousin got the jewel off Arianrhod.

Her father's ghost became even paler. "*Then we haven't got much time, daughter. If Mordred destroys my jewel and wears the Crown of Dreams at the Round Table, my knights will have no choice but to give him the throne of Camelot. The Crown chooses the rightful heir according to the old Pendragon bloodline, and if my jewel is missing there'll be no record of you. Mordred will be the only candidate.*"

Rhianna paused in her digging to stare at him.

"That's stupid! The knights won't give the throne to Mordred. They know I'm your daughter now – you were there at midsummer when the queen told everyone I was heir to the throne. Sir Bors and Sir Lancelot aren't going to let some silly magic crown decide who rules them! Don't they write important things like that down? They wrote down the treaty I made with the Saxons last year. Anyway, the throne's still yours! When you return from Avalon, you'll take the Crown back from Mordred, won't you?"

She tried not to think of what might happen if she failed her quest and couldn't bring her father back.

The king sighed. "*I can remember so little of Camelot. It's like a dream to me now. Maybe you are a dream, too? My daughter, who rides a fairy* horse and wields Excalibur... *it sounds like one of old Merlin's songs. And now Merlin's out of the way, it'll be easy enough for Mordred to wipe us both from history.*" His ghost faded again.

"Merlin's not dead yet." At least, she hoped not. Where was the druid when they needed him? But even a small hawk wouldn't be able to get through this wall of rock.

"*You can't rely on Merlin,*" her father said, frowning again as if trying to remember something else.

"Then I'd better hurry up and get out of here so I can remind everyone we exist, hadn't I?" she said, forcing a grin. She didn't like to see her father so sad. She hoped he would cheer up a bit once she got him back into his body.

Renewing her attack on the rubble, she jammed the spear under a boulder and leaned all her weight on it. The spear snapped, and she stumbled against the rocks, bruising her shoulder.

She flung the broken pieces of wood at the blockage in frustration. "Oh, this is hopeless! I'll never get out this way."

Suddenly, the air in the cave seemed less fresh. Rhianna sat down on the treasure to catch her breath and looked for her father's ghost, barely visible now in the shadows. What had he said?

Rocks are no barrier to a spirit.

"I know!" she said. "You can walk out through the rock the same way you got in here and find Elphin and Cai. They're in the woods two valleys away… or they were when I last saw them."

How long ago had she worn the crown and

seen her friends through the shadrake's eyes? She could have been lying buried under this mountain for days. Mordred might already have taken her father's jewel off Arianrhod and be sitting on the throne of Camelot. She shook her head, refusing to think of that.

"They saw you at Lady Nimue's lake when you chased Mordred and his men away in the summer," she continued. "So maybe they'll be able to see you again. Then you can lead them up here, and they'll bring the knights to dig me out."

It seemed so simple, she wondered why she hadn't thought of it before.

He gave her a worried look. "*I hate to leave you here in the dark with Morgan Le Fay, daughter. She is strong in this place. She might try to drag your spirit through the Gate.*"

Rhianna forced another grin. "She already tried, but I've got to die first and she can't kill me herself. Mordred had some candles down here. I'll find them when you're gone, and keep working on this side until my friends and the knights get here."

Her father's ghost reached for her hands. She felt a brief warmth as his fingers passed through hers. *"You'll make a stronger Pendragon than Mordred,"* he said. *"I'm proud to have such a daughter."*

Then he got up and walked into the rock, and the last glimmer of light from her armour died.

><><

Her father was proud of her. Even if she didn't get out of here, she'd die happy.

But she wasn't going to die. She wouldn't give Mordred and his witch mother the satisfaction.

She spent a bit of time searching for candles, but Mordred must either have taken them with him, or they had been buried under the rubble with the rest of her stuff. She didn't know how she would have lit them, anyway.

She worked more slowly in the dark, feeling around every stone before she removed it, in case she made a mistake and brought the rest of the mountain crashing down on her head. Sweat trickled down her back every time she heard an avalanche in the depths of the hill, but she didn't take off her Avalonian armour. Its magic had protected her so far.

Time passed. How much time, she had no way of telling, except by the ache in her arms and a terrible thirst caused by the dust in her throat. She wondered if Mordred had found out where she'd left her father's jewel yet. She kept thinking of her cousin marching through Camelot's corridors, and of Arianrhod's promise to guard the jewel with her life.

It was all taking too long. There had to be another way out.

She stopped to catch her breath and looked thoughtfully at Morgan Le Fay's body. Could she summon the witch's spirit, and trick her aunt into using her dark magic to make the rocks at the entrance collapse again? She shook her head. No, there was too much danger they would fall on her this time, and she no longer had the Crown or the mirror to do the summoning.

She clenched her fists. She hadn't come so far to die here alone in the dark. *Think, Rhianna, think.*

In the silence, she heard a faint dripping overhead. Of course – water! There had been a river outside the cave and a waterfall feeding it. Where had that water come from, if not out of the mountain?

With new hope, she worked her way back across the lair, stopping every few steps to listen carefully. When a drop of water landed on her cheek, her heart beat faster. She hitched up her chain and, carefully feeling for every hand and foothold, began to climb the rubble towards the sound.

"Don't fall," she muttered. "Just don't fall."

She climbed higher, glad that she couldn't see the void beneath her. After what seemed forever, she felt damp rock under her bare toes. Having no boots actually helped, and she laughed. That bloodbeard had done her a favour, taking them from her. But the rock here was more unstable. A whole handful came away, and she slid back down the rubble.

She pressed her face to the cliff, listening to the thud of her heart and the patter of stones falling into the depths of the mountain. The tinkling sounded louder now, coming from above – the music of Avalon. Hardly daring to believe, she looked up and saw a watery sunbeam shining though a small hole in the rock.

"Elphin…" she whispered.

She scrambled up the rest of the way and pressed her face to the hole. She sucked at the sweet, bright air and punched her fist through.

A great slab of rock went sliding away in a rush of green water.

She squinted into the sunlight. She had emerged at the top of the waterfall, which tumbled down into a flooded valley. Four tiny horses picked their way upriver towards the blocked entrance to the cave. Two of the horses trotted on the surface of the water, leaving trails of mist, the one in front ridden by a small figure with a shining harp. The third horse splashed and stumbled over the avalanched rocks behind them, carrying Cai with his lance. Sandy swam riderless behind.

Rhianna's heart lifted. She waved her arms. "Elphin! Cai! Up here!"

But the roar of the waterfall drowned her voice. She looked at the slippery rocks leading down beside it and shook her head. She'd done enough mountain climbing for one day.

She pinched her nose and made a leap through the water into the sunlight.

Wind whistled in her ears…. trees flashed past… water roared around her… and she entered the river with a splash. She barely had time to take a breath, and she'd forgotten the chain, which weighed her down. But the thought of Mordred on his way to Camelot with the Crown of Dreams kept her going. She kicked strongly for the surface and came up gasping for air. She managed to grab a rock before her armour and the chain could drag her back down again. Clinging on with one arm, she gulped handfuls of the cold, clear water and laughed.

"I'm still alive, cousin!" she yelled. "Do you hear me? I'm alive!"

❧

Small hooves, glinting with Avalonian silver, trotted towards her over the water. A soft nose lowered and sniffed at her. *You are very wet*, observed her mist horse. *Evenstar's rider is worried. He thinks you are buried inside the dragon's hill.*

Rhianna wiped hair out of her eyes and blinked up at the cliff she'd jumped from. It was higher than she'd thought. Down here, she could barely hear Elphin's music over the noise of the water.

She laughed again. "Help me out, my beautiful one," she said.

The mare obligingly let Rhianna catch hold of her tail, trotted to the bank and pulled her out of the river. Rhianna lay in the mud, too exhausted to move, staring up at the sky. She felt like going to sleep. Then Alba whinnied, and the music stopped. Elphin's six-fingered hand pushed the mare's muzzle out of the way. His anxious face stared down at her.

"Rhia?" he whispered, his eyes the deepest purple she'd ever seen them. "Where does it hurt?"

"All over," she groaned, which was true. Now that she was out of the dragon's lair, every muscle ached and her cuts and bruises had begun to throb.

Elphin touched a bruise on her cheek with gentle fingers. His purple gaze took in the chain still locked about her ankle. "Don't move, Rhia. You might have broken something. I'll play my harp for you."

Cai's flushed face appeared on her other side.

"Damsel Rhianna!" he gasped. "What did Mordred do to you? We were really worried when we found Alba. We've been tracking you for days! Elphin's good at it, but there was some magic at work around those stones. Then the river flooded, and those sneaky bloodbeards hid their trail in the water. We only knew this was the right valley when we found poor Sandy trying to swim down it. Elphin used his magic to find the path around the waterfall, but when we saw the avalanche behind it we thought the worst... how did you escape?"

"Cai," she said, coughing up water. "Now you're making my ears hurt! I heard your music coming through the water and climbed out, of course... you didn't see my father's ghost then? I sent him to find you."

The boy shook his head.

Rhianna sighed. Obviously, the magic of the Lance alone wasn't strong enough to make the king's ghost visible to her friends.

"Never mind, I expect he's around somewhere. You found me, and that's the main thing... don't fuss, Elphin." She pushed her friend's harp away. "I'm all right. The last thing I want is to fall asleep now. *How* long did you say you'd been tracking me?"

"Three days," Cai said. "And a night."

Rhianna struggled to her feet. Were three days enough for Mordred to get to Camelot with an army and break through the gates? It had taken them and the knights three days to ride here the long way.

"We've got to hurry!" She swayed on her feet, but clutched Alba's mane before Elphin could make her lie back down again. "Where are Sir Lancelot and the others?"

"Dunno." Cai bit his lip and glanced at Elphin. "Still looking for us, I expect. Elphin wouldn't wait for them. He said they'd slow us down, and we had to find you before Mordred killed you."

Rhianna looked back at the collapsed cave and shuddered. "He left me in there to die," she said. "But it takes more than a few rocks to kill me."

She tried to vault into Alba's saddle and tripped over the chain. Elphin pressed his lips together, closed one hand around the manacle and played a ripple on his harp with the other. Sweat sprang out on his brow. The metal sparkled and melted from her foot.

Rhianna stared at the shining puddle in the grass and let him help her up on her mare.

"Your magic's getting stronger," she said. "You couldn't do that for my mother's chain in the summer."

"He'll do any kind of magic for you," Cai muttered. "Where are your boots?"

"Buried in the shadrake's lair somewhere, I expect – I'm not going back for them now." She turned Alba impatiently. "We have to find Excalibur and the knights and get back to Camelot as soon as we can. Mordred's got the Crown of Dreams. If we don't stop him, he's going to destroy my father's jewel and all its secrets, and use the crown to wipe King Arthur's name from history!"

◅❿▻ 10 ◅❿▻

Dragons

A finger of rock did point the way
To mountain high at close of day,
Where deep inside the dragon's hoard
Harp and Lance shall find the Sword.

Since none of them knew which way the knights had gone, they decided to look for Excalibur first. If they returned to the place where the shadrake had attacked her friends, Rhianna thought she would remember the way to the red dragon's lair from there. She wasn't sure what they would do if they found the shadrake waiting for them, but she'd think of something.

Elphin and Cai wanted to know everything, of course. What Mordred had said to her, and exactly how she'd escaped. As they trotted back downriver, Rhianna told them most of it. She didn't tell them how scared she'd been when the roof collapsed, or what her father's ghost had said about his jewel containing something about the Grail. She wanted to ask Merlin about that, if the silly bird ever turned up again.

"So the Crown killed Morgan Le Fay?" Elphin said thoughtfully. "I wonder why?"

"Because she's an evil witch, of course," Cai said. "I hope it kills Mordred as well! Chaining Damsel Rhianna in the dark like that and leaving her to die… just wait till I see the traitor again! I'll knock him off his horse and chain *him* in the dark, see how he likes it." He swung his lance around to demonstrate, and Rhianna ducked.

"Careful," she said, laughing as her armour glittered in response. "Or Mordred will be out of a job."

Cai flushed. "Sorry."

"Your armour must have saved your life in that cave," Elphin said. "A good thing those bloodbeards didn't take that off you as well as your shield and your boots. Maybe Father's smith put more magic into it than we thought."

"A good thing she wasn't carrying Excalibur, you mean," Cai said. "Or Mordred would have the Sword of Light now, never mind the Crown."

"If I'd had Excalibur, his men would never have captured me in the first place, you dolt!" Rhianna said with a smile. She frowned at a track that led away from the river up into the hills. "This way."

"Are you sure?" Cai said.

"Of course I'm sure. I've been this way before."

When she closed her eyes, she could see the cave with its rocky finger as clearly as when she'd worn the Crown of Dreams and spirit-ridden the shadrake. The only trouble was, everything looked different from the ground. Trees and hills kept getting in the way.

"What if the dragon doesn't want to give Excalibur back when we get there?"

"Then you'll have to prove you can use that lance you carry, won't you?" she said, wishing the boy would shut up for once and let her concentrate.

Cai went quiet.

They rode in silence for a while. Around them, the woods steamed in the sun, reminding Rhianna of the dragons flaming the knights. She felt a bit guilty when she thought of how worried they must be about her. But once she got Excalibur back, she might be able to use its magic to let them know she was all right.

Recognising another landmark, she urged Alba into a canter. Cai kept up well enough on the big grey, and even Sandy didn't get left too far behind without a rider to carry. But it was obviously going to take them longer to reach the dragon's lair than it had taken the shadrake to fly there. The sun was going down behind the hills by the time they reached the old stone circle where the bloodbeards had captured her.

She slowed Alba, her neck prickling in memory. She had a sense of being watched… then something small and feathered zipped past her ear.

Rhianna's hand flew to her empty scabbard. Remembering she didn't have Excalibur, she drew her rusty dagger and stared at the shadows between the stones looking for an enemy. But this time it was not a bloodbeard arrow. Instead, a small, blue-grey falcon landed on the end of Cai's lance.

"It's Merlin!" Cai said, nearly dropping the lance as his horse danced sideways.

Alba shook her silver mane. *He nearly made me mist*, the mare snorted.

Rhianna scowled at the bedraggled little bird in a mixture of relief and annoyance.

"Merlin! Where have you *been*?"

The merlin opened its beak and screeched at her.

She shook her head, amused. "It's no good scolding me – I can't hear a word you're saying. You'll have to wait until I've got Excalibur back."

The merlin kept on scolding. Cai blinked at it in surprise. "He says you're a very foolish girl, and you're lucky your soul's not trapped in Annwn with Morgan Le Fay's by now," he reported. "Spirit-riding a dragon is dangerous enough, let alone a shadrake!"

Elphin nodded. "He's right about that, Rhia."

The shining spear lets the bird talk to the human boy, Alba informed her.

She made a face, feeling a bit left out.

"Just because *he* couldn't manage it..." she muttered, remembering how the druid had tried to borrow the shadrake's body after Morgan Le Fay had ambushed them when they first came over from Avalon.

The merlin screeched again, and Cai's eyes went wide. "Oh Damsel Rhianna, this is bad! He says Mordred's used the Crown to call an army of ghosts out of Annwn and is crossing the Summer Sea. Opening the dark Gate caused a flood, so he can take his boats right across the marshes. They'll be at Camelot by tonight."

A chill went through Rhianna. "Let me talk to him," she said. She held out her wrist for the merlin, but it refused to leave Cai's lance, which glittered faintly in the last of the sun.

"Mordred must be taking a short cut,"

Elphin's eyes whirled violet. "We might be able to catch him on our mist horses. But if the roads are flooded, the knights will have to go the long way round – their horses can't gallop over water like Alba and Evenstar can." He listened to the druid again. "Merlin says the knights headed back to the border so they wouldn't get trapped in Dragonland by the floods. We should go and meet them, Rhia."

She looked back the way they had come and gathered up Alba's reins. "No. I can't fight Mordred without Excalibur."

"But what if *we* get trapped in Dragonland?" Cai wailed.

"Alba and Evenstar won't get trapped," she said impatiently. "You'll just have to wait here with Sandy until the roads are open again."

Cai paled.

"I've got a better idea," Elphin said, fingering the spiral pathfinder around his neck. "Merlin, does this stone circle work like the one at Camelot?"

The bird cocked its head and eyed the stones. It fluffed up its feathers and chattered something. Cai looked a bit relieved.

Elphin nodded. "He says it's very old and some of the stones are broken, but it still has power. Between us, we might be able to use it to open the spiral path and transport the knights through to Camelot's circle before Mordred gets there."

"Then what are we waiting for?" Rhianna said. "Someone go and fetch the knights, while I get my sword back from that dragon."

Of course Elphin and Cai refused to let her face the dragons alone, and started an argument over who should stay to protect her. In the end, they decided to send Merlin back to the knights with the message. Cai wrote it on a piece of bark, with much advice from the merlin and face-pulling, while Rhianna fiddled with Alba's mane and stared impatiently at the hills.

"You don't have to write a song," she said. "Just tell them to follow my merlin to the stone circle and meet us there. At this rate, Mordred will be sitting on the throne of Camelot before you're finished."

"Writing's more difficult than you think, Damsel Rhianna," Cai said with a frown. "I can't remember how to spell all the words."

"Does that matter?" She glanced at Elphin.

"Don't look at me, Rhia," her friend said.

"Writing's a human thing. In Avalon we just have our songs, and they're hard enough to learn."

Rhianna sighed. She must ask Arianrhod to teach her how to read and write when they got back to Camelot. If Arianrhod was still alive after Mordred had finished with her.

She clenched her fist on her empty scabbard and tried to be patient with the squire.

Eventually, after more finger-pecking and scolding from Merlin, Cai was finished. He rolled up the message and tied it to the bird's leg. The little hawk fixed Rhianna with a blue-eyed stare and gave a final screech. Then he took off and flew away over the treetops.

Rhianna watched him go with mixed feelings. "What did he say?" she asked, pushing Alba into a canter.

"Never mind," Elphin said. "Let's hurry up and get Excalibur back before it gets dark. Which way now?"

Rhianna pointed to the mountains, and they set off again.

❊

The track wound up and up, disappearing into shadow and then emerging into the light again. Rhianna wondered if she'd got the wrong mountain. But as the sun began to set, she saw the finger of rock standing against the red sky, just as she'd seen it through the shadrake's eyes. Thankfully, there was no sign of the shadrake or the red dragon it had been fighting.

Relief filled her. "That's it!" she said, pushing Alba into a gallop. "The lair's up there!"

"Wait for us, Rhia!" Elphin called behind her. "The dragon might be at home."

Cai's horse and Sandy got left behind on the steep slope, but Rhianna did not slow her pace. Evenstar raced at her side, a blur of white and mist. Her friend struggled with his bag as they galloped, trying to free his harp and ride at the same time.

As Alba clattered up the final rocks, she smiled grimly and drew the little dagger she'd stolen from the shadrake's treasure. She paused at the cave mouth.

It smells bad in there, her mare snorted.

"I know, my darling. You should have smelled the shadrake's lair."

I am glad I did not, Alba said. *You still stink of it.*

Rhianna grimaced as she headed the little

horse into the cave. She planned on riding straight in. But as the rock closed over her head, her heart began to thud and her breath came faster. She halted Alba and stared into the mountain, clutching her dagger in a suddenly sweaty fist as memories crowded in.

Chained in the dark... boulders falling all around...

Elphin stopped his horse beside her and put a sympathetic hand over hers. "Let me go in and get Excalibur," he whispered, dismounting. "Look after Evenstar for me."

Rhianna gripped her dagger tighter. "I'm not scared," she said.

He nodded. "I know you're not, but that little dagger's not going to be much use against a dragon. I've got my harp to protect me."

"But I'm the Pendragon! I should go.

The dragon won't hurt me."

"We can't be sure of that, Rhia. It stole your sword, remember. And don't forget Mordred's wearing the Crown now…"

While they argued in fierce whispers, Cai caught up. He was puffing almost as much as his horse, but he still had the Lance of Truth safely braced on his stirrup.

"Is the beast in there, Damsel Rhianna?" he called. "Do you want me to slay it for you?" His voice echoed around the rocks.

"Shh!" they hissed together.

Too late. The grey mare stumbled over the rocks at the entrance, sending stones sliding down into the lair with a loud, echoing clatter. Cai gripped the Lance tightly so it wouldn't follow. He stayed in his saddle, but the damage was done.

From inside the hill came a deep, grumbling roar. Sparks fizzed out of the cave, followed by a lick of flame. Alba danced sideways, shaking her mane. *The human boy woke the dragon*, she said.

Rhianna pulled herself together. "Get back!" she warned, as the red dragon that had stolen her sword rushed out of the shadows towards them.

It exploded into the sunset with a glitter of red scales and golden smoke.

"YOU WILL NOT STEAL MY EGGS!" it roared, swinging its great snout at them.

But one wing was torn, and the creature seemed unable to take off. It was limping from a nasty gash in one foreleg, leaving a trail of yellow blood. This gave them a chance to take cover behind the rocks.

"Eggs?" Cai whispered.

"The dragons must be breeding," Elphin whispered back. "Careful, Rhia – if they've got eggs in there, they'll protect their young before everything else."

She turned Alba to face the creature and took a deep breath. "I am Rhianna Pendragon!" she called. "You remember me, don't you? We don't want your eggs. I just want my sword back. If you let me have it, no one will hurt you, I promise."

The dragon shook its great head and belched flame at her.

"YOU DO NOT WEAR THE CROWN, PENDRAGON MAID. I DO NOT HAVE TO DO WHAT YOU SAY."

"Keep it talking, Rhia," Elphin whispered. "I'll go inside and find Excalibur." He shrugged his harp off his shoulder. Playing a gentle tune to work the invisibility magic they'd used to escape the Saxon camp last year, he disappeared into the shadows.

The dragon blinked at Rhianna and Cai in confusion. "WHERE HAS THE OTHER HUMAN GONE?"

"There are only two humans here," Rhianna said with a smile. Which was the truth, since Elphin was an Avalonian.

"I SAW THREE OF YOU."

The dragon limped around the finger of rock to peer behind it. Evenstar misted and reappeared down the hill where Sandy had fled, confusing it still further. It shook its big head and sank down to the ground with a groan.

"MY LEG HURTS. MY WING HURTS. THE OTHER PENDRAGON CALLS US TO FIGHT, BUT I CANNOT FLY."

Rhianna thought guiltily of how she'd sent the shadrake to its lair, and felt rather sorry for the red dragon. She glanced at the cave. Elphin had still not emerged. At least the dragon had not tried to roast them yet. But she felt so helpless without her sword, and it was getting dark down in the valley. Soon, they would not be able to find their way back down the mountain to the stone circle.

"Come on, Elphin, come on," she muttered, not wanting to disturb the dragon now it had settled.

Something black flew across the rapidly sinking sun. The dragon raised its head again, distracted. There had been two dragons in the ambush. Had the shadrake killed the other one? Or was it still inside? She looked at the lair again, her heart twisting in sudden fear for Elphin.

Cai gathered up his reins and pointed the Lance of Truth at the injured dragon. The magical weapon glittered in the last of the sunlight. "Go and get your sword, Damsel Rhianna," he said. "I'll keep an eye on the beast for you."

Gratefully, she dismounted and patted Alba. "Stay here with Cai," she whispered to the mare. "I'm going to see what's happened to Elphin."

She waited until the dragon looked up at the sky again, and made a dash for the cave. This time she did not let herself stop at the entrance, though her heart beat faster as the rock closed around her. She broke into a sweat under her armour and wondered what would happen if she took a wrong turn in the dark.

No, don't think of that.

She felt her way around a turn in the tunnel, which led down steeply. Her feet dragged slower with every step, but worry for her friend overcame her fear. Then her armour began to glimmer, showing her a dark pile of treasure reaching almost to the roof of the lair.

"Elphin?" she called. Was he digging through it?

At the sound of her voice, the glittering pile she'd thought was treasure stirred. A bright eye opened and blinked sleepily at her. She caught her breath and stumbled backwards, clutching her dagger.

The second dragon!

"I'm Rhianna Pendragon!" she said quickly. "I won't hurt you. I just want my sword back."

The dragon sighed and lifted its head. "THE DARK DRAGON HURT MY

MATE," it said. "BUT WE DID NOT LET IT STEAL OUR EGGS."

Rhianna felt bad again. She'd been responsible for bringing the shadrake here.

"The dark dragon didn't want your eggs. It was looking for my sword. If you let me have Excalibur back, you'll be safe and we'll leave you in peace."

Where had Elphin got to? Her heart began to pound again. Avalonians could not die, but they could be hurt in the world of men. If he'd been burned by the dragon's fiery breath, she didn't know what she would do.

She was about to ask the creature if it had seen him, when there was a rattle from the back of the cave and she heard the tinkle of her friend's harp. She breathed easier as the dragon lowered its head again and its eye closed.

"Move slowly, Rhia," Elphin whispered. "I can't play my harp and look for Excalibur at the same time. I can keep this one quiet, but I can't do much about its mate outside. Is Cai all right out there?"

"He's fine," Rhianna said, edging around the sleeping dragon. As she joined Elphin at the back of the cave, the sweat came again. The dragon's bulk looked exactly like the rocks that had blocked the tunnel in the shadrake's lair and trapped her inside...

"I'm here, Rhia," Elphin said softly, touching her arm.

She gave him a grateful smile as the memory faded.

She concentrated on looking for Excalibur, rather than thinking about the rock above her head. With Elphin's music filling the lair, it wasn't too bad. She wondered what they'd do if the sword lay beneath the eggs the dragon was sitting on.

Then her armour brightened again, and she saw Excalibur's white jewel poking out from under the dragon's tail. She breathed a bit easier, closed her left hand about the hilt and gave a firm pull. The jewel flared silver under her hand, and straightaway she felt stronger.

She grinned at Elphin. He grinned back.

Then they heard the flap of large wings followed by a yell from outside the cave. "Cai!" Rhianna said, running for the exit.

◁◀ 11 ▶▷

Druid Beacons

Fire blazed from every druid hill
Calling men afar, their blood to spill.
Over the sea Mordred's army did ride
While the living drowned on its ghostly tide.

They hurried out into the sunset to find the tops of the mountains on fire. A black-winged silhouette swooped through the orange smoke, terrifying the horses.

"The shadrake!" Rhianna gasped, gripping Excalibur tighter. "Where's Cai?"

She looked anxiously for Alba. The two mist

horses and Sandy shivered behind the finger of rock. She couldn't see Cai's grey mare with them and peered over the cliff edge, afraid she might see her friend's broken body far below.

Then Elphin pointed to the far side of the peak, where the boy bravely sat his horse in front of the injured red dragon, which pressed itself to the ground and hissed at its enemy. "Looks like that shadrake got more than it bargained for," he said with a smile.

Cai's horse reared as the creature swooped towards it. The squire lowered the Lance of Truth and set his heels into the grey's sides. He galloped across the plateau, yelling a challenge.

The human boy is brave, Alba said.

Rhianna shook her head. "He's going to get himself killed, you mean! What does he think he's trying to do?"

The shadrake had caught Cai's glittering lance in its talons, and the squire was lifted out of his saddle as he refused to let go. He clung determinedly to the shaft with both hands, his short legs kicking wildly in the air. The dragon flapped strongly, but could not get much height because of its awkward burden. The grey mare galloped off in panic.

"Hold on, Cai!" Rhianna shouted, scrambling over the rocks. She made a grab for the boy's dangling feet, but missed.

Cai shouted something at her. Elphin ran his fingers over his harp, but the music was drowned by the shadrake's roars. He shook his head. "Sorry, Rhia. My magic still doesn't work very well against creatures of Annwn."

Rhianna stood on the highest rock and raised Excalibur so that the blade flashed red in the last of the sun. "Let him go!" she ordered, wondering if her cousin was using the Crown to spirit-ride the beast.

The shadrake circled clumsily, then came back. The trailing lance rattled against the rocks. Cai still clung to it, looking terrified.

"Let go, Cai!" Rhianna yelled. "Jump! Don't worry about the Lance. I'll make the creature give it back."

This got the shadrake's attention. It made another clumsy turn and peered down at her. Its eyes glowed in respect.

"YOU SPIRIT-RODE ME."

"Yes," she said, shivering at the memory.

"LIKE THE OLD PENDRAGONS USED TO."

She smiled. "That's right. Let my friend go."

The shadrake circled in confusion. "THE

OTHER PENDRAGON SAYS I MUST BRING HIM THE GLITTERING SPEAR AND THE SHINING SWORD."

"The other Pendragon is not here," Rhianna pointed out. "Is he calling you? He'll be angry if you don't go to him right away. And my friend's fond of his food – it'll be hard work carrying him across the sea. And if you drop the lance in the water the other Pendragon won't be able to find it again."

"THAT IS TRUE."

The creature opened its claw, and both the lance and Cai fell.

Too late, Rhianna realised she should have told the dragon to land first. The shadrake circled once more, spooking their remaining horses. Then it gave a final shriek and flapped off into the dusk.

Elphin and Rhianna raced over to Cai, who lay in a crumpled heap at the base of the rocky finger. Elphin reached for his harp. But as they approached, the squire scrambled to his feet and gave them a shaky grin.

"Worried you that time, didn't I?" he said.

"Cai!" Rhianna scowled at him. "You could have been killed! Why didn't you let go of the Lance?"

"Because that shadrake was trying to steal it, of course! Besides, Merlin told me the knight who carries the Lance of Truth can't die. So I had to hold on to it, didn't I? Otherwise the beast would've iced me, for sure."

"You mightn't be able to die when you're carrying it, but you could still have fallen and broken your neck!" Rhianna said. "Look at Mordred. He's not dead, but he's missing a hand and has a crippled leg. What good would my champion be, if he can't fight duels for me? And now you've lost your horse."

"Well I wasn't hurt, was I? And we've got Sandy back, so I can easily ride him again until we find the mare. My boots just got a bit singed when the beast flew over the beacon, that's all." Cai looked at her feet in their filthy rags and grinned again. "At least I've still *got* boots."

Rhianna grimaced at the reminder, then realised what else Cai had said. *When the beast flew over that beacon.* She looked at the fiery sky in horror. "Those are the druid beacons, aren't they?" she said. "If my mother's lit them to call for help, Mordred must already be across the Summer Sea!"

Cai nodded. "They go all the way across the water to Camelot," he said in awe. "I've never seen them all lit up before."

"Then we've no time to waste. Is the Lance of Truth all right?"

"It's one of the four Lights, remember?" Cai said with another grin. Then he sobered. "I would've killed that dragon for you, Damsel Rhianna, if my silly horse hadn't galloped off. Sandy's not scared of dragons. Do you want me to kill the other one?"

She frowned at the red dragon, which they had all forgotten in the excitement. It crouched at the entrance to its lair, watching them warily. Elphin played a gentle chord on his harp. The dragon stretched out its torn wing with a sigh and lowered its snout to the rock.

"No," she said, still feeling sorry for the creature. "It's not the dragons' fault that Mordred sent them to ambush us and steal my sword. Whoever wears the Crown of Dreams controls the dragons, so when we get it back we should be safe enough. Besides, its mate is sitting on eggs in there. I don't think it'll follow us… will you?" she asked the red dragon.

"OUR CHILDREN ARE MORE IMPORTANT TO US THAN HUMAN BATTLES," it said. Then its eyes closed and it began to snore gently, letting out puffs of smoke.

The dragon dreams of eggs, Alba snorted. *It is silly. Apples are much nicer.*

"Half of Dragonland will able to see those beacons," Rhianna said, her stomach twisting with fresh anxiety as she mounted Alba. "We've got to get back to the stone circle. I just hope the knights haven't tried going back by road."

"They wouldn't leave us behind, Damsel Rhia," Cai said. "They'll come, don't worry."

"That depends if they can read what you wrote," she said. "Are you sure you explained Elphin's going to open the spiral path to take everyone to Camelot using the stone circles so we can catch up with Mordred?"

The boy bit his lip again. "Sort of… at least, I expect they'll guess the magic path will be quicker. You said not to write a song about it, Damsel Rhianna."

"You did, Rhia," Elphin said with a smile. The night breeze lifted his curls and the flames lit half his face, making him look very Avalonian.

"It isn't funny!" she snapped, tired and sore now that the action was over. "It's all right for you. Mordred's never going to take an army of ghosts through the mists to Avalon and steal your father's throne! I bet you don't even care what happens to poor Arianrhod, do you? Don't you understand? I left my father's secret jewel with her, the one Mordred needs to destroy before he can rule Camelot, and she's locked in the dungeon so she can't even *run away*."

Her voice had risen. The red dragon's tail twitched, and its talons clutched at invisible prey.

The dragon dreams of eating horses, Alba said nervously. *Maybe we should go now?*

"Then we'd better hurry," Elphin said, echoing her mare. Calmly, he bagged his harp, helped Cai up on Sandy, and mounted Evenstar. "Don't worry, Rhia, we'll stop him."

Rhianna sheathed Excalibur, suddenly very weary. At least the fiery sky would light their path.

They rode back to the stone circle in silence. Seeing no sign of the knights at the shadowy stones, she tried to persuade Elphin to open the spiral path immediately and take them back to Camelot. But he shook his head.

"We should at least give them until morning, Rhia. They mightn't be able to follow Merlin in the dark. If we go back through the stones, and the knights do come here looking for us, then they'll be even longer getting back. Besides, I'm not sure I can open the path without Merlin's help. This circle's very old, and there are echoes of dark magic here. I don't want to send everyone to Annwn by mistake, and anyway, you need some sleep before you face Mordred again."

She knew he was right, but it didn't make the waiting any easier.

Cai found firewood and whistled happily as he made a camp for them inside the stones. He'd brought along a burning brand from the last beacon, and used it to light their fire. He gave Elphin a proud stare. "See? We knights of Camelot can do without magic tricks," he said.

The Avalonian boy smiled. "What do you think lit that beacon?"

"Er... magic tricks?"

"Exactly. That's why Merlin went with the hawks, isn't it? So how would you have lit it on your own?"

"I'm not on my own, am I?" Cai said.

There seemed no answer to that. Rhianna leaned back against a stone and unwrapped the rags from her feet. She touched her blisters and winced. She hoped the knights would bring some spare boots with them, because she didn't fancy fighting Mordred and his army of ghosts with nothing on her feet. She bit her lip and started to wrap them back up again.

A six-fingered hand stopped her. The first trill from Elphin's harp made her stiffen. But then her feet stopped hurting and she felt warmer.

"Better?" her friend whispered.

She smiled at him. "I didn't mean to snap at you, earlier."

"It's all right. You're worried about Arianrhod. I am, too. We don't know very much about her, do we? I know you smashed the dark mirror, but what if she's still helping Mordred? Do you think she'll give him the jewel?"

Rhianna frowned. "No. At least, not willingly."

Cai gave up trying to tie his cloak between the stones to make a shelter and joined them. "I know I called her a witch's maid before, but Arianrhod's on our side. She kept Excalibur hidden back in the summer, remember – when we swapped the swords so I could take the wrong one to Mordred. If she were working for the dark knight, she wouldn't have done that."

Elphin nodded. "I agree, but there's something strange about Arianrhod. I sensed it when I played my harp for her the day she tried to take your pendant. I think she might have more to do with your quest than we realised. Why did King Arthur really take that jewel out of the crown, do you think?"

"To stop Mordred using it if he got his hands on it, of course. Merlin told us the Crown's magic wouldn't work properly without all the jewels in place..." Her voice trailed off.

"Mordred's already using the Crown. He's summoned an army out of Annwn. You wore it yourself, and you used it to spirit-ride the shadrake when it was trying to kill us, so the magic obviously works well enough. No Rhia, I think your father and Merlin were trying to hide a secret, and it must be a secret too dangerous for any man to know."

"Something about the Grail..." Rhianna whispered.

Elphin looked sharply at her. "What makes you say that?"

She shook her head. "Just something my father's ghost said. He couldn't remember what, though. If this secret's supposed to be too dangerous for men to know, then why did he tell my mother to give the jewel to me?"

Cai grinned. "And since when are you a man, Damsel Rhianna?" he teased. "Even if you dress like one."

Her cheeks went hot, and Elphin smiled. "Your father must have made his jewel into a pendant, something only a damsel would wear, to keep it out of Mordred's hands," he said gently. "If it does contain the secret of the Grail of Stars, then we have to stop Mordred getting hold of it at all costs. King Arthur told Guinevere to give it to you, but he obviously wasn't too worried if Arianrhod saw it. I wish we knew why she was left outside Camelot as a baby."

"I know!" Cai blurted out. "Maybe

Arianrhod's half fairy, and that's why Elphin likes her so much…" He flushed at the Avalonian boy's purple look. "Sorry, Damsel Rhianna, but mothers often abandon their babies if they think a fairy fathered them – didn't you see anything in the Crown about her?"

She tried to remember if she'd learned anything about her friend. But she'd worn the Crown for such a short time, and she'd been too busy spirit-riding the shadrake to look for any other secrets.

"What I'd really like to know is who *Mordred's* father is," Cai continued. "Don't suppose you saw that when you wore the crown, Damsel Rhianna? Lady Morgan would never tell anyone."

Elphin raised an eyebrow. "Did you see who Mordred's father was, Rhia?"

Rhianna shook her head, distracted.

"Maybe you can find out when you wear the crown again?" Cai said cheerfully. "The squires took a bet on it, and we'd all like to know."

"Why don't you ask Mordred when you see him?" Rhianna said, her head spinning. "I've got more important things to think about now than squires' gossip."

The two boys glanced at each other. "We should all get some sleep if we're planning on fighting a battle against Prince Mordred and his army of the dead of tomorrow," Elphin said, and strummed his harp softly to make the fire burn brighter.

Rhianna rolled herself into her cloak with a sigh. Had she made a very big mistake, leaving her father's jewel with Arianrhod?

She woke from a nightmare of being buried in the shadrake's lair to a chill, damp dawn. Their fire had gone out. Smoke from the druid beacons hung above the trees, and she couldn't see her friends. She snatched out Excalibur and leaped to her feet.

"Shh!" Elphin said, jumping down from one of the mossy stones. "Someone's coming."

Her friend's Avalonian ears were sharper than hers. Very faintly now, she heard the drumming of horses' hooves. But even accounting for the distance and the gloom, she could only see a small party, not the proud troop of knights who had ridden out from Camelot.

"Where's Cai?" she said.

"Gone to meet them." Elphin pointed to

the young knight cantering through the trees on Sandy to meet the riders, his lance glittering in the dawn light.

"Why didn't you wake me?" Rhianna said, snatching up Alba's bridle.

"Because you needed your sleep, and they're coming here anyway." He put a hand over hers and stared at her with his violet eyes. "And I wanted to get you alone for a moment."

Her skin prickled. She wondered if he was going to kiss her again, as he had at the midsummer feast.

But he touched the spiral pathfinder he wore around his neck and said, "I don't know how Arianrhod fits in yet, but I've been thinking about that jewel of your father's, and I'm wondering if it might contain directions to the Grail Castle."

Rhianna frowned. "But my father never found the Grail of Stars!" she protested.

"So everyone thinks. The knights failed in their quest to bring it back to Camelot. According to our songs, the only ones who saw it are dead now. But we know both the Sword and the Crown can be used to contact the dead. Maybe the knights who saw the Grail told Arthur their secrets after they died? That jewel might well contain the only knowledge we have of how to find the fourth Light."

She stared at him. "And Mordred's going to destroy it!" she whispered. Then she remembered how she'd mentioned her father's secrets in the shadrake's lair. "Unless he decides to use it first..." She couldn't decide which would be worse – her cousin wiping King Arthur's name from history, or finding the Grail of Stars before she did.

"We mustn't let him get hold of it, either way." Elphin said, squeezing her hand. "I'll help you all I can. But I have to warn you, Rhia, my magic won't be much good against an army of Annwn. I can help you fight Mordred and his bloodbeards, but only the Lights have any power over ghosts."

She pulled herself together. "Then Cai and I will have to deal with them between us, won't we? The ghosts aren't important. It's Mordred we have to stop... oh, why don't they hurry *up*? What's Cai doing now?"

She watched the knights gather around the squire, their horses snorting in the cold air. The grey mare was with them, looking exhausted, her reins broken. The boy seemed to be telling them everything that had happened since they split up, pointing up the mountain towards the red dragons' lair and waving his lance about excitedly. Finally, he pointed to the stone circle. The knights turned their horses and galloped towards her and Elphin.

Rhianna hurried to saddle Alba, aware that Elphin's violet gaze still lingered on her. But she hardly had time to think about what he had said. Her head spun with images of her cousin seated on the throne of Camelot wearing the Crown... Annwn's ghostly warriors bringing the Grail of Stars to him... Arianrhod clutching the black jewel saying, "I'll guard it with my life"...

Alba nudged her. *Evenstar's rider is worried*, her mare reported.

"He's not the only one," Rhianna muttered. "We have to get back to Camelot before

Mordred gets hold of that jewel!"

She led the mare across the circle in such a hurry, her mist horse almost trampled the merlin as it glided low across the circle to perch on the nearest stone. It had a fat mouse trapped in one claw, which it proceeded to swallow in three bites.

"That's better," sighed the druid's spirit. "Can you actually hear me now, Rhianna Pendragon? Or have those dragons scrambled your brain?"

"Merlin!" she said in relief. "Where are the rest of the knights?"

"Never mind. We haven't much time, so just shut up and listen for once. This circle has gaps in it because of the fallen stones, which makes it dangerous because you could easily lose your way in the mists. When Elphin opens the spiral path, I'm going to have to stay on this side to make sure Morgan Le Fay doesn't lure you all off the path into Annwn. Remember what I told you about the Crown of Dreams? If Mordred's got into Camelot and restored Arthur's jewel to the crown, you'll have to be very careful. Best thing you can do is delay him until I get there, and—"

"Rhianna Pendragon!" boomed a voice. A big horse cantered across and stopped nose-to-nose with Alba. Sir Bors dropped out of the saddle and crushed her in one of his unexpected hugs. "Don't you ever, *ever* go off on your own in enemy territory like that again!" He held her at arm's length and looked her up and down. "What happened to your boots?"

Rhianna started to laugh. She couldn't help it. The laughing turned into tears, and she sniffed them back hurriedly. All the knights were watching, as well as her friends and the merlin.

"Never mind my boots," she said, raising her chin. She rested her hand on Excalibur's hilt. "What happened to Sir Lancelot and the rest of the knights? I sent a message telling you all to come to the circle. The roads are flooded."

Sir Bors glanced at Sir Bedivere. He coughed awkwardly. "We couldn't read half of it," he admitted. "Lancelot saw the druid beacons lit up last night, and all he could think of was the queen, so we said we'd stay and look for you so he could ride back to Camelot and help her. Don't worry, Damsel Rhianna. They got across the river before it burst its banks. They'll ride as fast as they can."

"We'll be faster." She swung into Alba's

saddle and glanced at Elphin. He clutched his spiral pathfinder and nodded.

The knights, who had all done this before, took their places behind the Avalonian boy as he led the way around the circle. The mist horses' manes shone silver in the gloom. Cai's lance glittered. Excalibur's jewel glowed.

The merlin finished scraping mouse fur off its beak and called, "I'll fly back the long way and meet you at Camelot. Don't do anything stupid until I get there, Rhianna Pendragon!"

The little hawk spread its wings and began to fly around the circle in the opposite direction, making Rhianna dizzy every time it flashed overhead. The back of her neck prickled as the air inside the circle began to sparkle. Dragonland with its damp hills and its mossy stones disappeared.

For a few breaths, she was alone with only her mist horse's sweet scent and the magic of the spiral path around her. She patted Alba's neck. "Let's hope it's not raining at Camelot," she whispered to the mare, and drew Excalibur in case they had to fight immediately.

Then the mists parted, and she saw her friends and Sir Bedivere and the other knights turning their horses in confusion. Alba snorted and picked up her hooves in surprise.

It is very wet!

Rhianna's heart sank. They'd emerged in the stone circle where they'd picnicked in the summer. But instead of being on a dry hill an easy half day's ride to Camelot, the stones were surrounded by water gleaming under a stormy green sky for as far as they could see.

"Go back, quick!" Elphin turned Evenstar,

his mist horse's silver-shod hooves skimming the surface, while the other horses splashed and floundered behind him. But as the last knight appeared from the stones, the path closed with a final sparkle.

Elphin clutched his spiral and stared warily at the water. "I'm sorry, Rhia," he said. "Merlin's closed the path. We're trapped."

Dark Knight
at the Gates

Mordred sat his black stallion outside the gates of Camelot and gazed up at the battlements. He had dreamed of this moment all year. Admittedly, in his dreams the gates had stood open to welcome him, rather than being shut in his face. But that was a small point, easily put right now that he wore the Crown of Dreams.

He adjusted the crown on his head and threw back his cloak so that his armour shone in the dawn. He had tied the reins around the stump of his right wrist so that he could grip his war-axe in his good hand, and before leaving the boats, he'd washed his hair in the floodwater that by now had hopefully drowned Arthur's knights.

"How do I look?" he asked his bloodbeard captain.

"Very kinglike, Master," the man said.

Mordred smiled. "Have you got the girl's things?"

The bloodbeard lifted a pair of small deerskin boots and the battered Pendragon shield they'd taken from his cousin when they'd captured her in Dragonland.

"Good. Then let's wake Camelot's lazy squires!"

Mordred waved his axe. At his signal, one of the bloodbeards blew a loud blast on a horn. The warriors of Annwn, surrounding the hill below the walls, howled eagerly and rattled their ghostly shields with pale swords. Those warriors that were out of reach of the Crown's magic stayed invisible, of course. But an eerie green mist rose out of the flooded ditches, making the sound even more frightening.

At Mordred's side, Uther Pendragon's ghost bared his teeth at the castle and shook his rusty sword. "Guinevere!" he roared. "Where are your manners, girl? Open up! I want to see the lass my son took to his bed, the one who couldn't give him an heir."

"Get lost, traitor!" A lanky dark-haired squire scowled down at them from the battlements and raised his bow. The weapon trembled as he took aim, and his arrow glanced off Mordred's axe to fall limply on the path.

Mordred laughed. "Is that the best you can do?"

The boy yelled something else, and a line of young heads appeared along the wall beside him. More arrows rained down – mostly way off target, but one went through Uther's ghostly body to land shivering in the grass. His green horse snorted and danced sideways.

"Not bad," Uther commented. "If I'd still been alive, that arrow might have killed me."

"Maybe it'd be wise to move back a bit, M-master?" said the bloodbeard captain, sheltering under the Pendragon shield.

"Oh, stop cowering like a scared damsel!" Mordred snapped. "Nothing can harm me while I wear the Crown of Dreams – watch!"

He rode his stallion forward until its nose touched the huge wooden gates, and spread his arms wide. He stared up at the young defenders. "Well, go on then!" he called. "Be heroes! Kill me… if you can."

The dark-haired squire had a good try. His next arrow flew straight for Mordred's exposed throat.

Mordred closed his eyes and concentrated on the jewel of Annwn. It warmed against his forehead, and there was a bright green flash on the other side of his eyelids. It made his head throb. But when he opened his eyes again, the arrow lay in two pieces in the mud, and the boy was staring at his broken bowstring in confusion. The other squires quickly ducked back behind their battlements.

Mordred laughed. "See? None of your

weapons can harm me while I wear the Pendragon crown. What's your name, boy?"

"Gareth," the lad said, sullen now.

"Well Gareth, as you know I'm Mordred Pendragon. King Arthur's daughter lies dead and buried in Dragonland. That means the throne of Camelot is mine now, since I'm the only one left alive with Pendragon blood. That's how it works, isn't it old man?"

He glanced at Uther and smiled at his grandfather's nod.

"Now then, Gareth. Run and fetch the queen for me, and maybe I'll let you be my squire when I'm king. You're not a bad shot with that bow of yours, considering. Better than that so-called champion my cousin brought with her to Dragonland. Fine lot of use he was, when we killed his princess."

The boy's gaze fell on the Pendragon shield in the captain's hand. He paled. "Princess Rhianna's dead…?"

"That's right. And all her knights and her little friends by now, too… just as you and your friends will be before tonight, if you don't hurry up and do what I say."

Gareth's head disappeared. The lad was gone such a long time, Mordred wondered if he would need to give the idiot squires another demonstration of his power. Using the crown to turn aside the arrow had already given him a splitting headache.

He closed his eyes with a scowl. But before he could call on the magic again, the gates creaked open. He tensed, half expecting more arrows. But his Aunt Guinevere had come to welcome him herself, still in her nightgown with her copper hair loose and flaming in the rising sun. She clutched a knight's cloak around her... one of Lancelot's, no doubt.

She took one look at the Pendragon shield and the boots dangling from the bloodbeard's hand, and gave a little scream of fury. A dagger flashed out from under the cloak, and she launched herself at Mordred.

"Murderer!" she shrieked.

He was so surprised, he didn't have time to raise his axe. He might have expected such behaviour from his cousin, but not from his Aunt Guinevere, whom he'd held captive all last winter and beaten the spirit out of – or so he thought. His bloodbeard captain was caught by equal surprise, unable to draw his sword because he still held Rhianna's boots and shield.

Uther's hand shot out in an attempt to catch the queen's wrist. The old man moved fast, though of course as a ghost he could not touch her, and her blade passed right through the dead warrior to strike at Mordred. But the magic of the Crown saved him again. The jewel flared green, and his aunt staggered backwards. The dagger spun from her fingers and disappeared into the nearest ditch. The queen collapsed before Mordred's horse, her bright hair spread out around her head like a fan.

A shocked hush fell.

Everyone stared at Mordred, waiting to see what he would do.

This was going even better than he'd hoped. He smiled and dismounted. Passing his axe to his bloodbeard, he limped across to Guinevere and knelt beside her.

He drew off his gauntlet with his teeth and laid his palm on her brow. She was still breathing – but that could be turned to his advantage.

"My poor aunt!" he said in a concerned tone. He looked around and spotted the dark-haired squire who had tried to kill him earlier hovering at the gates. "Don't just stand there, Gareth!" he snapped. "Find someone to carry the queen up to her bedchamber. Tell her maids to make up a fire to keep her warm. Oh, and while you're at it, send my mother's ex-maid down to me – the dark girl with the witch-mark on her cheek. She's still here, I understand."

The squires glanced uneasily at one another.

"She's in the dungeon," Gareth said eventually. "Is the queen…?"

"Dead? No, not yet. But the maid must attend me as soon as possible so we can get the formalities over with. Once I'm king, I'll be able to use the Crown's magic to heal Guinevere."

The squires whispered again. Nobody seemed to know what to do. Then two ancient knights came staggering out with a stretcher and gently lifted the queen on to it. They gave Mordred black looks as they staggered back inside with their burden.

They left the gates open. It wasn't exactly a royal welcome, but the squires reluctantly stood aside to allow him through.

"Good!" Mordred said, taking his horse's reins. Ordering Uther and his ghostly army to stay outside to guard the castle, he beckoned to his bloodbeards. "Let's go and see if Arthur's throne fits."

Ghost Warriors

Camelot stood against the flood,
Her walls surrounded by lakes of blood
And ditches filled with demons dread,
When a damsel rode back from the dead.

"Where's the road gone?" Cai said.

The knights blinked about them in despair, while their horses pawed at the flood. Poor little Sandy stood on the highest part of the hill with water up to his belly, snorting suspiciously at the swirling green weed.

"Crazy fairy boy must've brought us to the wrong stone circle," muttered Sir Agravaine.

"No." Sir Bors pointed to the familiar white towers, rising out of a green haze on the horizon. "Look, there's Camelot, right where it should be – except there's a dirty great lake between us and the queen. We'll just have to do some swimmin'! Make sure your packs are secure, tie your cloaks around your waists, and keep your swords out of the water. I don't like the look of that green stuff."

It smells bad, Alba agreed.

"Can the horses swim that far?" someone asked. "And what about the ponies? There might be currents."

"Mist horses don't need to swim," Rhianna reminded them.

But no one was listening to her. The knights were trying to decide whether the Roman road would be passable, and if they should wait for Sir Lancelot and his men before they challenged Mordred.

"We'll be stronger together," Sir Bors said. "If the road's passable, Lancelot shouldn't be long. Two days at most."

"We haven't got *two days*!" Rhianna stared in frustration at Camelot's towers – so near, and yet so far away. Was her cousin standing on the battlements right now, laughing at them? "Aren't you worried about what Mordred might be doing to your families?"

"Of course we're worried, Damsel Rhianna," Sir Bors said. "But if Mordred's already at Camelot, and I'm afraid it looks like he is, then a couple more days won't make much difference."

"It'll make all the difference!" Rhianna said. "You don't understand! If Mordred destroys my father's jewel and wears the Crown of Dreams at the Round Table, then we've *lost*. My father can never come back, because Mordred will be king of Camelot and will wipe King Arthur's name from history, and mine, and probably most of yours as well."

The knights muttered among themselves.

"Maybe the Saxons will help us?" Sir Agravaine suggested. "They've got boats. If we can reach one of their villages, we might be able to get word to Cynric."

"We haven't time to look for Saxons," Cai said, picking up his feet in alarm. "This water's getting deeper. If you don't make up your minds soon, we'll have to swim just to find the stones again. Elphin's got Merlin's pathfinder, hasn't he? Surely he can find a way through this by magic?"

The men looked at the Avalonian boy in hope. "Can you lead us along safe paths through this flood, lad?" Sir Bors asked.

Elphin clutched the druid spiral. His eyes whirled purple as the water began to lap at the stones, and Rhianna knew how brave he was being because no Avalonian could swim. "Cai's right, Rhia," he said. "My magic will be more use here. I have to stay and help the knights."

She thought of them all trotting in circles after Elphin to find a safe path through the flood and took a deep breath. "Then I'll ride across the flood and delay Mordred until you get there," she said.

Sir Bors shook his head. "Over my dead body! I promised your mother I'd not let you out of my sight. You've already been kidnapped by bloodbeards and buried alive in a dragon's lair. I'm not goin' to lose you within sight of Camelot. If you ride across that water, Rhianna Pendragon, I'm warning you now I'm swimmin' right after you if I have to hang on to your horse's tail the whole way across. You're not going alone."

"*I'll* go with her," Cai said, holding the Lance of Truth clear of the water. "I've got the second Light and I'm supposed to be her champion now."

The horses were beginning to roll their eyes and plunge about as the water touched their bellies. To Rhianna's surprise, the other knights seemed to think this was a good idea.

Sir Bors frowned. "Sandy can't gallop over water. Don't be silly, boy."

Cai's face fell.

"You can ride Evenstar, Cai," Elphin said, making the boy's face brighten again. "I'll ride Sandy to find a path for the knights. I'll look after him for you, don't worry."

"I only want to get my father's jewel from Arianrhod before Mordred does," Rhianna said. "I've got Excalibur back now. We'll stay out of Mordred's way until you arrive."

She could always use the time to find out if her mother knew anything about the secrets stored in Arthur's jewel.

Sir Bors gave in, and the boys quickly swapped mounts. Elphin held the Lance of Truth, while Cai squeezed himself into the mist horse's saddle. The Avalonian boy passed him the lance and whispered something into his horse's ear, then splashed through the water to rescue Sandy. Evenstar whinnied, and Alba snorted. It sounded suspiciously like the two mist horses were laughing at them, but Rhianna was too worried to smile.

Before the knights could change their minds, she set her heels to Alba's sides and headed the mare across the green flood towards Camelot. She heard Cai gasp as Evenstar leaped after her.

They galloped through glittering spray, faster than any ordinary horse could go. At first Cai clung to Evenstar's mane with the Lance of Truth jammed under his arm, looking terrified. But as the water stayed safely under the mist horses' hooves, he relaxed. Rhianna cast an anxious glance over her shoulder, but Evenstar seemed to be behaving himself. She gave the squire an encouraging grin.

"This is great!" he yelled. "No wonder you keep these fairy horses to yourself."

"Just don't fall off," Rhianna warned. "Because I'm not stopping to fish you out."

Tell him not to tug on the reins like that, Alba said. *Evenstar won't run away with him.*

Rhianna passed this on. "And don't drop that lance!" she added.

Cai just nodded, having no breath left to reply.

They reached the Roman road, which still looked passable in places. They saw some soggy sheep standing on it up to their knees in water and bleating for help. All the lower ground was flooded. The river that ran past Camelot looked more like a sea.

She wondered if the flood reached through the mists between worlds, and if it had flooded Avalon, too. What about the crystal caverns, where her father's body lay waiting for her to bring him the four Lights so he could return to the world of men? She had a horrible vision of swimming through crystal tunnels filled with water, the air in her lungs running out before she found the way to his sleeping body…

"Damsel Rhianna!" Cai called, interrupting her dark thoughts. "Look! Isn't that the Saxons?"

She realised they'd reached the bridge leading to Camelot. Or where the bridge should have been. Ahead of them, Camelot's hill rose out of the green water. She breathed a sigh of relief. She'd been afraid they might find the castle underwater, too. But then, of course, Mordred would have no throne to sit on –

even her cousin wasn't *that* stupid.

She could see no sign of Mordred or his bloodbeards. But an unnatural green mist hung above the flooded ditches, and Cai was right – Saxons in soggy furs were trying to reach the castle, led by a huge man with yellow braids and a golden torque around his neck.

Rhianna's heart lifted in recognition. "It's Chief Cynric! Let's find out what's going on."

"Careful, Damsel Rhia," Cai warned. "Don't forget those sneaky Saxons used to fight on Mordred's side."

"They signed a peace treaty with me," she said, drawing Excalibur. "They'll let us through, don't worry."

Cai bit his lip and readied the Lance of Truth. They rode up the hill side by side to join the men.

As they approached the first ditch, both Excalibur and the Lance of Truth gleamed brighter. The white jewel under Rhianna's hand warmed, and her skin prickled. The air turned ice cold.

I do not like this mist, Alba said. *It smells bad.*

Rhianna realised that the ditch contained more than water. Shadows writhed and hissed in the bottom. As they got nearer, two ghostly warriors rose out of the ditch, grabbed a Saxon by the throat and dragged him down beneath the green mist. They heard a thrashing and growling, like dogs fighting over scraps. He screamed horribly. A thin twist of darkness rose into the air like a torn rag, and howled as it vanished across the flood.

The other Saxons drew back, making signs against evil.

"Chief Cynric!" Rhianna called, ignoring the ghosts. "Have you seen Prince Mordred? Will you fight for me against him?"

The men whirled, swords raised. They stared at the two mist horses as if they had appeared from the sky. "Odin save us!" one muttered. "Caught between Mordred's devils and the Wild Hunt!"

"We're not the Wild Hunt," Rhianna said, fighting a giggle at the thought that he could mistake her and Cai for great heroes. "Don't you recognise me? Mordred stole my shield, but I've still got Excalibur."

"Princess Rhianna...?" The big chief strode across and stared at her in disbelief. He reached for her foot and warily touched the flesh showing between the rags. "She's alive!" he said.

"Hey, get your hands off her!" Cai said, jabbing the big man with the Lance of Truth until he stepped back. The other Saxons growled and jostled closer. Cai glared at them too, his lance ready to fight them all if need be.

Rhianna waved him away, a bit worried he might spear someone by accident. "It's all right, Cai," she said. "The treaty still stands... doesn't it, Chief Cynric?"

The Saxon chief stared wonderingly into her face. He looked at his men. Then he snatched her out of the saddle and swung her around in joy. "Mordred was lying. The Pendragon Princess is back from the dead!"

They moved out of the green mist, back to where the Saxons had made their camp. Over bowls of hot soup, they exchanged information.

It seemed the Saxons had seen the druid beacons on fire. Knowing this meant Camelot was in trouble and needed help, Cynric had recalled as many men as he could from the fields, crammed them into boats and rowed straight there. But many people and animals had drowned in the floods, and the villagers needed the Saxons' help to save their stranded families. By the time they'd arrived at Camelot, the dark knight and his men had already taken charge.

"Prince Mordred was already at the gates, Princess," the big man said. "I'm sorry. We did what we could, but he left his devils to defend the ditches. You saw what happened back there. The same thing happens every time we try to get near Camelot's walls. They're already dead, so we can't kill them. But they can tear our souls screaming from our bodies. It's impossible to get past even the first ditch, and Odin only knows how many more of the devils are hiding in the mist between here and the walls."

"But how did Mordred get inside?" Rhianna said, dismayed. She stared up at the dark knight's eagle banner flying from Camelot's highest tower. "Was he wearing the Crown? Did he use its magic?"

"Magic enough." Cynric grunted. "He had your dragon shield and your boots. He told everyone you were dead and showed them to the queen. Then there was this bright green flash, and she fainted, or worse... sorry, Princess, but they had to carry her back inside. Then the gates opened and he went in after her. We haven't seen him since."

Rhianna turned cold. If Mordred had

killed her mother, she'd never forgive herself for taking all the knights out of Camelot.

"That's because the guards will have dealt with the traitor," Cai said. "Especially if they think he killed Damsel Rhianna and hurt the queen!"

"I'm not so sure," Cynric said. "He had some of them bloodbeards with him. Not many, but enough to keep order inside if all Camelot's knights have gone off to Dragonland, as you say."

"If the guards don't kill him, the squires will!" Cai said fiercely. "They know the story of how he killed King Arthur. Gareth hates Mordred. He'll do it."

"They're probably dead by now, too," Cynric said glumly. "Poor brave lads."

Rhianna stared up at the closed gate and clenched her fists.

Mordred wanted to use the Crown of Dreams to wipe her father's name from history and take the throne. But if King Arthur had not existed, then neither would the court at Camelot, which he had built, so there would be no throne for him to take.

It was so crazy, she laughed.

The Saxons gave her sympathetic looks. "Poor maid," they muttered. "It's the shock, you know... Lost her father, and now maybe her mother too..."

"Where are the knights?" Chief Cynric asked Cai in a low tone. "Don't tell me they all drowned in the floods, like Mordred claims?"

"They'll be here, don't worry," Rhianna said, sobering. "They're just slow, as usual. They had to go the long way round."

Cai, who had been giving her a worried look,

grinned in relief. "Yeah, we rode right across the flood! It was brilliant fun. Elphin let me borrow his fairy horse, and he's riding Sandy. I hope he keeps him safe. At least it's a bit drier up here…" He frowned at the castle. "So how are we goin' to get inside, Damsel Rhianna? Do you want me to challenge Prince Mordred to a duel?"

"It's not a bad idea," Chief Cynric said, looking at Cai with more respect. "If you can lure the little rat out here, we might be able to grab him for you."

"I'll duel with the dark knight if you want me to, Damsel Rhianna!" Cai said bravely.

She smiled at his determined expression. "No – there isn't enough dry ground left for you to tilt on, anyway. I've got a better idea."

She took Chief Cynric aside and quickly explained what she wanted him to do.

He gave her a doubtful look.

"Are you sure you wouldn't rather wait for the knights, Princess?" he said. "It'd be safer."

"We haven't time to wait!" Rhianna said. "I've got to get my father's jewel from Arianrhod before Mordred destroys it, and this is the only way I can think of to get inside. Just don't tell Cai until we get up there. I don't think he's going to like it very much."

She could tell Cynric didn't like her plan, either, but he didn't have any better ideas. They made their preparations quickly. She remounted Alba and drew her sword. She waited until Cai joined her on Evenstar and gripped Excalibur more tightly. *"I call on the knightly spirits bound to this sword,"* she whispered. "*I need you to fight for me now!*"

The jewel on Excalibur's hilt brightened, and its blade glimmered. The air around her rippled as the spirits of the men who had been knighted by the sword and later killed in battle joined them. Maybe she did not need the living knights to win this battle. She saw the Lance of Truth glimmering too. Her friend's eyes shone with excitement.

"Straight up to the wall, fast as you can," she muttered to Cai. "No heroics."

The boy bit his lip. The Saxons had lent him a helmet, which was a bit big. When he nodded, it slipped down over his eyes.

"Can you see in that thing? she asked.

"Not much," he admitted.

"Probably just as well," Cynric muttered.

Rhianna straightened Cai's helmet, checked

the Saxons were ready and raised Excalibur in the air. "Charge!" she yelled.

As their horses approached the first ditch at full gallop, the mist rose to surround them with an icy chill. Like before, she glimpsed shadows writhing inside it. Frost formed on Alba's mane, and she wondered if they might freeze to death before they got past the ghostly warriors.

A long, shadowy arm reached up to grab her rein. The little mare misted to avoid it. Excalibur brightened and its hilt warmed under her hand. She brought the sword down on the arm and heard a wail of pain. The shadow fell apart before her eyes. The arm twisted out of the ditch, curled up like a burning leaf and vanished in a puff of smoke. The rest of the shadow rose after it into the sunlight and went howling back across the water towards Dragonland.

She looked anxiously at her sword and laughed. Excalibur's blade still gleamed brightly. At least she didn't have to worry about blooding the blade in *this* battle. Ghosts did not bleed.

Beside her, she saw Cai spear another ghostly warrior with the Lance of Truth. The same thing happened. When the magical weapon touched it, the shadow disintegrated, smoked in the sun and fled back to Annwn.

"We can kill them!" she shouted, swinging Excalibur more confidently at another ghost and taking off its head. "Four Lights stand against the dark, remember? And we've got two of the Lights!"

Out of the corner of her eye she saw the dead

knights in their shimmering armour battling the ghostly warriors of Annwn in the ditches. The strength of a hundred men filled her. She laughed and looked hopefully for her father's spirit, but could not see him. She practised using her sword in either hand, swapping it over each time they took a breather. Her blood sang, and she began to enjoy herself.

As they jumped the last ditch and galloped up the hill with the Saxons running behind, Mordred's ghostly warriors howled and launched a final attack. She glimpsed eyeless helms and maimed limbs, horrible scars and gaping wounds – the injuries that had killed these men and sent their souls to Annwn. Shadowy axes and swords swung at Alba and Evenstar, but glimmered through the two mist horses without harming them.

They had almost reached the walls when a tall, ghostly warrior wearing a winged helm stepped out of the shadows right in front of Rhianna. He had the bearing of a king, and his eyes gleamed with curiosity as they studied her.

"So, this is my infamous granddaughter," he growled. "You're brave enough to have fought your way through my army, that's for sure. But a girl cannot be the Pendragon. Let that young fool Mordred sit on the throne for a few years, and come with me back to Annwn where there is no pain. I'll make sure Lady Morgan looks after you."

"Never!" Rhianna yelled, swinging Excalibur at his head. What had he called her? Granddaughter? That meant he was part of the Pendragon family she'd come to the world of men to find... except he was dead now.

She wondered why he hadn't been taken to Avalon when he died, like King Arthur.

The ghostly warrior ducked. "That's no way to treat your old Grandpa Uther," he said with a chuckle, drawing his rusty sword and leaping towards her. "If you want a fight, I'll teach you a few tricks."

"I'll teach *you* some tricks, you mean!" Rhianna said, swapping Excalibur to her left hand and telling Alba to mist past him.

The ghost of Uther Pendragon spun round in confusion and squinted at her. While he was distracted, Cai swung the Lance of Truth at his ankles from behind. Uther tripped over the lance and stumbled backwards down the slope into the ditch, where Alba trampled him with her enchanted horseshoes, sending him after the other ghosts.

He forgot to look behind him, her mare said. *No wonder he is dead.*

Rhianna grinned. She heard a yell of warning from Cai, and swung Excalibur to behead another shadowy warrior whose long fingers had knotted around Chief Cynric's neck.

"Thanks," he grunted as the shadow wailed away. The Saxon chief grabbed Alba's tail and held on grimly as she pulled him out of the ditch.

Rhianna checked Cai was safe, and risked a look behind.

Now that their leader had gone, shadowy warriors were pouring out of the ditches behind them to flee back across the water in a green cloud. She saw ghostly horses with them, and felt a bit sad. Those poor horses had already carried their riders into Annwn once.

"Yah!" Cai said, shaking his lance after them. "Run, you cowards!"

The Saxons had re-formed in the shadow of the wall. They looked up grimly at Camelot's high battlements. Rhianna's arms ached from swinging her sword, and her hair crackled with frost. Despite the chill of Annwn in the ditches they had crossed, she was sweating under her armour. But they'd done it. Only two of Cynric's men had been lost to Uther's warriors as the Saxons fought their way up the hill.

Cai flopped over Evenstar's neck and rested the Lance of Truth on the ground with a sigh of relief. "I couldn't skewer Mordred if he stood right in front of me," he groaned. "So what's the plan, Damsel Rhianna? Are we goin' to climb the wall now? Because I think I need a rest first."

Rhianna sheathed Excalibur so that its magical light died. She checked that nobody was watching from above before she dismounted. She unbuckled her scabbard, strapped the sword to Alba's saddle and took the reins over the mare's head.

This was the part of her plan she did not like so much.

"Dismount," she told Cai. "Let Evenstar loose, and hide that lance somewhere."

The boy looked puzzled. "But what if I need it inside?"

"It'll be safer out here. So will Evenstar. He'll go and find Elphin and tell him where we are."

The boy looked as if he might argue. But then he slipped off the mist horse's back, scrambled into the nearest ditch and covered the Lance of Truth with fallen leaves.

Rhianna felt tempted to do the same with Excalibur. But the Sword of Light had to be inside the castle for her plan to work. She might not get out again so easily once she was through the gates.

Her sweat had cooled, making her feel shivery. While Cai was busy hiding the Lance, she kicked what remained of the rags off her feet and passed Alba's reins to Chief Cynric. "Don't mist, my darling," she whispered to the mare. "This man will make sure you get to your stable."

Why can you not take me to my stable? her mare snorted. *I am very sweaty. I need grooming.*

"I know you do, my darling. Cai will groom you. I have to see someone first."

She took a deep breath and held her hands

out towards the Saxons, wrists pressed together. "All right, tie me and make it look good. If Mordred thinks I'm your prisoner, he'll let you in."

◄◗ 13 ◗►

Prince of Camelot

A traitor sits at the table round,
Prince of Camelot, as yet uncrowned.
But only the true and rightful heir
Shall rule the knights who gather there.

Last year, Rhianna had ridden into Camelot while her father's people cheered and showered her with white rose petals from the walls. This time, everyone watched in silence as Mordred's bloodbeard captain led her, bound and barefoot, across the courtyard. His other hand clutched Excalibur in its red scabbard.

The Saxons followed, scowling under their damp furs. In their midst, a small warrior wearing an oversized helmet cast worried glances at Rhianna.

She hung back a little on her leash. "Stop looking at me," she hissed. "You'll give us away."

The bloodbeard gave the leash a tug. She bruised her toes on the steps, but bit back her angry words. *Act meek*, she told herself. *Then he'll think you're beaten and will forget to be careful.*

She lowered her head so her hair hung in tangles across her face and limped a bit. The captain looked down at her bare feet and chuckled. "Missing your pretty boots, Princess?

You won't need them in the dungeon. No place to run down there."

Rhianna hoped he would take her straight down to the cells so she could talk to Arianrhod and find out what had happened to her father's jewel. But no such luck.

As they passed the dining hall, the bloodbeard turned to the Saxons and growled, "What are you lot still following me for? I think I can handle a barefoot damsel! Go and get drunk or something. No doubt Prince Mordred will reward you later for your treachery."

The small warrior in the oversized helmet hesitated. The others hustled him along with them into the dining hall, calling for mead. Two frightened maids ran in to serve them, casting Rhianna nervous glances on the way.

"That's right." The bloodbeard chuckled at

their shocked expressions. "Take a good look at your princess – not so proud now, is she? This is what happens to damsels who defy Prince Mordred. Tell all your friends."

Rhianna kept her head down so she wouldn't catch the girls' eyes. They were used to seeing her looking scruffy after she'd been sword training with the squires. It didn't matter what they thought, but she wished she could ask them about her mother. She hoped Mordred had not hurt the queen.

While the bloodbeard was distracted, she twisted her hands against the rope. Chief Cynric had only tied the knot loosely, and she had the other end clutched in her hand so it would come undone quickly. But she needed to pick her moment.

"Right – come on, you!" the bloodbeard

jerked her leash again. "I don't know how you got out of that dragon's lair. But now you're here, Prince Mordred will want to see you. Turns out we've got a small problem, so you might be of some use after all."

Rhianna's heart beat faster as they turned down the corridor leading to the Great Hall. A small problem? Maybe she wasn't too late to stop Mordred taking her father's throne.

The big double doors stood open. Her cousin sat in King Arthur's seat, slumped over the Round Table, his head resting on his arms and his dark curls shadowing his face. Sunlight poured through the hole in the roof, illuminating the Crown of Dreams, which encircled the central slot where Excalibur could be inserted into the stone. The crown flashed with colour, its large green jewel swirling with Annwn's shadows.

As she tried to see if her father's jewel had been restored to the Crown, Excalibur began to glow in response. Startled, the bloodbeard held the sword at arm's length. He cleared his throat. "Er, M-master...?"

Mordred looked up, squinting at the sun and all the flashing jewels. "What is it now?" he snapped. "I thought I told you not to disturb me in here—"

When he saw Rhianna, he snapped alert. His gaze flew to the sword in the bloodbeard's hand, then back to her. A slow smile spread across his face as he took in her bare feet, her tangled hair, and the rope binding her wrists.

"Well well, this is a surprise, cousin! You're proving remarkably difficult to kill." He jerked his head at the bloodbeard. "For Annwn's sake, give that sword to me before it swallows your soul, and get the girl away from it!"

The bloodbeard pushed Rhianna into the nearest chair and slid Excalibur in its scabbard across the table. But the Round Table was so big that the sword didn't slide all the way across. It came to rest touching the Crown of Dreams. The blue stone of the table began to hum, and both the Sword and Crown brightened as they touched.

Mordred pulled a face at the glowing crown and struggled to his feet. He limped around the table, holding on to the backs of the chairs for support.

As he came closer, Rhianna saw dark shadows under his eyes and a ring of weeping black blisters around his head. She winced, realising they had been made by the Crown of Dreams.

Mordred looked exhausted. "What are you staring at, cousin?" he snapped. "It's hard work wearing that Crown, you know. A damsel like you would never manage to control the magic. Be thankful I found it first."

"I wore it in Dragonland," she reminded him, unable to play the meek prisoner any longer. "And I used it to spirit-ride the shadrake! That's more than you can do, isn't it?"

Mordred laughed. "Still got a bit of fight left in her, I see. Leave us, and lock the doors behind you. My cousin and I have unfinished business."

"But Master…" the bloodbeard protested.

"Leave us, I say!" Mordred scowled and pressed his palm to his forehead, where the largest blister wept sticky fluid into his eyes. "She's unarmed and bound. I have the Crown and the Sword. What's she going to do? Kill me with her bare toes? I'll call if I need you."

Rhianna bent over her hands and started to work the knot loose. When the bloodbeard left, she'd get her chance. Once the doors were locked, the only way in or out of the hall would be through the roof hole, which was impossible without wings. It would be just her and Mordred and two of the Lights. But she'd need to move fast to get hold of them both before the dark knight did, and the knot had been pulled tighter on her way here.

The back of her neck prickled as footsteps passed behind her. Not yet... with her head down and her hair over her face, she couldn't see what her cousin was doing. She heard him mutter something to the bloodbeard.

Then the doors slammed behind her.

She tugged desperately at the rope, trying to pull her wrists free. But before she could get the last loop off, Mordred's hand twisted in her hair and pulled her head back.

"What are you up to, cousin?" he hissed into her ear.

Rhianna gave up on the knot and twisted out of his grip, leaving copper strands in his fist. She scrambled on to the table and dived for Excalibur with her bound hands. He cursed and grabbed her ankle, pulling her back. She sprawled facedown and blooded her nose on the stone, but managed to hook the scabbard towards her.

She awkwardly drew Excalibur two-handed in a shower of sparks. The sun coming through the roof hole dazzled her. Her blade flashed, reflecting the colours of the crown.

Mordred still gripped her ankle, surprisingly strong for a one-handed cripple. She kicked to free herself and swiped at him blindly with her sword.

He ducked and laughed. "Careful, cousin. Don't want to blood your blade, do you?"

"Neither do you, if it's *your* blood," Rhianna pointed out, swinging at him again.

But it was awkward, lying on her stomach with her ankle captive and her wrists still linked by the rope. Her arms ached from fighting her way up the hill, making her wish she hadn't shown off so much when dealing with the ghosts.

As she twisted round to use her teeth on the stubborn knot, her cousin grinned and raised his stump. There was a dark blur in the corner of her eye. Before she could react, a black gauntlet flew from his belt towards her. The gauntlet tugged her bonds tight again and clamped around her wrists to stop her freeing herself. Ice flowed up her arms – cold, so very cold. Her fingers went numb on Excalibur's hilt. Though she tried her best to hold on to it, the sword slid off the table and clattered to the floor.

The gauntlet, oozing its rotten flesh, did not let go, and she realised where she'd seen it before. It was Mordred's missing hand, which her father had chopped off during the battle at Camlann just before the dark knight killed him. His bloodbeards had been carrying it the first time she'd met them, when their captain had used it to torture Sir Bors in the Saxon camp. It contained the shadow magic of Annwn.

All the strength ran out of her. Mordred dragged her off the table and pushed her back into her chair. She tried to get up again but could not fight the shadow magic without her sword and sank back in despair, shivering.

He smiled down at her. "That's better," he said. "Amazing how powerful Annwn's magic can be when you know how to use it properly. I've learned a few tricks since we last met, thanks to my mother. And now I think it's time we had a little chat."

He picked up Excalibur and limped back to his seat. While Rhianna struggled to shake off the gauntlet and free her wrists, her cousin laid the sword before him on the table and put on the Crown of Dreams. The jewels on both Lights brightened. He smiled at her.

"I'm glad you got out of that cave, cousin.

I didn't like to think of you buried in there – it wasn't my idea. You can blame my mother for that. I expect you're the reason my shadrake failed to get hold of Excalibur and the Lance of Truth, as I told it to do, but no matter. The Sword is here now, and you're just in time to help me summon the knights of the Round Table so they can crown me the new King of Camelot."

"They'll never make *you* king!" Rhianna said, a flicker of hope returning. If Mordred summoned the knights, they would arrest him.

"Ah, but that's where you're wrong. I wear the Pendragon crown. They'll have no choice. But for some reason they won't come when I call. You know the secret of summoning them, don't you? My mother tells me Excalibur can summon the spirit of anyone who has ever sat at the Round Table, living or dead. Help me call the knights who knew me when I sat here as a prince of Camelot and Arthur's favourite, and I'll make sure the queen is looked after. I don't like killing family unnecessarily."

"You killed my father!" she reminded him through gritted teeth, seeing that he meant to get the dead knights to crown him while Sir Bors and the others were delayed by the flood. "You're a traitor, and I'd rather die than help you."

"That could be arranged, if you continue to be stubborn," Mordred said, frowning at her. "Though your friends will die first, slowly and painfully. Be sensible for once, cousin. I've destroyed your father's jewel and changed history. The little maid was ready to die because of you. So why not keep your remaining friends and family alive by helping me?"

Rhianna turned cold. She stopped trying to get the gauntlet off her wrists. "What have you done with Arianrhod?" she demanded. "If you've hurt her..."

Mordred's smile widened. "The girl's either very brave or very stupid. She told me she'd promised you she would guard that jewel with her life, and I hate to see anyone break a promise."

Rhianna leaped to her feet with a cry of rage, but still couldn't free her wrists from the dark fist. She eyed Excalibur's blade. Maybe she could distract Mordred long enough for her to run around the table and impale the gauntlet on the sword...

"*Courage, daughter,*" said a familiar voice.

"Your maid is not dead."

"Father!" she gasped as King Arthur's ghost glimmered into view beside Mordred's seat. She was relieved to see him back from Dragonland and its gate to Annwn. But if history had been changed, how long would he be able to stay? "Be careful – Mordred's destroyed your jewel!"

Arthur frowned at the crown on the dark knight's head, then reached over his shoulder and tried to pick up Excalibur. His ghostly hands passed through the sword, but Excalibur's blade brightened and the crown flashed green.

Mordred winced and raised his hand to his head.

"Take off my crown, traitor, and let my daughter go!" Arthur commanded. *"Or I'll cut off your*

other hand when I return to the world of men."

Her cousin flinched. To Rhianna, her father looked more solid than he had in the shadrake's lair, but Mordred obviously couldn't see him as well as she could. He must have been able to hear him, though, because he laughed.

"You do that, uncle – *if* you return! I think we're going to have a long wait, though, before you can pick up your sword again... A very long wait, if you're relying on your daughter to find the Grail of Stars, which no knight has ever found and lived to tell the tale. So how can anyone expect a damsel to succeed?" He laughed again. "Especially alone, without her friends. Merlin won't escape the shadrake this time, and her fairy prince seems to have vanished off the face of the earth along with all your fine knights. No doubt the lad has seen sense and ridden back through the mists to Avalon by now."

Rhianna's heart thumped. "That's a lie! Elphin would never abandon me." But she couldn't help thinking of her friend leading the knights through Annwn's green flood, and the Lonely Tor that led to Avalon, only a day's ride away.

Seeing the doubt on her face, Mordred chuckled. "Are you so sure of that, cousin? I wear the Crown now. I can see through the shadrake's eyes, remember."

"Only if you can spirit-ride," Rhianna said. "Which you can't."

"Maybe I've learned how," Mordred snapped back. "Come, shadrake!" he called, raising his arms to the hole in the roof. "Come to your new Pendragon!"

A shadow passed across the sun. Her cousin looked up with a triumphant smile.

Rhianna's stomach tightened as huge wings blocked the light. But the dragon flapped on past. As Mordred squinted after it, a small, feathered missile dived through the hole above the Round Table and flew into the dark knight's upturned face, knocking the Crown askew.

"Merlin!" she gasped in relief.

Her cousin flung up his arms to protect his eyes, and the gauntlet's grip on her wrists loosened as he lost control of the shadow magic. She thumped it against the table, and the horrid thing dropped to the floor.

In a heartbeat, she had dragged off her remaining bonds, danced around the empty chairs, snatched up Excalibur and leaped on to the table. She thrust the blade into the slot that

Merlin had made for it long ago, and ghostly knights long dead shimmered into view all around the hall.

"Who summons us?" they breathed.

"I do!" Rhianna said quickly, before her cousin could speak. "I summon you to aid your king, Arthur Pendragon, guardian of the Round Table and rightful ruler of the world of men!"

The knights blinked at King Arthur's ghost. "Our king!" they whispered. "Our king has returned to Camelot... what is your command, sire?"

"*Throw the traitor Mordred out of here*," King Arthur ordered. "*He has dared to wear my crown, but he will never be king of men while my spirit survives.*"

Mordred, meanwhile, staggered from his seat and stumbled around the hall, pursued by the screeching merlin. The ghosts crowded around him. He bumped into pillars and tripped over a chair as the crown slipped over his eyes. He backed into a corner, fending off the pale knights. "Get away from me," he growled. "*I'm* your Pendragon, not Arthur! Don't you recognise me? I'm Prince Mordred, son of the king's sister, Lady Morgan Le Fay, and I wear the Crown now! You have to obey *me*..."

Rhianna closed her eyes to concentrate on the sword's magic. "Sir Lancelot?" she called. "Sir Bors? Sir Bedivere? Can you hear me? It's Rhianna! I'm at the Round Table. Where are you?"

She held her breath. If Sir Bors and Sir Bedivere were still following Elphin through the floods, would they be able to hear her?

"Right outside!" boomed a voice at the door,

making her jump. "Hold on, Damsel Rhianna, we're coming."

The double doors burst open. Sir Lancelot and Sir Bors rushed in with the other knights who had ridden to Dragonland. Their armour dripped and they left wet footprints across the floor, but their weapons were dry. Cai stood behind them with his oversized Saxon helmet in his hand, grinning. Rhianna grinned back in relief. She left Excalibur in the table and jumped down, looking for Elphin.

She'd forgotten the dark fist.

As she jumped off the table, it flew up from the floor and seized Excalibur's hilt. The ghostly knights disappeared. In the shadows, Mordred jerked his right arm. The sword came out of the table with a shower of blue sparks and flashed straight for Rhianna's throat.

She staggered back against a pillar, where the sword pricked her chin. She swallowed in fear as something warm trickled down her neck.

Blood, she thought in horror. *Blood on Excalibur's blade.*

14

Shadow Magic

Two Lights shone bright in Camelot's hall
Where a dark knight sat among them all.
When Sword is set against the Crown
Then shall Mordred be struck down.

Everyone froze, staring at Rhianna and the blade the dark fist was holding to her throat. Despair filled her. Now she couldn't take Excalibur back to Avalon for her father. Even if she found all four Lights, she could not complete her quest.

Mordred struggled to his feet and struck the merlin a blow that sent the poor little hawk tumbling across the floor. He adjusted the crown, which had slipped over one eye, and spat out a feather. Before the knights could stop him, he limped towards Rhianna and grabbed her wrist, pulling her in front of him.

"Nobody touches me!" he said, twisting her left arm up behind her back. "Lay your weapons on the floor and let us walk out of here. And keep that crazy bird off me as well, or your princess joins my mother in Annwn. I mean it."

With the dark fist and the sword following her every move, Rhianna had no choice but to shuffle with her cousin towards the door. The merlin lay on the floor under the table where

Mordred had knocked him, wings spread and panting. She couldn't see Elphin. Where was he when they needed his magic? She heard the clash of swords in the corridors outside and wondered if the Saxons had changed sides yet again.

When she thought of how stupid she'd been to let go of Excalibur, she felt like crying. Then she got angry. This was her father's castle! Mordred had no right to threaten her inside Camelot.

"Don't worry about me," she choked out. "It's only shadow magic. Arrest him!"

The knights stared uncertainly at the dark fist holding the sword to her throat. Sir Lancelot took a step towards Mordred, who raised his right arm. The fist jumped sideways, knocking Lancelot's sword from his hand before returning swiftly to Rhianna's throat.

"I'm not bluffing!" he warned as Lancelot hugged his wounded wrist. "That's my right hand holding Excalibur, the one King Arthur chopped off at Camlann. It's been to Annwn and back, and I know how to use the shadow magic now."

"He's only trying to scare you!" Rhianna spluttered. "He won't kill me. He knows he'll never get out of here alive if he does."

The knights muttered angrily. But none of them dared approach the dark knight.

"That's better," Mordred said. "As you can see, my fist holds the Sword of Light. That means I command your knightly spirits now. So lay down your weapons and get down on your knees! And someone bring me my horse and the Lance of Truth. I know it's here somewhere, if the little champion is around. Don't make me look for it, or it'll be the worse for your princess."

The knights glanced at Rhianna again, but whoever held Excalibur controlled them. Slowly, one by one, they laid their swords on the mosaic floor and dropped to their knees. Cai cast her an apologetic look and hurried outside. Another squire went running towards the stables.

"Oh, for goodness' sake!" she said as Mordred dragged her past the kneeling knights, into the corridor that led to the courtyard. "I can't believe you're just going to let him walk out of here! He killed my father remember? Pick up your swords, you fools, and arrest the traitor!"

Sir Bedivere shook his head at her as they passed. "Your life is more important, Damsel Rhianna," he said. "Don't do anything rash.

We can't fight Mordred while he's got two of the Lights – the spirit magic is too strong. But Cynric's still outside. The Saxons aren't controlled by Excalibur's magic, don't worry."

"Those two-faced barbarians won't get in my way if they know what's good for them," Mordred growled as he hustled Rhianna down the corridor.

The fighting had stopped. Rhianna wondered who had won. She made it as difficult as she could for Mordred to drag her along, slowing him down as much as possible to give the Saxons time to get into position.

An out of breath Cai waited outside in the courtyard with the Lance of Truth. A small group of bloodbeards stood warily near the open gates with their horses. The shadrake crouched on the battlements, watching every movement with its red eyes. When he saw no sign of the Saxons, Mordred relaxed slightly and pushed her down the steps towards his men.

"Strap that lance to my horse's saddle and get down on your hands and knees," he ordered Cai. "I need a mounting block, and you'll do nicely."

"Don't do it, Cai!" Rhianna called. "Go and get Elphin. Tell him to bring his harp."

"Forget it," Mordred said with a laugh. "Avalonian magic doesn't work against the power of Annwn, as your fairy friend knows."

The squire stopped. His hands trembled as he aimed his lance at the dark knight. "*I'll* save you, Damsel Rhianna!" Teeth gritted in determination, he advanced towards Mordred. But since Rhianna had knighted Cai with Excalibur in the summer so that he could be her champion, he had the same problem as the other knights. With the sword held by the dark fist controlling his spirit, each step the boy took was slower than the last.

"Stop!" Mordred said in alarm, dragging Rhianna in front of him again.

Sweat broke out on Cai's brow. His face twisted in pain as he fought the magic, but he kept the Lance of Truth pointed at the dark knight and managed another step.

"I command you by the power of this Sword that controls your knightly spirit to stop!" Mordred yelled, a flicker of fear in his eyes. "You're the Pendragon's champion, aren't you? I hold Excalibur, which means you have to obey me now, not her! Do what I told you, or your princess dies, here and now."

Mordred's bloodbeards closed around their

prince and Rhianna. The knights were still weaponless, watching helplessly from the top of the steps.

Cai's shoulders slumped. He carried the lance over to the black stallion, mouthing "sorry" as he passed her. Was he really under Mordred's control, or only pretending to be? This was getting ridiculous.

She jerked her elbow into Mordred's stomach and stamped down hard on his lame foot with her heel. This might have had more effect if she'd been wearing her boots, but Mordred doubled over in pain and grunted as his crippled leg gave way.

Before he could recover, Rhianna ducked under Excalibur's wildly waving blade and grabbed the dark fist in both hands. It twisted in her grip and froze her hands, but she had anger on her side and prised the black fingers open one by one.

"Give me back my sword!" she yelled at the dark knight. "I'm not scared of you!"

"You should be," Mordred hissed as his captain helped him up. "You'll be sorry you did that, cousin. You can't fight magic."

"I've been fighting magic all my life," Rhianna growled back through gritted teeth. "What do you think I had to do growing up in Avalon?"

As soon as her fingers touched the white jewel on Excalibur's hilt, it flared brightly. Freed from Mordred's control, the knights shook their heads as if waking from a daze. They picked up their weapons and staggered down the steps into the courtyard to help Rhianna with her struggle against the dark fist.

Mordred retreated behind his bloodbeards and raised both arms to the sky. The green jewel at the front of the Crown glowed, and the shadrake swooped down from the battlements, its shadow darkening the sun.

He laughed. "See?" he called. "This crown gives me the power of the ancient Dragonlords! Keep the silly lance, if you want. I don't need the Light made by the hands of men. The Crown and the Sword should be enough for now to make people obey me. When I find the Grail, I'll be invincible!"

"You'll never find *that* without King Arthur's jewel, traitor!" Cai said scornfully, swinging the Lance of Truth at the dark knight.

Mordred scowled and turned to deal with the boy. Cai's lance sparkled through the air, in danger of skewering Rhianna. While her cousin was distracted, she wrenched Excalibur from the dark fist's grip and yelled at the knights to help Cai. Seeing that she had her sword back again and could look after herself, they at last tackled the bloodbeards.

Rhianna leaped towards the dark knight, meaning to put Excalibur to *his* throat and make him give her the Crown. But before anyone could touch him, her cousin fell to the ground and began to thrash about, clawing at his head as Arianrhod had done in the chapel before they had set out for Dragonland. Seeing they could not win, the surviving bloodbeards abandoned their prince and fled for the gates.

The knights gathered warily around Mordred, forming a ring of swords. Annwn's green jewel brightened still further, and the crown began to smoke. Mordred groaned and thrashed some more. Then his back arched, he gave a final spine-tingling scream, slammed to the ground and lay still. The Crown rolled from his head, and the dark knight's spirit twisted up over the wall and vanished.

As everyone stared at the dark knight's body, a wild shriek raised the hairs on Rhianna's neck. There came a rush of wings, and the shadrake swooped into the courtyard making everyone duck. The horses reared in terror and bolted out of the gate.

"I WILL TAKE THIS NOW, PENDRAGON," the creature's familiar voice boomed in her head.

Rhianna tightened her grip on Excalibur and threw herself over the Crown, yelling a warning to Cai to keep a good hold of the Lance. But the creature did not try to steal any of the Lights this time. Instead, its scaly claw grabbed Mordred's fist from where she'd cast it aside. Before anyone could react, the dragon had escaped over the wall with its prize.

She climbed to her feet, shaking. She eyed the Crown, wondering if she dared put it on and call the dragon back. No, she wasn't ready yet for another battle with magic. Let the dragon take its treasure – her cousin wouldn't be using his dark fist to torture anyone else now.

The knights had dropped to the ground when the shadrake attacked, covering their heads with their shields. They gave Rhianna a sheepish look and turned their attention back to Mordred. Her cousin lay rigid, his face still twisted with its final scream. Sir Bors poked him with his sword. The dark knight did not move.

"Is he dead?" she asked, her stomach doing strange things.

Sir Lancelot bent over the motionless body and put a finger to the dark knight's neck. He frowned, then looked up and nodded. The others relaxed slightly.

Sir Bedivere sighed. "The Crown must have killed him," he said. "There's an old druid's tale that says it will kill anybody who tries to take the throne unlawfully, but we've never seen its magic in action before."

"It killed Morgan Le Fay too," Rhianna told them, staring at Mordred. She still could not quite believe he was dead.

"Serves the traitor right!" Cai said fiercely, gripping the Lance of Truth. "I wish you'd let me kill him for you though, Damsel Rhianna. It don't seem real he was killed by magic like that. Is Excalibur all right?"

She examined Excalibur's blade, reminded of the blood. But with Mordred dead, maybe it wouldn't matter so much if she couldn't take her father his sword when she went back to Avalon? She could always leave Excalibur at Camelot with her mother until the king returned to claim his throne.

Chief Cynric arrived at the gates with a bloodbeard's head dangling from each hand. The big Saxon's axe dripped blood, and he was grinning. "Caught these two devils running off. Guess Prince Mordred won't miss them now. Do you need any more help, Princess?" he asked. "It's a bit wet outside still – you won't be having any jousts for a while, but we'll soon get the place cleaned up for you. What happened in here? Looks like the Wild Hunt hit it."

Rhianna looked around the courtyard with its scorch marks, dead bloodbeards and scattered weapons. "Magic did," she said with a grin.

While everyone argued about whether the Crown's magic had really killed the dark knight or he'd finally died of his old battle wounds from Camlann, Queen Guinevere appeared at the castle door. She wore a nightgown and her bright hair was still tousled from her pillow.

Her frantic gaze swept the courtyard. When it reached Rhianna, she let out a gasp of relief and rushed down the steps towards her. "Oh, my brave darling! Thank God. I could hardly believe it when I woke up and they said you were back. He told me you were *dead*! He had your shield and your boots…"

Rhianna's heart lifted in equal joy to see her mother recovered. She laughed. "I still had my armour, Mother. It's magic, remember?"

"I know, but I've been so worried." Guinevere held back her hug at the sight of the bloodstained sword in Rhianna's hand. "I see you've been fighting again... I hope that's Mordred's blood?"

The knights glanced at each other. Nobody corrected her.

"We've got King Arthur's crown back, my lady." Sir Lancelot picked up the Crown of Dreams and handed it to her. "It was in Dragonland with Mordred, just like Princess Rhianna said. I think there's a few jewels missing, but it still seems to work. It rejected Mordred when he tried to use it to claim the throne."

The queen gave a funny little smile as she took the crown. She touched the green jewel of Annwn, drew a deep breath and looked around the courtyard. "Where is the traitor?" she said in an icy voice. "Bring him to me."

Sir Lancelot rested a hand on her arm. "Prince Mordred is dead, my lady," he said.

The queen frowned. Then she spotted Mordred's body lying in the shadows and pushed the knights aside.

"Stay back, Your Majesty!" Sir Bors warned. "It might be a trick."

The queen stared down at the twisted body of the dark knight. "I think my champion has fought enough battles to know whether a man is dead or not," she said, making some of the knights chuckle. "Get the Saxons to build a pyre for him. We need to call a meeting of the Round Table to discuss what to do about the mess Mordred's floods have left behind.

Cai, go inside and fetch out that merlin before it soils the floor. Rhianna darling, you're excused. Go and have a bath and get changed. We'll talk about this later." She frowned at Excalibur's soiled blade. "You'd better get your squire to clean your sword as well. Your father would never leave it in that state after a battle."

Cai opened his mouth to protest. "I'm a knight now, not a squi—"

"Do you want to sit in another boring meeting?" Rhianna hissed, and he shut up again.

‹✦›

While Cai rescued the panting merlin from under the Round Table, Rhianna kept her hand on Excalibur's hilt in case the druid wanted to say something to her. But the poor bird didn't even look capable of flying, let alone explaining how she was supposed to complete her quest now that Mordred had destroyed her father's jewel and blooded Excalibur.

"Where's Elphin?" she asked as the big doors boomed shut behind the knights and the guards took up their position outside, spears crossed.

"I think he's with Arianrhod," Cai mumbled, avoiding her eye.

Rhianna frowned. "We could have done with his help earlier. Mordred almost cut my throat out there." She touched the wound and shuddered, only now realising how close she'd come to death.

"I'm sure Elphin will play his harp for you when he's finished helping Arianrhod," Cai said more brightly. "Shall we go down to the dungeon and see if they're still there?"

They settled the injured merlin in the hawk mews on the way, and for once the druid made no protest about belonging in Rhianna's room instead. Her stomach tightened as they turned down the steps to the dungeon. The guards had gone, and all was silent below. She remembered how she'd left her friend a prisoner down here when they set out on their quest. If Mordred had hurt Arianrhod, she would never forgive herself.

The door to the cell stood open. Torches burned brightly inside, showing them the maid fast asleep on the bed. A new bruise showed on her cheek, but she was smiling as she dreamed. Elphin slumped on a stool at her bedside, his head bowed over his harp and his curls shadowing his face. He was sound asleep, too.

The sweet scent of Avalonian magic lingered in the air.

Rhianna saw blood on Elphin's fingers, and the angry words she'd been saving for him fled. She took the harp from his lap and gently set it on the floor.

Cai opened his mouth, "Huh! The lazy—"

"Shh!" she said. "He's exhausted. Don't wake him."

"Do you think there's anything left of King Arthur's jewel?" Cai said. "Elphin might be able to mend it, like he mended the Lance of Truth in the summer."

The same thought had occurred to Rhianna. She checked under the pillow, unsurprised to find no sign of the pendant. She cast a quick look around the cell and sighed. "We can ask Arianrhod what happened to it when she wakes up. The important thing is, Mordred didn't get hold of my father's secrets. My mother's got the Crown now – that'll keep Camelot safe until we get back. I've got something else to take care of first."

Cai brightened. "Lunch?" he said hopefully. "We missed it earlier."

In spite of her worries, she smiled. "No, I want to go up to the lake. I need to talk to Lady Nimue."

"But Damsel Rhianna, all the knights are in the meeting, and what about the floods? You can't go out riding so soon! What if there's trouble?"

"Mordred's dead. His ghost-warriors have gone back to Annwn, and the Saxons have taken care of his bloodbeards. The floods must have gone down if the knights got through.

And if you're worried about that promise I made my mother, not to go out riding without my armour, my sword, and at least one knight… well, I've got Excalibur and my armour, and I believe you told the queen you're not a squire any more."

Cai drew himself up and retrieved the Lance of Truth from the passage. "I'll ride Sandy," he said with a grin. "I want to make sure Elphin hasn't taught him any fairy tricks while he was off in those mists."

◅⫷ 15 ⫸▻

Funeral

That night they built a funeral pyre
To burn the traitor in cleansing fire.
Arthur's jewel to the Crown restored
May bring back Camelot's rightful lord.

They paused just long enough to pick up
Rhianna's boots and Pendragon shield,
which Mordred had tossed into the armoury
once they'd served their purpose. Then they
saddled their horses and trotted out of the

gates into a pink and gold sunset.

Around the castle, floods reflected the luminous sky as far as they could see. Only the Lonely Tor was visible above the drifting mist that lingered over the water. The ditches, which had been full of howling ghosts on their way up to the castle, swarmed with Saxons clearing up after the battle.

Chief Cynric passed them, cheerfully dragging a dead bloodbeard by his feet. "Funeral pyre tonight, Princess!" he called.

Rhianna's stomach turned at the thought of watching her cousin's body burn. But Cai grinned and called back, "Make sure you build it high for Prince Mordred!"

"High as Camelot's towers!" the Saxons promised.

Sandy seemed none the worse for his

journey along the spiral path with Elphin. He seized the bit between his teeth and trotted boldly ahead towards the river.

Alba snorted. *The Saxon pony thinks he is a mist horse now. But he cannot gallop over water like me. Can we leave him behind again?*

"No, my darling," Rhianna said with a smile. "Not this time. I promised my mother."

A yell from Cai distracted her. Sandy came splashing back out of the water, shaking his mane.

"The bridge is still underwater, Damsel Rhianna!" Cai called. "We'd better go back to the castle. It'll be dark soon, anyway, and we don't want to miss Mordred's funeral. We can always go to the lake and look for the fish-lady tomorrow."

She frowned at the swollen river. She hadn't

considered they might not be able to get as far as the lake. Maybe she should have told Cai to ride Evenstar again.

"No," she said. "I've got to ask her what to do about Excalibur before anyone tries to clean it—"

"So! You have finally blooded your blade, Rhianna Pendragon," called a silvery voice from the water, making them both jump. "I thought it would only be a matter of time."

A large tail splashed, and the fish-lady from the lake surfaced in a swirl of green hair. Sandy shied, and Cai almost dropped the Lance of Truth into the water.

"Careful, young champion," Lady Nimue warned in an amused tone. "I might just decide to accept your offering this time."

Cai recovered his balance and scowled

at her. "I haven't finished with it yet," he said. "I need it to protect Damsel Rhianna."

"Protect her from what?" Nimue sat on the flooded bridge and splashed her tail in the river. The pink sunset glittered from her scales. "I see no enemies for you to fight out here. Prince Mordred's bloodbeards fled back across the Summer Sea with those devils he called out of Annwn. I drowned a few, and the Wild Hunt will take care of the rest when it gets here at midwinter. Let me see that sword." She held out a webbed hand.

"Stay back!" Cai said, pointing his lance at her. "What are you doing out of your lake, anyway? You can't just sit on that bridge drowning people, you know. We'll get a lot of visitors at Camelot now Prince Mordred's dead."

"Prince Mordred's dead?" Nimue paused, her turquoise eyes going distant. "Are you sure?"

"Of course we're sure!" Cai said. "Arthur's magic crown killed him, because he tried to kill Damsel Rhianna and make himself king of Camelot. We're burning his body tonight."

The fish-lady frowned. "Then make sure you burn all of it."

"We're not stupid. And you still haven't told us why you're not in your lake."

"Stop it Cai," Rhianna said. "It's obvious how she got here. She swam downriver with the flood." She took a deep breath and blurted out, "Lady Nimue, can you clean Excalibur like you did last time – after King Arthur blooded it in battle and his knights returned the sword to your lake? My father's ghost has vanished again, so I still need to take it back to Avalon for him."

The fish-lady's turquoise eyes narrowed. "Bring the sword here."

"Careful, Damsel Rhianna!" Cai warned.

But Rhianna was already trotting Alba across the swollen river to the flooded bridge. She held out Excalibur, keeping a firm grip on the hilt in case the fish-lady tried to take it to her underwater cavern again.

Nimue ran her webbed fingers along the blade and frowned. "This is your blood," she said.

"Yes..." Rhianna swallowed in memory. "But you cleaned it last time, after my father chopped off Mordred's hand in the battle – and that was Pendragon blood, too. Please try, Lady? Mordred's spirit isn't in the hilt this time, so it's only the blade that needs doing."

"I could try," Nimue agreed. "But you'll have to offer the sword to me properly, like your father told his knights to do when he was dying, so I can pass it on to someone else after it has been cleansed."

Rhianna frowned. "But I need Excalibur if I'm going to look for the Grail of Stars!" She tightened her fist possessively on the hilt. The thought of not finishing her quest, now she had come so far, made tears spring to her eyes.

"I can see you're not ready to give up your sword," Nimue said with a sigh. "There's no need for me to do anything. Just polish it as normal. The blood won't be a problem."

"But I thought you said I mustn't blood the blade if I wanted to take Excalibur to

Avalon?" Rhianna snatched back the sword in anger. "You mean all this time I've been trying to be careful, fighting dragons and bloodbeards and Mordred without getting blood on my sword, and now you're saying it doesn't matter?"

The fish-lady smiled. "It does matter. But only if it's someone else's blood. When your father used Excalibur to wound men, he lost power over them. That's how Mordred was able to kill him at Camlann, and I didn't want you falling into the same trap. You've done amazingly well. You have three of the Lights now. If Arthur's spirit is still not ready to return to his body, then you may indeed need to look for the fourth – but I must warn you, no one has ever managed to take the Grail of Stars into Avalon."

"Then I'll be the first!" Rhianna said, lifting her chin and meeting the fish-lady's luminous gaze.

Nimue smiled again. "I can see your spirit remains strong. Perhaps you are ready for the final stage of your quest... You remember the riddle I asked you when you first visited me in my lake? *What is the secret of the Crown of Dreams?*"

Rhianna frowned. "I already answered that one... the Jewel of Annwn. It's the big green one at the front that contains the secret of dragon riding and opens the gate of Annwn, so it's hardly a secret."

The fish-lady laughed. "You only answered part of it. Every jewel in that crown contains its own secrets, and every Pendragon adds new knowledge to it. If any of the stones are missing, its wearer can't see the whole picture. Your father's jewel was missing when you wore the Crown of Dreams in the shadrake's lair. If you are to find the Grail and complete your quest, you'll need to wear the crown with your father's jewel restored. But be warned, Rhianna Pendragon – you might not like what you see."

"Then Elphin was right! My father's jewel does contain the secret of the Grail of Stars! But Mordred told me he destroyed it... so how can I find the fourth Light now?"

"The jewel was not destroyed," Nimue said.

The fish-lady's eyes reflected the last of the light, and in their blue depths Rhianna saw a luminous swirl of a horse's mane.

Evenstar comes! Alba whinnied, pricking her ears.

Rhianna's heart leaped in hope. Elphin

came trotting down the hill with Arianrhod clinging to his waist. His dark hair tangled with the maid's, whose head rested on his shoulder.

A pang of jealousy made Rhianna's fingers tighten on her sword. Then relief that Arianrhod was recovered took over, and she waved. "Elphin! Over here!"

He trotted straight across the river to join them, his mist horse's enchanted shoes kicking up pink spray. "*Faha'ruh*, Nimue. *Faha'ruh*, Rhia," he said, checking her over for injury. His violet gaze paused at the scab on her throat, and his eyes darkened. Then he smiled. "What are you doing out here talking to the Lady of the Lake? You're supposed to be safe in Camelot."

"Safe?" She blinked at him in disbelief. "Didn't you hear how Mordred got hold of

Excalibur, made all the knights kneel to him, and nearly killed me? He got blood on the blade. I had to do something about it… where *were* you, Elphin?"

"Missed me, did you?" he said, teasing now.

"I missed your magic! I thought Lord Avallach sent you out from Avalon to look after me?"

"Mordred was wearing the Crown of Dreams and using the Jewel of Annwn. I couldn't challenge him. My magic doesn't work against Annwn's dark powers. But I'm here now, and Arianrhod's got something for you."

He smiled as his passenger reached into her dress and pulled out a familiar pendant. Except the stone was not black any more. In the dusk it glowed pink and red, picking up the colours of the sunset. It dangled from a new cord woven out of Evenstar's mane.

Rhianna stared at it, her heart beating faster. "My father's jewel!" she said.

She'd been so stupid. Why hadn't she realised her cousin would lie to her?

"I promised to keep it safe for you my lady, didn't I?" Arianrhod said with a little smile. "So now you can put it back into your crown and complete your quest. Then King Arthur will return to Camelot, and everything will be right again."

"And I'll be able to see my father's secrets," she said, turning to ask Nimue what other knowledge the crown contained.

But with a splash of her tail, the fish-lady was gone.

❁

"But I don't understand," Rhianna said to Arianrhod, as they rode back up the hill to the castle. "However did you hide the jewel from Mordred?" She thought of their conversation in Dragonland. "Are you a witch?"

"Don't be silly, Rhia," Elphin said.

"But you're keeping secrets from me again, aren't you?" Rhianna continued, still annoyed that everyone seemed to think she needed protecting from the truth. "If you won't tell me how you were able to hide my father's jewel from the dark knight in a locked cell, I can always find myself another maid."

Arianrhod blinked.

"It's all right, she doesn't mean it," Elphin said, playing a quick ripple on his harp. "She's just fought an army of ghosts, saved Camelot from Mordred, and played another riddle game with Lady Nimue. She's tired."

Rhianna sighed as the music soothed her nerves. "Just tell me the truth," she said. "If you turn out to be Elphin's long lost sister, or you're a druid like Merlin and want to live in the body of a bird, I won't mind. I've already got one grumpy hawk. You can keep him company."

Arianrhod giggled. "I never keep secrets from you, Lady Rhia. I didn't know the truth myself, until I saw it in your father's jewel."

"You can see my father's secrets?" Rhianna's stomach fluttered.

"With Elphin's help," Arianrhod admitted. "I had a dream of my mother when Elphin played his harp for me in the dungeon."

"Arianrhod's mother was a Grail maiden,"

Elphin explained. "She had a baby, but she wasn't allowed to keep it in the Grail Castle because none of the maidens who look after the Grail of Stars are supposed to have children. So when her baby was born, she brought the child to King Arthur in secret. Your father promised Arianrhod's mother he'd look after her baby, and arranged for his knights to find Arianrhod abandoned on the hillside so nobody would think her special. It's all in the jewel… you'll be able to see for yourself when the Crown's mended."

Rhianna stared at Arianrhod with fresh eyes.

"Have you seen the Grail of Stars?" she asked, excited. "What does it look like? Do you know the way to this Grail Castle?"

"She was just a baby, Rhia," Elphin said gently.

The maid bit her lip. "I can't remember anything before I came to Camelot, my lady, I'm sorry. But hiding your pendant was easy enough. You remember how we fooled Mordred with the lookalike Excalibur in the summer? When Gareth warned me Prince Mordred was on his way down to see me, I simply hung a dark stone from my jewellery box on the chain around my neck and pretended it was the real one."

"But wasn't Mordred suspicious after the trick we played on him last time?" Cai interrupted. "He was pretty angry about that fake sword I took him at the North Wall."

"He ordered his bloodbeards to destroy all my other jewels, too," Arianrhod admitted, touching the bruise on her cheek. "They smashed them with their axes."

"So how did you hide the real one?" Rhianna insisted.

"I swallowed it," Arianrhod whispered. "I'm sorry, my lady, but it was all I could think of to keep it safe for you."

"We've been waiting for it to come out the other end," Elphin added, wrinkling his nose. "Good job I had my harp to help."

"Yeuch!" Rhianna held the jewel at arm's length and grinned.

⁂

Later, they all stood around the funeral pyre as flames leaped into the starry sky. The night had turned frosty, but the Saxons had built the pyre so high that it warmed the whole courtyard.

It seemed everyone had come out to watch

Mordred's body burn. The knights guarded the pyre with crossed lances. Wrapped in a fur-lined cloak, the queen stood with Sir Lancelot. She held the Crown of Dreams on a purple cushion.

Rhianna could feel the heat of the fire on her cheeks from where she stood near the back of the crowd. Even so, she shivered as the dark knight's body began to smoke.

Elphin gave her a concerned look. "We can go back inside, if you're cold," he whispered. "No one will mind."

"No," Rhianna said, setting her jaw. "I want to make sure he's really dead this time."

She half expected her cousin to jump out of the fire and charge at her with his battleaxe in his hand, yelling curses. But the flames licked along his crippled leg and burned up his hair, and all that happened was the fingers of his remaining hand curled.

He killed my father, she reminded herself as the smell of roasting flesh reached them. *He betrayed his king and the Round Table. He deserved to die.* It wasn't as if they were burning him alive. So why did she feel this upset?

"He won't be coming back from that," Cai said in a satisfied tone.

"The shadrake took his fist," Rhianna reminded them, thinking uneasily of Lady Nimue's warning to make sure they burned all of him. "When the Crown's mended, I'll have to make the dragon bring that back so we can burn it, too."

"I think Damsel Rhianna's missing the dark knight already," Gareth said, giving Elphin a sly look. "I reckon she had a soft spot for Prince

Mordred – you lost a rival there, fairy boy."

"I did *not* have a soft spot for Mordred!" Rhianna drew Excalibur, making people at the back of the crowd look round and frown at them.

The merlin, which had been dozing on Cai's wrist, opened a sleepy eye. "Put Excalibur away, Rhianna Pendragon," he grumbled. "I'm not feeling well enough to talk to you yet. Mordred has quite a punch."

"Not any more, he doesn't," Rhianna said, pointing Excalibur at Gareth. "You take that back, Squire Gareth."

The boy took a step backwards and raised his hands. "Steady… I didn't mean it. I'm just glad Mordred's dead at last. I'd have killed him myself if he hadn't been wearing that magic crown. Who helped keep your precious jewel safe, anyway? Would have saved us all a lot of trouble if you'd told us what we were really meant to be guarding from the dark knight."

"You could have stopped Arianrhod swallowing it!" But she smiled, because Gareth could just as easily have betrayed her friend to Mordred. Realising she was being silly, she sheathed her sword and touched the pendant hanging around her neck. It glowed gold and orange in the firelight. *Her father's secrets.*

She could feel Arianrhod at her elbow, watching her. The maid had promised to take the Crown to the smith in the morning to get the jewel reset. Then Rhianna would be able to wear the third Light, and they could start looking for the Grail to bring her father back from Avalon. She hadn't seen King Arthur's ghost since Mordred had blooded Excalibur's blade at the Round Table. Did that mean it was no longer in the world of men?

"I'm sorry, Father," she whispered. "We're going to find the Grail soon, and then I'll return to Avalon for you, I promise—"

"Did you think I'd miss my nephew's funeral?" said an amused voice.

She caught her breath as her father's spirit strode through the crowd towards them. People turned to frown and blink at the ghost as it slipped past them. He looked more solid than Rhianna had ever seen him look before, and her heart leaped in hope. Maybe three Lights were enough to restore his soul to his body, after all?

He walked up to her and touched the scab at her throat, making her shiver. Then he closed his hand about the pendant. *"Give it to me, daughter,"* he whispered.

She stared at the ghost in amazement. The jewel did not drop through his fingers as she'd expected, but glowed bright gold in his strong fist.

Shivering a little, she let him lift the pendant over her head. Arianrhod started and peered uncertainly at the ghost. She blinked and dropped a quick curtsey. "Sire!" she breathed.

"King Arthur!" Cai yelled, pointing.

The merlin almost fell off his wrist. The bird opened one eye, looked hard at the ghost, and stuck its head back under its wing with a sigh. "That's all we need," Merlin grumbled. "A ghost everyone can see."

"King Arthur?" Gareth said, staring in disbelief at the ghost.

One by one, heads turned and people whispered in amazement. "King Arthur's back!"

they shouted. "Make way for the king!"

A path opened up through the crowd. As everyone watched in amazement, her father walked up to where Sir Lancelot stood with the queen, gently took the Crown of Dreams from Guinevere's cushion and pushed the missing jewel into place. It sparkled as he did so, lighting up his face. He held the crown aloft for all to see. Guinevere stared at the ghost and pressed a hand to her mouth. Sir Lancelot stiffened.

With great ceremony, King Arthur's ghost carried the Crown of Dreams back through the crowd to Rhianna. He smiled at her and settled the third Light gently on to her bright hair.

"It's time you knew Camelot's secrets, daughter," he said. *"Then you can complete your quest."*

DARK SPIRIT

The smoke rising from the funeral pyre in Camelot's courtyard made Mordred feel sick. Through the shadrake's eyes, he caught a final glimpse of his blackened corpse in the flames. They were burning his body so he couldn't go back!

His triumph at finally managing the spirit transfer turned to fury. It might have a crippled leg and only one hand, but it was *his* body. He tried to make the dragon dive at the figures in the courtyard. But the stupid creature flapped higher into the night, ignoring him.

He ground his teeth, and was alarmed
when a cloud of ice appeared in front of
him. Then he felt the dragon's powerful
wings carrying him away from his enemies.
Mordred gave in. Let them burn his crippled
human body! He didn't need it any more.

As the shadrake carried his spirit over
the Summer Lands, he sneered at the silly
villagers herding their animals to higher
ground. The floods had caused more chaos
than he'd realised. Arthur's knights would
be kept busy cleaning up for weeks.

They flew across the Summer Sea, faster
than any boat, and the hills of Dragonland
flashed beneath him. It was like being on the
back of a runaway horse. Mordred felt some
of the same terror. Then he remembered
he didn't have his body any more – a spirit

couldn't fall off and get hurt, could it?
He relaxed a bit and began to enjoy the
ride. He wondered where the creature was
taking him.

They turned up a river, and he recognised
the valley leading to the shadrake's lair.
Of course. The waterfall gushed out of the
cliff just as he remembered, and the entrance
was still blocked by boulders. Uther and his
ghostly warriors waited outside, fully visible
to the dragon's eyes.

The shadrake showed no sign of slowing
down. It carried him straight through
the wall of roaring spray. He had another
moment of fear when he thought it might
crash into the cliff and kill them both.
Then the gate of Annwn appeared, and the
creature landed on a shadowy ledge outside.

His mother's spirit waited at the gate, glimmering green and very angry. The shadrake folded its wings and hissed ice at her. "Hello, mother," Mordred said, knowing he couldn't hide from the witch's gaze.

"What do you think you're doing?" she demanded.

"Spirit-riding the shadrake, of course," Mordred said, pride creeping into his voice. "If you'd taught me how to do this earlier, I might be sitting on the throne of Camelot by now."

His mother sighed. "You won't be sitting on anything ever again, if what Uther tells me is true. The girl has not only got hold of the Crown, but restored her father's jewel and will soon know everything about us. Foolish boy! Whatever possessed you to leave your body behind at Camelot? Didn't you realise Arthur's knights would burn it so you couldn't go back?"

"It wasn't much use to me, anyway," he muttered. "It could barely walk, let alone fight. That's why my cousin and her friends kept getting hold of the Lights. But things will be different now. Once I've learned how to ride this dragon properly, I'll go back and deal with her."

"And you think you can control that creature, do you?" the witch hissed.

Mordred remembered the terrifying flight across the sea and through the waterfall. "My cousin spirit-rode it, and she's only a damsel. How hard can it be? I just need a bit more practice, that's all."

"Ha!" his mother spat. "Not even Merlin

could control the shadrake. If not for me, the dragon would have carried your spirit straight into Annwn by now. But all is not lost. Part of your body still survives, thanks to Arthur. Show me."

At first he couldn't think what she meant. Then he remembered his dark fist, which the shadrake had snatched from the courtyard when his spirit jumped aboard. He concentrated, and the creature's claw reached into its pouch and dragged out the fist. It looked rather the worse for wear after his cousin had grappled with it for Excalibur, and it smelled terrible. Rotting flesh oozed out of the gauntlet.

His mother's lip curled as she examined it. "Not pretty, but it'll have to do. There should be enough of your body in that glove to keep

your spirit tethered in the world of men.
You can use shadow magic for the rest."

Mordred stared at her in alarm. "But
I don't want to be tethered—"

The witch muttered a spell under her
breath that made Mordred remember the
pain of dying. The shadrake beat its black
wings, and he felt something give his spirit
a kick. With a sickening lurch, he fell into
what remained of his old body.

Rotting flesh closed around him, crushing
him into a tiny dark space. He couldn't
breathe. He couldn't see. He could no longer
even hear the noise of the waterfall outside.

He started to panic. Then something
touched the gauntlet, and his mother
whispered, "Use the shadow magic, my
son. Make yourself beautiful again," and he

realised he could wriggle his fingers. The fingers of his *right hand*, the one Arthur had chopped off in the battle.

He stretched carefully, growing a right arm and then a shoulder. He added some muscles and grew a left arm to match. He spent some time on his face, determined not to make it too boyish or give it any scars. Then he grew two straight, strong legs. He stood up slowly and opened his eyes.

He felt fantastic. Only his right hand in its battered black gauntlet reminded him of his old, crippled body. But at least he had a right hand again. He imagined the fingers around Rhianna's throat and clenched them tightly. Green rot leaked out of the glove.

His mother looked him up and down with a critical eye, making him remember to add some clothes – a black tunic with his double-headed eagle embroidered in silver thread, a cloak, decent boots and a silver torque around his neck.

"Not bad," she said. "Seems you've learned something from that Crown, after all. Your cousin will hardly recognise you. Now, before you meet her again there are some things you need to know. No weapon except one of the Lights can harm your shadow body, so don't worry about Arthur's knights. Nor can fire, or anything else that harms flesh. But take good care of your right hand. That is still mortal. If it is destroyed, then your spirit will have nowhere else to go except to join me in Annwn for all eternity. This is your last chance in the world of men, my son. Don't waste it."

Mordred grinned. He looked down at the dizzying drop no sane man would attempt, spread his arms wide and sprang out through the waterfall. He landed on his feet, knee-deep in the river and shook his hair. The icy water barely bothered him. He laughed. He hadn't felt this good since the day he'd killed King Arthur.

"What are you all staring at?" he yelled at Uther's warriors, his voice echoing in the cliffs. "I am Mordred Pendragon back from the dead, and I have need of you."

"I hope you don't expect us to help you find the Grail of Stars?" Uther said, frowning. "Because that thing can kill spirits as well as bodies." The other ghosts muttered uneasily.

"No." Mordred smiled as he splashed to

the bank. "We'll let my cousin do the hard work this time. There's only one place she'll go when she finds it. We ride to Avalon."

ABOUT THE AUTHOR

Katherine Roberts' muse is a unicorn.
This is what he has to say about her...

My author has lived in King Arthur's country for most of her life. She went to Bath University, where she got a degree in Maths and learned to fly in a glider. Afterwards she worked with racehorses, until she found me in 1984 and wrote her first fantasy story. She won the Branford Boase Award in 2000 with her first book *Song Quest*, and now she has me hard at work on the Pendragon series, searching for the Grail of Stars.

You can find out more about Katherine at www.katherineroberts.co.uk

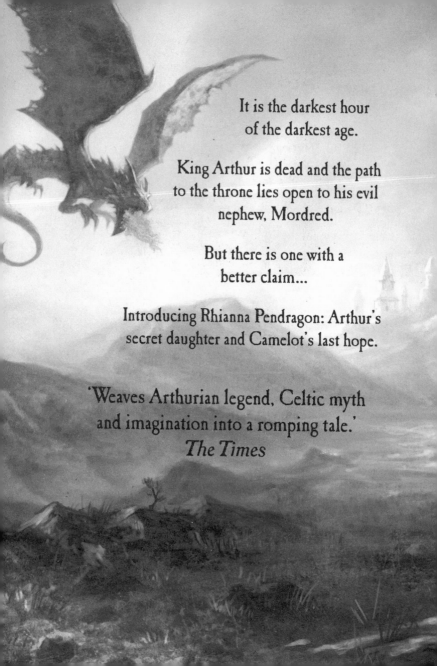

It is the darkest hour
of the darkest age.

King Arthur is dead and the path
to the throne lies open to his evil
nephew, Mordred.

But there is one with a
better claim...

Introducing Rhianna Pendragon: Arthur's
secret daughter and Camelot's last hope.

'Weaves Arthurian legend, Celtic myth
and imagination into a romping tale.'
The Times

Available now...

PENDRAGON LEGACY

⊰ BOOK 1 ⊱

SWORD
OF
LIGHT

The quest for Camelot's survival continues...

King Arthur's daughter Rhianna Pendragon
has faced dark magic, ice-breathing dragons
and mortal danger to win Excalibur, Arthur's
sword. But Excalibur is just one of four
magical Lights that Rhianna must find in
order to restore her late father's soul to his
body and bring him back to life. Now she
must head into the northern wilds in search of
the second Light, the Lance of Truth, before
her evil cousin Mordred claims it.

But Mordred is also holding her mother
Guinevere captive – can Rhianna stay true to
her quest for the Lights and save the mother
she's never known, before Mordred wreaks
his terrible revenge?

Available now...

PENDRAGON LEGACY

BOOK 2

LANCE OF TRUTH

Coming soon...

GRAIL OF STARS

by KATHERINE ROBERTS

Rhianna has found three of the four Lights and defeated Mordred. Only the fourth Light, the Grail of Stars, has the power to restore the king's soul to his body and heal the mortal wound Mordred gave him at the battle of Camlann. But the Grail has vanished from the world of men. Can Rhianna unlock the secrets of the Crown of Dreams to discover the Grail's whereabouts and bring her father back to life?

October 2013 Hardback
ISBN 978 1 84877 853 5